Later Stages

Later Stages:
Essays in Ontario Theatre from the First World War to the 1970s

Edited by Ann Saddlemyer and Richard Plant

A publication of the
Ontario Historical Studies Series
for the Government of Ontario

Published by the University of Toronto Press
Toronto Buffalo London

Printed in Canada

ISBN 0–8020–0671–X (cloth)
ISBN 0–8020–7624–6 (paper)

Printed on acid-free paper

Canadian Cataloguing in Publication Data

Main entry under title:

Later stages : essays in Ontario theatre from the First World
War to the 1970s

(Ontario historical studies series, ISBN 0380-9188)
Includes bibliographical references and index.
ISBN 0-8020-0671-X (bound)   ISBN 0-8020-7624-6 (pbk.)

1. Theatre – Ontario – History – 20th century.
I. Saddlemyer, Ann, 1932–   .   II. Plant, Richard.
III. Series.

PN2305.06L37 1996   792'.09713'09045   C95-932729-0

This book has been published with the assistance of funds provided by the Government of Ontario through the Ministry of Culture, Tourism, and Recreation.

University of Toronto Press acknowledges the financial assistance to its publishing
program of the Canada Council and the Ontario Arts Council.

Contents

The Ontario Historical Studies Series

For many years the principal theme in English-Canadian historical writing has been the emergence and the consolidation of the Canadian nation. This theme has been developed in uneasy awareness of the persistence and importance of regional interests and identities, but because of the central role of Ontario in the growth of Canada, Ontario has not been seen as a region. Almost unconsciously, historians have equated the history of the province with that of the nation and have often depicted the interests of other regions as obstacles to the unity and welfare of Canada.

The creation of the province of Ontario in 1867 was the visible embodiment of a formidable reality, the existence at the core of the new nation of a powerful if disjointed society whose traditions and characteristics differed in many respects from those of the other British North American colonies. The intervening century has not witnessed the assimilation of Ontario to the other regions in Canada; on the contrary, it has become a more clearly articulated entity. Within the formal geographical and institutional framework defined so assiduously by Ontario's political leaders, an increasingly intricate web of economic and social interests has been woven and shaped by the dynamic interplay between Toronto and its hinterland. The character of this regional community has been formed in the tension between a rapid adaptation to the processes of modernization and industrialization in modern Western society and a reluctance to modify or discard traditional attitudes and values. Not surprisingly, the Ontario outlook has been, and in some measure still is, a compound of aggressiveness, conservatism, and the conviction that its values should be the model for the rest of Canada.

From the outset the objective of the Series' Board of Trustees was to describe and analyse the historical development of Ontario as a distinct region within Canada. The Series includes biographies of several premiers and thematic studies on the growth of the provincial economy, educational institutions, labour, welfare, the Franco-Ontarians, the Native Peoples, and the arts.

In *Early Stages: Theatre in Ontario, 1800–1914* (1990), Ann Saddlemyer and her contributors described the emergence of theatre as an accepted and prosperous part of Ontario culture. In *Later Stages*, Richard Plant, Ann Saddlemyer, and their collaborators have defined and illustrated the intricate pattern of Ontario theatre from 1914 to the 1970s, the second phase of the 'great adventure of theatre' in this province. During these years a new hierarchy of theatrical values became accepted, only to be challenged in the 1970s. Amateur theatre flourished; new regional theatres were built; the Shaw and Stratford Festivals became major professional centres. Stagecraft, design, and theatrical organization became increasingly complex and costly, a process that had little impact on the incomes of actors and playwrights. The vitality of the contemporary theatrical scene in Ontario is the fruitful legacy of the years encompassed in *Later Stages*.

Richard Plant, Ann Saddlemyer, and their colleagues have written a lively and scholarly work that will broaden our understanding of the cultural history of modern Ontario. We hope that it will encourage others to explore others aspects of the evolving beliefs, attitudes, and values embodied in our culture.

The editors and the Board of Trustees are grateful to Richard Plant, Ann Saddlemyer, and their colleagues for undertaking this task.

GOLDWIN FRENCH
PETER OLIVER
JEANNE BECK
J.M.S. CARELESS
Chairman of the Board of Trustees

Toronto
August 1993

The corporation known as the Ontario Historical Studies Series ceased to exist 31 August 1993. This volume, the last in the Series, was completed and approved for publication before 31 August 1993.

Acknowledgments

Apart from the assistance of those who have been thanked by the authors of individual chapters or are included in the bibliography, a study such as this could only be undertaken with the help of a great many scholars whose efforts, often unacknowledged, frequently unknown, have provided the foundation on which theatre and social historians can build. This volume, like its predecessor, *Early Stages*, has been almost ten years in the making, and over that period has drawn upon the enthusiasm and expertise of many members of the Association for Canadian Theatre Research / L'Association de la Recherche Théâtrale au Canada, as well as of archivists throughout Ontario. We are grateful to the Master and Fellows of Massey College and to the Public Archives of Canada for permission to quote from unpublished materials. Special thanks must go to the University of Toronto School of Graduate Studies for a grant-in-aid. We have benefited from the assistance and advice of the following in locating illustrations: Patricia Beharriell; Louise Chaput, National Film Board; Tim Fort; Dennis Gannon; David Gardner; Darcy Gordon; Margaret Houghton, Hamilton Public Library; William Hutt; Frederick Kern; Stephen Mecredy, Fort Henry, St Lawrence Parks Commission; Martha Mann; Christopher Rosser; Don and Juliana Schnurr; Helen Smith; Mary Ainslie Smith; Anne Sutherland, Special Collections, Metropolitan Toronto Reference Library; and Lisbie Rae. Most of all, we are grateful for the wise advice and editorial skills of Dr Goldwin French, Dr Peter Oliver, and Dr Jeanne Beck and the patient faith of the Board of Trustees of the Ontario Historical Studies Series.

Contributors

Eric Binnie earned his Ph.D. at the Graduate Centre for Study of Drama in the University of Toronto and teaches theatre arts at Hendrix College, Arkansas. He has published work on Charles Ricketts and on modern Irish drama. His teaching interests are modern drama, theatre history, and Shakespeare.

David Gardner is a professional actor, director, teacher, and theatre historian who earned his doctorate from the University of Toronto. He has performed in London's West End, toured with the Old Vic Company, played with the Stratford Festival, and made numerous appearances on radio, film, and television. He was artistic director of the Vancouver Playhouse (1969–71) and spent ten years as a producer/director with CBC television. Former Theatre Officer of the Canada Council, he also chaired the committee that formed the National Theatre School. His scholarly work includes articles in numerous books and periodicals. In 1993 he was named an Honorary Member of the Association for Canadian Theatre Research.

Alexander Leggatt is Professor of English at University College, University of Toronto. He is the author of several books and articles on drama, particularly that of Shakespeare and his contemporaries. From 1975 to 1980 he reviewed English Canadian drama for the *University of Toronto Quarterly*'s annual *Letters in Canada*. His claim to be the only living actor to have appeared in two Merrill Denison plays was probably never accurate, and must be outdated by now.

Heather McCallum established the Theatre Collection at the Metropolitan Toronto Reference Library. She has produced (with Ruth Pincoe) the *Directory of Canadian Theatre Archives* (1992), is on the board of

directors of the Theatre Museum and has been for many years an active
member of the Association for Canadian Theatre Research, the International Federation for Theatre Research and the International Association
of Libraries and Museums of the Performing Arts (SIBMAS).

Martha Mann – theatre, film, and television designer – still treasures
books given to her as birthday presents by some of the people her chapter is about. She decided to become a theatrical designer listening to conversations in her parents' house – all the interesting ones were about the
theatre. She is winner of six Gemini Awards for television design, has
received several Dora nominations and has won American television
awards as well. The best-known of her designs are those for *Anne of
Green Gables* and *The Road to Avonlea*; two recent designs have been
Macbeth at Stratford and *A Fitting Confusion* at Stratford and Edmonton. Awards in the Central and the Western Ontario Drama Festivals
bear her name. She has been head of design at Hart House Theatre and
the Graduate Centre for Study of Drama for almost twenty years.

Richard Plant, co-founder and co-editor of the journal *Theatre History
in Canada / Histoire du théâtre au Canada* and former president of the
Association for Canadian Theatre History, has published extensively as
a bibliographer, drama critic, and editor. Also a director and sometime
actor, he teaches in the drama department at Queen's University and in
the Graduate Centre for Study of Drama at the University of Toronto. He
is working on a book on Canadian drama, and with John Ball has published a new edition of the *Bibliography of Theatre History in Canada*.

Ann Saddlemyer, Master Emerita of Massey College and Professor of
English and Drama at the University of Toronto, was editor of *Early
Stages: Theatre in Ontario 1800–1914*, co-founder with Richard Plant
of the journal *Theatre History in Canada*, founding president of the
Association for Canadian Theatre History, and a founding board member of Theatre Plus Toronto. She has published on twentieth-century
theatre and drama, especially that of Canada and Ireland, serves on
numerous editorial boards, and is a sometime actor and theatre critic.
Her current teaching and research interest is women in theatre.

Robert B. Scott, co-winner of the first annual Heather McCallum Scholarship for Canadian Theatre Research in 1988, is Professor and program
director, Media Arts, in the Film and Photography Department of Ryerson Polytechnic University. He has had a long-standing interest in
Ontario theatre history, beginning with his 1966 MA thesis, 'A Study of

Amateur Theatre in Toronto, 1900–30,' at the University of New Brunswick, then his M.Phil. at the University of Toronto (1968), and continuing
to date in his current research on developing an interactive multimedia
daily-performance calendar for twenty-eight towns and cities in Ontario
between 1914 and 1967. He has recently completed his doctorate at the
Graduate Centre for Study of Drama at the University of Toronto.

Rex Southgate – actor, teacher, and director – is a professor of English
at Ryerson Polytechnic University. While a member of the Stratford
Festival company for three years, he won a Tyrone Guthrie Award. In
early days, he appeared with such companies as the Canadian Players,
the Neptune Theatre, and the Manitoba Theatre Centre. In earlier days,
he appeared on the stage of Hart House Theatre and with the University
Alumnae Dramatic Club.

Anthony Stephenson was born in England in 1937. After receiving his
BA from Cambridge University in 1960, he worked in London until
1964. He began postgraduate work at the Graduate Centre for Study of
Drama at the University of Toronto in 1968, receiving his MA in 1969
and his Ph.D. in 1975. He is currently Professor Emeritus in the Department of Theatre at York University. In addition to his scholarly writings,
Professor Stephenson, under the pseudonym Anthony Quogan, has published four detective novels.

Ann Stuart has a BA and an MA from the University of Toronto and has
been in stage management at the Stratford Festival since 1977. She was
stage manager of *The Tempest, Two Gentlemen of Verona, Hamlet,
Homeward Bound, Macbeth, Phaedra, The Changeling, Ned and Jack,
Barren/Yerma*, and *Virginia*, starring Maggie Smith, which transferred
to the Haymarket Theatre in London, England. She has also stage-
managed for the Grand Theatre, Theatre Plus, the Royal Court Theatre,
at Canadian Stage, and for Tarragon Theatre. She began her career at
Hart House Theatre with Robert Gill.

Ross Stuart, whose doctoral thesis at the Graduate Centre for Study of
Drama, University of Toronto, was a stylistic analysis of productions on
the open stage at Stratford, Ontario, teaches theatre at York University.
He has written extensively about Canadian theatre for *The Encyclopedia
of Music in Canada, The New Canadian Encyclopedia, The Oxford
Companion to Canadian Theatre, Touring and Founding in North
America*, and his own *The Development of Theatre in the Prairie Prov-
inces*. His writing has also appeared in periodicals such as *Canadian
Theatre Review* and *Canadian Drama / L'Art dramatique canadien*.

Later Stages

Introduction

RICHARD PLANT AND
ANN SADDLEMYER

The pattern of Ontario theatre in this century can best be captured not so
much through the hierarchy of formal narrative as through the image of
the wheel, each spoke representing a different critical approach, history
continually turning back on itself while pointing to future events and
ambitions. It is not inappropriate that we end our story in the early
1970s, when the production of *The Donnellys* signalled yet another
change of direction. For the wheel spins its way through James Reaney's
energetically episodic, mythical-historical trilogy of western Ontario as
a prevailing image of continuity and change, constancy and fluidity, just
as many of the same subjects and persons turn up again and again in the
following chapters, moving throughout the province in and out of the
rapidly growing hub of Toronto. Thus, the reader will find similar
themes in chapters dealing with subjects as various as professional companies, variety acts, university training, amateur productions, design
concepts, and even archival collections.

Much of the impetus for change in the twentieth century was a reaction to the conservative tastes of largely middle-class Ontario audiences,
who continued to cling to inherited attitudes: entertainment was a (frequently suspect) fringe benefit of hard work and virtuous living; the
local and home-grown was innately inferior to imports from New York
and London; familiar forms, subjects, and plays preferable to (and much
more respectable than) the unusual and experimental.[1] The result was
the continued success of touring companies and visiting performers
(later, a fascination with television entertainment[2]), who were eventually
challenged by an increasing number of determined local mavericks dis-
daining commercialism and populism, some even repudiating traditional
standards of technical skills and creativity. Paradoxically, both attitudes
can be discerned in the amateur activity that flourished alongside the
professional, with allegiance to British playwrights and training on the

Theatre in Ontario villages: Schnurr's Hall, Linwood, exterior as it appeared circa
First World War

one hand and a growing sympathy with the arts and little theatre tradition on the other. It is no surprise that many of the 1967 centennial
projects harkened back to the amateur pageants of the nineteenth
century.

Indeed, as David Gardner and Ross Stuart point out, the variety of
fare representative of theatre in the previous century continues through
to this day. What is different is the process of marginalization that has
occurred along the way, in part a result of the ambitions of nineteenth-
century Ontarians eager for theatres of their own, partly the effect of a
rigid application of the definitions and expectations of twentieth-century
culture. Increasingly, the acceptable definition of drama became the
written word performed by actors polished by recognized training and
apprenticeship, reinforced by technical standards achievable only in
dedicated theatre spaces under professional directors, before a sophisticated audience with a strong sense of social and religious propriety. No
wonder that Toronto found it necessary to appoint a censor in 1913,
and that by 1932 even amateur theatre had become codified by the
social élite of the Dominion Drama Festival (DDF). No wonder also, as

Schnurr's Hall, Linwood, completed in 1910 and in use for over 50 years for films and live shows such as the Bell Ringers Co. (1927), the Harmony Kids (including Joyce Hahn, 1939), and the Luther League in 'Raggedy Nan' (1956). Interior showing artefacts recently found in hall: painted flats attached to stage left and right wing area, drops with local advertising, and 'scenic view'

Alexander Leggatt reminds us, that the characters of Robertson Davies, like those of James Reaney, lament 'the tyranny of organized virtue.'

As the attitudes, codes, and conditions refined and proliferated, so did the labels. The inclusive perspective that promoted the multifariousness of the previous century's theatrical entertainment was replaced by the new age's exclusive topography, which identified and ordered genres in a hierarchy of low to high art. The less respectable, such as burlesque in its twentieth-century strip-tease naughtiness, and the 'formless,' such as variety and vaudeville, joined other 'low art' such as the circus, pushed out of 'theatre' by privileged genres that fulfilled recognized artistic principles, reaffirmed the ruling socio-political ideology, or were deemed to be morally or intellectually enlightening. The hierarchy of values and standards was adopted by amateur companies and the fledgling Dominion Drama Festival without much consideration as to its appropriateness for such activities. However, the marginalized forms did not disappear, except for instance from the attention of historians. They continued, as David Gardner's chapter shows, in different 'not-theatre' performance spaces. As well, first radio and then television, with their respective abilities to compartmentalize types of entertainment, picked up popular variety forms, broadcasting them alongside high-art genres. Ironically, the narrowing of the 'theatre' definition increasingly characteristic up to the 1960s has since gradually given way to a postmodernist broadening of vision that is bringing circus and many other performative genres back into 'theatre.' The wheel turns again.

Following changes in taste and custom, the identification of performers and companies also altered with time. No longer, for example, was 'combination troupe' a meaningful term; that late-nineteenth-century designation was replaced by nomenclature for different production configurations, such as 'repertory' or 'stock,' which returned from earlier times in various conjunctions: for instance, resident stock, summer stock, summer rep, touring rep or touring stock. Such terms not only changed their sense over time, but some had greatly different meanings dependent on their derivation: for example, the English 'stock' referred to a company of permanent players attached to a specific theatre who performed a repertory that changed each night; essentially 'stock' differentiated them from a company of touring players. However, in America 'stock' could refer to a company performing a single play for a specified run. The company's attachment to a given theatre might be very short; in fact, the company might be touring from town to town almost daily. 'Stock' could also derive from contractual arrangements within a company; in essence, players had 'stock' in the company, determined by either financial investment or particular lines of business (roles), and were paid accordingly. Yet none of these is quite what anyone meant in Ontario in 1960 when referring to the Red Barn Theatre as 'summer stock' or to a theatre that operated on the basis of a stock of flats, stock of plays with stock characters, and stock of actors. The authors of these chapters have explained such terms when they felt it necessary, but readers may still need to keep in mind that language changed with its subject.

Perhaps the most far-reaching changes came with the increased commercialization of entertainment, which was accompanied by the restrictive use of the word 'professional' – a distinction debated no less heatedly in the arts than it is in the sporting world. Although constantly in use from the turn of the century, 'professional' has had many different alignments in Ontario theatre. For many people in the 1920s, 'professional' was synonymous with corrupt commercialism and the foreign domination, particularly American economic control, of our theatre. One can see how this definition helped the formation in the 1930s of an amateur 'national' theatre – the élitist DDF – under the sanction of those in the seats of Canadian power. But for the Leftist Progressive Arts Club and the Workers' Theatre in the 1930s, professional carried several different resonances: concern for the development of theatre craft as 'work' that should earn its rightful wage; fundamental antipathy to capitalist aspects of the prevailing theatre system; an alternative to the amateur movement, which was seen as an organ of the ruling class. The post–Second World War period saw professional associated with the vigorous movement by artists in Canada to earn a living from their theatre craft that brought about the consolidation of unions, such as Equity, ACTRA (Alliance of Canadian Cinema, Television and Radio Artists), and IATSE (International Alliance of Theatre and Stage Employees) with their sense of professional. Ironically, in the late 1960s and 1970s, the 'alternative' theatre movement combined the 'union' impulse, particularly in branches of the craft, such as playwriting, whose formal organization had lagged behind, with a return to a somewhat 1920s sense of professional, associating the term with establishment exploitation and oppression. Individuals in this movement repudiated amateurism, saw themselves as locked out of the existing profession, and worked hard at forming a definition of professional that was based on Canadian identity.

Clearly, by the turn of the century, battle lines had already been drawn between large commercial ventures (be they Shakespearean and melodramatic extravaganzas or vaudeville) and the art or 'free' theatres in Europe dedicated since the 1880s to reform of the theatre and the empowerment of the playwright. Small was beautiful, and simplicity was uplifting; poetry was a purer motive than profit. Dublin's Abbey Theatre, with a cast drawn from dedicated patriotic amateurs, a mandate to encourage indigenous playwrights, and in W.B. Yeats a major symbolist poet as apologist, proved the perfect model for North American idealists. Yeats himself toured North America in 1903–4, lecturing on the 'Theatre of Beauty,' and later, in 1919, promulgated his theories from the Hart House stage; the Dublin company's first tour, led by Lady Gregory, was in 1913–14 (the Toronto censorship board refused permission for their production of Shaw's *Shewing Up of Blanco Posnet* [14 April 1914]) and was followed by frequent visits through the 1920s and 1930s. Thus, the Little Theatre movement was born, with strong leanings towards the indigenous and the amateur; paradoxically, the art theatre and its offshoot, the theatre guild, tended to embrace the professional in the sense of refined craft – although 'without profit.'

When Vincent and Alice Massey drew up their plans for Hart House Theatre, the Abbey Theatre was prominent among their models. When Roy Mitchell, a member of a group of visionaries in the Toronto Arts and Letters Club, became the first director at Hart House, the little theatre concept and the experimentalism of the European art theatre merged. Mitchell's 1926 handbook and alarm *The Creative Theatre* mingled the results of staging and scenic experiments with theosophy and an urgent denunciation of commercialism as a betrayal of the mystery of art. Similar goals were held by playwright and director Herman Voaden, who also gained experience at Hart House Theatre and the Arts and Letters Club, and whose Playworkshops of the 1930s and 1940s explored what he termed 'symphonic expressionism.'

Hart House Theatre was situated in the heart of the University of Toronto, and Mitchell's plan for the miraculous theatre of the future, like Voaden's later, included training – of both the actor and the audience. In the meantime, Hart House Theatre offered apprenticeship for amateur groups aspiring to professionalism, opportunities for indigenous playwrights, and social acceptability for both audience and artist. In 1926–7 Vincent Massey triumphantly produced two volumes of *Canadian Plays from Hart House Theatre.* When the Dominion Drama Festival was established, he was an enthusiastic supporter, and many of its performers and directors were drawn from Hart House regulars. When appointed in 1949 to co-chair the Royal Commission on National Development in the Arts, Letters, and Sciences in Canada – the report that was to lead to the formation of the Canada Council, thus a new phase in the development of theatre – Massey returned to his early ideal of an indigenous culture, albeit strongly shaded by British overtones and a continuing emphasis on social values.

Not surprisingly, therefore, both at Hart House Theatre and within the DDF, training became synonymous with British standards, reinforced by invited teachers and DDF adjudicators from England. Some, like Esme Crampton, remained to teach at Stratford and elsewhere. Others, like Dora Mavor Moore, received part or all of their training in England and, on returning, became teachers in turn. The groups they founded, whether amateur or quasi-professional, tended to be based on English models rather than – perhaps in defiance of – theatre south of the border. Still, American theatre exerted its own influence, just as it had during the borderless tours before the First World War. The Provincetown Players, Eugene O'Neill, and George Pierce Baker, among others, were strong forces in the little theatre movement. The Workers' Theatre drew on New York, and professionals such as David Pressman, for at least part of their training and program. Whatever the cause, most workshops and courses, even within the CBC, continued a tradition of imitation of British Theatre that began with garrison and amateur theatricals of the nineteenth century (this in spite of the continued popularity of American stars and the more educational tent settings of Chautauqua). Not until after the Second

World War would the legendary Robert Gill – himself trained in the United States – prepare a generation of accomplished actors for the Canadian stage, radio, and television. Ironically, it was under the leadership of Michel Saint-Denis, the famous French actor and director who founded the London Theatre Studio and the Centre Dramatique de l'Est (France), and later was an adviser and co-director of New York's Juilliard School, that Canada's National Theatre School was finally established in 1960. Saint-Denis had first been asked to stay in Canada and develop an idea for a professional theatre school after adjudicating the 1952 DDF finals.

Similar trends can be observed in the precursors of the Stratford and Shaw festivals. Earle Grey and Mary Godwin, a husband-and-wife team who were touring with Barry Jones and Maurice Colborne's English players and were stranded in Ontario by the war, established an influential outdoor Shakespeare festival at Trinity College in Toronto that ran between 1946 and 1958. Their idea was to stage Shakespeare in accord with the 'original intention,' an idea that was in the air: in the 1930s, noted English scholar G. Wilson Knight experimented with Shakespearean productions at Trinity, and in the early 1940s, equally distinguished English professor G.B. Harrison did the same at Queen's University. It was Dora Mavor Moore and Robertson Davies who encouraged Tyrone Guthrie to accept the challenge of creating Stratford's theatre, while Brian Doherty, whose own play *Father Malachy's Miracle* had been a success in New York and England, first encouraged a group of amateurs to establish a theatre honouring Bernard Shaw and, later, his (primarily British) contemporaries.

The hierarchy of standards and values employed by theatre critics and accepted by theatre-goers thus encouraged the preference for the imported over the indigenous or community-based, professional over amateur, legitimate over variety, verbal or stylized over experimental or diffuse. Too often theatre historians and educators have reinforced these biases, thereby overlooking materials and theatre practice that legitimately belong within the story of our culture, skewing the received picture by too much dependence upon written reports or published criticism. A marked example of this neglect can be seen in the following pages, where the impressive and overwhelming contribution of many more women – as playwrights, actors, directors, producers, and teachers – is overlooked because unrecorded.

Similarly, these biases combined with the predominance of the English language have meant that theatre in non-English immigrant communities, as well as among our Native people and in the Franco-Ontarien community, has been and remains greatly neglected. The current *Bibliography of Theatre History in Canada: The Beginnings through 1984 / Bibliographie d'histoire du théâtre au Canada: Des Débuts – Fin 1984* lists a mere fifty scholarly articles or books on Native theatre up to 1985, including Ed Buller's valuable bibliography. Only recently (1992) has the Franco-Ontarien community received its first published book-length study, Mariel O'Neill-Karch's *Théâtre franco-ontarien: Espaces ludiques* (Vanier: L'Interligne 1992), which, like the very short *Le théâtre du Nouvel-Ontario – 20 ans* (Sudbury: Edition TNO, 1991), begins its subject at about the time our volume's coverage ends. Publication of any scholarly account of early Franco-Ontarien theatre is impossible until more fundamental research is done.

In 1991 William Lau completed his MFA thesis, 'Chinese Dance Experience in Canadian Society: An Investigation of Four Chinese Dance Groups in Toronto.' Two book-length studies of Ukrainian theatre in Canada appeared respectively in 1961 (in Ukrainian) and 1984 (in both English and Ukrainian). Robin Breon, among others, has made a start at the long history of black theatre. But enormous pioneering work remains to be done because the amount of theatre activity in many of these communities is large. Much of it has come since the early 1970s. Still, in the Toronto Chinese community of the 1930s, for instance, three Chinese opera houses operated on the basis of professional touring companies; this was in addition to local Chinese stage activity. Yiddish theatre has almost a century of history in Toronto, and Hungarian theatre was especially active in the 1950s. Scarborough and Thunder Bay have been homes of Finnish theatres and Hamilton of a Lithuanian group. Ukrainian theatre developed in Sudbury during the first decade of the century and in Toronto notably after 1956. And we should not forget the founding of the vigorous professional company Le Théâtre du P'tit Bonheur (now Théâtre français de Toronto) in 1967. These chapters contain some references to such activity, but troublingly few. However, as theatre scholars appear who are fluent in the respective languages and as the process of recovering discarded or otherwise uncollected records develops further, these hitherto marginalized histories will be celebrated too in volumes such as this.

Since the 1950s, with the building or renovation of major theatre buildings, such as the O'Keefe and St Lawrence centres in Toronto, the Grand in London, and the National Arts Centre in Ottawa, and with the establishment of two major theatre festivals, came an evolution in not only stagecraft but theatrical organization rivalling in complexity the great touring companies of the nineteenth century. The role of artistic director has become increasingly important, as has his (still rarely her) relationship with funding bodies. Recollect that even the Abbey Theatre was subsidized from its inception; idealism in the arts tends to cost money. (An interesting case study is that of the Ottawa Stage Society, which evolved into the Canadian Repertory Theatre and required sponsors; another is the controversial commercial sponsorship of the DDF.) The larger, the more elaborate the theatre space, the greater the need for audience support. Government support came with the establishment of the Canada Council; this in turn led to yet another level of potential censorship. Boards of directors were deemed necessary, not only to ensure accountability of public funding but to raise funds and battle threatening deficits. As with the CBC, government subsidy and corporate sponsorship threaten autonomy in the theatre, a situation frequently exacerbated by self-censorship.

The need to feed demanding structures and vast buildings has done little to assist the performers: stardom still tends to be accorded to visitors from elsewhere, while the vast majority of Canadian actors must still supplement their meagre earnings with jobs outside the theatre. Similarly, despite Canada Council grants and occasional workshops, playwrights have received little more encouragement since the 1930s, when the Playwrights' Studio Group was grudgingly allowed the Hart House Theatre stage. Not until 1971, when the Playwrights' Co-op was founded, was there promise of the printing and vitally important distribution of scripts beyond the pages of *Curtain Call* or Samuel French's catalogue of plays for amateurs.

The First World War marked an end to the expansion of theatre as Ontarians knew it in the nineteenth century. The early 1970s signal yet another sharp turn in the story of theatre in Ontario. In 1969, the opening of the National Arts Centre in Ottawa, which might be seen as a culmination of the regional theatre building that began in 1958 with the Manitoba Theatre Centre, raised hopes for a new entirely Canadian version of the touring production, a promise supported the following year by the opening of the St Lawrence Centre in Toronto. Although the DDF was dissolved in 1970 (and, as Theatre Canada, sputtered to an end eight years later), a stronger, healthier regional organization, Theatre Ontario, replaced it in 1971. Tired but debt-free, the New Play Society was dissolved in 1971, on its twenty-fifth anniversary. But Theatre Passe Muraille (1968) was followed by Canadian Place Theatre Stratford (1969), Factory Theatre Lab (1970), and the Tarragon, Truck, and Toronto Free theatres (all in 1971). If further assurance of fresh blood and feistiness was required, Toronto's Festival of Underground Theatre in 1970 provided it, while the opening of the Third Stage (1971) promised new experimental productions at the Stratford Festival. Nathan Cohen, arguably the most influential critic in English Canada, died that year, but two playwrights' conferences led to the establishment of the Playwrights' Co-op and a call for strong representation of indigenous drama in professional theatre. Nineteen seventy had seen the establishment of the Council of Drama in Education, the Ontario Multicultural Theatre Association (representing sixty companies), and the New Czech Theatre in Toronto. Shortly to come were LIP and OFY grants, encouraging a proliferation of young, enthusiastic, often short-lived theatre groups. The new wave had begun, and with it a re-evaluation once again of standards, tastes, and practice.

Although the early 1970s seem an appropriate cut-off point for this volume, any simultaneous ending is impossible for the various elements that constitute such a complex history as the theatre's. The early seventies' 'alternative' theatres have different engendering and sustaining forces, hence different trajectories, from those of the summer theatres or the amateur theatres, which are different again from such trajectories as the development of criticism, the work of individual playwrights, particular companies, or design in the theatre. We have taken this complexity into account in allowing all our authors their own voices. Consequently, readers will find some elements traced through to different dates from others and, since the parts of the story are at different states of research development, readers will also find chapters of different lengths.

The histories of the past two decades of Ontario theatre are now being written by a new generation of well-trained scholars. But there are still many gaps to be filled before we can be confident of a fair, comprehensive assessment of the entertainment of Ontarians through two centuries. Playwrights such as James Reaney have found 'poetry in archives'; we need theatre collections and memoirs, more informed theatre criticism, a broader (and deeper) approach to the concept of 'history,' and a greater range of acceptable topics for scholarly research with which to conceptualize what it is and has been to be a participant in the great adventure of theatre in Ontario.

NOTES

1 By 1914 more Ontarians lived in the city than the country, the vast majority in Toronto; as late as 1967, over 90 per cent of immigrants came from the United States and Europe.
2 The 1961 census records that, of the 1,640,750 dwellings in Ontario, 1,350,483 had television sets and 1,085,575 had passenger cars. From the beginning, television transmission overlooked national boundaries.

1 Professional Performers and Companies

ROBERT B. SCOTT

Between the First World War and Canada's centennial in 1967, professional theatre in Ontario underwent a profound transformation. At the turn of the century, the province was almost entirely dependent on imported American and British touring companies, except for a group of indigenous independent travelling troupes that played primarily to smaller communities. Without a professional theatre of their own, aspiring Ontario artists were forced to pursue careers on foreign stages. Many achieved immediate success and returned occasionally as stars of touring productions. However, unlimited expansion and fierce competition between the 'barons of Broadway' – (Marc) Klaw and (Abe) Erlanger, heads of the New York–based Theatrical Syndicate, and their rivals, the Shubert Brothers – had weakened the touring system. Furthermore, the rising popularity of movies and vaudeville as well as increased production and travel costs further contributed to the decline of 'the road,' reducing the number of companies and their itineraries. In addition, Canada's participation in the war intensified the demand for economic and cultural independence and spurred the growth of amateur 'little theatre' organizations as an alternative to the commercial stage.

During the 1920s, American and British resident stock companies attempted to replace the dying touring system, but they succumbed in turn to the arrival of the 'talkies' and of radio, which brought entertainment directly into the home. In the wake of the stock-market crash of 1929, road and resident companies all but vanished from the province, leaving Toronto as the only regular stop-over on the old circuits.

For many communities across the province, the vacuum in live entertainment was filled by local amateur organizations. Founded partly in response to a Canadian desire for a national theatre,[1] these groups received encouragement as early as 1907 from Governor-General Earl Grey's dramatic competitions (1907–11) and later from numerous British actors, directors, and Dominion Drama Festival adjudicators who came to Canada in the 1920s and 1930s, bringing with them the ideals and principles of the national theatre movement in the United Kingdom. This British 'presence,' which might be seen as a further act of colonialism, nevertheless contributed immeasurably to English Canadians' quest for a theatre of their own. Their efforts were given impetus when Canada achieved nationhood under the Statute of Westminster in 1931, and culminated in the establishment of the Dominion Drama Festival in 1933. The DDF, together with the newly formed Dominion-wide public radio service, the Canadian Radio Broadcasting Commission (later the CBC), constituted the basis of the first truly national theatre, the former producing actors, directors, and other stage artists, the latter offering through radio drama an outlet for their talents on a scale hitherto undreamed. CBC stations in Toronto and Ottawa quickly became centres of radio drama production and developed a cadre of actors drawn from local amateur circles and from private stations. These performers also formed the nucleus of several professional theatre ventures in touring and summer stock in Ontario that emerged during the late thirties.

Throughout the Second World War, radio served as a potent instrument for promoting the war effort by broadcasting patriotic drama series, as well as military shows produced by the armed forces. When peace returned in 1945, radio performers joined returning veterans to set up a number of important professional companies during the late 1940s and early 1950s. By this process, they laid the groundwork for a vibrant indigenous professional theatre movement. Encouraged by the Massey-Lévesque Royal Commission on National Development in the Arts, Letters and Sciences (1951) – sometimes referred to as the Commission on National Defence of the Arts (against increasingly aggressive American cultural influences through movies and television) – professional theatre experienced unprecedented growth in companies and facilities over the next decade. By the time Canada celebrated its centennial in 1967, professional theatre in Ontario had become a vital cultural industry consisting of internationally recognized festivals at Stratford and Niagara-on-the-Lake, strong community theatre organizations in several cities, widespread summer stock, an energetic alternative theatre movement, university theatre programs, and a host of new or refurbished buildings for the performing arts. Over the period, theatre in Ontario also produced a steady flow of performers who achieved stardom, not only at home but also on the stages and screens of the world. Despite these accomplishments, the question remains whether, in the face of the increasing presence of American television and movies, one means of cultural domination replaced another.

One of the large-sized 'opera houses' along the lucrative Ontario circuit, the Savoy Theatre, Hamilton (post–First World War): after the show, photographers such as the noted Edwin Poole of St Catharines sold audience photos taken from the stage at intermission

The First World War: 1914–1918

British and American Touring Companies
At the outbreak of the First World War, New York theatrical interests supplied the bulk of entertainment for an estimated twenty large-sized 'opera houses' along the lucrative Ontario circuit.[2] Following much the same pattern established in the nineteenth century, touring companies proceeded along the rail lines that linked Ottawa, Kingston, Toronto, and Hamilton, going southward to St Catharines and Brantford and on to Buffalo, or westward to London and through to Chatham and Detroit. Another route headed northward from Toronto to Barrie, North Bay, Sudbury, Sault Ste Marie, the Lakehead, and the western provinces. Toronto, with seven commercial theatres,[3] acted as the hub of the Ontario circuit, through which all major road companies passed, whether bound for the West or home to New York.

Ontario theatre-goers treated this theatrical monopoly with ambivalence. Although it stood as a palpable symbol of economic and cultural domination, the touring system brought in some of the most illustrious performers of the day. In 1914, for example, to celebrate the 350th anniversary of Shakespeare's birth, two of England's finest actors, Sir Johnston Forbes-Robertson and F.R. Benson, as well as William Faversham, Canadian Margaret Anglin, and E.H. Sothern from the American stage, appeared on the circuit in lavish Shakespearean productions.[4] Even during the war the system managed to provide a galaxy of attractions, from the snappy jazz musicals of Irving Berlin and Al Jolson to performances by such distinguished actors as George Arliss, John Barrymore, Maude Adams ('the most conspicuous figure upon the English-speaking stage, the most notable woman in a nation of a hundred million'), and the indefatigable international star Sarah Bernhardt, on her eighth and final trip to Canada.[5] More often than not, though, the offerings from the touring system consisted of mediocre companies performing outdated melodramas, lavishly mounted extravaganzas, or flimsy musical comedies that mixed slapstick routines and spicy dialogue with dance numbers featuring lots of leggy 'ponies' (chorus girls). In fact, the popularity of musicals in Toronto prompted Sir Herbert Beerbohm Tree's manager to remark at the time, 'There are seven leg shows in the city (pardon the inelegant term – 'tis not mine) and after all, what is art against nature?'[6]

Not everyone found such attractions acceptable. Indignant citizens in Ottawa and Toronto established drama guilds to boycott such 'unwholesome' and 'vulgar' dramatic material.[7] In fact, so sensitive were residual Victorian tastes to anything suggestive that the Toronto police prevented Sam Bernard from singing 'Who Paid the Rent for Mrs. Rip Van Winkle?' in *The Belle from Bond Street*.[8] In London, local clergymen succeeded in forcing cancellation of a travelling production of *Damaged Goods*, based on Eugene Brieux's play about the ravages of venereal disease.[9] But community standards obviously varied, because in neighbouring St Thomas, the local theatre owner eagerly opened his doors to the production and even provided transportation to disappointed Londoners anxious to see the play.

It was, however, the American domination of the theatrical world that aroused the strongest resentment against the touring system. Canadian novelist and playwright Arthur Stringer proclaimed: 'Canada is the only nation in the world whose stage is entirely and arbitrarily controlled by aliens. It is the only country of continental proportions that depends on foreigners for that spiritual refreshment that may and must be derived from theatre entertainment.'[10] Stringer's was one of many voices. Concerns over Canada's cultural and economic sovereignty spurred business interests in Montreal and London, England, to form the British Canadian

Theatrical Organization Society for the purpose of importing English touring companies to counter 'the extent of American bookings throughout Canada.'[11] Under the scheme, Sir John Martin-Harvey, the ill-fated team of Laurence Irving and Mabel Hackney (they died in the sinking of the *Empress of Ireland* on their return home), and H.V. Esmond and his wife, Eva Moore, appeared in successive Dominion-wide tours, playing to overflow houses in 1914. However, war broke out in August and curtailed further development of the embryonic venture.[12]

During the war, British companies continued to tour the Canadian provinces on an independent basis. Among those seen in Ontario were three of the most celebrated proponents of the new national theatre movement in Britain – Harley Granville Barker, Sir Herbert Beerbohm Tree, and Mrs Patrick Campbell, whose productions illustrated the latest ideas and techniques in stagecraft, dramatic material, and acting styles from Europe.[13] Combined with visits by W.B. Yeats and the Abbey Theatre Players just before the war,[14] the appearance of these celebrities encouraged local little theatre advocates, such as Mrs Scott Raff at Toronto's Margaret Eaton School of Expression, to persevere in their efforts to establish a national theatre based on the British model.[15]

Also from the London stage came the versatile lyric stars Marie Tempest and Phyllis Neilson-Terry (leading lady at His Majesty's, London), as well as the diminutive Scottish entertainer Harry Lauder, F. Stuart Whyte's famous English pantomimes, and a host of traditional music-hall attractions that appealed to Ontario theatre-goers, many of whom were of British stock.[16] Companies from Britain also brought in the first contemporary war plays, such as the London hit *Under Orders* (Albert Cowles), the gripping German spy drama *The White Feather* (Lechmere Morral and J.E. Harold Terry), and its sequel *The Black Feather*, written by William A. Tremayne, one of Canada's few resident commercial playwrights at the time.[17]

These British troupes added a patriotic touch noticeably absent from the circuit in the years preceding the United States' entry into the war in 1917. In fact, some American companies appeared to be quite insensitive to the patriotic needs of Canadian theatre-goers during wartime. In one instance, *The Passing Show of 1917* at the Gaiety Theatre introduced a patriotic number, 'Goodby Broadway, Hello France,' complete with such features as the provocatively titled 'Bridge of Thighs' (presumably a gymnastic stunt staged by the chorus girls) and a display of international flags. Not only was the Union Jack barely visible, but the Canadian ensign was nowhere to be seen, an omission that led one reviewer to observe with typical Canadian politeness, 'This was doubtlessly a first night oversight.'[18] A louder reaction greeted popular American entertainer Al H. Wilson when audiences protested his inclusion of German characters in two of his shows.[19] Complaints were also launched against some road productions considered to be blatantly insulting to the British Empire and the war effort.[20] Even after the Armistice, antagonism ran so high that Toronto audiences walked out of a vaudeville performance that praised the bravery of American soldiers, but blatantly ignored the sacrifices that Canadians had made in the conflict.[21]

Anti-Americanism only added to the difficulties that New York road companies had to face during wartime travel along the Ontario circuit. They also had to contend with disrupted train schedules, unheated theatres (to conserve fuel), shortened itineraries, war taxes, and raids not only by local morality squads but also by military police rounding up recruitable young male patrons.[22] In addition, American companies met increasing competition from a wave of patriotic pageants and concerts by local church and school groups to raise war funds and to entertain the troops. Movie houses also cut into attendance by drawing large crowds eager to watch newsreels 'direct from the front,' the latest war dramas from Hollywood, or the work of Ontario-born performers comedienne Marie Dressler (née Leila Koerber of Cobourg) and 'America's Sweetheart,' Mary Pickford (originally Gladys Smith of Toronto) – two of the greatest movie stars at the time.[23]

In an effort to win back theatre-goers, American touring companies staged benefit performances for various war funds, admitted uniformed soldiers free to matinées, and inserted jingoistic songs into their performances. Most important, they began to feature Broadway personalities who could claim, either by birth or previous residency, some ties to Canada. A surprising number qualified, among them several illustrious stars originally from Ontario.[24] For example, Ottawa-born and Toronto-educated Margaret Anglin, whom Sarah Bernhardt called 'one of the few dramatic geniuses of the day' for her powerful interpretations of classical Greek and Shakespearean heroines,[25] returned to her home province twice during the war, first as Mrs Erlynne in a revival of her 1902 success, *Lady Windermere's Fan*, on 16–21 November 1914 (a performance described as 'a rare revelation of what exquisitely restrained emotional power can do') and then in Somerset Maugham's light comedy *Caroline*, on 13–18 November 1916.[26]

Gifted with a 'golden' voice, 'high emotional power,' a figure that could be both 'dainty' and 'imperious,' a demeanour that was at once 'robust' and 'graceful,' and an inner 'spiritual exaltation,' Anglin was able to infuse life into all her characters, whether they inhabited the mundane world of the kitchen, the drawing room, or the halls of kings.[27] Equally at home in tragedy and comedy, she was also instrumental in introducing the non-representational styles of Europe's 'new stagecraft'

Margaret Anglin as Ophelia

to productions of Shakespeare on the American stage; in addition, she brought a new approach to acting that she demonstrated in *Lady Windermere's Fan* by replacing 'old fashioned' soliloquies with 'more careful techniques to suggest by action what was previously explained by words.'[28]

Anglin returned to Ontario several more times over her long and active stage life, but dissatisfied by the increasing commercialism of the theatre, she withdrew from the limelight. She was seen for the last time on an Ontario stage in February 1943, when she appeared at Toronto's Royal Alex for an extended run of *Watch on the Rhine*. After a brief attempt at radio acting and a career as an actress-manager in the late 1940s, she retired to Toronto, where she died in 1958.

Anglin's Toronto visits during the First World War did a great deal to bolster the spirits of Ontarians at a time when patriotism was fading.[29] Julia Arthur (née Ida Lewis), a native of Hamilton and former leading lady with Sir Henry Irving, created a similar effect when, after a decade in retirement, she returned to the stage to star in a production of *The Eternal Magdalene* (Robert McLaughlin), seen in Toronto in March 1916. Arthur regarded the title role as 'the biggest, finest character' she had portrayed,[30] and she anticipated a successful tour; instead, she met mixed reactions, primarily because of the play's liberal attitude towards 'fallen' women. In Toronto, the *World* praised Arthur's acting and declared that she presented the character of The Woman 'in a most artistic and finished manner' and 'with great poise and deliberation'; the *Daily Star*, on the contrary, called *The Eternal Magdalene* 'a very nasty play' and reported that the local Social Survey Committee was to investigate its improprieties. Regardless of the play's morality, Arthur's return to her home province caused excitement among Canadians generally because, as Denis Salter has pointed out, 'one of *their* artists, no matter how distant she had been, was now making a newsworthy comeback.'[31] Arthur's screen performance as the murdered nurse, Edith Cavell, in the 1918 film *The Woman the Germans Shot* aroused even stronger nationalistic feelings, especially when Arthur declared at a special screening in Hamilton that, while she loved Americans, she still believed that 'once a Canadian, always a Canadian.'[32] Driven by a deep-felt sense of patriotic duty, Arthur also participated in a variety of benefit performances in the United States and even worked part-time as a Red Cross volunteer. All of these activities helped her regain her position as one of America's most respected actresses and prepared the way for the most memorable phase of her career in the 1920s.

Another actress from Ontario, Maude Eburne (formerly of Bronte) also created a flurry of interest on the circuit when, in the spring of 1916, she toured in Edward Peple's popular Broadway hit *A Pair of Sixes*.[33]

Called 'the greatest character comedienne of the century,'[34] Eburne had recently become 'the most talked about actress in New York' following her Broadway début as Coddles, a love-starved English maid at work in a fashionable uptown New York household.[35] Eburne's amorous advances on the unwilling butler and her antics using the new-fangled telephone were carried out with so 'deft and confident' a hand that at her opening in Toronto she won her own curtain call at the close of the second act. Within the year, Toronto audiences also saw her in two more comic vehicles, *A Pair of Queens* and *Here Comes the Bride*.[36] After playing opposite Fred Stone and Will Rogers on Broadway, Eburne achieved modest fame as a character actress in Hollywood, her best-known movie role occurring in *Ruggles of Red Gap*, which starred Charles Laughton. By the time of her death in California in 1960 at age eighty-five, Eburne had played in over one hundred films.

Another Ontario actor, William Courtleigh of Guelph, who had made his stage début with John Dillon's company in the 1880s, was still going strong in the war years. After engagements with Fanny Davenport in *La Tosca* and with James A. Herne in Herne's own profitable hit *Shore Acres*, Courtleigh became a featured performer with such important stock organizations as the Empire Theatre Stock Company, New York, and the Castle Square Theatre Stock Company, Boston, and also played opposite noted comedienne Grace George.[37] In February 1916, Courtleigh came to Toronto in George Scarborough's *Oklahoma*, starring the popular Broadway ingénue Lenore Ulrich.[38] Although the play proved to be just one more 'Indian' melodrama of the day, Courtleigh was unanimously praised for his performance as the Indian chief Quannaha, a type of character in which he had specialized since he scored his first Broadway success in *Northern Lights*.[39] At war's end, Courtleigh's 'fine voice and bearing'[40] were once more evident when he returned to Toronto, again with Ulrich, in one of the season's most popular hits, *Tiger Rose*, a saga of Canada's North West, by Willard Mack (né Charles W. McLaughlin in Morrisburg, Ontario). Courtleigh's stage career continued unabated for the next decade until his death in 1934.[41]

During the war, two other ex-Ontarians, Ned Sparks (né Edward Arthur Sparkman of St Thomas) and Rapley Holmes (variously reported as being born in St Marys, Guelph, and 'Western Canada' in 1867) appeared together with William Collier in Toronto in their Broadway success, James Montgomery's *Nothing But the Truth* (Royal Alex, 29 October–3 November 1917). Sparks, one of the brightest comedians on the New York stage, had established himself originally as 'a singer of sweet southern songs' in his first big hit, *Little Miss Brown* in 1912 (*Variety*, 10 April 1957). He also participated in several Broadway musicals, among them *Jim Jam Jems* (with Joe E. Brown) and Victor Herbert's *My Golden Girl*. Because of Sparks's support of the Actors' Strike of 1918, New York producers eventually refused to book him and he headed for Hollywood to try his luck in the movies. There, until his retirement in 1948, he made a name playing deadpan comic characters in a variety of major screen productions, including *Imitation of Life* and *Wake Up and Live*.[42] He died in California in 1957.

Sparks's partner, Rapley Holmes (son of a Methodist minister),[43] began his stage career in Winnipeg. An imposing figure at 6′4″, Holmes became a character actor on Broadway, playing the 'Western type' in hits such as *The Round Up* and *Arizona* (Augustus Thomas). Later Broadway success with Jeanne Eagels in *Rain* (Clemence Randolf and John Cotton, adapted from Maugham's *Sadie Thompson*), 'the greatest dramatic triumph of 1922,'[44] placed him among the top ten stage actors at the time. Ill health forced him from the stage and he died at Strathroy, Ontario.

While Ontario-born performers continued to achieve prominence on the professional stage during the war, a substantial number of young actors from the province gave up promising careers to enlist in active military service. One Toronto lad, James Rennie, cut short a successful stint with the Northampton Players of Northampton, Massachusetts, to join the Royal Flying Corps. While stationed at the University of Toronto, he and several other actor-recruits in the Overseas Training Contingent formed a small amateur theatre company to entertain their colleagues and the general public.[45] On his return to the professional stage after the Armistice, Rennie won immediate recognition for his acting in *Moonlight and Honeysuckle* (1919, opposite Ruth Chatterton), *Shore Leave* (1922, opposite Frances Starr), and *The Great Gatsby* (1926). During the twenties, he also performed with several stock companies, chiefly Jessie Bonstelle's Detroit Civic Theatre troupe and the Lyceum Players of Rochester, New York. Later, he played leading man to Katherine Cornell in *Alien Corn* (1933) and ended his career as Buffalo Bill in a London revival of *Annie Get Your Gun* in 1958. He died in New York City in 1965.

The accomplishments of these Ontario-born stars, especially Anglin, Arthur, and Eburne, served as excellent examples for young actresses and helped to establish life in the professional theatre as a respectable vocation for women, since, despite the advances made by suffragists and the contributions of women generally to the war effort, the attitude still persisted that females on the commercial stage were of the *demi-monde* sort.[46] Even Mary Pickford's mother was initially unwilling to allow her 'innocent babies to associate with actresses who smoke.'[47]

The exodus of young Ontario-born aspirants to the professional stage continued throughout the First World War; for Canadians at home, their successes were heart-warming. Toronto audiences could look with admiration on Nella Jefferis, a brilliant actress in the city's Arts and Letters Club theatricals and a product of drama classes at the Toronto Conservatory of Music's School of Expression conducted by Douglas A. Patterson, a prominent figure in amateur theatre circles at the time. In 1916, Jefferis won roles on Broadway with O.P. Heggie in *Little Man*, with John Drew in Pinero's *The Gay Lord Quex*, and with John Barrymore in *Peter Ibbetson*, and in California in Oliver Morosco's *Pamela* before ill health forced her to return home. During the 1920s, she performed with distinction for local stock companies in Toronto and with the vaunted Hart House Players, and then played a significant role in the establishment of the Dominion Drama Festival in 1932. For her untiring efforts in the service of theatre in Canada, the directors of the DDF instituted their major award for best actress in her name in 1936. She died in October 1944.[48]

Another Torontonian to emerge from local amateur ranks was Louise Catherine Proctor, a product of the Toronto College of Music, directed by Harold Nelson Shaw.[49] After graduation, Proctor acted in Maude Adams's 1900 production of *L'Aiglon* (E. Rostand) and Annie Russell's *A Midsummer Night's Dream* in 1906–7. During the war, she understudied Laurette Taylor in the popular *Out There* and Ruth Rose in Otis Skinner's production of *Mister Antonio*. Through the 1920s, Proctor appeared in a series of Broadway shows, reaching her theatrical zenith in the road production of O'Neill's *Ah, Wilderness!* opposite George M. Cohan in the 1934–5 season. By the late 1930s, Proctor was one of the mainstays of the Actors' Colony summer theatre in Bala, Ontario, and through the 1940s and 1950s she performed regularly on radio and television on both sides of the border. She continued to act on Broadway in a variety of significant productions, including George S. Kaufman's 1944 hit, *The Late George Apley*, until her death in 1967.

Also a product of H.N. Shaw's drama classes, Toronto's Walter Huston (Houghston) made his stage début in the School of Music's annual production in 1901.[50] Huston acted for the next five years in Canada and the United States with a variety of companies headed by such leading actor-managers as Richard Mansfield and George H. Summers. At the outbreak of the First World War, Huston was touring in vaudeville with his wife Bayonne Whipple, but his stage career accelerated in 1924 with his first performance on Broadway in Zona Gale's *Mr. Pitt* and in Eugene O'Neill's *Desire Under the Elms* that same year. Then followed a succession of star roles in *Elmer the Great* (Ring Lardner) in 1928,

Catherine Proctor as Hermia in *A Midsummer Night's Dream*

Dodsworth (adapted from Sinclair Lewis) in 1934, and *Knickerbocker Holiday* (Maxwell Anderson and Kurt Weill) in 1938. Huston's equally distinguished film career included title roles in *Abraham Lincoln* (1930) and *Dodsworth* (1934) and an Academy Award–winning performance in *The Treasure of the Sierre Madre* (1948), directed by his son John. Huston died in Hollywood in 1950.

Though not nearly so well known as Huston, Charles Fletcher, another of H.N. Shaw's graduates and 'a Toronto boy and proud of it,' became a familiar face in stock companies in Toronto and Hamilton during the period.[51] Fletcher got his start on the professional stage as a last-minute substitute in H.W. Savage's production of *Parsifal* in Toronto; he later joined Miss Henrietta Crossman, toured with Miss Lulu Glaser, and went on to perform with the celebrated Carleton Opera, Red Mill, and Merry Widow companies. His involvement with local theatre spanned the next two decades. He made his last stage appearance in Hamilton with the Grand Players, in October 1932.

Resident Companies

Without a professional theatre of their own, many home-grown performers like Charles Fletcher advanced their careers by working for visiting companies, notably resident stock organizations that had begun to appear as the road system declined.[52] More responsive than itinerant troupes to the tastes of audiences in their 'home' cities, resident organizations occasionally gave local actors the opportunity to perform in the hope of discovering new talent and increasing box-office interest. For instance, in Toronto during the summer of 1914 three organizations featured talent from the area. At Shea's, a company headed by vaudeville star Miss Adele Blood engaged child actress Alice Dunn of Toronto,[53] as well as two Kingstonians, popular second man Edmund Abbey (né Frank Abernathey)[54], and Hubert Osborne.[55] Abbey, a graduate of Upper Canada College and the University of Toronto, had started with Julia Arthur, and played stock in various companies from Spokane to Halifax until his death in 1930. Osborne was the purported author of the highly successful comedy, *Shore Leave*, the progenitor of Vincent Youmans's popular 1924 musical *Hit the Deck*. At the Princess Theatre, Miss Percy Haswell, a respected stock-company manager in her fifth season in Toronto, hired Charles Fletcher, by then making a name in local stock. Haswell also engaged child actress Violet Dunn (Alice's sister), who after a short illustrious career on Broadway married prominent Hollywood director Hamilton McFadden.[56] At the Royal Alex, Miss Jessie Bonstelle, in her second summer in the city and mentor of many young Broadway stars, including Katherine Cornell, acquired leading lady Louise Catherine Proctor, who by that time had several Broadway roles to her credit.

Of the three competitors seen in Toronto the summer war began, only Percy Haswell's company returned the following year, but after a desultory shortened season was replaced by the newly established Edward H. Robins Players. Robins, formerly in Belasco's *The Easiest Way* and a lead in the Canadian-made film *The Motto on the Wall*,[57] had been introduced to Toronto audiences the previous year by Jessie Bonstelle. His new aggregation quickly won the hearts of wartime theatre-goers by featuring veteran Canadian actor Eugene Frazier[58] and local juvenile lead Harry G. Lyons,[59] and by producing two 'Canadian' plays – *The Argyle Case* by Harvey O'Higgins (once a journalist in Toronto) and *So Much for So Much* by Willard Mack. Frank C. Priestland of Hamilton managed the Players in their early years and later established his own touring company, the short-lived Royal Alexandra Players in 1916.[60]

For the duration of the war, Robins continued to employ local talent and to spotlight the work of Canadian playwrights, a notable example being the production of Harvey O'Higgins's sensational thriller, *The Dummy*, which starred a local actor, Alfred Woodhouse, in the title role.[61] By the end of the war, the Robins enterprise had become the foremost resident operation in the province, and played the Royal Alex every summer until 1922.

Resident companies operating in such cities as Hamilton, Ottawa, London, and Brantford during the war were also ready to give promising young actors a chance. In Hamilton, for example, two companies, George H. Summers's Mountain Theatre (in its eleventh season, with William E. Blake and Carol Arden as the current stars) and the Temple Stock Company at the Temple Theatre, provided opportunities for several area actors. From Newmarket, Ontario, George Summers had the distinction of hiring Walter Huston, in the days before Huston had become one of the great stars of American stage and screen.[62] Summers's own fortunes suffered a serious set-back when fire destroyed the original Mountain Park Playhouse in December 1914, and he was left without a permanent home for his company. As a consequence, Summers had to take up a career touring as the hilarious hero of the comedy *In Walked Jimmy* (Mrs Mini Jaffa) in which he was billed as 'Canada's Foremost Comedian.' After a stint on Broadway in the 1920s, he became a writer of comedy sketches for the CBC and film scenarios. He died in 1941.

At Hamilton's Temple Theatre, several resident companies in succession drew cast members from a growing contingent of talented Ontario actors;[63] the most prominent were the familiar Charles Fletcher and Edmund Abbey, as well as Douglas Dumbrille, a Hamilton native who had started on the stage with the Joseph Sellman Players at the Savoy Theatre and went on to play D'Artagnan in *The Three Musketeers* on Broadway for several years in the 1920s. He also appeared in James K. Hackett's 1923 production of *Macbeth* and in motion pictures, most notably *The Enchanted Cottage* (Henry Arthur Jones).[64]

Ottawa could count three resident companies in operation in the summer of 1914.[65] But by the Armistice, summer theatre had disappeared from Ottawa. Several stock companies, however, did take up residence in the winter seasons to fill open bookings left unclaimed by the declining touring system. Beginning with Ralph E. Cummings and his troupe at the Russell in December 1914, Ottawa hosted the Roma Reade Players at the St George Theatre (November 1915) and the Rialto Dramatic Players at the Français in January and February 1917. The Rialto's engagement represents the last appearance of stock theatre in the city until the early 1920s.

In smaller towns, resident stock occurred even more rarely. Brantford, for instance, experienced only one such company, the Edmund Keane Players (formerly the Roma Reade Players) for a short engagement in the summer of 1917, the last until after the war. Fred G. Brown, an old Brantford boy, was a member of the company and sang two of his compositions.[66] Under the pressure of wartime economy, it is clear that resident companies were driven to major urban centres with populations large enough to sustain theatre activities.

Independent Touring Companies

Most communities might not have experienced live professional theatre at all during the war had it not been for the efforts of several small independent troupes that played to audiences off the well-worn track. The most popular were the Marks Brothers, based at Christie Lake, Ontario, north-east of Kingston.[67] In the 1880s, R.W. 'Bob' Marks had founded the business and eventually formed a partnership with his six younger brothers. Dedicated to providing 'honest and orderly' entertainment, their travelling troupes earned the respect of audiences not only in Canada as far west as Winnipeg but across the north-eastern United States as well. The appeal of their productions rested in the brothers' shrewd selection of play material (almost always well-tried melodramas), their realistic staging, their sensational manner of presentation, and a polished and integrated acting style perfected over years of performance on the road.

To provide cohesion and continuity to the organization, three of the brothers headed up separate companies, all with similar aims but each with its own character. R.W. Marks managed Company No. 1, which featured his wife, May Bell, a veteran of many years in stock at Watertown, New York, with brother George and his wife Daisy in supporting roles. Company No. 2 was managed by Ernie Marks, whose wife Kitty Marks was leading lady. Tom Marks led the third troupe, which included his daughters Arlie and Gracie. All three companies were on the road at the start of the war, their criss-crossing patterns so carefully planned that most towns in southern Ontario saw at least one (and in some cases all three companies) once each season. In fact, for the first year or two of the war, when touring organizations from the States came through less frequently, Marks companies stepped in at Kingston and Hamilton to provide a substantial share of the season's bill.

Of the few Ontario-based travelling stock companies that survived the economic hard times of the war, the Marks Brothers' organization was the most prominent and ambitious. Tom Marks, in association with his daughter Arlie, appeared on the Number 1 circuit until 1920, while his brother Ernie carried on to the fall of 1923. Although May Bell and Bob Marks retired from the road before the end of the war, May Bell's theatrical activities continued into the 1930s.[68] Arlie and her husband Lindsay E. Perrin attempted to revitalize the organization in 1922 by conducting an extensive six-year tour that took them from Washington State to Newfoundland and back again.[69] Their return home in 1928 ended what was rightfully claimed at the time as the longest tour recorded by a travelling company. While Arlie Marks and her players lasted for at least another year, they never achieved the glory enjoyed by the original Marks Brothers theatrical enterprise.

Several other family-owned and -operated independent troupes toured small-town Ontario in the early years of the war and helped to fill in the gaps in the touring system's bookings. One noteworthy company, Perry's Peerless Players, owned and managed by G. Herbert Perry and his wife (both from Moncton, New Brunswick),[70] crossed the province in the 1914–15 season, with Dan Malloy and Hazel Corinne, a native of Hamilton,[71] in the principal parts. The Perrys, in the theatrical business for over twenty years, had visited Ontario several times previously with their players and their other venture, the Hi Perry Minstrels.

Husband-and-wife teams also included H. Wilmot Young and Marjorie Adams, the principals of the Young-Adams Stock Company, which played each year at Cornwall's Fair Week before embarking on its annual tour of the north-eastern United States and the Maritimes.[72] The Young-Adams company continued touring into the 1920s, but it

Mae Edwards Players, Novelty Orchestra

did not travel so far afield, preferring to frequent the Peterborough-Kingston area.

Mae Edwards (born in Lindsay) and her husband Charles ('Charlie') T. Smith (a one-time vaudevillian in the Murray Mackie Show) also formed a theatrical partnership, the Mae Edwards Players, which was seen several times in the province during the war, including a record twenty-nine-week run at the Family Theatre, Toronto.[73] Noted for her elegant costumes and diction, Edwards led the company in a standard mix of melodramas and light comedies. Her aggregation also doubled as a novelty orchestra, performing vaudeville between the acts of its plays and at charity benefits. The activities of her company throughout the 1920s were varied and far-reaching. Not only did the Players perform extensively in the New England states and travel regularly around the Atlantic region (with long runs in St John's and Halifax), they also took a cross-continent tour as far as the Dakotas featuring the sensational melodrama, *Dope*, which portrayed the evils of the narcotics trade in North America. On their return to the east coast, several members of the cast went to Broadway, but the majority stayed with the company into the 1930s, supplying many tiny Ontario communities with their last taste of the 'real old-time travelling show.' When the company disbanded in 1935, Miss Edwards and her husband retired to her home town, where she died in 1937.

The Joe E. Machan Associate Players, a family business run by

Machan and his daughters Gloria and Rosalind, played small towns from Sault Ste Marie to Woodstock and Chatham, before circling back to Sudbury on their only major tour of Ontario during the war.[74] Over the next few years, Rosalind, who played children's parts in her father's company, worked in stock theatre in the United States and with the Garrick Players, Ottawa; meanwhile, Gloria found a career performing stock in Peterborough. In the early 1920s, the Machan sisters formed their own company and appeared briefly in eastern Ontario.[75]

The Montrose Tabloid Stock Company, yet another family troupe, briefly toured the province with an assortment of saccharine tragicomedies. Built upon the talents of Gladys and Lillian Montrose, the company also featured 'Pictures in Black and White,' in which the cast posed, tableau-fashion, in scenes from the Bible, a novel attraction that drew as many as 1200 patrons a night.[76]

At least twenty other small troupes made brief appearances immediately before and just after the outbreak of war,[77] but they failed to show again in the province. Typical of them was the Sarah Gibney Stock Company, which operated in the St Thomas–London area and opened the new Griffin's Theatre in Chatham in 1913. Following a tour of western and northern Ontario in the summer of 1914, the company headed out west, where it eventually folded.[78] Gibney herself turned to vaudeville (she played briefly in 1915–16 in Windsor[79]) and then to the Redpath Horner Chautauqua organization in Chicago, with which she achieved modest success. She later retired to Otterville, Ontario, where she continued her interest in theatre by directing local amateur productions.[80]

Road life was difficult at the best of times for independent touring troupes, but the war only added to their problems. In one instance, the Rose Black Comedy Company arrived in St Catharines (August 1914) to present *The Ocean Waves* and *The Suffragette*, only to find that the theatre was without a production crew because they had all enlisted. The company further suffered an experience not uncommon in the theatre when its business manager absconded with the company's money and stranded fifteen 'ponies' at a local hotel, which seized their luggage for unpaid bills.

By war's end, small independent road companies had virtually disappeared from the province. Their fate only confirmed what was now clear: in an age when 'the moving picture show' could offer audiences a wider range of experience and a higher level of performance for half the price, it no longer made sense to eke out a living on the road. And it is also clear that United States' interests dominated the new moving-picture industry just as they had the professional touring system. In fact, despite attempts to establish film-production facilities in Toronto,[81] the situation had reached such a point at war's end that local cinemas began cooperating with the Canadian government to show only British and Canadian films in an attempt to counteract American control.[82]

The 1920s

Trans-Canada Theatres, Limited
Almost before the smoke of the First World War had dissipated, a consortium of Canadian and British businessmen proposed the creation of a nation-wide theatrical touring system linked by the country's railways as a means of breaking the American monopoly of the road.[83] Under the name of Trans-Canada Theatres, Limited, the consortium began buying up theatre chains across the country, primarily those of Canadian impresario Ambrose J. Small in Quebec and Ontario and the United Producing Company's operations in Western Canada. Ambrose Small's disappearance in December 1919, just as the take-overs had been completed, added an ominous note to Trans-Canada's inaugural season.

By the spring of 1920, the organization's first attractions began to arrive in Ontario. Percy Hutchison and Martin-Harvey's daughter, Muriel, in *The Luck of the Navy*, followed by H.V. Esmond in his own play, *The Law Divine*, and finally Grace George in *The Ruined Lady*, all played to audiences appreciative of seeing Canadian-backed travelling companies. Over the next two seasons, Trans-Canada delivered a diversity of important attractions that included tours by Sir John Martin-Harvey, Nigel Playfair's innovative production of *The Beggar's Opera*, and Oscar Asche's extravagant *Chu Chin Chow* and *Mecca*. Trans-Canada also sponsored tours by two popular Canadian organizations – the Winnipeg Kiddies and the celebrated soldier revue, the Dumbells. However, in 1922 Trans-Canada had difficulty finding enough quality 'all-English' shows to fill its 125 theatres and eventually was forced to book such ragtag items as *Boob McNutt* (starring Peterborough's own Danny Simon)[84] and *The Unloved Wife* (matinées 'for ladies only') – ironically, the very kind of mediocre shows the consortium had intended to replace. By October 1923, after announcing a deficit of $100,000, Trans-Canada closed and thus ended another dream of a national theatrical touring system.

British and American Touring Companies
Undaunted by the collapse of Trans-Canada, numerous theatre companies from the United Kingdom continued to tour the province on an independent basis, convinced that there was still a market for British-style entertainment among the growing population of British immigrants. Foremost among these were Dublin's Abbey Theatre Players,

in Lennox Robinson's *The White-Headed Boy*, and the indomitable Martin-Harvey, who carried out annual nationwide tours in a variety of high-spirited romantic melodramas typified by his favourite, *The Only Way* (Freeman Willis). Another exponent of romantic drama, but new to Ontario, was Montreal-born Matheson Lang,[85] a world-travelling actor-manager who came through the province several times, twice in the widely acclaimed production of his own play, *The Wandering Jew*.

Late in the decade, when mass immigration from Europe and increased Americanization of Canada's economic and cultural life threatened British-Canadian allegiances, London's popular stage sent a wave of 'all-British' delights, including famed music-hall entertainers George Robey, 'the Prime Minister of Mirth,'[86] and the greatest of them all, the diminutive Scottish entertainer Harry Lauder who appeared seven times in Toronto during the decade.

Mingled with these nostalgic favourites came splendid Shakespearean productions by the Stratford-upon-Avon Festival company in 1929, under the direction of Bridges Adams, and Florence Reed's highly regarded *Macbeth* (with sets by Gordon Craig), whose new stagecraft techniques challenged the tired production styles held over from late Victorian theatre.

The new mood of rebellion that characterized the 1920s was perhaps best captured by Noel Coward in his clever revue *This Year of Grace* and whimsical satire *Bitter Sweet*, which came to the province late in the decade.[87] Starring in the former was Toronto's own Beatrice Lillie, who had begun her stage career in local amateur theatricals before establishing herself as 'the leading revue-comedienne' on the London stage and one of Coward's favourite leading ladies.[88] Lillie first appeared on the commercial stage in Toronto in the trend-setting *Charlot's Revue of 1924*,[89] the show in which she made her professional début in North America and achieved instant stardom for her sketch of an addle-pated troop leader whose marching commands created hopeless confusion among the ranks. Lillie scored another hit later in Vincent Youman's *Oh, Please!*, this time lampooning Broadway musicals by playing not only the principal parts but the chorus and audience as well.[90] One of the theatre's longest-performing comediennes, she entertained troops in the Second World War and starred for Coward into the 1960s, overriding her turbulent marriage to Sir Robert Peel. Through the years, Lillie's distinctive cross-dressing and straight-faced delivery of naughty innuendoes became her trademark and influenced a whole generation of young actresses. She died in 1985 at the age of ninety-five.

Of all the British-based touring organizations at work in Ontario during the decade, Maurice Colbourne's London Company was unquestion-

Maurice Colbourne Company tour of *Fanny's First Play*, Act 3, 1929

ably the strongest and most important influence in the province and indeed in English Canada. Colbourne first came to Ontario in 1926 to help organize the English Repertory Theatre in Toronto and to champion Shavian drama as a bulwark against the crassly commercial American theatre. In 1928, he formed his own company and took the banner of Shaw and his contemporaries on several Dominion-wide jaunts that included extensive tours of outlying Ontario communities in 1928, 1929, and 1930.[91] As a result, many audiences were given their first taste of 'modern' drama through productions that, in terms of the excellence of the acting and staging techniques, were uniformly well above those usually provided by the American touring system. The impact was immediate and profound: whereas the plays had met with rejection or in some cases outright censorship only a few years before, they now were enthusiastically embraced by little theatre organizations in community after community. Colbourne's influence did not end with the little theatre movement, for he went on to establish ties with Canada that lasted into the early 1940s with the continuation of his cross-country tours.

The work of Colbourne and other British companies in the 1920s signalled a broadening of theatrical tastes that was also reflected in the New York road productions, ironically at a time when the closing of theatres meant fewer people could experience them. Nevertheless, important works by new American and European dramatists became regular features along what remained of the circuit. For example, Charles S. Gilpin's pioneering production of *The Emperor Jones*, which played Ontario in 1922, stands as the first of Eugene O'Neill's plays to be seen on the road, but it is doubly significant because Gilpin was the first

Afro-American actor to star in a major Broadway show. The newly founded Theatre Guild of New York broke artistic as well as racial barriers with presentations of Dorothy and Du Bose Heyward's *Porgy* (with an all-black cast) and an ambitious uncut version of O'Neill's epic *Strange Interlude*. In addition, Eva La Gallienne and her highly respected New York Civic Repertory brought their road productions of Molnar's *Liliom* and Sierra's *The Cradle Song*, while Bertha Kalich in Sudermann's *Magda* and Nance O'Neill in Jacinte Benavente's *The Passion Flower* proved that imaginative and intelligent works tastefully presented and well acted could survive on the road.

Margaret Anglin, Julia Arthur, and Catherine Proctor, having reached maturity in their craft, achieved their finest hours on Broadway and the circuit during this period. Anglin's all-star touring revival of Sardou's *Diplomacy*, seen in Toronto in April 1928[92] and regarded as one of the great theatre events of the decade, brought together some of the best-known personalities of the day, including Charles Coburn, William Faversham, Jacob Ben Ami, Rollo Peters, Cecilia Loftus, and Tyrone Power, Sr, in what was for some of them their swan song on the legitimate stage. Anglin also added to her laurels by her performances of Greek dramas on Broadway – *Iphigenia in Aulis* and *Electra* – as well as *The Trial of Joan of Arc*, a forerunner of Bernard Shaw's more famous *Saint Joan*. Coincidentally, it was Anglin's fellow Ontarian Julia Arthur who performed the title role in the first American touring production of Shaw's masterpiece in 1924. For Arthur, whose comeback to the stage was already a major triumph, the role turned out to be the most successful she ever took on, and she visited several Ontario cities in 1925 as part of two trans-continental tours.[93] After two years on the road, Arthur retired again; she died in 1950.

Catherine Proctor gave several guest appearances with Vaughan Glaser's stock company in Toronto, before playing to rave reviews on Broadway in Maugham's *East of Suez* (with Florence Reed), and then in Tarkington's *Bristol Glass* and the Actors' Theatre presentation of Wilde's *The Importance of Being Earnest*.[94] Proctor was again seen in Toronto in a 1926 road production of Charles Coglan's *The Royal Box*, with Walker Whiteside.[95] An actress who always sought interesting challenges, Proctor appeared a year later on movie screens in several American cities during a trial run of *The Ghost Parade*, an Anglo-Indian motion picture about life in India.[96]

Proctor was only one of many Canadian actresses seeking their fortunes on the silver screen. The most successful was still Toronto's Mary Pickford, who received a tumultuous welcome when she returned to her home town with husband Douglas Fairbanks in 1924. By the end of the

Julia Arthur as Saint Joan, Princess Theatre, Toronto, 1925

1920s, Canadian actresses had taken the movie world by storm, winning Academy Awards three years running – Pickford for *Coquette* (1929), Norma Shearer for *The Divorcee* (1930), and Marie Dressler for *Min and Bill* (1931). The glamour of the Oscar ceremonies and the burgeoning Hollywood movie industry, however, stood in stark contrast to the demoralized state of the live stage back home in Canada. There, the Shuberts had already taken steps to turn their theatres from coast to coast into 'talkie houses' in order to capitalize on the spectacular popularity of motion pictures with sound. As American movie chains aggressively acquired playhouses for conversion into cinemas, Montreal and Toronto were the only communities left with any venue at all for live professional theatre. Furthermore, there is evidence that when Famous Players Canadian Corporation was taken over by Paramount Publix Corporation of New York, theatre companies were actively prevented from playing their houses, a policy that defied Canadian laws forbidding combines. Although protests were made and the federal minister of labour promised an investigation, nothing transpired.[97] As a result, the once grand live-stage circuit, despite its many faults, received its death blow.

Resident Stock Companies

After the First World War, resident stock theatre in Ontario experienced rapid growth as increasing numbers of American actors sought alternative employment to the shrinking touring system.[98] The presence in Ontario of so many American actors and companies, some all the way from the West Coast, underlines just how desperate the situation was becoming for theatre people in the 1920s. Faced with changing tastes and economic hard times, with the popularity of movies and the advent of radio, as well as increased costs of travelling and play production, American stock companies had to contend with a dwindling market and were forced to look for new audiences. With the decline of the New York–based touring system, Canada, which had always been a lucrative theatrical market, was thus regarded as a potentially profitable new field for unemployed companies.

In Toronto, a new permanent company headed by Vaughan Glaser took up residence at the Uptown in the fall of 1921.[99] Prominent in stock theatre in Columbus, Cleveland, and Detroit since 1903, Glaser had also worked on the circuit with Mrs Fiske in *Hedda Gabler* before the war. He expressed his determination to offer Toronto more than 'bedroom farces and sex plays,' and he dedicated his company to providing high-class family entertainment, mainly middle-of-the-road items and the occasional musical comedy to appeal to the younger generation. His annual Christmas pantomime rivalled anything seen on the touring stage and drew as many as 100,000 patrons during a run of thirty-four performances. Avoiding any serious drama, Glaser's company played to packed houses almost without exception over its seven-year stay in the city, establishing a record of over 2200 performances of 214 different plays.

Following the example of resident companies in the past, Glaser made a point of headlining Canadian talent, featuring the already familiar Catherine Proctor and Charles Fletcher, as well as Hamiltonian Fred Kirby, a fourteen-year veteran with the Glaser organization, and Lois Landon, a gifted actress and interpretive dancer from Toronto who later became Glaser's wife. Other Canadians appearing over the years included May Bell Marks, Peggy Piggot, John Holden, and Hal Thompson. Holden, who started with the Jessie Bonstelle Players, later founded the Actors' Colony Theatre, a highly successful summer-stock venture, which ran between 1934 and 1941 at Bala in Ontario's Muskoka cottage district.

Always an innovator, Glaser published an informative newsletter, *The Vaughan Glaser Players Bulletin*, opened a successful but short-lived branch operation in Hamilton in April 1925, and teamed up with O.P. Heggie and his English Players in Toronto for three summers in order to meet increasing competition from British repertory stock companies setting up in the city.

When the Uptown became a movie house late in the summer of 1926, Glaser moved his company to the smaller Victoria Theatre, where he continued to September 1928, except when temporarily relieved by the Malcolm Fassett Players in September 1927. Recognizing that his popularity had run its course, Glaser left the stage to pursue interests in radio and vaudeville in Toronto. After several unsuccessful attempts to revive resident theatre in the 1930s, he made his way to Broadway and then to Hollywood, where he found a career in the movies, his most notable role being Judge Cullman in *Arsenic and Old Lace* with Cary Grant. He died in California at the age of eighty-six.

Throughout his seven years in Toronto, Glaser had to compete not only with Broadway road shows, but also with a number of rival stock companies beginning with the H. Campbell-Duncan Players in May 1923 at the Grand Opera House and, at the Royal Alex, the Royal Players (headed by Norval Keedwell and featuring local amateurs Grace Webster and Basil Loughrane) in 1923 and the Metropolitan Players from Rochester, New York, in 1924. His first major challenge, however, came from the Cameron Matthews Players, who began a winter season at the Princess Theatre in February 1923 and offered a sparkling bill of works by Shaw, Pinero, Barrie, and Wilde.[100] This impressive new aggregation was headed by Matthews, formerly with Glaser and Mrs

Patrick Campbell. Matthews's next few seasons in Toronto were rocky
ones during which he temporarily lost control of his company to T.
Richard Maurice, his business manager, and faced a strong challenge
from the George Vivian Musical Comedy Company at the Regent in the
1925 spring season.[101] When former cast members Charles Hampden
and Hugh Buckler subsequently set up rival companies at the Comedy
Theatre and the Royal Alex respectively, Matthews recognized that the
Toronto theatre scene had reached its saturation point and embarked on
a cross-Canada tour between October 1925 and January 1926, which
unhappily failed to attract audiences, as did a less ambitious trip to the
West in the spring of 1927.

Despite his difficulties, Matthews was responsible for bringing to
Toronto several important actors besides Hampden and Buckler, among
them Ernita Lascelles (late of the Northampton Players), Pauline Armi-
tage (formerly with Beerbohm Tree) and Barry Jones, a young British
war veteran who had débuted brilliantly with F.R. Benson and later performed with the Glaser Players and Maurice Colbourne. Matthews also
introduced Jane Keenleyside of London, who, under the stage name Jane
Aldworth and later as Jane Mallett, went on to become one of Canada's
most noted comediennes.[102] Starting her career under Bertram Forsyth at
Hart House Theatre at the University of Toronto, Aldworth appeared
with various stock companies in Toronto and with the Actors' Colony
Theatre at Bala. In addition to being a star in the yearly variety show
Spring Thaw through the 1960s, she became a favourite on radio and
television in such popular domestic comedy series as *The Craigs* and
in dramatic roles for Andrew Allan's 'Wednesday Night' and 'Stage'
productions. A year after her death in 1984, the main auditorium at
Toronto's St Lawrence Centre was named after her in recognition of
her long-standing contributions to Canadian theatre.

Matthews's ties with Toronto did not end with his intense struggles to
win audiences in the 1920s. Following his travels westward and engagements with stock companies in the United States and Canada,[103] he
attempted unsuccessfully to revive his English Players in 1931 and 1932
and to establish the Toronto Repertory Theatre in the mid-1930s, around
which time he also opened a School of the Theatre. After working in
radio drama and with local amateur groups, he reportedly retired to
Barry's Bay, Ontario; he died there in 1958.

The intricate history of the Matthews-Buckler-Hampden period indicates how tenuous were the fortunes of stock companies in the rapidly
changing entertainment scene through the mid-1920s. What followed
was a gradual slowing and stabilizing of activities.

In the fall of 1926, the Empire Theatre opened its doors as a home of

resident stock in opposition to the Glaser company at the Uptown. Originally a movie and vaudeville house, the Empire had been acquired by
the Theatre Guild of Canada, a powerful organization that emerged in
the 1920s to support the on-going struggle for a quality professional
theatre in Canada. Two prominent local theatre personalities, Major
John Mood and his wife, were engaged to manage the theatre and to
establish a company with the assistance of Maurice Colbourne, from
Stratford-upon-Avon's Memorial Theatre and a recent hit in his American début as Denis in Shaw's *Saint Joan*. Colbourne secured an excellent group of performers, including Toronto actors Betty Brough and
Florence McGee from the earlier Cameron Matthews company. Directing duties were taken over by Victor Tandy, a product of the Birmingham Repertory Theatre and a former director of the English Players in
Boston.

The English Repertory Theatre fulfilled its aims of offering high-class
entertainment with a distinctly English flavour, much like its predecessors, but business at the box office did not materialize. In January 1927,
Tandy and Phyllis Coghlan (from repertory in Australia and England)
left the cast to set up a subsidiary stock company at Hamilton's Grand
Theatre, where a warm reception convinced the Toronto cast to join the
Hamilton contingent for the following year.

As a consequence, the Empire in Toronto presented an entirely new
company for the 1928–9 season, headed by veteran American trouper
Edith Taliaferro. Sister of film and stage star Mabel Taliaferro, Edith had
played Toronto many times before, most recently with the Robins company, and she brought to her current position a knowledge of local audiences that showed in her judicious choice of material. Less restrictive and
more ambitious than the English companies before hers, Taliaferro's
troupe offered a mixture of Pinero, Barrie, and Sardou with lighter pieces
from Broadway playwrights. The acting company too was more cosmopolitan and included American and English actors, as well as a liberal
sprinkling of Canadians, notably Edmund Abbey (earlier with the Robins
Players), Jane Aldworth (back from her tour with Cameron Matthews),
and Grace Webster (from Hart House and the Maurice British Players).

Although Taliaferro led the Empire to a successful season, fending off
competition from the Charles L. Wagner company at the Royal Alex in
the process, she did not return in the fall of 1929; instead, she moved
to the Victoria Theatre, where the management was struggling to replace the Vaughan Glaser Players. Slotted between the Savoy Musical
Comedy Company in the fall and the Lyric Musical Comedy Company
in the spring, Taliaferro played a truncated season with such headline
names as Georgette Cohan (daughter of George M. Cohan), but the com-

pany's lacklustre program and weak supporting cast failed to bring in patrons. In the meantime, at the Empire, Taliaferro's replacement, Marjorie Foster, who had been with the Holman Players in 1919–20, guided her company through an equally undistinguished season.

In the 1929–30 season, the Victoria ostensibly ceased to offer live theatre, except for a brief but fruitless attempt to turn it into a permanent home for the Dumbells. The Empire in contrast came back stronger than ever under the management of George M. Keppie and his leading lady, Marjorie Foster. Appearing in several minor roles was Cosette Le Gassick, who, as a local school girl, had made her début with Vaughan Glaser in 1923.[104] Under her stage name Cosy Lee, she was to become, along with her fellow cast member Jane Aldworth, one of Canada's best-known stage and screen personalities. John Holden, formerly with Glaser, joined the troupe late in the season, and under his direction the Empire Players continued over the next two years.[105] After that, permanent stock was absent from Toronto for another decade.

The history of resident companies in Toronto during the 1920s was extremely complex, as various troupes jockeyed with each other to gain supremacy. It is clear, however, that the city found it difficult to support more than one permanent company at a time. Those that offered a variety of fare were more likely to endure. Quite possibly, as a result of the wide range of entertainment brought in by the touring system and movie chains, the general public had become accustomed to a variety of attractions and found a steady diet of modern British and European dramatists was not to their liking.

The same pattern was discernible in Hamilton, where the coming and going of resident stock companies through the 1920s seemed nearly as frantic. In September 1918, a company made up of performers previously seen at the Temple and Lyric during the war established itself at the Savoy and ran a forty-two-week winter season, the first since the early years of the century. It played a wide array of theatrical works, the most popular being *Parlor, Bedroom and Bath* by Charles W. Bell, a former Hamilton lawyer who had turned to playwriting in New York.

Throughout its run, the Savoy company had to compete against popular touring attractions coming to the Grand Theatre, as well as a challenge from the Northampton Players of Northampton, Massachusetts, engaged by the rival Lyric Theatre in May 1919. When the Savoy company did not continue into the next season, attention focused subsequently on the Grand Theatre, where the Holman Associate Players took up residence in May 1920 under the direction of the company's owner and lead man, Arthur Holman, and his leading lady, Marjorie Foster, seen later at the Empire Theatre, Toronto. The Lyric immediately retali-

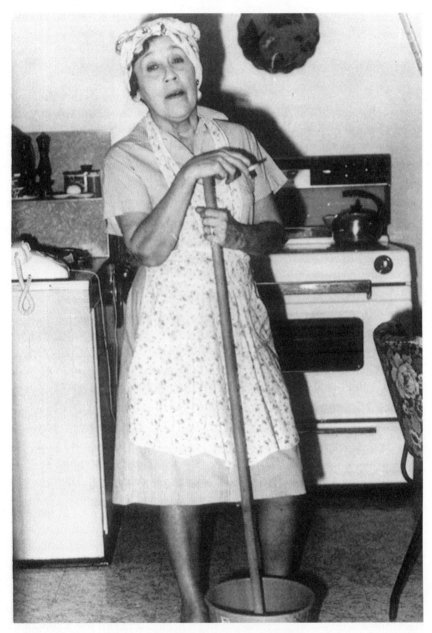

Cosette (Cosy) Lee began her lengthy career with Vaughan Glaser in 1923 and was still performing after the Second World War with stock companies such as the International Players.

ated with its own rival summer troupe, led by Harold Hevia of the Montreal Orpheum Theatre. Neither company lasted into the fall.

Resident stock again appeared at the Grand Theatre in the summer of 1921, when the William A. Grew Players provided a full winter of productions, after a successful stay in London the previous year. For the new 1921–2 season, Grew mounted a second company at the Majestic Theatre, London, which he alternated briefly with his Hamilton troupe. In addition to importing New York stars as headline attractions, he also sent his comic specialist James Swift on a brief tour of the province in *Charley's Aunt*. Grew found no enthusiasm for his innovations or brand of theatre and he withdrew his companies from Ontario in January 1922.

Several months later, in May 1922, Grew's place at the Grand was taken by the Milton–St Clair Resident Players, a company composed of actors mostly from the West Coast of the United States, which offered seven weeks of summer stock. The owner and controller of the organization, Jack Milton (born James M. Tuthill), had worked with George M. Cohan, the Essanay Moving Picture Company, and several road productions in Ontario. His partner, Robert 'Bobby' St Clair, billed as 'Canada's Peppiest Comic,' came from the St Clair theatrical family of California. The Milton–St Clair company began as the Imperial Players in Kitchener and opened there in the fall of 1921. The following January, the company under its new name located at the Griffin's Opera House, Guelph, for eight weeks with occasional excursions to Chatham, Owen Sound, and Woodstock. After its Hamilton engagement, the Milton–St Clair organization returned to Kitchener for a final run in January 1923 before it too disappeared from the province. Though their stay was short-lived, these performers from the West Coast provided stark evidence of how far actors were prepared to travel in their search for new markets for live theatre.

In the summer of 1923, the Lyric was the only theatre in Hamilton to present resident stock. The appearance of Hamilton native Jane Seymour as leading lady of the new company caused a great deal of local interest and merited a civic reception at the opening. With a program definitely geared to comic material, the new company had a profitable season. In October it moved to the Temple Theatre, and continued there for the next two years.

What followed was a succession of unsuccessful attempts to establish resident theatre in Hamilton. In September 1925, the Vaughan Glaser Hamilton Players occupied the Capitol Theatre, and offered a program of productions transferred from Glaser's Toronto operation. Audiences, however, were not impressed, and the company closed after sixteen weeks. Members of Glaser's unemployed Players promptly created the

Gladys Gillan Savoy Players and performed at the Savoy through 1926. When the Gillan troupe folded in November 1926, several actors regrouped as the Lyric Theatre Guild Players, a company that lasted only until February 1927.

The Lyric company's failure was apparently precipitated by the arrival in January 1927 of the English Players from Toronto's Empire Theatre to reopen the Grand, which had been closed since a fire in September 1926. Their anticipated arrival inspired one local drama reviewer to exclaim ecstatically: 'At last, after waiting for years, Hamilton has an English repertoire company in its midst, doing English plays.'[106] With director Victor Tandy and leads Phyllis Coghlan and Maurice Colbourne, the troupe undertook an ambitious program of British plays, and performed without interruption until April 1927.

That summer, the Lyric Theatre took bold advantage while the English Players vacationed and offered an eight-week season featuring Jane Seymour and stock actors from Toronto and Hamilton. Though they made every effort to attract audiences, even offering 'two for the price of one' ticket deals, they could not produce enough interest to extend their engagement.

The 1927–8 season in Hamilton got under way with two companies in residence – the English Players again at the Grand and the Shirley Grey Players at the Lyric. The latter closed after only four weeks, followed unaccountably by the English Players in December. It can only be assumed that, as in Toronto, the infusion of exclusively British drama into local theatre was not for the tastes of the general public.

Sadly, as a result of company closings over the period, many actors were stranded in Hamilton and had to take whatever employment they could. For example, Emmet Vogan, recently with the Gillan and Lyric companies, became master of ceremonies at the Temple Theatre for Abe Rosenthal's Tiny Town Follies – 'the greatest gang of baby stars ever seen in one show.' Others, like Frank Bond and Zora Garver (from the defunct Lyric summer troupe) and Florence McGee and Victor Tandy (of the English Players) ended up playing dramatic sketches between the feature films at the Tivoli. Tandy alone stayed in Hamilton and became drama coach at the Conservatory of Music and a moving force in the development of the Hamilton Players Guild.

Optimism for a permanent company ran high when a branch of the Galvin Players took up residence at the Grand in September 1928. The Hamilton troupe was one of six operated in the United States and Canada by the Galvin Producing Company. All were run on essentially the same principles – elaborate but tasteful advertising, solid management practices, and a tightly organized acting corps and efficient production methods. It was a family business founded by John A. Galvin at the National Theatre, Philadelphia, before the war. The Hamilton troupe was indeed a family affair, with Galvin's daughter Irene as leading lady and her husband, H.A. McAdam, born and educated in Toronto, as general manager. It had just been part of a phenomenal eighty-three-week engagement in Ottawa and anticipated a similar triumph in Hamilton. However, the absence from the company of Irene's uncle, Johnny Galvin, veteran comic actor and mainstay of the Ottawa contingent, combined with strong competition from touring attractions, forced it to withdraw in November 1928 and return to Ottawa. Several stranded cast members formed the Grand Players and continued to perform for two more weeks, but despite promises to be back after Christmas they never returned.

Hamilton was without resident stock until the Wright Players appeared at the Grand in October 1929. Part of a theatrical conglomerate containing a dozen distinct companies in various American cities, the Wright Players were headed by Lex B. Luce and Mary Ann Dentler, who planned a regular season in the city. However, the stock-market crash that same month forced owner W.H. Wright to withdraw the company after four weeks. Thus ended attempts to establish permanent resident stock in Hamilton in the 1920s. It would not be until 1932 that audiences would see another such endeavour.

Throughout the 1920s, the city of London also witnessed efforts to institute resident stock. The work of William A. Grew's Majestic Players at the Majestic Theatre in the spring of 1920, through the 1920–1 season, and into the fall of 1921 seemed promising, but when Grew set up a second company in Hamilton, he clearly overextended his resources, and both companies closed as a consequence. When the Grew Players left in January 1922, London did not see resident theatre again until the 1924–5 season, when a company of American stock performers led by Peggy Coudray and Edward Cullen presented a bill of romantic comedies and detective mysteries, as well as two musicals: *Irene*, for which they engaged twenty London girls to form the chorus line, and *Mary*, which featured Howard Blair, 'America's foremost female impersonator.'

In 1925, the venue and the company changed from the Majestic to the Grand, but Edward Cullen remained leading man; over the next three years, he played to a succession of leading ladies, among them London-born Lorna Perdue, and eventually reunited with Coudray in the 1927–8 season, the last for the company in the city. During its London stay, the company made several sorties to surrounding communities such as Galt and Woodstock; in fact, for a brief time Edward Cullen tried to set up a resident troupe in Chatham.

It was April 1930 when the next resident company came to London. Headed by Myrtle Bigden and John Driscol (formerly with Fiske O'Hara), the Imperial Players opened at the Palace Theatre after four years of resident stock in Toronto. By sharing the program with feature movies and changing plays twice weekly, the company managed to last for a month. No match for the new talking pictures (the first 'talkies' had already been seen in London that year), the Imperial Players disappeared, and resident stock was not seen in the city for the next twenty years.

Ottawa's experience of resident theatre in the 1920s paralleled London's to some degree, for it was not until several years after the war that each city welcomed its first company. In Ottawa, in September 1921, the Orpheum Players opened at the Dominion Theatre, under the direction of Harold Hevia (formerly of the Lyric Players, Hamilton). The organization began with a lively program of stock favourites, but in October the Dominion Theatre burned down, and the Players had to be relocated to the Russell Theatre for nine weeks. They then moved to the Family Theatre in January and played there until the end of their twenty-six-week run in March 1922. At that point, the whole company was reorganized under a new manager, Jack Soanes, and given a new name, the Garrick Players. It continued at the Family for the next ten months, but succumbed financially in December 1922.

A great deal of publicity preceded the opening presentation by the H. Campbell-Duncan English Players, Maugham's *Too Many Husbands*, at the Russell in October 1923. Following its auspicious première, the company (seen earlier that year at the Grand, Toronto) embarked on a season of ambitious productions that included Shaw's *Pygmalion*, Wilde's *The Importance of Being Earnest*, and Webster's *Daddy Long Legs*. Dwindling audiences, however, indicated that the company's reach far exceeded its grasp, and by December it too had ceased operations.

In February 1927, the Galvin Players at the Capitol Theatre began one of the longest and most successful engagements of a resident stock company outside Toronto during the period – 123 weeks of varied entertainment – carried out in the inimitable Galvin style, smoothly and efficiently, and with consistent quality. Wise management was also an important factor in the company's Ottawa achievements; it shrewdly negotiated to have the Capitol's name changed to the Galvin Theatre and thus established an enviable level of rapport with the community. Records are not yet available to explain why the Galvin Players left Ottawa in early December 1929, but possibly the stock-market crash forced the parent organization to retrench and recall its farflung subsidiaries. In any event, their departure from Ottawa brought to an end nearly three years of resident stock productions in the city.

The Galvins' place was quickly taken by the Oscar O'Shea Players in December 1929, and their theatre was renamed the Embassy. O'Shea, a native of Peterborough, had run his own company for thirty-seven years, seven of them in Milwaukee. His current leading lady was Frances Jean Robertson of Calgary; other Canadians in the cast were Emmet O'Shea, Oscar's brother, William Yule from Kingston, and, later, Mary Nancy Duncan, claimed in the Toronto *Telegram* to be 'the best-known Canadian-born actress in America.'[107] O'Shea's selection of plays was a happy combination of conventional stock repertory, including his personal favourite, *The Rosary* (Edward E. Rose), in which he had toured extensively. By April 1930, Nancy Duncan and Dwight Meade became leading actors, and the O'Shea Players continued at the Embassy for another year before they were ruined by the Great Depression.

Throughout the 1920s, Ottawa also received visits from several touring companies from Paris, France, that gained enthusiastic response from the city's French-speaking population. Beginning with the Grand Guignol Players in October 1923, Ottawa found itself to be an annual stopping point for the Théâtre de la porte St Martin each year until 1928. The visits became so popular that when the company did not return in 1929, the Ottawa Little Theatre invited the French Musical Company of Paris as a replacement, thereby enabling the tradition to continue for one more year.

Like other cities in the province, Kingston saw its first resident stock organization in September 1921, when the Rex Stock Company, following a successful trial run in Owen Sound the previous year, was brought to the Grand Opera House by Trans-Canada Theatres, Limited. Rex Snelgrove, owner and manager of the company, was an expatriate Englishman who had run the Wilson Avenue Theatre, Chicago. His wife, leading lady Zana Vaughan, had played stock theatre in Regina, Saskatoon, and on the West Coast; together they headed the cast, which spotlighted Kingston's own William Yule and Gloria Machan, daughter of Joe Machan of the original Machan Associate Players.

The Rex Company relied on an assortment of New York stage hits, along with vaudeville acts, in the style of the earlier travelling shows, and such gimmicks as play-naming contests. An unusual feature of the company's stay in Kingston was its procedure of playing the first half of each week in its home city of Kingston and shifting the production for the latter half to a community within easy travelling distance, initially Peterborough and then several months later Brockville.

The Rex Company played in the Kingston-Peterborough-Brockville area until January 1924 and then moved to St Catharines for the rest of the season. Following a stint in northern Michigan in the early fall of 1924, the company was again seen in St Catharines, where it arranged an

eight-week run at the Capitol Theatre. In December 1924, the Rex organization opened its next enagagement – and apparently its last – in
Chatham. Audiences were obviously pleased by Snelgrove's choice of
plays and players, for he and his company lasted from 25 December
1924 to 14 March 1925 before making their exit from the province.

The sporadic Ontario appearances of the Rex Company over three-
and-a-half years give some indication of the increasing difficulties that
companies experienced in obtaining bookings, as more and more theatres were turned into movie-houses. The Rex Company's system of
alternating between two cities, however, did offer a method for maintaining full employment over a season and keeping live theatre in towns
and cities otherwise no longer served by touring companies.

Another stock organization, the Jane Hastings Players, also attempted
to set up residency in the Kingston-Brockville area at about the same
time as the Rex Company. After several appearances in Brockville and
Kingston between September 1923 and September 1925, the Hastings
company finally secured the Grand Theatre in St Catharines as a permanent home for the 1926 spring season. Just when they were about to
finish their four-month engagement, a sudden and 'mysterious' fire
destroyed the building and all the company's props and costumes. In an
admirable gesture of generosity, former patrons arranged a benefit performance to help cover the company's losses. Over the next two years,
the Hastings organization revived and reorganized, playing engagements
in St Thomas and Brockville, as well as Ithaca and Lowville in upper
New York state.

In October 1928, Jane Hastings and Her Associate Players (as the
company was now called) made a triumphant return to St Catharines and
offered theatre-goers four weeks of up-scaled productions; nevertheless,
the company was forced to split its weekly bill of plays with the neighbouring city of Brantford, where it played an additional month at the
Brant Theatre. At the end of its run in April 1929, the Players vanished
from the province, another casualty of the severe economic times.

Though it was a small community, the town of Stratford attracted
Margaret Cameron and her company to the Majestic Theatre in the summer of 1921 to replace the usual vaudeville, which that season was not
up to the management's standards. Assisted by Jack Milton and Robert
'Bobby' St Clair (later to form their own company), the Cameron troupe
did manage to give a better-than-average level of performance of some
venerable Broadway hits and stayed until the end of the summer. In the
following summer, Margaret Cameron again appeared at the Majestic
with Harry Lockhard as her leading man. As with so many companies
during the 1920s, the Majestic Players were not seen again.

A small resident stock organization that seemed to possess more tenacity than others was the Marie Gladke Players, who performed in several cities during the period. One of their first and longest engagements took place in Kitchener, where besides introducing Jack Milton and 'Bobby' St Clair to local audiences and subsequently running in competition with them, the Gladke Players performed almost continuously from January to October 1921, except for a month when they alternated between Kitchener and Galt. Over the next three years, the company made brief appearances at Kingston, Kitchener, Brantford, and London, and for the last time in the province at Ottawa's Majestic Theatre in July 1925. Although it offered traditional stock theatre fare with the usual vaudeville between the acts, the Gladke organization never seemed to be able to secure a permanent booking, and during its short history, the company drifted into that undefined area between the legitimate and vaudeville stage. Marie Gladke herself exemplified the dogged persistence shown by many actress-managers working to establish careers in an often ruthless and demanding profession.

Independent Touring Companies
Efforts to revive independent travelling stock in the 1920s nearly always ended in failure; even the touring companies mounted by such experienced men as Edward H. Robins and William A. Grew, who knew the Ontario theatre scene intimately, did not do well. A few itinerant troupes, namely, the Marks Brothers companies, the Mae Edwards Players, and the Young-Adams partnership survived into the 1920s, but even they were increasingly curtailed in their efforts. However, several organizations did attempt to win audiences by presenting a different kind of fare. For example, the Dumbells, the great Canadian soldier revue, took to the road after the war and toured annually until 1933. A similar venture was the 1921 Ontario tour of *Mademoiselle from Armentières*, a funny and touching dramatization of army life at the front produced by the Varsity Veterans of the University of Toronto.[108] Although the theme had already been treated in such war dramas as *The Better 'Ole*, the play brought to local audiences a uniquely Canadian view of the events overseas.

Some troupes offered variety entertainment; the Pierrot Players, for instance, travelled from Stratford to Ottawa in February 1919, presenting 'the brightest scenes' from English musical comedies. The company was especially noteworthy because the featured performer, Eugene Lockhart, was a native of London, Ontario, who in his teens had performed with Beatrice Lillie[109] and by the age of twenty was on Broadway. Following his current tour, he went to Hollywood, where he became a famous supporting actor in over three hundred movies, the most notable being *The House on 42nd Street* and *Leave Her to Heaven.* He died in 1957.

One type of entertainment that did flourish in the 1920s was the Chautauqua, which packaged week-long programs of recitals, readings, one-person character sketches, and dramatic productions, and offered them on a subscription basis to small communities along a defined circuit.[110] Chautauqua made its first appearance in the province at Cornwall in August 1914, the highlight being a production of *The Taming of the Shrew* given by the Ben Greet Players. Greet found the experience of performing on the Chautauqua circuit to his liking, for he and his company played every summer from then through 1918. The Greet Players' successors included companies headed by Percy Vivian, Glen Walls, Alice Campbell, and Martin Erwin. In 1931, with the Depression in full force, the Chautauqua economized by cutting drama from the programs; one of the last recorded companies was directed by Duckworth Allison at Scott Park, Hamilton.

The 1930s

Surprisingly for a period so fraught with economic problems, touring companies in the 1930s offered the most mature and forceful productions yet seen on the commercial circuit. Some of the greatest entertainers on both sides of the Atlantic visited Ontario over the decade, and names such as Helen Hayes, Katherine Cornell, Sybil Thorndike, and John Gielgud all appeared in Toronto. Ontario-born performers on the international stage once again were well represented in touring productions coming into the Royal Alex. Over the decade audiences saw Jean Adair (born Violet McNaughton in Bruce County), one of Canada's most popular elocutionists,[111] together with Toronto's own Catherine Proctor in one of the decade's greatest moments when they teamed with George M. Cohan in the New York Theatre Guild's touring production of *Ah, Wilderness!* (Eugene O'Neill). The seasoned Bea Lillie was seen once more in Toronto, this time in *At Home Abroad.* Local actors Florence McGee and Patricia Godfrey appeared on the circuit for the first time, the former in Clifton Webb's production of *The Importance of Being Earnest*[112] and the latter in the trial production of Charles Morgan's *The Flashing Stream.*[113] Several of Ontario's most famous native sons also made their first professional appearances in the province during the 1930s. First was black actor Richard B. Harrison, born in London, who won acclaim for his portrayal of 'the Lawd' in Marc Connelly's Pulitzer Prize–winning play *The Green Pastures.*[114] Next came Raymond Massey, son of wealthy industrialist

Richard B. Harrison, whom Brooks Atkinson called 'an inspired man' possessed of
'spiritual radiance,' as 'the Lawd' in *The Green Pastures*

Chester Massey and brother of the future governor-general, who performed in the première of *The Shining Hour* (Keith Winter) with his wife Adrienne Allen; Massey later became best known for his television series *Dr Kildare* and for his title role in the film *Abe Lincoln of Illinois*.[115] Walter Huston, who had also played Lincoln with some success, was back in Toronto to present another of his famous creations, the title role of his Broadway hit, *Dodsworth* (Sydney Howard). Huston repeated his characterization of Dodsworth in the film version several years later. Another Ontario actor on the screen was David Manners (né Rauff de Ryther Acklom), a graduate of the University of Toronto. After a short time on Broadway he went to Hollywood where he acted alongside Katherine Hepburn and Barbara Stanwyck; his most memorable performance was in *Journey's End*.[116]

Resident Companies
Through the 1930s, resident stock virtually disappeared from the province, despite valiant efforts in several cities to keep it alive. In Toronto, when the vigorous Empire Theatre company under Marjorie Foster and John Holden closed in April 1931, after four years and over one thousand performances, Cameron Matthews and Vaughan Glaser stepped in. By alternating engagements at the Empire and Victoria theatres (rather than running in direct competition with each other), they were able to provide resident stock theatre almost continuously into the fall of 1932, when both companies disbanded.

The Empire then became home to the New York Theatre Guild's production of *Porgy* with the original all-black cast, until the manager walked out with the proceeds, and the run was cut short. After the company ceased operations, plans were announced to turn the building into a radio broadcast studio; instead, a new company of former Glaser and Matthews actors opened there under the direction of John Gordon, but it ran only two months and the theatre was eventually converted to a movie-house.

In the mid-1930s, with the Depression at its deepest, Cameron Matthews tried twice more to revive resident stock, once in December 1934 with the Toronto Repertory Theatre Company at the Royal Alex, and then in June 1936 with the Canadian Players at the Masonic Hall. But in both cases the companies disappeared very quickly.

Further efforts to set up resident stock in the city were made in 1935–6 by John Holden. After occasional performances at the Victoria Theatre, Holden established a winter company at Margaret Eaton Hall in February 1936 as a way of providing work for his regular summer players from the Actor's Colony Theatre: Jane Mallett, H.E. and Babs Hitchmann, Grace Webster, Isabel Price, and Robert Christie, all of whom were connected with local stock and radio theatre. But Holden's three months of Toronto productions were a prelude to more ambitious plans that led the company to Winnipeg, where it played each winter to the end of the 1939–40 season.

Two other attempts to initiate resident companies are worthy of note. The first, an engagement of a group of New York actors at the Victoria Theatre caused a minor sensation when some suggestive lines in their production of the popular Broadway musical *Sailor, Beware* offended the wife of the local Anglican bishop and the police closed it down because it was not 'conducive to the good morals of Toronto citizens.' The group's final play, *The Bishop Misbehaves*, may well have been a veiled form of retaliation.

The production of *Sailor, Beware* that spring (1936) is noteworthy for a more important reason; it afforded a young local actor, Robert Christie (1913–96), the opportunity to make his professional début. From this rather inauspicious beginning, Christie went on to become the dean of the Canadian acting community, a position he earned for his long career as an actor with the Holden Players and at the Old Vic before the Second World War and later as a major figure in the burgeoning stage, radio, and television world of postwar Canada. Diversely talented, he retired in the early 1980s from teaching in the theatre program at Ryerson Polytechnic Institute.

In the other attempt to establish resident theatre, Ross Millard started a company at the Toronto Island Aquatic Club in the summer of 1936. Its initial production, *A School for Husbands*, featured Judith Evelyn, a graduate of the University of Manitoba, a gifted member of the Hart House Players and CFRB radio drama group, and winner of the Tweedsmuir Prize in that year's Dominion Drama Festival. Although nothing more was heard of Millard's organization, Judith Evelyn went on to a lengthy and distinguished stage and screen career. She starred in the Broadway production of *Angel Street* opposite Vincent Price in 1941, and in the New York radio series *Helpmate*. She was later seen in a touring production of *A Streetcar Named Desire*, with Ralph Meeker, and in Alfred Hitchcock's film *Rear Window*.[118]

The only other professional company operating in Toronto during the 1930s, the Toronto Repertory Theatre (not to be mistaken for Cameron Matthews's week-long venture in 1934), was formed in 1937 by Melville Keay, head of the costume department at Hart House, and his wife Arden Keay, a well-known stage and radio actor.[119] Shocked by the closing of Hart House Theatre and the disbanding of the famous Hart House Players earlier that year, the Keays organized the new company in a determined effort to keep the Hart House tradition alive. They

Among Robert Christie's most notable roles was his Pedant in *The Taming of the Shrew* at the Stratford Festival in 1954, shown here in a Grant Macdonald portrait.

gathered together a small coterie of ex–Hart House Players, local actors, and people associated with the CBC and the arts community to socialize, discuss the theatre, and occasionally produce plays. The first activities of the new organization consisted of theatre classes, play readings,

Vincent Price and Judith Evelyn, *Angel Street*, December 1941

rehearsals, and Sunday salons – all held at the Keays' residence on Spadina Avenue. In June 1938 at Margaret Eaton Hall, the group gave its initial public performance, *The Enchanted April*, with Arden Keay in the role of Lady Caroline. The supporting cast included several familiar actors, notably Murray Bonnycastle from Cameron Matthews's recent company. Later that year, the players opened a full season at Margaret Eaton Hall capped off by a 'magnificent performance' of Maxwell Anderson's *Elizabeth the Queen*, with Arden Keay in the title role.[120]

In 1939, Fred G. Brown, a veteran vaudevillian from Brantford, took over the company and expanded its operations by forming a touring company, the Comedy Theatre Players.[121] The troupe was made up of many regulars from the Toronto Repertory Theatre and included Arden Keay, Dudley Doughty, Marjorie Frith, Mack Inglis, and Lambert Larking (the latter two from the old Empire Stock Company), as well as John Holden from the Actors' Colony.[122] The Players toured southern Ontario in Shaw's *Candida*, *The Curtain Rises*, and in Brown's own plays, *Is Marriage a Failure?*, *Cold Storage*, and *Quiet, Please*.[123]

Arden Keay, *Elizabeth the Queen*, Toronto Repertory Theatre, Margaret Eaton Hall, 27–28 January 1939

For members of the cast, life on the road was a pleasant change from the confines of a radio studio or the routine of stock theatre; at the same time, touring provided a way of augmenting the meagre salaries earned in radio, where, for example, Cosette Lee, one of Canada's foremost actresses, was paid $3.61 for each instalment of a weekly hour-long mystery show at CKCL or, at CFRO, where actors received the princely sum of $2.00 an hour.[124]

With the success of these touring activities, a twin subsidiary operation, the Mayfair Players, with Rance Quarrington as director, was established to tour eastern Ontario. Centred in Ottawa, the new company utilized acting talent from that city's theatre and radio community. The Comedy Theatre and Mayfair Players, working primarily on a contract basis with local service clubs and nurses' alumnae associations, provided theatre nights for special occasions and ranged as far as Kingston and Brantford.

Convinced that small-town Ontario could also support resident theatre, Fred G. Brown organized a permanent company, the Peerless Players, at the Capitol Theatre, Woodstock, in the spring of 1940. It opened as part of a program that included a Bette Davis movie and vaudeville acts.[125] How these attractions were meant to complement each other is not clear; in any event, none of them caught the fancy of local audiences, and the Peerless Players folded after a week and a half.

The failure of this experiment did little to affect the Comedy Theatre and Mayfair Players, who continued to take their popular brand of theatre to communities across southern Ontario. In the meantime, their parent organization, the original Toronto Repertory Theatre, maintained its position as the centre of a growing community of performing artists. Melville and Arden Keay also organized several 'June Cocktails,' year-end revues that featured local amateur and professional actors in skits parodying the past season's productions. In these affairs, the Keays joined forces with two of Toronto's best-known entertainers, Jane Mallett and Fred J. Manning, whose annual two-person show *Town Tonics* (with original music by Mary Morley), had satirized issues of the day and delighted audiences since 1931. The popularity of these revues was echoed years later in the annual *Spring Thaw* productions created by the New Play Society.

Except for the examples cited, radio drama and the Toronto Repertory Theatre with its two offspring, professional performers had only one other outlet for their talent – the numerous amateur theatre groups that had blossomed around the province during the 1930s. As amateur theatre increased in status after the establishment of the Dominion Drama Festival in 1932, it was not unusual for professionals to cross over into the amateur world, with the result that in Toronto, for example, the work of a variety of 'little theatre' groups such as Hart House Players was raised to a level that equalled, if not surpassed, many of the commercial productions downtown.

Other organizations that also recognized the educative value of the theatre were at work in the 1930s. With talk of social reform and political strife in the air all through the decade, proletarian groups entered into play production and dramatic education with the purpose of creating a protest theatre to counteract the bourgeois values embodied in both mainstream professional and amateur organizations. Beginning in 1932, the Workers' Experimental Theatre, a branch of the Toronto Progressive Arts Club, developed an agitprop troupe similar to those that sprang up in over sixty towns and cities across the country.[126] Its first production, *Deported*, was at the Ukrainian Temple in May 1932: two of the performers failed to show up, the curtain went up forty-five minutes late, and the play's ending was roundly criticized by party workers for being too defeatist. But it was the beginning of a powerful challenge to the prevailing political ideologies and theatrical practices.

Over the next year, dressed in standard uniforms of black pants, black shirts, and red kerchiefs, the crew and cast made three tours of southern Ontario, on one occasion being chased out of St Catharines as 'Moscow agents' for fomenting a riot at a local strike-bound cannery.[127] Following events such as this, the activities of the Workers' Experimental Theatre came under increasing official scrutiny. Thus, when the WET company presented *Eight Men Speak* (a collective work about an alleged attempt to murder imprisoned Canadian Communist leader Tim Buck) at Toronto's Standard Theatre in December 1933, the 'Red Squad' of the local police department banned subsequent performances, and theatre managers throughout the city were threatened with revocation of their licences if they rented their halls to the group.[128]

Realizing that their strident political tactics made them ineffectual and vulnerable, the WET reorganized into the Theatre of Action, a less doctrinaire group that represented the broad left and paralleled developments in Winnipeg and Montreal, where agitprop groups had become more experimental aesthetically and less radical politically. Beginning in 1935, the new organization entered a five-year period of high achievement in which it offered annual summer workshops led by directors from New York's Group Theatre and Neighbourhood Playhouse, held playwriting contests, and staged the Canadian premières of several 'anti-establishment' plays, including Sinclair Lewis's *It Can't Happen Here* in December 1938. In Toronto to oversee rehearsals, Lewis commented, 'I have never seen such enthusiastic people working on a play.' Despite its growing acceptance in the mainstream, which culminated in 1938 when the Theatre of Action won the Dominion Drama Festival with its production of John Wesley's *Steel*, the group continued to be dogged by controversy. Even its final production, Gogol's *The Inspector General*, which was presented as an anti-war play, caught the eye of a local Member of Parliament, who called for an immediate RCMP investigation of the group for supposedly engaging in 'subversive' activities.

Overall, the Theatre of Action was a vital force in its short history, and added a dimension of political comment that went a fair distance towards redressing the imbalance in the otherwise bourgeois and establishment interests underlying amateur and commercial theatre of the day. Whether it was because the company was dedicated to a political ideology deemed a viable alternative to that in power or because it offered opportunity to work in the unique agitprop style of production, the Theatre of Action attracted young intellectuals, among them Basya Hunter, Louis Applebaum, Lorne Greene, David Mann, Sidney Newman, Johnny Wayne, and Frank Shuster – all of whom later made their names in entertainment in Canada and abroad.

The Theatre of Action also prompted amateur groups such as the Toronto Jewish Little Theatre to try their hand at producing material arising out of the social-protest movement in the 1930s. The Jewish community in Toronto had always taken an active part in promoting social reform through the theatre, even early in the century when the Toronto Young Socialists had tried dramatics as a means of getting their message across. But this was only a facet of a rich tradition in Jewish theatre in the city. The first theatre serving the Jewish community was started around 1906.[129] By 1920, the centre of Jewish entertainment was the National (a 900-seat converted church, later renamed the Lyric) at the corner of Bay and Dundas. It became the home of touring Yiddish entertainers from New York and Europe, including well-known personalities Jacob P. Adler, Thomas Lefsky, and Ruth Shildkraut. The audiences were made up mainly of immigrant employees from the nearby garment district. When the Lyric was destroyed by fire in 1922, the focus of activity shifted to the Standard, a new theatre on Spadina Avenue that became the first Yiddish playhouse in North America. It hosted such performers as Maurice Schwartz, Berla Carlson, and Jacob Ben Ami, the latter as late as 1934. The Standard fought to remain a home for live theatre, but, like many other legitimate playhouses, it became a cinema (the Strand) and later, in 1945, a notorious burlesque house, the Victory.

Other immigrant national groups, primarily Chinese and Polish, brought in traditional theatre companies reflecting their native culture. As Dora Nipp points out, the Toronto Chinese community developed a highly active theatre, which included three Chinese opera houses in the mid-1930s.[130] Local Chinese performers took part in fund-raising shows during the Sino-Japanese and Second World Wars, and professional performers came to North America particularly during the Second World War. Some, like Lim Mark Yee, a renowned instructor in sword and spear dancing, stayed in Toronto. At an amateur level, the Ukrainian, Greek, Finnish, Italian, and Polish communities established dramatic societies in their respective native languages.

Judging from the tremendous amount of activity at the local level, community-based theatre in Toronto had reached a point in the 1930s where it began to supplant the commercial touring system. As local theatre grew in strength and stature, it provided a basis from which an indigenous Canadian professional theatre could emerge after the Second World War.

Other cities in Ontario did not experience the same upsurge as did Toronto in locally based commercial activity through the decade. Ottawa is a case in point. With the passing of the O'Shea Players in October 1931, the city saw its last resident stock company until after the Second World War. Even touring productions came less frequently, and by the mid-thirties they had all but stopped. Ottawans were not without live dramatic entertainment, however, since the city possessed a vital amateur community headed by the Ottawa Little Theatre, founded in 1913 and one of the most active and influential organizations of its kind in Canada. The Outaouais area also had French-language theatre from the various Cercles dramatiques at the turn of the century and later from groups such as Le Caveau.

Much the same pattern occurred in London and Hamilton. In both cities, touring productions from New York were reduced to a trickle by mid-decade, leaving local amateur organizations as the only source of live entertainment. Hamilton, however, did experience a brief resurgence of professional resident theatre in October 1932, when Jack Marco, long associated with the Broadway musical melodrama *The Candy Kid*, led a company at the Grand Theatre for a month-long run, playing three nights and a matinée each week. For theatre-goers, the occasion must have evoked memories of the early days of resident stock, since the cast included several veterans from that period, including Charles Fletcher and Grace Webster, familiar stock-theatre performers, and Stanley Brown, who had been in Hamilton with the Lyric and Gillan companies in the 1920s. After they closed at the Grand, the cast reappeared as the Savoy Stock Company at the Savoy several weeks later, but it also folded within a month.

To all intents and purposes, all major cities in the province outside of

Toronto had been eliminated from the touring circuit, and with the decline of resident stock companies, many communities were left with no professional theatre at all. It was this vacuum that amateur theatre filled so admirably, thereby helping to lay the groundwork for an unprecedented explosion of interest and activity in Canadian theatre following the war.

The Second World War: 1939–1945

When war was declared in August 1939, local theatre communities, both amateur and professional, were quick to respond. Those actors who did not immediately enlist set to work mounting productions of everything from Shakespearean drama to topical revues as a means of raising funds for the war effort and entertaining the troops. In Toronto, Roly Young, entertainment columnist for the Toronto *Telegram* at the time, assembled many of the original Dumbells for a wartime revue called *Chin Up* and embarked on a cross-Canada tour of camps and cities in December 1939. Often the armed forces worked in cooperation with local acting communities, as they did in the first major soldier variety show, *Ritzin' the Blitz*, which involved Melville Keay, Robert Baillie, and the Langley Active Service Auxiliary, a volunteer organization. Out of this production grew a second show, *Hittin' the Jackpot*, which included Cosette Lee and Mack Inglis in the cast and which lasted until 1946 as a principal vehicle for raising war funds.

Increasingly, the task of entertaining the military was assumed by the services themselves. The Army Show, its female counterpart 'all-girl' troop show Merry-Go-Round, and Meet the Navy, the sailors' answer to the soldier productions, all opened in Toronto in 1943 and toured camps and cities across Canada. Afterwards, both The Army Show and Meet the Navy headed to Europe and scored a hit with the armed forces. Meet the Navy even gave a Royal Performance in London. After VE Day, it continued to play military bases in Great Britain and Europe until disbanding in 1945. Meanwhile, The Army Show toured for two more years. Together, the three shows contributed to the training of many fine performers, musicians, and producers who went on to become well-known personalities in the entertainment world at home and abroad; they included Johnny Wayne and Frank Shuster (comedy team), Allan and Blanche Lund (dancers and choreographers), Victor Feldbrill and Eric Wild (orchestra conductors), John Pratt (professional comedian), and Ivan Romanoff and Carl Tapscott (choral leaders).

By broadcasting The Army Show over its national transmission service in Toronto, the Canadian Broadcasting Corporation provided another vehicle for bringing the talents of the armed forces to the public. At the same time in Toronto, the CBC Drama Department, under Rupert Lucas, opened up a new field for Canadian acting and writing talent when it created such successful war series as 'Canada Carries On,' 'Fighting Navy,' and 'L for Lanky.'[131] For these programs, the CBC drew on the large corps of Canada's best radio actors, among them Mercer McLeod, Howard Milsom, Vincent Tovell, Jack Fuller, John Drainie, Lloyd Bochner, Lister Sinclair, Peggi Loder, Francis Goffman, Pauline Rennie, Tommy Tweed, Robert Christie, Alan Young, and George Murray. Added to these luminaries were the popular stars of several long-running domestic comedies and soap operas, William Needles and Roxanna Bond, who played the title role in *John and Judy*, and Frank Peddie and Grace Webster in *The Craigs*, which ran for twenty-five years.

From a purely dramatic point of view, the most notable wartime presentations on CBC radio were from the celebrated *Theatre of Freedom* series, which brought to the air some of the most important stage and radio actors of the day in plays charged with patriotic enthusiasm and unashamedly democratic ideals and values. Canadian actors who participated in the series included Walter Huston in Drinkwater's *Abraham Lincoln*, Raymond Massey in *This Precious Freedom* (Arch Obler), Jane Mallett in *Pastor Hall* (Ernst Toller) and again in *Victoria the Great*, and Ivor Lewis in *This Is My Country* by the Canadian playwright John Coulter.[132]

CBC productions provided an essential service to Canadians by giving them a sense of purpose and involvement in the nation's destiny hitherto not conceivable in any other medium. Furthermore, the CBC's Drama Department gave the national network a world-wide reputation for excellence that has yet to be equalled. The CBC was, as well as any single organization can be in this vast country, the first truly national voice with an audience that stretched from sea to sea.

Complementing the patriotic programming on the CBC were a number of live attractions such as the Victory Star Shows that were organized to raise money and morale and that featured well-known movie and stage celebrities such as Pat O'Brien, Madeleine Carroll, and Canadian-born Hollywood actors Walter Huston and Walter Pidgeon. The Toronto Repertory Theatre company and its itinerant subsidiaries, the Comedy Theatre Players and the Mayfair Players, Ontario's only indigenous professional companies, also promoted the war effort by playing for local organizations that wanted to raise money for various relief funds. The parent Repertory Theatre maintained its Toronto base, producing plays at Hart House Theatre and Margaret Eaton Hall into the early war years with its regular cast of Arden Keay, Mack Inglis, Marjorie Frith, Dudley

Doughty, John Hayes, and Marie Fowler. Many of the same actors performed with the Comedy Theatre Players and the Mayfair Players, which continued travelling across Ontario in their popular presentations of Coward's *Hay Fever* and *The Curtain Rises* (B.M. Kaye). In 1941, when John Holden's Actors' Colony disbanded, the Mayfair contingent absorbed Holden and two of his actors, William Needles and Connie Vernon. The company also took on two English performers formerly of the Maurice Colbourne–Barry Jones Players, Vanda Hudson and Earle Grey, who had been marooned in Canada by the war.[133]

The Colbourne-Jones company was the only other organization on the road in Ontario during the war. It presented Colbourne's own play *Charles the King* and Bernard Shaw's newly revised *Geneva* in several cities as part of a coast-to-coast tour in 1939–40. Besides the two principals and Hudson, Grey and his wife Mary Godwin, the cast included Broadway star Jessica Tandy, as well as Lambert Larking, who had been with Colbourne at the old Empire Theatre, Toronto, in 1928. Both Colbourne and Jones played again in Toronto the following year, Colbourne in the touring Broadway production of Robert Sherwood's *There Shall Be No Night* and Jones in a CBC broadcast of Galsworthy's *Strife* as part of the stirring *Theatre of Freedom* series. The war ended Colbourne and Jones's appearances in Canada, but their presence at such a critical time helped to reinforce British-Canadian ties and stimulate pride in the two countries' mutual heritage.

During the early years of the war, the American touring system appeared unaffected by the conflict overseas and still brought in many distinguished performers from the New York stage. Once again Canadian actors figured prominently in road productions coming to the Royal Alex. Foremost was Raymond Massey in the title role of Robert E. Sherwood's *Abe Lincoln in Illinois* (November 1939). In the estimation of U.S. theatre historian Richard Moody, Massey's 'faithful and moving' portrayal of the American president was 'his greatest triumph.'[134]

Margaret Anglin also returned to her home province, as she had in the First World War, to help bolster patriotic spirits. Her current vehicle, Lillian Hellman's hard-hitting *Watch on the Rhine*, was the first play openly critical of American indifference to the dangers of fascism. In Anglin's hands, its effect was electrifying.

A Canadian actor making his first professional appearance in Toronto during the war was Alexander Knox, a native of Strathroy and a graduate of the University of Western Ontario.[135] His local début occurred in Katherine Cornell's much-praised revival of *The Three Sisters* (Chekhov), with Judith Anderson and Ruth Gordon, in April 1943.[136] Knox had begun his stage career in Boston in 1929; a year later he secured an

Alexander Knox, Strathroy-born actor and playwright

engagement with the Wyndham Theatre, London, England, and performed there with distinction during the 1930s. He first appeared on Broadway in *Jupiter Laughs* with Jessica Tandy in 1940. Knox also won accolades as a playwright and as a film actor, particularly for his title role in *Wilson* and in *Reach for the Sky*.

Another experienced Canadian actor to make a first professional appearance in Ontario was Margaret Bannerman, a Toronto native who was seen in Daphne du Maurier's *Rebecca* in November 1944.[137] After starting her stage career in Winnipeg, she achieved prominence as Lady Grayston in the original 1923 run of Maugham's *Our Betters*. Then followed extensive touring across Europe, Australia, and the United States. Her later roles included Mrs Higgins in the North American tour of Lerner and Loewe's *My Fair Lady* (1959–63) and parts in Hollywood films. She died in 1976.

During the war, Bannerman had also performed at the Royal Alex with a new resident summer company established there in 1940 by American producer Frank McCoy, the first since the 1920s. Made up primarily of American actors 'jobbed on' in New York and paid 'a buck a line,'[138] the cast provided the back-up for a parade of stage and screen stars that included Jose Ferrer, C. Aubrey Smith, Canadian-born Fay Wray (the hit of the movie *King Kong*), Gloria Swanson, and Estelle Winwood. It was Winwood's husband and the director of the company, Robert Henderson, formerly of the Hollywood Playhouse, who first opened up the cast to local professional actors, and in 1942 several from the defunct Actors' Colony company joined the Royal Alexandra Players. Their presence was immediately felt. For example, the American lead performer in *Petticoat Fever* regarded Cosy Lee as the best 'Kimo' he had ever acted opposite. In fact, by 1945 Lee had assumed the position of the central supporting female, while Earle Grey, Mack Inglis, and Jack Medhurst took on increasingly important roles. Nevertheless, the 'plum' parts invariably fell to New York actors, a situation that reflected the attitude that local talent was still considered second-class. That attitude was to change in the approaching postwar years.

The Postwar Years: 1945–1954

After the Armistice, a flood of servicemen and women arrived home looking for careers in the theatre, but few had the necessary training. To accommodate their needs, the federal government funded several university programs that allowed veterans and civilians alike to combine academic studies and theatre training. For example, the University of Toronto reopened Hart House Theatre after nearly a decade and hired Robert Gill, an experienced actor, director, and teacher from Carnegie Tech, to run the program.[139] Under his guidance, Hart House Theatre became a major force in developing new personnel for the country's burgeoning professional theatre. Graduates of his program included Anna Cameron, Barbara Chilcott, Donald and Murray Davis, Ted Follows, David Gardner, Barbara Hamilton, Eric House, William Hutt,

CBC Radio drama: Tommy Tweed (right) knocks out Lloyd Bochner (play unknown)

Charmion King, Leon Major, George McCowan, Kate Reid and Donald Sutherland.[140]

Another centre for training and developing young professionals was the CBC's Drama Department in Toronto, where Andrew Allan, national supervisor of drama production, brought together a remarkable company of radio actors.[141] Some, such as John Drainie, Tommy Tweed, Bernard Braden, Arthur Hill and his wife Peggy Hassard, Al Pearce and Lister Sinclair,[142] had performed for Allan in Vancouver. Others, such as regulars Frank Peddie, Jane Mallett, and Ruth Springford, started in local theatre or came from a growing number of radio schools.[143] Allan also drew upon the exceptional talents of Canadian radio dramatists Len Peterson, Joseph Schull, George Salverson, Tommy Tweed, Harry J. Boyle, Allan King, and W.O. Mitchell to provide the material for the popular *Stage* and *Wednesday Night* drama series. Between 1944 and 1954, several hundred people were employed in these series and over 250 plays were broadcast to thousands of people across the country.

The influence of Allan's CBC drama group in Toronto was not confined to the programs they produced. During the heyday of radio drama, actors and writers from the CBC were integrally involved in nearly every development in Toronto's theatre community, from establishing companies to directing and writing original works for them. However, with the opportunities afforded by the advent of television, the opening of the Stratford Festival, and the creation of the Crest Theatre, the tightly knit corps of actors was eventually dispersed and absorbed into the larger theatre community across Canada and beyond.

The most influential company to emerge in immediate postwar Toronto was the New Play Society, under the direction of Dora Mavor Moore with assistance from her son Mavor, a director and producer with the CBC. Recognizing that veterans interested in stage careers needed adequate training, the Moores formed the company as a professional but non-profit operation with assistance from Village Players alumni Don Harron, David Gardner, and Pegi Brown (who were acting students of Robert Gill at the University of Toronto) and CBC radio actors. Together they outfitted the small stage in the basement of the Royal Ontario Museum and opened in Synge's *The Playboy of the Western World* in October 1946. Over the years, the NPS established itself as the leading showcase for important Canadian plays, premièring such works as Lister Sinclair's *The Man in the Blue Moon* (1947), Morley Callaghan's *To Tell the Truth* (1948) and *Going Home* (1949), Harry J. Boyle's *The Inher-itance* (1949), and John Coulter's epic *Riel* (1950); this last, televised on the CBC in 1961, gained most attention because of Robert Christie's portrayal of John A. Macdonald.[144]

The list of artists with the NPS over the years reads like a 'Who's Who' of Canadian theatre and CBC radio and television drama. Fletcher Markle was by then a favoured playwright and producer on the CBC and in New York. John Drainie, judged the foremost radio actor in Canada, also appeared on Orson Welles's *Mercury Theatre of the Air*. The list also included Tommy Tweed, Bernard Braden, Frank Willis, Budd Knapp, Alfred Scopp, Alex McKee, Marion Misener, George Luscombe, Glen Burns, Ruth Springford, Charmion King, Jean Cruchet, Sandra Scott, Anna Cameron, Peter Mews, Lorne Greene, Drew Thompson, and a host of other actors who worked locally on stage and radio. In fact, there was hardly a performer of any stature who did *not* act in the company at one time or another.

Of particular interest was the development of the New Play Society's annual *Spring Thaw*, which appeared in 1948 and, except for a ten-year hiatus, regaled audiences in Toronto and on annual tours until 1985. The NPS also added a yearly yule-tide pantomime. Between them, these two institutions helped launch the careers of the most popular entertainers of the day, among them Eric Christmas, Giselle Mackenzie, Toby Robins, Robert Goulet, Dave Broadfoot, Barbara Hamilton, Don Francks, Lou Jacobi, Norman Jewison, and Jean Templeton. In addition, the shows provided an outlet for the writing talents of Mavor Moore, Lister Sin-

'The list of artists with the NPS over the years reads like a "Who's Who"' – literally so in the case of Mavor Moore's provocative and witty *Who's Who*, which he wrote and directed at the ROM Theatre in September 1949. Some of the cast: Robert Christie, Margot Christie, Toby Robins, Don Harron, Lorne Greene, Hedley Rainnie

clair, Don Harron, Johnny Wayne, and Dave Broadfoot, with original music supplied over the years by Lucio Agostini, Bobby Gimby, and Godfrey Ridout.

With the advent of television, the company established a school with classes in production, acting, and writing for the new medium. Some of broadcasting's most familiar names – Lister Sinclair, Andrew Allan, Robertson Davies, and theatre critics Herbert Whittaker and Nathan Cohen – taught there. Courses in theatre administration were conducted by Tom Hendry, energetic director of the Manitoba Theatre Centre, and Ed Mirvish, successful entrepreneur and future owner of the Royal Alex.

Given its many ancillary activities, the NPS continued until 1971 to perform dramatic works new and old with varying success, but always with characteristic energy. However, with Mrs Moore's energies dedicated to the new school and *Spring Thaw* becoming the company's main concern – and the main source of income – the NPS gradually withdrew from serious play production.

In 1951, the Jupiter Theatre, a company composed of many NPS regu-

A Herbert Whittaker design for Bertolt Brecht's *Galileo*, Jupiter Theatre, 1951

lars and with almost the same objectives, took up residence at the Museum Theatre and in effect assumed the role of the dramatic production branch of the NPS.[145] The new company's first presentation, an imaginatively staged production of Brecht's *Galileo* that opened in December 1951, gives evidence of the serious intention to make the Jupiter the principal theatre in Toronto. Director Herbert Whittaker, drama critic of the *Globe and Mail*, assembled some of the most prominent actors of the day, casting John Drainie, Lorne Greene, Margot Christie, David Gardner, and Hugh Webster in the principal roles. In that same season, the Jupiter courageously presented Toronto play-goers with *The Biggest Thief in Town* by Dalton Trumbo, an American playwright blacklisted by the McCarthy tribunals in the United States. The production spotlighted several future stars of stage and screen, Budd Knapp, Norman Jewison, and Gerry Sarracini. Then came Lister Sinclair's epic *Socrates*, a large-scale production that Esse Ljungh, CBC producer, handled with flair. Frank Peddie, CBC's best-known character actor played the title role, assisted by Paul Kligman, from the Wayne and Shuster radio show, and Christopher Plummer, Toronto-born and Montreal-trained star of the Canadian Repertory Theatre, Ottawa. The first season concluded with Jean-Paul Sartre's *Crime of Passion*, which

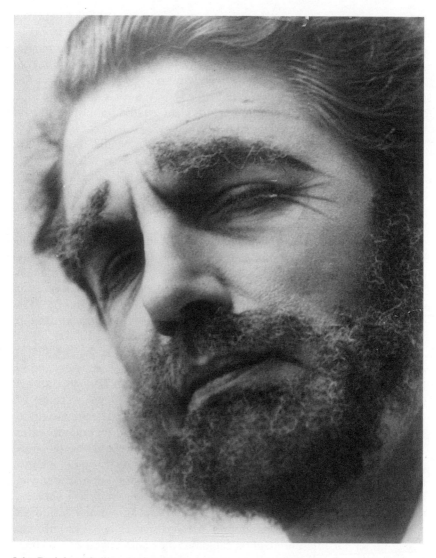

John Drainie as Galileo, Jupiter Theatre, 1951

featured British television actress Honor Blackman and a cast with Don Harron, John Drainie, and Lorne Greene.

For its three remaining years, the Jupiter continued to provide first Canadian productions of some of the best of the world's contemporary drama. Christopher Fry's *The Lady's Not for Burning*, with wonderfully comic performances by Don Harron (Richard), Christopher Plummer

(Mendip), David Gardner (Humphrey), and Eric House (The Chaplain) became an instant hit. The company also gave eloquent voice to Fry's poetry in *A Sleep of Prisoners*, which was taken on tour through Ontario and Quebec. In addition, the company introduced Pirandello's *Right You Are* and Anouilh's *Ring Around the Moon*, the latter starring Douglas Rain, whose performances in Winnipeg, at London's Old Vic, and at Stratford (as Alec Guinness's understudy) had established him as one of Canada's leading young actors.

The Jupiter also performed three more original Canadian plays – Ted Allen's *The Moneymakers* (which was later televised with Kate Reid, John Drainie, and Lorne Greene in the cast), *Blue Is for Mourning*, a sombre play by Toronto critic Nathan Cohen, and Lister Sinclair's story of Cape Breton life, *The Blood Is Strong*. Although it planned to mount two more new Canadian works, the Jupiter ran into trouble with its production of Coward's *Relative Values*, which it unwisely mounted at the Royal Alex in the same month that the new Crest Theatre company opened across town. Without adequate financial resources, a permanent home, or a cohesive ensemble of actors, the company could not hope to survive in the increasingly competitive entertainment scene in Toronto, so it closed abruptly in January 1954. In its short life, the Jupiter gave to Toronto some of its greatest theatrical moments during the period.

Toronto's Belmont Group Theatre, in contrast to the Jupiter, had a much longer history, with a lineage going back to the Theatre of Action in the 1930s, when the founders of the Belmont, Ben Lennick and his future wife, Sylvia Paige, first met.[146] Modelled on the Group Theatre of New York, the Belmont began in 1942 as the Toronto Theatre Group to bring new socially relevant plays to the city's Jewish community after Yiddish entertainment died out at the Standard. Eventually, the new company settled into the Belmont Theatre, changed its name accordingly, and entered into production – mostly of contemporary Broadway hits by authors from Schisgal to Saroyan. To help finance their venture, the Lennicks took bit parts at the Royal Alex and performed with their company on Sundays. To get around Toronto's 'blue laws' prohibiting live commercial entertainment on Sundays, they sold tickets in advance. Invariably, the house was full. During its formative years, the company played in every kind of space from tennis clubs to high-school auditoriums, but still managed to win such honours as the Civic Theatre Association's spring drama competitions and later a DDF best-actor award for Ben Lennick's role in *Awake and Sing*. Ben Lennick also set up and taught a summer acting course and introduced many young graduates, including Sean Sullivan, Sammy Sales, and Araby Lockhart, to Toronto audiences. The Belmont players also presented summer stock in Collingwood and dinner theatre at Mart Kenney's Ranch. About the same time, the Lennicks began a career on radio and television with their series *At Home with the Lennicks*. In 1954, they joined the Crest Theatre Company, and without their dynamic input the Belmont Group Theatre faded temporarily from the scene.

At least one other postwar venture had roots in wartime theatre. One of the subsidiaries of the Toronto Repertory Theatre, the Comedy Theatre Players, regrouped in 1945 with a new cast including Cosy Lee, her sister Enid Mills, Rupert McLeod, Val Carey, and Dennis Murphy and played the road until 1949, providing additional work for actors from the professional stage and radio.

A maverick organization, the Civic Theatre Association, established in 1945, is difficult to position in the professional-theatre movement in Toronto at the time, largely because it was not a theatre company in its own right but an umbrella organization for fourteen local amateur performing-arts groups. Brainchild of Roly Young, entertainment critic for the *Globe and Mail* at the time, the CTA was essentially Ontario's first postwar community theatre supported by subscription and donations.[147] According to the goals set by Young, the Association intended to offer non-élitist professional entertainment unlike the 'art' and commercial theatres in the city, to remain locally based, and to reject any link with a government-funded national theatre movement.

Needless to say, Young's blind populism and philistine attitudes put him at odds with groups such as the pro-nationalist Arts and Letters Club and Dora Mavor Moore's Village Players, which withdrew its membership to protest the CTA's anti-artistic aims. Nevertheless, Young persisted and the first production took place at Eaton Auditorium in November 1945, starring Anna Russell in *The Lady Intervenes*, a comedy by expatriate Arthur Stringer.[148] Though Young encouraged participation by member groups in ballet and opera, over the next three years the Association turned more towards dramatic performance. However, except for annual pantomimes and revues written by Young, CTA offered only one Canadian play, *Father Malachy's Miracle*, adapted from Bruce Marshall's novel by local playwright Brian Doherty. And although hundreds of local performers took part in productions, most were unknown and only a few were professionals. While the notion of a community theatre held some merit, the contradictions in Young's conception and execution doomed it to failure. His untimely death in January 1949 effectively brought the Civic Theatre to an end without its having welded Toronto's arts groups into any lasting relationship.[149]

While the postwar development of indigenous resident theatre in Toronto was an important sign of growing theatrical independence, the dream of a nation-wide Canadian touring system and control of the road still persisted. One of the first civilian touring ventures was undertaken by John Adaskin Productions, which took John Patrick's Broadway hit *The Hasty Heart* to Toronto, Hamilton, and London in December 1945, but without success. Over the next few years, tours of *The Drunkard* and *There Goes Yesterday*, produced by Murray and Donald Davis's Straw Hat Players, and of *Arsenic and Old Lace* and *One for the Road*, produced by Canadian playwright and impresario Brian Doherty, further indicate the impulse to establish a touring industry, but these ventures lacked the high-profile product, the serious financial backing, and the organizational structure to compete with the more efficient and aggressive American touring system or the new medium of television.

After the war, the American touring system continued to be the main supplier of commercial entertainment along the circuit, and as before, audiences in Toronto (the only city on the old circuit still regularly visited) had to be content to take what came their way. The expansion of transatlantic air flights in the postwar years was an important factor in speeding up cultural exchange between Europe and North America and opening new markets for the work of directors, performers, and playwrights on both sides of the ocean. Almost immediately after the war, the New York–based touring system took on a noticeably international look, as a significant number of attractions coming to Toronto either originated in Great Britain or featured British dramatic material and performers in American productions.

Though Shakespeare might have been the sentimental favourite among the classics from the British stage, Bernard Shaw won the day in terms of total productions. Many of Britain's great performers appeared in the city, among them Flora Robson, Michael Redgrave, Donald Wolfit, Maurice Evans, and John Gielgud, as well as Charles Laughton, Katherine Cornell, and Agnes Moorehead from the American stage. North America's infatuation with things British was also mirrored in productions of Noel Coward and Oscar Wilde, the latter being represented by *Lady Windermere's Fan*, which included in its cast Canadian actor David Manners. Having become disenchanted with 'the false life' in Hollywood, Manners had resumed his stage career for a short time, but eventually retired to California, without ever returning to Toronto, a city he once described as being 'more provincial than the village of Marmora.'[150]

The strong British presence in postwar North America balanced the reverse process occurring in London where, in 1955 alone, fourteen American plays and musicals were on the boards in the West End. But internationalism was not limited to the London–New York corridor.

Material from the French theatre began appearing on the touring circuit as well, headed by works of Cocteau, Rostand, and Giraudoux. Other countries were represented in a wide assortment of attractions showcasing their theatre's most celebrated dramatists and performers. Opera (from La Scala and the Metropolitan Opera in New York), Flamenco dancing (from Spain, performed by Jose Greco), ballet (from London's Sadler's Wells and the Ballet Russe de Monte Carlo), Afro-Caribbean extravaganzas (presented by Katherine Dunham), Yiddish-style 'bagels and yox' vaudeville (from New York State's 'Borscht Belt') – all formed part of the entertainment that paraded across the stage of Toronto's Royal Alex, which remained the city's main commercial house. However, the Eaton Auditorium and Massey Hall – even Maple Leaf Gardens, an ice-hockey rink – were called on more and more to handle the growing number of road productions.

As a result of the broadening influences of postwar life, a significant portion of the material coming from New York directly confronted social issues of the day, perhaps the most pressing of which was racism. Given the devastating effects of McCarthyism on the artistic community in the United States, it is a wonder that any material critical of American life would have been produced, but local theatre-goers did get to see such plays as *Strange Fruit* (directed by Jose Ferrer), *Call Me Mister*, and *Deep Are the Roots*, and productions of *Carmen Jones*, *Night Must Fall*, and *Anna Lucasta* by black performers struggling for racial equality and recognition on the legitimate stage. How Toronto audiences related to this material is a moot point, but one can assume that over the years they had learned how to 'read' entertainment out of New York as a barometer of American tastes and values and as a precursor of things to come in their own land.

If one form of entertainment dominated the commercial touring productions at the Royal Alex, it was the Broadway musical, a craze that led to the establishment of Melody Fair, a summer music theatre that opened in 1951 in a 1600-seat tent at Dufferin Race Park and then moved indoors to the Mutual Street Arena before closing down in 1954.[151] Every season, director Bertram Yarborough and manager Ben Kamsler assembled a permanent company headed by lesser-known but 'established and qualified' American musical-comedy performers brought in because the investors were convinced that the required proficiency of craftsmanship could not be found among Canadian actors. As a consequence, except for the occasional appearance of such actors as E.M. Margolese, Al Pearce, Alex McKee, and Josephine Barrington in supporting roles, local talent was relegated to the chorus and dance troupe. Even for such limited opportunities, dozen of aspiring performers attended try-outs every spring for parts in the ten-production seasons. And every spring, manager Kamsler launched a high-powered publicity campaign that included a regular fifteen-minute Sunday radio program on summer theatre in Ontario, as well as extensive feature stories and photos in the local press.

The popularity of Melody Fair effectively ended summer theatre at the Royal Alex. At the same time, the establishment of new professional companies in cities outside Toronto and the explosion of summer stock theatre began to attract a substantial audience. These developments signalled the beginning of a decentralizing process in which local communities became more involved in determining their own cultural destinies.

Ottawa

Ottawa's postwar professional-theatre era began in 1948 when Hugh Parker, a member of the Ottawa Drama League, and Harry Southam, publisher of the Ottawa *Citizen*, imported British director Malcolm Morley (from Montreal's Open Air Theatre and former DDF adjudicator) and four British professional actors to form the nucleus of the Ottawa Stage Society.[152] Local amateurs filled out the cast, and the new company opened a summer program that won such a favourable response that Parker mounted a winter season. In spite of the enthusiasm and general high level of ability, the company was split by personal differences. Parker, in ill health and $30,000 in debt, gave control of the company to Morley, Eric Workman, and Reginald Malcolm in the spring of 1949. With support from corporate sponsors, they founded the Canadian Repertory Theatre, which provided theatre of exceptional quality over the next seven years in Ottawa.

Much of the company's early success was due to the work of two young actors, Betty Leighton, a product of the Ottawa Little Theatre, and Christopher Plummer, 'discovered' by Morley at the Mountain Playhouse in Montreal.[153] Leighton, leading lady of the original Stage Society, continued to head the cast until 1952, when she was signed by Tyrone Guthrie to play at Stratford. She went on to become a remarkably versatile star performer with many of the country's major companies, from the Crest to Theatre Calgary and the Shaw Festival. Plummer acted in over a hundred roles in his two years with the company, before he left to act in repertory in Bermuda, on Broadway, at Stratford, and with a number of British and American companies; he also built a successful televison and film career, his most famous role occurring in *The Sound of Music*.

When Amelia Hall joined the CRT in 1950, it was as artistic director. Energetic and driven by a love of the theatre, she not only guided the

Amelia Hall as Lady Anne in *Richard III*, 1953 – the first woman on the Stratford Festival stage

company through its most productive years, but she herself gave some of the most memorable performances in its history. Like Betty Leighton, she too was invited to play in Stratford's inaugural season and, as Lady Anne to Alec Guinness's Richard III, she became the first actress to step onto the new stage – a fitting tribute for a great pioneer of the modern professional theatre in Canada. During her directorship of the CRT, Hall ran a demanding production schedule of a play a week, and each year engaged some of the country's most promising actors. The cast for the 1952–3 season was particularly strong and included regulars William Hutt, by then a star in summer stock and on CBC radio and television; William Shatner, whose acting with the CRT led to a professional career in American film and television, most recently as Captain Kirk in the long-running *Star Trek* series; guests Australian-born Max Helpmann and his wife Barbara (Davis) Chilcott; Donald Davis, director of the Straw Hat Players; comic Eric House; and well-known New York set designer Leif Pederson. When Hall left in 1954 to act in the Stratford company, the CRT went into decline over the next two years, despite 'pay-as-you-go' subscription plans and rousing performances by William Hutt, Eric Christmas, and David Gardner, the last in Robertson Davies's comedy *A Jig for the Gypsy*, one of the few Canadian plays produced by CRT. In the end, its ranks thinned by defections to the Crest, Stratford, and television, the CRT closed in 1956, bringing to an end a unique and vibrant period of Ottawa's theatrical history.

London
Because it possessed a large, well-equipped, but relatively unused theatre (the Grand) and a knowledgeable audience, postwar London suddenly found itself the jumping-off point for a series of pre-Broadway try-outs and transcontinental tours. John Gielgud, Michael Redgrave, and the Dublin Gate Players started their North American tours there; these attractions were followed shortly after by premières of several New York–bound commercial plays,[154] including *The Fourposter* (Jan de Hartog), in which London-born Hume Cronyn and his wife Jessica Tandy toured southern Ontario and later played a long run on Broadway. Cronyn and Tandy continued to score successes as a partnership and singly on stage, screen, and radio. Cronyn, who began his career at the Montreal Repertory Theatre while he was at McGill, has since been associated primarily with the American theatre, which in 1986 presented the Cronyn-Tandy team with a Lifetime Achievement Award.[155]

While London was enjoying its new-found reputation as a theatrical testing ground, it also welcomed its first resident company in over twenty years when the Shelton-Amos Players opened at the Grand in mid-August 1949. Hall Shelton was a well-known Broadway producer; his wife and partner Ruth Amos had acted with Toronto's Glaser Players in the 1920s and had recently played the Canadian west with a Calgary repertory company. For the next six summers, the Shelton-Amos Players offered London theatre-goers a wide selection of dramatic material, from romantic comedies and melodramas such as *Dracula* to ambitious productions of *The Whiteoaks of Jalna* (which featured Amos as the 104-year-old Gram), Williams's *A Streetcar Named Desire*, and Inge's *Come Back, Little Sheba*. While the cast remained primarily American over the years, two members were from Ontario. Walter Massey was of particular interest to Londoners, since he had been with the London Little Theatre and the UWO Players' Guild as a student at the University of Western Ontario.[156] Another of the famous Toronto family to go onto the stage, Massey had started acting professionally at the Niagara Falls Summer Theatre with Franchot Tone. The Shelton-Amos company also engaged Olga Landiak, 1948 winner of the Nella Jefferis best-actor award and a performer at Stratford in 1954. Both Massey and Landiak eventually found careers in television.[157]

Although the Shelton-Amos Players never returned to London, their attempts to revive resident stock signalled the theatrical boom occurring in the postwar years. At the same time, their demise provides a graphic illustration of the profound impact that the Stratford Festival had on professional summer theatre in nearby communities.

Towards Canada's Centennial: 1954–1967

The single most important event in Toronto's theatrical history following the war was the opening of the Crest Theatre in Toronto in 1954.[158] Its impact was momentous enough to silence or disrupt several established organizations, namely the Jupiter Theatre, the New Play Society, the Belmont Group Theatre, and the Toronto-based second company of Kingston's International Players. In terms of Toronto's theatrical life, the Crest represented a major shift from smaller 'shoe-string' operations to a full-scale commercial theatre organization with its own theatre (a converted movie-house on Mount Pleasant Road), its own permanent company, and a pledge to bring Toronto into the international theatre scene. Theatre, in other words, became 'big business.'

Leading figures in the creation of the Crest were the Davis brothers, Murray and Donald, who had made their name as founders of the Straw Hat Players summer theatre in the Muskokas.[159] Since existing theatres in Toronto provided only limited opportunities for full-time professional work, the Davises (their sister Barbara Chilcott was only peripherally

Donald Davis and Barbara Chilcott in *The Glass Cage*, a play written for the Davis family (Murray, Donald, and Barbara) by J.B. Priestley and staged at the Crest Theatre in 1957

involved) decided to establish a permanent year-round company. Following a sophisticated promotion campaign, the Crest opened on 5 January 1954 to great fanfare, and for the next thirteen years it provided Toronto with its most exciting theatre. But drama was found not just on the stage. Over its history, the Crest was the target of public invective that ranged from allegations of financial mismanagement to harsh criticism of its artistic standards. Proof of the Crest's contributions to local theatre lies not solely in its record of over 140 productions, but in the calibre of the personnel who brought the work to life on the stage.

Casts were made up of actors who had already demonstrated a high level of achievement in Toronto theatre with the New Play Society, the Jupiter, and the International Players. To their numbers were added leading players from the flourishing Canadian repertory theatres in Ottawa and Montreal, as well as from the Stratford Festival. In fact, nearly every major Canadian stage personality played the Crest at one time or another. In addition, Dame Edith Evans, Gwen Ffrangcon-Davies, Powys Thomas, and Frederick Valk were among the international stars who appeared at the Crest.

If there was a weakness, it could be found in the often uninspired selection of plays. Excursions into the politically or dramatically unusual were the exception. For the most part, true to its original intent 'to provide repertory theatre in Toronto comparable with the best of British repertory companies,' the Crest chose to produce work from the lexicon of conventional English and American drama – Agatha Christie, J.B. Priestley, Noel Coward – that found acceptance among the majority of theatre patrons. Given the tenuous financial position of the Crest, it could hardly do otherwise.

But there were artistic successes. Jack Landau's *The Three Sisters*, with Kate Reid, Charmion King, and Amelia Hall, and Douglas Campbell's colourful interpretation of *Antony and Cleopatra* are just two that stand out. And there were box-office successes, too, such as John Holden's production of *Anniversary Waltz*, which ran for seven weeks, and Barry Morse's treatment of *Salad Days*, which ran for seventeen, plus a respectable stay off-Broadway. In addition, the Crest did keep its commitment to stage at least one original Canadian play each season, premièring, among others, two of Roberston Davies's satirical comedies, *A Jig for the Gypsy* and *Hunting Stuart*, Marcel Dubé's prize-winning *Zone* in an English-language translation, and Mary Juke's delightful Rosedale comedy *Every Bed Is Narrow*. And the Crest could also boast of Barbara Chilcott's Hour Company, a group of young actors who toured high schools in the province and played to hundreds of thousands of students over the years.

Regrettably, all these artistically rich productions, revolving stages, changes of programs, and tours to Montreal, Vancouver, and New York did not attract sufficient numbers of paying theatre-goers. In its last days, the Crest instituted a permanent company in full repertory with

Toby Robins, Chris Wiggins, Ken James, and Bruno Gerussi in the cast. But progressively hostile reviews from the influential drama critic Nathan Cohen helped cause audiences to dwindle and debts to mount. In the summer of 1964, the Canada Council, which had funded the Crest for six years, decided not to continue supporting Crest productions on the grounds that they were found to be 'indifferent.'

This must have been the hardest blow of all for the Davises. Granted, the Crest had not always measured up to expectations, but of all the companies operating in Toronto over the decade, it had proved by its very longevity and the sometimes bold choice of plays and memorable productions that it had unequivocally earned the title of Toronto's civic theatre, the opinions of Nathan Cohen notwithstanding. Nevertheless, this public repudiation of the Crest's efforts seriously damaged its chances to become the resident company at the proposed St Lawrence Centre.

Its finances and reputation diminished, the Crest undertook a fund-raising campaign, the proceeds of which allowed it to continue for another season; but it produced only one hit, Hochhuth's *The Deputy*, in which Leo Ciceri and Joseph Shaw gave outstanding performances. Another season followed, but the resignation of Murray Davis and a disastrous production of *Hedda Gabler*, criticized by Nathan Cohen for its 'benumbing indifference,' brought down the curtain at the Crest for the last time.[160]

At this point, the fate of the Crest became inextricably bound up with that of another organization operating in Toronto at the time: the Canadian Players, established in 1954 partly as work for off-season Stratford Festival artists.[161] For eleven winters the Players travelled extensively in Canada and the United States, usually with two companies presenting different plays in different parts of the continent each season. Although it broke its ties with the Festival in 1957 and moved its headquarters to Toronto, the Players organization continued to tour on an independent basis until the growth of regional theatres and television began to provide a more comfortable living for actors. By 1964, faced with debt and the need to redefine its aims, the Players' board of management announced the appointment of Marigold Charlesworth and Jean Roberts, successful directors of the Red Barn summer theatre in Jackson's Point, as the new artistic directors.[162] For their first full season (1965–6), Charlesworth and Roberts acquired the Central Library Theatre and set up two companies, one in residence, the other on tour, for the fall season, with the two changing places in the spring. The company in Toronto in the fall of 1965 produced Eliot's *Murder in the Cathedral* and Frisch's *The Firebugs*, in which Douglas Rain gave a sterling performance. In the meantime, the touring troupe's production of *The Importance of Being Earnest* (Wilde) and *The Glass Menagerie* (Williams) were both well received in southern Ontario. However, receipts were down overall and the lavish productions at home and on the road had rung up a substantial deficit. The 1965–6 season was not a good one either for the Canadian Players' cross-town rival, the Crest. In 1966, the boards of directors of the respective organizations met to discuss a merger. Unfortunately, differences of opinion occurred and when Charlesworth and Roberts resigned, negotiations collapsed and the organizations disbanded.

Over the next year, several companies tried unsuccessfully to fill the gap created in professional theatre by this situation. For example, Dennis Sweeting of the Kawartha Summer Festival mounted several travelling productions that employed former Crest and CP actors, but was forced out of business by the Hydro Theatre fire in December 1967. Aries Productions set up at the CP's old home, the Central Library Theatre, but could muster only twenty or so customers on some evenings. Finally, though Marshall-Taylor Production's staging of *Fortune and Men's Eyes* by a U.S. touring company[163] at the Central Library Theatre turned a tidy profit for producer Bill Marshall, it was a 'one-shot' effort and he left to pursue other interests, later as one of the backers of the controversial 1969 production of *Futz* (Rochelle Owens) and the prime mover in the creation of Toronto's international film showcase, the Festival of Festivals.

When it became clear that no substantial replacement for the Crest or the Canadian Players was forthcoming, William Graham, Crest board chairman, spearheaded a move to set up a company called Theatre Toronto, which ran for two four-play seasons at the Royal Alex until 1969. Clifford Williams, the British director hired to lead the new company, caused distress among many members of Toronto's cultural community, especially because the four plays he had chosen for the initial season were, as theatre historian Denis Johnston has put it, 'preoccupied with homosexuality and sadism';[164] with the notable exception of full houses to witness John Colicos's extraordinary performance in Hochhuth's *Soldiers*, they drew only 54 per cent capacity.[165] When Williams's production of *Edward II*, complete with graphic scenes of torture, started the second season, it was more than the conservative audiences could bear and the board of Theatre Toronto quickly forced his resignation. Although British directors Richard Digby Day and Timothy Bond replaced Williams for the last three plays on the bill,[166] the productions were not sufficiently profitable to erase an $80,000 debt, and Theatre Toronto closed at the end of the season.

In 1970, Toronto Arts Foundation, an amalgam of what remained

Peter Needham and Irene Mayeska, *Champagne Complex*, Red Barn Theatre, 1959

from the Crest, the Canadian Players, and Theatre Toronto, was formed and designated as the first tenant of the new St Lawrence Centre of the Arts, headed by Mavor Moore. Ironically, Crest alumni/ae (minus the Davis family) dominated the new company in its first years.[167] Thus, it seems, the general opinion that the Crest should have been the first and rightful resident of the St Lawrence Centre was vindicated in an unexpected way.

Throughout the period when it dominated the burgeoning theatre scene in Toronto, the Crest had to face challenges to its unofficial claim to being Toronto's civic theatre.[168] An early pretender to the throne, Premiere Productions, started at the Avenue Theatre in January 1956. Established by Davis rivals Mervyn Rosenzveig and Stan Jacobson, Premiere Productions functioned as a winter operation for Red Barn actors and a venue to offer Toronto audiences a brand of New York–

style theatre that had disappeared when the old Belmont Group Theatre gave way to the Crest. Indeed, the Lennicks were very much involved in the present company, as were such local CBC and theatre notables as Bill Walker, Stan Francis, Sammy Sales, Larry O'Connor, Joyce Sullivan, Barbara Hamilton, and Wally Koster. When the company shifted to the Circle Theatre (on Yonge Street north of Eglinton) a year later, it did not survive. What took its place was a company organized by Terry Fisher, a Montreal impresario in the media business, who imported American performers Cornelia Otis Skinner, Arthur Treacher, Luther Adler, and Theresa Wright as star attractions, supported by casts of local actors. Fisher was ever the entrepreneur; in fact, when criticized about the Americanized tone of the productions, he admitted he was more dedicated to the Canadian dollar than to the Canadian play.[169]

Terry Fisher's involvement in local theatre lasted only one season, but his partner, Eric Greenwood, continued in Toronto, producing a modern-dress version of John Ford's '*Tis Pity She's a Whore* for the short-lived Black Watch Productions in March 1960. Rehearsed at the King Edward Hotel and staged at the Lansdowne Theatre, the production featured Walter Massey, formerly with the Niagara Summer Theatre. However, the play was generally ignored and the company was not heard of again.

For a short time in the 1950s and 1960s, the Lansdowne Theatre housed a number of theatrical ventures that met with varying degrees of success. Perhaps the most sensational production was staged in 1958 when the Playhouse of Toronto, Inc., a New York–based company, gave the North American première of Sean O'Casey's *Cock-a-Doodle Dandy*, with American actor Will Geer in the cast. Its 'violently anti-clerical' attitudes scandalized many Roman Catholics in Toronto, but stimulated ticket sales. As a pre–New York try-out, the production was moderately successful, but when it moved to off-Broadway, the play did not fare as well. The biggest hit by the Playhouse group came in 1960, when a production of *The Tunnel of Love* played to 53,000 customers during its eleven-week run.

High hopes surrounded the announcement in September 1961 that Antony Ferry, a drama critic for the Toronto *Star*,[170] and Harvey Hart, artistic director at the CBC (and later at the Crest), had received an extraordinary $10,000 Canada Council grant to help establish the Civic Square Theatre in the Casino Theatre, formerly a burlesque house opposite the new city hall. With populist aims curiously similar to those of Roly Young's earlier Civic Theatre Association, the company apparently saw itself as offering an alternative to the élitist direction of the Crest and intended to provide modern classics at a modest price. At the same time, it also set out to attract people away from television and back into the theatre by using the full potential of all the new media, including film.[171] As Hart stated in the Toronto *Telegram*, 'What we hope to have when we're finished is Total Theatre – theatre that utilizes every available trick and triumph of 20th century technology.'[172] To that end, the theatre was extensively renovated. Widely applauded for its goals, the Civic Square Theatre opened its first production, Ionesco's *Rhinoceros*, in January 1962, with a star-studded array of actors headed by Jeremy Wilkes, Corinne Conley, Timothy Findley (from the Stratford Festival company and now a noted novelist and playwright), Joseph Shaw, Jane Mallett, and Gerard Parkes. But despite its superb cast, the production did not attract audiences, nor did the next offering, *Do You Know the Milky Way?*, supervised by one of the CBC's top directors, George Bloomfield, and performed by Budd Knapp, an actor of growing prominence on the stage and radio.

Burdened with a record of unprofitable presentations, Ferry and Hart abandoned their proposed bill and resorted to bringing in star performers in one-person shows on Sunday evenings. Lack of public funds and of interest in these attractions eventually killed the Civic Square project. Again it was apparent that Toronto could not absorb another theatre company, even one so ambitious and with such promise. But in a period of increasing accountability to governments, shareholders, investors, and taxpayers, a company could not afford to live on ambition and promise alone.

Numerous other organizations searching for a niche in the city's busy professional-theatre world came and went through the period. Some, such as the Avon Theatre and Status Theatre Productions had a short life. Others with bold plans, like Arts Theatre Foundation, conceived by Eamon Martin, and Canadian Group Theatre, proposed by Montgomery Davis and Roy Higgins, never got off the ground. One company, the old Belmont Group Theatre, experienced a brief revival when the Lennicks, disillusioned with the situation at the Crest, returned and breathed new life into their dormant creation. Settling in at the 250-seat Hydro Theatre in 1966, they created several important hits over the next year, including a fourteen-week run of Schisgal's *The Tiger* and *The Typists*, and *Cindy*, which featured Donald Sutherland in one of his first professional roles. In December 1967, the fortunes of the Belmont Group Theatre took a turn for the worse when the Hydro Theatre burned and they lost $15,000 worth of costumes. Undaunted, the Lennicks leased the small 200-seat Central Library Theatre and continued there until 1969, when their association with the television series *Trouble with Tracy* became a full-time commitment. During their years with the Belmont, the Lennicks had tried to give Toronto audiences some taste of an alternative theatre – slight, not quite off-Broadway plays dressed up to look and sound 'socially relevant'; but if they were guilty of producing bland material, it may have had more to do with what Toronto audiences would accept than with what the Lennicks were able to present. However, the Belmont Group's major transgression may have been its ill-advised alignment with New York attitudes in a period of growing nationalism and pride in Canada's own theatrical accomplishments.

This problem was evident in other developments in the city during the pre-Centennial years. When the Bayview Playhouse, a former movie theatre, opened in 1965 as a venue for live theatre,[173] it featured Broadway musicals almost exclusively and, following a long-established pattern at the city's mainstream theatres, it hired American actors for the lead roles. This privileging of American commercial success proved to be the greatest impediment to the development of a truly Canadian theatre.

Until the opening of the O'Keefe Centre in 1960, the Royal Alex remained Toronto's only commercial home for visiting companies. But like some shabby, faded dowager, the Royal Alex seemed increasingly removed from the tumultuous times. Rarely did the work presented there inspire or stimulate, nor did companies passing through attempt the bold and daring; more often than not, the Royal Alex continued to supply its annual mixture of standard hits from Broadway and London's West End. During the middle to late 1950s, companies from Britain tended to rely on their specialties of light drawing-room fare and Shakespearean drama. The Old Vic's bill of *Twelfth Night*, *Henry V*, and *Hamlet*, presented in 1960, was noteworthy for having David Gardner, the only Canadian actor (in fact, the only North American) in the cast, along with budding star Laurence Harvey and John Neville, a future director at Stratford, Ontario. Generally, however, the decline in the quality of touring productions was becoming noticeable by the end of the decade. Even American companies began to show signs of decline. Faced with a massive exodus of talent to television and film, rising costs, and a shift of audience interest to off- and off-off Broadway and regional theatre, commercial interests in New York were forced into cost-cutting measures that often included sending second-rank performers on the road.

While touring productions declined in total, an unprecedented number of one- and two-person shows began to appear featuring such celebrities as Edith Piaf, Marcel Marceau, Bette Davis, and Vincent Price. Efficient in the sense that such attractions required low overhead costs, solo and duo performances had a venerable tradition of providing star actors with an opportunity to display their talents in a more intimate and direct way than when encumbered by the push-and-pull demands of a regular multi-actor drama. In another way, the genre also provided competition to increasingly popular cabaret and 'intimate theatre' entertainment; furthermore, the individual performer, capitalizing on his or her reputation, could probably fare better financially this way than as part of a performing company.

As fewer quality touring productions were available, management at the Royal Alex was forced to bring in more eclectic and varied programs, consisting of everying from magicians to mentalists. In fact, one outcome of the shortage of dramatic attractions was the increasing willingness of the management to book Canadian-produced shows. In addition to *Spring Thaw*, the Royal Alex presented Mavor Moore's *Sunshine Town* (an adapation of Stephen Leacock's *Sunshine Sketches of a Little Town*, Don Harron's *The Broken Jug* (an adaptation of Kleist's play), the college musical success *My Fur Lady*, another musical revue *Jubiliee* (starring Corinne Conley and Dave Broadfoot), as well as pre-Broadway try-outs for two productions from the Stratford Festival – an ill-fated staging of Marlowe's *Tamburlaine the Great* and more successful venture, Shakespeare's *Two Gentlemen of Verona*. In relative terms, the appearance of so many Canadian-based productions at the Royal Alex in the short period between 1954 and 1960 represents a significant breakthrough for the burgeoning Canadian professional theatre, especially when one considers that in the preceding half-century since it opened in 1907, only a handful of original Canadian works had made it to the stage of the Royal Alex. This current surge underlines the increasing pressure for Canadian work to be recognized and not to be relegated to the less prestigious theatres. But it also points up an undeniable irony about the reality of Canadian professional theatre – that in any other country, the main body of produced work is of that nation, not of another.

In the fall of 1960, when the new O'Keefe Centre opened its doors, the Royal Alex faced its first major competition since the days of the Grand Opera House and the Princess Theatre. At 2200 seats, the O'Keefe presented a formidable opponent. Its capabilities for handling mammoth shows were immediately apparent in its inaugural attraction, a lavish pre-Broadway trial production of a new musical, *Camelot*, which featured a star-studded cast of Julie Andrews (Guenevere), Richard Burton (Arthur), Canadian actor/singer Robert Goulet (Lancelot), and Roddy MacDowell (Mordred). The opening performance was a whopping 4½-hour marathon that found few patrons in the theatre at the final curtain. In their efforts to whittle the show down to size, Alan Jay Lerner (librettist) and Moss Hart (director) were both hospitalized, but their efforts paid off and the musical went on to Broadway where it became a huge success, running over two years. The season continued with a stellar bill, including Laurence Olivier in *Becket* (it grossed $100,000), Brendan Behan's *The Hostage* and *Impulse*, another Lerner and Loewe smash hit, *My Fair Lady*, and a summer of celebrity entertainers starring in their own shows – in all, twenty-nine separate productions between September 1960 and August 1961.

The Royal Alex tried to counter with its own array of popular attractions, beginning with a return engagement of the previous season's hit, *The World of Suzie Wong*, and continuing with a full program including a well-received production of Robertson Davies's full-length comedy *Love and Libel*, Lorraine Hansbury's popular *A Raisin in the Sun*, Peter Shaffer's *Five Finger Exercise* directed by John Gielgud and performed by Jessica Tandy and Brian Bedford (soon to become a star at the Stratford Festival), and appearances by England's Stanley Holloway and Cedric Hardwicke. Clearly it was 'no contest' when the Royal Alex tried to match the O'Keefe's ability to mount a full season. But the older theatre had certain advantages over its junior opponent. Quite simply, it could still offer a traditional theatrical experience in environs that audiences continued to appreciate. Thus, when it entered into an agreement with the American Theatre Guild to offer subscriptions for the following year, 21,000 subscribers signed up for the ten-show program. The O'Keefe, by contrast, was running into various difficulties. Even though it grossed over $5 million in its first two years, the Centre still ran up deficits, a situation that bears out the old adage about the theatre – that it is not the size of the house but the extent of the operating costs that dictates profits. Management of the O'Keefe Brewery Company, owner of the theatre, must have breathed a sigh of relief, therefore, when the city of Toronto accepted the Centre as a gift and assumed all further debts.

Whatever aspirations the O'Keefe Centre might have had about becoming a first-rate theatre were never realized, since in reality the Centre was forced into providing a wide assortment of rather pedestrian entertainments to cover costs. Dramatic productions eventually served merely as book-ends to a hodge-podge of Las Vegas night-club acts; it was also becoming clear that the theatre's cavernous stage dwarfed anything but the largest spectacles and that its vastness was really better suited for opera and ballet. Actually, both the Canadian Opera Company and the National Ballet soon made the O'Keefe their home, after finding the Royal Alex too small for their productions.

In the meantime, the Royal Alex experienced its own difficulties. In 1963, manager Ernest Rawley sensed that the days of the theatre were numbered. Touring attractions were scarcer, and he started filling in the gaps in his schedule with Canadian productions. An extended run of

Spring Thaw and the appearance of Gratien Gélinas's popular *Bousille and the Just* met with varying degrees of success at the box office, but try as he might, Rawley could not find the right combination of attractions. Finally, at the end of the 1962–3 season, the administrators of the Mulock Estate put the grand old 'Queen of King Street' up for sale. Local entrepreneur 'Honest Ed' Mirvish could not resist a bargain (it sold for $215,000) and bought the vintage theatre, restoring it to its Edwardian elegance over the summer of 1963. Whether an act of madness or bravery, Mirvish's purchase of the Royal Alex certainly presented him with a challenge, for he would have to compete not only against the O'Keefe but also against sixty-one other theatres operating in the city at the time. In the hands of its new owner, the Royal Alex entered a unique period in its history. Mirvish, a consummate 'bargain basement' retailer, decided early that the only way to fight the competition and win was to play their game, but better and cheaper. While the O'Keefe ploddingly offered the same spread of attractions from one season to another, the Royal Alex began to reflect more and more the Mirvish touch. Blending low-budget productions of current Broadway musicals and tried-and-true bedroom farces with pre-Broadway tryouts, some Canadian shows (*Spring Thaw* again, plus Brian Swarbrick's *Return to the Mountain*), and a summer of musical comedies, he kept the theatre financially viable through the seasons leading up to Canada's centennial in 1967. Meanwhile, the O'Keefe was running into trouble with the critics, who panned the highly publicized but wretched John Gielgud–Richard Burton productions of *Hamlet* in which Burton mumbled his way through the title role and Hume Cronyn as Polonius rescued the piece from complete failure. They also decried Arthur Miller's *After the Fall* as tedious. Nathan Cohen went even further, slamming it as 'a gross and odious play.' The incomparable but tragically besotted Judy Garland, who was all the rage just four years before, could hardly draw enough patrons to break even on her second appearance. And what befell Canada's own Feux Follet should have more rightly been the fate of other lesser productions, for the French-Canadian dance troupe had the ignominious distinction of having the smallest audience ever in attendance at the O'Keefe. By 1966, dramatic productions had fallen to one per year, the rest of the attractions being ponderous or, conversely, flimsy vehicles for aging stars.

As the country celebrated its centennial, a decidedly Canadian flavour could be detected in the program at the Royal Alex, which mounted a hastily-put-together production of *The Teahouse of the August Moon* (expertly acted by a Canadian cast) and a new play by Canadian humourist Eric Nicol, *Like Father, Like Fun*. At the O'Keefe, by contrast, there was no discernible acknowledgment of Canada's birthday. With more than a little irony, one realizes that in Canada's centennial year, except for the annual visits of the Canadian Opera Company and the National Ballet, not one item at the O'Keefe, the nation's largest theatre, was of Canadian origin, yet nearly every other nationality was represented, from the Red Army Chorus to the Ballet Africains. One must ask what purpose such an institution has in a country if it is so much in the hands of interests that do so little to support or promote that country's own culture. By way of contrast and to its credit, the Royal Alex at least made some effort to recognize Canada's centennial when it brought in that extraordinarily Canadian musical, *Anne of Green Gables*. Written by Don Harron for the inauguration of the Charlottetown Festival, the show rose above its sentimentality to represent to the world ever since what may be the quintessential qualities of being Canadian: a supreme sense of tolerance and understanding.

Outside local mainstream theatre lay a host of small professional and semi-professional groups whose main purpose was to provide an alternative to the politically and morally conventional productions of the city's highly commercialized (some might say 'Americanized') 'establishment' houses like the Royal Alex and the O'Keefe Centre. Many of these alternative companies arose in response to a concerted drive to establish a uniquely Canadian theatre and to increasing government funding for the arts (as recommended by the Massey-Lévesque royal commission of 1951). In their ideology, these companies represented a direct link to the 'beat' generation through the 1950s and 1960s, when social and political revolution was in the air, when the standards of the silent, postwar generation were found wanting. It was a time, too, when civil rights and antiwar demonstrations rocked the United States and when the attitudes and ideals at the very core of North American culture came under attack.

In its early stages, the beatnik culture in Toronto was reflected in the growth of new forms and venues of entertainment: coffee-houses and cabaret theatres offering a mixture of folk songs and satirical revues lampooning middle-class values; closet-sized intimate out-of-the-way theatres to encourage 'participatory' experiences; 'happenings' and other theatrically based experiments deriving from the Dadaists and surrealists and from the politically based theatre of social protest in the 1930s.

Some small companies, like the Producer's Playhouse, were dedicated to 'literary' theatre, giving readings and studio productions of current avant-garde plays that were treated more as academic curiosities than as instruments of social change. Others, like Adventure Theatre,

New Venture Players, and the Garret Theatre, were founded as forums for dissent and produced the works of such provocative playwrights as John Herbert, author of the controversial play on prison homosexuality *Fortune and Men's Eyes*.[174] These groups protested everything from housing conditions to abortion and represented nearly every political stripe and sexual persuasion. Most had a very short shelf life.

Added to all of this activity were numerous other small alternative operations (more often than not semi-professional or amateur) associated with the University of Toronto. Foremost among them was the University Alumnae Dramatic Club, founded in 1918, which gained new energies in the mid-1960s after it opened its new Coach House Theatre (a converted synagogue). Following such powerful productions as Pinter's *The Caretaker* (directed by Herbert Whittaker and acted with eerie perfection by Donald Ewer in the title role), the Club entered a period under the direction of Brian Meeson (later chairman of the theatre program at Ryerson), whose ingenuity brought new life and dramatic materials to the Club to the end of the decade.

In the vanguard of Toronto's alternative theatre was a small band of American performers and teachers who came north, some to escape the McCarthy persecutions or, later, the Vietnam draft, others merely to seek new opportunities. Some, trained at the Actors' Studio in New York, found the theatre in Canada firmly entrenched in traditional attitutdes towards acting and production and they set out to bring about change. Among the first Americans with Actors' Studio training to settle in Toronto was Al Saxe who founded the Studio Theatre in 1956. An acting teacher, he ran his classes on the Method system. Such an approach was a marked departure from that found in Toronto's older and more established schools, which were highly influenced by classical British training methods. Saxe had some evident success, and within a year or two, he had produced such well-known graduates as Anna Cameron, Toby Robins, Larry Solway, Joan Fairfax, and Sheila Billing – all of whom found careers in the broadcast industry. Saxe's Asquith Street studio later housed the First Floor Club, a typical beat-generation coffeehouse that offered jazz, folk music, poetry, and play readings and the occasional stage production. Also from the Actors' Studio, Eli Rill founded the Actors' Lane Workshop in 1957, the Studio Workshop in 1961, and then, with Janine Manatis, the more successful Playwrights' Studio, which trained Canadian actors Michael Sarrazin and Guy Sanvido. Another ex-member of the Actors' Studio, Leslie Charles, established the Actors' Theatre at the popular House of Hambourg cabaret theatre and jazz club in 1962.[175] The House had already made a name as a centre for innovative theatrical production with its long-running hit,

Jack Gelber's *The Connection*, in which several of Canada's best-known performers, among them Don Francks, Gordon Pinsent, Bruno Gerussi, and Al Waxman, acted early in their professional careers.

The Actors' Studio influence from the United States did not dominate the period entirely. In fact, the ideas of the 'new' British theatre were beginning to have a local impact. The Village Playhouse company, which appeared on the scene in 1961, insisted on producing the latest drama from Britain's 'angry young men' and approaching it with an appropriate style. Squeezed into a small eighty-one-seat hall on Laplante Street at the edge of Toronto's original artists' colony, the VP compiled an enviable record of first Toronto productions of works by John Arden and John Osborne, as well as the world première of Sean O'Casey's controversial *The Drums of Father Ned*, which had been banned in Dublin the previous year and caused a minor sensation locally. In spite of its tiny stage, the VP managed to attract an impressive array of local actors to the company, including Donald Ewer, Stellar Finlayson, Trudi Wiggins, Joyce Campion, Ken James, Pam Hyatt, Heath Lamberts, Jackie Burroughs, Peter Sturgess, and Barbara Chilcott. The same was true for directors, notably George Bloomfield and Sean Mulcahy.

The company was at its best in works that reflected protest and social change in contemporary life. But among the thirty plays in its two-year history were many concessions to audiences who found the recent British playwrights too challenging. Although the VP had established itself as the only place in town to give audiences a taste of what was happening in modern British drama, so many other groups had entered the market by 1963 that it was impossible to remain viable financially without a broader repertoire.

If the Village Playhouse was Toronto's Royal Court,[176] then Toronto Workshop Productions was its Theatre Royal, the home of Joan Littlewood's vigorous troupe. Undisputed leader of Toronto's alternative theatres, TWP was the longest-lived, the most productive, the most inventive, and the most ideologically consistent of all the alternative companies operating in the city through the 1960s.[177] On these points, even critics Nathan Cohen and Herbert Whittaker could agree. TWP resulted from the amalgamation in 1961 of two groups, the Arts Theatre Club of Basya Hunter, and Workshop Productions of George Luscombe. Hunter trained in the theatre in Montreal and with the local workers' theatre movement in the 1930s. Luscombe had just returned to Canada from a five-year apprenticeship with Joan Littlewood's Theatre Workshop in England. He joined Antony Ferry's play-reading circle, the 'Theatre Centre' at 47 Fraser Avenue, located in the heart of Toronto's industrial area, and became its artistic director in 1959, at which point the group's name was changed to Workshop Productions.[178]

Luscombe operated WP out of the small basement at 47 Fraser Avenue, where he put into practice Littlewood's ideas. Foremost was the concept of collective creation, a process by which the director and playwright (usually a writer-in-residence) worked up a basic guideline for characterization, dialogue, and situation and handed it over to the actors and technicians, who then improvised accordingly.

Acting styles also reflected the Littlewood rejection of conventional stage mannerisms in favour of the greater possibilities in mime, music hall, and the movement techniques of Rudolf Laban. The sheer physicality of the productions required performers to be actors, mimes, acrobats, singers, and dancers all rolled into one. Innovative staging became a trademark and some truly inventive props and sets brought unpretentious authenticity to the action. In dramatic terms, the results were visually and viscerally engaging, meant for a proletarian audience, not for high-brows.

The company's modus operandi was best typified by the first collective effort, *Hey Rube!*, an imaginatively conceived and presented work staged at the Fraser Street home in the spring of 1961. For the occasion, the tiny studio space was turned into a circus tent, with real bleachers (seating 110) and a 'big top,' a 35-foot parachute stretched overhead. The production drew two thousand over its run, and vaulted the company into immediate public attention.[179]

Over the next six years, Toronto Workshop Productions (as the group became known in 1963)[180] embarked on some of its most exciting ventures. For example, they established a summer company, Theatre 35, and toured cottage country with a program carefully geared to rural tastes and a cast that played its parts with appropriate rustic embellishments. TWP also produced two of its most distinctive works – *Before Compiègne* and *The Mechanic* – both by resident writer Jack Winter. The versatility of the company was neatly highlighted in the two productions, the first by its powerful social commentary, the second by its endlessly inventive staging. TWP also carried its work directly to the public by producing 'Theatre in the Square,' a program of free theatre in Nathan Phillips Square. TWP became deeply involved in the 1967 Centennial celebrations by taking its original production, *Hey Rube!*, on a university tour to Queen's and Western; it then inaugurated the Youth Pavilion at Expo 67 with its theatre-in-the-round production of *The Mechanic*; finally, it opened the Theatre in the Park outside the Exhibition Hall of the Festival Theatre at Stratford, where it presented a summer program of three plays.

Nancy Jowsey and George Luscombe devised a translucent panel onto which were projected images, including Georg Grosz's cartoons, for Michael John Nimchuk's adaptation of Hašek's novel *The Good Soldier Schweik*; Toronto Workshop Productions, 1969.

In 1967, TWP moved from its cramped quarters to a relatively spacious former automobile showroom at 12 Alexander Street, and consequently found itself more than ever in the public limelight. Over the next few years, TWP continued to be the most prolific and most vital English-language company in the country. Often underrated because of its leftist leanings, TWP did not waiver from its artistic objectives or from its commitment to be a voice of social commentary.

Of the numerous small professional alternative troupes to emerge in Toronto, few had their own performance spaces, but several small, well-equipped playhouses eventually were created to meet their needs. Centre Stage, for example, was founded in 1960 by Esther Solomon who, with the help of over a thousand volunteers, remodelled a former gym and over the next three years provided a series of programs and classes in performance and art-related skills in dance, opera, and theatre.[181] Centre Stage also housed a children's theatre (supervised by Ann Livingston) and an extensive theatre library and art collection supported by foreign consulates located in the city. Over its career, Centre Stage was the scene of many important local theatrical events, including the première of John Coulter's *Sleep My Pretty One*, the Bohemian Embassy's first annual *Village Revue*, the first Toronto productions of Tennessee Williams's *27 Wagons Full of Cotton* and Jean-Paul Sartre's *The Respectful Prostitute*, and the work of three young local directors, Leon Major, James Balfour, and Ray Lawlor. However, by the end of the summer of 1963, Centre Stage was no more. A victim of Toronto's expanding subway system, it was expropriated and demolished; but in its short history it had produced its own share of important moments in local theatre.

In 1964, another playhouse whose size also met the requirements for small-company productions was built into the Colonnade, a new complex of trendy shops and apartments on Bloor Street.[182] Daringly situated in the centre of the building's main lobby, the Colonnade literally brought theatre to the people, and with it came a whole new range of events, such as lunch-time productions to accommodate busy shoppers, students, and employees 'on the go.' Toronto Workshop Productions opened the theatre with its exciting collaborative effort *Before Compiègne*. From that moment, the theatre became the focal point for a variety of small companies, amateur and professional, who rented the space in order to take advantage of its proximity to a lucrative new audience. Halwyn Productions, a small professional company, made the theatre its home on several occasions, beginning with a lively adaptation of *Canterbury Tales* in 1964, later in a double bill of Genet's *The Maids* and Fried's *The Dodo Bird* (starring future television personality Al Waxman), and in a number of 'instant' or 'vest pocket' performances featuring Joyce Campion in lyric readings and dramatic excerpts aimed at noon-hour audiences. Merger Productions appeared to be the most adventuresome group, first with Maurice Evans's staging of Delaney's *A Taste of Honey* in tandem with *The Best of the Bunch* (featuring Victor Garber and Tim Devlin), and subsequent presentations of Jellicoe's *The Knack* and a bold foray into the taboo territory of homosexuality in John Burgess's play, *A Stranger Unto My Brethren*. However, independent productions of Kafka's *The Trial* (with Stellar Finlayson, Peter Sturgess, and Paul Soles), Genet's *The Balcony* (with Margaret Griffin and Henry Tarvainen), Strindberg's *Miss Julie* (with Jackie Burroughs in the title role, Bruno Gerussi, and Deborah Turnbull), and Joe Orton's *Entertaining Mr Sloane* rivalled anything produced by better-known companies at the theatre.

The Colonnade also became a favourite spot for children's theatre because its intimate design made it possible for audiences and performers to interact. In 1965, the first of many programs for young people was produced by Ernest Schwartz, an American director educated at Yale and founder of the Studio Lab Theatre.[183] And Susan Rubes, formerly of the Museum Children's Theatre, launched a series of productions inspired by Brian Way, co-founder of the Theatre Centre of London, England, whose methods of staging drama used professional actors trained to involve children to the point of active participation. The enthusiastic reception of these productions persuaded Rubes of the need to address the specific interests of youth audiences and led her eventually to found Toronto's famous Young People's Theatre.[184]

The Colonnade continued to be a lively theatre well into the 1970s, offering a wide range of activities for the young and the old. Of all the small theatres in the city, the Colonnade possessed by far the most consistent record of interesting material, sometimes bravely presenting works that otherwise would not have seen the light of day, including some important original work.

Only one other small theatre, the Poor Alex, could match the Colonnade's position as the busiest and most productive centre in the city.[185] The Poor Alex opened on Brunswick Avenue in 1964 slightly outside the fashionable shops, galleries, and studios called 'Mirvish Village,' an area rejuvenated by famous department-store owner 'Honest Ed' Mirvish. A 'poor cousin' of the more illustrious Royal Alexandra Theatre (which Mirvish had purchased in 1963), the Poor Alex brought the same kind of populist perspective to small-scale theatre that its namesake offered to the carriage trade downtown. Created out of an unused plastics factory warehouse, and fitted out with leftovers from the Royal Alex renovations, the little playhouse made a very serviceable and comfortable space for theatre companies seeking an inexpensive venue for their productions. Less sedate and more eclectic than the Colonnade, the Poor Alex became home to a wide assortment of organizations.

Among the first to take advantage of the theatre's trendy 'off-Bloor' ambience were the Broadview Barn Players, who over their eleven productions offered mainly nineteenth-century pot-boilers. In contrast, Aries Productions, bankrolled for $75 by a group of theatre people headed by Bruce Gray from London's Mermaid Theatre, presented more up-to-date plays, including first Toronto productions of Tennessee Williams' *Suddenly Last Summer* and *The Milk Train Doesn't Stop Here Anymore*, Edward Albee's *Who's Afraid of Virginia Woolf*, and Jean Anouilh's *The Rehearsal*, in which Sean Mulcahy gave an acclaimed performance. The company also won some notoriety for its presentation of Schnitzler's oft-banned sex play *La Ronde*.

In 1966, when the Barn Players and Aries Productions both deserted the Poor Alex, the Brunswick Avenue theatre was left without a sustaining artistic direction and it entered a period of decline. A few small companies continued to use the facilities, however. Foremost among them was the Theatre Company of Toronto, a group of non-Equity talent that over the period presented a series of rather off-beat but innovative works. Peter Mann, an important figure in this company, was a young producer/director/writer who also organized noon-time lunch theatre at the Colonnade and later opened the Bayview Playhouse.

The Joyce Society also periodically utilized the Poor Alex to celebrate various dates and anniversaries related to the literary world of James Joyce. Two of the narrators for these special events were media guru Marshall McLuhan and Canadian novelist Hugh Garner. Other groups, among them the Questors, the Q Players, the Masquers, and the Otterville Players, were responsible for first Toronto showings of William Inge's *Picnic*, John Osborne's *Look Back in Anger*, Jack Richardson's *Gallows Humour*, Charles Dyer's *Rattle of a Simple Man*, and Jean Genet's *Deathwatch*, as well as several original works by local playwrights; in addition, readings were given by the Compact Six, a group of James Reaney's disciples from the University of Western Ontario.

Increasingly, the Poor Alex became a haven for nondescript groups and bands of actors intent on 'doing their own thing' (however subjective that might be), rather than playing to an audience. By the spring of 1967, the sorry state of the theatre and the increasing inanity of the dramatic material performed there provoked criticism from all the local drama reviewers; it was, someone pointed out, 'the first time the critics agreed on anything.'

The Poor Alex never recovered its early respectability and it limped into the late sixties, at which point The Three Schools, an alternative arts-education complex, rescued it and brought back some of its former glory. Except for a brief time as home of the Tarragon Theatre, the Poor Alex has continued to be the site of small-scale theatre productions and an almost forgotten part of the Mirvish theatrical empire, except to a small group of inveterate theatre-goers.

While the companies operating at Centre Stage, the Colonnade, and the Poor Alex could not be classed as 'alternative' in quite the same sense as later organizations such as Theatre Passe Muraille, Toronto Free Theatre, Tarragon Theatre, and Factory Theatre Lab, they nevertheless were major forces in breaking traditional attitudes to production styles and dramatic content and they helped to lay the groundwork for the alternative-theatre movement that swept over the city by the 1970s.

Other Communities
Although other centres did not experience the same unprecedented

growth of professional theatre witnessed in Toronto during the 1960s, the postwar impulse to establish an indigenous professional stage was generally alive and well. Simultaneously, the Dominion Drama Festival and its nationwide structure for local amateur groups was in a decline. This is not to say that the move to professionalism ended the DDF (it was renamed Theatre Canada in 1970 and closed in 1978). On the contrary, various types of amateur theatre activity continued to flourish, often associated with local initiatives connected with the up-coming Centennial celebrations, and some of these in turn led to the formation of professional organizations. For instance, in smaller communities, where expanding cultural resources to commemorate the Centennial often meant building new sports arenas or recreational facilities, some of them actually contained a well-equipped theatre space that became home to local troupes. Other communities erected larger and more elaborate facilities designed specifically for theatrical performance on a commercial basis.

In Ottawa, the Theatrical Foundation of Ottawa replaced the Canadian Repertory Theatre in 1957 and for the next ten years acted as a combined booking and subscription agency that annually sponsored as many as ten touring productions of such companies as the Canadian Players, Spring Thaw, and the Metropolitan Opera. But when its offspring, the Towne Theatre, tried to create a community theatre in 1967, it failed to get civic support, even after two years of artistic successes. The Towne folded in 1969, the same year the National Arts Centre opened.[186] A three-theatre complex with both French- and English-language programming, the controversial Centre faced the responsibilities of serving several constituencies of Ottawa social and political life. In one light, the NAC might be seen as Ottawa's response to the 'regional' theatre development across the nation that had begun with the Manitoba Theatre Centre in 1958–9, and that saw the establishment of a professional theatre in most cities.

In London over the summers from 1955 to 1957, the New York Players, an American company, and the Trans-Canada Theatre Company, a Canadian company, attempted to become successors to the departed Shelton-Amos organization, but neither could accomplish the task. Except for occasional visits from touring productions on the circuit, professional theatre did not return to the city until the mid-1960s, when the UWO Campus Players' Summer Theatre (barely a semi-professional venture) staged several Canadian plays, including James Reaney's *The Sun and the Moon* (1965) and *Listen to the Wind* (1966). One of a growing number of university drama clubs across the country, the Campus Players attracted several young theatre activists who later became leaders in the alternative-theatre movement in Toronto. Martin Kinch, for example, went on to help establish Toronto Free Theatre; Keith Turnbull, the

Fiddler on the Roof (ink and pastel), Theatre London, designer Ed Kotanen, 1971

NDWT Company; and Paul Thompson, Theatre Passe Muraille.[187] The Campus Players were followed by a short-lived, but professional repertory company at UWO's Talbot Theatre Centre, and by Theatre London, formed between 1971 and 1975 out of the London Little Theatre. Theatre London has occupied the refurbished Grand Opera House since then.

The City of Hamilton, which had virtually no local professional theatre after the 1930s, continued without it until 1957, when Hamilton Theatre, Incorporated, was formed to produce four Broadway musicals each season. For the next decade, the company fulfilled its aims and became the closest thing to a community theatre seen anywhere in Ontario. The proximity to Toronto, the Shaw and Stratford festivals, and summer theatre in the Niagara region gave play-goers in Hamilton a wide variety of professional theatre to choose from, but there remained the urge to have a civic theatre of their own. By 1967, with Centennial fever in the air, Hamilton Place became a reality, serving as a community centre and a home for touring attractions.

Windsor, like many border centres, relied on its American neighbours to supply professional theatre over and above whatever touring companies might come its way. It was not until 1963 that a full-fledged professional company set up in the city. Called the Windsor International

Theatre Festival, it provided a single summer season of quite imaginative productions, but it could not surmount competition from Detroit and did not return. There was no other attempt at creating a local professional theatre until 1970, when a company based at the University of Windsor offered a summer program.

Chatham tried professional theatre in June 1951, when the Community Centre's Sylvan Theatre experimented briefly with 'theatre under the stars,' but audiences did not take to the idea. Another short-lived experiment occurred in November–December 1955, when a season of professional theatre was planned with actors from the Stratford Festival and Toronto. But after only two productions the company ceased operations. Major activity did not return until the Thames Theatre Dramatic Society shows undertaken by home-town product John Ford Taylor in the mid-1960s.

On 29 June 1948 in the ball room of Kingston's La Salle Hotel, Arthur Sutherland's International Players opened their first season of summer stock, which ended ten weeks later after a highly successful première of Robertson Davies's *Fortune, My Foe*.[188] Sutherland had been active in theatre at Queen's University with Davies and Lorne Greene during the 1930s, and had gone on to the American Academy of Dramatic Art, helped found New York's Imperial Players, performed in stock and the American Armed Forces, before returning to his home town as it was revitalizing after the war. Following a second summer, Sutherland, with Drew Thompson, opened a winter-spring season in Toronto's Leaside Collegiate. The International Players continued in both cities, sometimes with two companies simultaneously, and with occasional visits to towns in the Kingston area, until Sutherland died in September 1953. One further summer season in Kingston was mounted by Drew Thompson. Over the years, within a repertoire of light comedy, melodrama, and domestic drama, the Players' casts, a mix of Americans and about fifty different Canadians, had included Cosy Lee, Donald Davis, Joy Coghill, Timothy Findley, William Hutt, Charmion King, William Needles, Bernard Slade,[189] and Neil Vipond, all of whom went on to significant careers. But from 1953 to the end of the 1960s, Kingston was without professional theatre.

Kingston's experience mirrored the developments in professional theatre in many communities outside Toronto. Following a wave of activity during the postwar period evidenced in the rapid growth of summer stock and the establishment of the festival theatres at Stratford and Niagara-on-the-Lake, interest tended to wane through the early sixties, only to be revived in the years leading to Canada's Centennial and beyond. This second wave resulted in the formation of regional or civic theatres at

Sudbury (the Sudbury Theatre Centre and Kam Theatre), Thunder Bay (Magnus Theatre), Hamilton (Theatre Aquarius), St Catharines (Press Theatre), Peterborough (Arbor Theatre), Blyth (Blyth Festival), Grand Bend (Huron County Playhouse), Lindsay (Kawartha Summer Theatre), the Muskoka Festival, and the Petrolia Summer Theatre. In addition, vigorous French-language and Native Indian organizations and ethnic theatre companies, together with the first theatrical expressions from the gay, lesbian, and feminist communities, reflected the changing character of Ontario society and contemporary values, and at the same time enriched theatre with ethnic, racial, and gender diversity.[190] Added to these developments was the growth of theatre training, research, and study programs at several universities and colleges, including Toronto, Ryerson, Guelph, Windsor, Brock, and George Brown, and the establish- ment of archives and collections of materials related to provincial theatres and their histories, the most notable being at the Metropolitan Toronto Reference Library.[191] By the end of the 1960s, Ontarians had finally created a distinctive theatre they could truly call their own.

In the half-century of professional activity covered in this survey, a striking feature has been the persistent vision and the sustained effort directed towards creating a theatre independent from the commercial imported variety that has dominated the stage in Ontario. Despite the economic hardships of two world wars, the intervening Depression, and the constant intrusion of foreign cultural influences through radio, film, and television as well as theatre, that goal has been achieved – if the suc- cess of homegrown playwrights, actors, directors, and designers is any indication. It has been argued that these successes could not have been achieved without public funding and government policy dedicated to instituting a national theatre, a trend that began in the early 1930s with the establishment of the DDF and the CBC. The trend was accelerated by the formation of the Canada Council and various regional and local arts councils following the Massey-Lévesque royal commission recommen- dations of 1951. In this light, the subsequent explosion of activity in the 1960s and 1970s is in large part attributable to increased government support.[192]

In the ongoing discussion, however, two major arguments have been made against massive government funding: first, it breeds dependence on the public coffers and thereby kills entrepreneurial initiative; second, it locks companies into political, rather than cultural, agendas that serve the hegemonic interests that have controlled the province and the nation since the beginning. Yet the alternatives can be seen as equally disquiet- ing. While civic or community theatre flourished in the 1960s and

1970s, the 1980s has seen a reduction of government funding for the arts because of a widespread economic recession. In its place has come increased corporate sponsorship of cultural activities and a concomitant shift in ideology towards the production and marketing of the arts as a cultural industry.[193] Theatre in particular has come to be treated more and more like big business, as can be seen in the recent extravagantly promoted megamusicals *Cats*, *Phantom of the Opera*, *Les Misérables*, and *Miss Saigon*, in which spectacular stage effects and 'media hype,' rather than intellectual and artistic content, dominate production values.

Besides 'reducing' art to light entertainment, it has been argued, the corporatization of culture has produced other disturbing consequences:

- the exploitation and sensationalizing of cultural differences for profit, as in the much-touted September 1993 production of *Show Boat* at the new North York Centre
- the increasing difficulty for small companies to compete financially with privately subsidized blockbuster productions
- the co-option or marginalizing of diverse and alternative voices, as seen in the merger of Toronto Free Theatre and the Canadian Stage Company in 1988

If a lesson can be learned from Ontario's professional theatre history, it is that art production does not occur in a vacuum. From a postmodern perspective, one can see that the various forces that have promoted culture over the years have their own objectives. Such a position does not diminish what has been gained; it merely reveals that as theatre practitioners enter the next century and a period of increasing continentalism, they need to examine closely whom they serve and to what ends their efforts are directed.

NOTES

1 Denis Salter, 'The Idea of a National Theatre,' in *Canadian Canons*, ed. Robert Lecker (Toronto: University of Toronto Press 1991), 71–90.
2 This estimate includes a number of theatres in western Ontario identified by Orlo Miller (see London *Free Press*, 26 May 1962) and a list of comparable-sized theatres across the province compiled by John C. Lindsay in *Turn Out the Stars Before Leaving: The Story of Canada's Theatres* (Erin, Ont.: Boston Mills Press, 1983), 174. See also Theatre Ontario, comp., *Theatre Ontario; Theatre Identification Project, 1972* (Toronto: Theatre Ontario Personnel, 1972). Although the following gate receipts are not for Ontario cities, they provide some idea of the typical 'take' for a Western tour

of *Peg O' My Heart* in October and November 1914, and indicate, as the newspaper account states, that 'it pays to play in Canada':

Winnipeg	19–24 October	$6307.75
Moose Jaw	26–27 "	1244.00
Regina	28–29 "	1761.25
Saskatoon	30–31 "	1899.75
Prince Albert	2–3 November	912.25
Edmonton	5–7 "	3015.75
Calgary	9–11 "	4016.00

(New York *Dramatic Mirror*, 2 December 1914; see also ibid., 22 December 1917.)
3 The Royal Alexandra Theatre, the Princess Theatre, the Grand Opera House, Shea's Victoria, the Gaiety Theatre (a vaudeville house), Shea's Hippodrome (a vaudeville house), the newly opened Loew's Elgin and Winter Garden complex, the Lyric (a Yiddish theatre), and the Star (a burlesque theatre)
4 Forbes-Robertson visited Toronto (6–18 April), London (20 April), Hamilton (21–22 April), Kingston (23 April), and Ottawa (24–26 April); see *Saturday Night*, 3 January and 4 April 1914; see also Toronto *World*, 6 April 1914. Benson appeared in Toronto, week of 27 October 1913 and return engagement week of 5 January 1914 (*Saturday Night*, 25 October, 27 December 1913, and 3 January 1914; Toronto *World*, 28 October 1913 and 5 January 1914). Anglin performed in Toronto, week of 29 December 1913 (Toronto *Globe*, 20 and 27 December 1913; *Saturday Night*, 27 December 1913; Toronto *World*, 14 and 29 December 1913). Faversham played in Toronto, weeks of 29 December 1913 and 5 January 1914 (Toronto *Globe*, 20 December 1913; *Saturday Night*, 11 December 1913 and 3 January 1914; Toronto *Mail and Empire*, 29 December 1913; Toronto *World*, 5 January 1914). Sothern was seen in Toronto, week of 4 April 1914 (*Saturday Night*, 2 May 1914; Toronto *World*, 4 May 1914).
5 Arliss toured southern Ontario during the war years in a series of plays based on historic figures, including *Disraeli* (Hamilton, London, Peterborough, Kingston, and Ottawa, 7–11 September 1914), *Paganini* (Toronto, 22–27 November 1915; London, Hamilton, Kingston, and Ottawa, 27 March–1 April 1916), and *Hamilton* (Toronto, 31 December 1917–5 January 1918). John Barrymore appeared with Constance Collier in their great Broadway success *Peter Ibbetson* (Kingston, 11–12 March 1918; London, 15–16 March 1918; Toronto, 18–23 March 1918). The comment on Maude Adams was quoted in R. Moody, 'American Actors, Managers, Producers and Directors,' in T.W. Craik, general ed., *The Revels History of Drama in English, Volume VIII: American Drama* (New York: Barnes and Noble Books, 1977), 109. Adams toured the province in works by her favourite author, James M. Barrie, first as the lead in *Rosalind* and *The Legend of Lenora* (Toronto, 19–24 October 1914; Hamilton and London, 26–27 October 1914), and then as the heroine of *A Kiss for Cinderella* (Toronto, 10–15 December 1917; Ottawa, Kingston, Hamilton, and London, 17–22

December 1917). Bernhardt, 'The Divine Sarah,' stopped at Hamilton, Kingston, and
Ottawa, 22–24 November 1917. See John Hare and Ramon Hathorn, 'Sarah Bern-
hardt's Visits to Canada,' in *Theatre History in Canada / Histoire du Théâtre au
Canada* 2 (Fall, 1981), 110–16.

6 Hamilton *Spectator*, 2 December 1916
7 Toronto *Star Weekly*, 12 July 1913; Toronto *Globe*, 29 March and 20 April 1915, 6;
Toronto *World*, 19 April 1915
8 Toronto *World*, 26 October 1914; see also New York *Dramatic Mirror*, 4 November
1914.
9 London *Free Press*, 19 February 1916; New York *Dramatic Mirror*, 11 March 1916.
The play was cancelled outright in Stratford and money refunded (Stratford *Herald*,
19 February 1916, and Stratford *Beacon*, 19 February 1916). See also Malcolm Dean,
*Censored! Only in Canada: The History of Film Censorship – the Scandal Off the
Screen* (Toronto: Virgo Press, 1981), 22–4.
10 As quoted by Main Johnson in Toronto *Star Weekly*, 27 May 1915
11 Patrick B. O'Neill, 'The British Canadian Theatrical Organization Society and The
Trans-Canada Theatre Society,' *Journal of Canadian Studies* 15:1 (Spring 1980),
56–67.
12 Martin-Harvey performed in several Ontario towns in 1914, including Belleville
(2 February), Kingston (6–7 February), Guelph (9 February), St Catharines
(11 February), Woodstock (17 February), London (20–21 February), and St Thomas
(11 March), and played a week in Toronto (23–28 February). Laurence Irving and
Mabel Hackney were seen in Kingston (23–24 February 1914), Belleville (27 February) St Catharines (5 March), Toronto (9–14 March), St Thomas (17 March), and
Sudbury (24 March). Esmond and Moore visited Sudbury (23 February 1914), Renfrew (24 February), Lindsay (27 February), Kingston (7 March), St Thomas (11
March), and Woodstock (12 March). In London, Martin-Harvey made the following
comments: 'We are not satisfied with the condition of the theatre in Canada. It is too
much at the mercy of speculative men who send you what they choose and who are
not in touch with the Imperial Canadian ideals in the country. You have too many
companies which when they come across the line from the south suddenly become
all-British and who very frequently are not; and stars who are one week born in Calgary and the next in Indianapolis.' (London *Free Press*, 26 January 1914)
13 Granville Barker gave a lecture in Ottawa entitled 'Some New Ideas in the Theatre,'
evening of 12 November 1915 (Ottawa *Journal*, 6 and 12 November 1915) before
appearing on stage; he was seen in Toronto, week of 27 December 1915 (*Saturday
Night*, 15 December 1915, 6; Toronto *World*, 20 December; New York *Dramatic
Mirror*, 8 January 1916). Beerbohm Tree appeared in Toronto, night of 20 November
1916 (Hamilton *Spectator*, 21 November 1916; *Saturday Night*, 18 November 1916;
New York *Dramatic Mirror*, 2 December 1916; see also Toronto *Daily Star*, 25
November 1916, for Beerbohm Tree's views on the new medium of film). Mrs
Patrick Campbell played Toronto, 19–24 April 1915 (Toronto *World*, 12 April and

19 April; New York *Dramatic Mirror*, 5 May 1915; program: Metropolitan Toronto
Reference Library, Theatre Section). She performed in Ottawa, evenings of 26 and
27 April 1915 (Ottawa *Journal*, 17 April and 24 April; New York *Dramatic Mirror*,
5 May 1915). She also appeared in Kingston, evening of 28 April 1915 (Kingston
British Whig, 20 April and 22 April). Though booked into Hamilton and London, she
apparently never appeared (New York *Dramatic Mirror*, 5 May 1915). In the 1915–16
season, she returned to the province, playing in London, matinee and evening of
5 February (London *Free Press*, 29 January and 5 February 1916; New York *Dramatic
Mirror*, 11 March). She also appeared at Peterborough, 7 February 1916, and Hamilton, evening of 8 February 1916 (Hamilton *Spectator*, 29 January and 5 February).

14 Yeats lectured on the Irish Theatre Movement at Margaret Eaton School of Expression, Toronto, 13 February 1914 (Toronto *Globe*, 14 February). He visited Toronto
on two other occasions, speaking on 'The Old Culture Lost,' at the University of
Toronto, 13 February 1904 (Toronto *Globe*, 15 February); and on 2 February 1920,
'A Theatre of the People,' at the University of Toronto (Toronto *Varsity*, 30 January,
and Toronto *Globe*, 3 February 1920). The Abbey Theatre Irish Players of Dublin
appeared at Toronto, week of 20 April 1914 (Toronto *World*, 12, 19 and 20 April;
Saturday Night, 18 April). Local audiences received the program of plays with
decided enthusiasm, except when the players performed Synge's *The Playboy of the
Western World* and a committee of local Irishmen left the theatre after hissing loudly
throughout the production. Later that week, reaction to a proposed performance of
Shaw's *The Shewing Up of Blanco Posnet* was more pronounced, and the police
commissioner, in prohibiting the production, described the play as 'full of blas-
phemy, profanity and language of the lowest type' (Toronto *Globe*, 9 May 1914).

15 For a discussion of the the the rise of the little-theatre movement in Toronto, see Robert
B. Scott, 'A Study of Amateur Theatre in Toronto: 1900–1930,' MA thesis, University
of New Brunswick, 1966. 2 vols.

16 Tempest appeared in Toronto, week of 5 October 1914 (Toronto *World*, 3 and 5
October; New York *Dramatic Mirror*, 30 September) then in Brantford (12 October),
Hamilton (14 October), Kingston (15 October), and Ottawa (16–17 October). She
returned to Toronto, week of 15 November 1915 (Toronto *World*, 15 November;
Saturday Night, 13 November; New York *Dramatic Mirror*, 20 and 27 November).
In the 1916–17 season, she visited Toronto again, week of 25 December 1916
(*Saturday Night*, 23 December, p. 6; Toronto *World*, 23 December; New York
Dramatic Mirror, 30 December 1916 and 6 January 1917; advertisement: Metropoli-
tan Toronto Reference Library, Theatre Section). See also Hector Bolitho, *Marie
Tempest: The Great Lady of the Stage* (Philadelphia: J.B. Lippincott, 1937). Neilson-
Terry, daughter of the respected English actors Fred Terry and Julia Neilson, made
her North American début in *Twelfth Night* on Broadway in 1914. She followed this
performance with the starring role in the New York production of *Trilby* the same
year. She first appeared in Ontario in Toronto (6–11 September 1915) and then on
tour to London (13–14 September), Hamilton (15 September), Kingston (16 Septem-

ber), and Ottawa (17–18 September). She again performed in Toronto that season at Shea's (23–28 January 1916) and in a revival of the comedy *The Great Pursuit* (C. Haddon Chambers), with Jeanne Eagels and Marie Tempest (13–18 March). Her 1918 tour from Vancouver to Toronto in Maugham's *The Land of Promise*, a controversial play of Canadian life in the West, is documented by Robert G. Lawrence, 'The Land of Promise: Canada as Somerset Maugham Saw It,' *Theatre History in Canada / Histoire du théâtre au Canada* 4:1 (Spring 1983), 15–24. She completed her tour of Ontario, visiting such cities as London (4 February), Hamilton (5–6 February), Kingston (11–12 February), Peterborough (14 February), Ottawa (? February), and Sudbury (19 February and 1 May).

17 Albert Brown and his company gave *The Black Feather* its première performance on 11 September 1916 at the Royal Alex, Toronto (Toronto *World*, 12 September; *Saturday Night*, 9 September). Brown then took the play on tour through the province at least to 16 December. See also Murray D. Edwards, 'William A. Tremayne,' in Eugene Benson and L.W. Conolly, eds, *The Oxford Companion to Canadian Theatre* (Toronto, Oxford, New York: Oxford University Press, 1989), 567–8, and Murray D. Edwards, 'A Playwright from the Canadian Past: W.A. Tremayne (1864–1939),' *Theatre History in Canada / Histoire du théâtre au Canada* 3:1 (Spring 1982), 43–50.

18 Toronto *World*, 13 November 1917

19 Wilson ran into trouble first in *A Prince of Tatters*, Toronto, 18–23 January 1915 (see Toronto *World*, 18 January; New York *Dramatic Mirror* 3 March), and again in *As the Years Roll On*, 24 January 1916 (see New York *Dramatic Mirror* 15 and 29 January; advertisement: Metropolitan Toronto Reference Library, Theatre Section). Anti-German sentiments led the mayor of Toronto to propose to City Council that German-language teaching be discontinued at all collegiate institutes under the jurisdiction of the local board of education (see Toronto *World*, 23 February 1918).

20 Actor Taylor Holmes's recitation of Kipling's 'Boots' at the curtain of *His Majesty, Bunker Bean* at the Royal Alex, 19–24 February 1917, was not well received in Toronto, which had 'contributed so many "sons" as a sacrifice in this terrible war' (see New York *Dramatic Mirror*, 24 February and 3 March 1917). In a letter to the editor of the Toronto *Daily Star*, one reader decried 'films in the moving picture shows that laud American characters and hold up to ridicule Englishmen and women ... Everything American is lauded to the skies, from President to the soldier. This is all right for the United States, but entirely out of place in Canada' (Toronto *Daily Star*, 25 November 1916).

21 *Variety*, 25 April 1919

22 Productions in New York fell from 475 in 1907 to 172 in 1917 (New York *Dramatic Mirror*, 22 December 1917). A noticeable drop also occurred in the number of road productions seen in the province (London *Advertiser*, 13 October 1914; Ottawa *Journal* 19 and 26 December 1914, and 15 January 1915). By 1918, because there were only two trunk lines available to ship theatrical productions out of New York, as few as 51 plays were seen on the road in any one week (New York *Dramatic Mirror*,

19 January 1918). At 1 cent per ticket, war taxes brought in $52,000 a week from theatres, movie-houses, and race tracks in Toronto (Toronto *Daily Star*, 8 March 1916). In February 1918, Prime Minister Borden brought in a Dominion-wide policy to shut theatres down one day a week as a fuel-conservation measure (St Catharines *Standard*, 16 February 1918; New York *Dramatic Mirror*, 23 February, and 2 and 16 March 1918). At the Gaiety Theatre, Toronto, 1000 men had their papers checked while police watched the exits to prevent anyone from slipping out. The raid yielded 150 eligible men who were summarily marched to the nearest recruiting office to enlist (Toronto *Daily Star*, 9 March 1918).

23 Dressler, who appeared on screen with Charlie Chaplin in *Tillie's Punctured Romance*, also came to Toronto in her stage hit *The Mix Up*, 7–12 December 1914. Pickford was seen in numerous hits, including *Such a Little Queen* and *Cinderella*. A number of young Canadians found careers in the movies: Florence La Badie in *The Man Without a Country* (Toronto *Globe*, 1 December 1917); Alice Yorke ('Coodie' Hill of Toronto and later wife of B.C. Whitney) in the movie version of *The Chocolate Soldier* (Helen Avery Hardy, *Canada West Monthly* 6 (1909), 177; *Saturday Night*, 29 August 1914; Toronto *Globe*, 28 October 1929); Vida Ekkers of Toronto in *The Lash* (Toronto *Globe*, 24 October 1916); and Florence Rockwell in *He Fell in Love with His Wife* (London *Free Press*, 8 April 1916).

24 The list included Donald Brian of St John's, Newfoundland, famous as Prince Danilo in Lehar's *The Merry Widow* (1907), who appeared in Victor Herbert's *Her Regiment* at the Royal Alex (*Globe*, 6 March 1918); Brian had appeared in Toronto in *The Marriage Market* in April 1914. Touring companies also featured the work of a colony of expatriate dramatists from Canada writing for the New York stage, namely James Forbes, Edward E. Rose, Willard Mack, Charles W. Bell, George V. Hobart, and Harvey O'Higgins, whose plays were loudly proclaimed as 'Canadian' all along the circuit (see Scott, 'Study of Amateur Theatre in Toronto,' specifically pp. 116–17, and Robert B. Scott, 'A Study of English-Canadian Dramatic Literature 1900–1930,' Phil.M. thesis, University of Toronto, 1969). Writers such as Charles G.D. Roberts and Arthur Stringer were also part of the colony (see McKenzie Porter, 'Flashback: Arthur Stringer's Purple Life,' *Maclean's Magazine*, 9 February 1963, 28).

25 Bernhardt was quoted in the Toronto *Evening Telegram*, 17 November 1914. During the period, Anglin played several Shakespearean roles in New York and, following her 1910 success in *Antigone*, she won acclaim for her performances in *Medea*, *Electra*, and *Iphigenia in Aulis* in 1915 at the Greek Theatre in Berkeley, California, and later on Broadway. David Blum, *A Pictorial History of the American Theatre, 1900–1950* (New York: Greenberg, 1950), 100, 101, 103, 105, 138, 183, and 185

26 On her first visit she played the Princess Theatre, Toronto (*Saturday Night*, 14 November 1914; Toronto *Evening Telegram* 17 November; Toronto *World*, 8 November; New York *Dramatic Mirror*, 18 and 25 November). On her second visit, she appeared at the Grand Opera House, Toronto (*Saturday Night*, 11 November 1916; advertisement: Metropolitan Toronto Reference Library, Theatre Section).

27 Denis Salter, 'Margaret Anglin,' *Oxford Companion to Canadian Drama*, 24. See also Moody, *The Revels History*, 199–120); John Le Vay, *Margaret Anglin: A Stage Life* (Toronto: Simon & Pierre, 1989); Mary M. Brown, 'Entertainers of the Road,' in *Early Stages* (Toronto: University of Toronto Press, 1990), 144–5; and Blum, *Pictorial History*.

28 Toronto *Daily Star*, 17 November 1914. See also Salter, 'Margaret Anglin,' *Oxford Companion to Canadian Theatre*, 24

29 She was the subject of a five-part series in *Everywoman's World Magazine* in November 1916.

30 Toronto *World*, 19 March 1916

31 Denis Salter, 'At Home and Abroad: The Acting Career of Julia Arthur,' *Theatre History in Canada* 3:1 (Spring 1984), 1–35

32 'Julia Arthur Comes Back,' *Maclean's Magazine* (January 1916), 18–19; see also Hamilton *Spectator*, 26 March 1919. Arthur had married a Boston millionaire, Benjamin Pierce Cheney, Jr, in 1898. When she learned that the movie was to play in Canada she felt she should be present because it was her duty as 'a Canadian by birth.' She also appeared in Toronto at the matinée and evening screenings of the film at the Allen Theatre, 24 March 1919, where she gave a 'little speech' (Toronto *Evening Telegram*, 24 and 25 March).

33 She appeared in Toronto at the Royal Alex, week of 28 February 1916 (Toronto *World*, 27 February; New York *Dramatic Mirror*, 11 and 18 March; advertisement: Metropolitan Toronto Reference Library, Theatre Section); also in Sudbury, 11 April 1916 (Sudbury *Star*, 1 April); Renfrew, 11 April (Renfrew *Mercury*, 7 April), Cornwall, 17 April (Cornwall *Standard*, 30 March 1916), and Hamilton, 27 April (Hamilton *Spectator*, 22 April). She returned to the Royal Alex, week of 1 May 1916 (Toronto *World*, 30 April; advertisement: Metropolitan Toronto Reference Library, Theatre Section).

34 Toronto *World*, 27 February 1916

35 Toronto *World*, 29 February 1916

36 *A Pair of Queens* (Hauerbach, Brown, and Lewis) at the Royal Alex, 24–29 April 1916 (Toronto *World*, 23 and 24 April; advertisement: Metropolitan Toronto Reference Library, Theatre Section; also Blum, *Pictorial History*, 116, 119); *Here Comes the Bride* at the Princess Theatre, 19–24 November 1916 (New York *Dramatic Mirror*, 17 and 24 November and 1 December; Toronto *Globe*, 6 May, p. 9)

37 Johnson Briscoe, *Actors' Birthday Book: An Authoritative Insight into the Lives of Men and Women of the Stage Born between January 1 and December 31* (New York: Moffat, Yard, 1907), 2:150; see also Blum, *Pictorial History*, 94, and Weldon B. Durham, ed., *American Theatre Companies, 1888–1930* (New York: Greenwood Press, 1987), 73, 161.

38 *Saturday Night*, 5 February 1916; advertisement: Metropolitan Toronto Reference Library, Theatre Section. Courtleigh had played in a vaudeville sketch 'Peaches' at Shea's, Toronto, February 1908 (Toronto *Globe*, 11 February, p. 14).

39 Toronto *World*, 6 and 8 February 1916; Toronto *Daily Star*, 5, 7, and 8 February;
   Toronto *Telegram*, 8 February

40 At the Princess Theatre, 24–29 March 1919 (Toronto *Evening Telegram*, 25 March;
   New York *Dramatic Mirror*, 8 April; *Variety*, 14 March; Toronto *Globe*, 25 March;
   advertisement: Metropolitan Toronto Reference Library, Theatre Section)

41 He died at Brentwood Heights, California, 18 November 1934. See Burns Mantle,
   The Best Plays of 1934–35 (New York: Dodd Mead, 1948), 512. See also 'William
   Courtleigh' in Robinson Locke Collection of Dramatic Scrapbooks, itemized in New
   York Public Library, *Catalog of Theatre and Drama Collections*, part 3, Non-Book
   Collections (Boston: G.K. Hall, 1976), vol. 6.

42 *Screen World*, September 1958, 226

43 *Saturday Night*, 3 November 1917 and 28 May 1921. See also London Public
   Library, Theatre File, and the Robinson Locke Collection, *Catalog of Theatre and
   Drama Collections*, Volume 4.

44 Blum, *Pictorial History*, 112, 145; see also Gerald Bordman, *American Musical
   Theatre: A Chronicle* (New York: Oxford University Press, 1986), 346.

45 Toronto *Varsity*, 19 November 1917, 1; *Saturday Night*, 13 December 1919; Arts and
   Letters Club Archives: Newsletter, 22 January 1918. Horace Sinclair, who later
   appeared in *Fiddlers Three* in 1919, was probably another member of the company
   (see Toronto *Globe*, 6 December 1919, 15). It was the work of organizations such as
   this that later led to the creation of the famous Dumbells, an all-Canadian troop show
   that toured military bases in France and then re-organized as a successful civilian
   company in the 1920s and early 1930s. Rennie, formerly a student of Willard Mack,
   had made his first professional appearance in Canada, 8–13 December 1913, in *The
   Confession* at the Grand Opera House, Toronto (Toronto *World*, 7 and 8 December).
   Another Toronto actor, Malcolm Owen, associated with the Polt Stock Company in
   New Haven, Connecticut, left the stage in the early days of the war to join the British
   Army (Toronto *Globe*, 22 March 1915, 15).

46 Albert Auster, *Actresses and Suffragists: Women in the American Theatre, 1890–
   1920* (New York: Praeger, 1984). See also Tracy C. Davis, 'Actresses and Prostitutes
   in Victorian London,' and Jan McDonald, 'Lesser Ladies of the Victorian Stage,'
   both in *Theatre Research International* 13:3 (Autumn 1988).

47 Mary Pickford, *Sunshine and Shadow* (New York: Doubleday, 1959), 31

48 See Nella Jefferis file in Special Collections, Metropolitan Toronto Reference
   Library, Theatre Section

49 Douglas Arrell, 'Harold Nelson: The Early Years, c.1865– 1905,' *Theatre History in
   Canada / Histoire du théâtre au Canada* 1:2 (Fall 1980), 83–110. See also *Varsity*,
   17 October and 1 November 1899; *Saturday Night*, 8 September 1900, 9 May 1914, 2
   January 1915, 1 May 1916, 12 and 25 May 1917, 24 August 1918, 19 October 1918,
   3 December 1921, 20 May 1922, 23 and 30 September 1922, 15 November 1924, 15
   May 1926, 20 October 1928, 3 November 1928, 2 November 1929, 28 April 1934, 16
   and 23 February 1935, 28 July 1945; Toronto *Mail and Empire*, 6 July 1923, 16

December 1925; Toronto *Star*, 28 February 1935; Toronto *Telegram*, 7 June 1922; *Glaser Players' Bulletin* 1:14 (May 1922); Ralph Hicklin, Toronto *Globe and Mail*, 26 August 1961; Herbert Whittaker, Toronto *Globe and Mail*, 30 August 1967.

50 Scott, 'Study of Amateur Theatre in Toronto,' 38; Arrell, 'Harold Nelson,' 95; Denis Salter, 'Walter Huston,' *Oxford Companion to Canadian Theatre*, 275–6

51 *Glaser Players' Bulletin* 2:4 (13 September 1922), Metropolitan Toronto Reference Library, Theatre Section. Hamilton *Spectator*, 13 and 17 November 1915, and Hamilton Theatre Scrapbook, vol. TIII, p. 77, Hamilton Public Library

52 Besides providing a pleasant change of venue, resident stock afforded performers, many of them from prestigious American stock organizations, year-round employment at a time when the commercial theatre was declining. For theatre managers, the arrangement saved them from having to close down or make expensive conversions to movies in the off-season. Although they generally operated in the summer season, resident companies were not like modern 'summer' stock troupes performing in 'barn' theatres for vacation resort communities. Instead, they were regarded as extensions of the regular commercial-theatre season activities, and in some cases even established themselves as permanent companies the following winter. See Durham, ed., *American Theatre Companies*, 51, 53, for a further discussion of resident companies.

53 Daughter of Herbert L. Dunn, a Toronto lawyer, Alice was not as well known as her sister, Violet. Toronto *Star Weekly*, 11 June 1927

54 Toronto *World*, 21 July 1914; Hamilton *Spectator*, 22 July 1916; Toronto *Mail and Empire*, 24 March 1930

55 *Saturday Night*, 27 June 1914, 6 September 1924, and 15 October 1927; Toronto *World*, 16 June and 21 July 1914

56 Nancy Jane Haynes, 'A History of the Royal Alexandra Theatre, Toronto, Ontario, Canada, 1914–1918,' Ph.D. thesis, University of Colorado, Boulder, Colo., 1973, 213. See also Hamilton Theatre Scrapbooks, vol. 2, 514; Toronto *Star Weekly*, 11 June 1927; and Toronto *Mail and Empire*, 4 August 1930.

57 Toronto *World*, 21 February 1915

58 New York *Dramatic Mirror*, 16 March 1918

59 Lyons, son of Mr and Mrs J.H. Lyons of Toronto, later acted in movies with Francis X. Bushman and Beverly Bayne (Toronto *Globe*, 15 November 1919, 17).

60 Hamilton *Spectator*, 7 October 1916. Together with H. Webb Chamberlain, a member of the cast and a former manager of his own company (the H. Webb Chamberlain Stock Company), Priestland created the Royal Alexandra Players, which toured across the province in the fall of 1916. Chamberlain's earlier company had visited Peterborough and Kingston in the fall of 1914. See, respectively, Peterborough *Examiner*, 8, 13, 14, 16, and 17 October 1914, and Kingston *British Whig*, 15, 19, 20, 21, and 23 October 1914, and New York *Dramatic Mirror*, 11 November 1914.

61 New York *Dramatic Mirror*, 11 August 1917

62 David Gardner, 'George H. Summers,' *Oxford Companion to Canadian Theatre*,

509–10. In 1914, Summers also engaged Harry Reeves, a local boy, in *Nobody's Widow* (week of 15 June).

63 Hamilton had always been an active theatre town. One of the most sensational events in the acting community at the time was the murder of Ethel Kinrade, sister of Florence, a concert singer and acquaintance of James Baum, an American actor. Although Florence was a suspect, no evidence was found to convict her and she went on to a modestly successful career on the stage. Toronto *Globe and Mail*, advertising supplement, 13 August 1983, H11

64 Hamilton *Spectator*, 10 July 1924 and 30 November 1935

65 The Dominion Stock Company played the Dominion, 20 April–11 July 1914. The Lynne Yoder Company was at the Britannia, 1 June–13 July 1914. The Roma Reade Players performed at Drey's Arena, 6–11 June 1914. However, only one young actor from the city, Paul Doucet (a graduate of Ottawa University), appeared on the local commercial stage during the period (Ottawa *Journal*, 5 September 1914). After leaving a job as a bank employee in Ottawa, Rockliffe Fellowes, grandson of George Byron Lyon Fellowes, former MP, starred in *Brown of Harvard* and in a road production of *Within the Law* that toured Ontario in April 1914 (St Catharines *Standard*, 18 April 1914; London *Free Press*, 11 and 18 April 1914).

66 Brantford *Daily Courier*, 17 July 1917

67 Murray Edwards, *A Stage in Our Past: English-Language Theatre in Eastern Canada from the 1790s to 1914* (Toronto: University of Toronto Press, 1968), 41–8. See also Murray Edwards, 'The Marks Brothers,' *Oxford Companion to Canadian Theatre*, 332–3.

68 She acted with the Vaughan Glaser Players at the Victoria Theatre, Toronto, 25 December 1932–19 March 1933.

69 Brantford *Expositor*, 18, 20, 21, 23, and 24 February 1928. See also *Billboard*, 25 November 1922.

70 Stratford *Herald*, 30 September 1914

71 Hamilton *Spectator*, 20 March 1915

72 Cornwall *Standard*, 3 September 1914 and 9 September 1915

73 Robert Scott, 'Mae Edwards,' *Oxford Companion to Canadian Theatre*, 193–4

74 Sault Ste Marie *Star*, 7 September 1915. See also New York *Dramatic Mirror*, 5, 12, 19, and 26 February 1916. Following is the company's itinerary for 1915–16: Goderich, Victoria Hall, wk. 31 January, wk. 7 February; Sault Ste Marie, King's, wk. 13–18 September; Sudbury, Grand, wk. 19 June; Woodstock, Griffin's, 20–22 December; Woodstock, Griffin's, wk. 27 March–1 April; St Thomas, ?, 21–26 February; Hanover, ?, 11–12 February; Owen Sound ?, 14–19 February

75 Peterborough *Examiner*, 27 April 1923

76 Berlin [Kitchener] *Daily Times*, 5, 7, 13, 16, 21, and 23 October 1914; Peterborough *Examiner*, 28, 29, and 30 October 1914

77 The following companies made appearances in the province during the period: Baldwin Stock Co., Toronto (May 1914); Nancy Boyer Stock Co., London-Hamilton

(May 1914); Boyer-Vincent Stock Co., Kingston-Stratford-Goderich (Sept. 1914–
January 1915); Britannia Stock Co., Ottawa (May 1914); H. Webb Chamberlain
Stock Co., Kingston-Peterborough (October 1914); Ralph E. Cummings Stock Co.,
Ottawa-Sudbury-Peterborough-Hamilton-Toronto (December 1914–March 1915);
Colonial Stock Co., St. Catharines-Brantford (January–February 1915); Culhane
Comedians, Sault Ste Marie (December 1916); Dominion Stock Co., Ottawa (April–
July 1914); Empire Players, Kingston-St.Catharines (January–December 1915–16);
B.F. Forbes Comedy Co., Windsor (December 1916); Florence Johnstone Stock Co.,
Sault Ste Marie (July 1916), Peterborough (July 1917); Edward Keane Players (*see*
Roma Reade Stock Co.); Nellie Kennedy Stock Co., Peterborough (May 1914);
Leonard Players, Toronto (October 1914); Alexander Loftus and His English Co.,
Peterborough-Stratford-Sudbury, (March–April 1915); Frances McGrath Stock Co.,
Hamilton (July–December 1916); Frances McHenry Stock Co., Ottawa (May–July
1915); MacKay-Kemble Stock Co., Hamilton (April–July 1915); Phillips-Shaw
Stock Co., Toronto (May–July 1915); Princess Theatre Stock Co., London (April–
June 1914); Rialto Dramatic Players, Ottawa (January–February 1917); Roma Reade
Stock Co., Ottawa (May–June 1914), Ottawa (November–April 1915–16), Brantford
(July–August 1916); Mr Stewart and His Company, London (October–December
1914); Stoddart Comedy Co., London (June 1914); Clara Turner Stock Co.,
Kingston (May 1914); Windsor Permanent Players, Windsor (October 1915)
78 Chatham, Griffin's, wk. 24 November 1913–wk. 26 April 1914; Goderich, Victoria
   Hall, wk. 24 May 1914; Woodstock, Griffin's, wk. 8 June–wk. 10 August 1914;
   Owen Sound, ?, 7 September 1914; Goderich, Victoria Hall, wk. 8 October 1914;
   Kitchener, Grand, wk. 16 April–22 May 1915; Sault Ste Marie, ?, wk. 21 June–wk.
   26 July 1915
79 Windsor Permanent Players, Windsor, 4–26 October 1915; Gibney, Wilson, and
   Ward, Windsor, 14–17 June 1916
80 Woodstock *Sentinel Review*, 19 April 1924; St Thomas *Times Journal*, 19 January
   1924
81 At least three companies were at work locally in the period: William James and
   Sons (*Saturday Night*, 20 June 1914; Toronto *Globe*, 15 and 20 1914), Messrs
   Conners and Till (Toronto *Globe*, 15 June 1914), and United Features (Toronto
   World, 21 February 1915). In addition, the Canadian Academy of Music offered
   the first moving-picture acting course in the city (New York *Dramatic Mirror*,
   8 November 1915).
82 Toronto *Globe*, 9 April 1919. See also Dean, *Censored! Only in Canada*, 21–2, 25–8.
83 Patrick B. O'Neill, 'The British Canadian Theatrical Organization Society and the
   Trans-Canada Theatre Society,' *Journal of Canadian Studies* 5:1 (Spring 1980),
   56–67
84 Peterborough *Examiner*, 1 February 1922
85 He appeared at the Royal Alex, Toronto, the weeks of 4 and 11 October 1926
   (Toronto *Globe*, 2 October; Toronto *Mail and Empire*, 8 and 10 October; *Saturday*

Night, 2 and 16 October). See also David Gardner, '(Alexander) Matheson Lang,' *Oxford Companion to Canadian Theatre*, 290.

86 'Sir George Robey,' in Martin Esslin, ed., *The Encyclopedia of World Theatre* (New York: Charles Scribner's Sons, 1977), 230

87 *This Year of Grace* appeared at the Royal Alex, week of 13 May 1929 (*Saturday Night*, 11 May) and *Bitter Sweet* was seen there week of 14 April 1930 (*Saturday Night*, 29 March and 12 April). *This Year of Grace* also played Hamilton, 20, 21, and 22 May 1929 (Hamilton *Spectator*, 4 and 11 May) and London, 23, 24, and 25 May 1929 (London *Free Press*, 11 and 18 May). Lillie was another product of Toronto's girls' schools who ended up on the professional stage. She attended St Agnes College before leaving at age 15 to go trouping with her mother, a concert singer. See David Blum, *Great Stars of the American Stage: A Pictorial Record* (New York: Grossett and Dunlop, 1954), 116; *Saturday Night*, 22 November 1924; Montreal *Star*, 28 May 1966.

88 Denis Salter, 'Beatrice Lillie,' *Oxford Companion to Canadian Theatre*, 301. Lillie made her first stage appearance in *Jappyland* at Toronto's Princess Theatre in June 1907 (Toronto *Globe*, 6 and 12 June 1907). See also Scott, 'Study of Amateur Theatre in Toronto,' 127.

89 *Charlot's Revue of 1924* played the Royal Alex, week of 1 December 1924 (*Saturday Night*, 29 November). She also appeared in Toronto on film in *Exit Smiling*, week of 24 January 1927 (*Saturday Night*, 22 January).

90 *Oh, Please!* played the Princess Theatre, Toronto, week of 16 May 1927 (*Saturday Night*, 14 May, p. 7).

91 Some of the cities visited included London, 20, 21, 22 September 1928 (*Free Press*, 8 September); Peterborough, 19 January 1929 (*Examiner*, 12, 19 January); London, 21–23 January 1929 (*Free Press*, 12 January); Hamilton, 25, 26 January 1929 (*Spectator*, 19 January); St Catharines, 28 January 1929 (*Star*, 26 January); Woodstock, 29 January 1929 (*Sentinel Review*, 22, 26, 29, 30 January); Brantford, 31 January 1929 (*Expositor*, 19, 21, 26, 31 January); Kingston, 1, 2 February 1929 (*Whig Standard*, 25 January); Hamilton, 7, 8, 9 October 1929 (*Spectator*, 28 September and 5 October); Hamilton, week of 10 February 1930 (*Spectator*, 8 February); Hamilton, 30, 31 January 1931 (*Spectator*, 27 December).

92 *Saturday Night*, 28 April and 12 May. Anglin had been booked to appear in Toronto in *Billeted* in 1919, but because the New York trusts were paranoid about the possibilities of Bolshevik uprisings in Canada following the Great Strike in Winnipeg, they rerouted the production (New York *Clipper*, 4 June 1919) and played, instead, at Kingston, 29 May 1919 (Kingston *British Whig*, 26 May).

93 Toronto, weeks of 30 March and 6 April 1925 (*Saturday Night*, 28 March 1928); London, 13, 14, and 15 April 1925 (London *Free Press*, 11 April); Hamilton, 16, 17, and 18 April 1925 (Hamilton *Herald*, 28 March; 8, 17, and 18 April); Kingston, 22 April 1925 (Kingston *British Whig*, 11 April); Ottawa, 23, 24, and 25 April 1925 (Ottawa *Journal*, 18 April). Arthur also performed with distinction opposite Lionel

Barrymore in the Theatre Guild's New York production of *Macbeth* in 1921 (Blum, *Pictorial History*, 138).

94 She joined Vaughan Glaser's company to play in *Déclassé*, week of 22 May 1922 (*Saturday Night*, 20 May) and *The Great Divide*, week of 5 June 1922 (Toronto *Telegram*, 7 June). She received rave reviews in *The Morning American* and the New York *World* for *East of Suez* (*Saturday Night*, 30 September 1922). The New York opening of *Bristol Glass* was in the fall of 1923 (Toronto *Mail and Empire*, 6 July 1923). *The Importance of Being Earnest* played in June 1926 (*Saturday Night*, 15 May and 5 June).

95 *The Royal Box* played the Princess Theatre, Toronto, week of 15 November 1928 (*Saturday Night*, 20 October; advertisement): Metropolitan Toronto Public Library, Theatre Section).

96 *Saturday Night*, 2 November 1929

97 Ibid., 26 July, 2 and 23 August 1930

98 New York *Dramatic Mirror*, 28 December 1918

99 See Robert G. Lawrence, 'Vaughan Glaser on Stage in Toronto, 1921–1934,' *Theatre History in Canada / Histoire du théâtre au Canada* 9:1 (Spring 1988).

100 See Robert G. Lawrence, 'Cameron Matthews,' *Oxford Companion to Canadian Theatre*, 335.

101 George Vivian directed one of Ben Greet's companies on the Chautauqua circuit in the summer of 1914 (Durham, ed., *American Theatre Companies*, 220).

102 See Herbert Whittaker, 'Jane Mallett,' *Oxford Companion to Canadian Theatre*, 322–3.

103 He was director-manager of a stock company in Montclair, NJ, between 1929 and 1931. Toronto *Telegram*, 15 September 1931

104 Cosette Lee file, Metropolitan Toronto Reference Library, Theatre Section. Toronto *Star*, 8 January 1963 and 20 September 1976. She got her start in *The Trial of Mary Duggan* in Toronto and studied under Wallace Ford, Spring Byington, and Leo Carillo. She played in the first radio drama broadcast from Toronto's station CFCA in 1936, a mystery entitled *Vitrol*. Later she acted in the television series *Strange Paradise* and *Hatch's Mills* and at the Shaw Festival. She died in 1976 at 66.

105 One sad event occurred during the year; Edmund Abbey, one of the regulars of the company, died what can only be described as truly an actor's death, for after completing his lines in the play entitled *Thank You*, he collapsed at the final curtain (Toronto *World*, 24 March 1930).

106 *Spectator*, 15 January 1927

107 Toronto *Telegram*, 10 November 1932. Duncan also played with the New Empire Company at the Empire Theatre, Toronto, week of 14 November 1932 to week of 9 January 1933.

108 Toronto *Globe*, September 1921. The play was published serially in *Canadian Forum* between September and December 1921.

109 London *Free Press*, 1 July 1967

110 Sheilagh S. Jameson, in collaboration with Nola B. Erikson, *Chautauqua in Canada* (Calgary, Alta.: Glenbow-Alberta Institute, 1979). See also Sheilagh S. Jameson, 'Chautauqua,' *Oxford Companion to Canadian Theatre*, 91–2.

111 The production took place at the Royal Alex, Toronto, 25, 26, and 27 February 1935 (*Saturday Night*, 16 and 23 February; Toronto *Mail and Empire*, 16 and 23 February). Adair first appeared in Toronto as a headliner at Shea's Theatre, week of 12 November 1923 (*Saturday Night*, 17 November). In 1940 she appeared on Broadway in *Arsenic and Old Lace* and two years later was on tour on the Pacific Coast with Boris Karloff (Blum, *Pictorial History*, 243; London *Free Press*, 5 September 1942).

112 The production played the Royal Alex, Toronto, week of 13 March 1939; *Saturday Night*, 11 March 1939; Toronto *Star*, 14 March. McGee, born in Pretoria, South Africa, graduated from the Margaret Eaton School of Expression. She was a child actress with the Vaughan Glaser Players, with the Empire Theatre, Toronto, in *Treasure Island* (*Saturday Night*, 1 January 1927; *Curtain Call* 6:5 [February 1935]) and with the Maurice Colbourne British Players (*Saturday Night*, 20 October 1923); she also appeared as a regular in several Players' Club of Toronto productions at Hart House (see Scott, 'Amateur Theatre in Toronto,' 668, 680, 682, 684, and 687). She also appeared on Broadway in Lillian Hellman's *The Children's Hour* in 1934 (Blum, *Pictorial History*, 216).

113 *The Flashing Stream* played at the Royal Alex, Toronto, week of 20 March 1939 (*Saturday Night*, 11 March, *Curtain Call*, 5:6 and 10:6 [March 1939])

114 The production appeared at the Royal Alex, Toronto, week of 20 March 1933 (*Saturday Night*, 11 and 18 March, Toronto *Mail and Empire*, 11 March; Toronto *Star*, 18 and 20 March); see also Walter C. Daniel, '*De Lawd': Richard B. Harrison and 'The Green Pastures'* (New York, Westport, London: Greenwood, 1986); Blum, *Pictorial History*, 198, 199; and Robin Breon, 'The Growth and Development of Black Theatre in Canada: A Starting Point,' in *Theatre History in Canada / Histoire du théâtre au Canada* 9:2 (Fall 1988), 216–28.

115 The play was performed at the Royal Alex, Toronto, week of 5 February 1934 (*Saturday Night*, 3 February; Toronto *Mail and Empire*, 3 February). See also Robertson Davies, 'Raymond Massey,' *Oxford Companion to Canadian Theatre*, 334–5.

116 Manners appeared in *Journey's End* at the Tivoli Theatre, Toronto, week of 2 June 1930 (Toronto *Star Weekly*, 31 May 1930). He had appeared on the Broadway stage and at Toronto's Royal Alex (week of 19 November 1923) with the Theatre Guild Repertory Company of New York in its production of *He Who Gets Slapped* (*Saturday Night*, 17 November).

117 *Mail and Empire*, 2 May 1936

118 *Curtain Call* 7:9 (June 1936). See also *Saturday Night*, 20 December 1941, 21 and 28 February 1942; and Blum, *Pictorial History*, 243, 258, 267, and 269.

119 Melville Keay file, Special Collections, Metropolitan Toronto Reference Library, Theatre Section

120 *Curtain Call* 10:4 (January 1939). See also Melville Keay file, Metropolitan Toronto Reference Library

121 *Civic Theatre Magazine* 1:2 (November 1945). Brown had acted with the Roma Reade / Edmund Keane company in Brantford in July 1917. Brantford *Daily Courier*, 17 July 1917

122 Scott McClellan, *Straw Hats and Greasepaint: Fifty Years of Theatre in a Summer Colony* (Bracebridge, Ont.: Muskoka Publications, 1984), 1: 48

123 *Civic Theatre Magazine* 1:2 (November 1945), 26

124 Toronto *Star*, 8 January 1963

125 Melville Keay file, Metropolitan Toronto Reference Library. See also Woodstock *Daily Review*, 25, 29, and 30 May, 1 and 3 June 1940.

126 Toby Gordon Ryan, *Stage Left: Canadian Theatre in the Thirties, A Memoir* (Toronto: York University Press, 1982). See also Richard Wright and Robin Endres, eds, *Eight Men Speak and Other Plays from the Canadian Workers' Theatre* (Toronto: New Hogtown Press, 1976) and Sandra Souchotte, 'Canada's Workers' Theatre,' *Canadian Theatre Review* 9 (Winter 1976), 169–72; 10 (Spring 1976), 92–6.

127 Endres, Introduction, *Eight Men Speak*, xxv–xxvi

128 Ibid., xxvii–xviii. See also Eugene Benson and L.W. Conolly, *English-Canadian Theatre* (Toronto: Oxford University Press, 1987), 57–9.

129 For a fuller account of the history of local Jewish theatre, see Hye Bossin, *Stars of David: Toronto, 1856–1956* (Toronto: Canadian Jewish Congress, 1957).

130 Dora Nipp, 'The Chinese in Toronto,' in R. Harney, ed., *Gathering Place: Peoples and Neighbourhoods of Toronto, 1834–1945*, 147–75 (Toronto: Multicultural History Society of Ontario, 1985).

131 Sandy Stewart, *A Pictorial History of Radio in Canada* (Toronto: Gage, 1975), 67–95. See also CBC *Drama and Features: Five Years of Achievement* (Toronto: Canadian Broadcasting Corporation, 1941).

132 Geraldine Anthony, 'John Coulter,' *Oxford Companion to Canadian Theatre*, 116–18

133 Ross Stuart, 'Earle Grey,' *Oxford Companion to Canadian Theatre*, 248–9

134 Moody, 'American Actors, Managers, Producers and Directors,' in *The Revels History*, 135

135 London *Free Press*, 5 September 1942, 30 December 1942, 31 January 1942, 16 May 1951, and 1 July 1967. See also Blum, *Pictorial History*, 240, 246, 247, 248.

136 The production played the Royal Alex, 22–23 April 1943 (*Saturday Night*, 10 and 17 April).

137 The production played the week of 6 November 1944 (*Saturday Night*, 4 November). See David Gardner, 'Margaret Bannerman,' *Oxford Companion to Canadian Theatre*, 42.

138 Interview with Jack Medhurst, a cast member, in June 1986.

139 David Gardner, 'Robert Gill,' *Oxford Companion to Canadian Theatre*, 233. See also Ann Stuart, 'Robert Gill at Hart House,' *Tenth Anniversary of the Drama*

Centre, 1966–1976 (Toronto: Graduate Centre for Study of Drama, University of Toronto, 1976) 1.1 (1976), 12–13.

140 Susan Stone-Blackburn, 'Barbara Chilcott,' *Oxford Companion to Canadian Theatre*, 92. Herbert Whittaker, 'Donald Davis' and 'Murray Davis,' ibid., 132–4. William Toye, 'David Gardner,' ibid., 220. Eugene Benson, 'Barbara Hamilton,' ibid., 254. Neil Carson, 'Eric House,' ibid., 274. David Gardner, 'William Hutt,' ibid., 276–7; see also Herbert Whittaker, *Whittaker's Theatricals* (Toronto: Simon & Pierre, 1993), 148–55. Rota Herzberg Lister, 'Charmion King,' *Oxford Companion to Canadian Theatre*, 285. Denis W. Johnston, 'Leon Major,' ibid., 321–2. Timothy Findley, 'Kate Reid,' ibid., 463–4; see also Whittaker, *Whittaker's Theatricals*, 156–65. Neil Carson, 'Donald Sutherland,' *Oxford Companion to Canadian Theatre*, 515; see also *Whittaker's Theatricals*, 166–71. This list of 'graduates' from Gill's workshops was presented in David Gardner, 'Robert Gill,' *Oxford Companion to Canadian Theatre*, 233.

141 Murray D. Edwards, 'Andrew Allan,' *Oxford Companion to Canadian Theatre*, 14–15. N. Alice Frick, *Image in the Mind: CBC Radio Drama 1944 to 1954* (Toronto: Canadian Stage & Arts Publications, 1987).

142 Bronwyn Drainie, *Living the Part: John Drainie and the Dilemma of Canadian Stardom* (Toronto: Macmillan of Canada, 1988). Howard Fink, 'Tommy Tweed,' *Oxford Companion to Canadian Theatre*, 572. Fink, 'Lister Sinclair,' ibid., 498.

143 In Toronto they included Edgar Stone's early Radio Hall, Lorne Greene's Academy of Radio Arts, Ben Lennick's School of the Theatre, and later Sterndale Bennett's Canadian Theatre School and Marjorie Purvey's Toronto School of Radio (this last institution also being responsible for the Children's Theatre of the Air on CKEY). Queen's University, the University of Toronto, and Ryerson also had radio training activities.

144 Eugene Benson and L.W. Connolly, *English-Canadian Theatre* (Toronto: Oxford University Press, 1987), 68–9. For reviews of *Going Home* and *Riel*, see Ronald Bryden and Boyd Neil, eds, *Whittaker's Theatre: A Critic Looks at Stages in Canada and Thereabouts: 1944–1975* (Toronto: University of Toronto Press, 1985).

145 Terry Kotyshyn, 'Jupiter Theatre, Inc. 1951–1954: The Life and Death of Toronto's First Professional Full-Time Theatre,' unpublished MA thesis, University of Alberta, 1986. See also *Jupiter Theatre, Inc. What and Why It Is* (1954?), Jupiter Theatre file, Metropolitan Toronto Reference Library, Theatre Section.

146 Transcript of taped interview with the Lennicks, Ontario Historical Studies Series theatre project, Archives of Ontario. See also Belmont Group Theatre, Toronto Scrapbooks, Metropolitan Toronto Reference Library, Theatre Section.

147 Anton Wagner, 'Infinite Variety or a Canadian "National" Theatre: Roly Young and the Toronto Civic Theatre Association, 1945–1949,' *Theatre History in Canada* 9:2 (Fall 1988), 173–92

148 The important roles were to be taken by members of the Toronto Repertory Theatre,

namely Enid Mills, Karen Glahan, Rupert MacLeod, and Ray Hamstead, but they were actually performed by a cast of unknowns. *Civic Theatre Magazine* 1:2

149 Joe Jolley, director of the Association in 1947, made attempts to keep it going, but they proved futile. Jolley, however, went on to establish Theatre '49 and to direct plays for the amateur Plaquest Drama Guild. See Theatre '49, Toronto Scrapbook, 71–73, Metropolitan Toronto Public Library, Theatre Section.

150 Toronto *Star*, 13 October 1977. See also Charles Foster, 'David Manners: Hollywood's Canadian-born Star,' *Atlantic Advocate* 69 (1978), 50–7; Gregory Mark, 'David Manners Surrendered Stardom for Privacy and Peace of Mind,' *Films in Review* 28 (1977), 561–611.

151 Ross Stuart, 'Summer Stock,' *Oxford Companion to Canadian Theatre*, 511.

152 James Noonan, 'Canadian Repertory Theatre,' *Oxford Companion to Canadian Theatre*, 76. See also Theatre Collection, Ottawa Public Library.

153 Ottawa *Citizen*, 11 June 1949; Ottawa *Journal*, 12 May 1973. See Eugene Benson, 'Christopher Plummer,' *Oxford Companion to Canadian Theatre*, 421.

154 Productions: John Gielgud, Margaret Rutherford, et al. in *The Importance of Being Earnest* (Wilde), 23, 24, and 25 January 1947; Dublin Gate Theatre (Michael MacLiammoir, director) in *John Bull's Other Island* (Shaw), *The Old Lady Says 'No!'* (MacLiammoir), and *Where Stars Walk* (MacLiammoir), 15, 16, and 17 January 1948; return engagement, 24, 25, 26, and 27 March 1948; Michael Redgrave, Flora Robson, et al. in *Macbeth* (Shakespeare), 11, 12, and 13 March 1948; Madeleine Carroll, Conrad Nagle, et al. in *Goodbye, My Fancy* (Fay Kanin), 21, 22, and 23 October 1948; Judith Evelyn, Hurd Hatfield, et al. in *The Ivy Green* (Mervyn Nelson), 4 and 5 March 1949; Frederic March, Florence Eldridge, et al. in *Now I Lay Me Down to Sleep* (adapted from Louis Bemelman's novel), 31 January 1950; Hume Cronyn, Jessica Tandy, et al. in *The Fourposter* (Jan de Hartog), 16, 17, and 18 July 1951; Larry Parks, Betty Garrett, et al. in *Anonymous Lovers* (Vernon Sylvaine), 1 and 2 December 1952

155 Brian Smith, 'Hume Cronyn,' *Oxford Companion to Canadian Theatre*, 125–6

156 London *Free Press*, 2 January 1952

157 London *Free Press*, 25 April 1952, 10 April and 11 September 1954. See also Ottawa *Evening Citizen*, 25 April 1952.

158 Donald Davis interview by Mira Friedlander (includes Crest Theatre Chronology), *Canadian Theatre Review* 7 (Summer 1975), 34–51. See also Ross Stuart, 'The Crest Controversy,' ibid., 8–11, and Herbert Whittaker, 'Recollections of Achievement,' ibid., 12–23.

159 Jill Tomasson Goodwin, 'A Career in Review: Donald Davis, Canadian Actor, Producer, Director,' *Theatre History in Canada / Histoire du théâtre au Canada* 10:2 (Fall 1989), 132–51, and 'A Career in Progess, Part 2: Donald Davis Canadian Actor and Director, 1959–1990,' ibid., 12:1 (Spring 1991), 56–78. See also Herbert Whittaker, 'Donald Davis,' *Oxford Companion to Canadian Theatre*, 132–3, and 'Murray Davis,' ibid., 133–4.

160 Quoted by Eric Crump, 'Drama: English Canada,' in *Canadian Annual Review* 1966, 439

161 Canadian Players Scrapbooks, Metropolitan Toronto Reference Library, Theatre Section. See also Ross Stuart and Harry Lane, 'The Canadian Players,' *Oxford Companion to Canadian Theatre*, 74–6.

162 Eugene Benson, 'Marigold Charlesworth,' *Oxford Companion to Canadian Theatre*, 88; Timothy Findley, 'Jean Roberts,' ibid., 471

163 Bryden and Neil, eds, *Whittaker's Theatre*, 116–17

164 Denis W. Johnston, *Up the Mainstream: The Rise of Toronto's Alternative Theatres, 1968–1975* (Toronto: University of Toronto Press, 1991), 15. The four plays in the first season were Hochhuth's *The Soldiers*, Jean Basile's *The Drummer Boy*, John Hearn's *A Festival of Carols*, and Jules Feiffer's *Little Murders*.

165 Neil Carson, 'Theatre Toronto,' *Oxford Companion to Canadian Theatre*, 551–2

166 Digby Day directed Shaw's *In Good King Charles' Golden Days* and Goldoni's *The Servant of Two Masters*; Bond directed the final play, Frank Marcus's *The Killing of Sister George*.

167 *Canadian Theatre Review* 7 (Summer 1975), 9

168 Following is a partial list of professional and semi-professional companies that appeared in Toronto (except where noted otherwise) between 1945 and 1967 (Toronto Scrapbook and individual files, Metropolitan Toronto Reference Library, Special Collections): Actors Company – *see* Belmont Group Theatre; Actors' Lane Workshop (1957–9); Actors' Workshop – *see* Canadian Actors' Workshop; Actors' Theatre – *see* Toronto Actors' Theatre; Academy of Theatre Arts (1967?–?); Aries Productions (1964–7); Arts Club Theatre (1951–2); Arts Theatre Club (1959–60); Arts Theatre Foundation (1962); Avon Theatre (1964); B and B Productions (1948); Stanley Bell, Museum Theatre – *see* B and B Productions; Belmont Group Theatre (1948–67); Black Watch Productions (1960–?); Broadview Barn Players (1964–?); Canada Players (1945–60; Canadian Actors' Workshop (1961–?); Canadian Drama League Players (1946–7); Canadian Group Theatre (1965–?); Canadian Players – *see* Touring Players Foundation; Canadian Theatre Guild – *see* Holloway Bay Playhouse; Canadian Theatre School (1949–55?); Centre Island Association (1956); Centre Stage (1960–62); Civic Square Theatre (1961–2); Civic Theatre Association (1945–9); Comedy Theatre Players (1945–?); Comet Productions (no dates available); Crest Theatre (1954–66); Earle Grey Players (1948–58); Eric Greenwood / Terry Fisher Productions, Avenue Theatre (1957–8; First Floor Club (1959) – *see* also Studio Theatre; Forest Hill Players (1948–9); Hart House Players (1946–50); Haymakers (1946–?); Grenville Street Playhouse (1962; Halwyn Productions (1966–?); Holloway Bay Playhouse (1947–8?); House of Hambourg cabaret theatre (1959–60); International Players (1948–53); Intimate Theatre (1967–?); Jupiter Theatre (1951–4); Kingston Repertory Theatre – *see* International Players; Kool-Vent Theatre (1952–?); London Theatre Company (1954–5); Marshall-Taylor Productions – *see* Trio Productions; Masquers (1965–?); Mentor Productions (1967–?);

Merger Productions (1966–?); Midland Players (1949–?); The Moonlighters
(1965–?); New Play Society (1947–71); Odyssey Productions (1967–?); Penguin
Productions (1960–?); People's Repertory Theatre (1947–9); Plaquest Drama Guild
(1946–50); Playcraftsmen (1949–55); Playwrights' Studio (1964–?); Pocket Players
(1964–?); Premiere Productions (1956–?); Producers' Playhouse (1957–?); The
Questors (1964–?); Studio Theatre (A. Saxe) (1956–9); Studio Children's Theatre
(1965–9); Studio Lab Theatre (1969–76); Temple Players (1954–5) – see Belmont
Group Theatre; Theatre Company of Toronto (1964–?); Theatre '49 (1949–54);
Theatre Upstairs (1965–?); Toronto Actors' Studio (1963–?); Toronto Chamber
Theatre (1965–?); Toronto Repertory Company (1951–?) – see International
Players; Toronto Theatre Club (1946–50); Toronto Workshop Productions
(1959–?); Touring Players Foundation (1966–?); Verve Productions (1964–?);
Village Playhouse (1961–3); Village Revue, Bohemian Embassy (1961–7); Work-
shop Productions – see Toronto Workshop Productions; York Community Players
(1954–?); York Community Theatre (1958–?); York Drama Club (1949–?); Young
People's Theatre (1966–)

169 Avenue Theatre file, Metropolitan Toronto Reference Library, Theatre Section
170 Johnston, *Up the Mainstream*, 18–19
171 *The Varsity* (University of Toronto), n.d., in Civic Square Theatre file, Metropolitan
Toronto Reference Library, Theatre Section
172 *Telegram*, 25 November 1961
173 Bayview Playhouse file, Metropolitan Toronto Reference Library, Theatre Section
174 In fact, Ken Gass, founder of Factory Lab Theatre in 1970, had worked closely in
workshops at Herbert's own company, the Garret, and one can trace Factory Lab's
policy of dedicating itself to the discovery and production of Canadian plays back to
Herbert's influence.
175 The name Hambourg derived from a family of musicians in Toronto who had been
prominent in the city's musical life in the early 1900s.
176 So described by David Gardner in 'Drama: English Canada,' *Canadian Public
Affairs, 1963*, 470
177 Johnston, *Up the Mainstream*, 18–23
178 Ibid., *Up the Mainstream*, 18
179 Bryden and Neil, eds, *Whittaker's Theatre*, 87–9
180 Alan Filewod, 'Toronto Workshop Productions,' *Oxford Companion to Canadian
Theatre*, 557–8
181 Centre Stage file, Metropolitan Toronto Reference Library, Theatre Section
182 Colonnade Theatre file, Metropolitan Toronto Reference Library, Theatre Section
183 Alan Filewod, 'Studio Lab Theatre,' *Oxford Companion to Canadian Theatre*,
508–9. See also Johnston, *Up the Mainstream*, 198–204.
184 Joyce Doolittle, 'Young People's Theatre,' *Oxford Companion to Canadian
Theatre*, 596–7
185 Poor Alex Theatre file, Metropolitan Toronto Reference Library, Theatre Section

186 James Noonan, 'The National Arts Centre: Fifteen Years at Play,' in *Theatre History in Canada / Histoire du théâtre au Canada* 6:1 (Spring 1985), 56–8

187 See Johnston, *Up the Mainstream*, 55–6, 238–49, and 109–11, respectively.

188 Richard Plant, 'International Players,' *Oxford Companion to Canadian Theatre*, 279

189 Malcolm Page, 'Joy Coghill,' *Oxford Companion to Canadian Theatre*, 103–4. Harry Lane, 'William Needles,' ibid., 367. Eugene Benson, 'Bernard Slade,' 498–9.

190 Anton Wagner, 'Theatre in Ontario,' *Oxford Companion to Canadian Theatre*, 403–4

191 Benson and Conolly, *English-Canadian Theatre*, 110–13

192 Ibid., 68–73

193 Anton Wagner, 'Theatre in Ontario,' *Oxford Companion to Canadian Theatre*, 404

2 *Variety*

DAVID GARDNER

Ever since Greek tragedy was followed by the satyr-play, we have had two main thrusts in the theatre – the serious and the popular; high art and low; the 'legitimate' and the 'illegitimate.' Eighteenth- and nineteenth-century drama was leavened by the entr'acte and the afterpiece; gradually these divertissements evolved into a rainbow of new entertainment forms that we loosely group under the umbrella title of variety.

In nineteenth-century Ontario, 'legitimate' was a term still showing its connection to an English theatre influenced by the licensing acts and patent houses. It loosely connoted Shakespeare, poetic or other serious drama, and old comedy,[1] but by the twentieth century almost any well-crafted play would be classified as 'legit' (at least in the appropriately named showbiz bible, *Variety*). The 'illegit' seems harder to pin down, embracing as it does the circus, clowning, medicine and minstrel shows, vaudeville, burlesque, pageants, revues, cabaret, and musical comedy. But then, the nature of variety is its variety.

Usually, variety shies away from emotional complexities and difficult language. It is content to entertain. Music, movement, and knockabout humour are its stocks-in-trade. Even the Shaw and Stratford festivals have found it profitable to embrace the 'illegit' for its popular and festive appeal. Indeed, most of Ontario's non-profit theatres conclude their seasons with something to gratify the pleasure principle, either to bail them out financially or to leave a pleasant after-taste at subscription-renewal time. Not unexpectedly, Ontario's 1970 cabaret revues and dinner theatres paved the way for the move away from subsidization towards a self-sufficient commercial theatre, a potential confirmed in the 1980s and 1990s by such large-scale musicals as *The Phantom of the Opera*.

The First World War is a good jumping-off point for a survey of variety. It marks a tangible shift from colonial to indigenous aspiration.

(1) 'Essfest Der Kriegsgefangenen' (Carnival of the prisoners of war in Fort Henry, 1918). During the First World War, Ukrainian and Austro-Hungarian immigrants were interned with German prisoners of war at Fort Henry, Kingston, 1914–19. Among their activities were theatrical performances, circuses, carnivals, and an annual ceremony commemorating the sinking of the Germans' ship. The ceremony included a parade and the burning of a replica of the ship.

While one could attempt the numbing task of documenting all the imported vaudeville acts, the countless foreign musicals and comedy revues, and the innumerable circuses that continued to roll across the border, the focus of this chapter is the popular entertainments that Ontarians began to devise themselves after the war.

Circuses

The circus is the grand-daddy of variety; the early equestrian shows, which grew by incorporating clowns, acrobats, pantomime, trained animals, and other acts, eventually handed on the reins to Barnum (d. 1891) and then to Bailey (d. 1906). But before the Barnum and Bailey Circus was absorbed by Ringling's in 1918, they had one intriguing matinée in Ontario during the First World War when, on 8 October 1916, the YMCA Prisoners of War Service hired them to entertain German POWs at King-

(2) 'Eine Familie vorsintflutlicher Urtiere aus der Gattung Kaposiurius,' October 1916
(Primitive animals from the species 'concentration camp lowest-of-lowly officer';
'Kapo' is slang for a prisoner of war in charge of fatigue detail [*Grosse Brockhaus*])

ston's Fort Henry.[2] Two years later, the upstart Ringling Brothers created the 'Ringling Bros. and Barnum and Bailey Combined Circus' –
truly 'The Greatest Show on Earth,' setting the pace in North America
for more than a decade. By 1922 their consolidated 'Big Top' (tent)
show travelled on more than a mile of train consisting of a hundred railway cars.[3] But few people know that the train-master who organized this
feat was John A. McLachlan (or McLaughlin), a native of London,
Ontario.[4]

In 1956 John Ringling North made the painful decision to abandon
the big top forever. From then Ringling Brothers performed only in the
indoor sports arenas that had mushroomed across North America before
and after the Second World War (Toronto's Maple Leaf Gardens, for
example, had hosted circuses and rodeos since the 1930s), allowing the
circus to tour year-round. Gradually, McLachlan's hundred railway cars
were replaced by eighteen-wheelers, and the personnel travelled and

(3) 'Zulus' taking part in the prisoners' 'Barnum and Bailey' circus, October 1916. In back-left of the performance space prepared in the Fort quadrangle is the band; to the right are various performers, and on the upper level as well as in the foreground are audience members.

lived in a fleet of recreational vehicles, which became the transportation mode for all circuses for the rest of the century. Ringling's survived and Ontario cities welcomed them.

But if Ringling Brothers set the standard for large-scale circuses, the average Ontarian is just as likely to remember the more modest ones. Even during the dying fall of vaudeville, tiny circuses sometimes appeared on stage as one of the acts. Barton Brothers' Circus made such an appearance in April 1925 at Keith's (Loews/Capitol) in Ottawa.[5] From the 1930s to the 1960s the medium-sized Clyde Beatty Circus was one of those that visited Maple Leaf Gardens regularly. Few people who saw him will forget Emmett Kelly's sad clown balancing a feather on his nose and sweeping the spotlight under the rug. Beatty himself was one of the great animal trainers, and he was dressed like a silent film director in white shirt, boots, and jodhpurs when he stepped into the cage with the big cats. He died in 1965 at the age of sixty-two but the name of his circus was continued for many years.

Another regular Ontario visitor was the Shrine Circus, which has come annually since the early 1930s to raise funds for its twenty-two hospitals across North America. Until 1979 the Shrine contract went to Garden Brothers, an Ontario organization with offices in Toronto and winter quarters in Georgetown. Garden Brothers' three-ring indoor cir-

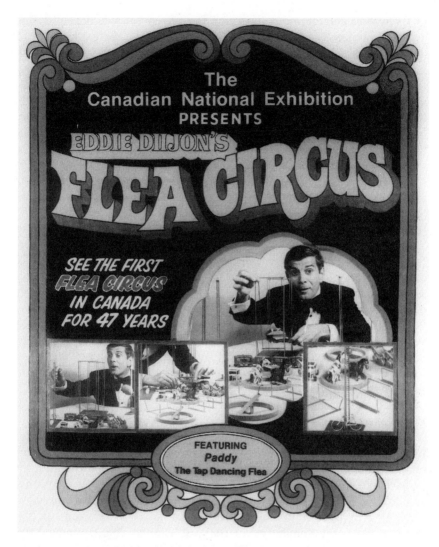

Eddie Diijon and his Flea Circus played eight shows a day at the CNE in 1975; he still tours his circus.

cus was launched in Toronto in 1938 by William Garden, a vaudeville actor, and in the 1970s and 1980s was run by his son, Ian M. Garden.[6]

There are still a few, old-fashioned, small 'high grass' rolling circuses or 'mud' shows, so-called because they set up their tent in the empty fields of rural Ontario, catering to communities with a population of two or three thousand and no competition from even a movie house. By the 1970s, Ontarians were taking a strong stand against the exploitation of animals. Russian circuses, deemed to have been offenders in this regard, have been coming to Ontario intermittently since August 1962, when a first cultural exchange tour made its North American début in Ottawa and then proceeded on to Toronto. Chinese acrobatic troupes followed in the 1970s, inspiring Québec's *Cirque du Soleil* to reinvent the form. Horses in the ring were replaced by bicycles and all the four-legged animals became two-legged ones.

However, not all circuses could be reconceived in this way. Toronto-born conjurer 'Eddie the Great' Diijon (né Denis, 1938–) was taught the art of training fleas in Hong Kong about 1961. After performing there for eight years at the Lai-Chi-Kok Amusement Park, he incorporated the fleas into a novelty nightclub act that he put on tour from Tokyo to Saigon. In 1975 he returned to Toronto to present his All-Canadian Performing Flea Circus underneath the CNE Grandstand for a pet-supply company. It was advertised as the first flea circus in Canada for forty-seven years, and it may well be the only performing flea circus now left in the world.[7] Audiences of no more than thirty to forty sit around a table-stage and peer through magnifying glasses to see Eddie's troupe of seven fleas balance on the high wire, perform triple somersaults, tap-dance, juggle, pull a toy locomotive, and engage in a grande finale chariot race. Only human fleas (*Pulex irritans*) can be used, because they live for approximately two years and it takes up to four months to train one. Between engagements, flea-master Eddie Diijon plies his trade as a magician.

Before we leave the world of animals we must recall that foggy, fateful night of 15 September 1885, when the most renowned of circus elephants, Jumbo, was struck from behind by an unscheduled freight train in St Thomas, Ontario. The world has never forgotten P.T. Barnum's Jumbo, nor has St Thomas. The fiftieth anniversary of his demise was celebrated in 1935 with a three-day gathering by the citizens of this Western Ontario community;[8] in 1985, St Thomas commemorated the one hundredth anniversary of Jumbo's death by unveiling a spectacular $60,000, forty-ton elephant sculpture on a bluff overlooking the western end of the city.

In most theatrical evocations of the circus someone walks a line on the floor pretending to be on the highwire. But Sudbury skywalker Jay Cochrane (1941–) has been doing the real thing since 1960. In 1974 he set a long-distance record at the CNE, and in 1995 he established a world record for height and distance, crossing the Yangtze River gorge in China.

Clowning

One of Garden Brothers' attractions is Rumpy the Clown (he gets his
name from a well-padded posterior), alias Roger Prystanski (1947–) of
Thunder Bay.[9] But not all of Ontario's clowns work in the circus. Robert
Carr (1884–1975) was born in Glasgow, the fourth generation of a
clown family. He came to Toronto after his First World War service as a
dispatch rider with a Canadian artillery unit, and after a dozen years with
Ringling Brothers and the Sells-Floto circuses, he became a fixture with
Eaton's Toyland, from 1932 until his retirement in 1967.[10] North Bay's
Orville Conliffe (1907–), alias Jo-Jo, is another clown outside the circus
fondly remembered from earlier in the century.[11] Topper the Clown
(Charles Colville, 1911–87), born in Hastings, Ontario, was a member
of Ring 17 of the International Brotherhood of Magicians and a familiar
figure at the National Arts Centre and Ontario Place.[12] During the Second World War, Toronto's Les Beazer (1915–77), who toured with
Conklin Shows, was billed at the CNE Water Show as 'the world's greatest high-diving aquatic clown.'[13] Bilingual Roger Clown (his real name;
1950–) came to Ontario from England when he was seven. In 1971 he
was named 'Citizen Clown' of Ottawa in a fifteen-minute black-and-
white, award-winning film documentary. The great French master
Etienne Decroux (1898–1991), teacher of Jean-Louis Barrault, Marcel
Marceau, and Jacques LeCoq, visited Toronto in 1958, giving a mime
recital at Eaton Auditorium. The bilingual Rocko (Wayne Constantineau), born 1947 at Espanola in Northern Ontario, studied mime and
clowning in the mid-1970s with Decroux and became his assistant
instructor during the master's final years. Constantineau is married to
Carmen Orlandis Habsburgo, whose clown Blip is a balloon-twister
extraordinaire. At corporate Christmas parties, she has been known to
sculpt a giant dragon utilizing 500–600 balloons.[14]

With the rise in the 1960s of street theatre and the rediscovery of the
age-old outdoor art of the busker, professional clowning in Ontario took
on an extended life. Since the 1970s it has developed a new artistic
thrust as clown companies began to emerge at the National Arts Centre
in Ottawa and particularly in Toronto. However, their story must await
another volume.

Medicine Shows

At one time there were 150 medicine shows on the road in North
America[15]; many entertainers, Buster Keaton among them,[16] got their
start with these caravanning pedlars. This commercial phenomenon of

the nineteenth and early twentieth centuries persisted in Canada with Thomas Patrick 'Doc' Kelley. Born in Newboro, Ontario, in 1865, 'Canada's King of the Medicine Men' travelled the rural areas of all nine Canadian provinces, the Dominion of Newfoundland, and thirty-seven American states from 1886 to 1931 with Kelley's Shamrock Concert Company.

Because the 'med-show' was free, showmen had to survive on their sales. Kelley's patent medicines carried the 'Shamrock' label and were considered reputable products. They included Shamrock Healing Oil, Liniment, Nerve Tablets, Tapeworm Remover, and Corn Salve, as well as Vigor and Passion Flower Pills supposedly made from Guru seeds, yak's milk, and 'the glands of young angora goats.'[17] The 'pitch' was integrated into the vaudeville-cum-circus entertainment. One performer, an aging tragedian with the unlikely name of Wellington Bun, put on one-man versions of Shakespeare's plays. Kelley's shows consisted of songs and soft-shoe dancing, slack-wire turns, comic juggling, card tricks, mind-reading acts, Punch and Judy routines, banjo-playing, and knockabout burlesque skits.

Performers had to be continually resourceful to attract and hold the potential customers, and Doc Kelley's biography credits him with two major contributions to the art of variety entertainment – the most-popular-baby contest and the now-immortal pie-in-the-face routine. Actually, the baby contest was popularized by Barnum in 1855, but the custard pie stunt seems to be original. This classic comic device could be said to have launched the twentieth century, and it certainly became an enduring trademark of vaudeville and silent-film comedies. The original victim, Kelley's comic dancer and banjo player, Jim Gay, was in Hollywood between 1911 and 1912 doing bit parts in two-reelers for Vitagraph Studios. He passed on the comic business to John Bunny, 'the screen's first big comedian.'[18] A year or so later, fellow Canadian Mack Sennett (1880–1960) picked up the idea for his Keystone comedies. The earliest surviving Sennett silent including a custard pie–throwing sequence was *A Noise from the Deep*, released 17 July 1913.[19]

'Doc' Kelley died on tour in Uxbridge, Ontario, in 1931.

The Minstrel Show

'Doc' Kelley also dabbled in minstrel shows. In 1894, he assembled Kelley's Ladies Minstrels for a series of winter tours and claimed they were 'The Only All-Girl Minstrel Show in The World!' Female minstrels have been labelled the forerunners of the 'girlie show,' and Kelley's minstrels were no exception. His 'Carload of Pretty Girls' was backed by a three-woman musical trio in the pit, and featured patriotic and mermaid production numbers, as well as flame dances and one Amazonian strong woman. They made money, but created amusing chaperoning problems.[20] Five winter seasons was as long as Kelley felt he could protect the virtue of sixteen young women on tour. However, his love of the minstrels continued. Between 1911 and 1921, in addition to his medicine show, he managed Kelley's Colored Forty and Kelley's Dixie Cotton Pickers, black troupes touring the rural heartland around the Great Lakes before and after the First World War.

Another small professional minstrel company was run by the Guy Brothers, who trouped from the United States to Canada often between the 1870s and 1920. During the First World War, September and October were regular dates for Kingston and Peterborough, while the Kitchener–Niagara Falls circuit welcomed them in December.[21]

Variety reported that there were still thirteen big minstrel companies emanating from New York during the 1912–13 season, but they virtually disappeared after the First World War. Commercially, the minstrel stars were absorbed by vaudeville and the musical-comedy revues that flowered in the teens and twenties. The exception to this rule was Al Jolson, who joined Dockstader's Minstrels in 1907 after he had spent time in vaudeville.[22] Jolson played at Toronto's Royal Alexandra Theatre during the week of 23 October 1916, supported by a cast of nearly two hundred, in his musical extravaganza *Robinson Crusoe Jr.*, in which he appeared in black-face as 'Good Friday.'[23] The minstrel show ended as it began, a solo black-face act.[24] But between Thomas D. Rice's 'Jumping Jim Crow' entr'acte in 1828 and Al Jolson's 'Mammy,' there had been a century of uniquely American entertainment rooted in plantation music and the comic parody of blacks. The principal reasons for the demise of the minstrel show were changing attitudes towards racial humour and the collapse of the form itself. Ironically, both these changes were precipitated in large part by the arrival of Afro-American entertainers into the field.

In 1866, with emancipation and the Civil War behind them, the most famous all-black troupe, the original Georgia Minstrels, was founded. Throughout the history of minstrelsy 'Georgia Minstrels' or 'coloured' became generic terms for black companies. For example, Honey-Boy Evans and his 'Georgia Minstrels' frequented the Ottawa Valley before the First World War, and even as late as February 1933, we hear of yet another reincarnation of 'Georgia Minstrels' on the stage of Ottawa's Capitol Theatre, with 'a hot-cha cast of 40 and Dixie's Hottest Jazz Band.'[25]

Increasingly, the nostalgic re-creation of life on a plantation became a black preserve, and subtly black performers infused new vitality and relevance into the form with the introduction of jubilee gospel music, spirituals, and, later, ragtime and Dixieland jazz. The travelling black companies flourished, especially when marketed by white managers like Kelley, and they created new black audiences. However, their success was marred by incidents of shocking discrimination: the constant denial of hotel accommodation; the use of their moving railway cars as targets for rifle practice; and even the occasional lynching for slight or manufactured pretexts.

Minstrelsy had reached a crossroads in the 1870s, when white minstrels found themselves being criticized for their lack of authenticity. Slowly these entertainers dropped the 'blackface' material and white impresarios and, in competition with the three-ring circus and variety music halls, moved the minstrel show towards the big musical and dance extravaganzas of the late nineteenth century. Ontario's minstrel celebrity George Henry Primrose (1852–1919), was instrumental in instituting the final phase of what has been called 'white minstrelsy.'

Primrose was triple threat: a singer (he introduced 'It's a Hot Time in the Old Town Tonight' in 1897),[26] and end-man ('Canada's Own Comedian'), he is remembered best as a consummate dancer. By 1914, near the end of his career, he was called 'The Man of the Velvet Feet.'[27] He is often considered to have originated the soft-shoe dance,[28] and when he appeared on his own in vaudeville his soft-shoe rendition of 'Lazy Moon' was hailed as a classic.[29] Primrose's 1908 tour of Southern Ontario featured soft- and wooden-shoe dances, and one of his production numbers in evening dress was called 'The Poetry of Motion.'[30] Hector Charlesworth recalls that 'even in old age his easy grace in leading a dancing ensemble was fascinating.'[31] In 1919, the year Primrose died, the Zeigfeld Follies paid tribute to the Minstrel Show in its Act One finale, with dancing star Marilyn Miller portraying George Primrose.

Much of the humour in late-nineteenth-century variety theatres was rough and racial, and it was not just blacks that were presented in stereotypical caricatures. As European and Asiatic immigration mushroomed, ethnic humour became increasingly distasteful. In 1909 the National Association for the Advancement of Colored People (NAACP) was formed in the United States[32] and the long uphill battle for civil rights was begun. Few people know of an earlier Ontario meeting in July 1905, when twenty leading Afro-Americans from fourteen states, denied accommodation in Niagara Falls, NY, relocated in Ontario at the Erie Beach Hotel in Fort Erie. Out of their three-day conference the Niagara Movement was born, advocating basic freedoms, integration, and the abolition of discrimination. After five years it merged with the NAACP.

Blacks also took an increasingly hard look at their own perpetuation of unrealistic images on stage. While black troupes catered more to the rural bias of minstrelsy with its gentle harking back to the warm and gracious South of pre–Civil War America, the comic clowns and servant-figures (such as Jack Benny's 'Rochester') were slow to lose their wide-eyed mannerisms and lackadaisical speech patterns. Eventually, the growing urbanization and sophistication of North America relegated the minstrel show to the periphery of the entertainment wheel and Afro-American minstrels went the way of white. The woebegone, sad-faced, West Indian comedian Bert Williams moved on, first to vaudeville, then to eight years with the Ziegfeld Follies, while others gravitated to landmark all-black musicals like Bob Cole and Bill Johnson's *A Trip to Coontown* (1898) and Eubie Blake and Noble Sissle's *Shuffle Along* in 1921.[33] *A Trip to Coontown* was polished in Ontario in 1898, 1899, and 1900 before its New York opening (9 April 1900),[34] and the Guy Brothers Minstrels presented their version at Hamilton's Grand Opera House (24 November 1898).[35] Eubie Blake brought *Shuffle Along* in person to the Royal Alexandra Theatre in the fall of 1923. Toronto audiences saw seventeen-year-old Josephine Baker in its cast and heard the hit song 'I'm Just Wild About Harry.'

In Ontario the black-face tradition died more slowly. Amateurs loved the minstrel show because it was a grand group activity. It is impossible to document the prolific outpouring of community minstrel shows in Ontario, for athletic, church, and service clubs from Kingston to St Marys were addicted to the burnt cork. The Hamilton Bicycle, Banjo and Mandolin Club, with C.L.M. Harris as its accompanist, was active in the 1890s, and the Toronto Lacrosse Club's Minstrel Show graced the Grand Opera House in January 1894.[36] In 1900, at the age of sixteen, Toronto's Walter Huston (1884–1950) made his second stage appearance as an end-man in a St Simon's Anglican Church minstrel event held at Toronto's Massey Hall.[37] Hamilton's Victoria Yacht Club Minstrels were sailing strong in 1902, and Toronto's Rowing Club Minstrels featured 'Canada's premier buck and wing dancer, Mr. Joseph Hill' in London, Ontario, on 8 May 1909.[38] The year before, another Torontonian, Edward W. Miller, wrote and published 'The Minstrel Show,' which had been performed in 1908 at Saint Anne's Church in Ottawa.[39] On 9 February 1918 (repeated 23 February) Toronto's Arts and Letters Club mounted their first and last minstrel show. Located then in their second home, the Assize Court room on Adelaide Street (later the short-lived Adelaide Court Theatre), they dubbed themselves 'The Old Court Minstrels.'[40]

Perhaps the most famous instance of minstrelsy associated with a

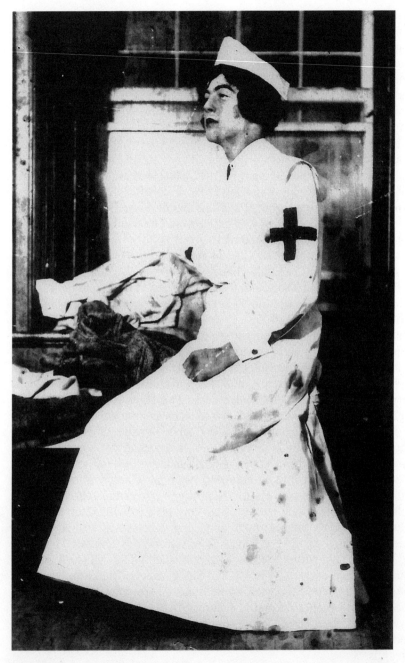

Gord Cassels in a so-called Minstrel Show, 1914, Royal Military College, Kingston

Toronto son was the show produced in January and February 1919 at Vladivostok, the eastern terminus of the Trans-Siberian railroad. Like Walter Huston, Raymond Massey (1896–1983) had his turn as a minstrel. Young Lieutenant Massey was an officer with a Canadian expeditionary force sent out to help the White Russians oust the Bolsheviks. Because of his acting prowess in a shipboard spy farce en route to Russia, Massey was asked to get up a variety entertainment for the allied troops in the area. He immediately remembered the Primrose and Dockstader Minstrels from their Grand Opera House visits to Toronto. While spending 1917–18 at Yale University as a military instructor, he had haunted New York and memorized the comedy routines of such Ziegfeld headliners as Fanny Brice, Leon Errol, and, particularly, Bert Williams. Within twenty-four hours a show was roughed-out and into rehearsal. 'The Roadhouse Minstrels,' as they designated themselves, opened early in 1919 after less than two weeks' rehearsal and performed on about twenty occasions. The twenty-three-year-old Massey, who had not yet ventured onto the Hart House Theatre stage or decided on a theatrical career, played Rastus, one of the end-men. He sang 'Nobody' and performed the 'Solo Poker Game' routine, both plagiarized from Bert Williams, and gave an interpretation of Salomé's dance – 'In the Shadow of the Pyramids.' With tongue in cheek, an American regimental paper hailed 'the all-star All-Canadian troupe ... the best Allied show yet produced in Siberia.'[41]

To celebrate St Patrick's Day week in 1924, the Winter Garden Vaudeville Theatre in Toronto staged a local Amateur Minstrel Frolic. It was produced by Victor Hyde of New York and arranged through the courtesy of owner Marcus Loew. Betty Ford, a member of the chorus, recalls lots of singing and highland dancing, but, with the exception of one minstrel number, the large cast of over forty did not 'burn the cork.'[42]

Some time during the 1920s and 1930s an itinerant pianist, Arthur Livingston Ashworth and his wife, Millie Bell, the sister of May Bell who starred with Ontario's Marks Brothers, organized a Children's Minstrel Show that toured Canada. The Toronto Kiddies ran for about ten years, doing comedy routines and creating music by strumming musical frying pans. Girls tied bells on their toes and did some bell ringing by shaking their feet, while Miss Bell appeared on a swing 'fitted with electric lights.'[43] Audience participation contests and quiz shows were part of the fun. But, of course, it had little to do with a true minstrel show.

Radio carried on the black-face tradition with the 'Amos 'n' Andy' show, which was launched in 1929. It ended in 1953, when ratings dropped and the NAACP was able finally to pressure it off the air. A tele-

St Catharines Steel 'Minstrel Show,' 11 May 1943

vision version in the 1960s featured black performers, but it was short-lived. Canada's radio contribution was 'The Four Continental Porters,' a Vancouver-based quartet of white male singers, two of whom doubled on piano and saxophone. For many years the CNR had hired only blacks as porters, hence it was ironic that 'The Four Porters' were heard as early as 1925 on the CNR's Radio Network (1923–32).[44]

One hears various claims for 'the last Minstrel Show in America,' but probably the palm should go to the Southern Melodians at the Main Street Calvary Baptist Church in Toronto's east end. It was started by the Men's Bible Class in 1936 to provide entertainment for people who 'couldn't afford a nickel to go to the local show.'[45] For more than twenty years the Calvary Minstrels 'blacked up,' but in deference to changing attitudes went white-face in 1969. While they remained a staunch, all-male aggregation, the evening often concluded with the thirty-man chorus decked out in borrowed evening gowns. In 1979, after forty-three years, their public minstrel show was quietly retired in tribute to its chief author, interlocutor Bill Sewell, and end-men Bill Moore and Harry Mitchell, all charter members who had reached their seventies and eighties. For four additional years the minstrels reappeared for semi-private church dinners before finally retiring in 1983.

Although the minstrel show was rarely seen after the Second World War, I fondly remember, in October 1947, being a member of the blackface chorus in the third act of Victoria University's 75th Annual Vic 'Bob.' We blacked up to sing 'Can't You Hear Me Calling Caroline' and 'Blue Skies' against the Tara-like backdrop of Victoria's front steps. Our performing director was Toronto-born Norman Jewison (1926–), yet to make his name in Hollywood. He sang 'Hogtown Blues,' one of the best of the original numbers, and would go on to compose and perform for *Spring Thaw*.

Vaudeville

Vaudeville was North America's most popular, mass, family entertainment form during the opening years of the twentieth century. Its audiences outnumbered those of the legitimate playhouses by ratios as high as ten to one.[46] When the great fifty-year cycle of theatrical touring (1874–1924) began to wind down, it was the vaudevillians who were able to hang on for a few years longer. Vaudeville competed directly with the legitimate theatre through syndicated chains and circuits of 2000 to 4000 theatres,[47] many of them newly built and air-conditioned, at a time when the older playhouses were in need of refurbishing. At the box office they charged 15, 25, and 50 cents for the best seats, compared with $2.00 or $3.00 to see a drama. Vaudeville's entertainment factor appealed more widely to recent immigrants and working-class families. Wives and youngsters could be included in the outing, and with musical, magical, acrobatic, animal, or dance acts, language was never a problem. Vaudeville was also cheaper to produce. Managers had to provide only the physical space of a theatre, musical accompaniment, and a few basic backdrops. The solo or family acts came prepackaged, and if they bombed one week there was always a fresh selection for the week following.

As this volume's predecessor *Early Stages* has described, the Shea

Magic shows have continued at both the amateur and professional levels long after vaudeville closed. 'The Charmed Rope,' by a magicians' group in Hamilton, Ontario, 20 October 1950

brothers introduced resident vaudeville to Ontario; their Toronto theatres were open twice a day, with eight high-class, twenty-minute acts obtained through Benjamin Franklin Keith and Edward Franklin Albee's United Booking Office. Drinking, smoking, whistling, and spitting were not permitted, and a watchful eye was kept on material that was blasphemous or smutty. But if Keith-Albee earned their sobriquet as the 'Sunday School Circuit,' they were anything but polite when it came to business. Through their Booking Office they controlled the hiring and firing of most performers, even forbidding them to perform on radio or place an ad in *Variety* magazine,[48] which was then out of favour. Movies, too, were generally unwelcome for many years.

The Keith-Albee cartel was challenged eventually by small-time, independent agents like William Morris and Marcus Loew, both of whom established bases in Toronto. In September 1909, Morris leased the Majestic Theatre (or Music Hall) on Adelaide Street at Bay.[49] By 1912 Marcus Loew had bought out Morris, and in 1916 Famous Players turned the Majestic into Toronto's first all-movie palace, the Regent.

We see in hindsight that small-time, turn-of-the-century vaudeville was the Trojan horse that carried the fatal motion-picture enemy. At first the short, silent, black-and-white moving-pictures were simply one more novelty in vaudeville's cornucopia of variety acts. But once the novelty had worn off, the two-reelers were moved unceremoniously to the end of the bill and used to empty the house for the next round of continuous live performance. Gradually, as the movies evolved into feature-length entertainments, the pattern was reversed. By the 1920s it was vaudeville programs that were being sandwiched between the new fad, double features. Crude sound and colour films had been available since 1907 and proper amplification since 1914, but in the 1920s they were held back by movie producers jealously guarding their stockpiles of silent, black-and-white product. Influenced by the growing popularity of radio, the near-bankrupt Warner Brothers (Jack Warner [1892–1978] was born in London, Ontario) decided to take a chance and make their pictures talk. On 6 October 1927, they gave the world *The Jazz Singer*, and audiences marvelled to hear Al Jolson's shadow sing and say, 'You ain't heard nothin' yet!'[50] By 1928 the 'talkies' were considered a commercial bonanza and the costly transition to sound began. Already, the vaudeville circuits and their theatre buildings were being absorbed in the creation of new film conglomerates like RKO, whose very initials spelled out the kind of mergers being made (Radio–Keith–Orpheum). Now there were extra expenses in shooting films in sound, and the cost of converting thousands of theatres was high, $10,000 to $30,000 per house.[51] Vaudeville was quietly smothered in this last frantic phase of the shift of syndicated wealth to movies. In addition, there were the wages for large orchestras and the sometimes exorbitant salaries for vaudeville stars, coupled with spiralling freight and railway rates. The growing appeal of free radio and the pleasures of the motor car finally combined with the stock-market crash of 1929 to sound the death-knell for most touring productions. Vaudeville stars like Eddie Cantor, Edgar Bergen, and Jack Benny began to desert to radio, while others like Ginger Rogers, Fred Astaire, and W.C. Fields soon became household names on the silver screen. Managers discovered that vaudeville was no longer necessary to bolster movie attendance. Many vaudeville performers also made the mistake of committing their famous routines to film,

From an earlier age: The unprepossessing exterior of the St Catharines Grand Opera House, a typical late-nineteenth-century theatre, which dates back to 1877 but was still in use in 1926 when fire destroyed its stage

which further diminished vaudeville's drawing power. Vaudeville, too, was tired by 1929 and no next generation was being trained in its skills. New animal acts and acrobats gravitated to the circus, while those with comedy, dance, and singing talents found their way into radio, film, or musical comedy. Although vaudeville was seen intermittently during the 1930s and even into the 1940s and 1950s (the Red Barn Summer Theatre at Jackson's Point ran vaudeville twice a week in 1952), cinema had superseded it as the twentieth century's primary diversion.

At its height larger Ontario centres like Ottawa, Hamilton and London had at least two theatres devoted solely to vaudeville, and Toronto many more than that. Smaller localities with only a single multi-purpose 'opera

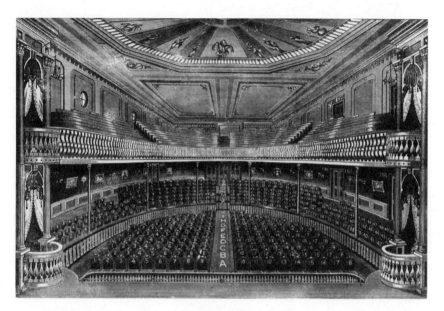

Seating diagram for St Catharines Grand Opera House

house' regularly included vaudeville's trained dogs and baggy-pants
comedians. In the end, in Ontario, it was this vast network of variety theatres that the movies inherited when they exchanged places. The legitimate playhouses and many of the small-town opera houses were able to
continue for a time with an eclectic mixture of movies, touring shows,
and local attractions. In some rare cases the amateur movement took over
a house, like London's Little Theatre at the Grand (1945), or, during the
1920s, resident dramatic companies returned to cities like Toronto for
seasons of weekly stock. The attrition rate for theatres was high. Usually
located on prime real estate, many of the older non-paying houses were
victims of decay or progress. The newer vaudeville-cum-movie palaces
survived the Depression primarily because the talkies (like the amateur
theatre) were affordable. When in turn the movies were challenged, first
by mid-century television and then by the multiplex and videocassette
revolutions of the 1970s and 1980s, a few of the older remaining vaudeville houses came free again and were restored for live performances
(primarily musical comedy). Genuine vaudeville revived on television,
especially with Ed Sullivan's twenty-three-year variety show (1948–71),
and it can still be found in the buskers' street festivals, in the lounge acts
of many holiday cruise ships, and in 'New Vaudeville.'[52]

Canada enjoyed a wave of theatre construction in the 1960s around its centennial celebrations. Before that the principal building spree was due to vaudeville. Toronto's position as 'one of the big tour cities on the road from New York through to Chicago'[53] meant that in the years between 1913 and 1920 six major Toronto theatres were built for vaudeville and, to a lesser extent, the movies. Miraculously, five of these six 'dream palaces' continued to exist into the 1990s. Even more amazingly, three of them were lovingly renovated and reopened in the latter months of 1989.

The principal eastern attack against the Keith-Albee empire came from Marcus Loew (1870–1927) and his championing of the mix of vaudeville and films. In 1913 Loew invaded the Toronto market by erecting a remarkable, seven-storey, double-decker theatre complex, the first in Canada and now the last to survive theatrically in North America. On the bottom was Loew's Yonge, all burgundy and gold and seating 1926 (now reduced to 1600 for increased leg-room). It became simply the Yonge in 1970 and Famous Players renamed it the Elgin in 1978. This flagship theatre opened on Monday, 15 December 1913, with the architect, Scots-born Thomas White Lamb (1871–1942), the 'Dutch' comedy team of (Joe) Weber and (Lew) Fields, and Marcus Loew, himself, as special guests. An added treat was the guest appearance of the twenty-five-year-old composer Irving Berlin who played piano and sang several of his ragtime hits.[54]

Two months later, on Monday, 16 February 1914, the second theatre (above the Loew's/Elgin) welcomed its first patrons. The Winter Garden's 1422 seats (now reduced to 1000) were filled, and the audience was delighted by the innovative decor. The Winter Garden played the same attractions as the lower house, but only in the evenings. Five minutes after a number finished downstairs its entire effects were whisked upstairs by a backstage freight elevator to appear in the 'atmospheric,' branch-and-trellis-covered upper theatre. On warm nights electric fans rustled the hanging leaves and magic lanterns. In 1928, with the heyday of vaudeville over, the Winter Garden was closed permanently. Its elevators, and grand seventy-two-step staircase were sealed off, and because it was not wired for sound it was not subject to the intermittent renovations any active movie-house must undergo. With great good fortune this untouched 'Sleeping Beauty' (as Herbert Whittaker called it) lay entombed in a dusty time capsule for more than fifty years. Downstairs, the Loew's/Yonge/Elgin became a first-run active movie-house until it, too, closed in 1981, by then a purveyor of lower Yonge Street's massage-parlour mentality. Using Lottario funds, these two historic vaudeville theatres were purchased 1 December 1981 by the Ontario Heritage Foundation, an agency of the Ministry of Citizenship and Culture, for $4.5 million. Painstakingly restored at a total cost of $29 million, they reopened 15 December 1989, exactly seventy-six years after Marcus Loew's original inaugural evening.

A bonus of the restoration project was the discovery in the Winter Garden fly-loft of 150 authentic but dirt-covered scenic drops. Carefully cleaned and retouched, they now constitute the largest single collection of vaudeville scenery in North America, and perhaps the world.

The Shea brothers answered Marcus Loew's competitive challenge with a magnificent new vaudeville theatre of their own, the mammoth 3200–seat Hippodrome, which opened 7 April 1914 on Terauley Street (now better known as Bay). Unfortunately, this ornate theatre was not destined to survive. Standing on the north-eastern corner of today's Nathan Phillips Square, it came down in January 1957 to be replaced by Toronto's modern city hall. The 'Hipp' was the home of high-class, two-a-day vaudeville. In this third house Shea-goers saw many of the greats, from Bob Hope and Elvis Presley, to Bill 'Bojangles' Robinson, Jack Benny, and the Dollie Sisters. They also applauded such Montreal entertainers as comedian Ben Blue (1901–75) and the 'French Bombshell' Fifi D'Orsay (née Yvonne Lussier, 1904–83), as well as London, Ontario's Guy Lombardo (1902–77) during the big-band era. Canadians complained when vaudeville was too Americanized.[55] To provide local colour there was often a 'plant' in the audience. 'Mr. Benny, I came clean from Hamilton to see you.' To which Jack would reply, 'No one ever came clean from Hamilton!'[56]

In addition to films and vaudeville acts, many of these First World War and early-1920s theatres included musical revues and 'cultural' shows. In its early years, Shea's Hippodrome was considered a 'presentation' house, featuring opulent productions 'of a symphonic, balletic or operatic nature.'[57] Jack Arthur conducted the orchestra and staged the spectacles, while ballet-master Leon Leonidoff was responsible for the choreography. It is not the last time we will hear of this exciting creative team.

Ontario's 'Mr Showbusiness,' Jack Arthur (1889–1971), was born in Glasgow and trouped with Harry Lauder as a child prodigy on the violin. He was brought to Canada in 1901, at the age of twelve, attended the Toronto College of Music on a scholarship and played violin with the Toronto Symphony when he was fourteen. As a youth he joined the Raymond and Poore vaudeville troupe in the United States as a fiddler, then at nineteen conducted the orchestra on a Mississippi showboat and, eventually, for George Primrose's minstrel show. Returning to Canada around 1910, Arthur began a career as orchestra leader and impresario for the Griffin theatre chain, moving on to Loew's Winter Garden in 1914–15. When N.L. Nathanson (1886–1943) and his associates launched the Famous Players (Canadian) Corporation, Jack Arthur was hired to become the Regent Theatre's orchestral conductor and stage director: 'It was here that he won early fame as the producer of atmospheric prologues and symphonic accompaniments for silent films.'[58] Also Arthur has been remembered for introducing pop concerts to Toronto during the intermissions at the Regent.[59] When Famous Players began its expansion in 1918, he was named director of all their stage and orchestra productions, which meant that Arthur eventually mounted shows for not only Shea's but many other Famous Players acquisitions.

Most vaudeville acts required music and the silent films, too, were rarely silent. The major combination houses (vaudeville and films) provided a ten- to twenty-piece orchestra. And if it was too expensive to keep the pit-band around the whole day, the resident pianist or organist took over to provide the hand-cranked photoplays with sound effects and a musical background appropriate to the action of the drama. In 1922 the Hippodrome installed a ten-ton Wurlitzer pipe organ, which used to rise majestically out of the orchestra pit. The spotlight would pick out Horace Lapp or Quentin McLean already in action at the keyboard. As Hilary Russell has pointed out, 'the theatre organ was cheaper and more versatile in the long run than a full orchestra.'[60] Its versatility included an amazing array of sound effects, everything from the lapping of waves to the galloping of horses, as well as the imitation of other musical instruments such as banjos, violins, and even tom-toms. Jeremiah ('Jerry') Shea died in 1943, but until 1942 he was able to keep vaudeville alive at Shea's long after all the other supposed combination theatres had switched to a policy of movies only. One newspaper item even dates the final vaudeville show at Shea's Hippodrome as occurring in 1952, with hoofer Gene Nelson headlining the bill.[61] The Hippodrome was closed on Boxing Day, 1956. The Wurlitzer was the sole survivor, transferred first to Maple Leaf Gardens and then, in 1971, to the Great Hall of Casa Loma.

The fourth of Toronto's six major vaudeville-movie theatres was the Allen (Danforth), on the south side of Danforth Avenue just east of Broadview. Designed by C. Howard Crane of Detroit, it opened in 1916. Unlike the others it was not built in Toronto's burgeoning downtown theatre district, the area running north from King Street to Dundas, and west from Victoria to John streets. The Allen was a new phenomenon, a local neighbourhood combination house. On one hand, it was like the Regent, a demonstration of 1916's growing equality between the movies and vaudeville; on the other, it was a sign of Toronto's physical expansion. Its vaudeville days, however, were short-lived.

Bernard Allen and his four sons, Jule, Jay-Jay, Herbert, and Sol, had come from Bradford, Pennsylvania, to Brantford, Ontario, in 1906. From there the Allen family pioneered Canada's first national chain of movie theatres. In the year of their arrival, they opened the Theatorium in Brantford, a store-front nickelodeon (odeon, Greek for theatre; nickel, the price of admission). A series of nickelodeons led to larger theatres and expansion across the prairies to Vancouver, then east to Quebec City, and finally into the northern United States and England. In 1919 they hired the esteemed Thomas Lamb to construct an 1800-seat, largely unadorned combination theatre in their native Brantford. Still extant, the Capitol (initially the Temple) has been declared a historic site and is known now as the Sanderson Centre for the Performing Arts. By 1920 the Allen family would own and operate forty-five theatres across Canada, nine neighbourhood ones in Toronto alone. But in 1922–3 the Allen balloon burst owing to overexpansion and Paramount Pictures' sudden withdrawal of their motion-picture distribution franchise. Famous Players bought the Allens' approximately fifty theatres for a reputed $5 million, and they became the initial core of Famous Players' current 225-theatre, 400-screen empire.

Allen's principal theatre in downtown Toronto would be known as the Tivoli. It opened 12 November 1917 and was demolished without a protest in 1965. Its silent-film days are remembered for their reserved-seats policy and the music of Luigi Romanelli's orchestra, with Roland Todd at the piano or organ. The Tivoli was built in answer to the Regent, that is, as a movie rather than a vaudeville house. Although it had no well-equipped stage, the Tivoli did present a decade or so of annual Christmas pantomimes. The choreography was again by Leon Leonidoff and his assistant, the dancer Florence Rogge.

The 1200-seat Allen Theatre (147 Danforth Avenue) has had a chequered existence. Renamed the Century in 1934 in celebration of Toronto's one hundredth birthday, it was then sold and rechristened the Music Hall during the 1970s.

The fifth and sixth of the Toronto vaudeville houses had their premières in 1920, and both were designed again by the dean of combination-theatre architecture, Thomas Lamb. Marcus Loew bought out Metro Pictures in 1920[62] and was in the mood to add a third neighbourhood theatre to his Toronto string, locating it once more on Yonge Street just south of Bloor, and calling it, appropriately, Loew's Uptown, seating 3000. The Greek-born entrepreneur Alexander Pantages, who was venturing east from his western strongholds, chose Toronto's downtown theatre district instead, building south of Dundas Square, between Yonge and Victoria streets. As was his wont, he simply named each of the vaudeville theatres in his chain after himself, but he made Toronto's Pantages the largest theatre in Canada (3626 seats). As John Lindsay has pointed out,[63] the two 1920 theatres were remarkably similar in design. With his first Canadian assignment at the Elgin and Winter Garden, Lamb had pioneered the long narrow entrance way (from Yonge Street), which allowed him to build the stacked theatres behind several store fronts on less-expensive land. This practical device was repeated with both the Pantages and the Uptown. The interior decoration derived from his Scottish heritage, with Lamb borrowing freely from the neoclassical vocabulary of Robert and James Adam.

The Uptown was the first in Toronto to show a talking picture, *Mother Knows Best*, in 1927, and the first to be partitioned into a multiple-auditorium cinema in 1969–70.[64] It remained a movie-house into the 1990s. But in its early days, Loew's Uptown had a higher profile for its original live entertainments than the Pantages. Vaughan Glaser's weekly stock company was there from 1921 to 1926, and 'The Show Place of Toronto' shared the talents of Jack Arthur and Leon Leonidoff with the Regent and Shea's theatres. 'Jack Arthur's Presentations' were also taken to Ottawa, Hamilton, Montreal, and other Canadian cities, with Leonidoff and Florence Rogge featured both as dancers and choreographers.[65] John Lindsay tells us that these 'presentations' were designed to be sent around the circuits to complement a particular movie and that 'original music was composed to add to the overall theme.'[66] Leonidoff and Arthur are said to have developed the precision chorus line together – girls of equal height who linked their arms and synchronized their steps, though it is extremely doubtful that they invented the kick-line. In 1929 Leonidoff and Arthur were wooed by the Roxy Theatre in New York. Arthur chose to stay, but Leonidoff went, forming first the Roxy-ettes and then the immortal Rockettes when he moved over to the world's largest theatre, the new RKO Radio City Music Hall (6200 seats), which opened in 1932. With Leonidoff gone, Jack Arthur imported Boris Volkoff from Chicago, assisting him to establish his Toronto ballet studio. Arthur remained with the head office of Famous Players until he took on new assignments during the Second World War. When the need for stage productions to accompany films evaporated, he channelled his orchestral skills into radio. Jack Arthur met and married his second wife Margaret Phillips (1912–79) in 1935.[67] Seventeen years later 'Midge'

Arthur went on from the Imperialettes to found the Canadettes, the renowned Ontario precision team of up to sixty female dancers who dazzled audiences at the Canadian National Exhibition Grandstand shows from 1952 to 1966.

Famous Players renamed the Pantages the Imperial in 1930. During the 1950s it was the first movie-house in Canada to install a cinemascope screen[68] and in 1973 it was chopped up into the Imperial Six. Then, almost by accident, the Imperial became the Pantages again and Toronto regained another, important, live stage theatre. The wheels of destiny began to revolve in October 1979 when the Imperial was listed for historical status.[69] In 1986, in an acrimonious tussle with Famous Players, Garth Drabinsky, then in charge of Cineplex Odeon, obtained the lease of half the Imperial Theatre from its American owner. By 1987, he was able to purchase this demi-portion for $4 million, and in March 1988 he acquired the whole theatre from Famous Players on the condition that it not be used to show motion pictures. Drabinsky immediately announced plans to restore the Pantages to its original name and grandeur, and devote it primarily to the showing of musicals. The 3626 seats were reduced to 2247 for increased audience comfort and the stage was enlarged to encompass the high-tech, international mega-hit *The Phantom of the Opera*, which reopened the sixty-nine-year-old theatre on 20 September 1989. Deservedly, the beautiful Pantages renewal was awarded two Architectural Conservancy Awards of Merit.

So, in the autumn of 1989, three superbly restored vaudeville houses, the Elgin, Winter Garden, and Pantages, with accommodation for nearly 5000 patrons, were added to the exquisite Royal Alexandra's approximately 1500 seats and the (Danforth) Music Hall's 1800, to create about 8000 available seats per night or 64,000 potential seat sales a week. Suddenly, Toronto was again Canada's commercial theatre centre and second only to New York in North America. But whereas, at the beginning of the century, Toronto had imported all its shows and been totally dependent upon New York, now it was capable of casting and mounting fully Canadian musical and dramatic productions drawn from an international repertoire, and supporting this commercial thrust with an increasingly vital, indigenous underlay. Vaudeville in Ontario may have died, but the musical and variety theatre was alive. And Canadians themselves were venturing more and more into the commercial bigtime with their own large-scale *Rock-a-bye Hamlet*, *Marilyn*, *Duddy*, *Durante*, and *Dreamland*. It was just a matter of time, perhaps, before the chemistry clicked and Toronto's *Kiss of the Spider Woman* production would complete the process of reversal from importation to exportation.

In concentrating on Toronto's six major vaudeville houses we have not forgotten similarly purposed theatres (usually under 2000 seats) in Ontario's other large urban centres: Bennett's and Loew's in London, where Guy Lombardo conducted his pit-band before forming his Royal Canadians; Bennett's (Temple; 1907–10), Loew's (Capitol; 1917–early 1970s), and Pantages' (Palace; 1921–early 1970s), all in Hamilton; or Ottawa's Russell (1897–1928), Bennett's (Dominion; 1906–21), and Loew's/Keith's/Capitol (1920–70).

Similarly, Ontario was rich with medium-sized opera houses or town halls, most of which were converted to include sound-film presentations. Any attempt at a comprehensive list would be bound to include Aylmer (1874–), Barrie, Blyth (Town Hall), Brampton, Brantford (Temple/Capitol, 1919–), Belleville (Capitol), Brockville (Brock), Chatham (Princess), Cobourg (Victoria Hall, 1860–, and Capitol), Cornwall (Capitol, 1928–), Drayton (Town Hall, 1902–), Fort William (Orpheum and Royal), Galt (Regent), Gananoque (Turner's), Gravenhurst, Guelph, Kingston (Grand, 1902–, Griffin's, Ideal, Strand), Kitchener (Berlin Opera House), Lindsay (Academy), Merrickville (Town Hall), Morrisburg, North Bay (Capitol), Orillia, Oshawa (Regent), Owen Sound (Classic), Paris (Capitol), Peterborough (Bradburn's Grand, Princess, Red Mill, and Royal), Petrolia (Victoria Playhouse, razed 26 January 1989), Port Arthur (Colonial), Port Dover, Port Hope (Music Hall), Port Perry, Rat Portage (Kenora) (Hilliard's), St Catharines (Allen/Capitol), St Marys, St Thomas (Bennett's and Duncombe's), Sault Ste Marie (Algoma), Stratford (Albert/Griffin/Majestic/Avon, 1900–), Sudbury (Capitol), Timmins (Palace), Walkerville (Tivoli), and Windsor (Allen/Palace and Loew's). The majority of these theatres came under Famous Players' operating banner of 'Capitol Entertainment,' founded in 1921, which undoubtedly accounts for the prevalence of the name 'Capitol' amongst them.[70] In Toronto, too, there were smaller neighbourhood theatres built to handle vaudeville as well as films, namely, The Beach, The Beaver (at Dundas and Medlund streets, which had a stock company in the 1920s that did *Uncle Tom's Cabin* at least once each year),[71] The Belsize (1927, later Donald and Murray Davis's Crest Theatre and currently called the Regent), the Bloor, Capitol, College, Garden, Gem (on Hanlan's Point, which burned down in 1909), Kum-C on Queen Street West, Madison, Parkdale, Radio City, Royal, St Clair, Standard (Yiddish theatre on Bay at Dundas razed to build the Ford Hotel), and the Strand (Yiddish theatre built to replace the Standard) on Spadina, above Dundas, renamed the Victory (burlesque) during the Second World War.

But vaudeville was more than theatres; it was people. Although the acts were primarily American, Ontario was privileged to witness a liberal sprinkling of British and French music-hall personnel, artists like

The O'Connor Sisters (Mary, Anna, Ada, Kathleen, Vera, Nellie), 1915

Sarah Bernhardt, Harry Lauder, Marie Lloyd, and Bransby Williams. As Robertson Davies has pointed out, this internationalism made Canadian vaudeville individual.[72] Ontario performers could appear in the entr'actes between the plays produced by local stock companies like those of George H. Summers and the Marks Brothers, but mainly the vaudevillians were obliged to go to New York, because that was where the booking offices were located and the tours originated. We know of the big turn-of-the-century vaudeville stars: the minstrel comic 'Cool' Burgess from Toronto and the soft-shoe dancer George Primrose; burlesque comedienne Marie Dressler from Cobourg; comic singers May and Flo Irwin from Whitby; Toronto's six saxophone-playing Brown Brothers, born on Simcoe Street;[73] and the six singing O'Connor Sisters from Mimico. Some of the less well-known were Toronto's Cleve Caswell, xylophonist,[74] Mabel Barrison, a musical-comedy soubrette, and comedienne Amelia Summerville, who once commented that all the best female comics on the stage today (1909) were 'Canucks.'[75] Victor Stone was a Toronto singer who sang first with the pun-titled vaudeville trio Stone, Wahl, and Jackson (Stewart Jackson was a fellow Canadian, but Miss Wahl was not). Later, Stone headlined a lavish musical fantasy called 'Clownland,' which played Shea's Victoria in 1914.[76] From Hamilton came Dick Wilson, famed for his amusingly happy drunk act and then, a TV alter ego, 'Mr Whipple.'[77] Wartime, too, created a brief flurry of specialty acts with particular emotional appeal for charity benefits. In 1917 one of these, called 'The Shrapnel Dodgers,' brought together four Canadian veterans, one blind, one missing an eye, one an arm, and another a leg, who played home-made trench instruments, and 'sang and narrated their war experiences.'[78] They played the Winter Garden the week of 10 September 1917. Another Winter Garden act was *Billet 13*, which appeared in October 1918, and featured three returned heroes, Jack Slack, George Picken, and James Neville, sharing their impressions of life at the front.[79] Even Lady Aberdeen, wife of Canada's former governor-general, was seen in vaudeville in 1918. In an act representing a lawn fête, she spoke on the effect of war upon children. Vaudeville also needed legitimate stars as headliners and many actors, especially those in decline, were unable to resist the financial rewards. Sarah Bernhardt set the pattern and Ontario contributed McKee Rankin from Sandwich, James K. Hackett born on Wolfe Island, and, in the mid-1920s, even Ottawa's distinguished Margaret Anglin. Usually they appeared on the vaudeville roster in a scene from one of their famous roles.

Toronto's Walter Huston (né Houghston, 1884–1950), however, would not make his mark on Broadway until he was forty. For him vaudeville was a training-ground. Passing himself off as an engineer with the Light and Power Company in Nevada, Missouri, Huston was 'found out' one night when he fouled up the town's water system by frantically pulling the wrong switch during a fire. Sensing it was time to return to the road, he answered an ad in 1909 for someone looking for a partner for a vaudeville sketch: Bayonne Whipple was fifteen years older and had a pet monkey.[80] They toured together in Canada and the United States continuously from 1909 to 1923; between 1914 and 1931 Bayonne became his second wife. Whipple and Huston were a light and charming comedy 'talking act,' which included song and dance. Three of Walter's sketches have been printed: *Spooks* (published in 1912), in which Huston sported a Charlie Chaplin moustache and portrayed a dapper portrait painter with an easel in hand, *The Outing*, and *The Fixer* (published 1916).[81] Huston is remembered, too, for a routine in which he simply sat on a park bench talking to an imaginary dog. In another sketch seen at Shea's Hippodrome, Walter entered a hat shop dressed in evening clothes, tipped his top hat to the audience, then tap-danced and sang a song he had composed called 'I Haven't Got the DO-RE-MI.'[82] Sophie Tucker raved about their act, which had been a hit in the regional theatres, but had trouble getting into New York.[83]

Finally, in 1923, Whipple and Huston played the Palace on Broadway, but in a bad spot. They never quite hit the top, and a year later Walter returned to the legitimate stage and true acclaim. Without his vaudeville training, however, he would not have been the sensation he was as the salty Pieter Stuyvesant in Maxwell Anderson's 1938 musical comedy *Knickerbocker Holiday* about seventeenth-century life in New York under Dutch rule. Directed by a youthful Joshua Logan, Walter Huston sang bawdy songs and did a silver-peg-leg dance with a line of Netherland chorus girls,[84] and then he stopped the show with his husky, haunting rendition of Kurt Weill's 'September Song.' Walter Huston's sister, Margaret, was also a singer, a trained classical soprano who gave concerts at Massey Hall and later became a vocal coach for John Barrymore, and the wife of the American stage designer Robert Edmund Jones. Huston's cousin Arthur J. was in vaudeville as well as being a pantomimist. One of his skits was titled *The Bug Hunter* (published in Toronto, 1921).[85]

Another splendid character actor from Ontario who cut his teeth in vaudeville was London's Eugene (Gene) Lockhart (1891–1957). From the age of seven to ten he toured in Canada and the United States with the 48th Highlanders 'Kilties' Band as a boy dancer. His father John Coates Lockhart, a concert singer, was the tenor soloist. Between 1917 and 1919 Gene toured with the Pierrot Players. He also wrote revues like *Heigh-Ho* (1921), *The Bunk of 1926*, and *How's Your Code?* (1932), and from 1927 to 1931 appeared with his actress-wife Kathleen Lockhart (née Arthur, 1893–1978) in a series of recital-revues. One of his sketches was even adapted for *Spring Thaw '51*. Lockhart, the ex–Toronto Argonaut player, is recalled musically for writing the lyrics with composer Ernest Seitz to 'the most successful popular tune in Canada's history' – 'The World is Waiting for the Sunrise' (copyright 1919).[86]

There were other writers from Ontario who created original, dramatic, musical, or comedy playlets for vaudeville, in search of fame and fortune. At its height, in 1916, there were twenty thousand vaudeville acts[87] and the market was hungry for those short ten-to-twenty-minute numbers. (In 1933, in contrast, there were only two hundred acts working full-time.) Some of the published and unpublished Ontario authors included William Courtleigh of Guelph, Irene C. Love of Hamilton (*Amateur Night*, 1908), Thomas E. Kyle in Toronto (*Picture House Vaudeville*, New York, 1911), Garnett Weston (*Too Much Smith*, Vancouver, 1915), Frank Mortimer Kelly (*The Sewing Circle Meets at Mrs. Martin's*, New York, 1916), and J.W. Conrad of Hamilton (*The Last Laugh*, 1921).[88]

The most successful Ontario vaudeville writer was James Forbes (1871–1938), who was born in Salem and educated in Galt. In addition to his American career as an actor, dramatic critic (in Pittsburgh and New York), press representative, and business manager, he wrote fiction. One of his short stories, 'The Extra Girl,' appearing in *Ainslee's Magazine*, attracted the attention of a fellow Canadian, the Montreal-born actress Rose Stahl (1870–1955). She commissioned Forbes to turn it into a vaudeville sketch. On 13 June 1904, at Proctor's Music Hall in New York, *The Chorus Girl* had its première and was an immediate success. Forbes and Stahl were turned into celebrities. Stahl trouped the sketch for two years, including an engagement at Shea's Yonge Street (26 September 1904) and climaxing with an appearance at the Palace in London, England, on 14 May 1906. On her return to North America, Forbes expanded the vaudeville piece into a four-act comedy, retitled *The Chorus Lady*. The production, which he directed, again starred Rose Stahl and opened at Broadway's Savoy Theatre, 1 September 1906, to run for a staggering 315 performances. On the road it continued to break box-office records in America and England (at London's Vaudeville Theatre, 1909) for five years. Stahl's part as Patricia O'Brien, a tough, slangy showgirl who 'sacrifices her own reputation to save her sister's'[89] signalled an end to Victorian strait-laced morality. James Forbes continued writing and directing plays until 1936. Several were seen in Toronto.[90]

Burlesque

There were three phases of burlesque. The first was the traditional caricaturing of a dramatic, musical, literary, or dance work. Shakespeare's plays were favourite subjects for ridicule in the nineteenth century, when *Julius Sneezer* (1872) or *Julius Snoozer* (published 1876) could appear as an afterpiece or in the final section of a minstrel show.[91] In twentieth-century Ontario burlesques concerning the flag debate, the liquor control board, and the Toronto Transit Commission had their political thrust, but they were gentle expressions of Canadian humour. And what was being burlesqued, especially through such annual year-end reviews as *Spring Thaw* (1948–71), were the stylistic traditions of drama, opera, ballet, and literature, and Canada's inherent lack, at that time, of any of these deeply rooted art forms. The emergence of indigenous ballet, theatre, and musical revue would prompt Connie Vernon and Peter Mews to dance *The Red Choux* (*Spring Thaw*, 1949), Ted Follows to take off Gratien Gélinas as *Tit-coq* (1951), or Don Harron's 1952 pastiche of 'An Original All-Canadian Musical!' called *Guys and Squaws*, with characters identified as Curley Bonspiel and Annie Oakville (you can't get a man with a pun). *Spring Thaw* reminded us through laughter that we were culturally bereft and, at the same time, praised us for moving in a proper direction. So it was in 1954 that we could enjoy *The Lady's Not for Frying* and a literary nod to Stratford entitled *Thif Bleffed Plot* (or *What You Will*) by Wm. Fhakefpeare and Mavor Moore (b. Toronto, 1919–).

Ontario's great gift to traditional burlesque was Marie Dressler (1869–1934), born Leila Marie Koerber in Cobourg. Because the booking agents were unable to pronounce her Austrian father's surname she took that of an aunt instead. Only a trained musician can spoof the prima donnas of opera and her early career was built around such contralto roles as Katisha in *The Mikado*. She starred in vaudeville (*The Banqueteers*, 1913) and revue (*The Passing Show of 1921*) before concluding her life as one of filmdom's most superb character actresses (winner of the 1931 Academy Award in *Min and Bill*). She played frequently in Canada, and her burlesque talents were given a very special airing on 12 October 1912 in Toronto. The Mutual Street Rink Arena had opened five days earlier with a week-long Musical Festival and a host of notable soloists. Marie Dressler the 'operatic comedienne' was the eagerly anticipated closing event. Her concert consisted of good-humoured 'comedy recitations' and 'imitations' of those who had guested during the week.[92] Spiritually at least, Marie Dressler was succeeded by the English-born, but Unionville-based, *Spring Thaw* favourite, Anna Russell (b. 1911). Now retired, she began her musical caricatures in Toronto, with Sir Ernest MacMillan's Christmas Box concerts. Describing herself as possessing 'one of the great voices of the decayed,'[93] Russell regularly reduced Wagner's Ring Cycle to twenty minutes of nonsense and turned the naked bagpipe into a thing of provocative mystery.

Literary burlesque survived, too, in such revue sketches as Beatrice Lillie's 'Mockbeth' (*Big Top*, 1942), and in Johnny Wayne and Frank Shuster's radio and television parodies on subjects like the Trojan War and *Julius Caesar* (Who can forget 'Martini?' – 'If I want two I'll ask for them' – and Calpurnia's immortal 'Juley, don't go!'?).

Grant Macdonald's portrait of Ted Follows as Launcelot Gobbo in *The Merchant of Venice*, Stratford Festival, 1955

One of the nineteenth-century fascinations with traditional burlesque had been women's impersonations of men in 'breeches roles.' When the actresses in flesh-coloured tights, or 'fleshings,' began to hold more interest than the antique dramas they were purportedly mocking, burlesque took on its second and more contemporary connotation as a girlie-girlie show. At its most raunchy, 'burleycue' went underground into the honky-tonk saloons and midway tents of Ontario's Fall Fairs,[94] or into independent, third-rate stag theatres where smoking was permitted, sawdust covered the floor, and boxing matches or mirrored 'billiards demonstrations' catered to the 'masculines.' One of the first dancers to be called a 'Burlesque Queen' was a chunky Canadian from Toronto, May Howard (née Havill), who ran her own company after 1887.[95] In line with the prevailing taste of the time, she stipulated that all her ladies had to weigh at least 150 pounds.[96] By the mid-1890s the 'beef trusts' were giving way to the lean and shapely ideal of the twentieth century.

By the turn of the century, variety in America had been tamed by the market-place and turned into the genteel family entertainment called vaudeville. Burlesque too, went through a cleansing process and a more sophisticated, mainstream version evolved. So-called clean burlesque was loud and lively, a colourful, rapid-fire revue of the kind of innuendo comedy disallowed by Keith-Albee, interspersed with lavish production-dance numbers and sometimes including 'tab-shows' (from 'tabloid') – condensed, potted versions of hit comedies, plays, or musicals. Tab-shows were also seen in vaudeville: a potted version of *The Bells* appeared at Shea's. The burlesque stages were peopled by 'top banana' clowns in checkered pants and statuesque chorines wearing as little as they could get away with. It was eyebrow-raising but fun; in Raymond Mander and Joe Mitchenson's words, 'wholesome vulgarity' for adults.[97] During the intermission 'candy butchers' extolled the virtues of chocolates or comic books from the stage, while associates in the aisles completed the transactions.

The Folies-Bergère in Paris featured an all-nude dancer in 1912,[98] but the first mention of public stripping-down is reported to have occurred in Montmartre at the Moulin Rouge on 9 February 1893. In America a lady named Odell is given credit for launching the striptease in 1907, at New York's American Theatre,[99] and next year, from March to November 1908, at the Palace Theatre in London, England, a Toronto-born woman caused intercontinental shock waves with her classical dance, 'The Vision of Salomé.'

Maud Allan (1883–1956) was the daughter of two physicians. Taken first to California as a child, she then trained in Europe as a pianist.

Inspired by Botticelli's 'The Return of Spring,' she became instead an interpretative dancer in the free Hellenic spirit of her contemporaries Ruth St Denis and Isadora Duncan. Miss Allan made her dancing début in Vienna in 1903 at the age of twenty. Her Salomé was created the year after Richard Strauss's 1907 musical drama. Performed in a skimpy beaded costume, her child-like 'dance of the seven veils' caused less consternation than the biblical implications of a fourteen-year-old Salomé kissing the head of John the Baptist and being sexually awakened by the experience. Ten years later, at London's Royal Court Theatre (12 April 1918), Maud Allan also portrayed Salomé in Oscar Wilde's play of the same name.[100] In 1908, the American dancer Gertrude Hoffman was despatched to London to pirate Allan's original dance composition. Hoffman returned and danced Salomé for a record twenty-two weeks, starting a North American craze that lasted for five years.[101]

The Salomé dance was banned in Toronto for a time but allowed back on the stage in 1909 when a sofa cushion was substituted for the papier-mâché head of John the Baptist.[102] Maud Allan, who had begun it all, kept the dance in her repertoire of classical and oriental pieces. From 1908 to 1930 she toured the world almost continuously, travelling to Russia, Africa, India, China, and South America and making at least four transcontinental trips across North America. In September and October 1916, Toronto's 'famous symphonic dancer' toured Ontario for the first time, bringing her own scenery, a forty-piece orchestra, and a corps of approximately twenty additional dancers to the Royal Alexandra (5, 6, 7 October 1916). Her 'Vision of Salomé' was accompanied by Schubert's 'Ave Maria,' 'The Blue Danube' by Strauss, and Grieg's 'Death of Ase' from Ibsen's *Peer Gynt*, amongst other selections.[103] Miss Allan acted in several plays in the 1930s and drove an ambulance during the Battle of Britain. Injuries sustained in a 1938 automobile crash in California ended her dancing career. She died forgotten, with no living relatives, in a rest home in Los Angeles at the age of seventy-three.

With the Salomé dance and the precedent of striptease, the way was open for total nudity on the stage. It came first not in the burlesque theatres, but in such spectacular, deluxe musical revues as Ziegfeld's *Follies*, the Shubert Brothers' *Passing Shows*, *Errol Carroll's Vanities*, and many others.

To compete, 'clean burlesque' went dirty and 'burleycue' metamorphosed into its third and final phase. By 1928 the runway was fashionable, and burlesque theatres abandoned any pretence of being family entertainment, resorting to a repetitious parade of strippers linked by a smutty emcee behind a microphone. There were some great artists: 'Her Sexellency' Sally Rand, swathed in white ostrich plumes, or Montreal's elegant Lili Saint Cyr, who took a bath onstage. Ontario's major cities, however, were more likely to see 'Boom Boom' Laverne, Tempest Storm, or 'Cupcakes' Cassidy on a regular basis. And the degrading spectacle of the bored and less-than-beautiful mechanically taking it off could be more dampening than titillating. The only new wrinkle was the introduction of male striptease in the 1970s.

Burlesque, whether clean or dirty, tended to be restricted to Ontario's larger cities. Hamilton's earliest roadhouse was the Star (later the Savoy), while Ottawa had its Casino (1909–29), later the Capitol, and its Family Theatre (1910–32), also known as the Franklin or Galvin. Toronto's two better-class houses became the homes of weekly stock in the 1920s: the Star on Temperance Street (later the Empire) and the New Gayety (built 1907) on Richmond Street West (later the Comedy). As an old-timer reminisced, you could see Bert Lahr or Eddie Cantor at the Gayety for only twenty-five cents![104] Striptease in Toronto was seen primarily at the Casino (1936–65) on Queen Street West, opposite the new City Hall, but also at the Lux (362 College Street) and the Victory on Spadina, formerly the Strand (1922–) and then the Golden Harvest Theatre.

Revues, Cabaret, and Musical Comedy

At the beginning of the First World War British performers were responsible for the morale of Canada's armed forces, simply because the Canadians were part of the British Army. By 1916, however, costs dictated that the Canucks entertain themselves, which they did to their great credit. By the end of the Great War the Canadian Army had over fifty divisional and battalion concert parties.[105]

In June 1916 Jack McLaren (b. Edinburgh, 1895–1988) of Goderich, Ontario, put together the renowned Princess Patricia's Canadian Light Infantry Comedy Company. Consisting of half a dozen actor-comedians and pianist Leonard Young of the 9th Field Ambulance, the PPCLICC was 'the first organized group of soldier entertainers in the World War I Canadian Corps.'[106] Similar troupes followed, some taking their names from their insignia patches: the Rouge et Noir (First Division), the See Toos (Second Division), the Little Black Devils (Winnipeg Rifles), the Woodpeckers (126th Company of the Canadian Forestry Corps), the Glengarrys (Canadian Scottish), and the Whizz Bangs (Canadian Artillery), to name just a few.

Control over the concert parties slowly shifted from the chaplains and priests, the Salvation Army, the Knights of Columbus, and the Red Cross to the YMCA, especially after 'Y' social director Captain Merton Wesley Plunkett ('his captaincy came from the YMCA'[107]) of Orillia (1888–1966) appeared in France in early September 1916. As a front-line comedian, a singer, and a natural leader, Plunkett earned affection and the authority to organize, creating new troupes such as the 'Y Emmas' (autumn 1916), the name pointing up the sponsorship of the YMCA, and the Fourth Division's Maple Leaf Concert Party. The latter boasted the talents of younger brother Al, the baritone 'crooner' (always dapper in top hat, tails, and satin-lined cape) and the First World War's most celebrated female impersonator, the six-foot-tall ambulance driver Ross Hamilton (1889–1965) from Pugwash, Nova Scotia. By the end of 1917 the YMCA had financed a Canadian network of twenty-five theatre (and silent-movie) spaces that operated almost continuously.

Merton Plunkett's most renowned troupe was, of course, the Third Division's Dumbells. Unlike the Princess Pat's Company, who came from and entertained their own regiment, the Dumbells (and the 'Y Emmas') were drawn from all the men serving in France and were available to all the troops.[108] This meant that standards could be enhanced and the cream of the crop gathered together. The artists rehearsed behind the lines and were excused from trench duties. However, the exigencies of war often dictated that they were pressed into service as stretcher-bearers.[109] By the time of the 1918 armistice there was even one hut at Mons set aside as a training centre and dubbed the 'Dramatic School.'[110]

The Dumbells' name came from their Third Divisional badge: red, crossed dumb-bells on a French-grey background. From their début in August 1917 at Guoy-Servis in Belgium they were a hit, and within two months were 'serving as a model to train others.'[111] Following the Passchendaele campaign (26 October–10 November 1917) and throughout the German spring offensive of 1918, the Dumbells 'supplied continuous entertainment day and night' in the rest area behind the line, winning 'a permanent place in the hearts of Canadian troops.'[112] With the Armistice some of the concert parties were disbanded, including the Princess Pat's Comedy Company. Plunkett was asked to absorb several of its stars into the Dumbells, who stayed in Europe until the spring of 1919 and mounted an all-male, pantomimic adaptation of Gilbert and Sullivan's *H.M.S. Pinafore*. They ran the show for some forty performances from 11 November 1918 at an opera house in Mons, and then moved to Brussels for a command engagement before King Albert of Belgium.[113]

Back home during the summer of 1919, Merton and Al Plunkett rehearsed a new, peacetime Dumbells song-and-dance revue, which was given a try-out in Owen Sound. The audience loved, it but impresario

Ambrose Small (1866–1919?) knew that the Dumbells would have to compete with the Ziegfeld Follies and advised an additional $12,000 worth of improvements in costumes, lights, and scenery. These changes made, *Biff, Bing, Bang* – there had been an American musical called *Biff! Bang!* by the U.S. Naval Training Camp in 1918[114] – opened in Small's Grand Theatre in London, Ontario, on 1 October 1919. Before Act One was over, Ambrose Small telephoned long distance, and stayed listening through to the ovation at the end.[115] He then booked the Dumbells for a sell-out eight weeks at his Grand Opera House in Toronto. Next spring there was another fifteen-week, capacity engagement in Toronto, an event unprecedented in Canadian theatrical history. It was followed by the first of twelve consecutive cross-Canada tours (until 1932–3), and it made stars of Ross Hamilton, Al Plunkett, and comedian 'Red' Newman.

On 9 May 1921, a second edition of *Biff, Bing, Bang* opened the Ambassador Theatre in New York and ran for twelve weeks, the first Canadian show ever to play on Broadway. The *New York Times* reported that 'It consists of about fifteen musical numbers and two skits, played with plenty of dash and lightning speed,' while the *New York Telegram* declared, 'No American soldier show seen in New York has *Biff, Bing, Bang*'s shape and vigor, nor its talent.'[116] The Broadway engagement led to an eastern United States tour, with advertisements informing the public that the Dumbells had played 'over 1200 times in France, Belgium and England, and 85 weeks in Canada.'[117]

In 1922 there were two Dumbells' revues. A 1921 dispute over the sharing of profits had caused a temporary rift.[118] The two stars, Ross Hamilton and Al Plunkett, remained loyal to Merton Plunkett and appeared with brother Morley in (the perhaps significantly titled) *Carry On*. Fraser Allan replaced Jack Ayre at the piano. The second company was built around some fourteen former Dumbells, including for a time Red Newman. The two companies tended to divide the country between them, one playing in the East and the other in the West. The Plunkett troupe called itself 'The Dumbells,' while the renegades became variously 'The Originals,' 'The Old Dumbells,' 'The Maple Leafs,' or 'Khaki Productions.'[119] In 1923 there were again two companies, Khaki's *Full O' Pep* in the West and Plunkett's *Cheerio* in the East; and in 1924 the Dumbells' revues had grown to three, *Oh, Yes, Let 'Er Go*, and *Ace High*. Additional performers were hired to supplement the casts, notably the English comics Pat Rafferty and Fred Emney. *Lucky 7*, *Rapid Fire*, *Thumbs Up*, and *Stepping Out* were the titles of the 1925 revues, and in 1926 they were *That's That*, *Three Bags Full*, and *Joy Bombs*.

The year 1926 also saw the opening of the four-hundred-seat, open-air Merrymaker's Stage on the beach of Sunnyside in Toronto, a favourite summer stop-over for Captain Plunkett's crew. Miss Toronto and Miss Winnipeg were added in 1926, and Captain Plunkett's mother was featured in the ninth annual revue, titled *Oo! La! La!* (1927).[120] By 1928 more women had been introduced for *Bubbling Over* and *Why Worry?*, creating an identity crisis in a wartime show that had been built around female impersonation. But the women remained for *Here 'Tis* (1928–9), *Come Eleven* (1929–30), *As You Were* (1931), and *The Dumbells* (1933). Finally, the expensive large-cast revues had to be shelved in 1933, defeated by the Depression, the death of vaudeville, and the increased competition from talking films.

Jack McLaren and some other Dumbells gravitated to radio, making guest appearances on the comedy spot in Merrill Denison's 'Maple Centre,' a forty-five-minute revue and dance-band program heard 1931–2.[121] McLaren was also a regular in the Arts and Letters Club revues of the 1930s, and in 1936 he teamed with Horace Lapp to produce *Click! Click! – A Revue* at Toronto's newly opened Eaton Auditorium (1931).[122] When the Second World War erupted, four of the Dumbells (Jack Ayre, Ross Hamilton, Red Newman, and Pat Rafferty) regrouped quickly to appear in *Chin Up*, the first Canadian revue of the new conflict. It was written and produced by *Globe and Mail* columnist Roly Young (1903–48). After two weeks at the Royal Alexandra in December 1939, it travelled to Montreal and several other Canadian cities.[123] Various Dumbells were involved in wartime shows like the *Lifebuoy Follies* (1945)[124] and a 1955 concert in Massey Hall reunited some of them briefly. In later years their memory was evoked in a few CBC radio and television documentaries, the last of which was George Salverson's *The Dumbells*, telecast 5 March 1978, which included footage of the four members then surviving.

Where Canada had its indigenous concert parties from 1916 to 1919, the U.S. Army abroad was entertained by the 'Over There Theatre League.' It was organized by the American theatrical profession and directed by James Forbes, the Salem, Ontario, playwright who had written *The Chorus Lady* from a vaudeville sketch. Willard Mack (né Charles Willard McLaughlin of Morrisburg, Ontario; 1878–1934) was another who launched his playwriting career in vaudeville and wrote sketches for the 1921 *Ziegfeld Follies*.[125] Both George White's *Scandals* (Ottawa, Russell Theatre, 1926) and the *Ziegfeld Follies* played Ontario in the 1914–30 period. Indeed, the *Follies* engagement at Toronto's Princess Theatre (week of 16 February 1914) provoked a backstage feud between a British-born chorine and her American counterparts, when in one number the Union Jack was waved to the detriment of the Stars and Stripes.[126]

Revue was sassy and sophisticated, denoting a new urbanity and the ultimate severing of links with the Victorian age. The smart set was becoming bored with vaudeville that was corny, rural, and based so often on racial humour. In order to compete, vaudeville subtly changed its tone. Acrobats began to perform in evening clothes and ballroom dancers joined the bill. Revue (or Review, as it was known before the word was Frenchified during the First World War) could be either intimate or spectacular, and seemed to divide along these lines depending on whether it was British or American. In 1924, the intimate British revue style made its début in New York (and Toronto), profoundly altering the whole concept of revue. In America it shifted the Broadway spectacular towards the Las Vegas–style night clubs or the Busby Berkeley films, and ultimately in the direction of the book musical. In Ontario the small revue became a way of life.

The catalyst was *Charlot's Revue of 1924*, an unpretentious compilation of sketches and musical numbers drawn from a series of André Charlot revues performed in London during the previous decade. At the centre was Canada's greatest revue artist, Ontario's own Beatrice Gladys Lillie (1894–1989), finally introduced to the North American public as the star she was. Bea was born in Toronto, of Irish, English, and Spanish-Portuguese descent (which may explain the dash of Salvador Dali about her). In the six or seven years before the First World War, the teenaged Beatrice Lillie had barnstormed about Ontario with her soprano mother Lucie (Shaw) and piano-playing older sister, Muriel. They called themselves 'The Lillie Trio,' and Bea sang (and yodelled) a refined series of ethnic ballads (Italian, Japanese, Amerindian, and so on), with appropriate costumes for each.[127] Muriel had been a prize-winner in the 1910 Earl Grey Musical and Dramatic Trophy Competition, and when the opportunity arose for further piano study in Germany, Bea was left behind in a boarding school. But the Great War intervened and twenty-year-old Bea rejoined her mother, this time in London. After a few turns on amateur nights and a brief sister act with Muriel, Bea auditioned for André Charlot's business manager and landed a little part in the singing chorus of a Charlot revue called *Not Likely* (October 1914). Charlot soon recognized that she was 'a natural-born fool,'[128] and started her out as a male impersonator in a succession of wartime revues. Sometimes in top hat and tails, sometimes in the uniform of a Canadian 'Tommy,' she honed her comic gifts. It was the soldiers on leave who made her a star, coming to see show after show. Bea was incorrigible offstage and on. She was frequently fined or fired for putting on silly moustaches or forgetting to button her fly. Once during *Bran-Pie* (1919) she wandered out into other people's sketches saying 'Pardon me, but you're wanted on the gramophone.'[129]

For America, Charlot put together *Charlot's Revue of 1924* starring Bea Lillie, Gertrude Lawrence, and Jack Buchanan. Bea stopped the show with Ivor Novello's 'March By Me,' sung by a very dignified Britannia 'who runs into trouble with her spear, her shield, her helmet and her feet.' Brooks Atkinson hailed her as 'quite simply the funniest woman in the world.'[130] It was *Charlot's Revue* that brought Bea Lillie home triumphantly to Toronto's Royal Alexandra for the week of 1 December 1924. She returned to Ontario many times in shows like *At Home Abroad* (1936), *Inside U.S.A.* (1949), and, in 1962, at Toronto's O'Keefe Centre, *An Evening with Beatrice Lillie.*

After André Charlot, Bea was most frequently associated with Noël Coward, and she introduced many of his most famous songs: 'World Weary' (1928), 'Mad Dogs and Englishmen' (1931), and 'I've Been to a Mahhhvelous Party' (1939), to name but a few. Her final show, *High Spirits*, was a musical adaptation of Coward's *Blithe Spirit* in which, as Madame Arcati, she sang 'I'm a Happy Medium.' With Arcati in 1964, Bea Lillie had been on the variety stage, on both sides of the Atlantic, for close to sixty years, a 'Delectable Zany' as Toronto critic Lawrence Mason called her,[131] remembered for her Eton Crop (hairdo), an enormous cigarette holder, her double and triple *entendres*, and an unruly set of pearls that spun round her body in descending spirals.

Other expatriate Torontonians included Margaret Bannerman (née Le Grand, 1896–1976), who made her West End début singing in a musical called *Tina* in 1915 and ended her career as Mrs Higgins in the 1959–63 North American tour of *My Fair Lady*, and Helen Morgan (1900–41), the smoky torch singer who created the half-caste Julie in both the stage and film versions of Jerome Kern's *Show Boat* (1927, 1936). Sitting atop an upright piano in a red dress, she was sadly memorable pouring out 'My Bill' and 'Can't Help Lovin' Dat Man.'

Another larger-than-life star of the time was Aimee Semple McPherson (née Amy Elizabeth Kennedy, 1890–1944), born on a farm south of Ingersoll, Ontario. The first 'to put evangelism and show-business together,'[132] Aimee built the ornate, still-functioning, 5400-seat Angelus Temple in Hollywood in 1923, and took her joyful religious message to mass rallies around the gospel circuit as far afield as Australia. She broadcast from a radio station within her Temple and even ventured directly into theatres (once filling the Albert Hall in London, but bombing out at Loew's Capitol in New York).[133] Her ability to generate publicity and bring sex appeal to the pulpit made her an object sometimes of satire. She was depicted in Moss Hart's Broadway revue *As Thousands Cheer* (1933) and Fanny Brice took her off as 'Soul Saving Sadie' in the 1934 edition of the *Ziegfeld Follies*.[134]

Beatrice Lillie in *Cigarette Land*, 1924

Edward (Ned) Sparks

Last but not least, before the Second World War, we have the deadpan comedian Ned Sparks (né Edward Arthur Sparkman, 1883–1957). Born in Guelph and raised in St Thomas, Ontario, he left home at eighteen to pursue a forty-five-year career on stage, screen, and radio. From juvenile leads in stock he graduated to character parts in over one hundred films.

Mainly he portrayed 'hard-boiled, cigar-chewing reporters or agents' in pictures such as *Gold Diggers of 1933*,[135] but he is remembered also as the caterpillar in the 1933 movie version of *Alice in Wonderland*. His gravelly voice and sour expression were distinctive and much imitated. Sparks also co-authored at least one comedy, *The Way Home* (1919), with the prolific Hamilton, Ontario, playwright and lawyer Charles W. Bell.[136]

While the Tommies in Europe responded to the First World War with concert parties, back in Toronto there were at least four major revue-musicals to support the war effort. On 28–29 January 1915 at Massey Hall, audiences could take in *Made in Canada, A Fantastic Extravaganza*. A year later the Winter Garden presented *The Belles of Boo Loo* (February 1916), which spoofed the Women's Home Guard.[137] Later that year, *The All-Star Revue* was advertised at the Park Theatre (Bloor and Lansdowne) in aid of French and Belgian refugees (week of 9 October). This all-Canadian production featured a symphony orchestra, cartoonist Lou Skuce, actor Farnum Barton and his company in *Waterloo*, dancing acrobats, and an attraction called 'at the cabaret.'[138] After the Toronto run they were scheduled to tour to the Atlantic coast. In 1917 *The Canadian Passing Show*, put together by Norman Fraser Allan, appeared at Toronto's Empire Music And Travel Club. Allan later played piano and wrote songs for the Dumbells' civilian shows, and often teamed with comedian Stanley Bennett. Another of Allan's works was *The Prince of Mah Jong* (Royal Alexandra, 12 May and 17 November 1924), in which a yachtsman's shipwrecked secretary is passed off as the prince of a south-sea island. A further postwar entertainment, the Varsity Veterans' play revue *The P.B.I.; or, Mademoiselle of Bully Grenay* (P.B.I. stood for 'Poor Bally Infantry'), was staged at the University of Toronto's newly opened Hart House Theatre on 10–12 March 1920. It proved popular enough to be taken on a southern Ontario tour, and repeated at the Princess Theatre and at Massey Hall.

Wartime touring was interrupted frequently because of coal shortages and the rescheduling of trains. To conserve energy the Federal Dominion Fuel Controller closed all theatres on Mondays during the winter of 1918 and announced 'Heatless Tuesdays' for homes and public buildings.[139] The Canadian Chautauqua Shows (1917–35), however, bypassed these problems by playing only during the summer months and in tents. They always had an uplifting variety component. Many Canadian youngsters in remote areas heard their first musical instruments at a Chautauqua Show. Although based in Calgary, the Canadian Chautauquas travelled annually to Ontario, and their tours lasted until the mid-1930s.[140]

The ambitious, but short-lived, Anglo-Canadian organization, Trans-Canada Theatres Ltd (1919–23), brought out a British revue *Hullo, Canada!* with impressive credentials.[141] It ran at the Russell Theatre in Ottawa, 12–15 October 1921, and played through until 20 May 1922 at many of Trans-Canada's recently acquired chain of theatres (including the six purchased from Ambrose Small on 2 December 1919, the day he disappeared).[142] An earlier charity revue in England, coincidently named *Hello Canada!*, featured such Canadian artists living in London as singer-dancer Phyllis Davis (1891–), Martha Allan (1895–1942, of Montreal Repertory Theatre fame) and Toronto's Margaret Bannerman.[143]

Perhaps because there were dark nights, the larger theatres welcomed local amateur events in the 1920s. The Canadian Operatic Society had a 'great success'[144] with a revival of Owen Hall's *Florodora* at Toronto's Princess Theatre (24 November 1924), and continued their winning streak a year later at the Royal Alexandra with *The Mikado*. Even canoe clubs dipped into the big time. The 'Alex' hosted the Parkdale Canoe Club's annual late-winter revue for a number of years (*The Jollies of 1923* through to *The Jollies of 1927*), and in 1928 Massey Hall welcomed the Toronto Canoe Club's *In Gay Paree*.[145] Loew's Winter Garden opened its stage to local talent on several occasions. In December 1922 Loew's sponsored *The Toronto Follies*, a two-hour 'whirly girly song and dance revue' that ran two weeks. This was followed in 1923 by the *Toronto Frolics* in February and *The Frolics of 1923* in October, the latter directed by a former New York vaudevillian, Victor Hyde. For St Patrick's Day week in 1924 he mounted *Amateur Minstrel Frolics*; he was back in June with the 'all–local' *Summer Bathing Revue*. One of the numbers featured just the legs of eight bathing beauties seated on a bench, the rest of their bodies masked by a drop-curtain. The Winter Garden also rented to the Junior Hadassah in September 1924 for a musical called *Springtime*.[146]

At Loew's Uptown, the American matinee idol Vaughan Glaser ran his professional weekly stock company between 1921 and 1926. In the 1922–3 Christmas season he put on the first of his hugely attended pantomime productions that tended to supersede F. Stuart-Whyte's wartime English pantomime company 'The Versatiles,' who had been a popular fixture in Southern Ontario during the 1914–18 years. Glaser produced four lavish pantos altogether for the 3000–seat Uptown: *Cinderella* (Christmas 1922–January 1923), *Babes in the Wood* (1923–4), *Mother Goose and the Gingerbread Man* (1924–5, also seen in Hamilton), and *Babes in Toyland* (1925–6). The *Cinderella* was reprised when Glaser moved his resident stock operation to the Victoria Theatre for the 1926–8 seasons. Although Famous Players had not renewed Glaser's Uptown

Theatre lease, preferring to concentrate on the growing market for films, they did supplement their flicks with musical stage presentations such as Jack Arthur's *Sunny Spain* (1929), choreographed by Boris Volkoff with Horace Lapp conducting the orchestra.

Vaughan Glaser's first two pantomimes had been written and directed by the English artist George Vivian, and for the holiday season of 1924–5 Vivian launched a rival pantomime (*Aladdin*) at the Regent Theatre. He followed this with a 1925 spring season of such musicals as Rudolf Friml's *The Firefly* and Victor Herbert's *The Only Girl* and *Princess Pat*. After Vivian was gone the Regent reverted to movies. The Victoria Theatre, too, hosted such musical-comedy stock companies as the Savoy-Victoria (1928) and the Lyric Musical Company (1929), which were interspersed during Vaughan Glaser's tenure. Glaser had included a handful of musicals as well in his regular Uptown and Victoria Theatre seasons, usually in April or May to conclude the theatrical year with a flourish. Probably the best remembered of these was the 12–17 May 1924 production of James Montgomery's *Irene* (also revived to close the 1925–6 season). In the cast and chorus were several notables: Toronto's Lois Landon (c. 1904–60), who would marry Glaser on 24 May 1927;[147] the Canadian-circuit star May A. Bell Marks, wife of Robert Marks, one of 'The Canadian Kings of Repertoire'; Violet Murray (1895–), the Glasgow-born music hall singer-dancer who had toured with Harry Lauder and would become a delight in Toronto show-business circles well into the 1980s as the 'Belle of the Gay Nineties';[148] and American choreographer Busby Berkeley, repeating his Broadway role in *Irene* as the dress designer Madame Lucy, as well as masterminding precision dance routines that eventually became synonymous with his name.[149]

The First World War had awakened a new sense of nationalism in Canada. With professional touring on the wane, the little theatre movement rose to fill the theatrical vacuum. Revue was an ideal way to express the saucy defiance of American morality and begin the subtle process of questioning British imperialism and Canada's colonial status.

In 1922–3 the Ottawa Drama League (destined to become the Ottawa Little Theatre in 1952) incorporated a dancing *Masque of the Seasons in Canada* into one of their bills of one-act plays.[150] At Rideau Hall a private revue, *Oriental Ottawa*, was presented during the 1924–5 season before a carefully screened audience. The revue had been written secretly by Governor-General Lord Julian Byng (1862–1935), with music drawn from the hits of the day and a few extra melodies composed by Mrs Fred Periera, the wife of Byng's assistant secretary. All the characters bore the names of streets in Rockcliffe, many of which 'are named after prominent families.' Clearly, the governor-general had some fun pointing up the foibles of members of the Ottawa upper class, whose attempts to spy upon, or ingratiate themselves with, the royal representative had made them quite ridiculous. Neither Lord nor Lady Byng took part in the actual performance, 'and it was months before the name of the author was discovered.'[151]

Back in Toronto, Hart House Theatre's second director, Bertram Forsyth, began to leaven the rather earnest repertoire of the Players' Club. In 1924 he put on *Playbills – a Georgian Revue*, which was his own 1922 reworking of an eighteenth-century travesty. To update it, Forsyth is reputed to have borrowed and condensed Fred Jacob's 'The Great Canadian Drama,' a January 1922 Arts and Letters Club one-act comedy that ridiculed the attempts to create an indigenous highbrow drama.[152] The Players' Club also had some laughs on 29–31 May 1924 with a burlesque called *Plays in the Air*, which metamorphosed into their charming *Cuckoo Clock Revue* in 1925. When the Players' Club severed its Hart House connections in the spring of 1925 to take up new quarters in the Margaret Eaton School of Expression's cosy McGill Street Theatre, they took this revue with them. William Milne and Bertram Forsyth were two of the principal contributors to the *Cuckoo Clock Revue*, which ran for only a single night in 1925 but seven evenings in June 1926. In February 1929 the *Cuckoo Clock Revue* was revived briefly in Hart House Theatre to raise money for a memorial fund to commemorate Bertram Forsyth, who had committed suicide in New York. The next Hart House director, Walter Sinclair (1925–7), presented William Thackeray's 1854 fireside pantomime *The Rose and the Ring* for the Christmas holiday seasons of both 1925 and 1926, and introduced a 1926 *Follies*. Director Carroll Aikins (1927–9) brought in adaptations of *Cinderella* and *Alice in Wonderland*, and Edgar Stone (1929–34) gave Hart House *The Wizard of Oz* (1929) and a *Mid-Week Frolic* (1933).

The Board of Syndics at Hart House also permitted some student productions. In 1928 *Honey Boy* appeared from the youthful team of R. Howard Lindsay and Maureen O'Mara.[153] Miss O'Mara was back in 1930. This eighteen-year-old University College student wrote the book, music, and lyrics for a 'fast action' revue *The Way of the World* (11–15 March). Bearing an ironic relation to a recent production of William Congreve's comedy by the Players' Club, this *Way of the World* was about 'flaming youth,' and filled with dancing coeds and their boyfriends. Fred Mallett (Jane's husband) was noticed in several skits and songs. Direction was by Edgar Stone and the costumes were by Hart House's resident wardrobe manager, Melville Keay. Howard Lindsay returned as well in 1930, giving Hart House another student musical comedy called *Whosit*. Its 'absence of amateurishness was nothing short of marvellous'; however, 'the salacity in dialogue [was] ... unmistakable.'[154]

Elsewhere on the campus at Victoria College, Class of 3T3 undergraduate Northrop Frye (1912–91) was contributing sketches for the 1930 and 1931 editions of the *Vic Bob*, which had been going since 1874, making it the oldest continuous variety entertainment in the country. Originating in Cobourg (before Vic moved to Toronto), it began as a party to honour the college caretaker Robert (Bob) Beare, and evolved into the traditional sophomore welcome of the freshman class. Toronto's medical students began their *Daffydil* tradition in 1895, caricaturing their professors in a Punch and Judy show. It took on its revue format in 1912 with an elaborate first production at Convocation Hall titled *Epistaxis. Dentantics* (originally *Dentactics*) grew out of a dental 'Stunt Night' in 1920 first called 'Noctem Cuckoo,' and the University of Toronto's engineers launched *Skule Nite* (or *Spasms Nite*) in 1921.[155] University College's *Follies* began in 1924 and welcomed Johnny Wayne (né John Louis Weingarten, 1918–90) and Frank Shuster (1916–) to its ranks in the 1936–41 period, and 'dancer' Patrick Watson (1930–) in 1949. Subsequently the *U.C. Follies* was joined by the more broadly based *All-Varsity Revue*, produced by Norman Jewison, which made its début on 10–15 January 1949.[156] Trinity College had a hit with Keith MacMillan's *What, No Crumpets!* (1947) and again, in 1949, with *Saints Alive*, a rare book show with libretto by Ronald Bryden.[157] Its unforgettable musical number was 'Does an oyster have a love life? / Is there passion in a clam?' The show was revived in 1952. A more recent University of Toronto revue was the *Pharmacy Show* (later *Pharmacy Phollies*), established 9 February 1962.

Queen's University revived its revue tradition in January 1935 with the *Campus Frolics*. Put together by Arthur Sutherland (who was to launch and run Kingston's International Players from 1948 to 1954), the cast included Robertson Davies as a melodrama villain and Lorne Greene singing 'Believe it, Beloved.'[158] The Queen's Glee Club, active since the 1870s, concentrated on Gilbert and Sullivan operettas until it changed its name to the Queen's Musical Theatre in 1969. Broadway musicals have been the name of the game since. At London's University of Western Ontario, *Purple Patches* saw the light of day in 1946;[159] in 1950 *Rye Riot*, an acronym for Toronto's Ryerson Institute of Technology, was created to celebrate the birth of the student union.

Toronto's Arts and Letters Club (1908–) was an influential, but informal and frolicsome, private men's club. In its early years, its personnel overlapped particularly with the Players' Club and those on stage at Hart House Theatre. Unashamedly amateur, their dramatic activities amounted at first to esoteric plays and Christmas revels, with the odd excursion into *Commedia dell'arte* (1913), minstrelsy (1918), and even a mummers' play (1920). On 20 April 1925, the Club's inclination to variety began to surface with the first in a long series of 'Artists' Jamborees.'[160] Then, after *One Bad Nite*, 'a revue of sorts' in 1929, the annual Arts and Letters Club revue tradition began in earnest (2, 3 April 1930). The first was called *April Foolies*, and was followed by *Spring Fever* (1931), *Sulphur and Molasses* (1932), 'a real spring tonic,' *Sap's Runnin* (1933), *Round the Corner* (1934), and *Sprig is Cub* (1935). It is easy to see why the direct line from these revues to *Spring Thaw* has often been traced. Although he was not credited until 1932, the writer/director/brainchild of these revues was Napier Moore (1894–1963). Born in Newcastle-on-Tyne, and editor of *Maclean's* for twenty years, Moore was a superb storyteller and humourist. With the exception of some war years (1940, 1942–4, and 1946), he guided a virtually unbroken string of fourteen revues from 1930 to 1948. Frank Peddie joined the crew for *Club Sandwich* (1937). Herman Voaden was said to be involved in *Date Pudding* (1936),[161] and in 1938's *So What!* Voaden's symphonic theatre was parodied in a sketch called 'Think of the Rocks,' written by James Dean and William Milne. In 1939 the revue switched from spring to autumn and its title *The Old Skit-Bag* echoed the war. The show in 1941 was called *Never Again*, which, supposedly, was Moore's refrain after every exhausting production was over. *Sixty Cycle* in 1948 was the last to bear the tidings that Napier Moore was the 'one and onlie begetter' of these unique entertainments.[162] A special tribute was held six years later, 25 September 1954, on the occasion of his retirement and departure from Toronto. Robert Christie, the distinguished actor and director, took up the directorial mantle for the next fifteen years or so. He was succeeded in the 1970s by the team of Professor J.N. Patterson Hume and Gary Hall.

The satiric-revue tradition in Toronto took a new professional direction with *Town Tonics* (1934–45). In a real sense it was the connecting link between the Arts and Letters Club revues and the New Play Society's *Spring Thaw*. Jane Mallett (née Jean D. Keenleyside, 1899–1984) was born in London, Ontario, and Frederic Manning (d. 1958) was a native of Windsor. Manning's skills as a baritone and a mime made him a comic institution at the Arts and Letters Club; Jane Mallett had brightened the 1920s Toronto scene (under the family name of Jane Aldworth) as an ingenue and comedienne with both the Vaughan Glaser and Empire stock companies, as well as Hart House Theatre. Jane and Freddie were to collaborate for ten years in *Town Tonics*, and always with a third partner, the pianist and singer Frances Adaskin (née Marr). Dorothy Goulding directed, Edgar Stone did the lighting and the costumes were supervised

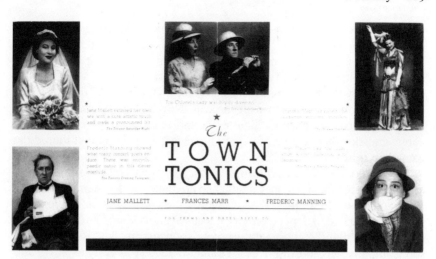

Flyer for *Town Tonics*, starring Jane Mallett, Frederic Manning, and Frances Marr

by Melville Keay. They opened at Hart House Theatre on 7 April 1934 for a single occasion that B.K. Sandwell called 'a sophisticated night' and a 'full evening of hilarity.'[163] The public demanded a repeat performance, which was held 30 May 1934 in the less-than-intimate Eaton Auditorium. In 1935 the Hart House runs were extended to two nights. There was an increasing shift in focus towards indigenous targets and away from items such as 'folk-songs of the Bronx' (1934). Original contributions came from Murray Bonnycastle, Margaret Ness, and Mary Lowrey Ross, amongst others. Jane's husband, Fred J. Mallett, a chemistry master at Upper Canada College, was added to the cast in 1937, and was still there in 1939 when a choral ensemble of twenty-nine ladies from the University Alumnae Dramatic Club sang and did calisthenics when *Town Tonics* again entered Eaton Auditorium. Wartime touring began in 1940, with dates in Hamilton, St Catharines, and Camp Borden.[164] In a 1942 article entitled 'Touring Is Fun,' Frederic Manning amusingly outlined the perils of playing one-night stands in school auditoriums across southern Ontario.[165] *Town Tonics* ended with the Second World War.

Jane Mallett contributed some *Town Tonics* bits for another spring revue called *Green Leaves* in 1938. Presented by the costumiers Melville and Arden Keay in the little theatre space in Toronto's Ward-Price Galleries on College Street, it boasted most of the familiar revue names of the 1930s and was hailed as 'lively and sparkling.'[166]

The Actors' Colony, John Holden's professional summer theatre in Bala and Gravenhurst, produced two revues. The first, *So This Is*

Canada, was seen in the company's initial season of 1934.[167] The second was *Haywire* (1941), the Colony's final stage production ever in Bala (their 1942 season consisted only of films). The core of the revue had been written originally in 1936 by Marjorie Price for a Hart House production by the Playwrights Studio Group, which is why the 1941 version in Bala had little to do with the war. New music and material were added by choreographer Ev Staples[168] and Connie Vernon contributed songs and sketches from a Masquer's Concert Party 'that had toured the Canadian military camps.'[169]

Mention of the Masquers brings us back to 1933 and the amateur theatre. During the Depression, Canada had no make-work scheme in the arts comparable to Franklin D. Roosevelt's Federal Theatre Project, so Ontario often had to depend either on wealthy individual patrons or on the first serious manifestations of corporate sponsorship. The Robert Simpson Company had an Employees' Dramatic Society as early as 1919, and Imperial Oil sponsored the Imperial Players Guild and their Spring Review (1938), as well as several radio programs. Bell Canada and Canada Packers had famous operatic societies, and the T. Eaton Company was particularly generous with its Girls' Club, the Santa Claus Parade (1904–81), the Margaret Eaton (née Beattie) School of Literature and Expression (1907–41), the Timothy Eaton Memorial Church (1914–), the Eaton Auditorium (built in 1931), the Eaton Operatic Society (1932–65), and the Eaton's Masquers Clubs (1933–c. 1946) in Toronto and Hamilton (as well as Montreal, Winnipeg, and Calgary). The Eaton's Masquers specialized in drama and revue. Like the Operatic Society, its membership consisted of Eaton's employees administered through a Recreation Department. Welsh-born Ivor Lewis, one of Toronto's leading amateur actors, was an Eaton's general manager; Jack Brockie was another sympathetic boss. Even before the Masquers were formed in 1933, Eaton's staff members had taken part in previous variety concoctions such as *Hello Springtime* (26 February 1927) and *The Treasure Chest* (1 November 1927).[170] Under the new focus of the Masquers, Toronto's one hundredth birthday was recognized with the *Centennial Revue* of 1934. Some of the other titles included *The Maskers [sic] Revue* (1935), *Knuts in May* (1936), and *Heigh-Ho!* (1938). The *Saturday Night* reviewer, Nancy Pyper, picked out Constance Vernon as the versatile performer who held *Heigh-Ho!* together;[171] Connie Vernon would reappear in the Masquers' wartime concert parties, *Haywire* at Bala, and the Canadian Army Show's 'Rapid Fire' E Unit in Holland and Italy, then return for a featured place in *Spring Thaw*. Born in Lancashire, Connie came to Canada when she was sixteen. One of her celebrated army-show appearances was in the Bathing Suit Contest. Alongside Miss Quebec and Miss

Ontario, Connie Vernon stood as Miss Unexplored Canada.[172] The Masquers' Canadian concert parties were one-night stands presented at military camps in various sections of the country. Returning late at night in trucks and buses the dedicated casts and crews still managed to show up for work at Eaton's the next morning. After VE Day, in June 1945, the Canadian Legion War Services sponsored ten civilian concert parties in a five-month overseas tour. The Masquers from Toronto and Montreal were amongst those chosen, and each troupe chalked up 115 performances, playing before more than 90,000 troops from Aldershot to Amsterdam, with stopovers even in Germany. Another familiar Toronto Little Theatre figure, Frank Rostance, was the producer for these overseas adventures. He had put together *June Cocktail – A revue* at Hart House in 1935.[173]

Renowned for its interpretations of Gilbert and Sullivan, the Eaton Operatic Society had begun as a choral society in 1919. In 1929 it celebrated its tenth anniversary with two hundred members.[174] The choir transmogrified into a full-fledged producing company in 1932, guided by T.J. (Tommy) Crawford from Scotland, its choral conductor since 1925. Crawford would direct the Eaton Operatic Society until 1947 and share his leadership abilities with the Victoria College Music Club from 1927 to 1942. Sometimes the members of one group crossed over to the other. Actor/teacher Charles Jolliffe (1913–91) was singing for the Vic Music Club in 1934. He recalled being hired as a store detective at Eaton's when they were in need of a Ko-Ko for their production of *The Mikado*.[175] Eaton's employee Lois Marshall starred memorably in the rarely performed *Princess Ida* in 1945, and the singing careers of Elizabeth and Howard Mawson were launched in the 1949–60 period, at a time when there were few professional opportunities available. They would go on, in the 1960s, to Savoy operettas at Stratford and musicals at the Charlottetown Festival, Elizabeth Mawson becoming one of the famous Marillas in *Anne of Green Gables*. Tommy Crawford was succeeded at Eaton's by Harry Norris (1948–50), who had worked in Britain with D'Oyly Carte,[176] then by three Ontarians, Godfrey Ridout of Toronto (from 1951–8), Lloyd Bradshaw from St Marys (1959–61), and Horace Lapp, born in Uxbridge (1962–5).[177] The demise of the Eaton Operatic Society is attributed to the death of its hard-working president, James Pryce, and the proliferation of operatic companies by the mid-1960s. As well as the Vic Music Club, Canada Packers, the Toronto Operatic Society, and the Simpson Avenue United Church aggregation, all of whom had championed Gilbert and Sullivan, two new light-opera groups emerged that would produce on a major scale: St Anne's Music and Dramatic Society and the still-active Toronto chapter of the Gilbert and Sullivan Society (1967–).[178]

At the other end of this corporate and subsidized spectrum was the 1930s labour response to the endemic unemployment of the age. The workers' theatre was a natural adjunct of the Communistic Progressive Arts Clubs founded in 1928 in several of the larger cities across Canada. Through their publication *Masses*, propaganda playlets were printed and produced, utilizing the street-theatre techniques of choral chant and stylized choreography. Still amateur, the politically left-of-centre clubs also entered the Dominion Drama Festival with ready-made plays like Clifford Odets's *Waiting for Lefty*. Although they made it to the finals, they felt out of place in the 'Love and Whisky' atmosphere and pro-British stance of the little theatre movement. The mobile Workers' Experimental Theatre in Toronto (1932–4) and its exciting successor, the Theatre of Action (1935–40), were inspired by the Group Theatre in New York and galvanized by their advocacy of the Stanislavski method of acting. Frequently the agitprop was leavened with evenings of revue and improvisation. In Toronto, Christmas, New Year's, and Sunday nights were favourite cabaret times. Sundays, particularly, attracted an audience because there was nothing else to do. Sandwiches, candies, and fruit punch were served. Beer or liquor were not yet permitted. Because many of the cabaret evenings were fund-raisers, a silver collection was taken.[179] One of the innovations was the introduction of the 1920s European expressionist technique of Living Newspapers. In America the idea had become associated with a controversial unit of the Federal Work Project, and it would be employed later by such stand-up satirists as Montreal-born Mort Sahl (1927–). In Toronto the *Living Newspapers* of 1937–9 elicited improvisations on topical subjects suggested by the audience, followed by open discussions between the spectators and the performers.[180] It is probably the first example we have of modern-day improvisation in Canada. Some of the Theatre of Action actor-comedians of the time included Syd Banks, Lou Jacobi, Ben Lennick, and Johnny Wayne and Frank Shuster. One of their most pertinent cabaret revues was the anti-fascist *Time Lurches On* (28–29 April 1939 at Toronto's Belvin Theatre), in which Hitler and Mussolini were featured in a sketch called 'The Chamberlain Crawl' and a song by Frank Gregory entitled 'The Syncopated Dictator.' Gregory turned out to be a bit of a 'discovery'; another of his songs, 'We're Socially Insignificant / But We Get Along,' became the theme song of their cabarets and usually opened and closed the performance.[181]

Of course, history was reflected not only in cabarets and revues, but also in pageants. The pageant (out-of-doors or in) was a between-the-wars variety phenomenon that strung together a series of spectacular elements, usually to illustrate some patriotic theme or commemorate a momentous occasion. The annual CNE Grandstand Show was one popular example of the entertainment to be gleaned from massing choristers, bands, dancers, and scenic efforts. Other pageants were more specific and geared to learning. On 25 April 1923 at Toronto's Parkdale Methodist Church, Minnie Harvey Williams's *The Romance of Canada* reminded Canadians of their debts to the pioneers.[182] A cast of five hundred gathered together in Sarnia, Ontario, on 18–25 July 1925 to present *The Great Historical Pageant*, which traced the span of history from creation to contemporary times in Sarnia and district.

Then, on 1 July 1927, Canada celebrated its Diamond (sixtieth) Jubilee with Ernie Dalton's staging of *Sixty Years of Confederation* at the CNE Grandstand.[183] That August at the CNE Coliseum, fifteen thousand attended Augustus Bridle's *Heart of the World*, heralding the triumph of peace and presented for an international conference on education. The pageant depicted sixty characters from Helen of Troy to Bernard Shaw and involved 1400 performers in a 'colourful mélange of ballet, pantomime, choral work and processional pomp.'[184] Bridle repeated the idea in December 1930, this time with a Christmas pageant titled *Light of the World*. There were others in Jubilee year: Amy Sternberg's *Canadian Historical Pageant*; True Davidson's *Canada in Story and Song* for children; and, at the Simpson Avenue United Church, Denzil G. Ridout's *United to Serve* examined the heritage of the United Church in Canada.[185]

The next marker to be honoured was Toronto's Centennial in 1934. Hart House director Edgar J. Stone et al. presented *Milestones of a Century: A Pageant for Toronto*; at the Royal York Hotel, Jesse Edgar Middleton put together *A Pageant of Nursing in Canada*. In 1937 George VI's Coronation year inspired another round of pageantry, this time in praise of the empire. London, Ontario, saw *Britannia*, written by Melburn E. Turner,[186] and Toronto witnessed Raymond Card's *Coronation Pageant*. Maple Leaf Gardens was the scene of a massive War Loan Pageant in late 1939, directed this time by Raymond's brother Brownlow Card and filled with military marches and countermarches.[187] In later years there would be isolated occasions such as Barbara Cass-Beggs's *A Festival Pageant* in 1964, an exploration of 'the folk and ritual origins of Christmas' held in Waterloo, and John R. Linklater's *Champlain*, produced 18 July 1970 by the Ontario Youth Theatre at Couchiching Park, Orillia, to mark the 400th anniversary of the explorer's birth.[188] But, generally speaking, by the 1960s, the cost factor began to militate against these gigantic spectacles and the appeal of history diminished beside the pyrotechnics of the rock 'n' roll concert.

In England during Coronation year (1937), dance-band vocalist Les

Allen (1902–96; born in London, England, but raised from infancy in Toronto) formed a vocal group called 'Three Canadian Bachelors,' which consisted of 'fellow countrymen Jack Curtis (lead), Herbie King (tenor) and Cy Mack (baritone and arranger).' They toured British variety theatres for three years.[189] Back in Canada in June 1937, CBC staff pianist Bert Pearl (1913–86; né Shapira) was asked if he could come up with a half-hour filler to follow the one o'clock news and time signal. The result was that beloved air-wave pot-pourri of light music and cheery banter, *The Happy Gang*, which survived for twenty-two years, until replaced by Tommy Hunter in 1959. Les Allen's seventeen-year-old nephew, balladeer-accordionist Eddie Allen, became a mainstay of the program in 1938 and would eventually host this most popular radio variety show for its final four seasons. All in all, The Happy Gang gave 4890 performances.[190]

Early radio comedy on the CBC was first in the hands of a western team called Woodhouse and Hawkins (Frank Deaville, b. 1905; Art McGregor, b. 1906),[191] followed by Alan Young (né Angus Young, 1919–) a soft-spoken British-born comedian in the Bob Newhart mould who came to Vancouver at the age of seven. Young got his break with CBC radio in the early 1940s on the West Coast, and then moved on to the role of the bumbling sidekick to 'Mr. Ed,' the talking horse, in the 1961–5 sitcom series. Finally, of course, Toronto's Wayne and Shuster would become the comedy stalwarts of the CBC network.

Another famous name from the golden age of radio was Andrew Allan (1907–74). However, not many remember his moment in the sun as a variety writer. In 1935 he co-wrote an intimate revue called *Oh, Yes?*, which was put on in Toronto by the Unnamed Players.[192]

We cannot leave the 1930s without mentioning the remarkable attention paid to child performers. One of the age-old escapes from the ghetto of poverty always has been through talent, and the 1930s was the heyday for amateur shows. NBC Radio set the pattern with Major Bowes' Original Amateur Hour (1934–52). (Bowes's Amateurs also toured; they played Ottawa's Capitol Theatre in November 1935.) A host of local 'talent nights' followed suit. Sometimes, too, there were cute fads like the 'Tom Thumb Weddings,' where children were dressed in formal clothes and put through mock marriage ceremonies, and 'Our Gang' look-alike contests (in 1928 Toronto winners got a part in a locally shot Our Gang movie, *Pie Eetin' Contest*).[193] Undoubtedly it was Hollywood that fanned the flames of child stardom. Certainly the twenty-three-year box-office success of Toronto child star Mary Pickford (née Gladys Smith, 1893–1979) paved the way for acceptance of youthful Canadian talent.

Josephine Barrington became known not only for her performances but as an influential acting and voice teacher as well as the founder of Barrington's 'Juveniles' (1931– c. 1948)

The 1930s was the decade that saw the beginnings of the Toronto Children Players (1931–59), Josephine Barrington's 'Juveniles' (1931– c. 1948) and Dora Mavor Moore's youthful Village Players (1938–46), all Toronto groups with a primarily dramatic focus, although often celebrating the Christmas holiday season with a musical comedy or a pantomime.

Strictly in the variety field, however, the Winnipeg Kiddies (1915–34) deserve to lead off. Their number varied from four in 1915 to twenty or forty on their Canadian, American, and Alaskan tours, depending on the nature of the engagement. They were frequent visitors to Ontario throughout the span of their existence. Mostly under thirteen, they were Canada's most famous juvenile troupe, and their '40 minutes of sure fire vaudeville' was seen two or three times a day between the double features.[194] A 1934 program lists eight acts and a special added attraction, Baby Joyce, 'The Broadway Baby Doll, Only 3 Years Old: Youngest Stage Star in the World.' Baby Joyce (McLachlan) indeed began performing at age three, but was five by the time this program was printed. She was a tiny trouper who sang songs, tap-danced, did handsprings, splits, head balancing acts, and one adagio number in which she hung onto an older girl's neck and was whirled around in an aeroplane spin.[195]

Another Prairies travelling act was 'The Harmony Kids,' two older boys and two younger girls named Hahn (Lloyd, Robert, Kay, and Joyce), who trail-blazed the Midwest and even made it to New York, with radio appearances on 'We the People' and 'Major Bowes' Amateur Hour.' Led by their father Harvey, the Hahns lived out of a home-made trailer and, during the Depression and early war years (1930–41), played guitars, banjo, and accordion, singing for their suppers in dancehalls, small theatres, and neophyte radio stations across the country. Although they played Toronto (Club Top Hat at Sunnyside) as well as Sudbury, Timmins, and Orillia, the real Ontario connection came later, in the 1950s, after they had disbanded. The lead singer, Joyce Hahn (1932–) grew up to become a featured television vocalist for *Cross-Canada Hit Parade* and the CBC's Variety Department, telecasting out of Toronto.[196]

One more between-the-wars trio of song-and-dance juveniles, this time based in Ontario, were the popular 'Little Raes of Sunshine,' Grace, Saul, and Jackie Rae. They were active in the late 1920s and early 1930s, performing for Jack Arthur as part of the Famous Players vaudeville circuit on the stages of the Uptown, Pantages/Imperial, and Shea's Hippodrome in Toronto, and points west. Saul Rae (1914–) in his tuxedo, was a teenage hoofer who went on to write songs and produce the *U.C. Follies* at the University of Toronto. He continued to entertain while working in Ottawa with the Department of External Affairs during the Second World War. On 29 December 1940 he was in the cast of the musical comedy pantomime *1066 and All That* at the Petawawa Army Camp, and for the Ottawa Drama League on 23–25 January 1941 he teamed with Amelia Hall in Noël Coward's tribute to English music

hall, *Red Peppers*.[197] The Ottawa Drama League also had a huge success
with a 1941 *Little Theatre Revue*, which was written and produced by
Saul Rae and Mr Evelyn Shuckburgh of the British High Commission.[198] In 1948 Saul collaborated with art critic Graham McInnes on
The Bytown Revue.[199] Father of the recent premier of Ontario, Bob Rae,
Saul's distinguished career in the diplomatic service saw him become
the Canadian ambassador to the United Nations, Mexico, and The Neth-
erlands.[200]

Saul's older sister Grace (d. 1959) retired early from 'The Little Raes'
to dance with Leonidoff in New York. His younger brother, Jackie Rae
(b. Winnipeg, 1922), had launched his show-business career in 1925, at
the age of three.[201] When he was ten, the 'Vaudeville Kid' headlined a
Christmas 1933 *Kiddies Revue* for Jack Arthur at Toronto's Imperial
(Pantages) Theatre, and as a teenager he worked part-time as a talent
scout for 'Ken Soble's Amateur Hour' on Toronto radio.[202] Awarded the
Distinguished Flying Cross in 1943 as a Spitfire pilot, Jackie Rae
returned after the war and kept alive his variety beginnings by producing
a CBC radio show called 'Broadway in Your Own Backyard.' This led to
other CBC producer assignments: TV shows for Wayne and Shuster, Mart
Kenney's Orchestra, and Gisèle MacKenzie and the *Mr. Showbusiness*
series (1954–5), based on the career of Jack Arthur. (Jackie also had
assisted Arthur in the early 1950s in producing the mammoth CNE
Grandstand shows.) Between 1956 and 1957 he hosted his own TV program, 'The Jackie Rae Show,' until he was promoted to head the CBC
Variety Department. Jackie left in July 1959 for the United Kingdom,
where he began an eighteen-year stint on British television with programs such as 'Jackie Rae Presents,' 'Chelsea at Nine,' and 'Saturday
Night at the Palladium.' Writing songs was a Rae tradition, and Jackie
had an international hit and a Nashville Award with 'Please Don't Go'
(1969) and made U.S. 'gold' when Andy Williams sang his 'Happy
Heart' in 1970.[203] Rae returned to Toronto in 1976 and ran Standard
Broadcasting's Canadian Talent Library from 1978 until it was merged
with a similar organization called Factor in the mid-1980s, thus helping
to groom and record a whole new generation of performers.[204] In 1981
he put together The Spitfire Band, nineteen musicians who re-created
the big-band sounds of the 1940s.

Almost at their birth on 28 May 1934 in Callander, Ontario, the
Dionne Quintuplets entered a bizarre world of international showbiz.
When they were just one year old, their father received an offer from the
Chicago World's Fair to exhibit them. Instead, the Ontario Liberal gov-
ernment, under Mitchell Hepburn, stepped in and placed them under its
guardianship, thereby reaping over a million dollars annually in royalties

from product endorsements.[205] Between 1936 and 1938 the Quints appeared in a series of 20th Century Fox feature films: *The Country Doctor* and *Reunion* (both 1936), and *Five of a Kind* (1938), all co-starring the Danish-born actor Jean Hersholt as the kindly doctor who guides their destiny.

Next to Winnipeg's Deanna Durbin (1921–), perhaps the most famous expatriate Canadian singing youngster was Bobbie Breen (né Jackie Boreen in Montreal, 1927, raised in Toronto), who began to sing professionally in 1933. Amateur contests led to his initial paid booking at Toronto's Silver Slipper Supper Club (on the South Kingsway) at the ripe old age of five.[206] After singing in several of Jack Arthur's Toronto revues,[207] Bobbie left Ryerson Public School to be taken on tour to Chicago and New York, where he was 'discovered' by Eddie Cantor and given national exposure from 1936–40 on CBS Radio. With his pure soprano voice and curly-headed good looks, he was snapped up by RKO Studios for twelve Hollywood musicals (1936–42) and promoted as 'the boy Shirley Temple,' until his voice broke in 1940. He went on to win a bronze star in the U.S. Army and, in the 1980s, ran a showbiz booking agency in Florida.[208]

We know more about songs and people than we know about Ontario's early, original operettas and musical comedies. We have the copyright registration years for about a dozen or so titles, but we lack exact production dates – if they were ever produced – and, therefore, information about them is difficult to trace. For many, we must be satisfied with a listing. In 1915, at Kingston's Grand Theatre (3, 4, 5, June 1915), there was a revival of the 'military opera' *Leo, the Royal Cadet*, first staged on 11 July 1889. In it a Royal Military College cadet leaves to fight the Zulus and returns to his lady-love with a Victoria Cross.[209] Another Canadian production (amateur) was *Miss Pepple (of New York)* (1910) by C.S. Blanchard with music by William Dichmont.[210] Written and staged in Winnipeg, it featured the seventeen-year-old Toronto student Margaret Bannerman as leader of the chorus. Launcelot Cressy Servos of Niagara-on-the-Lake wrote a series of 'operatic dramas' during the 1920s, all on historical themes: *Builders of an Empire* (1924) about Butler's Rangers; *They Laid the Foundation* (1920) concerning Frontenac; *He Also Built* (1924) regarding the 1837 Rebellion; *We Also Built* (1921); *Laura Secord* (1921); and *Madelaine of Verchères* (1930).[211] Edward W. Miller was based in Toronto and associated with St Anne's Church. He put together a minstrel show for the congregation in 1908 and then two operettas for younger audiences, *The Wishing Cap* (1920), 'A Fairy Tale' with music by Roger B. Priestman, and the delightfully titled *His Royal Shyness* (1927) in three acts (with libretto assistance by

Carleton L. Dyer and music by Miller).[212] From 1903 to 1929 the Hamilton lawyer Charles W. Bell (1876–1938) wrote many comedies and farces for the American market. One, at least, *Parlor, Bedroom and Bath* (1917), was a Broadway smash. He is credited, as well, with a quartet of musical comedies, although they might better be labelled comedies or plays with music: *Dear Angeline* (1922), *The Girl and the Prophet* (1924), *The Gypsy Queen*, and *Paradise Alley* (both 1925). *Angeline* and *Alley* were musical adaptations of previous dramatic pieces by Bell.[213]

Another prolific author-composer in the 1925–43 period was Torontonian K. Lottie Rimmer. Beginning with a one-act operetta, *Love in the Woodlands* (1927), she moved on to a three-act musical comedy, *Pink Pearls* (1929), an opera, *In Love's Dismay* (1929), and then an opera film, *A Flame of Fire* (1931). Her other libretti were *Polly Speaks* (1931) and *Raoul* (1938), with music by Edgar Flavelle and Sally Clements, respectively.[214] There was a 1929 spoof of anti-Bolshevik sentiments in Toronto that appeared in *The Canadian Forum* (vol. 9, no. 102); penned by Samuel H. Hooke, *The Tyrants of Toronto* was described as 'A (very) Light Opera by Gullem and Silliman' (or Gilbert and Sullivan if you say it fast).[215] Toronto in 1930 had two more silly-sounding 'dramatico-musical' compositions, *Belinda Biddle* and *Teetering Andy* (1930) by Arthur Leslie Carter,[216] while Kingston writers Bruce Cornock Robson and Jean-Julien Fortin came up with *Beloved Heroine* (1933), 'A Talking Picture Play ... with Music.'[217] Even (Sir) Ernest MacMillan (b. Mimico, 1893–1973) took to the stage in 1933 as music composer for Jesse Edgar Middleton's ballad opera *Prince Charming*. MacMillan had written an earlier comic opera, *Sweet Marjoram* (1912), with at least the title taken from *King Lear*.[218] Still in the romantic mode were *Melody Moon* (1934), a musical by Toronto authors Delbert R. Piette and G. Strickland Thompson, and *Melody in Maytime* (1941) by Keith Graham Macdonald of London, Ontario.[219] George H. Summers's son, Ambrose Gates ('Beau') Summers (named after Ambrose Small) had a career in radio and brief aspirations as a writer. His drama with music, *Court of Old King Cole*, was copyrighted in Toronto in 1937. Wartime saw two Toronto musicals appealing to patriotic instincts; Eva May Reid's *Shoulder Arms* (1940) and *Pull Together Canada* (1942) by Howard J. Reynolds et al., however, little is known about them.[220] The escapist revue would dominate the war years, and the Canadian musical per se would have to wait until the 1950s.

The Second World War was the watershed between the amateur and the professional theatre in Canada. Though the Dominion Drama Festival was suspended for the duration, the broader amateur movement

McKinnon Industries, 'Plant and Lord Mayor's Play,' April 194?: cast members amid flags of many countries (visible Soviet Union, USA, Finland)

turned to supporting the war effort. A Citizens' Committee was formed to provide entertainment for the troops in training. Under Jack Arthur's chairmanship it proved to be a vital national umbrella organization that arranged more than three thousand shows and earned Arthur an MBE (Member of the Order of the British Empire). The Toronto section was headed by the accomplished Nella Jefferis.[221]

There was a rash of light wartime revues and amateur shows that toured the military camps, the Active Service Canteens, and the hospitals of Ontario. They were voluntary efforts supported often by companies like Massey Harris, Bell Telephone, Sun Life Insurance, and Lifebuoy soap (*The Lifebuoy Follies*). In the Toronto area Nella Jefferis organized the *Merry-Go-Round*, an all-female concert party that gave over two hundred performances: one night every week, usually Thursdays, and one weekend a month to venture further afield, say to Kingston. Anna Russell was with them, and in her autobiography, *I'm Not Making This Up You Know* (1985), she tells of Canteen nights when she was paired with University Alumnae veteran Ruth Johnson in a series of 'nauseating Victorian duets.'[222] Russell in high heels, upswept hair, and feathered hat towered over the diminutive Johnson, who wore a walrus moustache and padded tails. The duo-piano team of sisters Dorothy Watkins (1896–1978) and Jessie MacDonald (née McCullough, 1900–78) provided the music.[223] In 1944–5 the *Globe and Mail* critic Roly Young came on board as *Merry-Go-Round*'s writer and director. Young's *Chin Up* revue in 1939 had been followed with *Climbin' High* (1940), *Funny Side Up*, and *Celebrity Parade* in the winter of 1942.[224]

Sterndale Bennett, director of the Eaton's Masquers, put together *Well, of All Things* for the Central Ontario Drama League (29 January–3 February 1940) at Hart House Theatre: one of the events satirized was the 1939 Royal Visit, and Jane Mallett and the Boris Volkoff Dancers made guest appearances.[225] Jane was also on hand for two revues produced by the Playwrights' Studio Group, *Keep It Flying* (2–5 October 1940) and *Flying Higher* (week of 13 October 1941), both again at Hart House. The skits and monologues were written by such Canadian dramatists as Winnifred Pilcher, Dora Conover, Rica Farquharson, and Lois Reynolds Kerr. At the two pianos this time were Charles Tisdall (later with *Spring Thaw*) and orchestra leader Dennis (Denny) Vaughan. In the supporting cast were names like Barbara Davis (Chilcott), Lloyd Bochner, and Peter Mews; the director was Arthur Gelber, destined to become a notable arts patron and executive officer for innumerable Ontario organizations. In *Keep It Flying* Boris Volkoff choreographed 'The Echo Youth' (an Indian fantasy). Montreal comedian John Pratt (soon to be starring in *Meet the Navy*) was another visiting artist.

A lesser-known group of volunteers were the Victory Entertainers, who 'criss-crossed Ontario' and may have been involved with the *Victory Revue* in Hamilton's Civic Stadium during the week of 31 August 1942.[226] In 1943, in North Bay, Doris Thomas wrote the *A.N.A. Revue*[227] and in 1945 Dora Mavor Moore's Village Players visited the camps with *Charley's Aunt*, starring Don Harron, Barbara Kelly, Budd Knapp, and the ubiquitous Jane Mallett.[228]

Ross Laver calculates that 1,086,343 Canadian men and women served full time in the army, navy, or air force during the Second World War.[229] The number indicates the potential impact of the Canadian Armed Services shows. At first the Second Detachment of the Royal Canadian Army Service Corps and some Royal Canadian Air Force personnel combined with the private sector to produce two editions of a musical revue called *Ritzin' the Blitz* (1941, 1942). It came to the Royal Alexandra Theatre (14 July 1941) under the direction of Private Jack Hennessey. Melville Keay appeared as a Ziegfeld chorine, and danced in a comic 'Minuet.' The Toronto concert pianist Clement (Clem) Hambourg (b. London, England, 1900–73) played both Chopin and a Rachmaninoff Prelude in appropriate period garb. He was detected as well in the Ziegfeld number in yards of tulle, a big hat, and horn-rimmed glasses. Other notables included future CFRB morning radio personality Wally Crouter (b. Peterborough 1924–), who sang a solo. However, after this one effort, the various branches of the armed forces went their separate ways.[230]

The RCAF's Second World War entertainments were reminiscent of British concert parties and somewhat more modest than *The Army Show* or *Meet The Navy*, but unlike those were aimed only at the various air-base populations. The organizing producer/director was Flight Lieutenant (later Squadron Leader) Robert Coote (1909–82), an English actor-singer who had enlisted in the RCAF from Los Angeles. All in all, there were seven touring troupes: two major variety shows and five smaller, portable units. *The Blackouts* (May 1943–September 1945) and *All Clear* (September 1943–6) were the grand ones, with casts of about thirty-five RCAF personnel, a mixture of comedians, singers, dancers, baton-twirlers, and magicians, plus a twelve-piece pit-orchestra. Rehearsed at Ottawa's Rockcliffe station and launched in Yorkton, Saskatchewan, *The Blackouts'* Canadian tour extended as far north as Alaska. Overseas it played the Comedy Theatre in London (1944), as well as RAF depots across Britain, and eventually entertained the troops in Belgium, Holland, France, and Germany.[231] Similarly, *All Clear* was invited to Washington, DC, and a series of U.S. bases, and later would be heard on BBC Radio. In Canada it toured extensively along the Atlantic coast. Often the smaller variety units were assigned to specific areas: *Swingtime* (September 1942–5) was seen in the Winnipeg district; *Joe Boys* around Vancouver; *Tarmacs* was an all-male concert party assembled in October 1943 from Canadian airmen stationed in the United Kingdom.[232] Another all-male unit called itself *Airscrews*; the Women's Division (WDS) production was known as *W-Debs* (June 1944–5). Both went overseas in 1944. 'Up, Up, Up, We Go,' with music by Dorothy Watkins and lyrics by RCAF Wing Commander Brian Doherty, was a wartime hit. The pre-war playwright Doherty would emerge after the conflict as one of Ontario's most important entrepreneurs. Some of the better-known Ontario entertainers included Jack Bickle, dancer-choreographer, Slim Burgess, comedian, Rex Slocombe, magician, Byng Whittaker, songs and skits, and musicians Kenneth Bray, Wishart Campbell, Neil Chotem, Lloyd Edwards, and Hyman Goodman.

'The Canadian Army Radio Show' was a thirty-eight-week CBC series produced from Montreal (13 December 1942 to 5 September 1943) by Rai Purdy (1910–). Its stars were Shuster and Wayne (the billing changed later), who also wrote most of its musical and comedy material. The radio success prompted a big, touring, stage version in 1943, *The*

Army Show, an answer to America's *This Is the Army* (1942–5). Jack Arthur, on loan from Famous Players, was its supervising producer; stage-management was by Don Hudson, later to direct a pantomime for the New Play Society as well as *The Big Revue* and the Wayne and Shuster series for CBC TV. The Army's 'big show,' as it was nicknamed, rehearsed in Toronto, first at George Street School and then at Shea's Victoria, where it opened on 2 April 1943. A lively, lavish combination of sketches, dance numbers, and songs, it crossed Canada twice by train that spring and summer, playing to great acclaim in public theatres or at military installations. The radio shows continued to be broadcast, as well, each week from a different army base. Once more Sergeants Shuster and Wayne wrote the sketches and most of the song lyrics, with music supplied by Captain Robert Farnon (b. Toronto, 1917) and additional melodies from Freddie Grant. The orchestra was conducted again by Geoffrey Waddington. Male singers included Jimmie Shields, Roger Doucet, Gordon Blythe, Andrew MacMillan, Russ Titus, Denny Vaughan, plus Brian and Dennis Farnon, brothers to Robert; the Canadian Women's Army Corps was deeply involved, notably singer Corporal Raymonde Maranda. Private Peter Mews was featured in many of the skits along with comediennes Sergeants Connie Vernon and Mildred Morey. The older, established dance team of 'The Marquettes' (Sergeant Hal Seymour and Corporal Lynda Tuero) had several solo numbers. Also high-stepping through the choreography of Aida Broadbent (of Vancouver and Hollywood) were Lance-Corporal Everett Staples and Privates Gwen Dainty and Lois Hooker.[233] Toronto's Lois Hooker is remembered today as Lois Maxwell and James Bond's favourite secretary, Miss Moneypenny.

By the end of 1943, after its triumphant seven-month run, there was talk of taking *The Army Show* to Broadway.[234] Instead, it was broken into five self-contained units, three musical-comedy revues (with small combos) and two larger variety shows (with big bands), and all were sent overseas. These five sections were sub-divided into smaller segments, so that eventually there were approximately thirty-two separate units in the field, many with unique names like 'You've Had It,' 'Pardon My Glove,' 'The Haversacks,' 'Combined Ops,' 'Rapid Fire,' 'About Faces,' 'Fun Fatigues,' 'Play Parades,' 'Khaki Collegians,' and '*Après la Guerre*.' Six weeks after D-Day (in mid-July 1944), 'Wayne and Shuster and their colleagues of the Canadian Auxiliary Services went into action as close as possible to the battle areas.'[235] Like the concert parties of the First World War, they played wherever they could, on portable stages (sometimes built on gasoline drums or even live ammunition cases)[236] and usually in the afternoons, when there were no blackout restrictions. However, in January 1945, 'the two comic sergeants were sent back to Canada and assigned to prepare new units,' thus being 'denied their fond dream of putting on a show in conquered Berlin.'[237] Wayne and Shuster had come a long way since they met in 1930 at the ages of twelve and fourteen and collaborated on a fund-raiser for their Boy Scout troop. At Harbord Collegiate (from 1932 to 1936) they had organized a revue called the Oola Boola Club. After their U. of T. days in the *U.C. Follies*, their fifteen-minute household-hints radio show, *The Wife Preservers* (CFRB, 1941), marked their entry into professionalism. A weekly CFRB variety program, *Co-Eds and Cut-Ups*, followed next, and led to network exposure on the CBC's *Blended Rhythm* (1942), sponsored by Buckingham cigarettes. By the end of the year they had enlisted as privates.

The expanded Canadian Army Show overseas required additional personnel. Music director Robert Farnon, originally a trumpeter at Humberside Collegiate and later heard on *The Happy Gang*, 'became one of the Big Three band leaders with the Allied Forces (along with Glenn Miller and George Melochrino)' specializing in composition and orchestration, and 'profoundly influencing the style and sound of popular music.'[238] There were added comedians also, like the sad-sack mime Doug Romaine (1916–71), Frank Munro in his pork pie hat, and Margaret Ackroyd (née Cross), who had launched her musical-comedy career with Gracie Fields numbers before turning to hillbilly songs. Magicians were also front and centre, smoothies like Sergeant-Major Ron Leonard (b. Toronto, 1923), and Stewart James (1908–) from Courtright, Ontario, who is renowned now as one of the great creators of original magic tricks.[239]

Feelings ran high after the war. There were riots as the Canadian troops waited impatiently to be demobilized. At Guildford, *The Army Show* performers rallied to put together one last extravaganza called *Rhythm Rodeo*, which blended music and such 'Calgary Stampede' attractions as chariot races and stage-coach rescues. It played seven days a week for several months to over five thousand servicemen and women per show.[240]

Canada's London hit was the Navy Show. Although it, too, could be broken down into smaller units for visits to hospitals and camps, *Meet the Navy* was a big slick musical revue that survived basically intact when transferred from Canada to Britain and Europe. The Ontario connection was considerable. It rehearsed for three months at Hart House Theatre, 44 of its cast of 130 came from Toronto,[241] and, like *The Army Show*, it previewed at Shea's Victoria (2 September 1943). The Navy Show was memorable for the youthful dance team of Alan Lund and

Blanche Harris, the forty Wren (WRCNS) dancers drilled to 'Rockettes' perfection and the semi-professional comic trio that had sharpened its techniques in the Montreal Repertory Theatre's *Tin Hat(s) Revue*: Robert Goodier, Lionel Murton, and John Pratt. Goodier repeated a 'cruelly funny' routine he had been doing since 1933, satirizing a woman dressing before a mirror,[242] and Pratt's deadpan rendition of 'You'll Get Used to It' was destined to become a Canadian legend.

The meteoric history of *Meet the Navy* is quickly told. After previewing in Toronto and Brantford, it opened in Ottawa's Capitol Theatre (15 September 1943). As Ruth Phillips wrote in her York University thesis about *Meet the Navy*, 'No one could believe that a Canadian group could stage such a good show!' The cast travelled (and lived) in a fifteen-coach CPR train. It is estimated they logged 10,000 miles and played to 500,000 on their September 1943 to September 1944 trek back and forth across the nation.[243] Again there was talk of a New York engagement for this Broadway-style show. But the idea was vetoed in favour of a north/south tour of Britain. Beginning October 1944 in Glasgow, it ended at the Hippodrome on Leicester Square, 1 February 1945. London's opening-night, sell-out audience literally stood and cheered. Noël Coward remarked afterwards, 'I was going to say it was up to professional standard, but really it was above it.'[244] Canada had a first hit in the West End. The London booking of six weeks was extended to three months (1 February–7 April 1945). In June 1945, a few weeks after VE Day (8 May), the company was flown to Paris for a ten-day performance before the GIs under the aegis of the USO. *Time* magazine rated the various service shows and placed *Meet the Navy* first, followed by the United States's *This Is the Army* and *Winged Victory*. Following Paris, it was Brussels for two weeks, Amsterdam for eight (the Canadians were there), and, finally, Oldenburg in occupied Germany for four weeks and the show's closing night, 12 September 1945.[245] *Meet the Navy* had played for two years and ten days. But the company was not disbanded. Elstree Studios put it on film. A hackneyed backstage plot was concocted as a clothes-line for the musical-comedy numbers and shooting began in November 1945. But reactions to the film were mixed. Still, *Variety* called it 'the Best Musical Picture ever to come out of Britain,' and audiences turned out in droves.[246] The RCN Benevolent Fund received $200,000 from the movie's box-office receipts, more than some Canadian films earn at today's rates.

The entertaining of troops did not end with the Second World War. United Nations 'police actions,' as in the Korean conflict (1950–3), and the many peacekeeping missions around the world since, have kept the Canadian Armed Forces active. In response, National Defence Head-

'Whizz Bang Revue,' 1946: Cecil — ? John — ? Vin — ?

quarters has organized regular Las Vegas–style variety shows in the tradition made famous by Bob Hope. In Korea *Army Show* regulars like Wayne and Shuster, Margaret (Cross) Brenton, Ron Leonard, and Doug Romaine performed not only for the Canadian Forces but for English,

Australian, and New Zealand troops as well. They played out-of-doors, primarily, or in quonset huts, one appropriately named the Maple Leaf Theatre.[247] Two of the many newcomers in Korea were dancer Zena Cheevers and magician and MC Ross Bertram. Over the years the places Canadian variety performers have visited have included Cyprus, Damascus, Egypt, Israel's Golan Heights, West Germany, and even Alert Bay at the North Pole.

I said that the Second World War was the watershed between the amateur theatre and the professional. But it does not mean that the postwar community theatres stopped producing revue. In Ottawa the Drama League (OLT) continued the Saul Rae tradition with Hugh Parker's *The Crystal Garden* (1947), 'A Pantomania of Our Time,' and *The Bytown Revue* (1948). Especially active were the team of Graham Campbell McInnes and Norman Gilchrist. They had been noted first for their 1942 *Little Theatre Revue* and would go on to create *Come-By-Chance* (1950), a salute to the new province of Newfoundland, and the musical *The Last Best West* (1951).[248] The London Little Theatre ended its 1945–6 season with a revue, a mix of minstrel show, Indian powwow, female impersonation, dancing *à la* 'rockettes,' original music-hall numbers, and a collegiate barbershop quartet. The whole grab-bag was produced with 'zippy' pace by Ken Baskette, the Grand Theatre's business manager.[249]

Between 1945 and 1949, Roly Young produced four seasons of the semi-professional Civic Theatre (Association) in Toronto. Young's predilection was for musical variety. Now he poured his energies into a series of original pantomimes, all at Hart House Theatre and aimed at youthful Christmas audiences. Sometimes he marshalled a cast of a hundred actors, dancers, and singers, guided by professionals like Jack Medhurst (design), Bettina Byers (ballet), and Joe Jolley (direction). Titles included *Gone With the North Wind* (1946), *Aladdin '47*, and *Cinderella* (1948). In the spring of 1948 he also penned *Music All the Day*, based on the life and music of Stephen Foster.[250] On the eve of *Cinderella* (24 December 1948), Roly Young died of a heart attack at forty-five.

After his untimely death, the holiday pantomime tradition was picked up for several years by the New Play Society's professionals. English revue artist and comedian Eric Christmas (b. London, 1916–) arrived to direct and star in *Mother Goose* (1949–50) at the Royal Alexandra Theatre. He impersonated Dame Mother Goose, while Jack Medhurst curled himself inside the waddling papier maché bird that produced the golden eggs. For the NPS's second full-scale panto at the Alex, Don Hudson directed *Babes in the Wood and Bold Robin Hood* (1950–1). Boris

Volkoff choreographed and Samuel Hersenhoren conducted. Getting the laughs were Ron Leonard, Doug Romaine, and Lou Jacobi, while singing the songs and looking stunning in her mini Robin Hood outfits was Principal Boy Gisèle Mackenzie (née La Flèche, in Winnipeg, 1927). The NPS pantomimes ended with *Peter Pan* (1952–3) and *Cinderella* (1953–4), both at Eaton Auditorium. Toby Robins (1931–86) donned the flying harness and Jacqueline Smith lost her glass slipper to Peter Mews's Prince Charming. Robert Goulet was the footman.

Of course, the major event of postwar variety in Ontario was the New Play Society's phenomenal musical revue *Spring Thaw* (1948–71). For twenty-three years it set the pattern in English Canada, a pattern that was imitated but never quite duplicated. Whereas the Arts and Letters Club revues and *Town Tonics* played to the little theatre intelligentsia, *Spring Thaw* went public, attracting a new, popular audience, hundreds of thousands annually who had never seen a stage production before. The question of identity became a postwar spiritual quest. The lack of flag and anthem and indigenous culture were suddenly important. The right show at the right time, *Spring Thaw* tickled those particular nerve endings. The secret of its success was corny charm and unremitting topicality. The jokes were about Rosedale, the TTC, our antiquated blue laws, and silly politics. We also laughed in recognition of our tender first attempts at opera, ballet, and Shakespeare.

Opening night, appropriately, was April Fool's Day, 1948. When Hugh Kemp's dramatization of Hugh MacLennan's novel *Two Solitudes* was not forthcoming, there was need for a last-minute replacement. The first collective thought was 'Off on a Holiday,' a show about the cast's projected summer vacations, but Andrew Allan suggested a return to the *Town Tonics* revue mode and even came up with a title. 'You might call it *Spring Thaw*,' he said, echoing all those other pre-war rites of spring.[251]

There were really two *Spring Thaws*. The first belonged to Mavor Moore; the second to all the other directors and entrepreneurs who cashed in on the name and turned out *Thaws* that fluctuated wildly in quality and style from year to year. Mavor's *Thaw* is the one that is remembered fondly. It was, as he maintained, a review (not a revue) of the local and national events just past. Over the years there were a legion of writers involved in the sketches and lyrics, familiar names like Lister Sinclair, Pierre Berton, Tommy Tweed, Lyn Howard, Norman Jewison, Margaret Ness, and Eric Aldwinckle. Robert Fulford, himself a contributor, once noted that, with the country's lack of popular playwrights, the revue 'had become all by itself the national dramatic art form.'[252] For the first decade Mavor shared directorial duties only with Robert Christie. The music came from two pianos, usually with Marian Grudeff

Spring Thaw, 'Simpson and Delilah,' a spoof of Simpson's and Eaton's department store war, starring Paul Kligman, Andy MacMillan, Robert Goulet, and Barbara Hamilton

and Charles Tisdall at the keyboards. Peter Mews handled the décor, as well as all those Diefenbaker imitations. Other early stars, in addition to Jane Mallett, Connie Vernon, Pegi Brown, Don Harron, Lou Jacobi, and Mavor himself, were Robert Goulet, Barbara Hamilton, Anna Russell, Dave Broadfoot, Rich Little, Don Francks, and Toby Robins, amongst many many others. The stage version of Charlie Farquharson (at th'Ex) was introduced during *Spring Thaw* in 1952[253] and Dave Broadfoot's Member from Kicking Horse Pass found his stump in 1954.

In Toronto *Spring Thaw* opened in the underground crypt of the Royal Ontario Museum (ROM), moved on to such movie houses as the Avenue (Eglinton and Avenue Road), Fairlawn, and Radio City, then the Crest, Royal Alex, and Bayview Playhouse. The first show ran for only three nights, but by 1957 *Spring Thaw* celebrated its tenth anniversary with a record-breaking 171 performances, playing from April into August. It was scheduled that year to open the Royal Alexandra's fiftieth-anniversary season, tour Canada, and even venture overseas to England. But Mavor and his mother had a fight. Dora had never liked *Spring Thaw*.

'Chess Is Hell,' *Spring Thaw*, 1968 (Ed Evanko, Rita Howell, Diane Hyland, Dean Regan, Roma Hearn, Bob Jeffrey, Jack Creley)

She felt it detracted from the New Play Society's more important work. Mavor stepped down as the producer and the extended tour was cancelled (*My Fur Lady* filled in at the Alex). Mavor became the drama critic for the *Evening Telegram* and Mrs Moore gave the revue franchise to others. After a couple of years under Alan Lund, *Spring Thaw* began to flounder, having an especially sour season in 1960 under the *My Fur Lady* team. Mavor took control again in 1961, and paid his mother and the NPS $15,000 for the show's title and rights of production. Many of the old favourites came back; it was Mavor's *Thaw* once more. He tried to keep some control over the next five years and achieved a victorious first national tour in 1964 with *The Best of Spring Thaw*. His protégé Leon Major had been given the reins for an Ontario *tournée* in 1962, but Leon's glossy concept for the fifteenth-anniversary production in 1963 was assailed by the critics. Where two pianos had once sufficed, there was now a full orchestra and production values to match. Fulford called the show 'pompous' and 'fantastically overblown,' and observed that in the intervening years a 'satire industry' had developed around the world and like any boom may have overextended itself.[254] Mavor shifted his interests and became the founding artistic director of the Charlottetown Festival for its start-up year (1965). His abdication from *Spring Thaw* was complete when he leased the rights to Robert Johnston (1966–9), to Howard Batemen and John Uren in 1970, and to Robert Swerdlow in 1971. Johnston had been a ROM usher for the initial 1948 *Thaw*, and had successfully managed the 1964 and 1965 tours. He enjoyed a great Centennial year in 1967 when Don Harron wrote the show single-handedly around the theme of Canada's history. Also Dinah Christie and Catherine McKinnon made their coast-to-coast débuts that year. It was the 1970 show that was the capper. Retitled *Spring Thaw '70 Is a New Bag*, it starred Salome Bey and Rosemary Radcliffe at the Bayview Playhouse. But the new generation tried to meet the challenge of *Hair* with a ballet featuring a totally nude Adam and Eve (Alan Jordan and Nicole Morin). The purists were aghast. After a heavy-rock version at Global Village in 1971 called '*Hey Thaw* or something,' Mavor pulled the plug. Twenty-three consecutive years came to a close. Both *Spring Thaw* and the NPS were put into the deep freeze.

Alongside Mavor and Dora Mavor Moore, the other postwar Ontario founding figure to have lasting impact was the Toronto-born Irish-Canadian lawyer Brian Doherty (1906–74). Many people remember Doherty's 1937 dramatization of Bruce Marshall's novel *Father Malachy's Miracle* (and its healthy runs on Broadway and the West End), his founding of the Shaw Festival (1962), his help with the Canadian Mime Theatre (1969–79), and his early association with the Irish Arts Theatre in Toronto. Fewer recall his other contributions. In 1940 he became a co-producer with Frank McCoy at the Royal Alexandra, taking several of the Alex's summer shows to the Savoy Theatre in Hamilton. Abandoning his law practice in 1941, Doherty served as a wing commander in the RCAF, where he penned the lyrics for 'Up, Up, Up, We Go.' After the war Brian Doherty almost single-handedly restored theatrical touring in Canada. As an impresario he brought over a series of important British productions. When these large-scale UK tours proved less than profitable, he turned his attention to the Ontario scene and to variety. First he assisted Murray and Donald Davis in the launching of the Straw Hat Players summer theatre in Muskoka, and then formed with them the New World Theatre Company, which was to be based in London, Ontario. It mounted a single touring production of *The Drunkard* (1948–9) which the Davis brothers followed with *There Goes Yesterday* (1949–50). They were the first indigenous Canadian entertainments to tour since the army, navy, and air force shows.

Initially a Straw Hat Players production, *The Drunkard; or, The Fallen Saved* was a comic revival of a nineteenth-century temperance drama that was then breaking records in Los Angeles. What made *The Drunkard* a delight was the overblown acting (audiences were encouraged to boo the villain) and the inclusion of period song-and-dance routines. One bar-room quartette sang 'Why Did They Dig Ma's Grave So Deep?'; Barbara Hamilton and Beth Gillanders clutched lace handkerchiefs for 'Whispering Hope,' while John Pratt and the elegant Australian revue artist Murray Matheson (1912–94) soft-shoed their way through 'Pretty Little Pansy Faces.' All this was to rescue Murray Davis from the demon drink, which was wrecking the lives of his distraught wife (Charmion King) and addled daughter (Araby Lockhart). *The Drunkard* travelled from Montreal to Victoria with a swing through Ontario (Ottawa, Kingston, Peterborough, Oshawa, Simcoe, Hamilton, St Catharines, Kitchener, Brantford, and London). It also dipped down into Buffalo and Detroit, with an extended stopover in Chicago.

There Goes Yesterday covered roughly the same itinerary, with an added two weeks at Toronto's Royal Alexandra. More ambitious than *The Drunkard*, it was an eclectic musical cavalcade that surveyed the first half of the twentieth century, from the Gay Nineties through Noël Coward and 'Brother Can You Spare a Dime?' to the Second World War. Murray Matheson wrote and compiled the British, American, and Canadian material, and directed. Again he and Pratt were the smooth headliners, with the Hart House / Staw Hat Players in strong support. *Merry-Go-Round* pianists Dorothy Watkins and Jessie MacDonald provided the two-piano accompaniment, while singer Theresa Gray, and the dance team of Dennis and Maxine, gave it extra spice. Once more the tour enjoyed critical and financial success along the familiar routes reopened by Brian Doherty.

In 1950, Doherty took over the Red Barn Summer Theatre's third season at Jackson's Point. The 'Barnstormers' mounted an eight-week series of *Crazy With the Heat* revues. Again John Pratt starred; the musical backup came from another Montrealer, Roy Wolvin, whose songs and music would later adorn *My Fur Lady*. Doherty's Red Barn revue season evolved into one more touring show, *One for the Road*, which opened in Ottawa (6 November 1950) and played Toronto and Montreal over the winter of 1950–1.

Also in the summer of 1950, Eric Christmas and Betty Oliphant (later of the National Ballet) put together *Showtime*, a lavish musical revue with a cast of six men and six women, including Toronto's music-hall comedian Al Harvey (1907–). They had planned to play in town halls in four separate Muskoka communities, but, after drawing badly their first week, switched strategies and booked the show into twenty different area resort hotels and made a slight profit.[255] Incidentally, Al Harvey's métier, British music hall, had not been seen in Canada for twenty years until George Formby and his wife Beryl arrived in 1949. The

'Lancashire Lad with the ukulele' made three spectacularly successful Canadian tours in 1949, 1950, and 1954.[256]

Equally memorable in 1949 was Rogers and Hammerstein's *Oklahoma!* at the Royal Alex. This 1943 hit was the symbolic beginning of the ranks of postwar imported musicals that paraded through Ontario in the second half of the twentieth century. At first it seemed that Richard Rogers and Oscar Hammerstein II wrote everything. Then it was Alan Jay Lerner and Frederick Loewe, followed by Stephen Sondheim in the 1970s. The American musicals gave way to the British invasion of Andrew Lloyd Webber in the mid-1980s, and in Toronto at least, a refreshing policy of homegrown productions in a string of handsomely refurbished theatres.

In the 1950s the Royal Alexandra was the only available playhouse equipped to handle international musicals, with Maple Leaf Gardens serving occasionally for special events and cult concerts. Elvis Presley was at the hockey arena on 2 April 1957 and the Beatles for two sold-out nights in September 1964. But the first postwar attempt to produce American musicals in Toronto was in the middle of the Dufferin Park raceway (now the Dufferin Mall) by Melody Fair (see p. 224) in 1951. Seeing the danger of attempting shows out-of-doors, Melody Fair borrowed the idea of a tent from the Chautauqua tours – Tyrone Guthrie borrowed it from Melody Fair for the Stratford Festival.[257] They presented musicals in-the-round (a favoured performance mode in the early 1950s), with seating for 1640 (about 100 more than the Royal Alex). Melody Fair opened slowly with Edwin Lester's *Song of Norway*, starring Irra Petina of the Metropolitan Opera. Business picked up with Lerner and Loewe's *Brigadoon*, which followed next.[258] Their *Paint Your Wagon* (week of 6 July 1953) was a summer theatre première. Although it starred London's Gene Lockhart, generally the directors and leading performers were American-born, with only the chorus cast in Toronto. Gradually Canadians like Kathryn Albertson, Josephine Barrington, Glenn Gardiner, Sylvia Grant, Alexander Gray, E.M. 'Moe' Margolese, Alex McKee, Joan Maxwell, and Doris Swan were seen in small roles and, in the final two years, luminaries such as Barbara Hamilton and Robert Goulet were featured. Melody Fair moved its tent to the CNE grounds in 1953 (1800 seats), but the noise of racing cars and 'tractor pulls' defeated the singers. Also, the Royal Alexandra began competing by importing summer musicals with strong companies. Finally, in 1954, the Melody Fair venture went bankrupt in the 5000-seat Mutual Street Arena, which Marie Dressler had opened in 1912.

The summer-musical idea shifted, on occasion, to the Brant Inn in Burlington, which boasted an 'under the stars' dancehall, the Sky Club, overlooking Lake Ontario. For example, on 27 June 1956, the Brant Inn mounted a floor-show version of Rogers and Hammerstein's *South Pacific*, directed by Ian Dobbie.[259] Then, back in the Toronto area between 1957 and 1961, the tent concept was revived in suburban Dixie Plaza. Once more famous Broadway musicals like Irving Berlin's *Annie Get Your Gun* (1946), Cole Porter's *Silk Stockings* (1955), and George Gershwin's *Porgy and Bess* (1935) were seen at the 2000-seat Music Fair. With the tent heated to 70 degrees, performances at the Dixie Music Fair continued into September. The noted tenor Alan Crofoot (1929–79) of Toronto scored there in 1957 as Nicely-Nicely Johnson in Frank Loesser's 1950 hit *Guys and Dolls*.

The British tradition of small-scale musicals should not be forgotten. They have been an inspiration to Canadian creators and set attainable goals for our entrepreneurs. One of the most delightful of these British imports was Julian Slade and Dorothy Reynold's *Salad Days*, the light-hearted musical pastiche about a magic piano that made everybody dance. Toronto's Toby Robins picked up its North American rights and produced an initial Ontario version in September/October 1956 that enjoyed a run of more that seven weeks, five at Hart House Theatre, one at the Royal Alex, plus a tour to Montreal and Ottawa. Toby's husband Bill Freedman teamed up with the director Barry Morse and two New Yorkers to co-produce a revival. *Salad Days* reopened at the Crest Theatre in September 1958 and transferred successfully for a three-month, off-Broadway engagement at the Barbizon-Plaza Hotel, opening 10 November 1958. Brooks Atkinson in his *New York Times* review praised Barbara Franklin and Richard Easton as the young lovers, Powys Thomas as the mysterious tramp, Walter Burgess as the dancing mute, and June Sampson as the ballet dancer.[260]

The 1950s was also the decade when Ontario's own book musicals began to appear. Toronto teacher Court Stone composed the music for at least three, usually in script collaboration with his mother Louise Stone and/or his brother Arthur. In 1951 there was *Farmer in the Dell*, followed in May 1952 by a rural satire *So Long Silas* and, in June 1957, by *Muskoka Holiday*, the tale of a dashing European at one of our holiday resorts. These semi-professional productions were seen in Toronto, although *Muskoka Holiday* earned a November revival in Richmond Hill.[261] At the London Little Theatre, Will Digby tackled the subject of a witch who comes from Hell in *Up She Goes*,[262] and between 1954 and 1958, S. Alec Gordon of Belleville penned eight childrens' musicals based on fairy tales and one operetta on a native theme.[263]

The big professional event was *Sunshine Town*, Mavor Moore's musical adaptation of Stephen Leacock's 1912 *Sunshine Sketches of a Little*

Town. Aired first in 1954 on CBC Radio and later on CBC TV, it was produced in an elaborate stage version by Mavor in the winter of 1954–5. As well as writing and directing, he was responsible for the lyrics and music. Mavor acknowledged a tendency to blend Gilbert and Sullivan influences with American sounds to create his Canadian musical mix.[264] *Sunshine Town* opened at the Grand in London, Ontario, travelled to the Royal Alex in Toronto, and on to His Majesty's in Montreal. It was a most amiable concoction, with a full chorus, brightly coloured period sets and costumes, and a picnic hamper of delicate humour and pretty songs. Act One climaxed with the paddle-steamer 'Mariposa Belle' running aground. Fifty Sunday passengers on a tilt was no mean accomplishment for set designer Jack McCullagh. The Lunds staged the dances and the cast included such *Spring Thaw* veterans as Pegi Brown, Robert Christie, and Robert Goulet (as Peter Pupkin's friend and the reporter for the *Newspacket*). Sid Adilman reported in 1975 that *Sunshine Town* had 'received at least one production in Canada every year' since 1955, and there was another in 1978 at the Banff Festival.[265]

Mavor had less success in 1956 with his staging of *The Optimist* despite a seven-week run at the Avenue Theatre in Toronto (13 September–3 November 1956). However, Don Harron felt that Mavor's musical adaptation of Voltaire's satirical *Candide* was 'more humorous and tuneful' than the same-year version by Lillian Hellman and Leonard Bernstein in New York.[266] Certainly Mavor's predated theirs. Originally titled *The Best of All Possible Worlds*, it had been heard on CBC Radio on 9 January 1952. Robert Goulet (b. 1933, Lawrence, Massachusetts, raised in Edmonton) finally came into his own as a leading player portraying Candide. It was revived on CBC TV (17 January 1968) under its first title, *The Best of All Possible Worlds*.

With money lost during *The Optimist* run, Mavor's goal of producing a series of new native musicals lay dormant until 1964, when he became the founding director of the Charlottetown Festival. His input into *Anne of Green Gables* and adaptations there of Elmer Harris's *Johnny Belinda* (1968–9, 1974–5, 1983) and Frances Hodgson Burnett's novel *[Little Lord] Fauntleroy* (1980–1) were highlights for the island institution. Always interested in opera (he directed for the Canadian Opera Company between 1959 and 1963), Mavor's most important contribution to musical theatre was his 1967 collaboration with Jacques Languirand on the libretto for Harry Somers's *Riel*.

In January 1957 the New Play Society reverted to plays, presenting Don Harron's dramatization of Earle Birney's novel *Turvey*. Later Norman Campbell (b. in Los Angeles of Canadian parents, 1924) and Harron turned *Turvey* into a musical, *The Adventures of Private Turvey*

(1966), and a revue, *Private Turvey's War* (1970), both for Charlottetown. Harron and Campbell were capitalizing on the triumph of their musicalization of Lucy Maud Montgomery's *Anne of Green Gables* in 1965. We perhaps have forgotten that Norman Campbell initially produced *Anne of Green Gables* for black-and-white television in 1956 (on the CBC's 'Folio') and again in 1958. Toby Tarnow was the first Anne, while Margot Christie and John Drainie created Marilla and Matthew Cuthbert. Norman Campbell's previous CBC musical was Eric Nicol's *Take to the Woods* ('Folio,' 1955), a delightful spoof on summer camps in the Rockies.

CBC television made its Toronto début two days after Montreal (8 September 1952) with a panoply of entertainers on its initial telecast, from Glenn Gould to Uncle Chichimus (John Conway's bull-headed puppet supposedly patterned after Mavor Moore, the first head of CBC TV).[267] To compete with the six-year-old American networks, the CBC embarked on a series of variety shows. In his book *The Pierce-Arrow Showroom Is Leaking*, Alex Barris mocked their blandness, including among his examples of twenty-three 'faceless, bloodless titles,' *The Big Revue*, *After Hours*, *Four for the Show*, *Showtime*, *Swing Easy*, and *Parade*. He makes the somewhat debatable point that there were only 'a handful of shows named for people,' citing Wayne and Shuster, Juliette, Tommy Hunter, and Joan Fairfax. Despite the CBC's cautious approach to stardom, showcases like *Pick the Stars* and *Singing Stars of Tomorrow* gave newcomers such as Ottawa's Paul Anka (1941–) and impressionist Rich Little (1938–) their first national TV exposure.[268] Regrettably few 1950s variety artists were adequately promoted nationally or well sustained by Canada's relatively small population. Once dropped by one of the networks, performers had difficulty finding comparable outlets. But, although regional stage musicals and the banquet and 'Club Date' circuit may have been less satisfying options, at least the variety personalities could now have a career in Canada, almost for the first time.

A whole generation of comic talent was fostered by CBC TV in the 1950s and 1960s. Some of the new funny faces were actor-singer Jack Duffy (a wonderful Sinatra look-alike who was hired as a regular in sketches on the Perry Como Show), Max Ferguson (radio's 'Rawhide'), Al Hamel, Larry Mann, Alfie Scopp ('Clarabell the Clown' on *Howdy Doody*), Gordie Tapp ('Cousin Clem' on *Country Hoedown*), Jean Templeton, and Billy Van [Evera], among many others. CBC regulars Wayne and Shuster took off when Ed Sullivan hired their literate slapstick for an unprecedented sixty-seven engagements between 1958 and 1970. Other Toronto comedy writer-producers such as Lorne Michaels (1945–) and the team of Frank Peppiatt (1928–) and John Aylesworth

(1929–) also cut their teeth on CBC TV variety shows (for instance, *The Hart [Pomerantz] and Lorne Terrific Hour* (1969) and *Here's [Jack] Duffy*) before heading below the border to create *Saturday Night Live* and *Hee Haw*.

Television variety, which peaked during the 1950s and 1960s, is remembered especially for its roster of exceptional singing personalities and Ontario was well represented. Two TV vocalists who had their christening on CBC Radio as 'Microphone Moppets' were Shirley Harmer (b. Oshawa, 1932–) and Tommy Common (b. Toronto, 1934–85). Shirley fronted Sunday night's *Showtime* for three years (1954–7), with Robert Goulet as co-star. Boyish-looking Tommy Common, often compared to Eddie Fisher and Pat Boone, succeeded Charlie Chamberlain in 1972–3 on *Don Messer's Jubilee*, but died tragically by his own hand.[269] Also from Toronto was Tommy Ambrose (1939–) whose career has included gospel singing, club dates, and commercial jingles. The third 'Tommy' – Hunter – (b. London, Ontario, 1937–) began playing his guitar on CBC TV at the age of nineteen, before anchoring his own 'gentlemanly' country and western show for an amazing twenty-seven years (1965–92).

Phyllis Marshall (1921–96), a fourth-generation Canadian of black, French, Mohawk, and Irish ancestry, was a singer of smoky blues and jazz. She sang with Percy Faith's orchestra, toured with Cab Calloway, and was the very first performer to appear on English-language television in that historic *The Big Revue* broadcast of 8 September 1952. Under contract with CBC TV, she starred regularly on *The Big Revue* (1952–4) and *Cross-Canada Hit Parade* (1956–9), before branching out into 1960s nightclub work in Canada and Britain, as well as dramatic roles at the Crest Theatre and on television.[270]

Before becoming a regular on *Candid Camera* and Lucky Strike commercials, Dorothy Collins of Windsor (née Marjorie Chandler, 1926–94) was featured vocalist on *Your Hit Parade* in the United States (1950–9). She had been discovered as a band-singer in Detroit, where her Canadian father worked for Chrysler.[271] Mezzo-soprano Joyce Sullivan (née Solomon, Toronto, 1924–) sang for both the Leslie Bell and Carl Tapscott Singers, as well as handling the introductory chores for several CBC radio and TV programs.[272] Another CBC singing host was Billy O'Connor (b. Kingston; 1914–), whose father had been a minstrel with Lew Dockstader. Billy's *Late Show* (1954–6) served to find torch singers like Sylvia Murphy, Rhonda Silver, and Vanda King (CTV's *Diamond Lil*, 1969), but his greatest dicovery was undoubtedly 'Our Pet' Juliette (née Juliette Sysak, Winnipeg, 1927–). Juliette's highly rated show was seen on CBC TV from 1956 to 1966.

It is impossible to document all the variety performers who had their moments in the television spotlight. They ranged from the Video-ettes (Mabel and Art Guinness), a bell-ringing duo who also coaxed tunes out of balloons, bottles, and saws, to the disarmingly funny comedian, Scottish-born Billy Meek (1923–). In the late 1950s and early 1960s CBC seemed to do nothing but variety. Revue artists and dancers crossed over from *Spring Thaw*, Melody Fair, and the Charlottetown Festival. Television had added another performing outlet that helped establish a truly professional working infrastructure in Ontario.

For all the increased encouragement at home, there were still Ontarians who gravitated to the musical comedy stages of the United States in search of professional recognition. Patricia Drylie of Toronto is such an actress-dancer-singer. She was seen in Charles Strouse, Thomas Meehan, and Martin Charnin's *Annie* (1977) at Hamilton Place in 1980 as the cartoonish child-hating head of the orphanage. Ballad singer Priscilla Wright (1940–) of Strathroy had a winning recording at age fourteen with Warrick Webster's 'Man in the Raincoat' in 1954. It brought her appearances on CBC TV, *The Ed Sullivan Show* (1 July 1955), and with Elvis Presley in a U.S. movie short and at several of his concerts.[273]

The 1950s were also marked by the advent of variety shows at the Stratford Festival. Most of the Festival's audience would be unaware that the Stratford company has regularly held a weekly private cabaret in the Avon Theatre's upper lounge, where the actors enjoy a beer and let off steam after the performances. An amazing amount of stand-up comedy and vocalization occurs. At the close of the very first Stratford season, Don Harron put together a parody of *Richard III* and *All's Well That Ends Well* that was performed on the thrust stage. Reportedly, Alec Guinness was shocked at the Canadians' irreverence (or perhaps it was seeing comedian and stage-manager Jack Merigold wearing his costume as the hunch-backed king).[274] Stratford's more formal variety tradition can be dated from 22 July 1957, when McGill's satiric musical *My Fur Lady* was booked into the Avon Theatre for forty performances. It probably triggered Tyrone Guthrie's five-year excursion into Gilbert and Sullivan during the early 1960s and the possibilities of late-night fringe revues. The first of these was *After Hours* (11–15 August 1959). Staged by Norman Jewison, who later served on the Festival's board of directors, it was produced by Bernard Rothman, Ian Ross, and Alex Barris, with script supervision by Frank Peppiatt – a good cross-section of the movers and shakers of the time. *After Hours* starred Jack Creley, Norma Renault, Don Francks, Allan Blye, Pam Hyatt, and Betty Robertson. In years to come, Pat Galloway, Tom Kneebone, Dinah Christie, and Roderick Cook, among many others, would light up the revue stages in various inns and 'niteries,' at both Stratford and Niagara-on-the-Lake.

Revues were bound to have their imitators and, in 1955, Jane Mallett Associates (Jane, Don Harron, and Robert Christie) planned an autumn version of *Spring Thaw*, originally to be named *Fall Freeze*. Possibly fearing a cool response, Don came upon a title he liked better in a line from *A Midsummer Night's Dream*: 'the poet's eye in a fine frenzy rolling.'[275] *Fine Frenzy* opened at Toronto's Avenue Theatre on 18 October 1955 for a relatively short three-week run. Harron wrote most of the material and Bob Christie got it on its feet.

Not every revue succeeded. *Collector's Item* failed dreadfully at Hart House in October 1957, primarily owing to lack of promotion,[276] and, surprisingly, the elaborate cross-Canada tour of *Jubilee*, assembled in 1959 by the *My Fur Lady* team, was not a box-office success, despite Brian Macdonald's spirited staging and complimentary reviews.[277]

The Crest Theatre chose this moment to celebrate its fifth anniversary by finally getting into the revue field. Appropriately titled *This Is Our First Affair* (the first Crest revue), it opened New Year's Day, 1959, for a month's run. Jane Mallett, Phyllis Marshall, Corinne Conley, Meg Walter, Eric House, John Baylis, Joseph Shaw, and Igors Gavon were the principals and Donald Davis directed. Nathan Cohen, who as Ross Stuart said, 'simply could not be objective when dealing with the Crest,' shafted it as 'a scrawny and mirthless amusement.'[278] In May of the same year the Crest also tackled its first original musical, *Ride a Pink Horse*, with book and lyrics by Jack Gray and music by Louis Applebaum. It was a talky effort about an archaeologist's search for a centaur, and ended with Jack Creley appearing gloriously as the mythological half-human, half-horse. For the closing of its 1960 season the Crest responded to the current civil-rights unrest by presenting an imported production, *African Holiday* (opened 23 May), headed by Brock Peters. For the next two years the Crest rented out its end-of-the-season slot to Mavor Moore for *Spring Thaw* '61 and '62; in May 1963 the Crest hosted Barbara Hamilton (1926–96) in *That Hamilton Woman*, a marvellous revue she put together for herself. Tom Kneebone gave support and Alan Lund directed. The Crest had success with its Christmas offering, *Mr. Scrooge*, first seen in December 1963 and repeated in 1965. Richard Morris, Dolores Claman, and Ted Wood adapted Dickens's *A Christmas Carol* and Murray Davis staged it. The last Crest musical was *Evelyn* (opened 13 May 1964), a *Charley's Aunt* spin-off about a hapless Englishman named Evelyn who wins a scholarship to a women's college in the United States. Tom Kneebone starred with Pat Galloway.

Clap Hands was a private Toronto revue that had a five-year life span and is fondly remembered. There were three editions, two at Hart House Theatre (1958, 1959), and the 1962–3 one that toured England, all pro-

Clap Hands: Canadian Revue, 1959 (Sheila Billing, Betty Leighton, David Gardner,
Araby Lockhart, Eric House)

duced by Araby Lockhart and directed by Robert Gill. They contained
material selected and edited by Eric House, whose taste shaped the
shows into a nice blend of lemony satire and delightful nonsense. The
various editions contained music by Ray Jessel, Marian Grudeff, Ben
McPeek, and Sue (Davidson) Polanyi. The sketches and blackouts were
written by Robert Fulford, James Knight, Kildare Dobbs, and the 1986
Nobel prize–winner John Polanyi, among others. Noted for his wry wit,
Polanyi contributed a monologue for *Clap Hands* '58 that he had written
at Oxford, called 'The Open Mind.' He also collaborated with his wife
Sue on the lyrics of a saucy Mozartian ditty about the upper classes,
entitled 'The Blue Book.' Merry-Go-Round pianists Dorothy Watkins
and Jessie Macdonald were joined at the keyboards by Elizabeth
Mackay, and Ed Bickert accompanied on guitar. In addition to Araby
and Eric, the initial 1958 cast included Peter Mews, Betty Leighton,
Dave Broadfoot, and Donna Miller. That shoestring show was hailed as

'the sleeper of the season' and it ran an unexpected five-and-a-half weeks to good houses. Its second year was just as successful at the box office, although the critics were harsher.[279] The 1962–3 England tour included five weeks in Wolverhampton, Oxford, Cambridge, Torquay, and Brighton, as well as three months in London, where it opened in the Lyric Hammersmith and then was picked up to inaugurate the new Prince Charles Theatre in Leicester Square.[280]

Toronto's first new theatre building in forty years was the O'Keefe Centre, a watershed between 'big,' that is, generally 'establishment' (imported American or English) shows, and 'small,' which has meant indigenous or local since the 1960s. As early as 1936, Roly Young had written two articles for *The Mail and Empire* lamenting Toronto's lack of a municipal opera and ballet house.[281] In 1954, responding to a 'Challenge to Industry' issued by Mayor Nathan Phillips, E.P. Taylor, the head of the O'Keefe Brewing Company, offered to build a large, multipurpose auditorium for the performing arts. As eventually scheduled, the O'Keefe Centre opened on 1 October 1960 with the world première of Alan Jay Lerner and Frederick Loewe's *Camelot*, starring Richard Burton, Julie Andrews, and Robert Goulet. Over the years, the O'Keefe Centre has served as a roadhouse for the best and not-so-best in British pantomime, American musical theatre, and international stars. Its vast size and dubious acoustics have always been criticized. The 3211 seats were said to be necessary to draw the major international attractions and to keep prices competitive. As well, one can note in its defence that the Centre's acoustics were often defeated when visiting productions brought along their own incompatible sound systems. Occasionally, Canadian productions have been seen there, mainly from the Alan Lund years at the Charlottetown Festival, shows like the *Feux-Follets, Ballade, Johnny Belinda, Kronberg: 1582*, and *Anne of Green Gables*. Then, too, individual Canadian stars of international calibre have commanded audiences at the O'Keefe: singers like Paul Anka, Robert Goulet, Monique Leyrac, and Anne Murray; the magician Doug Henning; impressionist André-Philippe Gagnon; and comedians Beatrice Lillie and Jim Carrey.[282] They were, of course, often the same stars who were capable of drawing a crowd at the CNE's Grandstand shows or the 'Imperial Room.'

When the Royal York Hotel opened in 1929, the Imperial Room was its elegant supper club. Thirty-four years later the dance floor was removed, and from 1963 to 1988 the Imperial Room became a Las Vegas–inspired performance-space that played a nightclub role in Toronto's variety scene. More modest in scale than the O'Keefe Centre or the CNE Grandstand, it attracted a sophisticated, supper-and-show

crowd in search of big-name movie and recording stars, stand-up comedians, and spicy revues. The Four Lads were an early attraction in February 1963 and impressionist Rich Little was welcomed the week of 28
June 1964. After 1969 the bookings were handled by talent agent and
master publicist Gino Empry, under whose encouraging eye a host of
Canadian talent and home-grown revues has appeared.

In great contrast, during the 1960s Toronto acquired its first cabarets
and coffee-houses, intimate spaces where customers could sit at a table,
sip a little something, and take in either a revue or a folk-singing performance on a tiny raised stage. Clement Hambourg, whom we met earlier
in *Ritzin' the Blitz*, should be honoured for beginning the tradition in
Toronto. His basement House of Hambourg (1946–63), immortalized in
Banuta Rubess and Nic Gotham's jazz play *Boom, Baby, Boom!* (1988),
was the city's first after-hours jazz club following the war.[283] On Friday
nights during the summer of 1962 Clem invited the zany *Village Revue*,
a show borrowed from the Bohemian Embassy (1960–6) to enliven the
proceedings.

Pierre Berton has described the 'BoEm,' once mistakenly listed in the
yellow pages under 'Consulates and Foreign Representatives,' as the
city's 'quintessential coffee house of the '60s.'[284] These unlicensed,
herbal tea and cappuccino venues attracted the university crowds and the
sandal-shod 'hippies,' because Ontario's drinking age was still twenty-
one. When the age was lowered to eighteen in the 1970s, the licensed
clubs hired away the artists for higher fees and the coffee-houses all but
disappeared. Coffee-houses were not limited to Toronto, of course.
Ottawa had Le Hibou. London had the Cuckoo's Nest and Change of
Pace. Stratford boasted The Black Swan (a favoured home for Cedric
Smith and the Perth County Conspiracy). Of many in Toronto, only the
Bohemian Embassy put on revue. Tucked away on St Nicholas Street, a
laneway behind the Sutton Place Hotel, the 'BoEm' was run by Don
Cullen, writer, comic actor (especially on the Wayne and Shuster Show),
and amateur impresario. As he said, it was 'a catchall for anybody who
had an interesting idea that might loosely be described as artistic or
intellectual.'[285] Along with the Thursday night poetry readings, jazz
concerts, folk music hootenanies, and 'happenings' (remember those
eggs fried in a bathtub?), the Embassy attracted comic performers like
Barrie Baldaro, Carol Robinson, Warren Wilson, and David Harriman,
who, together with Cullen, created the spasmodic *Village Revue*. British-
born Baldaro, a mainstay of Jack Greenwald's Café André revues in
Montreal, had relocated to Toronto. In the next few decades, Baldaro,
Cullen, and Roy Wordsworth would become a constant three-quarters of
the quartet responsible for several local, updated revivals of *Beyond the*

Fringe (1967–8, 1980, and 1986). Toronto had seen the influential *Fringe* revue with its original British cast in 1962 at the O'Keefe Centre. In addition to its House of Hambourg dates in 1962, the irreverent *Village Revue* was invited the following summer to turn Equity and play the Theatre-in-the-Dell, which it did from July to September 1963. The sketches included take-offs on *Lawrence of Arabia*, a BBC announcer at the Royal Wedding, the Peace 'Corpse,' and the FLQ. The invitation to the Dell had been extended by the Ottawa-born actress and agent, Sylvia Shawn, once described as 'the mother of cabaret theatre in Canada.'[286]

The Dell Tavern and Spaghetti Restaurant had opened in 1947, but in 1962 Willie De Laurentis was persuaded by producer Sylvia Shawn and director Ray Lawlor to turn the upstairs room into a 130-seat cabaret theatre for plays. It opened on 12 June 1962 to reasonable houses, but was often dark between shows while plays were being rehearsed. The long-running success of the *Village Revue* during the summer of 1963 convinced the De Laurentis brothers to run Theatre-in-the-Dell themselves as a revue house akin to Julius Monk's Upstairs at the Downstairs in New York. This they did most successfully from 1964 to 1986, when they retired and the Dell reverted to its original function as a grocery store, with a Chinese restaurant up top. Sylvia Shawn left in May 1964, but returned several times to co-produce cabaret revues with them. Willie De Laurentis had been a flute, clarinet, and saxophone player with the Ottawa Symphony, the Metropolitan Opera, the Royal Alexandra Theatre Orchestra, and several Toronto dance bands. His first revue was *The Conformists* (opening 18 June 1964), a CBC Workshop production directed by Bill Davis, with Norman Ettlinger and Paul Wayne. It was followed in late July with *Umm!*, a Sylvia Shawn presentation featuring Zoe Caldwell, Jean Templeton, Art Jenoff, and Don Arioli. Only Zoe got reasonable notices. But in September 1964 the Dell had its first big hit, *Actually, This Autumn* (the retitled Stratford fringe revue, *Surprisingly, This Summer* imported from the Victorian Inn).

This series had begun in 1963 as *Suddenly, This Summer* at Stratford, starring Pat Galloway, John Church, and Roderick Cook, who also directed. So prevailing was the show that it changed its seasonal title once again to *Warmly, This Winter* and went on into 1965 to play more than 250 times. The Dell enjoyed another six-month run with *Ding-Dong at the Dell* (beginning 20 April 1965), the revue that introduced Tom Kneebone and Dinah Christie (b. London, England, 1943–) to its patrons and to each other, along with Gary Krawford. It was devised by Roderick Cook, staged by Walter Burgess (the Mute in *Salad Days*), and sparkled to the music of Ben McPeek. For Herbert Whittaker, Tom Kneebone appeared 'as if he just broke through the shell.'[287] Dinah

Christie, whose entertainment career had begun in 1956 when she worked as a 'call boy' (not a call girl, she insists) at Stratford, was right at home in the satirical *'This Hour Has Seven Viewers.'* She had come to national prominence as the singing co-host of the CBC current-affairs show *This Hour Has Seven Days* (1965–6). McKenzie Porter, writing then for *The Telegram*, predicted that 'there is no reason why half a dozen revues of this nature should not be on a stage six nights a week in the suitably licensed establishments of our lively city.'[288] It was a prediction that would come true, but not until the mid-1970s.

Then the Dell ran into a string of badly received revues, some by important comic performers like Pam Hyatt, Dave Broadfoot, and John Cleese of Monty Python fame.[289] A local effort, appropriately titled *For Whom the Dell Tolls* (January 1967), was dismissed as 'an evening of staggering mediocrity.'[290] Ron Chudley and Diane Stapley wrote and starred in *T.O. for Two* (January 1968), a mini-epic that took Toronto from Muddy York to the present. Jokes about Upper Canada and Havergal colleges abounded, but 'Sailing Up the Dirty Don' was deemed a highlight.[291] September 1968 saw *You Blow Yours, I'll Blow Mine*, which began with a balloon inflated to enormous size and exploded: something to do with inflated egos and pretensions. It 'had an undertow of horror,' according to Gail Dexter in the *Toronto Star*,[292] and indeed, among the topical, anti-establishment numbers were some about bored sophisticates riding with motorcycle gangs, what to wear while committing murder, and a stripper who dressed as a nun. In *She-rade* (August 1969), five female impersonators camped it up. The show had moved to the Dell after three weeks at Global Village, an early 'alternative' musical theatre occupying the space vacated by the Bohemian Embassy. One of the items featured a topless striptease down to boxer shorts.[293]

The bounds of nudity were being tested and the Age of Aquarius was about to dawn in Toronto with the musical *Hair*. But from 12 November 1969 to March 1970 at the Dell, there was a tastefully nude Adam and Eve dance from Czechoslovakia. It was part of a 'Creation of the World' segment in the magical Black Box Theatre that had been a sensation at Expo 67. This highly original black-light show drew its techniques from the Japanese Bunraku tradition of invisible operators moving puppets and objects. With the addition of ultraviolet light and black masking, the operators disappeared and the glowing objects took on a life of their own. There was a memorable moment, for example, when two chairs made love. It was new to Canada and an obvious influence on the Hamilton puppeteer Diane Dupuy (1948–), who would go on to found the Famous People Players in 1974.[294] The Garden of Eden dance probably inspired the notorious nude scene in the 1970 *Spring Thaw*. Writing in *The Telegram*, McKenzie Porter was aghast at the drastic changes in Toronto's famous revue over the past two seasons, labelling them 'hippy harmonies.'[295] And so the 1960s ended at the Dell. But its golden decade lay just ahead, to be launched by *The Noel Coward Revue*, subsequently retitled *Oh, Coward!* (1970)

Despite its centrality, we must not leave the impression that everything variety in Toronto's 1960s happened at the Dell. As early as April 1960 Mark Furness had attempted cabaret theatre at the enticingly named 'Speakeasy,' but, in true Ontario fashion, he could not get a liquor licence. Still, he ran a production of *The Boyfriend* there for three weeks.[296] In 1961 Old Angelo's spaghetti house on Elm Street offered Dave Broadfoot and Jean Templeton (then married) in *Well-Rehearsed Ad-libs*. Between the comedy sets, seventeen-year-old Dinah Christie made her professional début as an intermission vocalist. Dinah would again be Upstairs at Old Angelo's in November 1965 with *The Decline and Fall of the Entire World as Seen Through the Eyes of Cole Porter*, while Dave Broadfoot would return in 1973–4 with *Take a Beaver to Lunch*. By the 1970s Old Angelo's would parallel the Dell in terms of attractions. Revues also appeared occasionally during the mid-1960s at the Poor Alex and the Colonnade theatres. From November 1965 on, the Bayview Playhouse became a transfer house and regular showcase for intimate musicals such as *She Loves Me* (Bill Cole and Barbara Hamilton, 1965), *You're a Good Man Charlie Brown* (Derek McGrath as Linus and Grant Cowan as Snoopy, 1967), *Jacques Brel Is Alive and Well and Living in Paris* (1968), and a rock version of Shakespeare's *Twelfth Night*, dubbed *Your Own Thing* (1968).

Global Village (1969–76), with its obvious echoes of Marshall McLuhan's 1968 book *War and Peace in the Global Village*, was founded in 1969 by Montreal composer-pianist Robert Swerdlow (1939–) and his wife at the time, the New York dancer Elizabeth Szathmary (1938–). Between 1969 and 1975, they put on fifty-two productions, often with the directorial assistance of Roy Fleming. Global Village also hosted the important two-week Festival of Underground Theatre (FUT) in August 1970. But, basically, the Swerdlows sought to encourage musical theatre in their 194-seat, early 'alternative' theatre space, and they stressed improvisation and works-in-progress. Global Village's big hit was *Justine*, starring New Jersey–born Salome Bey, who had settled in Toronto in 1964 and remains one of the city's musical glories. *Justine* opened in 1970 for a Toronto run of eight months, followed by another seven in New York, the only Canadian musical to have an extended stay off-Broadway. Retitled *Love Me, Love My Children* in New York, it was recast except for Salome Bey, who won an Obie Award.

There were other highlights to be noted in the 1960s. Tom Jones and Harvey Schmidt's delightful musical *The Fantasticks* moved into the cosy Central Library auditorium (the former winter home of the Red Barn Summer Theatre) on 29 October 1963 for a resounding six-month run. The producers Marigold Charlesworth and Jean Roberts continued at the Central Library Theatre with a December 1964 production of *Cindy-Ella*, an all-black musical adaptation of the Cinderella legend starring Phyllis Marshall that ran for twenty performances.[297] In the spring of 1968 the Central Library warmed to *Here Lies Sarah Binks*, a six-handed musical version of Paul Hiebert's novel. It was a Jane Mallett Associates production, with script by Don Harron, direction by Robert Christie, and a wonderful performance by Jane Mallett.

During the mid-1960s, there were professional mini-musicals for children emanating from the ROM's basement theatre. In 1963, Susan Rubes's Museum Children's Theatre (which would evolve into Young Peoples' Theatre) presented Chris Wiggins's adaptation of *Sleeping Beauty* (with music by John Fenwick), and in 1966 an original piece, *Please Don't Sneeze* (music by John Sims). The Toronto broadcasters Dodi Robb and Pat Patterson became a winning team with a series of light-hearted musical works. Their first was *The Dandy Lion*, which opened January 1965 and played for five months, featuring eleven-year-old Reed Needles (son of Bill) in a circus with a friendly lion.[298] They followed *The Dandy Lion*, which was destined to become an international favourite, with several other teeny-bopper hits, notably *Henry Green and His Mighty Machine* (1967), *Red Riding Hood* (1968), and *The Popcorn Man* (1970), with Jack Northmore delightfully right in the title role.

On the expatriate front, Don Francks (b. Burnaby, BC, 1932–) made his Broadway début starring in the title role of *Kelly*, but the musical closed after a single performance on 16 February 1964. That same year Rich Little came to national prominence following a guest appearance on *The Judy Garland Show*. In Canada his recording of John Diefenbaker ('My Fellow Canadians') sold 10,000 copies.[299] Toronto-born Christopher Plummer (1927–) co-starred with Julie Andrews in the Hollywood film treatment of *The Sound of Music* in 1965. Robert Goulet won a 'Tony' Award in 1968 for 'Best Actor in a Broadway Musical,' playing the not-so-shy photographer in *The Happy Time*, the musical made from Robert Fontaine's affectionate novel of a French-Canadian family living in 1920s Ottawa.

The Canadian-composed musical *Baker Street* came to the O'Keefe Centre from 20 January to 6 February 1965 between its baptism in Boston and the Broadway opening (16 February). Producer Alexander Cohen, who booked shows for the O'Keefe from 1959 to 1964, hired

Raymond Jessel and Marian Grudeff to write the music and lyrics. Jessel (b. Wales, 1930–) was a freelance orchestrator-arranger for the CBC who had come to Canada with his family in 1953.[300] Between 1957 and 1963 he collaborated with pianist Marian Grudeff (b. Toronto, 1927–) on the lyrics and music of many *Spring Thaws*.[301] Their songs for the *Baker Street* Sherlock Holmes musical were written 'in the *sprech-stimme* that had worked so well for Rex Harrison in *My Fair Lady*.'[302] Herbert Whittaker in the *Globe and Mail* found the 'light, charming music closely integrated with the dramatic action,' but Glenn Litton writing in *Musical Comedy in America* stated that the lyrics were too prosaic for the detective's prodigious intelligence, and their melodies were insipid.[303] Still *Baker Street* ran for over eight months on Broadway, and another critic called it 'one of the best musicals in the 1960s.'[304] Grudeff and Jessel also teamed up to create the Charlottetown musical *Life Can Be – Like Wow!* (1969), a free-wheeling adaptation of Molière's *Le Bourgeois gentilhomme*, in which a rich, would-be hippy (Peter Mews) enters the world of the flower children only to be duped by Speed, the owner of a discothèque (Dean Regan).

Another *Spring Thaw* writer, Stan Daniels, joined Norman Campbell in adapting Molière's *The Misanthrope* into a television musical called 'The Slave of Truth' for the CBC's *Festival* series. It was seen in 1965, starring James Douglas, Leo Ciceri, Toby Robins, and Joseph Shaw. Daniels had written songs for Jack Arthur as well as scripted an unsuccessful West End revue, *Not to Worry* (1962). He departed for Hollywood in 1968 and became the TV series writer for *Taxi*. The well-known CBC playwright Len Peterson (b. Regina, 1917–) put together a revue titled *All About Us* for the Manitoba Theatre Centre in 1964. Ontario saw it on tour in 1965, courtesy of the Canadian Players. It was one of the first entertainments to have a distinct multicultural feel.

Centennial year was celebrated in London, England, by actor Louis Negin and a wayward group of Canucks. Negin assembled *Love and Maple Syrup*, a miscellany of Canadian poetry, prose, and songs about love that they put on early in January 1968, first for a single night in a pub in Highgate and then for a week at the Round House theatre in Camden Town. The show touched a chord for Canadians abroad, who flocked to hear the poetry of Irving Layton and Leonard Cohen, selections from the novels of W.O. Mitchell and Margaret Laurence, and the songs of Joni Mitchell and Gilles Vigneault. Negin was encouraged to bring his compilation home, and it opened 8 July 1969 in the Studio Theatre of Ottawa's National Arts Centre for a run of about twelve weeks. There were criticisms: too many bits and pieces; a patchwork without a unifying point of view; too many words and not enough music;[305] but the audiences came. *Love and Maple Syrup* tried its wings in New York at the Mercer-Hansberry Theatre (opened 7 January 1970) and the response was perhaps predictable. Clive Barnes in the *New York Times* declared it 'a little too cute by three-quarters,' and asked, 'Have you ever actually tasted maple syrup?'[306]

Sex and rebellion were in the northern air during the summer of 1969. While *Love and Maple Syrup* played at the NAC, Peter Mandia (later to establish Theatre Aquarius in Hamilton) joined with Vic Spassove to mount a rival revue at Ottawa's Le Hibou coffeehouse. Its succinct and provocative title was *Up Yours!* (21–28 July 1969).

There were even stirrings at Stratford. The Festival equated the 'make love, not war' years with the last profligate days of the Roman Empire, developing a controversial musical version of Petronius Arbiter's *The Satyricon* for the Avon Theatre. It opened, perhaps symbolically, on the 4th of July, 1969. John Hirsch pulled out all the stops to make the satiric orgy exotic and spectacularly decadent. The budget soared and by the end of the season Hirsch would resign and Jean Gascon would be left solely in charge. Later, in 1972–3, the songs and Tom Hendry's lyrics for *The Satyricon* were recycled intact for a new New York musical called *Dr. Selavy's Magic Theatre* by Richard Forman.

The socio-sexual revolution reached its mainstream apogee with the tribal–love rock-musical *Hair* (1967, revised 1968). Its thirty seconds of total, frontal nudity at the end of Act One were to become a milestone that has reverberated ever since in stage and film production. Equally revolutionary in terms of theatrical practice was the new concept of 'franchise' productions: fresh, local mountings of established musical hits in various cities around the world, rather than the cumbersome and often second-rate apparatus of touring the show. Ontario's production of *Hair*, directed by its authors Gerome Ragni and James Rado, was rehearsed in Toronto and played at the Royal Alexandra for a year and a bit (from 29 December 1969 to 3 January 1971). The cast of thirty were drawn from an audition call that attracted over a thousand hopefuls. As in each of the ten productions of *Hair* around the globe, they were named after a tribe – the Mississaugas in Toronto. Many of *Hair*'s young players, and that includes those who were substituted over the year, found their way into the profession – talent like Taborah Johnson, Gale Garnett, Frank Moore, Tobi Lark, Avril Chown, Dorothy Poste, Jonathan Welsh, Colleen Peterson, Terence Black, Brenda Russell (née Gordon), Wayne St John, Robin White, and Mary Ann MacDonald. Most memorable were the show's songs, composed by then thirty-seven-year-old, Montreal-born jazz pianist Galt MacDermot (1929–), remembered for his collaboration on the score of *My Fur Lady* a decade earlier.

In the autumn of 1970, while *Hair* was still playing at the Royal Alex, another interesting youth musical, *The Me Nobody Knows*, slipped into the Crest Theatre. Based on the collective writings of 125 children living in a New York ghetto, it was represented by a largely unknown teenage cast gathered from high schools around Ontario. Its group sales, however, were handled by entrepreneur-to-be Marlene Smith.[307]

Mention of Marlene Smith links us to the Elgin / Winter Garden complex and the newly restored musical-comedy theatres of Toronto's 1980s and 1990s. Utilizing the franchise concept pioneered by *Hair*, Smith would turn *Cats* into the first of the locally produced, commercial mega-hits. Theatre-in-the-Dell inspired a second decade of revues that were, in turn, superseded by the stand-up-comedy phenomenon of Yuk Yuk's, the rich sketch-comedy tradition of Second City, and a host of other troupes. Finally, Global Village's *Justine* pointed the way towards an ambitious wave of small-to-middle-scale, indigenous Ontario musicals. And so our chapter ends, as it began, *in medias res.*

Traditionally, the mood of light entertainment is light. Variety is 'the spice of life,' or maybe its dessert, but not the main course, not the meat and potatoes of the theatre. Still, many a bitter truth has been made more palatable with satiric seasoning or clever sugar-coating. Variety remains a vital front-runner of the theatre, capable of mirroring the changing headlines quickly, and often with great impact and immediacy. By the end of the 1980s, much of variety's saucy sweetness had gone uncharacteristically sour as it reflected, among other things, the era's moral and political cynicism, the fragmentation of the nation, the damage to our ecology, and the spectre of AIDS. But the pleasure principle is strong and sometimes stronger than our fears. We continued to trust in the insightful gifts of silly laughter, rousing song, and antic dance. As Ontario tumbled into the last decade of the twentieth century, the cry still went up, 'Send in the clowns.'

NOTES

1 Ida Van Cortland address to University Women's Club of Ottawa (c. 1918), Tavernier Collection, Theatre Department, Metropolitan Toronto Library, 4
2 Handmade poster outlining the afternoon program in German; National Archives of Canada #C113500. See also YMCA Prisoners of War Service letterhead, NAC #113499
3 Gene Plowden, *Those Amazing Ringlings and Their Circus* (New York: Bonanza Books, 1967), 134
4 Earl Chapin May, *The Circus from Rome to Ringling* (1932; reprint, New York:

Dover Publications, 1963), 316. In Plowden's history, p. 175, the name is spelled McLaughlin.

5 Hilary Russell, 'A Theatre's Diary 1919–1970,' National Historic Sites Service, unpublished manuscript, 8

6 *Globe and Mail*, 19 February 1979, 6; Toronto *Sunday Star*, 17 February 1980, 28

7 Toronto *Sunday Star*, 4 March 1979, B4

8 Toronto *Star*, 17 September 1983, A10

9 Toronto *Sunday Star*, 27 May 1979, B6

10 Toronto *Star*, 24 October 1975, A8

11 Ibid., 24 and 25 August 1977, C8

12 Ibid., 10 August 1987, A8

13 Ibid., 18 October 1977

14 Telephone interview with Wayne Constantineau, 21 March 1991

15 Abel Green and Joe Laurie, Jr, *Show Biz: From Vaude to Video* (Garden City, NY: Permabooks, 1983), 83

16 'A Hard Act to Follow,' TV special on the life of Buster Keaton, PBS TV Network, 28 November 1988

17 Thomas P. Kelley, Jr, *The Fabulous Kelley: Canada's King of the Medicine Men* (Don Mills: Paperjacks 1974), iii, 2. See also his 'The Great Gu-Zamba Is Coming,' *Canadian Magazine*, 19 October 1974, 14.

18 Kelley, *The Fabulous Kelley*, 109

19 *Globe and Mail*, 7 June 1986, A6

20 Kelley, *The Fabulous Kelley*, 92ff.

21 Private records held by Robert Scott

22 Robert C. Toll, *On With the Show* (New York: Oxford University Press, 1976), 350–1

23 Toronto *Star Weekly*, 21 October 1916, 20

24 Robert C. Toll, 'Show Biz in Blackface: The Evolution of the Minstrel Show as a Theatrical Form,' in *American Popular Entertainment*, ed. Myron Matlaw (Westport, Conn.: Greenwood Press, 1979), 22, 31

25 Hilary Russell, unpublished daybook for the Capitol Theatre, 13

26 Eugene Tompkins and Quincy Kilby, *The History of the Boston Theatre 1854–1901* (Boston and New York: Houghton Press, 1908), 453

27 Toronto *Star Weekly*, 31 January 1914, 26–7

28 *The Oxford Companion to American Theatre* (New York and Oxford: Oxford University Press, 1984), 558

29 Harlowe R. Hoyt, *Town Hall Tonight* (Englewood Cliffs, NJ: Prentice-Hall, 1955), 163

30 London *Free Press*, 18 April 1908, 15; 22 April 1908, 2

31 Hector Charlesworth, *More Candid Chronicles* (Toronto: Macmillan, 1928), 313

32 Toll, *On With the Show*, 351

33 'Blacks in American Theatre and Drama,' *Oxford Companion to American Theatre*, 82ff.

34 Mary Brown, 'The Canadian Connection,' *Theatre Studies* 24/25 (1977–9), 115

35 Mary Brown, Hamilton performance calendar.

36 Hamilton *Spectator*, 15 July 1926, 70; *Saturday Night*, 13, 27 January 1894, 6

37 Toronto *Sunday Star*, 6 September 1981, C7

38 Hamilton *Spectator*, 24 November 1956, 30; London *Free Press*, 1 May 1909

39 Patrick B. O'Neill, 'Checklist of Canadian Dramatic Materials to 1967,' *Canadian Drama* 9:2 (1983), 410

40 Arts and Letters Club Scrapbooks, courtesy of archivist/librarian, Ray Peringer

41 Raymond Massey, *When I Was Young* (Toronto: McClelland and Stewart, 1976), 191, 196, 215–20

42 Toronto *Star*, 6 August 1981, F2, and telephone interview, 10 November 1989

43 Arthur Livingston Ashworth papers, *Winter Rain* MS 1953, NAC MG 31, D20. The pages are generally unnumbered.

44 Warner Troyer, *The Sound & the Fury, An Anecdotal History of Canadian Broadcasting* (Rexdale, Ont.: John Wiley and Sons Canada Limited, 1980), 59–60; also Sandy Stewart, *A Pictorial History of Radio in Canada* (Toronto: Gage Publishing, 1975), 37, 40

45 Toronto *Star*, 16 April 1979, A3, and telephone interview, 16 November 1989

46 John E. DiMeglio, *Vaudeville USA* (Bowling Green, Ohio: Bowling Green University Popular Press, 1973), 11

47 Ibid. Two thousand theatres playing vaudeville exclusively plus many more. John C. Lindsay, *Turn Out the Stars Before Leaving* (Erin, Ont.: Boston Mills Press, 1983), 68, quotes Gerald Lenton's estimate of 4000 theatres.

48 Green and Laurie, *Show Biz*, 101

49 *Saturday Night*, 11 September 1909, 14

50 Green and Laurie, *Show Biz*, 68, 102, 258

51 Hilary Russell, *All That Glitters: A Memorial to Ottawa's Capitol Theatre and Its Predecessors*, Canadian Historic Sites, Occasional Papers in Archaeology and History, No. 13 (Ottawa: Information Canada, 1975), 80

52 Toronto *Star*, 4 June 1988, F24; *Globe and Mail*, 25 July 1987, C11

53 Lindsay, *Turn Out the Stars*, 27

54 Toronto *Telegram*, 16 December 1913, 23.

55 *Saturday Night*, 3 September 1898, 6

56 Quoted by Alan Howard in a lecture at Glendon College 23 February 1984

57 Stan Helleur, 'Farewell to Shea's,' *Mayfair Magazine*, March 1957, 62

58 *What's New?* (Famous Players), January 1953, 2

59 'Jack Arthur,' *Encyclopedia of Music in Canada* (Toronto: University of Toronto Press, 1981), 36

60 Hilary Russell, *All That Glitters*, 78

61 Toronto *Star*, 22 May 1979, A15

62 Green and Laurie, *Show Biz*, 245

63 *Turn Out the Stars*, 98

64 *Globe and Mail,* 10 October 1977, 8; *What's New?* (Famous Players), Spring 1970, n.p.

65 Photo caption, *What's New?*, 30 January 1945, 6

66 Lindsay, *Turn Out the Stars,* 73

67 Toronto *Star,* 5 September 1979, D22

68 Lindsay, *Turn Out the Stars,* 87

69 Toronto *Star,* 14 January 1988

70 See 1924 Capitol listing advertisement, *Ottawa Citizen,* 30 August 1924, 15. List also compiled from reference to Lindsay, *Turn Out the Stars,* 174; Russell, *All That Glitters,* various pages; and *What's New?*

71 Toronto *Star,* 24 February 1964, 7

72 Robertson Davies, *The Enthusiasms of Robertson Davies,* ed. Judith Skelton Grant (Toronto: Macmillan of Canada, 1979), 15

73 Toronto *Star Weekly,* 31 January 1914, 27

74 *Saturday Night,* 20 June 1914, 6

75 Helen Avery Hardy, 'Successful Canadian Players,' *Canada West Monthly* 6:3 (July 1909), 173

76 Toronto *Star Weekly,* 31 January 1914, 26

77 Toronto *Star,* 8 February 1982, D1

78 *Show Biz,* 172

79 Toronto *Globe,* 8 October 1918, 6

80 Crescence Krueger, grand-niece of Walter Huston, 'Caterpillar to Butterfly,' unpublished essay on Walter Huston, University College Drama Programme, University of Toronto, 1985, 5

81 O'Neill, 'Checklist of Canadian Dramatic Materials to 1967,' *Canadian Drama* 9:2, 499

82 Krueger, 'Caterpillar to Butterfly,' 5 and 6, memories of her grandmother, Walter Huston's niece

83 Sophie Tucker, *Some of These Days* (Garden City, NY: Doubleday, Doran and Co., 1945), 153

84 *New York Times,* 21 October 1938, 26

85 Fred Allen, *Much Ado About Me* (Boston, Toronto: Little, Brown and Company, 1956), 189. O'Neill, 'Checklist,' *Canadian Drama* 8:2 (1982) 290

86 Toronto *Sunday Star,* 17 June 1984, A24

87 *Show Biz,* 357

88 Drawn from Patrick B. O'Neill, Mount St Vincent Canadian Drama Collection (1984), 37, 33, 15, and *Canadian Drama* checklists, 8:2, 296, and 9:2, 499

89 *Oxford Companion to the American Theatre,* 143, 266

90 *The Travelling Salesman* (1908) at the Princess Theatre, 19 September 1910; *The Commuters* (1910) at the Royal Alexandra, August 1916; *Sweet Genevieve* (1916), performed by Marie Dressler and Co. in Toronto, 19 May 1916; *The Making Over of Mrs. Matt* at the Grand Opera House, 30 April 1917; and *The Famous Mrs. Fair*

(1919) at the Princess Theatre, 1 February 1922, as drawn from Robert B. Scott, 'A Study of English-Canadian Dramatic Literature 1900–1930,' Phil.M. thesis for University of Toronto, 1969, 142–5. See also O'Neill, 'Checklist,' *Canadian Drama*, 8:2, 257.

91 Claudia D. Johnson, 'Burlesques of Shakespeare: The Democratic American's "Light Artillery,"' *Theatre Survey* 21:1 (May 1980), 57
92 Toronto *World*, 12 October 1912, 8
93 Toronto *Star*, 13 November 1982, F7
94 Hamilton *Spectator*, 12 August 1905, 18
95 Laurence Senelick, 'Burlesque Show, American,' *Cambridge Guide to World Theatre* (Cambridge, New York: Cambridge University Press, 1988), 134–5, with photograph
96 Toll, *On With the Show*, 222
97 *Revue, A Story in Pictures* (New York: Taplinger Publishing Co., 1971), 38
98 Lawrence Senelick, 'Nudity on Stage,' *Cambridge Guide to World Theatre*, 721
99 *Show Biz*, 89
100 Maud Allan, *My Life and Dancing* (London: Everett & Co., 1908). Two sections are devoted to the Salomé dance, at 120ff. and 125ff. See also Felix Cherniavsky, *The Salome Dancer* (Toronto: McClelland and Stewart, 1991).
101 *Show Biz*, 30, 40, 76
102 Mary Shortt, 'Victorian Temptations,' *The Beaver*, December 1988 / January 1989, 13
103 Toronto *Star Weekly*, 23 September 1916, 21, announcing the 5–7 October engagement
104 Toronto *Star*, 29 May 1985, A2
105 This section is indebted to Patrick O'Neill, 'The Canadian Concert Party in France,' *Theatre History in Canada / Histoire du théâtre au Canada* 4:2 (Fall 1983), and 'Entertaining the Troops,' *The Beaver* (October–November 1989, 59).
106 Jack McLaren as told to Stephen Franklin, 'A Funny Thing Happened on the Way to the Trenches,' *Weekend Magazine* 17:47 (25 November 1967), 26–8. The six original PPCC were Jack McLaren, Bill Cunningham, Fred Fenwick, Percy Ham, Tom Lilley, and Stan Morrison.
107 O'Neill, 'Entertaining the Troops,' 60
108 Ibid.
109 Larry Worthington, *Amid the Guns Below* (Toronto, Montreal: McClelland and Stewart, 1965), 64
110 Charles W. Bishop, *The Canadian YMCA in the Great War* (Toronto: YMCA, 1924), 155
111 O'Neill, 'The Canadian Concert Party,' 200
112 O'Neill, ibid., 201, and 'Entertaining the Troops,' 61
113 Patrise Earle, *Al Plunkett: The Famous Dumbell* (New York: Pageant Press, 1956), 63–8

114 Daniel Blum and John Willis, *A Pictorial History of the American Theatre 1860–1976*, 4th ed. (New York: Crown Publishing, 1977), 173

115 Earle, *Al Plunkett*, 72–73

116 Alexander Woollcott, ' "Biff, Bing, Bang" Has Dash,' *New York Times*, 10 May 1921, 20. Herbert Whittaker, ' "Dumbells" Rag: From Vimy to Broadway,' *Globe and Mail*, 27 June 1977, 17

117 Advertisement, *New York Times*, 8 May 1921, section 6, p. 1

118 Patrick B. O'Neill, 'The Dumbells,' *Oxford Companion to Canadian Theatre* (Toronto, Oxford, New York: Oxford University Press, 1989), 188. See also Earle, *Al Plunkett*, 77–9.

119 The Maple Leafs were at Cobalt, in Northern Ontario, 7–18 November 1921, and at the Theatre Royal, North Bay, 19 November 1921, in *Camouflage*. This same production had been at the Empire Theatre, Saskatoon (20 September 1920), billed as Captain Plunkett's Maple Leafs. In the Toronto Winter Garden program for *Love Letters* (Spring 1990), an unnumbered page shows old programs for *Full O' Pep* and identifies the producer as Khaki Productions, with a cast of fourteen 'Old Dumbells' and star Red Newman, who rejoined the Plunketts later.

120 Patrick B. O'Neill, early draft for 'Saskatchewan Theatre: Early Years a Golden Age,' *Saskatoon Star-Phoenix*, 29 March 1974, 9

121 Dick MacDonald, *Mugwump Canadian* (Montreal: Content Publishing Ltd., 1973), 98–9

122 O'Neill, 'Checklist,' *Canadian Drama* 9:2 (1983), 405

123 *Curtain Call*, 11 December 1939, 39. See also Hector Charlesworth, ' "Chin Up" Cheers in War Time,' *Saturday Night*, 16 December 1939, 18.

124 O'Neill, 'The Dumbells,' 188

125 David Ewen, *New Complete Book of the American Musical Theater* (New York, Chicago, San Francisco: Rinehart and Winston, 1970), 585

126 'Flag incident at Princess Theatre leads to strike of chorus girls from United States: Girls know now that this city is part of Canada,' *Toronto Star*, 18 February 1914, 1

127 Beatrice Lillie, *Every Other Inch a Lady* (New York: Dell, 1973), 40–4, 62. See also James Dugan, 'Ungilded Lillie,' *Maclean's Magazine*, 15 July 1948, 33, and the 1909–10 advertisement for Bea Lillie as a 'Character costume vocalist, impersonator, and fancy dancer,' Toronto *Evening Telegram*, 6 December 1924, 27

128 Lillie, *Every Other Inch a Lady*, 85

129 Ibid., 95

130 Ibid., 150–3. Atkinson is cited in Donald Jones, 'Historical Toronto: Toronto's Bea Lillie,' Toronto *Star*, 5 August 1989, M4.

131 Dr Lawrence Mason, 'Toronto acclaims Beautiful Beatrice,' *The Globe*, 5 April 1936, 5

132 Greg Rothwell, 'Sister Aimee's mix: Showbiz and Evangelism,' Toronto *Star*, 24 June 1989, M27

133 Michael Collins, 'Sister Aimee: A Canadian Evangelist Took the Roaring '20s by

Storm,' *The Beaver*, June/July 1989, 32. Ben M. Hall, *The Best Remaining Seats* (New York: Bramhall House, 1961), 227–9

134 Stanley Green, *Broadway Musicals of the 30's* (New York: DaCapo, 1971), 86–7, and Ewen, *New Complete Book of the American Musical Theater*, 601

135 Ed Gould, *Entertaining Canadians: Canada's International Stars 1900–1988* (Victoria, BC: Cappis Press, 1988), 278–9

136 O'Neill, 'Checklist,' *Canadian Drama*, 8:2 (1982), 194. O'Neill also lists a quartet of musical plays by C.W. Bell on p. 195.

137 Hilary Russell, *Double Take* (Toronto: Dundurn, 1989), 114

138 Advertisement, Toronto *Star Weekly*, 7 October 1916, 21

139 *Kitchener Daily Telegraph*, 13 February 1918, 1

140 Sheilagh S. Jameson, *Chautauqua in Canada* (Calgary: Glenbow-Alberta Institute, 1979), 1, 143

141 *Hullo, Canada!* was presented by Albert de Courville of the London Hippodrome; written by de Courville and Wal Pink, with music by Frederick Chappelle and Herman Darewiski. It boasted a cast of 70, with a gaiety beauty chorus of 40 or 50 (depending on which advertisement you read). Two of the stars were the notable revue comedians Shirley Kellogg and Harry Tate. See Public Archives of Canada MG281, 139, vol. 17.

142 Mary Brown, 'Ambrose Small: A Ghost in Spite of Himself,' in *Theatrical Touring and Founding in North America*, ed. L.W. Conolly (Westport, Conn. and London, Eng.: Greenwood Press, 1982), 77–88

143 Robert G. Lawrence, 'Phyllis Davis,' *Oxford Companion to Canadian Theatre*, 134. I am grateful as well to Robert Lawrence for providing me with dates and itinerary for the British 1921–2 tour.

144 'Florodora great success,' *Evening Telegram*, 25 November 1924, 23

145 *The Globe*, a series of photos herald the 'Jollies of 1927': 21 February, 7; 22 February, 12; 24 February, 15; and 26 February 1927, 16. The show is reviewed by Lawrence Mason, 'Music and the Drama,' 1 March 1927, 14. For *In Gay Paree*, see Mason, ibid., 2 March 1928, 2.

146 Russell, *Double Take*, 115–17

147 Robert G. Lawence, 'Vaughan Glaser on Stage in Toronto 1921–1934,' *Theatre History in Canada / Histoire du théâtre au Canada* 9:1 (Spring 1988), 68, 71

148 Frank Rasky, 'Gay Ninetie's Belle is still kickin',' Toronto *Star*, 11 May 1978, C6

149 Souvenir program, Great War Veteran's 'Benefit Night,' *Irene*, Monday, 12 May (1924)

150 M.D., 'The Little Theatres: The Ottawa Drama League,' *Canadian Bookman*, February 1923, 32

151 Jeffery Williams, *Byng of Vimy, General and Governor General* (London: Leo Cooper / Secker & Warburg, 1983), 297–8. I am indebted to Paula Vachon, archivist-librarian at Rideau Hall, and to Professor James Noonan, Carleton University, for research assistance with *Oriental Ottawa*. See also Colonel H. Willis-

O'Connor, *Inside Government House* (Toronto: The Ryerson Press, 1954), 22–3, and cast photo, p. 37.

152 Nathaniel A. Benson, 'Varsity's Little Theatre,' *University of Toronto Alumni Bulletin*, February 1952, 6

153 O'Neill, 'Checklist,' *Canadian Drama* 9:2, 381

154 G.N., '*Whosit*, Hart House Theatre,' *Canadian Forum* 10 (March 1930), 226–7

155 Information about the various campus revues is drawn from *Dramatis Personae: Amateur Theatre at the University of Toronto 1879–1939*, prepared to accompany a University of Toronto Archives exhibit, 6 October 1986–5 January 1987, 4, 10, 11.

156 The *All-Varsity Revue* was sponsored by the Students' Administrative Council (SAC) and performed at Hart House Theatre. Musical arrangements were by Bob Cringan, Bud Priestman, Cliff Braggins, and Ida Mae Nicholson. I am grateful to Norman Jewison's assistant Liz Broden for this information.

157 Francean Campbell Rich, 'Keith MacMillan,' *Encyclopedia of Music in Canada* (1981), 584

158 Erdmute Waldhauer, *Drama at Queens from Its Beginnings to 1991* (Kingston: Typecast, 1991), 24

159 Leonard R.N. Ashley, *The History of the Theatre* (New York: Crown Publishers, 1968), 848

160 Arts and Letters Club Scrapbooks for 1925, courtesy of archivist, Ray Peringer

161 Michael Spence mentioned this at Herman Voaden's funeral, 2 July 1991

162 Arts and Letters Club Scrapbooks

163 B.K. Sandwell, 'The Town Tonics,' *Saturday Night*, 14 April 1934, 23

164 Jane Mallett's scrapbook materials, courtesy of Araby Lockhart

165 Frederic Manning, 'Touring Is Fun,' *Saturday Night*, 12 December 1942, 38–9

166 Nancy Pyper, 'Masquers and Revuers,' *Saturday Night*, 7 May 1938, 9

167 Scott McClellan, *Straw Hats and Greasepaint: 50 Years of Theatre in the Summer Colony; Vol. 1: The Actors' Colony Story, 1934–42*, (Bracebridge, Ont.: Muskoka Publications, 1984), appendix, 52. William S. Atkinson wrote it first as a three-act farce in 1926. See O'Neill, 'Checklist,' *Canadian Drama* 8:2 (1982), 186–7

168 O'Neill, 'Checklist,' *Canadian Drama* 9:2 (1983), 437; telephone interview with Everett Staples, 18 December 1989

169 McClellan, *Straw Hats and Greasepaint*, 49

170 Robert B. Scott, 'A Study of English Canadian Dramatic Literature 1900–1930,' M.Phil. thesis, Graduate Centre for Study of Drama, University of Toronto, September 1968, 139

171 7 May 1938, 9

172 Personal interview with Constance Vernon, 12 August 1979, Canadian *Army Show* reunion, Royal York Hotel

173 Frances Douglas, 'Some Notes on Masquers Overseas Tour,' *Canadian Review of Music and Art* 5 (February 1946), 39–42; O'Neill, 'Checklist,' *Canadian Drama* 9:2, 453

174 John Huston, 'A History of the Eaton Operatic Society 1932–1965,' unpublished
    essay submitted to the author, University of Toronto, 1985, 1
175 Personal interview with Charles Jolliffe, 21 November 1977
176 Huston, 'History of the Eaton Operatic Society,' 5–6
177 Don Sedgwick, 'Eaton Operatic Society,' *Encyclopedia of Music in Canada* (1981),
    292
178 Huston, 'History of the Eaton Operatic Society,' 9–10. I am indebted, too, to
    Warren Hughes of Costume House, who informed me that while the Toronto
    chapter of the Gilbert and Sullivan Society began producing in April 1967 (with *The
    Mikado*), they had started 20 years earlier, in December 1947, as an appreciaton
    society.
179 Toby Gordon Ryan, *Stage Left: Canadian Theatre in the Thirties* (Toronto: CTR
    Publications, 1981), 94, 193
180 Ibid., 146
181 Ibid., 187–90, photo 192
182 *The Brock Bibliography of Published Plays in English 1766–1978*, ed. Anton
    Wagner (Toronto: Playwrights Press, 1980), 334
183 Corelli, 'The Toronto that used to be,' Toronto *Star*, 24 February 1964, 7
184 'Tremendous audience applauds big pageant,' Toronto *Star*, 10 August 1927, 21
185 O'Neill, 'Checklist,' *Canadian Drama*, 9:2, 476. *The Brock Bibliography*, 108, 267.
    Ridout was assisted by E.J. Pratt, Ernest MacMillan, and others.
186 O'Neill, 'Checklist,' *Canadian Drama*, 9:2, 409, 477, 489
187 Raymond Card, 'Drama in Toronto: The Forgotten Years 1919–1939,' *The English
    Quarterly* 6:1 (Spring 1973), 78–9
188 *The Brock Bibliography*, 88, 203
189 Eugene Miller, 'Les Allen,' *Encyclopedia of Music in Canada* (1981), 15. Obituary
    notice: 'Cy Mack, 74, radio entertainer,' Toronto *Star*, 16 June 1979, C26
190 Dick Brown, 'Knock, Knock. Who's There?,' Toronto *Star Weekend Magazine*,
    1 November 1975, 28 and 30
191 E. Austin Weir, *The Struggle for National Broadcasting in Canada* (Toronto,
    Montreal: McClelland and Stewart, 1965), 275, photo opposite p. 128
192 O'Neill, 'Checklist,' *Canadian Drama*, 8:2 (1982), 198
193 Ripley's 'Believe It or Not,' Toronto *Star*, 1 February 1986, F10. Russell, *Double
    Take*, 117–18. George Gamester, 'Scratch 'n' Laugh tickled Old T.O.,' Toronto
    Star, 19 July 1989, A2
194 Unidentified newspaper advertisement
195 Program for City Hall, Yorkton [Saskatchewan], 7 and 8 February 1934. Personal
    letter to the author from Mrs Jody Flye (née 'Baby Joyce' McLachlan), Edmonton,
    7 November 1977
196 See recollections of Robert H. Hahn (b. 1920), *None of the Roads Were Paved*
    (Markham, Ont.: Fitzhenry and Whiteside, 1985); photographic section after
    p. 141

197 *Curtain Call*, January 1941, 3, and May/June 1941, 3. See also Amelia Hall, *Life Before Stratford* (Toronto: Dundurn Press, 1989), 46.
198 *Theatre Canada* 37 (November/December 1957), 3. See also Hall, *Life Before Stratford*, 47.
199 O'Neill, 'Checklist,' *Canadian Drama* 9:2, 405
200 Judy Steed, 'Premier Bob: He's not just another Rae of sunshine,' Toronto *Star*, 29 September 1990, A1, A10
201 George Gamester, 'Names in the News: Whatever became of ... Jackie Rae,' Toronto *Star*, 24 October 1978, A17, and telephone interview with Jackie Rae, 27 July 1992.
202 Constance Olsheski, *Pantages Theatre, Rebirth of a Landmark* (Toronto: Key Porter Books, 1989), 63 (advertisement). Laurie Deans, 'That's Entertainment: The Vaudeville Kid comes back and finds a townful of talent,' Toronto *Sunday Star*, City Magazine, 15 January 1978, 7
203 Mark Miller, 'Jackie Rae,' *Encyclopedia of Music in Canada* (1981), 792
204 Gamester, 'Whatever became of Jackie Rae,' and telephone interview with Rae
205 Larry Zolf, 'The longest debauch in Canadian history,' Toronto *Star*, 11 January 1992, F12
206 Mitchell Smyth, '"Boy Shirley Temple" remembers TO,' Toronto *Star*, 22 February 1987, D4
207 Gould, *Entertaining Canadians*, 34
208 Material culled from Smyth article, Gould entry, and George Gamester, 'Names in the News,' Toronto *Star*, 26 April 1975, C1, and 3 March 1980, D6. The *Encyclopedia of Music in Canada* (1981) erroneously says Bobbie Breen died in England in 1972 (see 'Prodigies,' 777c, and 'United States of America,' 951e). Smyth's interview with him occurred in 1987.
209 Revival written by George Frederick Cameron, music by Oscar Telgmann (Kingston: Henderson, 1889). See Erdmute Waldhauer, *Grand Theatre 1879–1979* (Kingston: The Grand Theatre, 1979), 10–13; Richard Plant, 'Drama in English,' *Oxford Companion to Canadian Theatre*, 153; Ross Stuart, 'Musical Theatre,' *Encyclopedia of Music in Canada* (1981), 656, and Patricia Beharriell, 'Oscar Telgmann,' 908. More than 150 performances were given over 40 years. It was still being produced in the 1920s.
210 'Musical Theatre,' *Encyclopedia of Music in Canada* (1981), 657, and Stephen Willis, 'William Dichmont,' 269
211 O'Neill, 'Checklist,' *Canadian Drama* 9:2, 460–1. Music for Servos's operatic dramas was by Don Sebastian de L'Estrilla, a pseudonym for Hubert Shorse.
212 Ibid., 410
213 O'Neill, 'Checklist,' *Canadian Drama* 8:2, 194–5
214 Ibid., *Canadian Drama* 9:2, 446–7
215 *The Brock Bibliography* (1980), 173

216 O'Neill, 'Checklist,' *Canadian Drama* 8:2, 218

217 Ibid., 9:2, 451

218 John Beckwith, 'Sir Ernest MacMillan,' *Encyclopedia of Music in Canada* (1981), 582–3. See O'Neill, 'Checklist,' 9:2, 409, for *Sweet Marjoram*.

219 O'Neill, 'Checklist,' 9:2, 434 and 386 respectively

220 Ibid., 444–5

221 Famous Players Theatres, *What's New?*, July 1952 and January 1953, 2. Rica McLean Farquharson, 'Wartime Drama in the British Empire: Canada,' *The Theatre Annual*, New York (1944), 16

222 Anna Russell, *I'm Not Making This Up You Know* (Toronto: Macmillan of Canada, 1985), 96

223 Interview with theatre historian Agatha Leonard, 22 September 1977

224 Anton Wagner, 'Infinite Variety or a Canadian "National" Theatre: Roly Young and the Toronto Civic Theatre Associaton, 1945–1949,' *Theatre History in Canada* 9:2 (Fall 1988), 178

225 Agatha Leonard interview

226 Obituary notice, 'Edward Bromley, entertained servicemen as singer-comedian,' Toronto *Star*, 11 May 1983, A12. See also 'Best ever, declare crowds at opening show of revue,' *Hamilton Spectator*, 1 September 1942, 11.

227 O'Neill, 'Checklist,' *Canadian Drama* 9:2, 482

228 Don Harron at the Dora Mavor Moore memorial service, Sunday, 27 May 1979

229 Ross Laver, 'The Ties of Blood: War Made Canada Change Direction,' *Maclean's*, 4 September 1989, 42

230 Material culled from advertisement, 'Soldier-actors make hit in ritzin' the Blitz Show,' *The Globe* (Toronto), 15 July 1941, 20; Rose Macdonald, '"Ritzin' the Blitz" revue bright and tuneful show,' *The Telegram* (Toronto), 15 July 1941, 31; and the Royal Alexandra Theatre program.

231 Sam Levine, 'RCAF Blackouts,' *Encyclopedia of Music in Canada* (1981), 795

232 Rica McLean Farquharson, *The Theatre Annual (1944)*, 17. I am indebted also to *All Clear* performer Marguerite Fournier (née Le Blond) for an interview 9 August 1986 and for access to her scrapbooks; and to Elaine Campbell for material from the RCAF paper *Wings*. Much information was drawn from Anon., 'Spread Joy up to the Maximum,' *Wings Abroad*, 28 June 1945, 4, 8. See also David Gardner, 'The Blackouts,' *Oxford Companion to Canadian Theatre*, 53.

233 Cast drawn from *The Army Show* program

234 John Berke, 'The Army Show,' *Encyclopedia of Music in Canada* (1981), 32

235 Clyde Gilmour, 'How Wayne and Shuster Helped Win the War,' *Leisure Ways* (April 1985), 13

236 Stewart James, *Stewart James in Print: The First Fifty Years*, ed. Howard Lyons and Allan Slaight (Toronto: Jogestja Ltd, 1989), 383

237 Gilmour, 'How Wayne and Shuster Helped Win the War,' 14

238 George Gamester, 'Names in the News:' What ever became of Robert Farnon?
    Toronto *Star*, 10 March 1977, D1.

239 Kenneth Bagnell, 'Up to Their Old Tricks,' *Imperial Oil Review*, Fall 1991, 16. See
    also James, *Stewart James In Print*, 211–13, 359–61, 383–5.

240 'Rhythm Rodeo' interview with Ron Leonard at the Canadian Army Show Reunion,
    Royal York Hotel, Toronto, 12 August 1979. Interview with James Hozack about
    his *Army Show* memories (17 February 1977). See also Russ Whitebone, *Showman:
    The Russ Whitebone Story* (Fredericton, NB: Fiddlehead Poetry Books and Goose
    Lane Editions, 1986), 82–3 re *Rhythm Rodeo*.

241 Ruth Phillips, 'The History of the Royal Canadian Navy's World War II Show *Meet
    The Navy*,' MA thesis, York University, March 1973, 6

242 Interview with Robert Goodier, 1 June 1979. See also Beverley Baxter, 'This Was
    Something More Than a Show,' from London *Evening Standard* in Phillips, 'His-
    tory of *Meet the Navy*,' after p. 27.

243 Phillips, 'History of *Meet the Navy*,' 14, 16, 20

244 Canadian Press release, '"Meet the Navy" Resounding Hit at Hippodrome,'
    1 February 1945, included in Phillips, 'History of *Meet the Navy*,' after p. 27

245 Ibid., 24–7

246 Advertisement in Famous Players' *What's New?*, October 1946, 12; photos from
    Meet the Navy on p. 7

247 Margaret Brenton, as told to Eva Watt, 'My Visit to Korea,' *The Scarboro Mail*,
    7 April 1955, 1, 2

248 O'Neill, 'Checklist,' *Canadian Drama* 9:2, 428, 405. *The Bytown Revue* was
    written by Graham McInnes and Saul Rae.

249 John H. Yocom, 'London Little Theatre Gay Revue Ends Season in New
    Playhouse,' *Saturday Night*, 8 June 1946, 30–1

250 Wagner, *Theatre History in Canada / Histoire du théâtre au Canada*, 9:2 (Fall
    1988), 191–2

251 John Gray, 'More Laughs to the Square Revue,' *Maclean's*, 5 May 1962, 52

252 Robert Fulford, 'On Satire: The Country Changed, but Spring Thaw Didn't,'
    Maclean's, 4 May 1963, 57

253 *Vic Report* 5.1 (Fall 1976), 5

254 Fulford, 'On Satire,' 57–8

255 'Theatre,' *Saturday Night*, 28 February 1950, 21; Margaret Ness, 'The Theatre Tips
    a New Straw Hat,' *Saturday Night*, 4 July 1950, 9; and 'End-of-Season Round-up,'
    Saturday Night, 12 September 1950, 22

256 Jack Winstanley, 'George Formby carried on love affair with Canada,' Toronto
    Star, 22 March 1986, F8

257 Maurice Lucow, '$75,000 gamble pays off for Toronto Angels,' *Financial Post*,
    9 August 1952, 7; Tom Patterson and Allan Gould, *First Stage: The Making of the
    Stratford Festival* (Toronto: McClelland and Stewart, 1987), 82, 84

258 Lucow, '$75,000 gamble,' 7

259 Alex Barris, 'Barris Beat,' *Globe and Mail*, 19 June 1956, 20, and advertisement, ibid., 22 June 1956, 9

260 Brooks Atkinson, 'Theatre: Musical frolic,' *New York Times*, 11 November 1958, 24

261 Margaret Ness, 'Now We're Writing Musical Comedies,' *Saturday Night* 67:38 (28 June 1952), 12. See also Herbert Whittaker, 'Showbusiness,' *Globe and Mail*, 10 June 1957, 30, and 'Musical revived' *Globe and Mail*, 26 October 1957, 13.

262 Ness, 'Now We're Writing Musical Comedies,' 12

263 O'Neill 'Checklist,' *Canadian Drama* 8:2, 267

264 Mavor Moore, 'Who Is History?,' speech given at Association for Canadian Theatre History conference, Victoria, BC, 27 May 1970

265 Sid Adilman, 'Eye on Entertainment: Mavor Moore's musical in its 20th year,' Toronto *Star*, 31 December 1975, D10. Peter Perrin, 'Mavor Moore,' *Encyclopedia of Music in Canada* (1981), 642

266 Martha Harron, *Don Harron: A Parent Contradiction* (Toronto: Collins Publishers, 1988), 195–6

267 Gordon Sinclair, 'Memories,' *Once Upon a Century: 100 Year History of the 'Ex'* (Toronto: John H. Robinson Publishing, 1978), 33

268 Alex Barris, *The Pierce-Arrow Showroom Is Leaking: An Insider's View of the CBC* (Toronto: Ryerson Press, 1969), 95–9

269 Mark Miller, 'Tommy Common,' *Encyclopedia of Music in Canada* (1981), 209. See also Peter Goddard, 'Fallen singing star Tommy Common a Canadian tragedy,' Toronto *Star*, 16 August 1985, A2

270 Helen McNamara, 'Phyllis Marshall,' *Encyclopedia of Music in Canada* (1981), 597. See also Stephen Franklin, 'Phyllis Marshall's Swinging Comeback,' *Weekend Magazine*, 21 November 1964, 10–12, and telephone interview, 9 November 1992.

271 Gould, *Entertaining Canadians*, 56

272 Mark Miller, Peter Goddard, 'Joyce Sullivan,' *Encyclopedia of Music in Canada* (1981), 899

273 Sid Adilman, 'Eye on Entertainment: Canadian teen who sang with Elvis starts her comeback with new disc,' Toronto *Star*, 17 May 1992, C2. See also Helen McNamara, 'Don Wright,' *Encyclopedia of Music in Canada* (1981), 1015.

274 Telephone interview with Eric House, 10 November 1992

275 Harron, *A Parent Contradiction*, 188

276 Herbert Whittaker, 'Showbusiness,' *Globe and Mail*, 26 October 1957, 13

277 John Kraglund, 'Is Vancouver's loss Toronto's gain?,' *Globe and Mail*, 25 July 1959, 15; Louise Bresky, ' "Jubilee" takes swipe at Tories, culture,' Toronto *Star*, 6 July 1959, 20

278 Ross Stuart, 'The Crest Controversy,' *Canadian Theatre Review* 7 (Summer 1975), 10. Nathan Cohen, 'The mirthless birthday,' Toronto *Star*, 5 January 1959, 19

279 Ron Evans, 'Clap Hands – But Rarely,' *The Telegram*, 15 September 1959, 36

280 The 1959 cast of *Clap Hands* included Araby Lockhart, Betty Leighton, Sheila

Billing, Eric House, Al Pearce, and David Gardner; the 1962–3 London cast featured Araby Lockhart, Corinne Conley, Eric House, Dave Broadfoot, Jack Creley, and Peter Mews, with Assistant Stage Manager Douglas Chamberlain stepping in on occasion.

281 Roly Young, 'Rambling round with Roly,' 'Wanted – one opera house,' *The Mail and Empire*, 4 February 1936, 12, and 'If I had a million,' ibid., 2 June 1936, 12

282 Hugh Walker, *The O'Keefe Centre* (Toronto: Key Porter Books, 1991), appendix E, 287–91

283 Ruth Pincoe, 'Clement Hambourg,' *Encyclopedia of Music in Canada* (1981), 407–8. Banuta Rubess and Nic Gotham, *Boom, Baby, Boom!* in *Canadian Theatre Review* 58 (Spring 1989)

284 Pierre Berton, 'Toronto the good becomes T.O. the naughty,' Toronto *Star*, 3 August 1991, E3. For consulate reference see Victor Paddy, 'Writers' Talk,' *The [Imperial Oil] Review*, Fall 1988, 10. For information on coffee-houses, see *Encyclopedia of Music in Canada* (1981), 205.

285 Paddy, 'Writers' Talk,' 10

286 Blaik Kirby, 'The mother of cabaret, Sylvia Shawn is back,' *Globe and Mail*, 24 November 1977, 19

287 Herbert Whittaker, 'Showbusiness: Dell revue is a pleasure,' *Globe and Mail*, 23 April 1965, 11

288 McKenzie Porter 'pays a ding-dong visit to the Dell ...' *The Telegram*, 26 April 1965, 5

289 Herbert Whittaker, 'Showbusiness: A bit of everything from Cambridge,' *Globe and Mail*, 18 January 1966, 13

290 Urjo Kareda, '"The Bell Tolls" for mediocrity,' *The Varsity*, 27 January 1967, Review Section, 2

291 Urjo Kareda, 'Miss Stapley and Mr Chudley announce T.O. for Two,' *Globe and Mail*, 6 January 1968, 24

292 22 August, p. 29

293 Blaik Kirby, 'The boys in the Dell: A clumsy costume parade,' *Globe and Mail*, 12 August 1969, 11. *She-rade* was also known as *Facad* and *Les Girls* when it played at the Global Village.

294 Diane Dupuy with Liane Heller, *Dare to Dream* (Toronto: Key Porter Books, 1988), 38, mentions Ms Dupuy spending a rehearsal month with Mikulas Kravjansky, the director of the Black Box Theatre.

295 21 March, p. 77

296 'Open Speakeasy theatre in Toronto, sans booze,' *Variety*, 20 April 1960, 149

297 Eric S. Rump, 'Drama: English Canada,' *Canadian Annual Review for 1964* (Toronto: University of Toronto Press, 1965), 457

298 Joyce Doolittle and Zina Barnieh, *A Mirror of Our Dreams* (Vancouver: Talonbooks, 1979), 85

299 Gould, 'Rich Little,' *Entertaining Canadians*, 168–9

300 Richard Friedman, 'Canadian's a musical medic: Raymond Jessel's lyrics keep Broadway show going,' Toronto *Star*, 24 July 1979, D3

301 Elaine Keillor, 'Marian Grudeff,' *Encyclopedia of Music in Canada* (1981), 395–6

302 Cecil Smith and Glenn Litton, *Musical Comedy in America* (New York: Theatre Arts Books, 1981), 254

303 21 January 1965, 11; *Musical Comedy in America*, 254

304 Emory Lewis (*Cue*, 23 February 1965) cited in Keillor, 'Grudeff,' 396

305 Gordon Stoneham, 'Too many bits, pieces leave vaguely sour taste to Love and Maple Syrup,' *Ottawa Citizen*, 9 July 1969, 25; William Littler, 'Beavers could do it better than Love and Maple Syrup,' *Toronto Star*, 9 July 1969, 24

306 8 January 1970, 47

307 *Scene* 7:35 (8–14 November, 1970), 20

3 Summer Festivals and Theatres

ROSS STUART

Summer theatre in Ontario is Neil Simon and Shakespeare. It is student theatre, summer stock, outdoor pageants, and world-renowned festivals. Performances take place in parks, barns, historic opera houses, and modern theatres. There have been theatrical performances in the summer months for more than a century, beginning in the 1880s with vaudeville on the Toronto Islands and spectacular pageants at the Canadian National Exhibition.[1] However, summer theatre as we know it today really began in the 1930s in the Muskokas. In the late 1940s professional summer theatres opened in resorts from the Thousand Islands in the east to Crystal Beach in the west, from Jackson's Point, Peterborough, and Port Carling in the north to Niagara Falls in the south. The influence of the Stratford Festival and later of the Shaw Festival destroyed these strawhat theatres. The new summer theatres of the 1960s and 1970s were community-supported, non-profit ventures with unique mandates: for example, Blyth for new Canadian plays and Theatre Plus (Toronto) for challenging plays from the modern international repertoire.

Summer theatre never flourished in Toronto. Ernest Rawley, manager of the Royal Alexandra Theatre, following the earlier example of the Edward H. Robins Players' summers in residence from the end of the First World War until 1922, produced seasons of summer stock from 1940 to 1948, presenting everything from Shakespeare to operetta.[2] When Rawley ceased summer operations, Earle Grey, a Dublin-born actor and director, and his actress wife, Mary Godwin, decided Toronto needed a serious summer theatre. The Earle Grey Players first began performing outdoors in the quadrangle at Trinity College on the University of Toronto campus in 1946.[3] Although the Earle Grey Shakespeare Festival, as it was known after 1949, lasted until 1958, it was never a match for the more prestigious Stratford Festival. Musicals were no more successful. Toronto's Melody Fair (see p. 193) opened in 1951 in a

Earle Grey Players Shakespeare Festival, *The Merchant of Venice*, North Terrace,
Trinity College, University of Toronto, 1951. Ontario has a history of outdoor or tent
Shakespeare from Ben Greet's innovative early-twentieth-century tours to more recent
park festivals in Ottawa, Toronto, Hamilton, and elsewhere.

1600-seat tent at the Dufferin Park raceway, and closed four years later,
housed indoors in the Mutual Street Arena.[4] Although Canadian-owned,
Melody Fair was modelled after the American chain of summer musical
theatres and employed Americans as directors and leading performers,
supported by Canadians, many of them drawn from the Royal Conservatory of Music. Robert Goulet was in the company in 1954. A similarly
unlucky endeavour, Music Fair, 1958–60, performed in a 2000-seat tent
in Toronto's suburban Dixie Plaza.

Summer theatre took root in the countryside, in cottage areas and
resorts. The earliest ventures tended to be rustic and amateur, like the
one at Bon Echo (now a provincial park) near Tweed. Performances
were given in the evenings for guests at a hotel run by Flora Macdonald
Denison, journalist, novelist, and suffragette.[5] They were produced by
her son, playwright Merrill Denison, who took charge of the hotel after

Babs Hitchmann and John Holden, Actors' Colony Theatre, c. 1936–7

his mother's death in 1922 and continued to operate it until 1928. Merrill Denison first launched his backwoods theatre in 1918 at the cost of nineteen dollars. Each summer there were three performances a week from mid-July until late in August. The audience sat outdoors in semicircular rows around a rough wooden platform that was hung with simple muslin stage curtains and lit by four floodlights. Performances had an impromptu *commedia dell' arte* flavour. The actors were members of the hotel's staff who had been hired in part for their theatrical ability. Guests were also encouraged to join in the merriment. The plays, which Denison supervised and occasionally helped script in collaboration with his actors, were topical skits about the lodge and its residents. Denison envisioned Bon Echo becoming a Canadian version of the Lake Chautauqua cultural centre, but that was not to be. When Denison gave up managing the hotel, its summer theatrical activity ended.

John Holden helped inaugurate what has already amounted to over half a century of theatre in the Muskoka Lakes region when he founded his own company, the Actors' Colony Theatre, in 1934.[6] Holden, an experienced actor-director, established his model for Canadian straw-hat theatres in the tiny Muskoka community of Bala, about equidistant from Port Carling and Gravenhurst. Holden chose Bala because his adopted sister and her husband owned an inn there where his company could stay free of charge. Bala was also the home of Dunn's Pavilion, a popular dancehall for big bands that had helped to make Bala an entertainment centre for prosperous summer residents from many miles around. He turned the town's hall, Victoria Hall, into a makeshift theatre and during the first season offered three performances of a different play each week; attendance totalled twelve hundred. One production was Holden's own comedy, *City Limits*.

Of the ten performers who made up a typical Holden company, most were young radio actors or people with stock experience, such as Eric Clavering, Babs Hitchmann, Bob Thompson, Lauriel Wood, Muriel Dean, Leonard Howe, Ella McBride, Donald Stewart, and Ray Phelps. Isabel Price, a founding member of the company and the only person other than Holden to return every season, acted and served as business manager. In later seasons Robert Christie, Jane Mallett, Josephine Barrington, Budd Knapp, Pam Haney, Thomas Palmer, Lorraine Bate, Betty Boylen, Wayne Van Sherk, Everett Staples, and Grace Mathews joined the company as replacements for those who decided not to face the rigours of another summer of stock.

Some of Holden's first company appeared in plays in Toronto during the off-season, but they were back in Bala for the summer of 1935. The ten-play repertoire contained several recent Broadway successes. Over the years Bala audiences saw plays such as *The Show-off, Elizabeth Sleeps Out, A Wise Child, Blind Alley, The Patsy, Petticoat Fever, Wind and the Rain, Rope, Accent on Youth,* and *There's Always Juliet.* The second summer season ended with a successful special performance at the Royal Muskoka Hotel, which was followed up the next year with regular Monday evening performances at the fashionable Bigwin Inn resort on Lake of Bays.

The publicity manager of the Bigwin Inn was a friend of the influential Richardson family, owners of the Dominion Theatre in Winnipeg. After a visit east to see Holden's work, the manager of the Dominion engaged the company for a season of winter stock in Winnipeg, and so the John Holden Players, as they were now called, began their inaugural season in Winnipeg in September 1936, becoming in the process the last remaining professional stock company in Canada. The Winnipeg engagement proved a success; a planned eight-week season stretched to twenty-four weeks and lasted until March. Holden and his actors then returned to Bala, with the regular weekly engagement at the Bigwin Inn, for a ten-week season.

After a second Winnipeg engagement that lasted thirty weeks, Holden needed to recruit several new actors for the summer in Bala. He also renovated Victoria Hall, enlarging the wings and improving the lighting. However, set designer Everett Staples still had to cope with peculiar visual problems like the two pillars in the centre of the stage. Following his next Winnipeg season, Holden brought ten new faces to Bala, including William Needles. In fact, there were only three hold-overs: Price, Staples, and Holden himself. The 1939 half-hour performances were broadcast nationally over the Richardson-owned radio station CJRC in Winnipeg.

The 1939–40 season was the last one for the John Holden Players in Winnipeg, although they continued to perform in Bala for the next two summers. Among Holden's last crop of new actors were Peter Mews, Mavor Moore, and Austin Willis. Attendance in 1940 totalled twenty-five thousand. The final production at Bala and the Bigwin Inn was *Haywire*, an original revue. But Holden felt that he could no longer work with so many of his actors going off to join service shows. He returned to Bala for the last time in the summer of 1942, presenting a season of movies.

Port Carling was a town of about five hundred, but there was a summer population of more than fifty thousand in the triangle between Bracebridge, Gravenhurst, and Port Carling. It was in this picturesque rocky area of the Muskoka Lakes that the Straw Hat Players, Ontario's best-known summer stock theatre, was born.[7] Its roots, like those of other

Canadian theatrical ventures of that period, were in Hart House Theatre, at the University of Toronto. Hart House was run by the legendary Robert Gill, and the students that he trained in the period after the Second World War were the nucleus of the contemporary Canadian theatre.

In 1947 Gill took some of his Hart House protégés, including Donald and Murray Davis and Charmion King, with him when he went home to the United States to direct at the Woodstock (New York) Summer Theatre. With their training at Hart House and that brief introduction to summer theatre, the Davises and their sister Barbara Chilcott organized the Straw Hat Players, and recruited fellow students Araby Lockhart, Eric House, and Ted Follows. Like other children of wealthy parents, the Davises had spent their summers in the Muskokas and that was where they chose to establish their theatre. Muskoka in the 1940s was close to the big city of Toronto, but was also a tranquil self-contained world that still attracted an annual migration of summer residents from as far away as New York. It was a natural spot for summer theatre, with a large potential audience, many of them accustomed to attending theatre, and little competition.

There had been the Bala Players in 1947, advertised as Ontario's only producing summer theatre.[8] Featured performers were Cosette Lee, Mack Inglis, and Charles McBride, who then left the area to found the Holloway Bay Playhouse at Crystal Beach on Lake Erie in 1948. The Rotary Club of Bracebridge sponsored the Mark Shawn Players, led by Mark and Sylvia Shawn. The company appeared at the Town Hall in Bracebridge in the summer of 1948, performing, among other plays, *Night Must Fall*. Henry Kaplan directed for the Mark Shawn Players; William Hutt made his professional début with them.

The Davises launched the Straw Hat Players in 1948. With the assistance of producer Brian Doherty, their company, which included Barbara Hamilton and Beth Gillanders from Vancouver, a veteran of the Everyman Theatre and Theatre Under the Stars, played a series of one-night stands around Lake Simcoe and the Muskokas before finally settling in for a season alternating between Huntsville, Gravenhurst, and Port Carling. Home base became Port Carling's 280-seat Memorial Hall, a building originally constructed in 1905, but subsequently extensively remodeled in 1952. The melodrama *The Drunkard* successfully opened a season of weekly summer stock featuring mainly tried-and-true comedies (*Papa Is All*, *Blithe Spirit*, and *Dear Ruth*). Robert Gill, under the pseudonym Donald Leroy, directed one play. The season ended with a national tour of *The Drunkard*, again organized by Brian Doherty.

In 1949 James Hozack, the business manager of Hart House Theatre, began the first of many seasons as manager of the Straw Hat Players.

Set design for *Mandragola*, designer Carolyn Souter, Straw Hat Players

The company stopped performing in Huntsville because it was felt that the exhausting forty-mile journey could not be justified for one performance a week. Instead half the week was spent in Port Carling and the other in Gravenhurst. The second season ended with another extended tour, this time of an original revue called *There Goes Yesterday*, featuring John Pratt, Murray Matheson, Murray Davis, Charmion King, and Araby Lockhart. In 1950 Pratt left to join Brian Doherty in running the Red Barn Theatre.

The Straw Hat Players continued to divide their time between Port Carling and Gravenhurst until 1952, when two separate companies were formed, one in each town. Peter Potter, the director of Glasgow's Citizens' Theatre ran one company, and Russell Graves, a teacher from Florida State University, ran the other. The Davises went on to found the Crest Theatre in Toronto late in 1952, and what with the Crest and acting engagements in Stratford, New York, and England, Donald Davis had little time to devote to the Straw Hat Players. Murray Davis had the bulk of the responsibility for both the Straw Hat Players and the Crest Theatre. Increasingly in this period, the Davises left the running of the summer company to others.

Pierre Lefevre and John Blatchley came from England to serve as principal directors in 1953 and 1954. Henry Kaplan, George McGowan, and Brian Maller from the Crest also directed. The Straw Hat Players were rich in talent: Max Helpmann first appeared in 1952 and both directed and acted; Robertson Davies directed *Ten Nights in a Bar-room* in 1955 and his own comedies *Fortune, My Foe* and *Overlaid* were produced in 1950 and 1952 respectively. Other performers included Kate Reid, Toby Robins, David Gardner, Kay Hawtrey, Gordon Pinsent, Ken Pogue, Honor Blackman, Deborah Cass, Dawn Greenhalgh, Amelia Hall, Jennifer Phipps, and Jackie Burroughs.

By 1952, seasons had lengthened to ten weeks. Although there was the occasional Shaw or Shakespeare, summer audiences preferred light comedies, and the 1954 repertoire was typical: Giraudoux's *Amphitryon 38*; a Russian farce, *Squaring the Circle*; Coward's *Fallen Angels*, Roussin's *The Little Hut*, Ustinov's *The Indifferent Shepherd*, Rattigan's *The Deep Blue Sea*, Machiavelli's *Mandragola*, and *Straw Hat '54*, a revue. Marian Grudeff, who later co-wrote the music and lyrics for Broadway's *Baker Street*, was musical director for the revue, which starred Jack Medhurst and Barbara Hamilton.

With Donald at Stratford and Murray coping with the Crest, the Davises finally relinquished control of the Straw Hat Players after the 1955 season. However, Port Carling's Memorial Hall did not remain empty. Two of the Crest's backstage staff (and Hart House Theatre veterans) William Bennett and Wilf Pegg put together a company like the first one, using many students, and presented a season. Meg Hogarth, who had played Ophelia in Robert Gill's Hart House *Hamlet*, was featured along with Donald Sutherland, Fred Euringer, John Douglas, Timothy Findley, and Rex Southgate. Joseph Furst was the principal director for a season that included such plays as *The Rainmaker*, *The Male Animal*, *Sabrina Fair*, *My Three Angels*, *I Am a Camera*, *The Tender Trap*, *East Lynne*, and Araby Lockhart's *As I See It*. Gravenhurst remained dark that season and the company performed only in Port Carling. The following year, L.C. (Toby) Tobias and James Hozack took over Port Carling, while a different management failed to complete a season in Gravenhurst.

In 1958 another Davis restored the name of the Straw Hat Players to the Muskokas. William Davis, a cousin of Donald and Murray, and his friend Karl Jaffray, both then students at the University of Toronto, recruited a company. Donald Davis opened the season by directing *Castles in the Air*, and Murray Davis closed it two months later, directing *Papa Is All*. Although the season was light and undemanding, it did succeed in re-establishing the Straw Hat banner in Port Carling. During

Alfred Mulock and Steffi Lock, founders of the Red Barn Theatre, on the set of *Voice of the Turtle*, July 1949

RED BARN THEATRE

Drawing of the Red Barn Theatre (1973)

their time in the Muskokas, Davis and Jaffray restored the two-company concept, with one group playing in Port Carling and another in Gravenhurst, with limited tours to other centres. Ron Hartmann and Peter Deering directed and actors included Patricia Carroll Brown, Timothy Findley, Nancy Kerr, Gordon Pinsent, Austin Willis, and Ken Pogue. *Private Lives, The Long, the Short and the Tall, Marriage Go Round, Every Bed Is Narrow, Wedding Breakfast,* and *Bus Stop* were some of the plays produced.

Davis and Jaffray continued to run the Straw Hat Players until the end of the 1961 season. Then, once again, the Straw Hat Players name was reinvented as an essentially university company, which was led for the next three years by a team headed by artistic director Peter Wylde, a modern languages student at the University of Toronto. Another young University of Toronto graduate, Alan Hughes, took over as producer at Port Carling for two seasons, 1965 and 1966, hiring Nicholas Ayre to direct young professionals and students. Next came a company called Theatre 21, which kept theatre alive in Port Carling for three more years, primarily under the direction of Edwin Stephenson. In 1969 Stephenson recruited a young actor-director from Timmins who had been trained in

New York, Michael Ayoub, and his actress-wife Mary Bellows. They would write the next chapter in the history of theatre in the Muskokas.

With the success of the original Straw Hat Players, similar ventures began at Lake Simcoe, in the Thousand Islands, in the Kawarthas, in Midland, and in the Niagara Peninsula. The Red Barn, the International Players, the Peterborough Summer Theatre, the Niagara Barn Theatre, and the Niagara Falls Summer Theatre were very similar in repertoire and purpose, and featured many of the same actors and directors.

Jackson's Point on Lake Simcoe was never as fashionable as the Muskokas, although it was a busy summer resort. But the Red Barn Summer Theatre, which opened there in 1948 in an actual nineteenth-century barn, converted into a 360-seat theatre, never seemed to succeed, no matter who was in charge or what was being presented. Producer Alfie Mulock brought in a company of Americans, supported by Canadians, and hoped to perform year-round.[9] However, by the end of his first and last season, the Americans were gone and an all-Canadian company, featuring Johnny Wayne and Frank Shuster, was appearing in *Boy Meets Girl.*

In 1950 Brian Doherty took over the Red Barn theatre with the assistance of Montrealer Roy Wolvin, who directed an eight-week season of musical revues by the 'Barn Stormers,' starring John Pratt. Doherty returned the following season, but this time with new co-producers – Amelia Hall, Bruce Raymond, and Silvio Narizzano, all from the Canadian Repertory company in Ottawa – and with yet another approach. Standard summer-stock fare, such plays as *Life with Father, Charley's Aunt*, and *The Man Who Came to Dinner*, replaced revue as the staple of the repertoire. But the Red Barn was still not attracting audiences. After two years of neglect, it reopened in 1954 with producers Mervyn Rosenzveig and Stanley Jacobson in charge and Leon Major as director. They were followed the next year by a twenty-five-year-old Toronto-born actor-director, Douglas Henderson.

The one high point of the Red Barn's history was the management of Marigold Charlesworth and Jean Roberts from 1959 to 1962. For the most part the repertoire was conservative, consisting of such proven staples as *The Tunnel of Love, The Moon Is Blue* and *Bell, Book and Candle*. The producers lost money the first season, but the following year they made a profit of $3000. In 1961–2, they launched an inaugural season in Toronto and followed that by engaging two summer companies, to perform alternately at the Red Barn and the Orillia Opera House. This expansion proved financially disastrous, and Charlesworth and Roberts could not mount another season. Patricia Carroll Brown and her Harlequin Players then tried their luck, and managed to keep the theatre open until 1966.

Stage design by Grant Macdonald for première of Robertson Davies's *Fortune, My Foe*, 1949, by International Players, Kingston. Macdonald made his living as a commercial artist working for such firms as Tennants in London, England, doing portraits of stars in their productions. In Canada, he did a commissioned series of portraits at the Stratford Festival. A collection of over 500 of his theatre portraits at the Agnes Etherington Art Gallery in Kingston is a unique chronicle of theatre history.

Two men – Drew Thompson from Ottawa and Arthur Sutherland from Kingston – began Kingston's International Players, which lasted from 1948 to 1955.[10] Thompson was one of the company's leading actors (in the first five seasons he appeared 365 times). A graduate of the University of Toronto, Thompson became committed to theatre while a member of the Everyman Theatre in Vancouver. Sutherland, who provided the real inspiration behind the founding of the International Players, was a graduate of the American Academy of Dramatic Art in New York and had had some experience in summer stock in the United States. Together they launched an eleven-week season on 28 June 1948 using the LaSalle Hotel Theatre, which was really the hotel's ballroom. The final show that year was the première of Robertson Davies's *Fortune, My Foe*, designed by Grant Macdonald. As their name suggests, the International Players tried to recruit actors from all over: England,

New York, California, Chicago, Colorado, North Carolina, and various points across Canada were represented over the years. A solid professional core company was then supported by the best local amateurs. To boost attendence, performances were often 'pay-what-you-can.'

More than two hundred actors got their start in Kingston, and many went on to distinguished professional careers in this country. Stalwart members of the International Players included Cosette Lee, Josephine Barrington, Roland Bull, Neil Vipond, Rod Coneybeare, Jillian Foster and Bernard Slade (who later married), Hugh Webster, and Timothy Findley. Joy Coghill directed in 1950; Vernon Chapman acted for the company and served as the principal director for the following two years. In 1952 and 1953, seasons stretched from February to December and there were often two International Players' companies operating simultaneously, one in Kingston and one on tour. The International Players also presented winter seasons at the Leaside High School in Toronto. But Arthur Sutherland died suddenly in September 1953 of a coronary thrombosis at the age of forty-two, and the International Players ceased to exist after one further summer season.

The Peterborough Summer Theatre opened in 1949 with *Fortune, My Foe*.[11] Although other summer theatres, notably the Straw Hat Players and the International Players, had staged his plays, Robertson Davies worked most closely with the Peterborough Summer Theatre until 1953, directing a number of plays, including *Ten Nights in a Bar-room*, *Arms and the Man*, *East Lynne*, and *The Silver Whistle*. In addition, as a tribute to Peterborough's centennial, the Peterborough Summer Theatre presented Davies's unorthodox view of the lives of the famous pioneer literary ladies of the area, *At My Heart's Core*, with his wife Brenda Davies originating the role of Frances Stuart. Michael Sadlier directed.

In fact it was Michael Sadlier, an Irish-born Canadian producer and director, who really ran the Peterborough Summer Theatre for the nine seasons that it was in operation. In addition to Peterborough, Sadlier operated a company composed mostly of Canadians who performed each winter in Bermuda.

Sadlier imported the feature performer of his inaugural 1949 Peterborough season from England. Bramwell Fletcher led a company of Canadians, including Robert Christie, Margot Christie, Anna Cameron, William Needles, and Catherine Procter. In 1951 and 1952 the Peterborough Summer Theatre worked in conjunction with the Niagara Falls Summer Theatre under a plan formulated by Michael Sadlier and Bruce Yorke whereby two companies would play alternating weeks in Peterborough and Niagara Falls. They recruited some of the best young talents available, among them Kate Reid, William Hutt, Christopher

Peter Mews as Charlie's Aunt, Peterborough Summer Theatre, 1951

Plummer, Barbara Hamilton, Charmion King, Richard Neilson, Josephine Barrington, Amelia Hall, Gerry Sarracini, and Brenda Davies, with Henry Kaplan as the principal director.

Robert Gill served as resident director (and upon occasion as an actor) for the Peterborough Summer Theatre's 1953 season. However, the Stratford Festival was already draining away talent: in 1953 the two leading performers, Harry Geldart and his wife Margaret Braidwood, came from England. By 1954, when Gill performed for the last time with the Peterborough Summer Theatre in *Come Back, Little Sheba*, Geldart was back, this time as resident director, with his wife as star. Geldart continued to be associated with the Peterborough Summer Theatre until 1956, when he served as producer, with directing assistance from Eric Christmas, who had first joined the acting company in 1954. The Peterborough Summer Theatre lost money each of its final three seasons, so it came as no surprise when Michael Sadlier announced in May 1958 that the theatre would not reopen.

The Niagara Barn Theatre grew out of the Midland Players with director Jack Blacklock, who had studied drama at Queen's University, the Royal Conservatory of Music, and Columbia University.[12] He was head of dramatics at Forest Hill Collegiate in Toronto when he first became involved in summer theatre. His Midland Summer Theatre, which had opened in 1948, was billed as Canada's only municipally sponsored theatre, as it was a project of the Midland Parks Commission. The Midland Players, recruited from Toronto's New Play Society and the Forest Hill Players, presented nine plays in the first season, performing each of them four times a week, and followed this with a short winter season in Toronto. Blacklock and the Players were back at Midland in 1949, but the following year they moved to the more populous Niagara peninsula, to Allanburg near the Welland Canal, and became the Niagara Barn Theatre. That first season in an old barn lasted seventeen weeks, longer than that achieved by any other summer theatre in Canada. In 1952 Blacklock moved his company once again, but this time only a short distance, to Vineland beside the Queen Elizabeth Way, six miles east of St Catharines. The Prudhomme brothers of Vineland built Blacklock a 450-seat playhouse adjoining their motel and garden centre. Although most of the building was new, it did incorporate parts of a century-old barn and was designed to resemble a barn. It was also 'air-cooled' through the hot Niagara summer, but heated to allow performances in the late spring and early fall. There was even a rehearsal hall.

Although the Niagara Barn Theatre's repertoire relied heavily upon such plays as *Natalie Needs a Nightie*, *Apple of his Eye*, *Nothing but the Truth*, and *I Remember Mama*, Blacklock had particular success with an original comedy by S.G. Bett, the music master of Ridley College in St Catharines. *Haywire Holiday*, a farce set in a Muskoka lodge, was a favourite of the 1951 season and was actually held over. Blacklock later produced another play by Bett, *Minerva's Monday*.

The Niagara Barn Theatre occupied Prudhomme's theatre for two seasons before moving for the final time in 1954 to Stoney Creek on the

Mr. Roberts, Garden Centre Theatre, August 1962

outskirts of Hamilton. Blacklock launched a season that stretched for thirty weeks, opening in April with *Charley's Aunt* and continuing with a new play every week until November. However, the strain of producing such long seasons of weekly stock took its toll, and Jack Blacklock gave up after the 1954 season. His theatre was taken over by a young actor from England, Donald Ewer, who confidently launched a full season in 1955, but had to close the Niagara Barn Theatre for the last time after only seven unprofitable weeks.

Prudhomme's theatre in Vineland lasted much longer. Bernard Slade and his wife Jillian Foster assumed control, with Warren Hart, an American actor, as their partner, and christened their new venture the Garden Centre Theatre. Slade and Foster, drawing on their experience with the International Players as well as the Niagara Barn Theatre, knew what summer theatre audiences wanted. Their inaugural season in 1954 consisted of such staples as *The Philadelphia Story*, *The Four Poster*, *For Love and Money*, *Light up the Sky*, and *Private Lives*; the one dramatic highlight was the controversial *A Streetcar Named Desire*. But after only one draining twenty-five-week season running the Garden Centre Theatre, Slade and Foster had had enough.

Following two additional unsuccessful seasons, John Prudhomme finally decided to bring in two experienced Americans, producer Nat

Godwin and director Robert Herrman, who had run a similar playhouse in New York state in 1956, the previous summer. Godwin left as early as 1959, but Herrman stayed until the theatre closed permanently in 1966. He served as producer, directed frequently, and even acted upon occasion, while his actress wife Terry Clemes was a featured performer and assisted her husband in running the theatre. Under the Herrmans, the Garden Centre Theatre hosted a large number of package tours from the United States and also imported television and film personalities to star in Canadian productions. Zazu Pitts appeared there in *The Solid Gold Cadillac*; in 1963 Raymond Burr broke box-office records in *Oh, Men, Oh, Women*. For the most part the Garden Centre repertoire consisted of such light comedies as *Pajama Tops* and *The Little Hut* or sentimental dramas like *Mr. Roberts* and *Raisin in the Sun*. During a production of *Cat on a Hot Tin Roof* in 1958, the theatre burned down. However, the Herrmans were not superstitious; when they reopened the following year, it was with another production of *Cat on a Hot Tin Roof*. The new Garden Centre Theatre was a 916-seat air-conditioned building with its own shops and storage areas and the latest in theatrical equipment. In the winter the building could be transformed into a curling rink.

But by then the summer-stock era was rapidly drawing to a close in Canada. The costs of hiring stars, booking package tours, and operating a commercial theatre that was not eligible for Canada Council grants led to a deficit of almost $13,000 in 1962. Herrman threatened not to reopen the next season, but did manage to struggle through for four more years, as he watched the nearby Shaw Festival prosper. The Garden Centre theatre premises eventually burned down in 1968 and were never rebuilt.

The Niagara Falls Summer Theatre opened in 1950 in a school auditorium with a production of *Harvey*. For the first two seasons the producers included Bruce Yorke, Michael Sadlier, from the Peterborough Summer Theatre, and, most important, Maud Franchot, an American. Plays included *Dream Girl*, directed by Henry Kaplan, and Robertson Davies's *At My Heart's Core*. In 1952 Maud Franchot took over sole management and began to import stars to work with a resident company of Canadians and Americans. Franchot Tone, who was Maud Franchot's nephew, opened the 1952 season in *The Petrified Forest*, while Eli Wallach and Maureen Stapleton appeared later that summer in *The Rose Tattoo*. Maud Franchot gave up after the 1953 season, which set attendance records but still lost money. In 1954 and 1955, a new Niagara Falls Summer Theatre featured the London Players, led by Leslie Yeo, who presented seasons of summer stock between winter tours and regular engagements in Newfoundland.

Summer stock was disappearing by the mid-1950s, a victim of the success of Stratford on the one hand and the appearance of television on the other. Yet theatres continued to open. Chatham tried professional theatre in 1951, when the community centre's Sylvan Theatre experimented briefly with 'theatre under the stars,' but audiences did not take to the idea. Another short-lived venture occurred in 1955, when a season of professional theatre was planned with actors from the Stratford Festival and Toronto. But after only two productions the company ceased operations. Many straw-hat veterans joined forces in 1956 in the unsuccessful Centre Island Playhouse on the Toronto Islands, where managers John Pratt and Bernard Rothman scheduled a season of typical light summer fare performed by experienced actors in a converted movie theatre. Andrew Allan directed several productions, including the season opener, *The Little Hut*, which starred Toby Robins, Jack Creley, and George McGowan. John Holden directed the final play, the comedy *Wake Up Darling*, featuring Barbara Hamilton. The Sun Parlour Playhouse in Leamington, a small town thirty-three miles from Windsor, opened the same year, and lasted for three seasons. Manager Errol Fortin, a Detroit television producer, brought the young American actress Martha Henry to Canada for the first time to appear at the Sun Parlour Playhouse. Starting in 1956, London's Grand Theatre hosted two seasons of summer theatre featuring the Trans-Canada Theatre Company, later renamed the Maple Leaf Theatre. It was not until 1963 that a full-fledged professional theatre was established in Windsor. Called the Windsor International Theatre Festival, it provided a single summer season of quite imaginative productions, but it could not surmount competition from Detroit and did not return. There was no other attempt at creating a local professional theatre until 1970, when a company based at the University of Windsor offered a summer program.

The founding of the Stratford Festival in 1953 effectively destroyed summer stock. Stratford was an event; stock was ad hoc. Stratford was polished and professional; stock was often slapdash and amateurish. Stratford was culture with international pretensions; stock was show business on a decidedly provincial scale. Yet Stratford drew heavily upon the people who had learned their craft in stock. From the Straw Hat Players came Donald Davis, while William Hutt was a Niagara and Peterborough veteran. Kate Reid had performed with the International Players and Amelia Hall with the Red Barn. Two of the first Canadians to direct at Stratford, Leon Major and George McGowan, had worked at Muskoka and Niagara.

Although the Stratford Festival was the brainchild of local journalist Tom Patterson, it was shaped by Anglo-Irish director Tyrone Guthrie. Initially, Guthrie had agreed to come to Stratford to give advice solely

Grant Macdonald's portrait (1958) of Eleanor Stuart as Calpurnia in *Julius Caesar*, Stratford Festival production of 1955

because he wanted to see how Canada had changed since the 1930s, when he had directed a radio series in Montreal.[13] However, he quickly saw that Stratford offered him the chance of a lifetime to create his ideal of a Shakespearean theatre. The thrust stage that Guthrie and his long-time collaborator Tanya Moiseiwitsch developed has been Stratford's crowning glory. It has been emulated but not surpassed in theatres around the world. The Guthrie-Moiseiwitsch stage has the general shape and features of the Elizabethan platform stage surrounded on three sides by a Greek-style auditorium. The thrust stage encourages spectacle and movement, characteristics Guthrie exploited to the full, beginning with his first season, which consisted of two contrasting plays, *Richard III* and *All's Well That Ends Well*.[14]

To establish itself, the festival needed credibility and that meant stars and high standards. Alec Guinness became Guthrie's star attraction, with fellow English actors Douglas Campbell, Michael Bates, and Irene Worth (American, but working extensively in Britain) for support. High production standards were guaranteed by Tanya Moiseiwitsch as designer and by three experienced English technicians: a production manager and the heads of the wardrobe and properties departments. Everyone else onstage and backstage that first Stratford summer was Canadian.

Guthrie then made a final decision that was to have a major impact upon the festival's enduring appeal. He wanted the festival to be truly festive, to have a holiday spirit. Stratford was Shakespeare, but it was also picnics by the Avon River and feeding the swans. Guthrie decided that a huge tent theatre would provide the appropriate atmosphere and solve the problem of finding a suitable home for his stage.

Tom Patterson, who was the festival's general manager, faced several financial crises during the winter of 1952–3. But by the time Alec Guinness stepped out onto the thrust stage as Richard III in July 1953, there was no question that the Stratford Festival was a success, a fact confirmed for the dubious by enthusiastic reviews from New York critics. That first season lasted six weeks, one more than planned, and attendance was sixty-eight thousand; the 1982 season was almost four times as long and attendance in the three festival theatres exceeded five hundred thousand. Over the years, the Stratford Festival has been criticized for its politics, its international outlook in a more nationalistic age, and the uneven quality of its productions, especially of Shakespearean tragedy. However, in statistical terms at least, Stratford has been an unqualified success and a tribute to the foresight of its founders.

Guthrie liked to conceive, not consolidate; he enjoyed launching brave new ventures, but not running them. His chosen successor was a

Stratford Festival tent, 1953

young English director, Michael Langham, who had made his festival début directing *Julius Caesar* in 1955. However, it was Langham's inspired production of *Henry V* in 1956, the year that he succeeded Guthrie as artistic director, that confirmed the wisdom of Guthrie's choice. Langham interpreted *Henry V* in a distinctively Canadian manner using Anglo-Canadians in the English parts and Quebec francophone actors as the French, thus turning the final act into a celebration of Canadian unity. A young Montreal actor, Christopher Plummer, played Henry. During his long tenure, from 1956 to 1967, Langham provided the kind of careful guidance that allowed the festival to mature.

Probably the most important event during these years was the opening of the permanent building. After the 1956 season the tent was struck for the last time and cut into pieces for souvenirs. Construction then started on a new building that would incorporate the ambiance of the tent with every necessary modern theatrical amenity. Toronto architect Robert Fairfield won awards for the resulting design. Although the building was constructed during Michael Langham's time, it was the physical embodiment of many of Tyrone Guthrie's cherished principles. The stage had to be the physical and psychological centre of the building. In fact the theatre was simply created around the original concrete shell on a hill overlooking the Avon River. Guthrie believed that the theatre should be circular, with the stage the focus for the entire building. The audience section is in one arc, which contains the lobbies and other public areas. Another section of the circle contains all the administrative offices. Finally, the last segment is the world of the artists – the dressing-rooms, shops, and storage areas, along with a rehearsal hall and green room. Guthrie believed this section was the most important because it was used from morning to night. Therefore, Fairfield provided a wall of windows, with the best view for the actors and technicians.

To accommodate over twenty-two hundred spectators, a necessity if the theatre were to generate enough box-office revenue to support a classical repertoire, Fairfield had to incorporate a wide 220-degree arc in the auditorium and include a low balcony. Yet he managed to retain the intimacy of the tent, with no seat being further than sixty-five feet from the stage. The Moiseiwitsch/Guthrie stage remained unchanged and, in fact, it has undergone only essentially minor improvements up to the present. The new building had superb acoustics and eliminated the shriek of train whistles and the hammer of rain that had plagued productions in the tent, while full climate control solved the problem of heat and humidity. Fairfield even managed to retain some of the visual aspect of the tent partly through the design of a fluted roof. The new Stratford Festival theatre was built in less than a year and opened in the summer of 1957, with Christopher Plummer starring in *Hamlet*.

Not only did Langham master Guthrie's difficult thrust stage, he also managed to recruit and retain a distinguished company particularly strong in character actors. As much as Guthrie had, he realized the importance of star appeal. Among the actors Langham brought in were Jason Robarts, Jr, Julie Harris, Tammy Grimes, Paul Scofield, Zoe Caldwell, and Alan Bates. However, he was convinced that Stratford had to develop its own stars. Under Langham, actors such as William Hutt, Douglas Rain, Tony Van Bridge, Kate Reid, Frances Hyland, Leo Ciceri, Martha Henry, and Bruno Gerussi rose to prominence. He also gave Canadians George McGowan, Leon Major, and Jean Gascon the chance to direct on the thrust stage. English-born Brian Jackson, who settled in Stratford as head of properties in 1955, and Canadian Marie Day became designers.

The Stratford Festival grew year by year under Langham, but this growth was carefully controlled to avoid overstretching human or financial resources. In 1963 the festival acquired the thousand-seat proscenium Avon Theatre in downtown Stratford, which it had used since 1956. The Avon had been built early in this century for touring productions and vaudeville before being turned into a cinema. The first notable productions at the Avon were a series of Gilbert and Sullivan operettas,

Grant Macdonald's portrait of Frances Hyland as Isabella in *Measure for Measure*, Stratford Festival, 1954

brilliantly staged by Tyrone Guthrie. The Avon has been an important addition to the festival, allowing it to produce plays there that are better suited to a proscenium or that appeal to a smaller audience.

The post-Langham history of Stratford is as full of drama offstage as on. Taking a typically Canadian stance, the festival board appointed two successors, Jean Gascon from French Canada, assisted by John Hirsch from English Canada, but they were temperamentally and artistically dissimilar, and Hirsch resigned after the 1969 season, leaving Gascon in sole control until 1974. Ironically, under Gascon, a Canadian, Stratford found itself increasingly isolated from the newly nationalistic theatre that was emerging across the country.[15]

The appointment of a young English director, Robin Phillips, to replace Gascon threatened to aggravate this schism. However, Phillips actually improved matters by recruiting many performers from the alternative theatre. He also proved to be a brilliant manager, who made the festival into a financial success, partly through the use of such stars as Maggie Smith and Peter Ustinov. Until 1980, Phillips ran the immense Stratford Festival almost single-handedly. The board of governors then mishandled the search for his successor and provoked a crisis.[16] Finally, John Hirsch agreed to serve as artistic director for five years. It was Muriel Sherrin, however, who actually organized the 1981 season and saved the festival. Hirsch's inheritance was twofold: long-overdue physical improvements to the festival's theatres and an almost unmanageable deficit. In 1986 he was succeeded by John Neville, the highly respected English actor and director who had served his Canadian apprenticeship as artistic director of two major theatres, the Citadel in Edmonton and the Neptune in Halifax. Neville managed to restore fiscal harmony and, for once, there was a smooth succession, to longtime Stratford director David William. An Englishman, William was an enthusiastic supporter of Canadian drama, but the recession of the early 1990s and increasing competition for audiences caused declining attendance and forced him to reduce the number of productions. He nurtured the career of director Richard Monette, who was appointed artistic director designate in 1992 and given a year to work closely with William before assuming full command and responsiblity.

While Stratford struggled through the 1980s, the younger Shaw Festival was reaching maturity. The Shaw Festival started without fanfare and without imported stars and directors as the brainchild of Brian Doherty, all-around lover of the theatre and author of the play *Father Mulachy's Miracle*, which had been presented in New York and England. Doherty, a resident of Niagara-on-the-Lake, managed to persuade a wealthy friend, Calvin Rand, an American businessman who lived near him in the summers, that a festival devoted to the plays of George Bernard Shaw made sense. The Shaw Festival was Brian Doherty's creation, but it was Calvin Rand, who became president of the Shaw Festival board in 1965, who nurtured it and made it grow.[17]

Influential Canadian radio producer Andrew Allan, a man with a long-standing love of theatre and considerable directing experience, agreed to run the Shaw Festival in 1963. The cast of *Spring Thaw* put on a performance to raise vital operating funds. Then, with his assistant, Sean Mulcahy, Allan staged a three-week professional season consisting of *You Never Can Tell, How He Lied to Her Husband, A Man of Destiny,* and *Androcles and the Lion.* Although budgets were limited, the make-shift auditorium was improved by air-conditioning and the addition of an apron to enlarge the stage. In 1964, risers for the seats were installed, but the stage remained inadequate. Nevertheless audiences continued to increase. In 1964 a young English actor-director, Christopher Newton, appeared for the first time in Niagara-on-the-Lake as Hector in *Heartbreak House* and Mr. A in *Village Wooing.* The acting company grew stronger with the recruitment of several experienced performers, who soon became part of the Shaw Festival family. These included Joyce Campion, Norman Welsh, Denise Fergusson, Betty Leighton, and Gerard Parkes. In his three seasons at the helm, Allan transformed the Shaw Festival from a rather quaint idea into a thriving reality.

During the one year, 1966, in which Barry Morse ran the Shaw Festival, he helped change a modest tribute to Shaw into a major theatre. He expanded the season to nine weeks and his reward was a 50 per cent increase in attendance. Thanks to his role in the popular television series *The Fugitive,* Morse attracted a great deal of attention to the young festival. He presented a cross-section of Shaw's plays: *Man and Superman, Misalliance,* and *The Apple Cart,* and recruited a strong company, including a talented young Englishman, Paxton Whitehead, who was teamed with Zoe Caldwell. Pat Galloway played Ann in *Man and Superman* before leaving to begin her long stay at Stratford. Fine character actors like Patrick Boxill, Sandy Webster, Tom Kneebone, Hugh Webster, and Sheila Haney took the supporting roles. Finally, Morse himself established a Shaw Festival tradition by both acting and directing.

Paxton Whitehead was artistic director of the Shaw Festival from 1967 until 1977, and during that period succeeded in getting the festival a new theatre. It had been clear for many years that the company needed a new home with modern production facilities if it were to increase box-office revenue and improve standards. Ron Thom of Toronto designed the new theatre, located on vacant federal land at the edge of town. Thom created a building of red brick, natural wood, and glass, set amongst carefully landscaped grounds, dominated by full-grown trans-planted trees that provided camouflage for the squat exterior and helped the theatre to harmonize with its surroundings. The building is constructed on a number of different levels and opens naturally to the outside in as many places as possible to let in light. There are several patios and porches, with bars and cafés. In addition to these audience amenities, the building contains administrative and production offices and shops, where scenery, properties, and costumes are built. The auditorium, which also utilizes wood and warm colours, seats 830 and has excellent sight-lines and acoustics. The stage is a traditional proscenium, the arrangement deemed most suitable for the work of Shaw and his contemporaries. The much-praised new theatre officially opened in June 1973, with Paxton Whitehead appearing in *You Never Can Tell* opposite Stanley Holloway.

Whitehead also took the Shaw Festival on tour. A co-production agreement with the Manitoba Theatre Centre allowed the festival to accept an invitation to appear at Expo 67. *The Philanderer* played a two-week engagement at the Kennedy Center in 1973. That same year, *You Never Can Tell* went to five cities in the United States and Canada. The Shaw Festival's 1974 production of *The Devil's Disciple*, starring Alan Scarfe, was one of the first Canadian productions in recent years to play at the Royal Alexandra Theatre in Toronto. Touring before or after the season helped win new audiences for the festival; at the same time, it enabled Whitehead to offer his actors the same kind of long-term contracts they could get at the Stratford Festival.

After years of increasing criticism about the quality of productions at the Shaw Festival, Paxton Whitehead resigned at the conclusion of the 1977 season. Following Whitehead's resignation, the board was unable to agree upon a successor, and Richard Kirschner served as producer in 1978. Kirschner, who had worked at Lincoln Center and the American Shakespeare Festival had come to Niagara-on-the-Lake as executive director in 1976. Then Christopher Newton was appointed artistic director, but he would not be available until 1980. Veteran Shaw Festival actor-director Leslie Yeo agreed to take Newton's place in 1979, and helped change the direction of the festival. Yeo redefined the Shaw Festival as more 'festival' than 'Shaw.' Instead of emphasizing Shaw's plays, he chose to vary his repertoire with works from some of the hundreds of writers who were alive during Shaw's extended lifetime. He also launched a lunch-time theatre to exhibit Shaw's often unproduced shorter plays. Balancing a popular Shaw play, *You Never Can Tell*, with a more unfamiliar one, *Captain Brassbound's Conversion*, he filled in the season with plays by Shaw or by his contemporaries.

After going to the United States from his native England, Christopher Newton had starred on Broadway in *The Knack*. His work as an actor culminated with a season at the Stratford Festival in 1968; the following year he went west to lead Theatre Calgary into full professional status.

Two years later he began the difficult task of revitalizing the Vancouver Playhouse. Newton faced an equal challenge in Niagara-on-the-Lake. To assist him he brought many of his Vancouver associates to Ontario: Cameron Porteous came as designer; so did many performers, Nora McLennan and Goldie Semple, among them. However, it was Heath Lamberts, an actor with a special gift for comedy and experience in theatres across the country, who emerged as the real star of the company.

Newton established a firm artistic policy right from the beginning. He wanted to develop a creative atmosphere for a strong company of actors. That meant the Shaw Festival had to be a pleasant, harmonious place in which to work. It also meant that each season actors had to be able to tackle a variety of demanding roles. Newton therefore formulated a number of policies regarding repertoire. Usually he schedules four plays for the Festival Theatre; one of these is a major Shaw play like *Saint Joan*, *Heartbreak House*, or *Pygmalion*. Another is a farce, such as Ben Travers's *Banana Ridge* or *Rookery Nook*. The last two choices are selected from plays by Shaw's contempories or plays about that period. This list has included Wilder's *Skin of Our Teeth* and the phenomenally successful *Cyrano de Bergerac*, starring Heath Lamberts, which was revived twice at the Shaw Festival, in 1982 and 1983, and in 1984 was remounted as a subscription attraction at the Royal Alexandra Theatre. The repertoire at the Court House, which was redesigned into a functional three-quarter-round theatre, includes lesser-known Shaw plays like *The Simpleton of the Unexpected Isles* and such works of more limited appeal as Noel Coward's *The Vortex*, which was the first of the Festival's 'Risks' series, presented as a workshop in 1983 and then brought back as a fully mounted production the following year. Newton also schedules compact productions of musicals such as *The Desert Song* or *On the Town* and mysteries like *Death on the Nile* in the small proscenium Royal George Theatre, a one-time cinema that had housed the Canadian Mime Theatre from 1969 to 1977.

Other summer theatres could not compete with Stratford and Shaw; they could only offer alternatives. In the 1960s and 1970s non-profit theatres with local boards of directors opened in many of the same places as the straw-hat theatres of old. Each tried to find its own niche and develop a unique mandate. The Red Barn Theatre never managed to do this and continued to struggle on from season to season; there were almost annual changes of management, with everyone from director Bill Glassco to talent agent Karen Hazzard trying to make a success of it. In contrast, the Muskoka Festival, the successor to the Straw Hat Players, prospered and has gone on to run companies serving Port Carling, Gravenhurst, and Huntsville.[18]

Michael Ayoub came to the rescue of theatre in the Muskokas in 1972, when he opened the Port Carling Summer Theatre. A season of safe plays like *Butterflies Are Free* and *Charley's Aunt* actually made a profit. However, this encouraged Ayoub to expand too quickly and he lost all his money during the 1973 season. This time, summer families and full-time residents got together to save the theatre. They formed the Muskoka Foundation for the Arts and hired Michael Ayoub as artistic director and Michael Cole, a local, as general manager. Ayoub established a model that he followed for many years: two separate companies, one doing two musicals and the other two plays, each performing half a week at the Gravenhurst Opera House and the rest of the time at the Port Carling Memorial Hall. He also encouraged Canadian writing, with the emphasis on new Canadian musicals. Blaine Parker wrote several musicals for Muskoka, including *Rhythm and Madness*, *City Light Blues*, and *Sweet and Wicked Adeline*. Jim Betts's *Thin Ice*, a hockey musical, was very popular. In 1979 both musicals were Canadian: *Flicks* and *Eight to the Bar*. In 1992, Ayoub was succeeded by former Huron Country Playhouse and Stage West artistic director Ron Ulrich.

The oldest of the new summer theatres, the Kawartha Summer Theatre, in Lindsay, was the last theatre left in Canada producing a different play each week. Although Lindsay had been a touring stop, it had never had its own theatre, despite having a suitable venue, the Academy Theatre, which was built in 1893 for visiting attractions and local productions. In 1931 this building was remodelled as a cinema, but by 1959 it was vacant and awaiting demolition. Then a group of local business people formed the Academy Theatre Foundation to save the building. After undergoing extensive renovations, the Academy Theatre reopened in the fall of 1964. The first Kawartha Summer Festival was held the following year, with actor Norman Welsh in charge. Welsh recruited a strong company: Jack Creley, for example, directed *Private Lives*, which starred Joyce Gordon and Paul Harding, supported by Patrick Boxill and Pat Armstrong.

Dennis Sweeting, a native of Calgary who had served as manager of the touring Canadian Players, first began his long association with the Kawartha Summer Theatre in 1966. Sweeting's second season, in Centennial year, revealed his growing interest in Canadian plays when three of the nine productions were Canadian: Arthur Murphy's *The First Falls on Monday*, George Blackburn's Ottawa comedy, *A Button Is Missing*, and *The Newsman*, a comedy about a Northern Ontario radio station, by Martin Lager, a former Torontonian then living in Lindsay. The rest of Sweeting's season was typical summer-stock fare such as *See How They Run*, *Bell, Book and Candle*, and *Ten Nights in a Bar-room*. But excessive rain and the distraction of Expo 67 kept the tourists away, and the theatre incurred a substantial deficit.

After the spectacular failure of a multimedia festival in 1969, the festival quickly re-engaged Sweeting and, with the assistance of his wife Maggie as administrator, he remained in charge for more than two decades. Although he used crowd-pleaser Neil Simon plays to win back his audience and pay off the deficit, Sweeting emphasized Canadian plays by writers such as Allan Stratton, David French, Aviva Ravel, Jack Northmore, Munroe Scott, Alden Nowlan and Walter Learning, and Peter Colley. Anne Chislett's *The Tomorrow Box* premièred in Lindsay. Sweeting's successor, Brian Tremblay, had served as his assistant and continued Kawartha's support of Canadian writers.

The Huron Country Playhouse, which has advertised itself as the most successful summer company in Canada, the Stratford and Shaw festivals excepted, concentrates on proven successes.[19] Founding director James Murphy, then a University of Guelph professor, and William Heinsohn, who became executive producer, were operating a small company in Toronto, the Gate Theatre, when they decided to open a summer theatre in the resort town of Grand Bend on Lake Huron. Just outside of town they found an old barn on three-and-a-half acres of ground. When the barn could not be converted easily, the theatre opened in a tent. Their first season, 1972, consisted of proven summer-stock plays, such as *The Little Hut, Dirty Work at the Crossroads, Dial 'M' for Murder*, and a play for children, *Sleeping Beauty*. Attendance during the six weeks totalled over ten thousand.

Thus encouraged and with growing support from the community, Murphy established a board of trustees, and after two more seasons in the tent the Huron Country Playhouse moved into a new theatre, designed by architect Peter Smith and constructed out of barnboard. The original barn was converted into workshops, a rehearsal hall, dressing-rooms, and audience areas, and eventually included a small licensed performance space, Playhouse II.

In 1974 the Huron Country Playhouse started a touring program; selected productions played engagements in such places as Owen Sound, Meaford, Kincardine, Fergus, Seaforth, Hanover, and Sarnia, in addition to their runs in Grand Bend. Although this venture proved costly and physically draining and was eventually abandoned, it did a great deal towards making the playhouse known to a large number of people in the surrounding area. The Huron Country Playhouse remains a popular commercial theatre dedicated to staging proven Broadway and English successes. It does not have a particularly adventurous repertoire, but it has developed a loyal audience. There has been little change in policy under successive artistic directors Aileen Taylor-Smith, Ronald Ulrich, Steven Schipper, Sandy MacDonald, and, especially and most successfully, Tony Lloyd, formerly of the Sudbury Theatre Centre.

The Gryphon Theatre in Barrie is a regional theatre in concept, yet forced to operate only during the summer months. Brian Rintoul, formerly a stage manager at the Stratford Festival, headed a group who launched the Gryphon's first season in July 1970 in a church hall. The season lasted nine weeks and featured six typical summer-stock plays like *There's a Girl in My Soup*, *The Mousetrap*, and *The Fantasticks*. The new company lost $3000 and could not mount a second season, but it had planted the seed. Community leaders then took over the struggle to establish a full-time regional theatre by organizing the Georgian Foundation for the Performing Arts and presenting a second and third summer season in the same space. In 1973 the Gryphon Theatre moved into the new theatre at Georgian College, which had been designed with the assistance of Rintoul and Myles Allison, an architect and governor of the Georgian Foundation. Gryphon has continued to use this comfortable, well-equipped suburban facility ever since. Rintoul also helped to expand the work of the Gryphon into the winter by engaging young performers to tour schools. Under a succession of artistic directors including Sean Mulcahy, Ted Follows, Vernon Chapman, and Virginia Rey, the Gryphon fought off bankruptcy and tried to attract local audiences. Veteran actor James B. Douglas, who took charge in 1984, finally managed to bring the deficit under control and restore stability.

The St Lawrence Summer Playhouse, a theatre-in-the-round, opened in 1967 in a tent on the banks of the St Lawrence River in Gananoque, near Kingston. It was created by Lee Tommarello, an American director, and Kingston broadcaster Gerry Tinlin, and featured amateurs instructed by professionals from the United States and Canada, performing popular musicals and comedies. The theatre moved to a Kingston park in 1969, where it lasted until 1976, when it was succeeded by the amateur Kingston Summer Theatre. Greg Wanless, an actor-director and veteran of the Stratford Festival, resurrected summer theatre in Gananoque in 1982. His Thousand Islands Playhouse presented an audacious selection of plays, including *The Beggars' Opera* and *Comedy of Errors*, performed in repertory in a large upstairs room at the local rowing club. The Thousand Islands Playhouse was initially semi-professional, relying heavily upon student help from the Queen's University Drama Department, but has since become one of the most successful of the new summer theatres.

Links between post-secondary educational institutions and summer theatres began with the relationship between the Straw Hat Players and the University of Toronto. In addition to the Queen's–Thousand Island Playhouse link, York University and Wilfrid Laurier University have sponsored seasons in Orillia. The Laughing Water Festival in Meaford and Theatre Collingwood were associated with Ryerson University. Moonlight Melodrama in Thunder Bay, which specialized in melodramas, was founded by Confederation College theatre instructor William Pendergast in 1972. Summer theatres provide students interested in theatre with practical experience; the theatres gain an energetic, useful, and inexpensive labour pool.

The two most important contemporary summer theatres are Toronto's Theatre Plus and the Blyth Festival. Theatre Plus founder, director-writer Marion Andre, came to Toronto from Montreal after resigning from the Saidye Bronfman Centre when the board cancelled his proposed production of *The Man in a Glass Booth*. Andre's action was a matter of principle, and that uncompromising attitude characterized the theatre he founded in Toronto. Theatre Plus, which Andre began in 1973, was not 'straw hat' theatre. It performed provocative plays that question society. An engaged, committed theatre, it was prepared to challenge its audiences with a variety of plays from the modern repertoire, such as Brian Friel's *Freedom of the City*, Trevor Griffith's *Occupations*, Peter Nichol's *Privates on Parade*, James Saunder's *Bodies*, Friedrich Dürrenmatt's *The Physicists*, and David Rabe's *Streamers*. Andre also presented classics by Ibsen, Chekhov, Wedekind, Anouilh, Giraudoux, Tennessee Williams, and Arthur Miller.

Although the compact 458-seat Jane Mallett Theatre (formerly called the Town Hall) in the St Lawrence Centre was not originally designed as a theatre, Andre managed to turn it into a flexible home for some of Canada's finest talent. His designers included Michael Eagan, Robert Doyle, Lawrence Schafer, Maxine Graham, John Ferguson, Hilary Corbett, Phillip Silver, and Terry Gundvordahl. Leading actors at Theatre Plus included Martha Henry, Jennifer Phipps, Alan Scarfe, Richard Monette, Lynn Griffin, Frances Hyland, Douglas Rain, Kenneth Welsh, Tony Van Bridge, and Neil Dainard. Kurt Reis directed several productions, as did Malcolm Black, who was named Andre's associate artistic director in 1984 and his successor in 1986. Black was succeeded by Duncan McIntosh, who brought the ideas of repertory performance and a resident company with him to Theatre Plus from his work at the Shaw Festival. Unfortunately, Theatre Plus stopped production in the middle of the 1993 season, a victim of the changing face of Toronto theatre.

Before Blyth, no summer theatre devoted to Canadian plays had survived. Keith Turnbull began his fruitful collaboration with James Reaney by directing *The Sun and the Moon* in the summer of 1965 at the

University of Western Ontario. The following year, in the new auditorium in the Althouse College of Education, Turnbull produced a five-week season of Canadian plays, including Reaney's own staging of *Listen to the Wind*. From 1974 to 1976, Toronto Workshop Productions presented three month-long summer seasons in Stratford, with performances taking place outdoors on a platform stage near the Festival Theatre. Stratford's Black Swan Coffee House also presented Canadian plays. In 1966 John Palmer founded the Little Vic Theatre in Stratford and premièred two of his own plays there. Palmer and Martin Kinch together launched Stratford's Canadian Place Theatre in 1969, but that venture like all the others died when it failed to attract the Stratford audience. From 1974 to 1977, Joseph E. McLeod, a theatre and English teacher, ran the second Peterborough Summer Theatre, dedicated to producing only Canadian plays and employing only Canadian actors, directors, designers, and technicians.[20]

Precedent, therefore, suggested that the Blyth Festival would fail. Blyth was also a most unlikely location for a theatre, a small farming community without spectacular scenery to attract tourists. Therefore, the Blyth Festival has never performed first and foremost for visitors, as has Stratford fifty miles down the road. Blyth productions speak directly to the community, to the townspeople and farmers in the area. In turn it is these people, normally not theatre-goers, who have provided the Blyth Festival with solid support through the years. Local residents attend the plays, provide homes for the company, and hold auctions to raise funds and organize popular country suppers. The other part of Blyth's mandate is the development of new Canadian plays. In this regard, the Blyth Festival is one of the most focused and committed of all Canadian theatres.

James Roy, a theatre graduate of York University and a native of Blyth, started the Blyth Festival in 1975 with the assistance of his wife, playwright Anne Chislett.[21] The third co-founder was Keith Roulston, who had come to Blyth in the early 1970s to edit the town newspaper. Both Roy and Roulston were influenced by an important theatrical event that had taken place in 1972 in nearby Clinton, when Theatre Passe Muraille's Paul Thompson and his company developed what became *The Farm Show*. This collective creation was first presented in a local barn for the community and similar collectives were an important part of the Blyth repertoire, especially in the early seasons. Theatre Passe Muraille veterans like Thompson, Janet Amos, Anne Anglin, David Fox, Ted Johns, Layne Coleman, and Clarke Rogers have acted and directed in Blyth.

The Blyth Festival uses the upstairs theatre in the Memorial Hall, which was built between 1919 and 1921 as a tribute to the dead of the

First World War. Having housed a variety of predominantly amateur events over the years, it gradually deteriorated and was almost totally unused when Helen Gowing and other locals undertook its repair. They arranged for a new roof, fire escapes, and modern electrical wiring. Over the years the Blyth Festival has made further improvements. In 1979 more than $100,000 went into renovations, which included air-conditioning. A new wing was added in 1980 to house a box office, dressing-rooms, an art gallery, and much-needed storage space. In addition, the small balcony, which had originally been declared a fire hazard, was brought up to modern safety standards to accommodate ever-increasing audiences.

James Roy began Blyth's first season with Agatha Christie's proven thriller *The Mousetrap*. However, much to his surprise, the original play that season, based on Harry Boyle's *Mostly in Clover*, did better at the box office. That settled it; after that Blyth concentrated on new plays. Some of these plays have been collectives about the history of the region. Others have been adaptations of stories by such celebrated local writers as Harry Boyle and Alice Munro. Two have been particular successes, Peter Colley's mystery, *I'll Be Back before Midnight*, which has been performed throughout the country, and Anne Chislett's award-winning *Quiet in the Land*, an intense drama of conflict within a tightly knit Amish community. The musical *Country Hearts* was staged twice and then taken on a post-season tour. Another musical, *The Dreamland*, was produced later by Canadian Stage and the National Arts Centre. Ted Johns, who has acted at Blyth, has been one of the festival's most prolific playwrights. Among Johns's plays produced at Blyth, *He Won't Come in from the Barn* also played in Toronto and *The School Show* and *St. Sam and the Nukes* were taken on extended tours.

Janet Amos, a member of the original *The Farm Show* and an experienced Blyth actor, became artistic director in 1979. While maintaining its traditional goals, Amos helped the festival to grow, improve its production standards, expand its facilities, and attract increasing numbers of visitors from outside the community. She was concerned about finding five or six worthwhile original plays every season. For that reason, she began presenting suitable plays from other theatres, such as Gratien Gélinas's *Bousille and the Just*, and began to workshop new scripts. When Amos left after the 1984 season to become artistic director of Theatre New Brunswick, she was replaced by her assistant, Katherine Kaszas, who led the Blyth Festival to new attendance records. Kaszas in turn was succeeded by her assistant, Peter Smith, in 1991.

The success of the Blyth Festival led to the birth of another generation of summer theatres. The Port Stanley Summer Theatre on Lake Ontario,

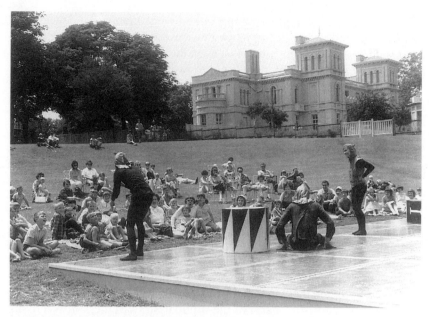

Cockpit Theatre, Hamilton, 8 July 1968, an outdoor summer venture typical of the late 1960s' break with conventional theatre spaces and forms

near London, started in 1978. Peterborough's Arbor Theatre, under John Plank, became fully professional in 1979. The Lighthouse Festival in Port Dover, near Simcoe, opened in 1980, using a renovated town-hall theatre. The Town Hall Theatre in Cobourg's historic Victoria Hall chose as its inaugural production, in 1983, a play called *Tracks* by bp Nichol and Mary Barton, directed by a veteran of the Red Barn, Burton Lancaster. Among others, there are the Upper Canada Playhouse in Morrisburg, the Showboat Theatre in Port Colborne, and the Stage Company in Midland. Summer theatre in Ontario north and west of 'cottage country,' with the exception of university centres, such as Sudbury, must await a further population explosion.

Stratford was not alone: beginning in the late 1980s, many summer theatres faced a crisis brought about by increasing costs and decreasing audiences. The Shaw Festival had serious deficits for several seasons before recording a profit in 1992. The Arbour Theatre stopped producing in 1992 and imported shows from other theatres. Theatre Plus almost closed permanently in August 1992, but was saved temporarily by zealous fund-raising. Even the reliable Blyth Festival experienced a severe decline in attendance that same summer. Reasons for this crisis included the recession, additional taxes such as the GST, the high cost of travel, rising ticket prices, and declining government grants. Audiences now had so much to choose from: mega-musicals in Toronto, sports phenomena such as the Toronto Blue Jays, even the corner video store.

One area of continuing popularity, however, is outdoor theatre. Since 1949 at Oshweken, near Brantford on the Six Nations Reserve, members of the Native community have presented one of a cycle of eight short plays chronicling the history of their people. Performances take place in the evenings on an island in the middle of a lagoon. Skylight Theatre in North York's Earl Bales Park, modelled after Joseph Papp's Shakespeare in the Park in New York, opened in August 1980 with a free professional production of *The Little Prince*. Skylight was totally supported by money from governments, corporations, and individuals, but even with a permanent amphitheatre, it could not compete with *The Dream in High Park*. This was the name given by Toronto Free Theatre in 1983 when it launched an annual free outdoor production of one of Shakespeare's plays to give young professionals experience acting Shakespeare for audiences of more than a thousand people a night. *The Dream in High Park* has some of the excitement of performances in the Stratford tent and much of the rustic charm of the original Straw Hatters. It is a living celebration of the past, present, and future of summer theatre in Ontario.

NOTES

1 Robert Sward, Toronto *Star*, 3 July 1983, A13. Colleen Gross, 'A Below-the-Belt History of the CNE,' *Toronto Life*, August 1983, 21–2

2 See Royal Alexandra Theatre clipping files, Metropolitan Toronto Reference Library, 1940–9

3 Ross Stuart, 'Earle Grey,' in Eugene Benson and L.W. Conolly, eds, *The Oxford Companion to Canadian Theatre* (Toronto: Oxford University Press, 1989), 248–9

4 Programs in Metropolitan Toronto Reference Library

5 'Bon Echo Inn,' advertising pamphlet, c. 1929. See also Dick MacDonald, *Mugwump Canadian: The Merrill Denison Story* (Montreal: Content Publishing, 1973).

6 See Scott McClellan, *Straw Hats and Grease Paint: Fifty Years of theatre in a summer colony; Vol. 1* (Bracebridge, Ont.: Muskoka Publications, 1984)

7 See Straw Hat Players clipping file, Metropolitan Toronto Reference Library.

8 Information on these theatres can be found in the Cosette Lee and Margaret Ness collections in the Metropolitan Toronto Reference Library. See also Amelia Hall, *Life Before Stratford* (Toronto: Dundurn, 1989) and Keith Garebian, *William Hutt: A Theatre Portrait* (Oakville, New York, London: Mosaic, 1988)

9 See Red Barn clipping file, Metropolitan Toronto Reference Library, and Amelia Hall's *Life Before Stratford*.

10 See International Players clipping file, Metropolitan Toronto Reference Library, and Richard Plant, 'International Players,' *Oxford Companion to Canadian Theatre*, 279.

11 See Peterborough clipping file, Metropolitan Toronto Reference Library.

12 See Midland and Niagara clipping files, Metropolitan Toronto Reference Library.

13 Tyrone Guthrie, *A Life in the Theatre* (London: Hamish Hamilton Ltd., 1960), 314

14 There are many worthwhile books and articles on the Stratford Festival, as indicated in John Ball and Richard Plant, eds, *The Bibliography of Theatre History in Canada* (Toronto: ECW Press, 1993). In particular, see Tyrone Guthrie's *A Life in the Theatre*; James Forsyth's *Tyrone Guthrie* (London: Hamish Hamilton Ltd., 1976); Tyrone Guthrie, Robertson Davies, and Grant Macdonald's *Twice Have the Trumpets Sounded* (Toronto: Clarke, Irwin and Co., 1954); Tom Patterson (with Allan Gould), *First Stage: The Making of the Stratford Festival* (Toronto: McClelland and Stewart, 1987); and John Pettigrew and Jamie Portman, *Stratford: The First Thirty Years* (Toronto: Macmillan, 1985).

15 See Ross Stuart, 'The Stratford Festival and the Canadian Theatre,' in Leonard Conolly, ed., *Theatrical Touring and Founding in North America* (Westport, Conn.: Greenwood, 1982).

16 See Martin Knelman, *A Stratford Tempest* (Toronto: McClelland & Stewart, 1982).

17 See Brian Doherty, *Not Bloody Likely: The Shaw Festival 1962–1973* (Toronto: J.M. Dent, 1974); and Shaw Festival, *Celebrating!: Twenty-Five Years on the Stage at the Shaw Festival* (Erin, Ont.: Boston Mills Press, 1986).

18 *Scene Changes* 6:6 (July/August 1978) contains useful articles on several contemporary summer theatres.

19 See *Huron Country Playhouse: Tenth Anniversary of Celebration* (Grand Bend, Ont.: Huron Country Playhouse, 1981).

20 Information on these theatres can be found in appropriate clipping files in the Metropolitan Toronto Reference Library.

21 See Ross Stuart, 'Blyth Festival,' *Oxford Companion to Canadian Theatre*, 55–6; and *Special Memories: Blyth Festival* (Blyth, Ont.: Blyth Festival, 1988).

4 Amateur Theatre

MARTHA MANN AND
REX SOUTHGATE

The story of amateur theatre between 1914 and the 1970s is one of vigorous activity and considerable accomplishment. But it is also a story that sees a Canadian professional theatre beginning in, notionally, 1955, the same decade that also saw the climactic period of amateur theatre in the most artistically accomplished of the Dominion Drama Festivals.

In 1914, war came not at first as a grim drummer,[1] but as an occasion for patriotic fervour to which the world of amateur dramatics immediately responded. A defining difference between those earlier days and our own is the ready willingness to raise charitable funds through public performance. The taste of what was charitable, dramatic, and patriotic all at once can be savoured when we read that, under the patronage of the Duke and Duchess of Devonshire (the war-time governor-general), the Ottawa Drama League presented *The Tyranny of Tears* by Hadden Chambers, preceded by a quartet of the 207th Battalion playing *God Save the King*, 'tableaux, pyramids and camp scenes' by Ottawa Boy Scouts, all in aid of the Ottawa Boy's home, '54 of whose boys are in the Service Overseas.' In Toronto, a benefit performance of *The Mikado* at the Royal Alexandra raised money for the Mothers' Pension Fund. A special event saw various groups contributing to a reading of Thomas Hardy's difficult and gloomy play *The Dynasts* to buy an ambulance for the Red Cross.

The war disrupted things, not least the tours of British (though not American) companies. A fairly flourishing amateur elocutionary and dramatic scene faded. The Toronto Musical and Dramatic Club bowed out with the production of the Canadian play *Houses of Clay* at the Columbus Hall under the auspices of the Women's Art Association. Vincent Massey directed his brother Raymond – and Walter Bowles of future radio fame – in Galsworthy's *The Pigeon* before all went off to war. The gentlemen becoming increasingly absent, the ladies came to the fore. They had always been prominent in this world, but now they took over as a commanding presence that would not dissolve after 1918: the University Alumnae Dramatic Club in Toronto dates from 1918; such figures as Martha Allan of Montreal, Dorothy Goulding and Dora Mavor Moore of Toronto, Dorothy White of Ottawa, Catherine Brickenden of London, Lady Tupper of Winnipeg, and Caroline Crerar of Hamilton were to be the pillars of amateur dramatics.

The woman's hand was everywhere evident in the patriotic presentations that abounded. The IODE (Imperial Order of Daughters of the Empire) sponsored *The Golden Age*, an opera by the Canadian J. Nevin Doyle at the Royal Alexandra in aid of the war effort. At Massey Hall, J.P. Buschlen's *The Belgian Nurse* and *Made in Canada* – 'a fantastic extravaganza' held the stage. But these and many others were special events. The continuity of on-going groups was lost. The Margaret Eaton School lapsed, as did the Canadian Academy of Music. The Arts and Letters Club, founded in 1908, continued on for a time (wartime pieces: Lord Dunsany's *The Glittering Gate*, Rabindranath Tagore's *The Post Office*, the members' own *Love and the Artists*, and Synge's *The Shadow of the Glen*). But only the Dickens Fellowship, with its own adaptations of the novels, and the Toronto Conservatory (Nella Jefferis) stayed active. Much of what did get produced was original. Canadian playlets abounded. The patriotic enthusiasm in evidence, unlike the more imperial themes of the Boer War, took on a particularly Canadian colour.[2]

In 1919, Ontario was uncomfortably poised between the rural and the urban – farms began to be abandoned rather than new land cleared and the towns were growing apace. It was still the age of steam, and railways were the thing. With the twenties came more cars, better roads, and more telephones; amateur productions increased at least in part simply because it became easier to do them. Participants and spectators began to have more free time and the means to get to a theatre. People still had to make their own entertainment – and expected to do so. There were still touring companies, but only in the larger centres. The movies had arrived (in 1925, 275,000 people – half the population of Toronto – saw some ninety-four movies), it is true, but only with the talkies from 1929 on did Hollywood establish its huge popularity, which would continue unchallenged through the thirties, the forties, and into the fifties. There was still breathing space for the amateur theatre to thrive.

In Ontario's many large towns and small cities (a population of 15,000 constituted a city), amateur theatricals could exist without concern for trains and cars. And in towns there was still a forming sense of identity, a desire to say that you were part of a place, that you belonged.

This was culture, though the term never occurred to the participants any more than 'heritage' did. As the theatrical adventure began, people must have been quite unselfconscious about it in a way that is difficult to conceive fifty years on with our tortured concern for identity.

Before 1914 and the Great War, and for a good time thereafter, organizations set up for other purposes put on plays as an ancillary function. Clubs put on plays, elocution classes put on plays, schools put on plays, the women's movement put on plays (a Mrs Ray Levinsky wrote *The Other Women* for presentation by amateurs at Massey Hall in Toronto under the auspices of the Political Equality Club in 1915) and, of course, churches put on plays. Not all churches, certainly – too many Ontario denominations still remembered in spirit the Puritans' closing of the London theatres in 1642. Until 1914, the 'Doctrine and Discipline of the Methodist Church of Canada' prohibited theatre attendance as sinful. But that changed: in 1931, the Young Peoples' Council of the United Church produced a book of carefully screened plays, and two years later the Young People's League of the First United Church in Hamilton was emboldened to produce *Applesauce*. On the other side of the fence, Catholic churches put on Catholic plays for Catholic purposes: in Toronto, plays from the De La Salle and Loretto Players sought a wider audience.

But the more liberal (or lackadaisical, Anglicans in particular) churchmen frequently became enthusiastic thespians. The musical expression to be found in choral singing often led to an interest in dramatic expression as well. The church was the godfather to the stage, frequently providing both focus and physical venue. Indeed, the Anglican Young People's Association formed its own competitive drama festival in Toronto in 1926. Some thirty-five entries were reduced to thirteen for the festival at Hart House Theatre. Nine years later, Mona Coxwell had to decide among seventeen similar plays at the Margaret Eaton Hall. And some of these productions found their way to the early Central Ontario Drama League festival.

But that still lay ahead. In Toronto and vicinity, amateur theatre burgeoned after the war: in 1919, the Arts and Letters Club, the Garrick Club, and the Eaton's Recreational Club all produced plays. The early twenties saw the Chester Players, the Manor Players, the Studio Players, the Players of the Little Theatre Upstairs, the Public Library Players, four 'ethnic' groups, and some thirty church groups make their first appearances. The Dickens Fellowship continued, while the Associate Players of the Margaret Eaton School returned. The art guilds and the IODE were active. Pageants were popular: Havergal College, still in what subsequently became the CBC building on Jarvis Street, gave one of its

Cast of *Aunt Susan Tibbs of Pepper's Corners* as staged by Melville Church in Melville,
November 1919, and Stouffville, January 1920

pageants the unfortunate title of *The Tale of the Tarts*. Some more modern works were done, but Shakespeare, Gilbert and Sullivan, and light
one-act plays were still the favourites.

Canadian voices were beginning to be heard though. Raymond Card's
General Wolfe was produced in 1922. The indefatigable W.S. Milne was
recognized for his play *Geranium* in 1922, presented by the St Andrew's
Players from his own church. The Heliconian Club and the Toronto
Women's Press Club presented plays by their members. The Arts and
Letters Club presented three plays by Fred Jacob and two by Merrill
Denison; Mazo de la Roche had her early plays performed by the Club.
The Canadian Literature Club and the Theatre Arts Group encouraged
new works. The period from 1925 to 1931 was one of great accomplishment as well as remarkable growth in the amateur-theatre movement. By
1930, there were some seventy producing groups in Toronto, fifty of
them associated with churches.[3]

Perhaps some of the old Protestant zeal, increasingly less confident in
its faith, spilled over into the enthusiasm for amateur theatre that grew in
the twenties. Churches could put on plays as part of the social gospel.
What had always been notorious could now become respectable. And

Hamilton Cathedral Holy Name Society, *The Upper Room*, April 1924

respectability was important. Music had always been respectable, but not so drama. The church, and somewhat later the community, was to provide a validation for the amateur theatre.

And, as in war work, the effort was charitable. Money could be raised through performance. This was a familiar tendency, if not a venerable tradition, for earlier generations. Indeed, the Garrick Club in Hamilton, to which the later and important Players' Guild of Hamilton traced its roots, was founded by professional men in 1875 – again under vice-regal patronage, the Marquess of Lorne – to raise money for various charities through the presentation of musical and theatrical events. This it did for some thirty years. Throughout the twenties and thirties, the Dickens Fellowship in Toronto frequently filled the six-hundred-odd-seat Jarvis Collegiate Auditorium for monthly meetings or play productions, the proceeds from which they distributed to children's charities.

A career that exemplifies much of this type of activity is that of W.S. Milne (1902–79), and it is to be emphasized that he is only one, though avowedly a prominent one, among many. His is an Ontario career, too, as well as a Toronto one. After his arrival from Aberdeen at age eleven, Troop-leader Milne of the 31st Toronto Baden Powell Boy Scouts of Old St Andrew's Church on Jarvis Street wrote a Scout play called *Unforeseen Circumstances*. This marked the beginning of his career at a church that had a theatrical arm, the St Andrew's Players, with which he would have much to do, directing for them and appearing in plays such as J.M. Barrie's *Alice-Sit-By-the-Fire*. Attending the University of Toronto, Milne appeared in Bertram Forsyth's *The Tempest* at Hart

House Theatre. He joined the Dickens Fellowship for *Nicholas Nickleby*, and worked at the Toronto Conservatory with A.J. Rostance, Raymond Card, and W.A. Atkinson. In London, at the University of Western Ontario, he appeared with the London Drama League in St John Ervine's *Mary, Mary Quite Contrary* and with the Half Way House Theatre. He directed, and appeared as Polonius, in a *Hamlet* at Western that starred the young Alexander Knox. Following *Geranium* in 1922, Milne's next play, *The Failure*, produced at Hart House Theatre, won an award from the Women's Canadian Club. In 1926, with an MA from the University of Toronto, he became a teacher and then head of the English Department at Northern Vocational School in Toronto, where he continued for thirty-four years.

At his school, and with the massive help of his wife Lillian as designer, Milne soon set about organizing what was to become the Norvoc Players, of which more will be said later. His first production was *Twelfth Night*, in which he played Malvolio. He joined the Arts and Letters Club. In the thirties he became a strength in the Central Ontario Drama League and was one of those who reorganized it after the Second World War. In addition to directing for all the groups so far mentioned, he also managed to work for the University College Players' Guild, Victoria College, the University Alumnae Dramatic Club (UADC), and the North Toronto Theatre Guild. Through church, school, university, and community Milne was a tireless enthusiast for the theatre, on which he centred his life, a total exemplar of involvement in amateur dramatics.[4] His path was a little different, however, from that of the 'little theatre,' which must be our next concern.

After the war Ontarians, perhaps a little later than elsewhere, began to hear another drum, that of the 'little theatre' movement.[5] What does this term imply? People set out to put on plays for fun, but some amongst them are always going to discover an unsatisfied seriousness within themselves and seek to perform sterner stuff. To call your group a little theatre was to be vaguely high-minded, to assure yourself that you were interested in the literature of the theatre and aware of currents other than the commercial trends, and that you were important municipally. It was the vague expression of a sense of community uplift.

The movement derived from the organization of little theatres in the United States in 1909 as the American Drama League, in response to the same impulse that was to see the formation of the British Drama League in 1919. All this might be said to hark back to André Antoine and his Théâtre Libre, started in Paris in 1887, to be followed by Otto Brahm and his Freie Bühne in Berlin in 1889 and by J.T. Grein and the Independent Theatre Society in London in 1891. All three were formed to produce Ibsen's *Ghosts*, which could not find a hearing in the commercial theatres because of its unorthodox and unpalatable realism. Thus, the tradition of the art theatre had arrived to provide stages for writers for whom the commercial theatre was not ready. Strindberg, Hauptmann, and Zola were to follow Ibsen. Grein was to introduce Bernard Shaw to the world and, in the last year of his life, provide a direct link between the larger theatrical world and the Dominion Drama Festival by being its second distinguished and popular adjudicator. Any number of Ontario towns were soon to have 'little theatres.'

Toronto had a model for their emulation in Hart House Theatre. Left unfinished at the outbreak of war, Hart House itself, the great benefaction of the Massey family to the University of Toronto, had been taken over as an officers' training centre. Down in the bowels of the building, a rifle range had been contrived with its butts set between two of the massive supporting pillars of the building. Seeing this after the war, Alice Massey was struck by how much the pillars suggested a titanic proscenium arch, and so Hart House Theatre was born in 1919 with a stage that always seemed too wide for such a low ceiling. This theatre was to become a lodestar for Ontario's little theatres.

The 'House' was meant for male undergraduates, and the theatre was the only place in the building where women were welcome for the next forty years. Newly rediscovered (1992) architect's drawings[6] of the decor of the theatre demonstrate the keen interest both Vincent Massey and his wife Alice took in the furnishing and equipment of the theatre – there are copious notes in both their handwritings on these drawings. Hart House Theatre was technically very advanced for its day. Its crushed-glass cyclorama was one of the few on the continent, and its lighting board, then located on the stage, was one of the largest in North America.

When, several years later, the Ottawa Drama League was raising money to build a home for itself, 'a theatre as good as Hart House in Toronto' was the rallying cry. Unlike those in Toronto and Ottawa, most amateur drama groups – new ones were forming almost daily – had to use existing school and parish auditoriums. The University of Toronto Players' Club, an outgrowth of the Victoria College Players' Club formed in 1916 under the aegis of Vincent Massey, became the principal tenant of Hart House Theatre and, under the professional directorship of Roy Mitchell, embarked on a pattern of yearly productions that was to continue until the outbreak of the Second World War.

Though university theatre is not this chapter's concern,[7] it is important here to clarify the position of the Players' Club. Hart House Theatre was very much a 'town and gown' theatre: membership in the Players' Club was conferred on those actors invited by a succession of directors to perform on its stage. The actors were from the community and not strictly the university. In this sense, not only the physical theatre but its operation was a model for others to follow. This was particularly true in the matter of prepaid subscriptions to a year's series of plays. The Hart House 'season' consisted of eight plays, but gave particular value for the money as the casts were full of keen, accomplished actors rather than nervous undergraduates. In the early days, these people maintained a rather superior dedication to pure amateurism, though some were professional veterans, and others, like Randolph Crowe (Norman Roland), Florence McGee, Raymond Massey, and Judith Evelyn, eventually left to establish careers in New York and London. Still others, like Andrew Allan, Frank Peddie, and Jane Mallett, became the leading members of the first professional theatre in Canada, radio. Later, students did appear in these productions, but only in minor parts.

This Hart House Theatre of the twenties set a fine example that has taken on an almost legendary aura, but that did not stop, though it somewhat diminished, the work of the Arts and Letters Club. Many of its people became part of the Players' Club at the university, including the first director, Roy Mitchell. The Arts and Letters Club was busy at this time removing itself to St George's Hall, where Vincent Massey was the first president and the architect Henry Sproatt had given the club a permanent small stage in the 'Elizabethan' great hall. Pat Mitchell, Roy's wife, was successfully to stage *Ten Nights in a Barroom* there, both 'seriously' and as a burlesque. The stage tended to become a focus of the club in the twenties, with Napier Moore's *Spring Revue* particularly popular. Under the direction of Frank Hemingway and often featuring Ivor Lewis, at one time its president, the Arts and Letters Club increasingly produced Canadian scripts such as Ferguson's *Campbell of Kilmhor*, Francis's *Birds of a Feather*, Campbell-Duncan's *Last Orchard*, and Bertram Brooker's *The Dead Should Sleep*. Lewis also appeared in *The Poacher*, a Welsh play by J.O. Francis directed by Edgar Stone in 1936, and in *Napoleon Crossing the Rockies* by Percy MacKaye the next year. In fact, Lewis seems to have appeared in almost everything and despite the demands of a responsible position at Eaton's, where he eventually became a director, must have been Toronto's premier amateur star. In three months, from November 1929, Lewis appeared in Galsworthy's *Loyalties* for Hart House Theatre, Masefield's *Good Friday* for the Canadian Drama League, and Parker's *Pomander Walk* for the UADC.

Other people much in evidence were the Cards — the talented architect and writer Raymond, together with his brother Brownlow and Patricia, the latter's wife. No sooner had they organized a theatrical group at

Ivor Lewis received the best actor award for the Kentuckian 'Lark' in the Arts and
Letters Club production of *Napoleon Crossing the Rockies*, 1936

St Barnabas's Chester church on the Danforth than they emerged from the church as the Chester Players. From this they proceeded to involvement with the Dickens Fellowship and their own Canadian Drama League. This latter organization specialized in staging the 'set' high-school play for three nights at the Eaton Auditorium before touring it to the schools. They may have gotten the auditorium because Patricia Card ran a theatrical costume business whose main client was Eaton's Santa Claus Parade. (The radio voice of Eaton's Santa Claus was H.E. Hitchmann, star character actor and stage manager from the Earl Grey Competitions, the Toronto Conservatory, and Hart House Theatre.) A noteworthy production was that of John Masefield's *Good Friday*, which toured from chancel to chancel and was revived annually, featuring Ivor Lewis, Dora McMillan, Harold Hunter, Norman Green, and Frank Peddie. Raymond Card essayed some Canadian hagiography in his play *General Wolfe*, written for the Chester Players in 1922.

Another stalwart, almost institutional group in the twenties and thirties was the Dickens Fellowship of Toronto, founded in 1903. From their first performance, *The Cricket on the Hearth*, in 1905, their public activity centred on the production of plays. But it was not, strictly speaking, a dramatic society; rather, the Fellowship was a study group whose principal objectives were to promote knowledge of, and to popularize, the novels of Charles Dickens, which they found was best done by presenting them in dramatizations.

Great encouragement was given to local authors to write dramatic versions of the novels. Horatio (Ray) Purdy's version of *Oliver Twist* was revived several times, as were a number of dramatizations of the same novel by other writers. The Fellowship eventually covered most of the Dickens canon, including a full length *Nicholas Nickleby* in 1922, *The Chimes* in 1929, *Little Dorrit* in 1931, and *Barnaby Rudge* in 1936. As a rule they did two full-length plays in a season, in a variety of theatres – Hart House, Margaret Eaton Hall, and various high schools – as well as public performances of 'scenes' that often raised money for children's charities.

The driving force of the Dickens Fellowship was the Rostances. Alfred J. Rostance, English by birth, taught manual training in the Toronto school system and was an accomplished actor who looked in life the perfect Dickens character. He acted, directed, and designed. But the real talent was Frances Rostance. She too was an extremely accomplished performer, but she also wrote a great many of the scripts for the organization. Her adaptation of *A Christmas Carol* became a standard performed all over North America. (Recently, in a junk shop in Brantford, we were looking at an interesting picture frame, holding a picture we were assured by the proprietor was of a very famous Polish actor, the leading light of the Cracow Municipal Theatre at the turn of the century. We knew better. It was 'Daddy' Rostance as Fagin in the Dickens Fellowship's *Oliver Twist* of 1934.) The Dickens Fellowship still exists, but has reverted to what it started out to be, a study group, although it still occasionally performs dramatized readings at its meetings.

Analogous to the Dickens Fellowship was the Shakespeare Society, started in 1930 and soon producing plays to test the theories of critic G. Wilson Knight. A Shakespeare series was produced in the early thirties: *Romeo and Juliet, King Henry IV, Part I, Hamlet, King Henry VIII* (with A.J. and Frances Rostance as well as Norman Roland), *Othello,* and *The Tempest. Henry VIII* was repeated for the Dominion Drama Festival in 1936.

Quite radically different in outlook and intention from these companies was the Theatre of Action in Toronto. It, and other similar groups, including its more radical Toronto forerunner the Workers' Experimental Theatre, grew out of Progressive Arts Clubs across the continent. Members aggressively sought to demonstrate a distinction of things Canadian from those American and British and to make the general population more socially aware. This theatre of the left was created by such academics and artists as Stanley Ryerson, Jean 'Jim' Watts, Frances Loring, Florence Wyle, and Dorothy Livesay. A somewhat sterner figure also involved was Ed Cecil Smith, yet to gain his fame as commander of the Mackenzie-Papineau Battalion in the Spanish Civil War. The Theatre's first production was Odets's *Waiting for Lefty.* From this experience the group realized it needed to improve, and arranged a summer theatre school for itself in New York, headed by David Pressman of the Neighborhood Playhouse. Years later, Johnny Wayne (he and Frank Shuster paid five dollars each to attend the school) stated of the experience: 'I'd say it's probably the most professional company we've ever been involved with.'[8]

Under Pressman, until 1940, the group produced some dozen plays, including Gogol's *The Government Inspector, Steel,* a notable staging of *Roar China,* and George Sklar's *Life and Death of an American,* directed by the young Daniel Mann of later Hollywood fame. The titles alone indicate their purpose. Their production of the pacifist Irwin Shaw's *Bury the Dead* was a provocative experience for the DDF in Ottawa in 1937. As a curtain-raiser to their original presentation of *Bury the Dead* and a relief from their hard political line, the Theatre of Action had done *Les Femmes savantes* – which gave them something in common with the ladies of the UADC, who always remember this very mannered piece as the first play they produced back in 1918. The group's last production was Steinbeck's

Typical postwar community theatre play-reading group, St Marys Little Theatre, 1952

Of Mice and Men in 1940. With the war, the Theatre of Action's time had come and gone; different action was called for.

Other groups started up during the twenties throughout the province, though the arrival of the Dominion Drama Festival in 1933 spurred the greatest growth: the Border Theatre in Windsor (1934), the Kitchener-Waterloo Little Theatre (1935), the Little Theatre Guild of St Thomas (1934), the Woodstock Little Theatre Guild (1934), the Niagara Falls Little Theatre Guild (1938). ('Guild,' one of those ubiquitous but difficult terms, seems to have felt medieval, supportive, and reassuring, but it also echoed the Drama Guild of New York and other similar references.) Not to be left behind, the Forest Hill Village Art Guild opened their little theatre, appropriately called Bessborough Hall, with Ian Hay's *Tilly of Bloomsbury* in 1934. Another new venture was Dickson Kenwin's Little Playhouse Academy of Dramatic Art. To establish himself as a teacher of acting, Kenwin had turned a Victorian drawing-room into a miniature theatre, which he opened with three Canadian playlets. In contrast to this small venture was the Ottawa Drama League, which by 1928 was into its seventeenth season, doing six subscription plays a year under its director Rupert Kaplan in its own theatre, and by 1935 had further increased its membership.

But beside the success and sophistication of Ottawa it is perhaps best

Community theatre workshop (Hamilton, 1953), one of many postwar initiatives to improve the level of theatre activity. This voice session, under little-theatre and university auspices, was part of a summer training program.

to remember that there was still a considerable naïvety about the theatre. At a performance for the Red Cross of a Barrie one-act play at College Street United Church, it had to be diplomatically indicated to the cast that including titles and stage directions in the performance was not the usual thing. A learning process was at work.

The Depression seems to have had little effect on the growth of amateur theatre. There was some decline in audiences, lost to the increasingly popular and much cheaper movies, but for the most part amateur theatres survived. What is even more noteworthy is the survival of the businesses that had emerged to support the amateur theatre.

Costume-hire companies – such as Malabar, a Winnipeg company that had expanded to Montreal and Toronto, Patricia Card Costumes, and the rental department of Hart House Theatre – flourished. All advertised their ability to ship anywhere. These firms also supplied fancy dress and masquerade costumes for events like skating carnivals, so they were not entirely dependent on the theatre. Elsewhere in Ontario other firms rented costumes; the Hamilton telephone book of 1928, for instance, had three such listings.

Scenic studios also existed, though little information has survived about them. The Evans' Scenery Company in Toronto could apparently supply scenery for all the popular Gilbert and Sullivan operettas as well as various stock sets and set pieces. Independent scenic studios did not reappear as viable businesses again until the 1970s, and then strictly as suppliers to the professional theatre. Coleman Electric, Specialty Lighting, and Avenue Lighting all listed themselves as theatre-lighting specialists, and two companies offered sound equipment for rent. Mona Coxwell managed the local branch of Samuel French, the theatrical publishers, largely to supply texts for the amateurs.

Most of these commercial interests that supplied the theatre survived the Depression, but with the exception of Malabar, they were sold, merged, or disappeared into other organizations by the end of the Second World War. The costume stock of Hart House Theatre was bought by Patricia Card, and the company went through two subsequent ownerships. But some of the costumes were still circulating in 1974 when their last owner, 'Robinson Plays,' retired from business and the remainders were sold for rags.

The first attempt to organize amateur theatre nationally – across the continent – came from a somewhat unlikely source: Earl Grey, the ninth governor-general. Interest in amateur theatricals was not unknown in vice-regal circles. Lord and Lady Dufferin, who could be said to descend from a theatrical family (his great-grandfather was Richard Brinsley Sheridan), had introduced theatricals to the social life of Ottawa in the 1870s when they had a small proscenium stage built into the ballroom at Rideau Hall. In 1906 Earl Grey, now best known as the donor of the Grey Cup awarded in the Canadian Football League, suggested the idea of an annual competition 'to advance and encourage the sister Arts, Music and the Drama, throughout the Dominion of Canada.'

There were five Earl Grey Musical and Dramatic Trophy Competitions held from 1907 to 1911: two in Ottawa and one each in Montreal, Toronto, and Winnipeg. The idea was to determine the best amateur performance. But in the opinion of Dora Mavor Moore, then a student at the Margaret Eaton School, who appeared in the 1910 and 1911 competitions, they had more to do with 'pointless socializing' than with dramatic art. After Earl Grey's recall, the competitions floundered. Amateur theatre faded back into regional isolation, but the seed of the idea of a national dramatic competition had been sown.[9]

It was to bear fruit as the Dominion Drama Festival. The impetus for this event came from the appointment of the Earl of Bessborough as governor-general in 1931:

One of the most interesting things from our point of view, that we have read about the Earl of Bessborough, our new Governor-General, is that he and his family are tremendously interested in the stage. Stanstead Park, the Earl's country estate in Sussex actually boasts a model theatre of its own. Originally a farm building, it has been reconstructed by the Earl's design to seat five hundred people and has as complete an equipment as would be found in any professional house ... It will be welcome news to every Little Theatre group in Canada to learn that our new Governor-General has so keen an interest in the stage, and we can only trust that our activities here will supply in some measure the pleasure which his own small theatre gave him and which he is foregoing in order to serve the Empire as the representative of His Majesty in our Dominion. Hart House will look forward eagerly to Their Excellencies' first visit to Toronto and it will be with some pride that we will introduce our own theatre and its record of performances.[10]

Bessborough's frequent attendance at the theatre soon attracted that Canadian aristocratic practitioner of the amateur theatre, Vincent Massey, who, forestalled in his political ambitions by the Bennett victory of 1930, was at a loose end.

Massey quickly became Bessborough's confidant and collaborator in the scheme to create 'an annual Dominion of Canada Drama Festival.' Bessborough had drafted a complex and somewhat grandiose plan, which he forwarded to Massey in the summer of 1931. The main thrust involved two tiers of competitors, junior and senior, to be screened by local adjudicators, who would select ten to proceed to the provincial trials. Four winners from each province would then proceed to a final in Ottawa that would coincide with exhibitions, classes, and demonstrations. Interestingly, Bessborough foresaw what would become one of the major problems with the DDF. He urged the 'simplest of scenic effects' to try to ensure that everyone competed on an equal footing.

Bessborough's vision was a noble one, as he himself indicated: 'The drama can be made not only an artistic but a great educational influence. I visualize a movement that might develop into a great Drama League, Dominion wide. The keen and growing interest in the little theatre and repertory movement extending as it does right across the Dominion from Ottawa, through Winnipeg and Vancouver, is proof in my mind that a movement for national drama might be born.'[11] Plans and counter-plans were now being exchanged between the governor-general and Vincent Massey. News of the great project soon became public knowledge; Mona Coxwell enthusiastically commented:

Has the time arrived for Canada to hold a national Little Theatre tournament? It was a subject we heard discussed with some animation by a group of people keenly interested in the theatre in this country and the consensus of opinion was in favour of such an event, with Toronto as the 'logical location.' The geography of the country was pointed out as a difficulty – could we expect people to travel from British Columbia, from Nova Scotia or even from Manitoba to compete with groups established here? Los Angeles sends its players to New York for just such an occasion and Dallas, Texas, does the same, but could we hope that the Victoria Theatre Guild, Esquimalt, for example, would cross the continent in the hope of wresting a trophy from the amateur actors of the east?

And what about awards? There should be a cup, of course, to be held by the winning group for one year, and to be competed for again at the next tournament. Then there should be a cash award for the best presentation of a published or an unpublished play, and a further award for the next best presentation. The contest should be open to all non-professional groups. There would necessarily be an entrance fee payable by each group at the time of registration. But each group might receive a stated number of tickets without charge, to be disposed of as it saw fit and at a price that it may choose. Each group must supply its own scenery, properties and special lighting effects.

Could it be done? If carried out the idea has great advantages, not the least of which is that we learn what others are accomplishing and benefit by their experiences. Here in Toronto one seldom runs across anyone who has ever seen what is being done in the little theatre in Ottawa, or Montreal, or Sarnia, much less Winnipeg or the cities at the Coast. It would be a stimulating and encouraging venture and we hope the day is not far off when it may be brought to pass.[12]

Massey's next problem was to raise the $10,000 that Bessborough felt was needed to get the festival off and running. Massey suggested his friend Henry Osborne, a founder of the Ottawa Drama League, as the director of the festival.

On 29 October 1932, a meeting was convened at Rideau Hall. The Ontario delegation involved the undoubted leaders, both social and actual, of the major amateur theatres in the province, including D. Park Jamieson of Sarnia, Caroline Crerar of the Players' Guild of Hamilton, Catherine Brickenden of London, Rupert Davies of Kingston, and Dorothy White of the Ottawa Drama League. The principal result of this meeting was the acceptance of Vincent Massey's motion that there should be a Dominion Drama Festival. Vincent Massey was to become its first president.

The regulations and regional structuring of this new festival were the first things to be sorted out. On Massey's recommendation, the whole structure of the festival was simplified, the levels of competition set at regional and dominion, and the junior and senior categories eliminated. There was a great deal of discussion that produced amusing correspondence about what was amateur and what was not, though it had been made very clear to everyone that the DDF was for amateurs. Out-of-work professionals were not welcome, but actors who had given up the profession entirely were acceptable. Was hiring costumes from professional supply houses acceptable? The rules committee had to pass judgement on all sorts of such queries. A particularly shocking, because to many people disappointing, rule was the prohibition of curtain calls – to remind everybody that serious work was afoot! A competition assumed a scoring system: 'Adjudicating at all festivals is being done on the following system. Acting, 50 marks. Production, 35 marks. Stage presentation, 15 marks. *Acting*: This will cover characterizations, audibility of speech, variation in tone, emphasis, gesture and movement. *Production*: Interpretation of spirit and meaning of the scene; team work, general pace and variation of tempo, grouping and movement, making of points and sense of climax. *Stage presentation*: stage setting, properties and lighting, costumes and make-up.'[13] Mona Coxwell, again, had the highest of expectations:

Taken in its broadest objective the Festival means the creating, finally, of a national drama. This in turn, presents a magnificent opportunity for the Canadian playwright, and for all concerned with the allied arts of painting, stage designing, costume designing, lighting and decoration. Names will emerge from obscurity, national recognition will be given to men and women who have needed this outlet for their work. History has been made for the Little Theatre in Canada and a movement begun which will unite the interests and increase the friendship and understanding of Canadians from the farthest east to the farthest west.[14]

She finds a particular reason to approve the new element of competition: 'Acting groups which had little incentive beyond the enjoyment gained and the entertainment given may now strive to excel in the regional competitions.' People will try harder so as to win prizes. (The idea of competition and prizes in the theatre is as old as the Greeks and as new as the Genies, Doras, Jessies, Geminis, Tonys, Oscars, and Oliviers.) But races are not being run, plays are being presented. The whole athletic analogy, bolstered by all the talk of tournaments and teams, even play-offs, was a dangerous business, opening the way for many invidious distinctions or, worse, popularity contests.

These problems, however, lay in the future. Now drama and its people were organized right across the continent into twelve regions, Ontario into three of them. The awkward size of Toronto necessitated a Central Ontario Drama League, to be organized by Edgar Stone, which controversially became a festival for city groups and made difficulties for communities to the north that were central but not urban. The Western Ontario Drama League of the DDF, organized by D. Park Jamieson, was made up of the many smaller cities and larger towns to the west of Toronto; the Eastern region, supervised by James A. Roy, consisted of the more sparsely peopled area to the east.

The first annual set of regional competitions pared ninety English and twenty French plays to the eighteen English and six French invited to the final festival on 24 April 1933. Obviously, not everybody went to the DDF. Not everybody even tried to go – much amateur activity continued quite apart from it. But over the years from 1933 to 1970, with a seven-year gap for the Second World War, the twenty-nine Dominion Drama Festivals throw other amateur theatrical activity into the shade. We can be reasonably sure that what is heard of because of the festivals not only was representative of what was being done, but also was the best, at least according to the standards established.

The kind of plays that were produced, and the kind of material that was expected by the fledgling DDF, may be seen from a list of suggested short or one-act pieces thoughtfully supplied to groups by the DDF in 1933. For those interested in the classics, five scenes from Shakespeare, two from Sheridan, and one each from Congreve and Goldsmith. Three European plays were suggested. Canada almost achieved parity with the United States: nine Canadian to twelve American items, five of which were Eugene O'Neill playlets. But the great preponderance, and a sure indication of the taste of the times, were the seventy-five British plays. At the head of the list were A.A. Milne, Harold Brighouse, Philip Johnson, and J.M. Barrie. Not far behind were J.B. Priestley, F. Sladen-Smith, John Galsworthy, St John Ervine, Stanley Houghton, Miles Malleson, and Vernon Sylvaine. These were the authors – together with Thornton Wilder and Edna St Vincent Millay – who were produced again and again, fading in popularity only after 1950.

The amateur theatre, particularly within the DDF, took itself seriously when it came to sociability and society at large. This attitude is often disparaged by a later age uncomfortable with anything that smacks of social distinction (and perhaps less socially adept as a result). In 1931 Hart House Theatre could announce that there would be 'tea at four as usual in the Green Room' and that the 'staff will be at home to its friends.' And even in 1942, afternoon tea would also be served in the Green Room at the Grand Theatre in London. London never stinted socially, as may be seen from this description of social arrangements for the 1939 regional festival:

Among the enjoyable features of the Festival were the entertainments arranged by the London groups for the visiting players and out of town guests. Each day tea was served by the London Drama League, the Half-Way House Theatre Group and Meredith Players, at the theatre. On Thursday noon, Mrs. G.A.P. Brickenden gave a luncheon at her house in the country for the adjudicator and the members of the executive. On Saturday a luncheon was held at the London Hotel for all the competing groups and after a short discussion of business details, Colonel H.C. Osborne, the honorary director of the Dominion Drama Festival, gave a most delightful address dealing with the Festival last year and this year. On Thursday night, Mr. and Mrs. Arthur Brickenden entertained at Dorindale for the competing casts on that night; on Friday night Mr. Stanley Meredith entertained at 'The Barn' for those taking part in the plays being presented that evening; and on Saturday night everyone gathered at a supper party at the London Hunt Club to celebrate the success of the Festival and to wish Mr. [Rupert] Harvey good-bye.[15]

So important was Vincent Massey that even his vacation plans were reported as theatrical news in the 'Heard in the Foyer' column of *The Curtain Call*: 'The Honourable Vincent and Mrs. Massey, who have been holidaying in Bermuda, are expected to return next week.'[16] A remarkable feature of any festival program is that the space devoted to the names on the organizing committees equals and sometimes surpasses that given the participants. And as the DDF's organization grew, so did the list of names. The names had to have their reward, and this was of course overwhelmingly social. The biggest reward of all was the vice-regal touch and the trip to Ottawa:

The awards were made at Government House on the Sunday afternoon following the Festival, and thus happily brought to a close the second event in one of the most successful competitive enterprises ever sponsored in Canada.

It would be impossible to separate the Festival proper from the social events which are so essentially a part of it. Social contacts begin in the foyer of the Ottawa Little Theatre, in which the Festival is held, and this is the great rendezvous where one meets all the players in all the teams from one end of the country to the other. The Ottawa Committee is hospitality itself – its members spare nothing to make the visitors welcome and happy during their stay. They meet trains at unearthly hours in the morning, drive new arrivals to the homes in which they have arranged to have them billeted, give them tea each day in the foyer of the theatre, and endeavour in every way possible to add to their enjoyment and see to their welfare. It is a gay week. Their Excellencies entertain little groups of players at Government House each afternoon; Colonel H.C. Osborne, the Honorary Director, opens his charming home and entertains luncheon guests each day; there are teas at the Country Club and everyone has a cocktail party to go to before dinner and there is always a gathering somewhere after the final curtain, where the discussion of the evening's performances goes on long into the night. One occasionally found a haven of quiet in the big swimming pool at the Chateau Laurier the morning after a late party, but just as likely as not when one was basking peacefully under a sun lamp after a refreshing swim, someone would push a head up from under water and call out: 'What did you think of the show the So-and-So's put on last night?' and the discussion began all over again.[17]

Such was the glamour of the DDF in the otherwise dirty thirties. Where now would you find an amateur theatre audience targeted like this: 'Let Elizabeth Arden help you look your best at the DDF'?[18]

The eastern region of the province took strength from the academic, institutional, and civil-service people of Ottawa and Kingston. These cities were the two poles of competition, providing in the Ottawa Little Theatre itself and in Convocation Hall at Queen's University two of the main venues of the festival. But the Eastern Ontario Drama League (EODL) was distinct in Ontario in that it managed on occasion to allow a French competition in its festival.

The first DDF regional festival ever, that of the Eastern Ontario Drama League in February 1933, was held in Convocation Hall. The Queen's University Drama Club presented *Gammer Gurton's Needle* (with Arthur Sutherland, later to organize the professional International Players in Kingston and Toronto), in competition with the Belleville Players' production of Harold Brighouse's *The Stoker*. A third entry was that of the St Peter's Players of Brockville, with the remarkable choice of *The Two Mr. Wetherbys*, written by St John Hankin in 1903, a dark and heavy Ibsenite play possibly never seen in an amateur festival before or since. Kingston presented an original play, *Rose Latulippe*, directed by its author Edward Wade Devlin, and the Ottawa Drama League presented two pieces, scenes from *Will Shakespeare* and O'Neill's *Ile* (very popular in the one-act competitions). Mr E.G. Sterndale Bennett, a name to be reckoned with as a director, first in Lethbridge and pre-eminently in Toronto, faced a challenging choice as adjudicator. He chose Ottawa – *Ile* first and *Shakespeare* second – which was a wrong choice in Kingston, as Vincent Massey was immediately to hear from the redoubtable Rupert Davies, publisher of the Kingston *Whig-Standard*:

We were not very well satisfied with Mr. Bennett, ... He seemed to start out very well but weakened towards the end. I had a very decided feeling, rightly or wrongly, that he was allowing his personal prejudices to influence him too much in his comments and decisions. I think you will agree with me that all things being equal it would have been much better to have given second place to Brockville or Kingston rather than to an Ottawa play which was so largely a one-woman show. Aside from the matter of choosing, in my opinion, Mr. Bennett's greatest weakness was in not giving systematic, constructive criticism on all points. On some plays he would dwell in great detail. Others he gave but brief attention.[19]

Massey suggested to Osborne that an invitation go to Kingston or Brockville as a third entry from eastern Ontario. A bad precedent was set and the tribulations of adjudication amply illustrated.

By the fourth festival in 1936, though still doing one-act plays, the participants were more varied. The Theatre Guild of Brockville echoed its first contribution with the *Folly of Faith*. Queen's entered four pieces: a Chekhov from the Drama Guild, a piece by the Faculty Players and two shows from the University Drama Club, one directed by Lorne Greene and one starring Lorne Greene (*Waiting for Lefty*) – an auspicious portent of future fame. Ottawa weighed in with three entries, including parts of *Winterset* and *The Late Christopher Bean*. Belleville sent both the Albert Players and the Young Thespians. Also represented, and giving some idea of the geographic expansion of the festival, were Kingston itself with *Legend* by Philip Johnson, Prince Edward County, Newcastle, and Cobourg, with two pieces.

The ninth festival picked up after the Second World War in Kingston, though why might be a little difficult to say, as five of its productions originated in Ottawa and Kingston was represented only by Arnold Edinborough's production of the inauspiciously titled *Wurzel-Flummery* by A.A. Milne. Ottawa's bulk in the EODL was always in evidence. Not only was there the mighty Ottawa Drama League and its junior adjuncts, but also the Ottawa Civil Service Recreational Association Drama Club and the Deep River Players (from the atomic-energy plant). Kingston's Domino Players and the Peterborough Little Theatre, sometimes supported by Brockville and Belleville, always mounted an effective skirmishing line against the overpowering Ottawa entries. Such courageous but unlikely places as Hawkesbury, Campbellford, Odessa, and Smiths Falls were occasionally heard from. But the small towns could not add the diversity to the festival that French entries did.

These came from Ottawa, Hull, Hawkesbury, and elsewhere, and the problem was how to accommodate them. Separate French festivals were held at the University of Ottawa in 1948 and at the Ottawa Little Theatre in 1949, where the groups involved were Le Caveau, La Comédie Nouvelle, La Groupe de l'Association St-Jean-Baptiste d'Ottawa, La Société des Concerts Brading, La Cercle Gascon de Hawkesbury, and Les

Acteurs de l'Institut Comédie Français, though the last two appeared only in 1948. Guy Beaulne first came to prominence directing Jean-François Reynard's *Légataire Universel* for Le Caveau in 1948, which earned him the best French production (the Robert Speaight) award in the DDF. He was to become a mainstay of the amateur theatre in French and an important adjudicator for the DDF.

Integration of the French plays into the main EODL festival was tried from time to time. In 1955 and again in 1958, Le Théâtre du Pont Neuf of Hull made a lonely appearance. *The House of Bernarda Alba* was presented by Le Théâtre de la Colline in 1962 and in 1963 Florent Forget had one play at least in his own tongue to judge, Le Théâtre du Pont Neuf's *Le Temps des Lilas*. The final festival at Woodroffe High School in Ottawa (1970) saw L'Atelier and Le Théâtre Populaire de Pointe Gatineau against only three English groups, two of which ironically presented translations from French – a Feydeau and an Anouilh. One other contribution was that of a Marcel Aymé piece by Les Compagnons de Hull in 1968.

One of the great strengths of the DDF, as well as one of its great trials, was its early and noble effort to be truly national, hence bilingual. Running a continent-wide drama festival in one language was difficult, running it in two almost impossible. Yet the DDF tried. Conceived very much in the mould of what Ontario considered to be Canadian and national, the DDF had no francophone among its original organizers, even for the Quebec regions. Quebec did have keen participants in time and French interest in the DDF increased, but the two solitudes were never really bridged. French participants remained aloof. The DDF was held in Quebec only once. When it was not held in Quebec, the organizers were always reluctant to admit the difficulty they had in getting an audience for the French evenings. Finding sufficiently bilingual adjudicators was always an added burden. In its own region, the EODL constantly faced these problems, which were somewhat mitigated by the Ottawa connection.

There seems little remarkable about EODL play choice over the years. One memorable entry, though, was that of the Lanark County Junior Farmers Drama Group of Perth, who seemed intent on preserving the values of hearth and home with their choice of *The Pie in the Oven* by J.J. Bell in 1949. By contrast, and in the way of challenging plays, Ottawa staged Graham Greene's *The Living Room* in 1961 and Pinter's *The Caretaker* in 1969; Domino essayed Miller's *The Crucible* in 1968, *Hedda Gabler* in 1959, and *Waiting for Godot* in 1963. The Belleville Theatre Guild presented *The Chalk Garden* in 1962. One of the true treats of the festival was rumoured to have been the appearance of

Roland Hewgill (best actor award) and Gordon Robertson in Domino Theatre's *Playboy of the Western World* (best play award), EODL Festival in Brockville, 1954. Robertson went on to be named best actor at the DDF final.

Rich Little as Bo Decker in the Ottawa Drama League's production of William Inge's *Bus Stop*.

But probably the pre-eminent figure in the eastern Ontario region through the forties and into the fifties was Robertson Davies. One might be pardoned for thinking the festival his playground. He first appears as a young man carefully reporting on the 1934 festival; his balanced and judicious description gives way, even then, to a certain magisterial asperity of tone, later to become much more familiar: 'Some slight dissatisfaction was felt when Mr. Harvey added to his already heavy duties those of literary critic. Of the plays which he condemned as badly written, two at least had been recommended by the Central Festival committee. Mr. Harvey's strictures on the works of A.A. Milne were felt to be unduly harsh, for although Mr. Milne's work is slight he has enjoyed sufficient success to exempt him from criticism as 'a dramatist who always lets you down.'[20] Davies's short plays became favourite festival fare: *Overlaid* won the Ottawa Drama League's playwriting contest in 1947 and *Eros at Breakfast* in 1948. A splendid production of the latter featuring Amelia Hall won the best Canadian play award (the Sir Barry Jackson Trophy) at the 1948 DDF.

The 1949 EODL festival in Brockville – and indeed the DDF at the Royal Alexandra in Toronto – were almost all-Davies affairs. The Ottawa Drama League won the regional festival with its presentation of his *Fortune, My Foe*. Defiant in defeat, however, was the Peterborough Little Theatre's production of *The Taming of the Shrew*, produced and directed by Davies himself and starring Brenda Davies. The regional adjudicator, Robert Speaight, occasioned much controversy by suggesting that this show was so remarkable and 'original' that it should go to the finals. It did, causing the adjudicator in Toronto, Philip Hope-Wallace, to express ironic mystification that the mere appearance of an actor in such a relatively small part as that of the Tailor should provoke a great gust of applause. The Toronto audience knew better, for they were acknowledging the protean efforts of Robertson Davies in all his new celebrity. His play, but not his production, won.

The next year Davies was back with a piece called *Voice of the People*, presented by Peterborough at the festival together with Synge's *The Tinker's Wedding*, directed by himself and again featuring his wife. And again he was opposed with his own work, this time by the Faculty Players of Queen's led by Arnold Edinborough directing Davies's 1947 play *Overlaid*. A further contribution to Peterborough was *At My Heart's Core*, specifically written for its 1950 centennial. Careful attention to the Peterborough Little Theatre's 1955 *Noah* would reveal one R. Davies playing the music! After Samuel Marchbanks had fled the eastern region for Ontario's Babylon, the Domino Players presented *Love and Libel*, the dramatization of Davies's novel *Leaven of Malice*. Carrying on his father Rupert Davies's work as a founder of the DDF, as a governor of that august body, as propagandist and adjudicator too,

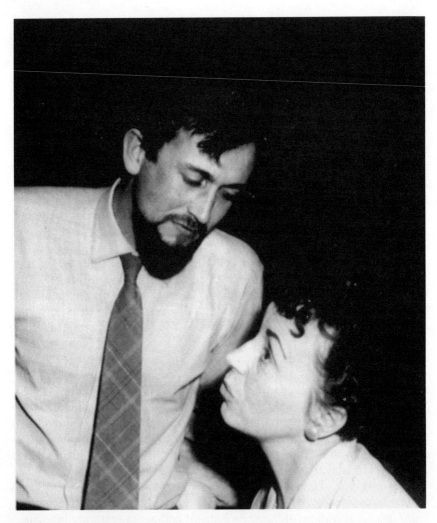

David Coleman and Kathy Roberts in Robertson Davies's *Love and Libel*, Domino
Theatre, Kingston, winner of three awards in the 1962 EODL festival, including best actor
(Coleman), best supporting actor (Roberts), and best director, Norma Edwards.

Davies accepted every challenge. But perhaps his noblest contribution to
the world of amateur theatre was, ironically, as a novelist: his dissection
of that world in his novel *Tempest-Tost* (1952) must stand as the finest
record of the amateur theatrical experience. Ever excoriating the shoddy,
this playboy of the eastern world surely used the festivals as they should
be used, giving to them much more than he took.

St Joan, London Little Theatre, 1947: Martin O'Meara, John Sullivan, Patrick Wells. The minimalist staging was typical of many entries to the Dominion Drama Festival, where curtain backgrounds were seen to equalize performance conditions for productions that had to travel.

In the western Ontario world during the First World War, J.S. Meredith of London had organized concert parties, and later established his Meredith Players at 'the Barn' – literally a barn on his own farm renovated as a small theatre. After the DDF had started, the Meredith Players, the Half-Way House Theatre, the London Drama League, and the London Community Drama Guild came together in 1938 to form what was to be the most formidable of all little theatres, the London Little Theatre. These groups had made some thirteen individual appearances at the Western Ontario Drama League (WODL) when in 1938 the LLT began its substantial contribution of twenty-three plays in all but five of the succeeding festivals with one of the great favourites of Ontario's amateurs, *The Late Christopher Bean* written by Sidney Howard. In time, its usual, conventional choices such as *Thunder Rock*, *Dear Octopus*, *On Borrowed Time*, and *The Rainmaker* gave way to ambitious and adventuresome plays such as *The Cocktail Party*, *Six Characters in Search of an Author*, *Hedda Gabler*, *As You Desire Me*, and, finally, the immense *Marat/Sade* in 1968.

Hamilton Community Players, *Everyman*, 1949

But London did not have it all its own way. The Sarnia Drama League, started by Herman Voaden in 1927 as the Drama Club of Sarnia, had been transformed by its great amateur impresario D. Park Jamieson, and by 1938, when the LLT emerged, had already produced thirty-eight shows. The Sarnia group was in the festival from beginning (*The Insect Play*, 1933) to end (*Sneaky Fitch*, 1970), making some fourteen appearances in all. The Players' Guild of Hamilton under Caroline H. Crerar had the most impressive record next to London, with twenty-two appearances. It was one of the few groups to do Shakespeare (scenes from *As You Like It*, 1937) in competition. Characteristically, it mounted solid, workable plays, but ventured into more advanced repertory in the fifties with *Murder in the Cathedral*, *The Importance of Being Earnest*, *Six Characters in Search of an Author*, and, in 1969, *The Killing of Sister George*.

Other cities too made their presence felt at the WODL. Kitchener-Waterloo Little Theatre (founded 1935) was a consistent performer, with such representative entries as *Elizabeth the Queen*, *A Doll's House*, *The Enchanted*, and finally (and appropriately) *No Exit*. Galt made a solid contribution, appearing some dozen times – and the staff of the Galt

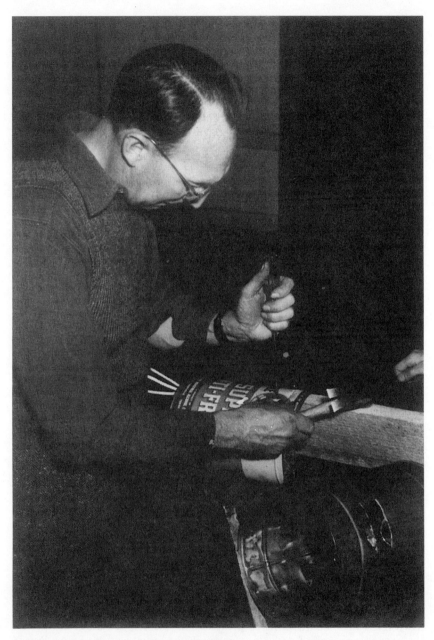

Post–Second World War technical adaptation in the community theatre: Arthur Fort makes lighting instruments from antifreeze cans (c. 1952)

Collegiate gave a strong impetus to Canadian material with its performances of Merrill Denison's work in 1933 and 1934. Woodstock was often there and Windsor, at first as the Border Theatre Guild (from 1934), while Brantford was big in the thirties and Simcoe in the fifties.

But the very predominance of these groups illustrates the problem with the amateur competitive festival. What about Wingham and Wallaceburg, Leamington and Burlington, St Catharines and St Marys? What, in particular, about the Ridgetown Players, featuring the young John Kenneth Galbraith, and their production of yet another *The House with the Twisty Windows*, by Mary Pakington, apparently the most popular play in Ontario in the early thirties? Sterndale Bennett had to screen twenty-three entries in the one-act festival of 1937, but only eleven in the next year, even though he had the help of Nella Jefferis. Were half the groups discouraged? Caroline Crerar reduced eighteen entries to five (but as usual, the big five – Hamilton, Kitchener-Waterloo, London, Sarnia, and Windsor) for the seventh festival, now of full-length plays, adjudicated by George Skillan of London, England, at the Savoy Theatre in Hamilton in 1939. (A theatre-goer paid $2.50 for the five shows and was assured that the ticket was transferable.) After the war, the pattern persisted – twenty-one entries in 1954, eighteen in 1958 and 1959. Could the fledgling groups from Elora or Goderich or Grimsby or Ingersoll or Tillsonburg compete with the numbers and resources of the larger theatres? The big groups sailed on; the smaller rose with enthusiasm and only too frequently sank with rancour and bitterness in envy of their wealthier neighbours. The LLT eventually had to modify its policy for the good of the festival after James Dean, the 1961 adjudicator, was more than warmly applauded when he announced that he had to give the victory to the LLT's *Hedda Gabler* because it was clearly the best, but that he was very reluctant to because the director, designer, and leading actress were professional. The LLT stopped entering plays directed by its professional director only to find competing groups paying for his services after he had left London!

Groups competed hard in western Ontario. They had more festivals than anybody else, continuing to 1942 and starting up again in 1946. Oddly, though Stratford was host to the western festival once (in 1959 at the Avon Theatre) it would appear to have had little interest in amateur theatre – a production of *The Hasty Heart* in 1954 did not get to the regional final – which perhaps says something about the difficulty the town itself has had adapting to professional theatre. If Stratford was not too conspicuous, the Scots were, through the entries of the St Andrew's Dramatic Society of Fergus and the Hamilton Gaelic Society Players.

Program cover, St Thomas Little Theatre, 1956

Program cover, Woodstock Little Theatre

Program cover, London Little Theatre, 1956–7 season

Chatham did not figure largely on the dramatic scene, but did give the festival appearances by Darcy McKeough and Peter Gzowski in the late fifties. The solid overall choice of plays seems notable – rarely is the ephemeral apparent. As to play origins, no particular pattern is discernible apart from the general drift away from the English and towards the American. All-American festivals occurred in 1955 and 1957, but on the other hand there were no American plays at all in 1968; in 1967 it was decided, however reluctantly, to have nothing but Canadian plays.

The name London Little Theatre was always a misnomer – from the outset there was very little that was 'little' about it. The four rival groups had become established in London during the twenties, and in 1945, after their 1938 union, they bought the Grand Theatre, at that time a Famous Players movie-house.[21] Legend maintains that the LLT was possibly the first amateur organization to own a full-size legitimate theatre.

The Grand had over 1800 seats (fewer after the two upper balconies were reduced to one), and for the next twenty-five years the LLT managed to fill most of them. From the outset the theatre's sheer size and the scope of the operation meant that a certain degree of professional input was needed. The theatre was an IATSE (International Alliance of Theatre and Stage Employees) union house, though the union had a mostly benevolent relationship with its employers. In the 'dark' weeks between LLT productions, the Grand continued as a 'road house,' as well as being the home of the London Symphony.

The London Little Theatre most clearly represented 'community theatre,' for its real success lay in its relationship to the community. It managed to cut across many social barriers in recruiting actors and technicians, for there was a certain *cachet* to appearing at the 'Grand.' Senior partners in eminent law firms, vice-presidents of London Life, and blue-ribbon cattle breeders who might have had doubts about appearing on the amateur stage in Toronto had no such inhibitions in London. Financial support came from local merchants – where else could you expect to see a 'Miss Adelaide' (*Guys and Dolls*) casually tossing about a very real six-foot-long white mink stole? The half-page story in the London *Free Press* gave the generous furrier ample reward. The local radio stations would always advertise for difficult properties. Furniture and dress shops eagerly supplied the requisite items.

But by 1957, the heavy production schedule made it apparent that the LLT had grown beyond an amateur management, and Peter Dearing was hired as artistic director. While Dearing added professional staff, his appointment did not radically change the amateur nature of the theatre. By 1960 it had in excess of 12,000 subscribers and an ambitious season of twelve productions, seven of them on the main subscription – including a musical comedy. The other five were a series of less widely appealing plays. This entire program was essentially sustained by volunteers. Later, the subscription series increased to eight plays and a musical. The likes of Brecht, Schiller, Ibsen, and Pinter began to find a place on the bill alongside the commercial shows. Space in old warehouses was found to do the new and experimental work.

Although the professional director wanted to keep pushing things in new directions, the amateur board of directors were happy to maintain things as they were. How to make the theatre the best that it could be for Londoners was subject to different interpretations: there was strain, and Dearing left in 1969. The theatre drifted with no director at the helm. In the argument about what to do next, the feeling that London should have the best even if it meant the end of the LLT prevailed. The board decided to turn this famous amateur theatre into the professional Theatre London, astutely phasing in the changes over three years beginning in 1971 under the new director Heiner Pillar.

The support that had sustained the LLT for nearly forty years continued. Board members, fund-raisers, some actors, and some technicians of the old dispensation treated the professional regional theatre as if it were still their own. It was a remarkable transition. Later Robin Phillips was to change the name, appropriately, to the Grand Theatre Company, as its old supporters raised the money to rebuild the theatre completely by 1978. But of course this change did not please everybody – a strong performance tradition dies hard. New amateur groups sprang up, the strongest being the London Community Players.

One of the stalwarts of amateur theatre in southwestern Ontario was Catherine Brickenden, whose name appeared when the London Drama League presented Rupert Brooke's *Lithuania* at the first Western Ontario final in 1933. Mrs G.A.P. Brickenden – 'Cissie' – was one of the provincial treasures of the amateur movement, a resilient and remarkable figure. Monied, she was the granddaughter of the founder of the McCormick Biscuit Company and so a figure of considerable social prominence in London – when she chose to be. For forty-five years she rode (side-saddle) to hounds at the London Hunt, of which she was honorary president. It was she who organized the elaborate social events when the festivals were held in London. Her picture, a formal social portrait, appeared in the 1937 program along with the adjudicators'. She entertained and organized lavishly.

Cissie Brickenden clearly seems to be the perfect illustration of all that was wrong about the social dimension of the amateur theatre in general and the DDF in particular. But in her the inherent contradictions of the social with the dramatic were held in a truly productive balance. She was called to Ottawa as one of the founders of the DDF. From her

Catherine Brickenden's *According to the Book* in Simcoe, Ontario, directed by Martin O'Meara

position within the London Drama League she was instrumental in founding the London Little Theatre in 1938. Her 1936 production of *Twenty-five Cents* by W. Eric Harris of Sarnia, a play that she found rather grim and for which she had no high hopes, won in London and went on to the DDF, where Harley Granville-Barker awarded her both the fourth Bessborough Trophy and the Sir Barry Jackson Trophy for the best play and the best Canadian work. After winning four more regional festivals for the LLT, it was suggested that she only be allowed to bring to the festival what she wrote. This she proceeded to do, returning with *A Pig in a Poke*, a very funny farce (not a particularly Canadian thing to write). But she returned now from Simcoe rather than London, for, deciding that she needed more room, she founded the Simcoe Little Theatre. (Her husband was a Norfolk County judge.) Not that she abandoned London: she simply spread her interests. The Simcoe Little Theatre proceeded to become a power, and her production of *The Boy Friend* in 1959 won another DDF. A passionate amateur in the full sense of the word, she distanced herself from the LLT when it hired a professional director in 1957. But she kept a watching brief and returned to her writing – her play *Zanorin* was produced by the Ottawa Drama League in 1957. Cissie Brickenden never retired – she was an amateur – but she retreated to her farm and her horses; clearly not typical, she was a remarkable doer.

Generally, the Toronto Festival, or more correctly the Central Ontario Drama Festival, was more ambitious than its cousins. It was superimposed on an existing and relatively sophisticated theatrical scene. It had its own special place in Hart House Theatre, its home from beginning to end except for one brief foray to Oshawa near the end of its days. The theatre at Hart House has its character, its advantages, but it was an afterthought, and so is reached through longish, turning, descending tunnels. It is a hidden place; you have to know it is there. It is all part of a mystique whereby year by year Toronto's theatrical mavens retreated to their underground enthusiasm.

An emphasis on original material is apparent in the Toronto festival from the beginning, with a quarter of the inaugural program consisting of original material. The first play presented was the one-act *Catalogue* by T.M. Morrow, 'a study of country life in the Ottawa valley,' staged by the Central High School of Commerce Evening Class in Dramatic Literature; this company was the creation of Herman Voaden, also responsible for another offering of the first festival, *Rocks*, his expressionistic play about Lake Superior. The third indigenous play of twelve festival entrants (reduced from thirty-three aspirants) was *The Paths of Glory*, about Ontario's own hero, General Brock, written and directed by Nathaniel A. Benson for the Ontario College of Education Drama Guild. Although this proportion of Canadian plays was not kept up, certainly writers such as Voaden, Benson, Morrow, V.L. Banks, Lois Reynolds, Leonora McNeilly, K.W. Edge, Margaret Ness, and John Coulter did get a hearing. In fact, in the last pre-war festival, six of the twelve plays were Canadian. The reading groups at the Toronto Public Library and the Beaches Library as well as the Playwrights' Studio Group generated much of this new material.

The first festivals in Central Ontario were dominated by the superior quality and multiple entries from Hart House Theatre and the Players' Club; for example, Edgar Stone's production of Miles Malleson's *Michael*, with W.A. Atkinson, Jane Mallett, and Robert Christie, which went on to win the Bessborough Trophy for best play at the 1934 DDF. There was considerable variety of groups in this urban festival. Stephanie Jarvis brought religious enthusiasm with her Miracle Players (and New Miracle Players). The Young Judaea Drama Group provided a program explanation of things Jewish for their play *Eyes*. The Unnamed Players struck a mysterious note and the Beach Roamers a rather nostalgic one. Dorothy Goulding's Junior Players opened the eyes of many children to the magic of the stage. The Welsh Dramatic Society was suitably Welsh. Once, a group from Port Credit struggled in from the west.

The city setting allowed for greater creative opportunities. Musicians and artists were readily available to lend their talents (Healey Willan, Sir Ernest MacMillan, J.E.H. MacDonald, R. York Wilson). The church groups from the Anglican Young Peoples Association could leave their churches for the theatrical milieu and so widen their horizon. At the same time, E.G. Sterndale Bennett and his Toronto Masquers could pursue their strictly theatrical aims all the more seriously. There was a floating pool of talent, not only of actors but also of directors: Edgar Stone, Sterndale Bennett, W.S. Milne, Nancy Pyper, and, much later, Herbert Whittaker. Directors identified with certain groups, but the groups often came unstuck and the directors travelled.

The resumption of the Central Ontario festival after the war coincided with a heightened interest in theatre by young war veterans and university students. Names of future celebrity roll off the cast lists, many of them to make places for themselves in the first generation of Canadian professional theatre – Michel Ney, William Hutt, William Kilbourn (Trinity College Dramatic Society); William Needles, Jack Medhurst (The Caravan Players); Arthur Hiller, Murray Davis, Henry Kaplan, Araby Lockhart (University College Players' Guild); Earle Grey (Arts and Letters Club); Jane Acker, Eric House (The Civic Theatre); Barbara Hamilton (Newmarket Dramatic Club); Ben Lennick, E.M. Margolese, Leo Orenstein (Belmont Group Theatre); David Gardner (UADC); Kay Hawtrey, Ted Follows (University of Toronto); Cosette Lee (Canadian Theatre Guild). True, these people were only passing through, but it is well to remember that they were there. And they were doing a variety of what you might expect – Thornton Wilder, Edna St V. Millay, a Canadian play, a native play, Odets, Coward, Pirandello, George Kelly, a Mexican play, another Canadian play, a Philip Johnson, another Odets, a third Canadian play, a Ruth Gordon, a Chekhov, another Coward, a Philip Barry, a Ben W. Levy. For the trend spotters, three Canadian plays, two Cowards, and two Odets.

The most productive period of the CODL, one dominated by the rivalry of W.S. Milne's Norvoc Players, James Dean's Playcraftsmen, and the University Alumnae Dramatic Club, came to an end with the fifties. Milne's last festival entry was *Mary, Mary Quite Contrary* by St John Ervine and Dean's was *All Summer Long* by Robert Anderson, both in 1960. Even more definitive for the festival was the final appearance of the 'Alum' – the UADC – with a very ambitious production of Congreve's *The Way of the World*. Not often did the festival aspire to Restoration comedy.

Toronto's Alumnae Theatre offers first staging in Canada of *Waiting for Godot*, 1957.
Left–right: Ivor Jackson, Kenneth Wickes, Fred Euringer, Powell Jones; directed by
Pamela Terry Beckwith

Milne's group, centring on Northern Vocational School, and the
UADC, retaining a closeness to the university, had been with the festival
since its beginning. Dean's group, drawn from Central Technical
School, had joined in 1934. Rivalry was intense among these three and
Herman Voaden's Central High School group. The four had the pick of
Toronto's aspiring and established actors and directors. Throughout the
fifties, the Playcraftsmen mounted solid commercial plays at a very
high standard: Noel Coward's *Marquise*, Williams's *The Rose Tattoo*
(in this production, Dean was first joined by the Tobiases – L.C. as
director and Frances, his wife, a talented actress), the very successful
production of Odets's *The Country Girl*, *The Italian Straw Hat*, Paul
Osborne's *On Borrowed Time*, and Robinson Jeffers's *Medea*. By contrast, the UADC taste was for more challenging, more artistic, and certainly less commercial choices. They had won the festival with T.S.
Eliot's *The Family Reunion* in 1953. Dean's *Rose Tattoo* won the next
year, when the Alumnae staged Christopher Fry's *Venus Observed*;

Chekhov's *Uncle Vanya* by the UADC followed and then Leon Major's production of the original Canadian play *Teach Me How to Cry* by Patricia Joudry, which won both the regional festival and the Bessborough Trophy at the DDF. The UADC offered two more original plays: Norman Williams's *To Ride a Tiger* in 1957 and James Reaney's *The Killdeer* in 1960, which went to the Vancouver DDF. In between, they introduced Canada to Samuel Beckett with *Waiting for Godot* and to the Spanish poet Lorca's *Yerma*.

Much of all this was ambitious and solid theatre. These were not the only groups, of course – prominent as well were the West End Players, the Sudbury Little Theatre Guild, and the York Community Theatre. Representative writers presented were Jean Anouilh, Noel Coward, and Bernard Shaw; plays such as Robert Ardrey's *Thunder Rock*, Terence Rattigan's *Separate Tables*, William Inge's *Picnic*, and J.B. Priestley's *Laburnum Grove* were typical. But things were changing. The professional theatre was quickening in Toronto – the better talents could now get paid. The faithful adjudicators of the British Drama League – Robert Speaight, John Allen, Andre Van Gyseghem, Cecil Bellamy, Richard West, and Richard Ainley, all of London, England – gave way to more familiar local, often CBC names. Typically, the new groups that came along were either impermanent gatherings of semi-professional actors or, more lastingly, a new breed of community theatre, usually suburban and with no illusions about reaching a wider audience than its own. The Richmond Hill Curtain Club was perhaps the most successful of these groups. Others were the Scarborough Theatre Guild, the Etobicoke Players, the Don Mills Players, and the Theatre Upstairs from North York. Older city groups were the Barn Players – which dated themselves from the Broadview YMCA in 1913 and won the DDF with Shelagh Delaney's *A Taste of Honey* in 1964 – and the Central Players. But what had started as a city festival had become a largely suburban one. Little was left at the centre.

A late and brave venture very far from that centre was the creation of a new region for the DDF in Ontario. The north as part of central Ontario, as conceived in 1933, was no longer viable, and in 1957 a northern region was set up as QUONTA – the Quebec/Ontario Theatre Association. This development was occasioned by remoteness – it was too hard to get to Toronto – and fairness – northern groups could not compete on equal terms when they did (though both the Sudbury Little Theatre and the Port Arthur Masquers acquitted themselves with credit).

The reason vociferously raised against the creation of QUONTA was that increasing the number of regions increased the number of regional winners who could not be invited to the finals. This aside, the arrangement

Community involvement created this huge sculpture for *The Lark* as staged by Sault
Theatre Workshop in Sault Ste Marie (1971). The figure was done by students at
Algoma College under direction of costume designer Evan Ayotte. It stands on a stylized
grillwork, symbolic of Joan's imprisonment, and represents the British lion resting its
paw triumphant on the shield of France.

was at best an uneasy alliance between French and English, and the Quebec groups withdrew from the festivals. The anchors of the region were
the Sudbury Little Theatre and the Sault Theatre Workshop. Other members (in 1967) were the Cambrian Players of the Lakehead (Port Arthur),
the Espanola Little Theatre, the North Bay Gateway Theatre Guild, the
Manitoulin Island Drama League, and the Laurentian Players in Sudbury. And as though to spite all the objections to the group's inception, it
frequently went to the final festival. It was a worthy northern fringe.

The festivals survived the sixties, but only just. It was too anarchic, too
individualistic a time. Gone were the receptions at Government House. In
1968 at Windsor, where his play *Fortune and Men's Eyes* had won the
Vincent Massey Medal (formerly the Sir Barry Jackson Trophy) as the
best Canadian work, John Herbert publicly refused to accept his prize,
damning the DDF as 'socializing dilettantes.' Organizations were in bad
odour. To organize, let alone patronize, a social event was increasingly
suspect, if not hypocritical. The social aspects of the festivals had to go.

'Wisdom' by Florence Wyle, one of fifteen Calvert Trophies, designed and sculpted
from various woods for the Dominion Drama Festival by noted artists Florence Wyle,
Frances Loring, and Sylvia Daoust

And money had now to be found. The DDF had always paid for itself, which meant that its governors had to be able to raise money. The entry fee to a festival for a group had been in the order of $20 before the war. While this had increased to $100, it hardly paid the expenses of the regionals, let alone the costs of transporting eight groups across the country for the final. The privilege of being president of the DDF in the 1950s reportedly meant $5000 in personal expenses. Commercial sponsorship was obtained from Calvert Distilleries in 1953. Sponsorship by a distillery still caused scandal, particularly when it was suggested the sponsor's products be used by the DDF. Calvert stayed with the festival until 1960, contributing some $15,000 a year and a set of thirteen figures carved in wood by Florence Wyle, Frances Loring, and Sylvia Daoust, one for each festival winner and known as the Calvert Trophies. So the intrusion of a sponsor caused considerable dislocation, but did keep the DDF going. When the DDF asked for yet more money, Calvert left and the Canadian Association of Broadcasters came on board and stayed until 1966, supplying some $20,000 a year.

But this was a new world. The (Vincent) Massey-Lévesque report on culture had come out in 1951, and the Canada Council had now been supporting the arts since 1957. Government money was forthcoming to the DDF for travel and training grants, but that was all. And that was not enough. By 1970 the DDF deficit was $36,000. It had established itself by its own efforts as a uniquely Canadian cultural institution, but that was not enough. Voices were raised in its defence (though not that of Robertson Davies) – but in vain. Whatever money was available was given to the professionals. The Dominion Drama Festival voted itself out of existence in 1970, after its last festival in Winnipeg.

A face-saving government operation called Theatre Canada replaced it and held further 'showcases,' the first a non-competitive one at the National Arts Centre in 1971. Besides that, Theatre Canada confined itself largely to training schemes and keeping groups in touch until its money was simply cut off in 1978.

And what of the Ontario government? Its official interest in community theatre goes back to an often overlooked theatrical pioneer named Jessie Beattie, whose job it was in 1935 to travel the province, 'arranging cultural recreation programs featuring amateur dramatics.' The government provided various supports over the years, such as the Ontario Drama Council of the Ministry of Education in 1960. But it was not until 1969 that a major step was taken with the organization of Theatre Ontario, a response to an expressed need in the province rather than a means to sustain the DDF. At first, the hope was that this agency could bring together amateur and professional by serving both. When this proved impractical, Theatre Ontario gradually became the arm of government that sustained community theatres. Through the seventies it disbursed some $800,000 in training grants. By 1980 its annual budget was $750,000.

There is no end to this story; amateur theatre still flourishes and always will. Theatre Ontario reported a membership of 283 groups in 1990, a phenomenal growth from 103 in 1980. As well as 87 groups in the Toronto region, 58 in the western, 44 in the eastern, and 26 in the northern, there are now 68 multicultural groups on Theatre Ontario's lists. There would seem to be a considerable future for the playmaking group as preserver and tutor of cultural traditions. As well, there seems ample opportunity for those who still want to get involved in putting on plays.

Some of these groups are formidable and important enterprises, particularly those that have managed to buy or build their own theatres. From 1960 to 1980 alone the Ottawa Little Theatre gave 183 full productions – though losing its old theatre to fire in 1970 and building a new one by 1972. Up to nine thousand Ottawans are members, producing ten plays a year with only a limited number of employees. The Domino Theatre not only serves Kingston, but tours to nearby towns from its handsome limestone building: it is an amateur regional theatre.

The continuing story of the Alumnae in Toronto is a phenomenon in itself. The women of what is now styled the Alumnae Theatre Company (men are still excluded from being members of the club) have built performance spaces successively in a coach-house, a warehouse, a synagogue, a church, and, finally, a handsome firehall on Berkeley Street. Here, in 1972, with the city's blessing and to the designs of Ronald Thom, they created the Alumnae Theatre: an intimate theatre, with gracious lobbies and a superior performance space on the third floor – the Elizabeth Mascall Studio – in an Edwardian fireman's billiard room. The Alumnae contrives to be a sort of respectable alternative theatre, entirely amateur yet offering an ambitious repertory of contemporary plays neglected by Toronto's professionals, with occasional classics and new Canadian work. Appropriately, they have often initiated and frequently featured women's writing, not only their own but such plays as those of Timberlake Wertenbaker and Caryl Churchill. The survival, perseverance, and continued renewal of this group is impressive: they have always paid their own way and made up with wit and intelligence – and a truly remarkable amount of hard work – what they may have lacked in resources and expertise.

Although often referred to as one, the amateur theatre has never pretended to be a training ground for the professional. What it has done, however, is provide aspiring amateurs with the opportunity to explore and expand their talent. A win at the festival often confirmed this talent and encouraged the young artist to continue. Certainly people did use the publicity and prestige of the DDF as a stepping-stone to professional theatre. It is easy to discover the names of the ten best-known actors in Ontario from amateur programs and laud the amateur theatre for producing them. But it is just as easy to look at the same programs and see the names of a future lieutenant-governor, an economist of world renown, one of Canada's leading psychiatrists, a future provincial treasurer, or one of Canada's pioneering heart surgeons to realize that first and foremost amateur theatre is a social activity – and although it has tried, and done its best, it has never really been the responsibility of the amateur theatre to create a national theatre or a national drama.

Theatre has always renewed itself. What began for the older amateur groups as something quite naïve, a response to natural prompting, addressed at first the international material available to the English-speaking world. The amateurs did not worry about finding their own voice, but rather devoted themselves to getting organized – something at which they succeeded only too well. But increasingly there were the demands that a Canadian voice be found. The groups responded; they sometimes tried hard, but their heart wasn't really in it. Either they did not have the imaginative energy or just could not make the jump to original work. They were not created for that. In their small towns they wanted to be 'big town,' to emulate what happened in London, New York, and even, latterly, Toronto. They wanted to copy – and still do; as groups and individuals they were content to copy. They wanted to be a remote reflection of metropolitan culture.

That it was 'culture' never really occurred to them – any more than that they were being too 'social' for their critics. Similarly, because they were doing it, it was presumably Canadian, but not, for the critics, Canadian enough. Such criticisms originated in the universities, but soon affected government agencies, who distributed financial aid. The groups were happy to accept the government's attentions, but they were now self-conscious and unsure of what was expected of them. The restless cultural bureaucrats tinkered the old drama festivals out of existence, but soon gave up on the amateurs when it became apparent that there was going to be enough money for a professional theatre.

That particular phase of amateur theatre is now over, as are the days of the DDF. The Bessborough Trophy hangs on an office wall in Ottawa; the Calvert Trophies are thought to be with whoever last won them. Hart House Theatre is almost empty now, given over to lectures and the annual student revues. And the redoubtable Mrs Brickenden has gone too – in 1993 at the age of ninety-seven. But even as she died, the theatre was renewing itself: a group called the London Community Players had just bought the Palace movie-house for a new home.

The amateurs are returning in growing numbers to what they had always done and have always wanted to do: 'have a go' – themselves and unassisted.

NOTES

1 Ann Saddlemyer, Introduction, *Early Stages: Theatre in Ontario 1800–1914* (Toronto: University of Toronto Press, 1990), 17

2 Robert Scott, 'A Study of Amateur Theatre in Toronto: 1900–1930,' MA thesis, University of New Brunswick, 1966. For this passage in particular, as for several others, we are indebted to Scott's thesis.

3 Ibid.

4 W.S. Milne Papers, Metropolitan Toronto Reference Library

5 See Scott, 'A Study of Amateur Theatre.'

6 These gouache on vellum drawings are obviously part of a set; the title page is missing. They are proposals for various decorative details and colour schemes for the auditorium. On deposit in the offices of Hart House Theatre.

7 See chapter 5 in this volume.

8 Toby Gordon Ryan, *Stage Left: Canadian Theatre in the Thirties* (Toronto: CTR Publications, 1981), 126

9 Betty Lee, *Love and Whisky* (Toronto: Simon and Pierre, 1982), 77

10 *The Curtain Call*, 4 March 1931

11 Earl of Bessborough, Speech to the Empire Club of Toronto, November 1931

12 *The Curtain Call*, 23 April 1932

13 *London Free Press*, 1 March 1933. This text may have been 'leaked' to the press. It is part of the DDF executive directive to the adjudicators.

14 *The Curtain Call*, 7 November 1932

15 Ibid., 19 February 1934

16 Ibid., 15 January 1935

17 Ibid., 21 May 1934

18 Ibid., April 1936, 10. This advertisement was used in DDF regional programs in the same year.

19 Lee, *Love and Whisky*, 109

20 *The Curtain Call*, 17 March 1934

21 For further information on the Grand Opera House, see Saddlemyer, ed., *Early Stages*, 235, 256.

5 *University Theatre*

ROSS STUART AND ANN STUART

Ontario universities have debated the role of theatre in higher education for more than a century. In some ways this began as an echo of the debate over the probity of theatre itself, as reflected in the austere Methodism prevalent in the province in the nineteenth century. John Wesley, the founder of Methodism, wrote that 'most of the present stage-entertainments sap the foundation of all religion, ... giving a wrong turn to youth especially.'[1] *The Doctrine and Discipline of the Methodist Church* (1898) expressly forbade 'attending theatres, ... patronizing dancing schools, [and] taking such other amusements as are obviously of a misleading or questionable moral tendency.'[2]

Late in the nineteenth century at the University of Toronto, one of fewer than nine post-secondary colleges and universities in Ontario at the time, theatre was synonymous with the notorious 'Hallowe'en nights': annual theatre evenings that regularly spilled over into vandalism and riot. Critic Hector Charlesworth would later recall how 'beasts' and 'rowdies' threw 'cabbages and boots at fellow students who took part in amateur theatricals.'[3] However, what 'was considered permissible amusement' on campus was no joke 'when professional performances were interrupted.' In 1877, Professor John H. MacKerras, a classicist and member of the senate of Queen's University, lectured on how theatre had 'fallen low' since the Restoration: 'The faculty of speech is the best part of drama and today the elocutionist, rendering selections from the greatest dramatists, [has] carried off from the theatre its *most* valuable – if not the *only* valuable quality which it possesse[s].'[4] The *Queen's Journal* records that this sentiment was greeted with applause.

And can we ever forget the trials of poor John Primrose, whose fate was chronicled for the moral uplift of Canada West in a sermon entitled 'Amateur Histrionics' (1858)?[5] 'John Primrose (as we shall call him)

From as early as 1828, when scenes of Terence's *Adelphi* were used by the Royal
Grammar School in York (Toronto) as a language exam, classical drama has been
present in education. In this photo, Euripides' *Alcestis* is staged by the Faculty Players,
Queen's University, 1943.

attracted attention by the skill which he displayed in performing the pre-
scribed exercises of his classes, and even succeeded in carrying off more
than one premium.' However John, 'who had a talent for elocution, was
induced to join a theatrical association.' Within a short time, 'the promising student degenerated into a ruined, aimless, spirit-broken man.' As
the author, Reverend R.J. MacGeorge concludes, 'Let "young Canada"
be warned by this lurid beacon.'

Student Drama: The English Model

The beginning of theatre on Ontario campuses had to be very earnest
indeed. Accordingly, the first noteworthy presentation at the University
of Toronto was Sophocles' *Antigone*, performed in classical Greek in
1882.[6] The student newspaper, the *Varsity* (25 November 1881), championed the idea, remarking that 'nothing perhaps has spread the fame of

Harvard so far as its representation of the *Oedipus Tyrannus* last winter.' In addition, the all-male university would have no trouble with casting because 'the non-appearance of women upon the Greek stage dispenses with their services.' Later the *Varsity* (9 December 1881) welcomed the forthcoming production as a 'refreshing and novel' change from 'the stereotyped annual College entertainments.' The fifty-member Glee Club acted as Chorus and sang to Mendelssohn's music. (The Glee Club, the first theatrical group on campus, had been founded in 1879.) The production was the inspiration of Professor Maurice Hutton, a brilliant classicist and later principal of University College, who played Antigone. Opening night, 11 April 1882, at Convocation Hall was an unqualified success, hailed by *Saturday Night* as 'the most ambitious cultural effort which Canada has seen.'[7] Drama had secured a respectable foothold at the university that it would not yield. The *Varsity* crowed, 'Oxford did it with less success and Edinburgh with less still.'

The *Varsity*'s references to Harvard, Edinburgh, and, particularly, Oxford, were germane; they indicate that associations such as the Oxford University Dramatic Society were already accepted as the model for dramatics within the university, and they would remain as such until very recently. In the English tradition, campus theatricals were permitted, and indeed encouraged when they had a perceived educational function, as long as they remained exclusively extracurricular and solely the responsibility of students. The university might offer facilities, and upon occasion interested faculty might participate, but no academic course credit of any kind would be given for putting on plays and no training of any sort provided.

There was not necessarily any qualitative difference between extracurricular and curricular student drama. What is significant was that for most of the participants, acting in plays was an enjoyable diversion from the pressures of undergraduate life, an avocation rather than a vocation. From clubs like the drama society of the University of Western Ontario might come future members of the London Little Theatre, but not theatre professionals. If university theatre could cultivate knowledgeable and articulate audiences, that was goal enough.

In the nineteenth century, special events often included the theatrical. On 12 December 1893, the new governor-general and his wife, Lord and Lady Aberdeen, were welcomed to the University of Ottawa in both English and French, as befitted the bilingual nature of that institution, still an affiliate of the Roman Catholic church, which had established it in 1848. The program included, as Lady Aberdeen recalled, musical events plus 'recitations, [and] dialogue between Brutus and Cassius etc.'[8] At what was then called the Western University of London, the first class of twelve in 1882 shared a residence with the boys of Dufferin College. To commemorate this milestone, Dr Darnell, principal of the school, wrote a satire on *HMS Pinafore*, which was performed by the boys under the direction of the physical-training instructor.[9] Before the First World War a highlight of every fall term at Western was the banquet in Huron College where freshmen treated seniors and performed music, dramatic scenes, charades, and class songs. The annual *Conversazione* evenings were another popular Western tradition in that period and always included an artistic component. Sporadic efforts at play production continued into this century at the University of Toronto, as at other colleges and universities. For example, Trinity College produced Aristophanes' *The Frogs* outdoors in 1902. One of the first formal drama clubs was the Women's Dramatic Club of University College, founded in 1905. It was devoted to using the plays of Shakespeare to teach voice culture, physical poise, and dramatic expression.[10] This organization was the nucleus of the University Alumnae Drama Club, begun in 1918, which has remained active to this day. Many men, by contrast, seem to have preferred less-esteemed theatricals. Burgon Bickersteth, warden of Hart House from 1921 to 1947, lamented the 'endless Faculty "shows" – very poor and rather vulgar skits got up annually by the Medical Faculty or the Engineers.'[11]

In contrast, Trinity College's Dramatic Society, founded in 1927, was typical of a creative college group. It presented a full-length play each year and entered university-wide one-act drama festivals, often with experienced directors such as Edgar Stone, Earle Grey, and Herbert Whittaker.[12] Of particular note were the Shakespearean productions of then faculty member G. Wilson Knight in the 1930s, which he used to test his theories, later expounded in critical works such as *The Wheel of Fire*. G.B. Harrison, another well-known Shakespearean scholar, did the same thing at Queen's University in the 1940s.

After an early failure in forming a drama society at Queen's, it was not until 1899 that the Queen's Dramatic Club (to be re-named the Drama Guild in 1925) was founded under the general direction of a member of the English Department, Professor W.S. Dyde. Yet the Ladies' Column in the student *Queen's Journal* still felt it necessary to denounce those who believed that the representation of drama would 'instil into the hearts of poor unsuspecting students that most terrible of all evils – the love of the stage.' Dyde hoped the club would help students learn more about Shakespeare, and began with *As You Like It*; every two weeks early in 1900 an act of the play was presented to club members. An anonymous history commemorating the Drama Guild's fiftieth anniversary in 1949 explained that these performances were private because 'the young student chosen for Rosalind was unwilling to don doublet and hose.' On alternate weeks the group studied *Julius Caesar*. Despite the club's seriousness of purpose, the *Journal* described meetings as 'a complete break from the formalism of class work and the rigidity of most other Society meetings.' The erstwhile female Rosalind did venture onto the public stage in consecutive years, playing Portia in *The Merchant of Venice*, act 4, and Gertrude in *Hamlet*, act 3, in what were called *Evenings with Shakespeare*, and which also included a piano solo, a recitation, and a dialogue.

The example of Queen's would be duplicated at other universities. Although 'university plays' had been a regular part of student life at Western, after the First World War, English and Music department staff helped to organize a Glee Club and a complementary Players' Guild. A Gilbert and Sullivan Society specializing in operettas followed after the next war. At the University of Ottawa there was a Drama Guild, which still exists. McMaster University seemed to prefer lighter entertainment. While it was still located in Toronto in the 1920s, the men students launched the 'McMasteriffics' to stage variety shows featuring ribald female impersonation.[13] After the university moved to Hamilton in the 1930s, the segregation of the sexes was broken with the formation of the Glee Club, but it was not until the 1950s that an active and ambitious Dramatic Society evolved along with an Operatic Society, which performed Gilbert and Sullivan. Drama clubs often competed with others on the same campus, and inter-university festivals took place from time to time.

In 1913, the first campus-wide theatre group, the Players' Club, was founded at the University of Toronto. Composed of university men, both graduates and undergraduates, the club, before its tenancy at Hart House Theatre, presented its productions in Burwash Hall, the dining hall of Victoria College's men's residence, where a raised platform formed a crude stage. The first production, directed by club founder and first president, R. Hodder Williams, a professor at the University of Toronto, was Ibsen's *An Enemy of the People*. The lieutenant-governor and other dignitaries came to ensure that, as the *Varsity* (15 December 1913) put it, 'The Club is not of the nature of the usual run of student theatrical organizations, whose objects often seem to be more in the line of providing amusement' but instead has 'serious aims.'

The second production was a double bill of Shaw's *The Dark Lady of the Sonnets* and Galsworthy's *The Pigeon*, the latter directed by Vincent Massey, who was club president for the 1914–15 season. Vincent described it as 'a great success' (it made $210.00 for the Red Cross), but brother Raymond Massey remembered his own performance as 'just awful.'[14] The work of the club was suspended during the First World War, but by 1917 Vincent Massey was trying to revive it. However, the first formal meeting of the syndics of the Players' Club is not recorded until 3 May 1919. When Hart House Theatre opened, the group was anxious to have productions there regarded as a continuation of its earlier work. Gradually, however, the link between the Players' Club, still very much a part of the university, and Hart House Theatre, very much a part of Vincent Massey, began to dissolve and was practically broken by 1921.

Hart House Theatre: The Massey Years

As Carroll Aikins, himself to become director of Hart House Theatre, recalled in *The Yearbook of the Arts 1928–29*, 'I remember ... the early years of Hart House,' when it was 'the scene of a genuine creative activity ... the beginning if nothing better, of a noteworthy dramatic movement.'[15] Massey envisioned Hart House as an art theatre in the tradition of the Abbey Theatre in Ireland, but never provided sufficient funding to realize this dream. Hart House was to be a 'little theatre,' in the 'arts theatre' tradition; it was definitely not to be a university theatre. Therefore, it is not surprising that it had a great influence on the little theatre movement in Canada, but almost none on university drama during the Massey years.

An élite audience attended the opening double-bill in the autumn of 1919. The critics made every effort to be kind, sometimes to the point of absurdity; the *Globe* reviewer commented, 'It was very difficult to follow the action although no doubt the roles had been well studied.' The theatre itself was exemplary, although its sub-basement location was uncommon and indicative of its being an afterthought, added to the existing student centre at Vincent Massey's behest and built with funds from the Massey Foundation. The intimate playhouse, seating 450, with proscenium stage and excellent acoustics, offered outstanding facilities for actors, technicians, and audiences. Its most serious shortcomings were the result of its subterranean location: there was only very limited fly space for hanging scenery, for example.

Vincent Massey met American-born Roy Mitchell, the man he chose to lead his theatre, at the Arts and Letters Club, where artists and like-minded people would gather. Possibly because he left a small body of written work, including his seminal book, *Creative Theatre*, Roy Mitchell is the best known of the theatre's six directors. Mitchell had attended the University of Toronto, but departed without a degree to work on various newspapers in Canada and the United States. Around 1914 he was in

New York City, where he directed several fringe productions and spent a year as technical director of the Greenwich Village Theatre, one of the 'little theatre' groups that were trying to revitalize the theatre scene.

Mitchell's productions were often remembered for their beautiful stage images, not surprisingly since they were sometimes designed or painted by members of the Group of Seven such as Lawren Harris and A.Y. Jackson. The words that appear most frequently in the reviews of these productions are 'light' and 'colour,' as in this description of Arthur Lismer's design for Euripides' *Trojan Women*: 'His use of colour particularly the clashes of crimson in the great stone walls added to the richness of the whole colour scheme. While the very beautiful colour combination in the costumes completed and enriched the whole picture. In the last scene the lighting impressed one with the technical possibilities of Hart House Theatre, and the bold use of deep shadowed high light gave a velvet depth to all the scenes.'

Merrill Denison, who had trained as an architect, also designed for Hart House, but he was to become more famous as a playwright. It had been the goal of the theatre from the beginning to present Canadian plays. By his second season Roy Mitchell had located two short plays, but both were intense dramas. Mitchell wanted a comedy to round out this Canadian bill, and he locked Denison in a room until he wrote down a story about the backwoodsmen near Bon Echo where he had spent much of his childhood. *Brothers in Arms*, as the work was called, became the most popular play to originate at Hart House Theatre. Denison went on to write other plays for Hart House, including *Marsh Hay* and *Contract*.

Roy Mitchell left Hart House Theatre after two seasons and spent the rest of his life working in New York. His replacement, Bertram Forsyth, was a graduate of Oxford and an active member of the Oxford University Drama Society. He had some experience as a professional actor and several of his plays had been mounted, though with very limited success. The prospect of a permanent job with his own theatre proved irresistible and he remained for four seasons, during which time he directed thirty-four of Hart House's thirty-six productions. His skill in training actors allowed the theatre to survive after his departure.

No doubt because of his own struggles as a playwright, Forsyth took up the cause of presenting Canadian plays and incorporated a 'Canadian Bill' of three one-act plays in each of his four seasons. He also directed the first full-length Canadian play to be performed on the Hart House stage. This was *The God of Gods* by Carroll Aikins, which had been staged by the Birmingham Repertory Theatre and thus had the cachet of international success.

Burgon Bickersteth, from his unique vantage point as warden of Hart

Carroll Aikins's *The God of Gods* as staged at Hart House Theatre, 1922. The play was first performed at the Birmingham Repertory Theatre, 1919.

House, commented in Forsyth's time upon what was to be an ongoing Hart House problem: its relationship to the student body of the University of Toronto. Undergraduates simply could not understand why they had such limited access to a theatre in their midst. Bickersteth observed that 'the undergraduates feel the theatre has been getting further and further away from them.'[16] Bickersteth deplored the fact that even 'recognized dramatic organizations ... such as those of Trinity College and Victoria College' were not always allowed 'a few nights during the course of the winter when they could put on their shows.'

Forsyth introduced a summer school, begun in 1923, which was sponsored by the department of extension. The course culminated in the production of one or more plays, which he presented at the end of the summer. Forsyth stayed at Hart House until 1925 before moving on to the Margaret Eaton School and finally to New York City, where he committed suicide in 1927.

The theatre's third director (1925–7) was another Englishman, Walter Sinclair, who had spent many years in Hong Kong, where he gained considerable experience directing the local amateur dramatic society. Sinclair was also a businessman, however, and that was part of the reason that Vincent Massey hired him. Theatre had been Sinclair's hobby; now it became his profession. He quickly solved one recurrent Hart House Theatre problem: he maintained excellent relations with Vincent Massey, whose tendency to meddle in affairs of the theatre had caused friction with previous directors. As well, under his management, Hart House

Vincent Massey as Pope Pius VII in Claudel's *The Hostage*, Hart House Theatre, 1924, directed by Bertram Forsyth

Judith Evelyn starred in Hart House shows and went on to an international career.
Grant Macdonald's portrait done in London, England, in 1947 captures a sense of her
remarkable presence.

achieved a temporary measure of financial stability. However, Sinclair was no more successful than his predecessors in dealing with an estranged student body. With little use of students in his casts, Sinclair's Hart House was closer to being a stock company than a university theatre.

When Walter Sinclair left in 1927 to take control of an American theatre at a much higher salary, Massey hoped he would return the following season. Massey, therefore, selected Carroll Aikins, playwright (Forsyth had produced his *The God of Gods*) and experimenter, as a temporary replacement. Aikins, director number four (1927–9) and the first person born in Canada to serve in that capacity, was a young man apparently with little common or business sense. He had bought an apple orchard in the Okanagan Valley and there started a school where students picked fruit during the day and put on plays in the evening. This unique but short-lived experiment, the Home Theatre, was Aikins's only experience running a theatre before his two-year tenure at Hart House. Although his seasons broke even financially and garnered respectable reviews, he received little support from students of the university and even less from Vincent Massey. His plan to train a new generation of actors to revitalize Hart House was only partly realized. In 1929, after moving to Washington, DC, he resigned from Hart House Theatre, and never again managed a theatre.

Aikins was succeeded by Edgar Stone (1929–34), the first director to come from within (he had served in several capacities and directed student shows). Stone was also the first Hart House director to begin to establish rapport with students, and he undertook a large schedule of plays, many of them featuring student actors. During Stone's tenure, in 1931, Dora Mavor Moore launched a company called the Hart House Touring Players to bring Shakespeare to schools.

After a year of guest directors, Nancy Pyper became the last Hart House director in the Massey period (1935–7). A woman of extensive amateur experience and immense energy, she brought many new ideas to the running of the theatre, but could not restore its sense of purpose in a changing world. After her departure, the theatre lapsed into a rental operation and opened itself more and more to student work. Now college and faculty groups enjoyed almost unlimited access to Hart House Theatre facilities. Massey himself had lost interest in his theatre as his diplomatic career expanded.

Early Practical Training

Theatre by the late 1930s was acceptable at universities in Ontario, but not the premise that participants needed more than energy and talent. To

The Comedy of Errors by a cast from the Normal School, Stratford, performed in City Hall, 1922

learn the rudiments of voice production, movement, and acting always seemed to pose the question, for what purpose? It was not respectable to train for the professional stage; apprenticeship was the preferred route for that. However, masters and schools of elocution did help the privileged young of Ontario's upper classes to learn civilized behaviour: manners, poise, good speech, dancing, music, and appreciation of art and literature. Schools such as the Toronto Conservatory of Music helped to endow the élite with the veneer of refinement, while incidentally providing for several a preparation for the stage.

Jessie Alexander was one of the first teachers at the Toronto Conservatory, beginning in the late 1880s. She taught elocution, using techniques she herself had learned from an English immigrant. Eventually she gave up teaching to spend a quarter-century touring Canada as a professional elocutionist, reciting dramatic and sentimental poetry and humorous stories. One of the last references to her is as a member of the advisory board of the Margaret Eaton School in the 1920s. Alexander also taught at Loretto Convent, where one of her pupils was Margaret Anglin, the famous Canadian actress, who was 'already pulling out the tremolo stops and showing signs of that dramatic temperament that carried her to fame.'[17]

Harold Nelson Shaw took charge of the small School of Elocution of the Toronto Conservatory in 1892. His first attempt at actual production came in 1894, when he directed Maurice Hutton in a second Greek *Antigone*, produced this time off-campus because Convocation Hall had been destroyed by fire. He was also involved at St Michael's College as director and actor. After *Antigone* the staging of plays was an increasingly important focus of his teaching, and he also appeared more frequently as an actor. In 1896–7 acting became an official topic of study at the School of Elocution.[18] By 1898 Harold Shaw had, like Alexander, abandoned his teaching career, and he moved to Winnipeg to begin life anew as Harold Nelson, actor-manager of an important prairie company.

The London Conservatory of Music was less daring than its Toronto counterpart. Under the careful, proper direction of Miss N. Topley Thomas, and with respectable affiliation with the Departments of English, French, and Physical Education at the University of Western Ontario, its calendar of 1921–2 advertised courses for teachers, 'General Culture,' and 'Artists' leading to certification examinations. The dramatic-art class included a section that incorporated 'practical training in acting and direction of plays and pageants.'

'Proper and respectable' were also adjectives applicable to the Margaret Eaton School. Her daughter-in-law described Margaret Eaton, Timothy's wife, as 'a talented amateur actress with a phenomenal gift for memorizing.'[19] The younger Mrs Eaton remembers seeing Margaret 'in the long ago nineteen-hundreds ... in Shakespearean roles in the theatre of the academy she founded.' The school opened in 1901 as the School of Expression and proved so welcome among fashionable Toronto that it incorporated in 1906 as the Margaret Eaton School of Literature and Expression. Although Mrs Eaton was patron, the school was the inspiration of a young Toronto widow, Emma Scott Raff (later Mrs George Nasmith), who also worked with University of Toronto drama groups. The school's first motto was 'A Sound Mind in a Sound Body.' However, in 1906, 'Mr Eaton had built a lovely, small copy of a Greek theatre on North Street, near the corner of the present Bloor and Bay streets,' which had emblazoned over the door, 'We Strive for the Good and the Beautiful.' Nasmith herself taught 'Voice Culture' and 'The Art of Expression.' One of her teachers in 1921–2 was a graduate, Dora Mavor Moore. The school, which was exclusively for young ladies and provided full-time and part-time instruction, stressed both physical culture and the arts, and study in the arts was both practical and intellectual. Graduates of the school might become teachers or simply more refined wives and mothers. Josephine Barrington, for example, a graduate in 1921, later established her own school and children's company and was a noted Toronto voice teacher.

But perhaps the best-known graduate was Dora Mavor Moore, who began her stage career in productions at the University of Toronto, where her father was a well-known economics professor. Raised in a culturally rich environment, she met important stage personalities, such as Sir Johnston Forbes-Robertson, W.B. Yeats, and Ben Greet, whose examples inspired her to pursue a life in the theatre. With her scholarships from the Margaret Eaton School, Dora Mavor enrolled at the Academy of Dramatic Art in London (the first Canadian to do so), then returned home for a short engagement with the Colonial Stock Company in Ottawa that same year. After playing minor roles in New York, she was hired by Ben Greet in 1914 to perform with his Woodland Players on the Chautauqua summer circuit, which that year included Cornwall.[20] During the war, Mavor returned to Toronto, directed plays for the Central Neighbourhood House in the Cabbagetown area, married army chaplain Captain Francis Moore, and accompanied him to England, where she became the first Canadian to appear with the Old Vic company, performing the role of Viola in Ben Greet's production of *Twelfth Night* in 1918.

Returning to Toronto after the war, she raised three sons (one being noted CBC broadcaster, actor, and writer Mavor Moore) and continued to involve herself in local theatre, acting at Hart House and founding the University of Toronto Extension Players in 1931, the Hart House Touring Players in 1932, and the Village Players in 1938. This last organization eventually became the basis of the famous New Play Society theatre company and school (1946–71) and of the annual satirical revue, *Spring Thaw* (first seen in 1948).[21] Much honoured and decorated in the years before her death in 1979, Dora Mavor Moore left a legacy of former student performers and directors who now form the core of modern Canadian theatre.

In 1919 the Margaret Eaton School affiliated with the Toronto Conservatory, and two decades later became the foundation for the School of Physical and Health Education at the University of Toronto.

It is ironic that, while religious leaders railed against the notion of women on the commercial stage, drama studies and productions at some of Ontario's finest private girls' schools became a major source of young talent for the acting profession, as Dora Mavor's early career indicates. Although many parents would no doubt have disapproved of their daughters being trained for the stage, a significant number of young ladies educated in Toronto girls' schools chose theatrical vocations. In addition to Margaret Anglin, Loretto Academy graduates included Ina Hawley of Belleville, a star with Augustin Daly, Fritzi Scheff, and James T. Powers,[22] and Kathleen MacDonnell of Barrie, who appeared with Mrs Fiske, Henry Miller, and Robert Edeson.[23] Several well-known actresses from abroad also received their early education in Toronto. For

Dora Mavor Moore as Viola in *Twelfth Night* with Ben Greet's company

Dora Mavor Moore, director

example, Lena Ashwell and Amelia Summerville,[24] both born in the British Isles, had been brought to Toronto for their education and went on to become leading figures on the British stage. The famous Viola Allen from Alabama attended Toronto's Wykham Hall before she made her professional debut.[25] In fact, Allen and the others were part of a trend in which many socially well-connected young ladies were actively sought out by managers and impresarios anxious to add respectability to their companies.[26]

There were also dramatic classes at schools such as the Canadian Academy of Music (formerly the Columbia Conservatory of Music) under the management of Stanley Adams and Ambrose T. Pike; and the Hambourg Conservatory of Music, which was directed by J.W. Stanislaus Romain.[27] However, many theatrical aspirants found training in little theatres, which offered classes and experience in acting, directing, drama, and stagecraft. Some of the best of these were the Toronto Repertory Theatre, the Dickson Kenwin School, the Cameron Matthews School of the Theatre, the Children's Players of Toronto (directed by Mrs Dorothy Goulding),[28] and Herman Voaden's Playworkshops at the Central High School of Commerce.[29] There were also many radio schools. The Radio Hall School of the Theatre (directed by Edgar Stone of Hart House)[30] was first, but later came Lorne Greene's Academy of Radio Arts, Ben Lennick's Canadian Theatre School, and Marjorie Purvey's Toronto School of Radio (which produced the Children's Theatre of the Air on CKEY). Queen's University, the University of Toronto, and Ryerson Polytechnical Institute also had radio training facilities. The CBC's Drama Department under Andrew Allan, national supervisor of drama production, provided experience and training for a remarkable company of radio actors after the Second World War.[31]

Robert Gill

Queen's University was leading the way to the future with its active summer school, launched in 1934, which taught practical theatre skills. Fully accredited university courses in theatre began to be offered in the summer of 1942. Finally, in 1947, three members of the English department were assigned to teach courses in a separate theatre department, the first in Ontario, with William Angus as director of drama. Angus, with a Cornell University doctorate in drama, and his wife and collaborator Margaret, a talented costume designer, were the most important contributors to drama education at Queen's from their arrival in 1937, when he accepted a lectureship in English.[32] Although hired to teach English courses, he devoted his time to working in many capacities with student theatre groups and became head of the practical summer school in 1938. Student theatricals at Queen's had already produced several noteworthy artists including Lorne Greene, who had graduated from Queen's in 1937, and Robertson Davies, who left Queen's for Oxford after a very active involvement in Queen's student theatre. Another graduate, and the first summer-school instructor, Herman Voaden, in *The Humanities in Canada* (1947) was predicting, 'As more instructors with a scholarly knowledge of the theatre and a thorough grasp of production techniques are added to the staffs of our universities, and as educators realize what their emphasis on theatre activity can contribute to society, there is no doubt that ... [a] large place will be given to drama.' Voaden was proved correct in the long run, but by 1947 the most famous university theatre in Canada was once again at Hart House, now under the legendary Robert Gill.

On 10 January 1946, the board of governors of the university moved to accept Vincent Massey's offer and take over Hart House Theatre. Warden Burgon Bickersteth was on the committee to hire a director and he recorded how impressed he was with the American selected, Robert Gill, 'who went through the Carnegie Tech Drama school, one of the best training schools in the world, and has since occupied many positions in university theatres.'

Robert Gill had graduated from Carnegie Institute of Technology (now Carnegie-Mellon University) in Pittsburgh, Pennsylvania, in 1933, winning a prize as best actor. His training had consisted of four years of acting, voice production, and stage movement, taught in the studio and in rehearsal, along with some experience in directing, theatre crafts, theatre history, and dramatic literature. After a succession of professional engagements as actor, director, and radio announcer, Gill returned to Carnegie to complete his MA in 1939; he joined the faculty in 1942 after further freelance professional work. From 1943 until 1946 he served as artistic director of the Pittsburgh Playhouse. He also worked in summer stock at the Woodstock (New York) Playhouse, which would become a model for Ontario's Straw Hat Players, launched by Gill's Hart House protégés in 1948. Gill had left the Pittsburgh Playhouse to return to Carnegie when he was offered the directorship of Hart House Theatre. Hart House was ideal for Gill; he would have his own theatre to run and could continue to teach.

Gill promised not to direct any plays before Christmas because he wanted to watch the various college societies perform first and cast the best available talent. As he told the students, 'he wanted to give definite instruction in acting and stage technique to those students who had the time and the wish to avail themselves of it. He made clear that the instruction would be similar to that given in any professional school and it would be hard work' (Bickersteth letters). It was perfectly clear that this was now a very different Hart House Theatre, one central to the university *and* about to provide training of the highest quality. Over a hundred students enrolled in Gill's practical courses during his first year.

The opening night of Gill's inaugural production was 27 January 1947. It could be argued that this was the most important evening in the development of a professional Canadian theatre before the opening of the Stratford Festival on 13 July 1953.

Robert Gill had a vision for Hart House Theatre and the ability to make that vision a reality. It is impossible to overestimate his contribution to the development of an indigenous professional Canadian theatre. The impact of his personality on the students around him was profound. Perhaps his greatest contribution was to instill in them a belief that a Canadian theatre *could* exist. As an American, he believed that summer theatres and local repertories could be started just as they had been in the United States. In addition to his belief in a bright theatrical future, Bob Gill provided his students with the most advanced training available in English Canada at the time and an opportunity to hone their natural skills and acquired techniques in excellent plays performed in a serious, dedicated atmosphere.

The system he established remained the same during his twenty-four-year tenure. Each year four shows were presented, except for the first and last seasons, when there were only two productions. In total Bob Gill directed seventy-one productions at Hart House Theatre. Almost all the plays done were classical, Gill's strength; only two were by Canadian authors. The seasons were planned as a whole. A large-cast show or one that required period costumes would be preceded by a small-cast show or one in modern dress. There was variety within each season, with plays designed to appeal to students of various university departments. All were performed in English, but there were works by French, Greek, and Scandinavian playwrights. Shakespeare and Shaw were the most popular authors. Gill wanted students to be able to see plays that they were studying in their classes. As Canadian plays were not a regular part of the curriculum at that time, it is not surprising that they were not part of Gill's repertoire. In addition, Gill excelled in his work with actors and directors; he had little interest or skill in working with playwrights.

Many aspects of the Gill regime at Hart House Theatre were influenced by the 'Carnegie Tech system.' At Carnegie, one learned theatre by making theatre. The focus was on the process of producing plays, with students being continually assigned cast or crew responsibilities of increasing challenge throughout their undergraduate years. However, unlike at Carnegie, all the activities of Hart House Theatre remained extracurricular. This placed a large burden on the students, because they were given no credit for their work at the theatre and had to keep up with their courses if they wished to graduate. However, it did give additional freedom to the director, who was able to bend the rules when exceptional talent appeared. Kate Reid (1930–93), one of the most illustrious names connected with Hart House Theatre, was never a student at the university, although she did study drama at the Conservatory of Music.

The early Gill years were the most exceptional. The Second World War had raised the cultural consciousness of Canadians and strengthened their desire for a theatre of their own. Many of the actors appearing in Gill's first productions were ex–service personnel exercising their educational option; this improved the quality of the productions by giving a greater age range than was usually possible when casting student shows.

Many of Gill's student actors became well known. In fact, they were

Barbara Allen (Barnett) as Ruth Gordon and David Gardner as Fred Whitmarsh in *Years Ago*, directed by Mary Pickford's nephew, John Mantley, a University of Toronto Alumnae entry in the 1949 Dominion Drama Festival

so familiar that at one point Bob Gill refused to name them in a newspaper interview because he felt they must be tired of seeing their names connected with Hart House Theatre. Among those who have gone on to distinguished theatre careers after passing through the stage door of Hart

House Theatre are William Hutt, Charmion King, David Gardner, Leon Major, Barbara Hamilton, Eric House, Donald Sutherland, and Donald and Murray Davis.

Robert Gill's system, though it produced good results and was very popular, did not satisfy everyone's needs and was not without its critics. James Reaney, a student at University College at the University of Toronto from 1944 to 1948, was impressed by the polished productions he saw at Hart House Theatre, but came to recognize this as American theatre-school technique and resent the lack of opportunity for Canadian playwrights. His informal Listener's Workshops in London, Ontario, in the 1960s were an attempt to explore a different kind of teaching and learning theatre, more improvisatory and less polished.

Drama Departments in Ontario Universities

The traditionalists for whom theatre was an extracurricular pursuit were losing, but the battle over the place of theatre within the university still went on. Although Robert Ayres, a pioneer prairie arts educator, was discussing the visual arts, his comments in *The Humanities in Canada* (1947) are apt:

It may be conceded that as an important part of the cultural life of a nation, Fine Arts, like literature, have a place on the university curriculum, though he would be a rash man who would demand for them equal rank in a general course. The question is, how far should the universities go? Should they limit themselves to a realization that education is not complete without a knowledge of the character and history of Fine Art as a basis of intelligent appreciation, having in mind the needs of students who will not become artists, and leaving to the art schools the technical training of those who will? Or should they go all the way and set up art schools of their own?[33]

That is the debate which has continued to this day in universities across Ontario. Gradually, the British model went out of fashion (although vestiges of it remain in universities such as Trent, Lakehead, Carleton, and Royal Military College where few if any courses in theatre are offered). With theatre itself generally recognized as important culturally, degree programs developed at more than fifteen post-secondary institutions province-wide, offering differing balances between 'studio' and 'study.' Drama departments stress 'education,' whereas theatre departments stress 'training.' The former offer the Bachelor of Arts, the latter the Bachelor of Fine Arts. The model for all these became largely American, not British.

Under William 'Doc' Angus, Queen's gave attention to Canadian playwrights. Joseph
Schull's *The Bridge* received its première at Queen's Summer Theatre, Kingston,
August 1948. (Cast: Margaret Dick, Cary Davids, Gordon Robertson, William Angus,
Helga Highfield, Lawrence Thornton)

Drama departments present the study of theatre as part of a liberal arts
education. The fiftieth-anniversary tribute to the Queen's Drama Guild
in 1947 also celebrated the inauguration of a new department at Queen's
'for instruction in the dramatic arts.' While recognizing that this was a
welcome 'sign of increasing interest in drama in this country,' the goal
of the department, it was emphasized, was to provide 'a purely cultural
study of dramatics.' It was a sign of the future: in 1976, the University of
Ottawa focused on 'the practical techniques and intellectual disciplines
of the theatre as a means of personal development';[34] the University of
Guelph department, as stated in a recruiting brochure from the 1980s,
aimed 'to stimulate thought and ... encourage development of artistic
and intellectual sensibility.'

A university update that shows the direction in which early theatre education has moved would not be inappropriate here, despite this volume's
stated cut-off date. Several Ontario universities developed BA programs,
but each department found its own unique strengths. Queen's jointly supports the periodical *Theatre History in Canada / Histoire du théâtre au
Canada* (now *Theatre Research in Canada / Recherches théâtrales au*

In 1954, Queen's Drama Guild took *The Patriots*, by Eric Cross to Woodstock.

Canada) with the University of Toronto, and has a valued, informal connection with the nearby Thousand Islands Summer Playhouse in Gananoque. Guelph has developed the best contemporary theatrical archives in English Canada, housing the papers of the Shaw Festival and many Toronto alternative theatres, and, building on this strength, now offers an MA in Canadian drama; as well, it publishes *Essays in Theatre* (which incorporates *Canadian Drama / L'Art dramatique canadien*, started earlier at the University of Waterloo), and its faculty includes the editor of *Canadian Theatre Review*, started at York University.

Brock, Laurentian, and McMaster universities offer more modest programs. Places such as Waterloo and Wilfrid Laurier have modern theatres that have served as arts centres for their communities. The University of Ottawa has the only bilingual program, although York University's Glendon College offers some courses in French. The department of theatre at Ottawa has had a special interest in new forms of theatre since it was founded in 1968. The University of Western Ontario has good facilities in the Talbot Theatre and Drama Workshop, but mounts only a handful of practical courses affiliated with the English department. Western has been the home of James Reaney, and the university helped to support a summer theatre in the 1960s where *The Sun and the Moon* and *Listen to the Wind* had their premières. At the University of Toronto, University College has a drama program offering some professional training, and there are nascent drama departments at both Erindale and Scarborough colleges of the University of Toronto.

However, the University of Toronto's distinction is as home to the Graduate Centre for Study of Drama, which awards MA and Ph.D. degrees in drama; many of its doctoral graduates are teaching and administering in universities across the country, in the United States, and abroad. Others are in positions that range from the professional theatre – dramaturge, director, playwright, designer, performer – through theatre critic to archivist or officer in various governmental and arts-support organizations. Begun in 1966, the Drama Centre has been led by a succession of distinguished scholars, from its co-founders Clifford Leech and Robertson Davies, to Brian Parker, Ann Saddlemyer, Ronald Bryden, Colin Visser, and Damiano Pietropaolo. A general interest in theatre history led to a specific interest in Canadian theatre history under Ann Saddlemyer. In fact, the Drama Centre helped to legitimize that field of study by helping to found the Association for Canadian Theatre History (now the Association for Canadian Theatre Research) and to co-sponsor its journal, *Theatre History in Canada*. During Saddlemyer's first years the Drama Centre also began publishing the international periodical *Modern Drama*, originally edited from the University of Kansas. Although the Drama Centre concentrates primarily on the academic study of theatre, since Parker's time it has encouraged the study of practice by offering workshops in movement, voice, and stage design by professionals such as Martha Mann, who is head of design, and inviting distinguished directors to direct plays in which the students perform. Hart House Theatre has been a union house since May 1929. Because of increased costs, the Centre no longer performs regularly there, although the theatre is still rented by it and other student groups on campus for special productions. As the Drama Centre was established in part to complement and support Robert Gill's extracurricular activities at Hart House, it is fitting that the Drama Centre's principal theatre, the former Central Library Theatre, is called the Robert Gill Theatre.

Certain universities in Ontario, following the Canadian example of the Universities of Saskatchewan and Alberta, began in the mid-1950s to teach the profession of theatre. York University in North York, Metropolitan Toronto, was originally an offshoot of the University of Toronto, becoming fully independent in 1959. The first student theatre was extracurricular: the Drama Club, founded in 1961 at York's original campus, Glendon College. The Drama Club hired Jack Winter and George Luscombe from Toronto Workshop Productions to give practical classes. The York University Players succeeded the Drama Club in 1965 and eventually moved into Burton Auditorium, a 613-seat thrust theatre on York's main campus. The York University Players began to fade with the arrival of the Theatre Program in 1968, although the program appointed a faculty adviser to support student activities.[35]

The focus of York University theatre became the curricular Theatre Program (changed to Department in 1971–2) in the Faculty of Fine Arts. The founding dean of the faculty was American. His choice for Theatre Program head was Joseph G. Green, a fellow American. And Green's first appointment was Don Rubin, still another American. The basic curricular philosophy of the York program, was, therefore, American. However, Green and Rubin both quickly became enthusiastic about things Canadian. Their next appointment was Mavor Moore, who came directly from establishing the St Lawrence Centre in Toronto and served at York until his retirement. In 1974, the Theatre Department launched *The Canadian Theatre Review*, with Rubin as editor and Green as publisher.

Although the original York program offered only the BA (Honours) degree, Green (and his successors) tended to hire professionals. By 1975–6 the degree of choice of many students and faculty, the BFA, was introduced. York's BFA program encompasses a strong professional training, balanced by a core of historical requirements in theatre. Supplementing this are courses taken within a Faculty of Fine Arts (with offerings in film, music, visual arts, and dance), and within the university at large. To complement the undergraduate program, York established a Master of Fine Arts degree in 1974–5 that includes one of the only graduate programs in acting in Canada as well as specialties in playwriting and directing. More than five hundred undergraduates and sixty graduates have completed York theatre degrees. Some have gone on to start theatres (the Blyth Festival, Buddies in Bad Times, and Necessary Angel are among the best known); some have continued to work regularly in theatre or television. Others have become theatre teachers, professors, or administrators. As with all theatre schools, probably the largest number of graduates ultimately found careers completely outside of the field.

While York is the largest professional school in Ontario, one of the most respected is Ryerson Polytechnic University (formerly Ryerson Polytechnical Institute), which has a program, begun in 1970, very much like the National Theatre School: high-quality training but without the university experience. Taking advantage of its location in downtown Toronto, Ryerson has developed close links with the professional theatre community.

The School of Dramatic Art at the University of Windsor dates back to 1968, although its founder, Professor Daniel Kelly, arrived ten years earlier to what was then still a Roman Catholic college. Windsor has strong programs in creative drama and musical theatre, and has run its own children's theatre. Although the school failed in an attempt to establish a professional theatre, it remains one of the key cultural institutions serving the entire city of Windsor.

Several community colleges in the Toronto area offer professional training, including George Brown, Humber, and Sheridan. That is still not all: there are many private coaches and small schools offering experience to the young actor. Some organizations, such as the Maggie Bassett Studio and Equity Showcase, focus on the professional actor. Performing-arts high schools, such as the Claude Watson School of the Arts in North York, have become increasingly popular in southern Ontario. And the Sears Collegiate Drama Festival (originated in 1946) has up to two hundred high-school groups participating each year from across the province. The final festival has been held for several years at Hart House, returning that theatre for a week each year to centre stage in student drama.

Theatre now belongs in the universities of Ontario: that is a living tribute to all the pioneers of the last hundred years.

NOTES

1 John Wesley, *The Works of the Rev. John Wesley, A.M.*, vol. 12, Letters (London: Wesleyan Conference Office, 1872), 128

2 A Committee Appointed by the General Conference, eds, *The Doctrine and Discipline of the Methodist Church 1898* (Toronto: William Briggs, 1898), 24

3 Hector Charlesworth, *More Candid Chronicles* (Toronto: Macmillan, 1928), 59

4 Quoted in Anonymous, 'The Queen's Drama Guild. 1899–1949' (Kingston: no publisher, 1949), 8

5 Rev. R.J. MacGeorge, 'Amateur Histrionics,' in *Tales, Sketches and Lyrics* (Toronto: A.H. Amour, 1858), 239

6 There had been sporadic productions in academic circumstances before this time, such as the presentation of acts 1 and 2 of Terence's *Adelphi* as part of the Latin exam at the Royal Grammar School in York on 23 February 1825.

7 Quoted by Donald Jones, 'Historical Toronto,' Toronto *Star*, 3 January 1987, M5

8 J.T. Saywell, ed., *The Canadian Journal of Lady Aberdeen* (Toronto: The Champlain Society, 1960), 40

9 John R.W. Gynne-Timothy, *Western's First Century* (London: University of Western Ontario, 1978), 88, 728ff.

10 Quoted in Harold Averill, *Dramatis Personae: Amateur Theatre at the University of Toronto 1879–1939* (Toronto: University of Toronto Archives, 1986), 3

11 Burgon Bickersteth quotations are from his unpublished letters to his family in England held in the University of Toronto Archives.

12 *A History of the University of Trinity College* (Toronto: University of Toronto, 1952), 179

13 Charles M. Johnston, *McMaster University: Volume I, The Toronto Years* (Toronto: University of Toronto Press for McMaster University, 1976), 48–9

14 Vincent Massey, Diaries (University of Toronto Archives), 29 January 1915; Raymond Massey, *When I Was Young* (Toronto: McClelland and Stewart, 1976), 104

15 Carroll Aikins, in Bertram Brooker, ed., *Yearbook of the Arts in Canada 1928–29* (Toronto: Macmillan, 1949), 47

16 Bickersteth, unpublished letter, 17 Febuary 1923

17 Jessie Alexander, *Jessie Alexander's Platform Sketches* (Toronto: McClelland, Goodchild and Stewart, 1916), xvi

18 The facts about Nelson are taken from Douglas Arrell, 'Harold Nelson: The Early Years,' *Theatre History in Canada / Histoire du théâtre au Canada* I (Fall 1980), 86.

19 Flora McCrea Eaton, *Memory's Wall* (Toronto: Clarke, Irwin and Co., 1956), 196

20 Cornwall *Standard*, 27 August 1914. This was the first appearance of Chautauqua in Ontario. Whether Dora Mavor actually performed with the company in Cornwall can not be determined from newspaper reports.

21 See David Gardner, 'The New Play Society,' *Oxford Companion to Canadian Theatre*, 379–80, and Herbert Whittaker, '*Spring Thaw*,' ibid., 500–1; also Gardner's chapter in this volume.

22 Walter Browne and E. De Roy Kock, eds, *Who's Who on the Stage, 1908* (New York: B.W. Dodge, 1908), 227–8. See also Daniel Blum, *A Pictorial History of the American Theatre, 1900–1950* (New York: Greenberg, 1950), 120.

23 *Billboard*, 16 April 1921. See also Toronto *Globe*, 28 January, 3 and 10 May 1913; Toronto *Star Weekly*, 28 March 1914; *Saturday Night*, 20 May and 16 December 1916; Blum, *Pictorial History*, 176.

24 Browne and De Roy Koch, eds, *Who's Who on the Stage, 1908*, 23, 418–19.

25 Katherine Hale, 'Some Prominent Players,' *Canadian Magazine* 17 (May, 1901), 40

26 Albert Auster, *Actresses and Suffragists: Women in the American Theater, 1890–1920* (New York: Praeger, 1984), 51

27 See Toronto *Globe*, 16 April 1913, 8; and 25 April 1914, 8.

28 Program, *Ladies in Retirement*, Hart House Theatre, Toronto, April 1947, directed by Dorothy Goulding. See also Toronto *Globe and Mail*, July 1947.

29 Anton Wagner, 'Herman Voaden's "New Religion,"' *Theatre History in Canada / Histoire du théâtre au Canada* 6:2 (Fall 1985), 191

30 'In those days actors were so anxious to get radio experience that it was possible for Edgar Stone to set up a non-broadcasting Radio Hall where he produced plays. Bob Christie and Rai Purdy were two of his successful students, and eventually Toronto stations transmitted some of these productions.' Sandy Stewart, *A Pictorial History of Radio in Canada* (Toronto: Gage Publishing, 1975), 102

31 N. Alice Frick, *Image in the Mind: CBC Radio Drama 1944 to 1954* (Toronto:

Canadian Stage and Arts Publications, 1987). See also Murray D. Edwards, 'Andrew Allan,' *Oxford Companion to Canadian Theatre*, 14–15.
32 Erdmute Waldhauer, *Drama at Queen's: From Its Beginnings to 1991* (Kingston: TypeCast, 1991), 21
33 Robert Ayres, in Watson Kirkconnell and A.S.P. Woodhouse, eds, *The Humanities in Canada* (Ottawa: Humanities Research Council of Canada, 1947), 220
34 'University of Ottawa,' *Scene Changes: Ontario's Theatre Magazine*, December 1976, 15
35 Susan McPhie, 'Theatre at York: The Early Years,' in *A History of Theatre at York: 1969–1989, York Theatre Journal* 31 (North York: York University Department of Theatre, 1989), 4

6 *Plays and Playwrights*

ALEXANDER LEGGATT

The range and achievement of playwriting in Ontario cannot be pictured fully in a chapter of this length, nor can 'Ontario' playwriting be altogether isolated from playwriting in other provinces or even – as will appear – other countries. But a few representative figures who have spent a substantial part of their working lives contributing to Ontario theatre may be examined, both as significant in their own right and as suggestive of the larger picture. The choice is not always easy, especially in the later period, but there is no question that the first playwright of the post-1914 era who claims our attention is Merrill Denison (1893–1975). The dramatic background against which he wrote may be sampled in the important two-volume collection *Canadian Plays from Hart House Theatre*, edited by Vincent Massey, which contain three of Denison's plays.[1] The authors are his literary contemporaries and their plays shared the Hart House stage with his. Their talent is variable, but one thing they share is a relative weakness in imagining a convincing community. There are dutiful reconstructions of the picturesque village life of French Canada. There are plays set in London and the English countryside, written by authors who may live in Canada but whose imaginations inhabit Pinero country. Isabel Ecclestone MacKay's clever melodrama *The Second Lie*, ostensibly set in a North American town with its drug stores and ice-cream parlours, includes in its cast a constable who is pure stage-English. A West Coast writer (and one of the early directors of Hart House Theatre), Carroll Aikins, contributes an Indian drama, *The God of Gods*, whose setting seems to have been made in Hollywood and whose natives come from central casting. The playwrights are groping, finding their most usable conventions in established writing from other communities, and lacking a strong sense of their own culture. In fairness, two exceptions may be noted: H. Borsook's *Three Weddings of a Hunchback*, whose surface liveliness and underlying melancholy bring its setting, a North American Jewish community, vividly to life; and Britton Cooke's *The Resurrection of John Snaith*, whose Ibsenesque structure now looks self-conscious, but which at least takes an attitude, a disillusioned one, to the spiritless Canadian town that forms its setting.

Against this background Denison's work, both in this anthology and in his own *The Unheroic North*,[2] stands out in high relief. There is a distinctive voice, dry and sardonic. The plays are well constructed, not just with the cleverness of a writer who has learned the basic tricks, but with the authority of one who knows what he wants to do with his medium. Most significant, there is a strong sense of community. Denison has staked out a particular territory – the unheroic North – and made it his own. The place names belong not just on a map but in an authentic country of the mind: Mud Lake, Cemetery Shoots, Dag's Hill; the aboriginal names that give poetry to the Ontario countryside are carefully filtered out. The characters' names are equally evocative: John Serang, Syd Yench, Cline MacUnch. Beyond the squalid cabins that are the usual stage settings we sense the tourist's North, the outdoor playground; but we sense far more strongly the grinding desperation of those who have to live there year in and year out, the almost subhuman condition to which they are reduced. As the city man remarks in *From Their Own Place*, 'They're all fourth generation, inbred pioneer stock gone to seed. All the good ones have had the guts to get out of the country. Only the dregs remain.'[3]

But what results is not the sort of morose playwriting that has made rural gloom such an easy form for the earnest writer and such an obvious target of parody. Denison shapes his material with a sharp, usually comic irony. It is no coincidence that his most popular and accomplished play, *Brothers in Arms*, is also the funniest. It also shows a certain detachment characteristic of the author. A city businessman, J. Altrus Browne, is desperate to get out of the woods to keep an appointment: he has to deal with the backwoodsman Syd White, slow, loquacious, tantalizing him with possibilities of help that turn out to be dead ends. The title reflects the discovery that the two were in the army together – Browne as the most officious of officers, Syd as the most intractable of privates. Syd's views on the army show him to be a shrewd innocent who was both out of his depth in the routines of the service and able to see through them, exposing their nonsense and their irrelevance to the business of killing Germans (Syd's unabashedly practical view of the war's aims). Set against the two men is Browne's wife Dorothea, who views the play's main themes, the North and the army, with an empty-headed romanticism born of the movies. The play is neatly constructed around a series of running gags, and builds, like a shaggy-dog story, to a deliberate anticlimax: Browne could have got out of the woods any time if he had known how to ask his literal-minded host the right question. Denison's satire is distributed even-handedly between the city and country characters; but it is difficult to avoid the suspicion that Syd and his friend Charlie are not quite such fools as they look, and that – at some level, not perhaps with full consciousness – they are stringing the city man along. If so, the balance is redressed in *From Their Own Place*, which begins with the convention of the gullible city folk and the shrewd rustics, then turns the convention upside down as the city visitor plays on the greed and stupidity of the three backwoodsmen and gets a set of furs – the object of the plot – for nothing.

The Weather Breeder both extends the range of Denison's vision and casts an interesting light on the most ambitious of the 'Unheroic North' plays, *Marsh Hay*. The play is based on a simple trick of character. Old John is happy only when predicting disaster; fine weather depresses him, and he is delighted when a storm apparently fulfils his prophecies by wiping out the summer's work on the farm and preventing his daughter and her young man from getting married. Characteristically, the play's final twist is an anticlimax: the storm to which it builds passes over harmlessly. The young people whose hopes are threatened by the gloomy old man and the inhospitable land suggest the conflict between life-affirming and life-denying characters that we will see more fully developed in Davies and Reaney. But the manner of the play is not solemn, and its mockery of Old John – the comic repetition of 'sour' with reference to him recalls the running gags of *Brothers in Arms* – suggests that for Denison the complainer can be as much a figure of fun as the romantic.

We need to remember this when we come to *Marsh Hay*. Its tone is darker than that of the one-act comedies, and its anticlimactic twist is a self-induced abortion. The central character is another complainer, John Serang (is the coincidence of first names significant?) to whom Denison's attitude is somewhat ambiguous. His constant repetition of the words 'fifty acres of grey stone' suggests a comic running gag, like the 'sour' of *The Weather Breeder*, but also seems intended to convey the numbing futility of the farmer's life; the tone, this time, is uncertain.[4] Serang is open to criticism – and is overtly criticized from within the play – as a self-destructive man whose misfortunes are in large measure his own fault, and who simply spreads misery around him. Yet he is also a strong theatrical presence; his first entrance is carefully prepared with a ritual clearing of the dinner table and a long, heavy silence. He dominates nearly every scene he appears in, and many of his complaints about the state of the country and the frustrations of farming carry real authority. He may be a life-denying character, but the opposition to him is stymied. The young people of the play are hardly vital figures. Their rebellion, such as it is, offers not the promise of a better life but casual sex, shotgun weddings, and settling down to a life as worthless as Serang's. The real opposition comes from his wife Lena, who gets liberal ideas from a city woman who stops by in a car (Denison's mother, in the real-life incident on which the play is based). Armed with these ideas, Lena insists on treating her pregnant unmarried daughter Sarilin with dignity, spends far more than she can afford on brightening her home, and declares that the baby will be born with pride, not simply made the object of social condemnation (as her neighbours insist) or of a shotgun wedding (as Serang plans). These unconventional notions have a large measure of the playwright's sympathy, and even Serang himself is grudgingly impressed. Yet there is something fuzzy in Lena's rebellion. The lady in the car is never seen by the audience, and Lena is not quite articulate about what she actually said. Her attempts to brighten the house have a certain sad irony – a calendar and fancy tea, for which the storekeeper overcharges her. Finally, on Lena's words 'Sarilin'll want her baby,'[5] there is a scream from the bedroom and the doctor has to be sent for. At the end of the play the house has relapsed into squalor and Sarilin is out on the tiles again. Serang, in a way, is satisfied; the girl's self-induced abortion 'showed pretty good sense'[6] – perhaps because it brought the family back down to a level he could understand. The structure of the play, with its return to square one, is so neatly ironic that it borders on black comedy. There is grim humour in many of Serang's tirades and in some of the secondary figures – notably the local shopkeeper, a one-man lynch mob who, when his intended victim walks on stage, starts presenting him with free cigars. This is recognizably the world of the one-act comedies, with a darker colouring and a more overt bitterness. Denison comes very close to identifying Serang's despairing cynicism as the view of the play; but (especially if we remember *The Weather Breeder*) there is a final ironic withdrawal even from the central character that helps to keep the play in balance.

The sympathy for human aspiration, however futile, that we detect in the middle scenes of *Marsh Hay* is developed in *Balm*. This time the setting is not the North but a boarding house in what could be any North American city. The theme, again, is frustration, but it is very differently handled. Miss Greyth, an old woman looking back on a life wasted in the service of conventional virtue, wants to adopt a child, on the model of a cut-out picture she has saved: 'A blue-eyed boy with black, curly hair, and a silvery laugh.'[7] To arrange the adoption, she has sent for a

Rawling's Rolling Road Show tent in Merrill Denison's *The Prize Winner*, Hart House Theatre, 1928

young social worker who, finding a half-demented old woman living in squalor, is hardly encouraging. As Miss Greyth gets more desperate, she lowers her demands: 'There might be one with a cross eye like mine. I'd take her.'[8] Her plea for even a damaged child becomes a plea for herself and all the misfits of the world – but Denison preserves his usual balance; when her friend Umine suggests 'a darkie,' that, for Miss Greyth, is going too far. The upshot of it is that the social worker offers to put Miss Greyth in a nice institution where she herself will be looked after, and the old woman throws her out. The play has Denison's characteristic economy and irony, but the vision is more compassionate than usual. He shows real affection for the stubborn eccentricities of the two old women (Umine is given to dosing her friend with 'Balm of Gillia' and mostly gloomy quotations from Burns) and even musters some sympathy for the social worker who '*was originally a very nice girl, but service and efficiency have about done for her.*'[9] In a situation that could have been played for simple pathos he shows a fine balance of humour, irony, and compassion. It is in many respects his richest play and one that deserves to be better known.

From the late twenties on, though Denison never quite abandoned the dramatic form and in fact became a prolific writer of radio drama, his creative springs seem to have dried up. *The Prize Winner* is a competent reworking of the hick-versus-city-slicker routine as a carnival manager tries to cheat a group of slow, stubborn, but brutal villagers, while the village idiot has the last laugh on all of them. The neat structure and the low view of human nature are the mixture as before, but the generalized North American setting denies the particularity that gave the Ontario plays their impact. The radio series *The Romance of Canada* shows Denison as a professional on assignment, turning Canadian history into a series of brief dramas, sometimes skilful but often flat and episodic. Occasionally the authentic Denison voice is heard, in satire on petty officials, in the wry acknowledgment that Laura Secord brought the British commander news he already had ('I might as well have stayed at home and baked'[10]), or in tales of failure like *Henry Hudson*. Another radio play, *On Christmas Night*, is notable only for the democratic emphasis it gives the Bethlehem story, with the kings deferring to the superior wisdom of the shepherds. This prepares for the last phase of Denison's playwriting career, a series of one-act plays addressed to American audiences on such themes as racial persecution (*An American Father Talks to His Son*), religious freedom (*Haven of the Spirit*), and woman's rights (*The U.S. vs. Susan B. Anthony*). High-minded and frankly didactic, these plays add little or nothing to Denison's stature as a dramatist, but they balance our view of him as a writer and as a man. The detached scepticism of the earlier Canadian plays might suggest that he was a cynic, and some of his gloomier pronouncements about Canadian theatre suggest that he allowed his career as a writer for the stage to peter out through sheer frustration.[11] But if the social idealism of the later work can fairly be read back into the earlier plays, then in his view of the meanness of the unheroic North we can see pain as well as sardonic laughter.

In almost every respect the work of Herman Voaden (1903–91) forms a contrast with that of Denison. Denison's idealism was focused on progressive social causes and (in the corporation histories to which he turned late in his career) the initiatives of imaginative businessmen. Voaden's idealism is spiritual, taking its power from a romantic view of the Northland. While he acknowledges the frustrations that life in such a land can bring, there is no real counterpart in his imagination for the scepticism of Denison: his work is visionary and celebratory. While Denison abandoned the theatre (or the theatre abandoned him), Voaden kept the faith. His output of plays is relatively small, but they form part of a full career as (among other things) teacher, theorist, and play anthologist. Through all his work there runs a remarkable consistency of purpose.

Earth Song is an early, radical departure from conventional theatre. An exercise in myth-making, it deals in a frank abstraction that gives it clarity and boldness of outline, while weakening its power to touch us, to convince us that it really speaks to the human condition. We are presented with Adam and Eve in an unpeopled world, defined by the seasons, the passage of day and night, suggestions of a rocky landscape and a pool – and, above all, the immense distances of sky and earth. The setting may recall Voaden's interest in Wagner, but the strongly marked seasonal rhythm – especially the evocation of the beauty of autumn – makes the play distinctively Canadian. The myth has lessons for its audience. Adam and Eve are incomplete without each other. When Adam seeks vision outside himself, he is blinded; when he embarks on a fresh journey of discovery, more attuned to the earth, he finds true godhead. Throughout, there is a suggestion of new life beginning as an old world is exhausted; beneath the abstraction we may detect the playwright's romantic view of Canada. *Wilderness*, produced in the same year, is apparently very different – a realistic setting in a village north of Lake Superior, a place of loneliness and deprivation, forms the background for the tragedy of a young man who dies in the woods. But while the hero's mother sinks into gloom, the girl who loves him dedicates herself to the magic vision of the land they both shared: 'I too shall hear the wilderness calling, calling my life into a great adventure. It will be my land. I'll belong to it. I'll be part of its winds and woods and rocks – part of its flashing Northern Lights. *Pause*. Though he's gone now he'll still be part of it. He'll still belong. And he'll be content.'[12] The young visionary (whose name, perhaps significantly, is Blake) never appears and his body is never found. The land has absorbed him. Symbolic touches in the staging – train noises and the shadow of a night-hawk – hint at a poetic vision beneath the surface realism, and in general the play is not so far as it may appear from *Earth Song* or the 'symphonic' plays[13] that were to follow. In fact, *Wilderness* was later reworked in that mode, as *Rocks*.

'Symphonic' drama as practised by Voaden is an experimental form in which devices such as music, lighting, dance, and choric voices are integrated with conventional dialogue to give a variety of perspectives on a single action. *Hill-Land*, an ambitious full-length work in this form, tells at one level a simple story of life passed down from one generation to the next. But it takes its time to unfold that story, and its main interest is in the spiritual forces behind the action, of which the chief is the land itself: 'The north-land is a young giant – clean and unfettered in his strength. He shall be mighty in the days to come, through the faith of his sons.'[14] The central figures – Paul, his mother, grandmother, wife, and son – are the subject of constant comment from choric figures – The Commentator, The Voice of Pity, The Voice of Hope, The Fatalist, High and Low Choruses. A dancer represents Death. The voices explore the pattern of longing and suffering, fear and exultation, that lies behind the action. In general, the (relatively) realistic idiom of the main characters is overpowered by the 'symphonic expressionist' machinery – as we see when the lovers Paul and Rachel meet:

Paul – (Strangely) – How do you do.
Rachel – (In the same mood) – How do you do.
(White light pours down on them ... as if the altar is glowing with mysterious flame. The music lifts into sublime assertion.)
The Commentator – (Exultantly) – These are marked and set apart. They shall be lifted to the god-life, through the glory of love born this moment, and their worship of the north-earth.[15]

The dialogue is of two shy young people, but the play's real business, as in *Earth Song*, is myth-making. Though Rachel later dies in childbirth, her love is seen as eternal and she is, like Blake in *Wilderness*, absorbed into the land.

Murder Pattern is more complex and concentrated. It tells the story of an actual murder in the Haliburton area, and its choric voices (First Earth Voice, Second Earth Voice, The Friendly One, The Accusing One) are juxtaposed with other voices that give us facts and dates, the circumstances of the story. This realistic level is more fully realized than in *Hill-Land*. The focus is on the killer, Jack Davis. Apart from his victim, who appears briefly, Davis is the only character in the play with a proper name; the others are abstractions. And even Davis is presented as a subject for experiment: 'An ordinary farmer of the north? No! A true subject to fit into our pattern.'[16] The pattern includes his relations with his family and neighbours, and beneath that his relations with the land. At first the country is seen as dark and brutal, almost a poetic version of Denison's unheroic North:

Shut off from the world to the south, life stood still. There was no fresh blood. Here and there, in the great solitude, life moved backwards, towards the animal, the grotesque, the warped and evil.
... Pity the isolate hill folk, fearful, estranged. They have no words to speak the terror of the gloom, and the silence, and the unending distances that wall in life from life.[17]

But as Davis languishes in prison, the North becomes an object of longing and the lyric beauty that was always woven in with the terror becomes the final, decisive mode of vision. Davis, released from prison to die at home, is absorbed into the land as Blake and Rachel were before him.

The combination of particular life and spiritual vision is seen very clearly in *Ascend as the Sun*. The hero, David, was born in 1903 (so was Herman Voaden) in a town by the Great Lakes. We follow him through the ordinary discoveries of youth – nature, friendship, art, love, disillusionment (romantic and religious). We leave him at the age of seventeen, finally winning through to a belief in the God in himself, an idea we can trace back to *Earth Song*. The surface of David's life has a Thornton Wilder ordinariness, but while Wilder showed his small-town characters to be universal precisely *because* they were ordinary, Voaden is more daring. David is surrounded by choric voices who proclaim him as the prototype of a new man for a new age. Even granted the tradition of the hero with humble origins, these two levels of the play never come together effectively, and its larger ambitions remain unrealized. It has, however, a smoothness and clarity of structure that make it seem more accomplished than Voaden's earlier work, and in some scenes the different levels of dramatization combine to produce interesting local effects. There is a scene at a dance, for instance, in which the awkward, inarticulate voices of the adolescents are juxtaposed with familiar dance tunes and with choric voices, both sympathetic and mocking, giving an engaging interplay of attitudes. In moments like this Voaden realizes at least one potential of his special form.

If the mocking, cynical voice of Denison finds ready echoes in our own distempered time, it is harder to reach a fair assessment of Voaden. His poetic language now looks strained and self-conscious, his experiments with form – as is often the way of experiments – look dated. But it may be said that any view of Canada that has no room for Voaden's key idea, the spiritual exaltation inspired by the land, is a sadly diminished view. (Robertson Davies, outwardly a very different writer, will return to this theme in his own way.) Above all, Voaden's determination commands respect. At a time when it must have been tempting to abandon Canadian theatre as a lost cause, Voaden had a positive, clearly worked-out vision.[18] Working with meagre resources, and with many other demands on his time, he pursued that vision. However we assess the aims or the result, we are bound to respect the spirit behind the enterprise.

Though Denison and Voaden both write of the North, between their satiric and spiritual visions there is little if any common ground. It was left to Robertson Davies (1913–95) to combine the two impulses; through his full and varied career he linked satiric observation of society with a respect for the inner life of the spirit and the imagination.

Norman Ettlinger, Max Helpmann, and Barbara Chilcott in Robertson Davies's *A Jig for the Gypsy*, Crest Theatre, 1954

Through his early work in particular this double vision is embodied in a conflict between 'the life-enhancing people' and 'the life-diminishing people.'[19]

In two early full-length plays the conflict is worked out in a British setting. A *Jig for the Gypsy* is set in the author's ancestral home, the border country of North Wales, an area that fascinated his imagination.[20] The tension between the gypsy fortune-teller Benoni and the politicians who want to use her magic for electioneering purposes is summed up by Conjuror Jones: 'These are bad old days for magic. Guarantees they want! And security they want, and the winds and stars hampered like a ram with his head in a bag.'[21] The politicians and their hangers-on, who want life organized and who wear 'the crotch-binding old trousers of other people's opinions,'[22] are sharply caricatured; but apart from one evocative scene at the end, a jig danced in a thunderstorm, the magic of the wiser figures is less fully realized. For that we have to turn to *King Phoenix*, set in the legendary Britain of Geoffrey of Monmouth, and its opposition of merry old King Cole and the glum archdruid Cadno. Cole's merriment, his love of drink and laughter, is related to the organic forces of the earth and celebrated in the John Barleycorn ballad that Reaney will later use for a similar purpose in *The Donnellys*. It also involves a submission, an acceptance of life, inimical to the hustling organizer Cadno, whose religion is significantly described as 'Druidical science.'[23] One way of describing the opposition of the two characters is conservatism against 'progress' – or as the shepherd Lug puts it, 'For the laughing man the skies stand still; only the dark and glowering man can push them on.'[24] In the end Cole dies as a sacrifice, but he dies to save his daughter's lover, and he lives on through her.

The conflicts thus introduced are worked out in Canadian settings in a series of plays that appeared between 1948 and 1950. They show Canadian culture as glum, provincial, materialist, and stiflingly respectable. The following exchange between mother and daughter in the one-act comedy *The Voice of the People* sets the tone:

MYRTLE: Mom, why can't I have a two-piece bathing suit?
AGGIE: Because it calls attention to your bust, that's why.
MYRTLE: Other girls have busts.
AGGIE: Well, you're not going to have one, and that's that![25]

In *At the Gates of the Righteous*, an exercise in quasi-Shavian paradoxes, a band of outlaws are seen as socially conventional and determined to find respectable careers. Even in Ontario, however, the positive energies of life are at work: the 'Psychosomatic Interlude' *Eros at*

Breakfast shows the age-old power of love stirring in the interior of a young man from a good Presbyterian family (literally the interior: the play is set *inside* the central character, a device Davies uses jokingly here and more seriously in later work). Davies's chief concern at this period, however, is the cultural bleakness of Canada: the problem of bringing art and culture to a materialist society that feels no need of them, and the dilemma of those who love art or who have talent, trapped in a country that does not understand their dreams. Once again, the conflict is between the life-enhancers and the life-diminishers, worked out this time through a distinctive local problem; and the result, as in *Marsh Hay*, is frustration.

Two complementary one-act plays dramatize this frustration. *Hope Deferred*, set in New France, shows the church blocking Frontenac's attempt to stage a performance of *Tartuffe*, but its application to Canada in the late 1940s is obvious. As Frontenac complains, 'if trade and piety thrive, art can go to the devil: what a corrupt philosophy, what stupidity for a new country!'[26] He surrenders to what Davies has called 'the tyranny of organized virtue,'[27] and the final tone of the play is bitter. The tone of *Overlaid* is boisterous and farcical, and its central figures are broad caricatures, but it deals no less seriously with the same theme. Pop, the self-professed 'bohemian set of Smith township, all in one man,'[28] is an eccentric old farmer who at the start of the play is dressed in top hat and work gloves, applauding wildly as he listens to the Metropolitan Opera broadcast from New York – much to the annoyance of his daughter Ethel, who has a headache and wants to get on with the ironing. Ethel's headaches are an excuse for denying Pop his pleasures, but do not stop her from working, merely giving her work a quality of surly martyrdom. When Pop gets a small windfall from an insurance policy, he determines to spend it on a spree in New York – opera, restaurants, and a burlesque show – in pursuit of his distinctive spiritual vision: 'God likes music an' naked women an' I'm happy to follow his example.'[29] The god in question sounds like Dionysus, the god of the theatre. Ranged against Pop are (to put it more solemnly than the play does) the forces of death: his insurance agent George Bailey, who would rather see Pop laid out in good order, with enough left for the heirs (George himself has a suspiciously nasty cough) and Ethel, who wants to use the money for a granite headstone. Ethel wins, but only after a debate in which the tone of the play becomes more thoughtful and Pop reveals deeper longings beneath his admittedly absurd idea of a spree in New York: 'I want what's warm an' – kind of mysterious; somethin' to make you laugh an' talk big, an' – oh, you wouldn't know.'[30] One thing the plays have in common is that the source of culture is located outside

Canada. *Tartuffe* is of course an imported play, and Frontenac's dream is given theatrical embodiment by the native girl Chimène, who bears the name of Corneille's heroine and who has trained as an actress in Paris. We might at first think that she embodies the strength of both cultures, but her native qualities are mostly mocked or deplored while her French training is admired. Pop's dream is located in New York; Smith Township has nothing for him, and perhaps in his comically garbled vision of the high life there is a touch of pathos: the dream is so obviously second-hand.

The problems of *Hope Deferred* and *Overlaid* are raised again in the full-length *Fortune, My Foe*, this time with more positive results. A young scholar, Nicholas Hayward, finding Canada a barren ground for his ambitions, is thinking of fleeing south; a refugee Czech puppet-master, Franz Szabo, is trying to establish himself in the new land. The stories of the two men illuminate each other. Szabo's friends help him put on a puppet play on the subject of Don Quixote. Though it is a scrappy version of his art at its fullest, it inspires deep excitement, even religious awe, in the characters who are capable of such feelings: the puppet theatre becomes a miniature temple of art.[31] Yet no sooner is the dream established than the parasites move in; the pattern is at least as old as Aristophanes. The most dangerous are a pair of professional educators who speak in the nasty jargon of their trade, and who want to use Szabo's puppets to spread the gospel of oral hygiene. Szabo has trouble understanding them; English he can cope with, but not pseudo-English. They want art to be scrubbed and orderly: the story of Don Quixote draws the protest, 'We can't show a play to children which has a maladjusted person as the chief character.'[32] They are finally driven away by the drunken professor Idris Rowlands, who – in a scene reminiscent of Jonson's *Bartholomew Fair* – attacks the puppet theatre with his cane, destroying the temple of art to save it from profanation. After an aborted performance before an uncomprehending audience, the theatre lies in ruins. But Szabo is not discouraged: 'I am an artist, you know, and a real artist is very, very tough. This is my country now, and I am not afraid of it ... So long as I keep the image of my work clear in my heart, I shall not fail.'[33]

His determination contributes to Nicholas's decision to stay in Canada. This decision, which ends the play, is more moving and persuasive for being hard-won, based not on glib patriotism but on a frank acknowledgment that 'This is not yet the kind of country a man loves; it is a country that he respects and worries about.'[34] Nicholas's final position is clear, but expressed with restraint: 'let the geniuses of easy virtue go southward; I know what they feel too well to blame them. But for some of us there is no choice; let Canada do what she will with us, we must stay.'[35] Two factors, one negative and one positive, support his decision. Throughout the play the most savage attacks on the spiritual poverty of Canada come from Idris Rowlands, and while he is allowed considerable eloquence, his views are finally devalued when Nicholas identifies the root of his bitterness as his own failure, and rejects him. More important is the setting of the play itself, Chilly Jim's bar, a place of freedom and civilization where even the absurd liquor laws of Ontario are suspended and characters as diverse as Rowlands and the tramp Buckety Murphy can mingle freely. The stage direction describing the set specifies that in the background we glimpse the Kingston skyline, '*one of the most picturesque prospects in Canada, and in this light, one of the loveliest.*'[36] There is, it seems, more beauty and civilized order in Canada than we might have thought.

The positive element is at first glance harder to discern in *At My Heart's Core*, a more sombre play set in Upper Canada at the time of the 1837 rebellion, in which the tempter Cantwell tries to destroy not the virtue but the peace of mind of three gifted women whose talents are suppressed by subservience to their husbands and the rigours of pioneer life. Avenging a social slight that seems to be largely imaginary (though his appearance is Byronic, his motives are those of Bevil Higgin in *Leaven of Malice*), he urges the women to think of the careers they could have had if only they had never come to Canada, and having filled them with hopeless longing, declares, 'These ladies will never, I think, know perfect content again.'[37] But two of the women are Susanna Moodie and Catherine Parr Traill, and Davies may be counting on our knowledge that both achieved distinction after all. The third, Mrs Frances Stewart, gains satisfaction within the play, by submitting – rather as Nicholas does – to the lot that is hers in any case, finding happiness in her husband's love. Stewart himself – witty, lively, and at ease in his world – dissipates the melancholy Cantwell creates and imposes an air of masculine authority at the end of the play. As in *Fortune, My Foe*, however, the positive note is restrained: Stewart shows a wry awareness of his imperfections as a husband and accepts that, while his wife may be content with him, there is no man who can fill 'the whole of a woman's heart forever.'[38] Moreover, the ease with which he dominates his little world may have been won at some imaginative cost. His robust declaration, 'we don't have the Devil in the nineteenth century, and we certainly don't have him in this country,' stamps him, in Davies's terms, as a man of limited vision.[39]

At My Heart's Core is the last in a series of plays written under the same impulse, though the frustrations of the artist surface again in a

lighter form in the entertainments written for Upper Canada College: in
A Masque of Aesop the artist is set upon by detractors who resent the
intrusion of art and beauty into their materialist lives, and in *A Masque
of Mr Punch* parasites with intellectual pretensions try to make an
ancient, popular, and cheerfully disreputable art serve their own sterile
visions. But for the most part, the plays of the 1950s turn to the exploration of inner states, a theme announced in *A Jig for the Gypsy*: 'If a man
wants to be of the greatest possible value to his fellow-creatures let him
begin the long, solitary task of perfecting himself. Look within, Edward,
look within.'[40] The looking within had already taken comic form in *Eros
at Breakfast*, and is developed more fully in *General Confession*; the
characters Casanova summons to act out the scenes of his life – Voltaire,
Cagliostro, the Ideal Beloved – turn out to be aspects of himself. In
Hunting Stuart a mild-mannered Ottawa civil servant, trapped in a stuffy
provincial life, is revealed as the heir of the Stuarts and returns from an
interior journey as one of his own ancestors, the Young Pretender. This
new incarnation, robust, arrogant, and charming, both reverses the personality of the man we have seen and suggests something that was
always latent there. There is also an ironic parallel between the two Stuarts, for both are in the same predicament, heirs to a royal tradition yet
living in squalor. The play's setting, a noble Victorian house full of
cheap modern furniture, suggests that the comment on the Stuarts may
also be a comment on Canadians, spiritually impoverished heirs of a
great tradition.

In 1960, Davies's *Love and Libel*, a stage adaptation of his novel
Leaven of Malice, failed on Broadway after being hacked about by 'collaborators' who thought they knew better than the playwright. Embit-
tered by the experience, Davies wrote very little for the stage till 1975,
when *Question Time* appeared.[41] The play takes up where *Hunting Stuart* and *General Confession* left off: this time the exploration is of the
Terra Incognita of the Canadian prime minister, Peter Macadam, lying
near death after a plane crash in the Arctic. His painful confrontation
with himself is combined, not always coherently, with an exploration of
the nature of Canada. Neither mystery is fully probed, but the play
makes it clear that both man and country need a deeper awareness of the
life of the spirit. Macadam is anatomized as brilliant but cold, a mere
intellectual whose mind always seems to be working a notch or two
beneath the thought of the play itself and who wins life in the end by
submitting to La Sorcière des Montagnes de Glace, a mysterious figure
who embodies (among other things) the spirit of the land. Similarly Canada, ruled by fussy bureaucrats (some good Ottawa jokes here) and
given to narrow-minded materialism, needs a sense of its own imagina-

tive depths, its combination of an ancient land and a European tradition. On this showing, the combination seems an artificial one, embodied in the figure of an Inuit shaman with a Scottish accent who trained in Edinburgh, as Chimène trained in Paris. In some respects Davies is still turned imaginatively towards Europe, as were the characters of *Fortune, My Foe, At My Heart's Core,* and *Hunting Stuart.* (So, more recently, are the central figures of the Deptford trilogy.) There is an odd, tell-tale reference to Peter Macadam sitting on 'the Treasury Bench.'[42] There is no Treasury Bench in Ottawa; Davies is thinking of Westminster. For all that, the attempt to come to terms with what Canada has to offer is more serious and extended than it was in the earlier plays, and shows Davies moving on from the tight-lipped acceptance that was all Nicholas Hayward could manage.

Neither Chimène nor the shaman embodies a convincing relationship between the native spirit of Canada and the culture of Europe. As though aware of this, Davies returns to the problem in *Ponteach and the Green Man,* an interior drama that is also (like the earlier plays, and unlike *Question Time*) a tale of artistic frustration. Major Robert Rogers, a British officer, dreams of the new land almost as Voaden's heroes do: 'a new land has a soul as well – perhaps a very old soul – and those who would find what is best in the new land must find its soul, and humbly embrace that soul.'[43] That is in part the message of *Question Time,* but Rogers's fate is more problematic than Peter Macadam's. He has written a play about the great chief Pontiac, with whom he identifies, and through whom he expresses his dreams. But (like *Love and Libel*) the play suffers the 'improvements' of collaborators and is savaged by the critics, who offer the playwright contradictory advice. The actors perform a sedate war dance to the tune of 'Over the Hills and Far Away'; and the glimpses we are given of the play itself (an actual work by the historical Rogers) show a sensibility as European as that of the early landscape artists who made Canada look like Sussex: 'Ye Groves and Hills that yielded me the Chace, / Ye flow'ring Meads, and Banks, and bending Trees.'[44] Rogers is finally a misfit who belongs neither with the English, whom he despises, nor with the natives, whose imaginations he can never fully enter and who, we are told, 'did not take him to themselves.'[45] At the end Rogers's play, and his dreams, seem to become reality as the set is transformed to a forest and Pontiac appears in the distance; but as Rogers tries to join the dream figure he is seized by sentries and marched off, confined to barracks.

The note of frustration is characteristic. It is perhaps the oddest feature of Davies's rich and varied career that, though his plays have been widely performed, they have never quite attained the critical and popular success his essays and novels have enjoyed; this, despite a love and understanding of the theatre that is one of the strongest currents in his work. Few Canadians have written so well *about* the theatre. Davies always approached the drama with a clear idea of what he wanted to say, and that may be part of the problem: a tendency to lecture, to pack the play with ideas the writer wants to air, may block the imaginative process more seriously here than in other forms. The achievement is considerable for all that; we see a lively and inventive mind, battling frustration, exploring its causes, but never finally giving in to it.

Original and idiosyncratic, James Reaney (1926–) none the less shares many affinities with his predecessors. Denison's interest in local material, Voaden's visionary and experimental qualities, and above all Davies's local application of the conflict between the forces of life and death – all these find their place in Reaney's distinctive vision. His long playwriting career also straddles the lean years of cultural deprivation of which Davies complains, when Canadian playwrights seemed to be sowing seed on barren ground, and the rich period that began in the early seventies, when a sudden boom in Canadian playwriting was matched with wide public acceptance. In the early sixties, when he first turned to the theatre, Reaney must have seemed an unlikely playwright. He was best known as a poet, difficult and private as modern poets tend to be. His dramatic work made few, if any, compromises with conventional expectations. In the slight but charming opera libretto *Night-Blooming Cereus* a group of villagers reveal their dreams at the opening of a plant that flowers once in a hundred years and then only at night. The bloom in the dark evokes the discovery of life within death that is the centre of the story: an old woman, pining for her lost daughter, learns that she is dead – but that the girl who has brought the news is her granddaughter. The setting is Shakespeare, Ontario, in the south-west region that Reaney (following Denison's example) has made a country of the imagination. A more difficult short piece is *One-Man Masque*, a collection of poems and prose pieces for a single speaker on a stage full of symbolic props. The portentousness of the work is summed up in the final line, 'Ladies and gentlemen, Life and Death are indeed difficult to define.'[46] The scrapbook technique, the suggestion of a man growing up, and the conflict of life and death will be refined and presented to greater effect in *Colours in the Dark*. *One-Man Masque* is at best an interesting false start.

The Sun and the Moon is rather more than that. The forces of life and death are embodied in the Reverend Francis Kingbird, who has in the past fathered an illegitimate child, and Mrs Shade – apparently an evangelist and social worker, actually an abortionist, literal and symbolic. The

manner is Southern Ontario Gothic, and the first two acts are finely evocative, especially the preparation for the magic night (recalling the special
occasion of *Night-Blooming Cereus*) when the sun and the moon appear
opposite each other. The village of Millbank and the wicked city of
Toronto are lifted lightly but firmly to the status of dream-places, and the
Gothic fantasy shades nicely into satire on the small-town congregation.
But in the last act the plot twists become arbitrary and the play veers
between fantasy and self-mockery. Still, though it must have seemed
very odd when it first appeared, *The Sun and the Moon* now looks like a
solid introduction to Reaney country, and Mrs Shade introduces a line of
splendid, paradoxical witch-figures who continue to haunt Reaney's
plays. Clearly identified as a negative, death-bringing force, she is also
witty and vital. When exposed at the end of the play, she is unabashed:
'Confess! I'm good to talk about. I'll last you a lifetime.'[47]

The same figure recurs in Madam Fay, the most powerful character in
The Killdeer, a drama about growing up and learning to deal with guilt.
We have two versions of the play, following Reaney's admission, 'I
don't think I'll ever get to the bottom of the story about the two girls and
the bird.'[48] The story is stranger than that of *The Sun and the Moon*, the
allegory more oblique. Once again, there is a difficulty in finding the
right ending: the second version is less convoluted and grotesque but
thinner, and the character of Madam Fay is unresolved. She has the same
dark wit as Mrs Shade, describing herself as

The woman that caused four deaths and one
Of the splatteriest nervous breakdowns I ever saw
And one blighted boy – my son – and one blighted girl –
My sister's daughter.[49]

She has, however, greater emotional depth and vulnerability. She
declares that she prays nightly to God not to forgive her, and she pleads
with her niece Rebecca:

Send me your hatred soon. Send me Hell
To consume me. To eat the wounded bird.
...
I don't want my wing to be fixed. I want
You to take a stick of wood and beat me to death!
Rebecca, Rebecca.[50]

Beneath the self-loathing and the drive to annihilation we sense a need
for love. In the first version she and Rebecca are reconciled. In the sec-

ond Madam Fay is simply driven out. Reaney has not, this time, found a way of satisfying the character's need for love while preserving her energy and integrity, and he simply gives up. He will return to the same problem in *Listen to the Wind*, and solve it.

The Killdeer is also notable for its evocation of the south-western Ontario setting. The bird of the title brings a whole world with it: it is, in Reaney's words, 'the very spirit of long walks in the fall or early spring over empty fields and deserted pastures.'[51] It is arguably more powerful in this capacity than as an element in the play's somewhat difficult symbolism. More evocative still is the conflict between Harry, whose growing maturity is one of the keys to the play, and his mother, whose home cooking reduces the things of nature to a sticky-sweet nightmare of 'pickled cherries, and candied pears, / Crystallized lemon rinds and glazed pumpkin blossoms,'[52] and whose parlour is enough to drive a bright young man crazy:

These brown velvet curtains trimmed with
One thousand balls of fur! Fifteen kewpie dolls!
Five little glossy china dogs on a Welsh dresser!
Six glossy Irish beleek cats and seven glass
Green pigs and eight blue glass top hats and
Five crystal balls filled with snow falling down
On R.C.M.P. constables. The little boys on chamber
Pots: Billy Can and Tommy Can't. That stove –
Cast-iron writhing and tortured curlicues![53]

The close reporting of detail, the balance between disgust and sardonic enjoyment – these help to create both a world and an attitude towards it, and show Reaney as a satirist in love with the sheer awfulness of his creation.

Harry's conflict with his mother is replayed in a less comic way in *The Easter Egg*, in which Kenneth is kept as an idiot by his stepmother Bethel (another Reaney witch), while Polly tries to free him by teaching him words – words that, as in some later plays, are valued for their own sakes. Bethel signals Kenneth with a ball, Polly with a piano. The terms of the conflict are clear and decisive at first, but the old problem of an arbitrarily convoluted ending spoils the play. In *Three Desks* the antagonists are Niles, a cold and unscrupulous young lecturer, and Jacob, a poetic old man who teaches Anglo-Saxon and believes in the second coming of Arthur. This time the battleground is a university office, and again the details of the setting are evocative: an overhead light globe with dead flies in it, a big stick for opening windows. We sense too the building around the office: echoing corridors, a drinking fountain, the Glee Club rehearsing in an empty hall. More overtly fantastic is the opera libretto *The Shivaree*, a comic reworking of the Persephone myth. The villain this time is the old miser Mr Quartz, whose wives have a suspicious habit of dying, and who cannot even remember the name of the girl he currently plans to marry.

The importance of words in general and names in particular is central to *Names and Nicknames*, the first in Reaney's series of children's plays. Old Mr Thorntree blights children's lives by giving them nasty nicknames. In the end words are used to defeat words, as Thorntree is battered into submission by long lists of names. This and the other children's plays – *Geography Match*, *Ignoramus*, and to a lesser extent *Apple Butter* – show Reaney experimenting more radically with theatrical form, using the free play of the childhood imagination for games, riddles, lists, and above all make-believe. In *Geography Match*, for example, the actors have to impersonate Niagara Falls. In his earlier plays Reaney sticks to the familiar surface conventions of drama – one character per actor, a set that represents one place. The relationship between these conventions and the fantasy and symbolism of the plays is not always an easy one, and the effect is often of a private dream world that seems real to the playwright, but may not be available to a general audience. In the children's plays Reaney develops a new freedom of dramatic idiom that allows, through a frankly unrealistic surface, a fuller exploration of inner realities, one that instead of excluding the audience invites their participation.

This experiment bears fruit in *Listen to the Wind*. Four children spending the summer in an Ontario farmhouse act out a flamboyant Gothic romance based on Rider Haggard's *Dawn* and interspersed with poems by Emily Brontë. In both the inner and outer plays the imaginative freedom of the childhood vision is exploited for theatrical effect: an actor running across the stage with a pair of antlers evokes a forest, a handful of maple keys a verandah on a summer afternoon. This time the arbitrary twists of the plot are acceptable as part of the convention of the inner play; unlike the characters of *The Killdeer*, the four children can act out a fantastic story yet still have convincing lives. There is also a significant relationship between outer and inner plays, revealed in the casting. The central creator is Owen Taylor, who is dying of a wasting disease and whose mother, unable to face his death, has deserted him. He brings her back for the play and casts her as the villainess, Lady Eldred. Through this character Mrs Taylor is able to act out the passions of her own strong but repressed nature, confronting the horrors that in her own life she retreats from. The need to face ugliness and pain is also suggested in the central test on the heroine of the story, Angela, who must kiss a doll made from the wishbone of Lady Eldred's murdered baby. When she does so the spirit of the baby releases Lady Eldred from her torment of guilt: 'You've been a wolf in the forest twice times seven years and now you will be freed ... For at last someone good enough has been found to kiss the rag doll you made of my bones – loving enough to lick the sores of Lazarus and gentle enough to weep for the scorpion.'[54] The relations between Angela and her tormentor Lady Eldred recall those of Rebecca and Madam Fay in *The Killdeer*, but this time Reaney manages to have it both ways. Mrs Taylor remains, convincingly, unreformed in the outer play and, just as convincingly, forgiven and released in the inner one. The inner play also embodies a more fundamental resistance to death. Owen (who plays the hero Arthur) and Harriet (who plays Angela) have thought of getting married; but Owen is now dying. Owen is using the play in part to keep himself alive, and at one point a crisis in the plot, in which Arthur apparently dies, corresponds to a crisis in Owen's illness. Finally, the children use the artist's prerogative of changing the ending: Arthur and Angela marry, acting out a desire that we sense will never be fulfilled in reality. Yet the final effect is not mere wish-fulfilment. The inner dream world of the play is given an authority more potent than daylight reality, and through it the children are, like Yeats's golden bird, liberated from time and placed in the artifice of eternity: '*they will never taste death again.*'[55]

Colours in the Dark is in many respects a period piece of the year 1967. It is a mixed-media presentation of the sort made popular that year at Expo – and in that sense is uncharacteristic of Reaney, who usually places the full burden on the actors and gives the lighting technician nothing much to do. In this contribution to the Centennial celebration (the play was commissioned for this purpose by the Stratford Festival) Reaney shows through images of his own life a boy growing up, and a country growing up. The particular and the universal meet in an amiable jumble: the Garden of Eden, Hitler, a boarding-house menu from Winnipeg. Earlier themes return, more clearly and simply stated. The boy goes through a dream of his whole life in a forty-day period when he remains in the dark, a victim of measles. In various ways he confronts and overcomes death, whether embodied in the traditional skeleton or in a killjoy professor who despises 'the imaginative point of view.'[56] He also grows up, and learns not just to apprehend but to interpret life: the elements of the recurring 'Existence Poem' (used also in the children's play *Ignoramus*) are at first just collected, as a child would collect pebbles: 'Pebble dewdrop piece of string straw.'[57] Later they are given meaning:

The pebble is a huge dark hill I must climb
The dewdrop is a great storm that we must cross
The string is a road that I cannot find
The straw is a sign whose meaning I forget[58]

But as the meaning comes, some of the poetic innocence of the childhood vision goes. The poem suggests that maturity involves loss as well as challenge; and the hero – like Angela with the wishbone doll – is tested by a confrontation with the ugly, a legless, armless 'baby' who horrifies him at first, then awakes his capacity for love. In its scrapbook technique, and in some of its themes, the play recalls *One-Man Masque*; but it is much livelier and more theatrical, and this time the private images, though they may not yield all their secrets, can touch and stir corresponding memories in a wider public.

The particular and the general are most powerfully wedded in the Donnelly trilogy: *Sticks and Stones, St Nicholas Hotel, Handcuffs*. This is local history, about a family in nineteenth-century Biddulph township, their conflict with their community, and the final massacre in which their house is burned and five members of the family are murdered. Reaney shows a researcher's interest in the particular, and the play is a scrapbook of facts, dates, times, and place names. Maps come to life, embodied by actors, farm implements become weapons, old songs acquire new meanings, and even the rituals of the Catholic church are pressed into service. Reaney's fascination with detail can seem obsessive at times, but at its best the trilogy uses the freedom of idiom developed in the children's plays to turn documentary into drama: as Mrs Donnelly walks from town to town collecting signatures for a petition to save her husband from hanging, the place names that mark her journey are juxtaposed with an inventory for the making of the gallows. Life is in a race with death. The power of the plays depends on Reaney's wedding the historical material to this central theme. The Donnellys are marked out as special in the first play, *Sticks and Stones*, which is (as the title suggests) much concerned with names. They are proud, imaginative, vital, whereas their enemies are prosaic and earthbound. Like Davies's legendary King Cole, they are associated through the John Barleycorn ballad with the organic life of the land. Mr Donnelly taunts one of his enemies: 'Having myself seven sons and a girl I ask you what children have you? What have you got between your legs, Cassleigh – a knife?'[59] Their home is a centre of love, unlike the grim, broken homes of their adversaries. Like the children of *Listen to the Wind*, they are also freed from death by the timelessness of art: or, as Mr Donnelly cheerfully announces, 'I'm not in Hell for I'm in a play.'[60] This is clearest in the last play, *Handcuffs*, when the stones representing the bodies of the five dead Donnellys are accompanied by living actors, suggesting their dual survival, in eternity and in the play – a convention that allows Jennie Donnelly one last dance with her mother.

Whether the parochial material of Ontario can inspire an ambitious playwright is a question that lies behind much of this chapter. For Denison and Davies, to write of this culture is to write of frustration; and when Voaden claims to be inspired by the land we may respect the claim but we feel a strain in the writing. That Reaney is inspired by his local material is self-evident; but the inspiration carries greater conviction as it is expressed not by a retreat into abstraction but by a close experience of the particular. A characteristic, indeed central passage in *The Donnellys* occurs half way through the second play, *St Nicholas Hotel*, in which the crippled Will Donnelly confronts the killer James Carroll:

There's one thing, Jim, that some people coming after will remark on. And that is – the difference between our handwritings. There is my signature. There is his. Choose. You can't destroy the way my handwriting looks, just as you can never change the blot that appears in every one of your autographs and the cloud and the smudge and the clot and the fume of your jealousy. There! the living must obey the dead! Dance the handwriting that comes out of your arm. Show us what you're like. Very well, I'll dance mine.
First Will, (fiddle), then Carroll, (trumpet), dance; the latter falls down in a fit. Placards displaying their signatures are held up for us to see.[61]

Writing becomes music, a cripple dances, an inner reality is revealed. The immediate purpose of the scene is to challenge the popular image of the Donnellys as bogeymen; at a more fundamental level, it shows Reaney's ability to find poetry in the local archives.

The sense of an inner life impinging on the surface of reality is also strong in *Baldoon*, written in collaboration with C.H. Gervais. A story of poltergeists that evokes the Lake St Clair region as vividly as *The Donnellys* evokes Biddulph Township, it shows, characteristically, a confrontation of vital and repressive cultures – in this case, the Shakers and the Presbyterians respectively – and creates in the central figure of McTavish a mean-spirited man who is finally made to come to terms with himself. *Wacousta!* shows again Reaney's interest in Gothic romance, but the story this time is flatly told and lacks the rich imagery of *Listen to the Wind*. Significantly, history proves more inspiring than romance in *The Dismissal*, about a dark episode in the past of the University of Toronto, and in *King Whistle!* about the Stratford Strike of 1933. In each case history yields the kind of hero Reaney had developed in *The Donnellys*, a cultivated and imaginative man defying repressive authority: William Dale in *The Dismissal*, 'Ollie Kay' (in real life, Oliver Kerr) in *King Whistle!* Dale and his fellow rebel Tucker are associated with the country: Dale, through his strong connection with his father's farm, Tucker through his talisman, a clam shell from Owen Sound. Dale's easy, manly relations with his father are contrasted with the hothouse coddling one of the students – young Willie King – receives from his mother. King is one of a number of historical figures who bring a grotesque comic vitality to *The Dismissal*; another is Sir William Mulock, alias 'Mole,' a picturesque old reprobate who shows that Reaney has not lost his gift for making his villains vital. *King Whistle!* is more diffuse, its hero not so clearly in focus; its main interest for a non-local audience is its evocation, through small details like a recipe for dried-pea soup, of the atmosphere of the Depression.

From *The Donnellys* on, much of Reaney's work was performed by, or in association with, the NDWT company, originating in the group of actors who first performed the Donnelly trilogy at the Tarragon Theatre in Toronto. The existence of such a company, dedicated to the work of a Canadian playwright, would have seemed impossible a few years earlier; so would theatres like the Tarragon, surviving, even flourishing at times, on a diet of Canadian drama. The development of a wide range of 'underground' or 'alternative' theatres in Toronto in the early 1970s, and the accompanying boom in local playwriting, is one of the most remarkable episodes in Canadian cultural history. But while the playwrights discussed so far have concentrated mostly on rural life, being themselves products of a largely rural society, the new playwrights are distinctly urban. While the collective creations of Paul Thompson and Theatre Passe Muraille take a documentary approach to local material (rural in *The Farm Show*, urban in *I Love You, Baby Blue*), most of the playwrights seem to reflect the international consciousness of the modern city, violent and alienated. They range in manner from the brash, inventive comedy of Hrant Alianak to the cold violence of Michael Hollingsworth; but a common factor is the creation of controlled fantasy worlds in which the familiar themes of role-playing, aggression, and the search for identity can be played out. Even so accomplished a play as George F. Walker's philosophical swashbuckler *Zastrozzi* seems finally to be taking place in the playwright's head, or (to put it another way) in a laboratory situation specially devised for a clear demonstration of the play's themes. The charitable view of such writing is that the surface of reality has been sacrificed for the essence; but the danger is that the playwright will lose contact with the life around him and lapse into solipsism. Other forms of art may thrive on such a vision, but the theatre is essentially communal, and when in the late seventies audiences dwindled and several underground theatres fell on hard times the cause may have been not just a natural flagging of energy but a self-defeating narrowness in the art itself.

One of the first major successes in the playwriting boom was *Creeps*, by David Freeman (1945–). It is one of the essential works of the tradition just described; but it rises above it in one important respect. The setting is not (as so often) a room that could be anywhere; it is the men's washroom in a shelter for cerebral palsy victims. This is a kind of club to which the 'creeps' of the play's title retreat from the shelter authorities, and in which they can talk freely. The result is a very specific and disturbing application of the old theme of frustration. Society treats these men as children, giving them useless jobs and entertaining them with 'Puffo the Clown' and 'Merlin the Magician.'[62] They are the subjects of a charity machine whose function is 'to keep the niggers in their place.'[63] But inside their distorted bodies are normal adults. Much of the play's verbal comedy is sexual, often violently so; this gives the language a coarse vigour that fits the setting, but it also suggests the whole range of normal urges frustrated by society's treatment of this particular minority. (*Creeps* takes its place in a distinctive Canadian mini-genre, plays about minorities, that also includes George Ryga's *The Ecstasy of Rita Joe* and John Herbert's *Fortune and Men's Eyes*.) The men band together against the outside world, evoked from their own point of view through images of self-satisfied middle-class homes and the empty merriment of service clubs. But within the group itself there are tensions. Each of the principal characters has a way of dealing with the common problem: Sam and Pete have taken the easy but sterile roles of charity recipient and protester respectively. Jim has become an Uncle Tom, cooperating with the authorities. Tom, the most positive figure, wants to be a painter and in the end he leaves the shelter to make his own career on his own terms. There is no easy optimisn in this ending, any more than there is in Nicholas Hayward's decision to stay in Canada at the end of *Fortune, My Foe*. We know that a real struggle lies ahead for both characters. But Freeman shows that the rage and self-pity he dramatizes so powerfully are not, in the end, enough.

The play's success cannot be accounted for merely by the fact that Freeman himself has cerebral palsy and is writing of something he knows first-hand. Sharp wit, acute observation, and an understanding of the irrational workings of emotion give the play an interest well beyond the autobiographical. These qualities are sustained in his later work, in which the society-versus-minority theme is left behind in favour of a closer look at the way people exploit and manipulate each other. Indeed, there is a sense in which *Creeps* is Freeman's most artificial work, for the characters are simplified slightly so that each can take a clear position in the argument, a necessary economy in a short play. *Battering Ram* examines its three characters at much greater length, and allows each of them to surprise and puzzle us. Virgil, a young paraplegic, has been brought home by Irene, who works in the hospital where Virgil is normally a resident, and who collects patients the way other people collect china dogs. Three-way tensions develop that include Irene's daughter Nora, who is about Virgil's age. Freeman has a sharp, malicious eye for the games people play with each other – feel sorry for me, watch me kill myself, you can't catch me. This is a familiar line in contemporary playwriting, though Freeman handles it expertly; the real interest lies in the depth of characterization. Irene, outwardly the most conventional and unsophisticated of the three – 'I'm just Glenn Ford movies and corn beef hash'[64] – is, once the ice is broken, quite matter-of-fact in her sexual demands and her refusal to let Virgil play the role of put-upon victim. Fast-talking and aggressive, given to startling jokes about his condition, Virgil becomes shy and tentative when introduced to alcohol, pot, and sex. Nora is the most elusive character. Her wit is as tough as Virgil's: she greets one of his appeals for sympathy with, 'So, Miss Calvin, if you would kindly help the handicapped by spreading your legs.'[65] But her early, defensive 'I have no fear of sick people, Mother'[66] suggests an inner unease, and her rejection of Virgil is succeeded in the end by a sexual interest that is no less powerful for being confused. All the characters are, in fact, uncertain of what they feel for each other. But in the stultifying routines of daily life – grilled-cheese sandwiches and old movies on television – they clearly need some kind of excitement, however perverse, and if there is one thing they want from each other it is attention. The playwright is articulate on this point, even if the characters – convincingly – are not.

The tensions of Freeman's *You're Gonna Be Alright, Jamie Boy* are those of a family in which the father (Ernie) tries to mould the others in his own images of them, images borrowed mostly from the television they incessantly watch. If this theme is handled a little glibly, there is plenty of compensation in the close observation of the family's slow, elaborate disputes over which program to watch and who gets which TV dinner. The favourite ploy is ostentatious surrender to the other side. The characters, like those of *Battering Ram*, are seen in some depth. Ernie looks like an aggressive monster, but has his own pathos and vulnerability; his wife Fran looks weak and passive but can get the knife in with the best of them. The two characters with some capacity for normal affection are the children Jamie and Carol, who in the end leave the house together in a gesture reminiscent of Tom's departure from the shelter at the end of *Creeps*. As the door slams, the TV set, which had been out of action, mysteriously repairs itself and what passes for normal life in the house resumes.

Flytrap returns to the three-character pattern of *Battering Ram*, as a surly middle-aged couple fight for possession of a young man. This time the character relationships are worked out rather mechanically, but the sour dialogue and the comic, desperate emptiness of the characters' lives – the woman, every night, puts out clean kitty litter and a saucer of milk for a cat who might one day return – show that Freeman's most characteristic talents are still intact.

Another playwright closely associated with the Tarragon Theatre is David French (1939–), though his work belongs to the larger tradition of modern dramatic realism. Freeman's plays could be set in almost any modern city; French's deal with particular, closely defined communities – beginning with *Leaving Home* and *Of the Fields, Lately*, linked stories of the Mercers, a transplanted Newfoundland family (like French's own) living in Toronto. Though they left the island years ago, their roots are strong. Their songs, stories, and dances bring the family past to life, and their friends and associates in Toronto have the same background. Yet when the father, Jacob, declares, 'there's only two kinds of people in this world – Newfies and them that wishes they was,'[67] we detect beneath the flourish a certain defensiveness. Jacob in particular is insecure about his working-class background and his lack of education; he is 'afraid of sticking out.'[68] He compensates by flamboyant, aggressive behaviour in which the 'Newfie' local colour is an inch thick: at his first entrance he is whistling 'I's the b'y.'[69]

In *Leaving Home* the tensions surrounding Jacob are the family ones implied by the title. He is always testing his sons' manhood, and half-hoping they will fail so as not to pose a threat to him. Billy, the younger and weaker of the two, is about to leave home through the conventional route of marriage, having got his girl friend pregnant; in the course of the play she has a miscarriage and it is not clear by the end whether the wedding will take place. Ben, the older brother, has a tenser relationship with his father, which finally explodes in a violent row. His leaving home is a decisive rejection of the past to which Jacob still desperately clings; at one point he tries to hang on to his son by showing him old family photographs. Given this material, the play could have been trite; and in some moments of excessively pat self-analysis and understanding, it is. It is saved partly by the sheer acuteness of its realistic observation. Billy, coming home from his last day at school, announces that he has cleaned out his locker and thrown away his gym things; he then helps himself to an apple from the fridge, and we see that he has not really grown up after all. But the play's main strength is the flamboyant energy of Jacob himself, which is lovingly realized and gives the play a constant vitality. The flamboyance gets closer to caricature in the figures of the bride-to-be's brassy, disreputable mother and her silent boyfriend. We may think at first that they have wandered in from a different play; but the comic energy that Jacob generates is enough to sustain this excursion into something like farce.

Against this background the change in tone in *Of the Fields, Lately* is remarkable. It is quiet, elegaic, delicate; yet it shows convincingly the next stage in the lives of the same characters. Ben comes home to find his parents alone in a new house, living peacefully together as Jacob recovers from a heart attack. The common changes of time are simply but powerfully evoked. But the old tensions remain, and are revived by Ben's return. Away from work Jacob becomes increasingly restless and miserable; Ben, realizing that his father needs to return to work to reassert his manhood, deliberately goads him into going back on the job, knowing it will mean his death, but knowing also that it is better for the old man to die with his pride intact. At the same time he eases his passage by telling him – falsely – that the reason for his own departure is that he has a girl friend. In the first play Ben showed a conventional drive towards truth and understanding; in the second he constructs a series of saving lies. So, in a sense, does the dramatist. The play is framed by two sequences beyond time: at the opening Ben recalls a key moment of his youth, his refusal to acknowledge his father after a baseball game in which Ben scored a great victory; he takes the incident as 'the emotional corner-stone of the wall between us.'[70] At the end of the play Ben and Jacob are on stage together again, after the news of Jacob's death; Ben asks the question he always wishes he had asked – 'How did you like the game?' – and Jacob *'lowers and folds his newspaper as though he has heard the question.'*[71] The play goes beyond surface reality to show a moment that never happened; yet the moment is both moving and honest, for it dramatizes Ben's deep need to imagine it happening. In the play as a whole French, without abandoning the wit and local colour of *Leaving Home*, adds a new depth of psychological observation. Jacob in particular is the character we know from the first play, but with a new and convincing vulnerability. His wife Mary describes his heart attack: 'Oh, I'm glad you wasn't here, my son. He'd never've wanted you to see him carried out, shivering, on a stretcher, all wrapped in blankets. It was all I could do not to turn away my head. He looked so *puzzled*.'[72] The precision of that last word is typical of the achievement of this play: the details are simple, the observation clear and compassionate.

In the Mercer plays the action is precipitated by familiar rites of passage: Billy's approaching marriage in *Leaving Home*, the funeral of a relative in *Of the Fields, Lately*. In his next two plays French shows characters in crises of a more specialized kind. This entails a shift in structure and interest, with plot tension supplanting character analysis to some degree. The consistent factor is the close observation of a special community. In *One Crack Out* the community is the underworld of Toronto, and the characters have a simplified vividness that, whatever it may owe to actual observation of the mean streets, seems to owe something to gangster movies. The central character is a pool hustler who needs to raise money fast, and who has to battle not only his adversaries but his own loss of confidence (the play began in French's mind as a play about writer's block). His final recovery of nerve through regaining his sexual self-respect is a bit glib; but in the early scenes the tightening of the screws is expertly done and the play builds a fine air of glittering menace from the rigid codes of the underground world. *Jitters* shows another specialized community, and another kind of underground: its tensions are those of a group putting on a play in a theatre not unlike the Tarragon. The result is a paradoxical celebration of the sheer madness of theatre: the tone is alternately farcical, satiric, and sentimental. The characters are neatly parcelled out to represent different stages of the profession, from the young actor making his début to the veteran actress who has made her name and is now in some danger of losing it. The more experienced the performer, the worse the jitters: 'You bet your life I'm a pro. You think a novice like Tom would stand here pleading? Begging and grovelling? He hasn't had the experience.'[73] This in fact represents the middle range; the older performers have passed beyond this simple panic to playing deep and complicated games with each other and with the rest of the company. To the natural insecurity of the profession French adds a distinctive Canadian dimension: the show is to be seen by a New York producer. His name happens to be Bernie Feldman, but it might as well have been Godot; everyone is obsessed with him, and he never arrives. To the worry about local success or failure is added the uncomfortable awareness that there is a bigger, tougher world elsewhere in which the standards are higher and the rewards greater. Does that other world matter? The play's answer seems to be that it shouldn't but it does. The problems of *Fortune, My Foe* and *At My Heart's Core* are still with us.

At this point all we can do is issue an interim report. Playwriting in Ontario, from depending on a few isolated individuals working against unnatural odds, has now become a thriving industry. But there is no sign of its settling into a complacent routine. The pressures of theatre that French dramatizes with such wit and affection are universal; and they link with other problems. French and most of his contemporaries are reporting, as Denison and Davies did, on a fragmented and uneasy society, full of transplanted cultures and isolated social groups, under the shadow of a powerful mass culture that emanates from the south and invades every area of our lives. French's title *Jitters* seems to refer to a world larger than the backstage world the play depicts. (It should be said in fairness that the play itself makes no such claim; but its popularity suggests that the kind of panic it shows is widely recognizable.) The more assertive playwrights, Voaden and Reaney, turn to nature, the past, and literature for a heroic vision that can be stated with confidence. At the moment they look like a minority, though a very significant one. The interplay between the heroic and celebratory, on the one hand, and the realistic and critical, on the other, is one of the fundamental processes of art. It has assured, and continues to assure, that Ontario drama is not just a vital form but a developing one.

Postscript

This chapter was designed to look at selected Ontario playwrights up through the 1970s. In retrospect, 1980 appears to have been a watershed. Of the playwrights discussed here, only David French has continued to write steadily for the theatre. In *Salt-Water Moon* and *1949* he continues the story of the Mercer family. Both plays move back into the past. The first, set on an August night in 1926, shows the courtship of Jacob and Mary. Appropriately for a play of beginnings, it is the simplest and most lyrical of the Mercer plays. The second finds the Mercers in Toronto at the time of Newfoundland's joining Confederation; as if in reaction to the simplicity of *Salt-Water Moon*, it has an old-fashioned generosity of structure recalling the plays of the period it depicts, combining the Mercers with a number of secondary characters and interweaving the personal drama with a sharp debate about the loss of Newfoundland's independence. Of the playwrights who came out of the underground theatres in the 1970s, George F. Walker has shown the greatest staying power. A key event of the 1989 Toronto season was the tremendous commercial success of *Love and Anger*, an attack on the smug, slick Toronto of the 1980s, a city (as one of the characters puts it) 'only satisfying to baseball fans and real estate agents.' To say that the audience was ready is an understatement; *Love and Anger* ran for months, sending a high-rolling decade on its way with a swift kick.

Nineteen-eighty saw the appearance of Judith Thompson's first play, *The Crackwalker*. Its tough, vivid, compassionate vision of life on the margins introduced a major new talent. Anyone who has seen Thompson read from her work knows that she does not just read the script; she becomes possessed by the characters. Her writing has the same quality:

she does not judge her people, she lives them. Native Canadians, whose stories have so often been told for them, speak for themselves in the work – at once hard-edged and playful – of Tomson Highway. The stories of these playwrights are still unfolding. In the smaller theatres, the free-wheeling, sometimes violent anarchy of the plays of the early 1970s has given way to more sharply focused political commitments – especially in the field of sexual politics. The feminist and gay perspectives are no longer the function of individual playwrights alone, but also of groups whose members draw strength from each other. The individual communities that make up Ontario's extraordinary ethnic mix are also being heard from. The most successful work in this vein so far has been Mustapha Matura's *The Playboy of the West Indies*, which, in transferring J.M.Synge's *Playboy of the Western World* to Trinidad, celebrates a culture as rich in language and witty in imagination as that of the Irish original. In general, the new playwrights may be said to have followed (consciously or not) the lead given by James Reaney: instead of worrying about the shakiness of Canadian culture as a whole, they find a smaller, more sharply defined community, and draw imaginative strength from that.

If at some time in the future a sequel to this volume takes the story up to, say, 2040, it is a safe prediction that the chapter on plays and playwriting will not be devoted, as this one was, exclusively to white male writers. It may also tell, for the end of the century, the story of playwrights working against tremendous odds: not the cultural bleakness that faced their predecessors, but the harsh circumstances of an economy that makes theatre increasingly hard to do. It is no coincidence that the name of one Toronto company is Buddies in Bad Times. Nor is it a coincidence that (as I write) that company has lasted for several years. Times may be bad, but, as Davies's puppet-master puts it, 'a real artist is very, very tough.'

NOTES

1 Toronto: Macmillan of Canada, 1926, 1927
2 Toronto: McClelland and Stewart, 1923
3 *The Unheroic North*, 80
4 It is worth recording that during the play's run in Hart House Theatre – which took place, somewhat belatedly, in 1974 – the phrase never once drew a laugh. But this may have to do with the skilful variations played on it by the actor, David Gardner.
5 *Marsh Hay* (Toronto: Simon and Pierre, 1974), A39
6 Ibid., A45
7 *Canadian Plays from Hart House Theatre*, 1:167

8 Ibid., 169

9 Ibid.

10 *Henry Hudson and Other Plays* (Toronto: The Ryerson Press, 1931), 149

11 See, for example, 'Nationalism and Drama' (1928), reprinted in William H. New, ed., *Dramatists in Canada: Selected Essays* (Vancouver: University of British Columbia Press, 1972).

12 *Wilderness*, in Anton Wagner, ed., *Canada's Lost Plays, III: The Developing Mosaic* (Toronto: Canadian Theatre Review Publications, 1980), 96

13 See Voaden's comments about 'symphonic' theatre in his 'Introduction' to *Murder Pattern*, in Wagner, ed., *The Developing Mosaic*, 100ff.

14 *Hill-Land* in *A Vision of Canada: Herman Voaden's Dramatic Works 1928–1945*, ed. Anton Wagner (Toronto: Simon & Pierre, 1993), 267

15 Ibid., 12–13

16 *Murder Pattern*, in Wagner, ed., *The Developing Mosaic*, 108

17 Ibid., 104

18 See, for example, Voaden's introduction to his anthology *Six Canadian Plays* (Toronto: Copp, Clark, 1930). Most of Voaden's anthologies aim to introduce students to a wide range of drama, but this one is deliberately restricted to plays set in the North, with exterior settings recalling the work of Canadian painters.

19 Davies applies these terms, which he attributes to Bernard Berenson, to Pop and Ethel in *Overlaid*. See his 'Epilogue' to *At My Heart's Core and Overlaid* (Toronto and Vancouver: Clarke, Irwin, 1968), 116.

20 First performed and printed in 1954, this play was, according to Davies, 'clear in my head' by 1938 and written in 1945. See Davies, *A Jig for the Gypsy* (Toronto: Clarke, Irwin, 1954), v–vi.

21 Ibid., 93

22 Ibid., 97

23 Davies, *Hunting Stuart and Other Plays* (Toronto: New Press, 1972), 115

24 Ibid., 168

25 Robertson Davies, *Four Favourite Plays* (Toronto and Vancouver: Clarke, Irwin, 1968), 41

26 *Hope Deferred*, in *Developing Mosaic*, 190

27 Ibid., 175

28 *At My Heart's Core and Overlaid*, 92

29 Ibid., 99

30 Ibid., 103

31 Davies's serious interest in puppetry can also be seen in his 1942 essay for the Peterborough *Examiner* on Tony Sarg, reprinted in *The Enthusiasms of Robertson Davies*, ed. Judith Skelton Grant (Toronto: McClelland and Stewart, 1979), 21–3.

32 *Four Favourite Plays*, 150

33 Ibid., 153

34 Ibid., 142

35 Ibid., 156

36 Ibid., 75

37 *At My Heart's Core and Overlaid*, 80

38 Ibid., 85

39 Ibid., 79. See Davies's note on this passage, 121.

40 *A Jig for the Gypsy*, 85

41 Besides *A Masque of Mr Punch* (1962) Davies was one of five authors contributing to the aborted *Centennial Play* (1966). His sections, the Prologue and the Ontario scene, once again suggest that Canada is a place more congenial to the banker than the artist.

42 *Question Time* (Toronto: Macmillan, 1975), 20

43 'Ponteach and the Green Man' (unpublished manuscript, Hart House Theatre, 1977), 66

44 Ibid., 68

45 Ibid., 58

46 *The Killdeer and Other Plays* (Toronto: Macmillan of Canada, 1962), 193

47 Ibid., 165–6

48 *Masks of Childhood* (Toronto: New Press, 1972), ix. This collection prints the second version of the play.

49 Ibid., 208

50 Ibid., 256–7

51 Ibid., 199

52 Ibid., 210

53 Ibid., 212

54 *Listen to the Wind* (Vancouver: Talonbooks, 1972), 110

55 Ibid., 112

56 *Colours in the Dark* (Vancouver: Talonplays with Macmillan of Canada, 1969), 65

57 Ibid., 19

58 Ibid., 32–3

59 *Sticks and Stones* (Erin: Press Porcepic, 1976), 152

60 Ibid., 49

61 *The St Nicholas Hotel: Wm Donnelly Prop* (Erin: Press Porcepic, 1976), 112–13

62 *Creeps* (Toronto: University of Toronto Press, 1972), 22

63 Ibid., 11

64 *Battering Ram* (Vancouver: Talonbooks, 1974), 27

65 Ibid., 81

66 Ibid., 10

67 *Leaving Home* (Toronto: New Press, 1972), 62

68 Ibid., 12

69 Ibid., 14

70 *Of the Fields, Lately* (Toronto: New Press, 1975), 1

71 Ibid., 112

72 Ibid., 32

73 *Jitters* (Vancouver and Los Angeles: Talonbooks, 1980), 36

7 Theatrical Design

ERIC BINNIE

As theatre is an illusion of reality, so colonial artistic expression is often a dream-like manifestation of the culture left behind. In its earliest forms, theatrical design in Upper Canada seems to have been merely nostalgic, primed by the memory of European theatrical conditions and driven by the desire to re-create well-established practices and effects as 'back home.' Almost immediately, however, the sheer exuberance and variety of the native landscape had its effect and was superimposed upon the memorial forms. Thus, in 1816 at a Kingston Amateur Society production, while 'the dresses were elegant and appropriate,' the scenery, specially prepared for the presentation, included a drop curtain representing a remarkable Ottawa landscape, the Falls of Chaudière.[1] Such harnessing of the purely local to the traditional has been central to both the great achievement of Ontario theatrical design and the obsession with identity that has always remained the shadow of the glory.

Very little is known about the visual aspects of theatrical production in Upper Canada during the eighteenth and nineteenth centuries. Such accounts as exist in newspapers, diaries, memoirs, and letters are mostly taken up with descriptions of the auditoriums themselves. Where there is any comment about the visual aspects of the stage, it is often concerned with the inadequacy of lighting, which would make detailed descriptions of settings or costumes impossible. Little known illustrative evidence remains of the stagecraft in Canadian-produced theatricals before the present century. What descriptive accounts there are, either in dramatic texts or in reviews, indicate considerable ingenuity, particularly in the representation of Canada and Canadian values. Thus, Frederick Augustus Dixon's *Canada's Welcome*, first performed at the Grand Opera House in Ottawa in 1879, contained the following scene: 'Those who should represent the divers Provinces in Confederation ... advancing to the tree where Canada lay concealed, drew her forth, and placed upon

Scenes from Raymond Hitchcock's touring *The Beauty Shop*, Kingston Grand Opera House, 1914. The elaborate staging is reflected in an equally elaborate, multipage fold-out program.

her a noble vestment and a wealth of golden maple leaves.' Similarly, the figure representing Ontario wears a head-dress of 'autumnal maple leaves and corn, emblematic of her agricultural wealth.'[2] While such representations seem visually pleasing, the entire text is jingoistic to the extreme, once again demonstrating both love of the homeland and the desire to create distinctive icons of the new identity.

This tension between colonial and native longings repeated itself up

Design (watercolour) by J. Tremain-Garstang, unidentified production, c. 1930

to the present century, when theatrical development in Ontario became closely linked to that other British transplant, the academic system. By the early twentieth century, the traditional British and American stock-company tours of Canada faced competition from radio and film, and were considered less profitable. This led to the formation of local companies for the presentation of serious drama, very much in the pattern of such innovative groups as the Abbey Players of Ireland. This part of the little theatre movement in Ontario was geared to innovative and experimental productions and was heavily influenced by the need to mount plays from very small production budgets. These considerations gave the presentations of such groups as the Arts and Letters Players of Toronto a new and distinctive look. The work of the Arts and Letters Players was continued after the First World War by Hart House Theatre in the University of Toronto, which, in turn, influenced other communities and universities to establish theatre in which purely commercial interests were eschewed.

Photographs of Hart House Theatre productions from the period between the war years indicate a heavy emphasis on silhouette settings and strong, dramatic lighting, using sharp contrasts of light and shade. Many of the early designers were painters whose names are now recognized as being among the outstanding Canadian artists of their day, famous for their colourful landscapes and vigorous sense of composi-

'Why, it's beautiful. It's far superior to any previously used in productions of this play,' said John Gielgud of Eric Aldwinckle's design for *This Mad World* at Hart House Theatre in 1936. Gielgud saw the show while on a Toronto visit after he had appeared in the London, England, staging.

tion: Lawren Harris, A.Y. Jackson, and Arthur Lismer, among others. At this time Canada had no training programs specifically intended for theatrical designers, so it was natural that many of the designers of this, and indeed the next, generation should have been drawn from those with training in the fine arts, the faculty and students of the Ontario College of Art. Thus, hand in hand with the development of professional theatre in Ontario went the growth of theatrical design as a possible career choice. Continuity can be seen in the fact that members of the faculty of the Ontario College of Art, principally easel painters who did occasional designs for theatre groups like the New Play Society or the Crest Theatre, drew from among their own students a new generation of artists who were to make theatrical design their chosen career.

Perhaps the most striking of the easel painters who made occasional forays into theatrical design was Harold Town. The effect of his brilliantly colourful, wittily conceived designs for *The Lady's Not for Burning* (1953) is still joyfully remembered by those who saw this production almost forty years ago. Some sense of his sympathetic yet spirited interpretation of the text can be gained from the three costume

Scene from *The House of Atreus* designed by Harold Town, 1964

drawings reproduced in *Theatre Arts* magazine at the time.[3] Interest-ingly, a later design project of Town's, *The House of Atreus* for the National Ballet of Canada in 1964, came about as a direct result of his critical response to Tanya Moiseiwitsch's designs for *Oedipus Rex* at the Stratford Festival. *Atreus* was an entirely indigenous creation, using a local choreographer, composer, and designer to establish a version of the ancient myth based on the capabilities and resources of the relatively new dance company. Critical responses to this ballet tended to run to either extreme, but, if nothing else, showed that the daring palette and sense of composition, so familiar in the works of the early Canadian colourists, were transferable to the Canadian stage.[4] Indeed, among the most consistently identifiable features of theatrical design in Ontario in this century has been the confident, but daring, handling of colour and colour symbolism.

Just as it was inevitable that many of the early designers had been trained in the fine arts, so it was natural that some of the most interesting design concepts for the early little theatre troupes (or the Jupiter Theatre, the Canadian Players, or the University Alumnae Theatre of Toronto) should come from directors or critics. One such figure was the remark-able Herbert Whittaker, now best known as a reviewer, but in his time a

The Lady's Not For Burning, Jupiter Theatre, 1953 (David Gardner, Richard Easton, Katherine Blake, Christopher Plummer, Donald Harron, Rosemary Sowby, Stanley Mann, Eric House)

fine director-designer. He is perhaps best remembered as a designer for his imaginative staging of *King Lear* for the Canadian Players' 1961–2 tour, using an Inuit setting and costumes. Of his design work in general, Jonathan Rittenhouse has given this perceptive evaluation: 'the innovative quality of the sets, the skilful use of limited space, as well as his spectacularly colourful or subtly shaded costumes, are the hallmarks.'[5]

While various little-theatre and university-theatre groups established a ground swell of interest in serious drama and provided a remarkable group of enthusiasts for any worthy theatrical venture, it was the establishment of the Stratford Festival in 1953 that brought international attention to the quality of theatrical design in Ontario. The history and organization of the Stratford Festival are discussed elsewhere in this study. Here it is important to examine the effect that the new company had upon theatre design throughout the province.

Familiar as we now are with thrust stages throughout the world, it is virtually impossible to imagine the impact of the remarkable shift in audience/stage relationship that Tyrone Guthrie and Tanya Moiseiwitsch effected with that initial concept for the festival stage. While the

Costume designs (ink and watercolour) for O'Reilly and O'Rourke played by Tom Kneebone and Larry Beattie in *The Ottawa Man*, Crest Theatre, designer Clare Jeffery, 1958

William Kurelek stage design for *Christmas in the Market Place*, Evergreen Stage Co.,
December 1961

stage has since been modified, and the original tent replaced by a permanent building, the basic spatial dynamic by which members of the audience seem to enjoy a close, almost confidential, relationship with the
actors, has remained as Guthrie first proposed it in his desire 'to produce
Shakespeare on a stage which might reproduce the actor-audience relationship for which he wrote.'[6]

The simplicity of the permanent features of the festival stage and the
variety of entries onto the acting area allow for great pageantry and
movement, inviting designers to concentrate on costuming and processional properties. Over the years there have been some very imaginative
uses of set pieces on the stage, but the effectiveness of the productions
has always depended for their main visual impact on the movement of
costumed actors through space and light, giving the constantly changing
stage pictures a feeling of depth, of plasticity, which, at best, has had
audiences gasping for pause enough to appreciate each shifting detail.

Given Moiseiwitsch's early background at the Abbey Theatre in Dublin with memories of Edward Gordon Craig's infinitely adaptable but
relatively neutral screens, and Guthrie's experience with the immediacy
of effect achieved in his platform stagings at the Edinburgh Festival's
Assembly Hall, it is hardly surprising that, from the very first productions of *Richard III* and *All's Well That Ends Well* in 1953, a style was
established that threw the design emphasis onto the effectiveness of

William Hutt in the title role of the Canadian Players' *King Lear*, the first of several Lears in his distinguished career. Designed by Herbert Whittaker, inspired by director David Gardner's idea of a northern setting

costumes in light and motion. Though the opening of two new stages, the Avon in 1966 and the Third Stage in 1971, has provided greater scope for set designers, the centre of design operations and the signature of the Stratford style has remained in costume design.

It is often assumed that what has set the Stratford style apart from theatrical design at other theatres is the sheer scale of the production budgets, the length of preparation time, and the army of backstage craftspeople. It is undeniable that the size of the operation has its effect,

Set design by Herbert Whittaker for the Canadian Players' *King Lear*, 1961

but it does not define the look. Reading over comments in interviews and exhibition catalogues one is struck by how often respect for the text is mentioned as the starting-point of the Stratford design process. Looking back on the first twenty-five years, Tanya Moiseiwitsch writes: 'It is the designer's aim to interpret the script in close collaboration with the director, the actors, the colleagues in the workshops who contribute their skills and their knowledge of materials.' This sentiment is repeated by Daphne Dare: 'The designer's focus must always be the text itself, and because the text is always so rich and evocative, instead of competing with it, the designer needs only to support it;' and by Susan Benson, discussing preparatory work: 'I like to read through the script three or four times when possible and study the background of the play as thoroughly as time allows.'[7] Though there have been many interesting period transpositions of the plays over the years, this respect for the text as a starting principle is still very evident in most of the design work at Stratford.

For the first four years of the Stratford Festival, Tanya Moiseiwitsch designed all of the productions, then she started to introduce other Canadian and British designers: Marie Day, Robert Prévost, Mark Negin, Desmond Heeley, Brian Jackson, Leslie Hurry, and others. While each of these designers has the highly individualized style one would expect,

Large banners and colourful costumes accentuate the movement of relatively few performers in *Richard III*, creating a sense of battle on an essentially bare but architectonic stage in the tent at the Stratford Festival. Directed by Tyrone Guthrie and designed by Tanya Moiseiwitsch in 1953.

their productions did have something in common. At this remove it is difficult, and perhaps unnecessary, to distinguish the provenance of specific elements. Suffice it to say that this group of designers around Moiseiwitsch established certain practices that became standard at Stratford: close reading of text and period; familiarity with relevant masterpieces of Western painting; emphasis on illustrative characterization in design renderings; frequent use of paint, dyes, and applied decorations to give texture and age to costume materials; extensive use of skilled specialists in the workshops for such items as armour, jewellery, wigs, masks, and props; and, always, a deep concern for the effects of light and movement on materials – a sense that the floor of the festival stage was a canvas, a background, upon which the actors painted their characters.

From the beginning there was a dedication to the training of apprentice designers. It is remarkable that many of the backstage craftspeople from the early years took the methods and knowledge they gained at Stratford

'Anna in Hell' (played by Dana Ivey) costume design (pencil, watercolour, and gouache) for Canadian Players' *The Firebugs* by Mark Negin, 1965

to influential positions in other theatres or training programs; for example, Robert Doyle to the unique costume-design program at Dalhousie University, Martha Mann to Hart House Theatre and the Graduate Centre for Study of Drama in the University of Toronto, and Hilary Corbett to the Shaw Festival at Niagara-on-the-Lake. This emphasis on Stratford as a training ground for young designers has continued to the present day, par-

'Quayside in Alexandria' (coloured ballpoint pen, wash, and pencil crayon) for *Caesar and Cleopatra*, Shaw Festival, designer Leslie Hurry, 1975

ticularly encouraged by two recent design supervisors, Daphne Dare and Susan Benson. It would be fair to say that, without in any way underestimating the creative abilities of any one individual designer, a person can go into a great range of different types of theatre, witness many different styles of design throughout the province and across Canada, and say, at a glance, 'Stratford-trained,' not with any niggling imputation of stale uniformity, but simply from observing a sense of completeness, a richness of approach, of respect for materials used.

What has created that Stratford look? It might be useful to look more closely at the work of some of the early designers. The Tyrone Guthrie production of *Oedipus Rex* that Tanya Moiseiwitsch designed in 1954, and that went on tour to the Edinburgh Festival in 1956, brought the Stratford company to international attention. The production used masked actors in costumes that exaggerated human proportions with the use of elevated sandals and padded robes. The effectiveness of the costume design derived from her use of subdued, earthy tones for the chorus figures, so that they seemed almost part of the blighted city, and clearer, truer tones for the costumes of the principal characters. The fabrics seemed to have considerable weight and volume, so that Oedipus, in his

King Oedipus (W.B. Yeats version) in 1955 staging by the Stratford Festival. Designed by Tanya Moiseiwitsch, directed by Tyrone Guthrie. Eleanor Stuart as Jocasta, Robert Goodier as Creon, Douglas Campbell as Oedipus, surrounded by Chorus

heavy-looking, pleated robe, half resembled some great fluted column, solid but somehow vulnerable and exposed. The immense folds of the robe were beautifully shaded through the use of pigment, so that, while the actor's presence had great visual clarity on stage, one was also aware of his inevitable fate. The darker shadows of his garment swirling around his feet almost seemed to will his fall, his final expulsion from the city. Those who saw the production can never forget the image of the blinded king fumbling his way forward to clasp his two little daughters into the folds of his great robe. It was a memorable coup-de-théâtre that defined the essence of that ancient tragedy. Simultaneously, it drew the theatrical world's attention to the new Canadian company, and to the importance that it obviously placed on the contribution of design to the whole production process.

Desmond Heeley began designing at Stratford in 1957, coming there from a design background at the Royal Shakespeare Company in England. Engaged in theatre work since the age of sixteen, he is essen-

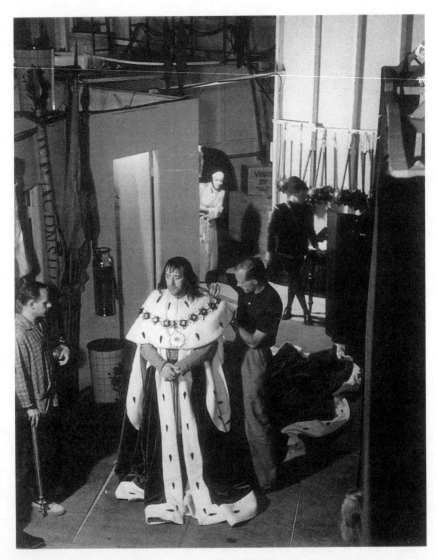

This National Film Board photo, made in conjunction with the NFB film *The Stratford Adventure*, captures a moment backstage preparing Alec Guinness for his role as Richard III in the Stratford Festival tent in 1953. Dressing Alec Guinness is Gordon Jocelyn; at the back, looking on, is Amelia Hall. Stage manager Jack Merigold is on the left; the other actor is unidentified.

tially a hands-on designer who knows his materials, what they can do, and how they can be modified to achieve many desired effects. His costume drawings show his wonderful skill in characterization and in the manipulation or distressing of fabrics to achieve richness of effect. Discussing his own tendency to go back to paintings of the Old Masters for ideas, he says: 'That's what all this does. It teaches you a language so you can say things in fabric and form and colour.'[8] One might profitably say this about his own design sketches, which go so far to help an actor visualize character, posture, and period. Looking at his 1967 design for *Richard III*, for example, what actor could fail to appreciate the uneasy mixture of single-minded aggression and bird-like fragility in the malformed back under the immense weight of the cloak, or the desperate pathos represented in the crippled, in-turning foot?

Another influential English designer brought to Stratford by Moiseiwitsch was Leslie Hurry. First coming to the festival in 1964 to design *King Lear*, he later designed there fairly regularly as well as at other Canadian theatres such as the Shaw Festival. His style is appropriately characterized in the memorial catalogue from The Gallery, Stratford, exhibition of 1982, where he is described as 'a painter for the stage.'[9] Like Heeley's, his designs were painterly in the best sense of that term, so that, at a glance, an actor could tell much about the character concept, while the design assistants also had enough information to re-create the life of the costume. Particularly gifted in the texturing of materials, he was a master at the application of layers of fabrics, hand-painted details, and superimposed decorations to achieve brilliant patinas of colour and shadow as his costumes were caught in motion. His design for *Caesar and Cleopatra* for the Shaw Festival (1975) provides a good example of his typically encrusted decorative technique. For all the simplicity of the basic dress, he gives the actress what she needs to know to create that creature – half curious child, half quintessential temptress, which is Shaw's expressed intention. It is interesting that for this, his last work in Canada, he moved from the vast resources of Stratford to the relatively restrained possibilities of the Shaw Festival, yet still created a most memorable and visually stimulating production.

Other fine designers worked at Stratford in the early years, but these three, Moiseiwitsch, Heeley, Hurry, and their assistants set the pattern: meticulous attention to text and period detail; study of the great painters of the past; renderings that were often close to caricature in their desire to aid an actor's interpretation; techniques of layering pigments and decorative details to the point where costumes seemed to take on lives of their own. These methods have remained the ideal for much theatrical design in Ontario and throughout the country, though changing times

The Winter's Tale, Stratford Festival, 1978. Designed by Daphne Dare, lighting by Gil Wechsler, directed by Robin Phillips and Peter Moss

have meant that later designers, schooled towards this ideal, have often had to learn short cuts or alternative approaches.

The first major change at Stratford came in 1975 with the appointment of Daphne Dare as head of design. A superb designer in her own right, she worked very closely with the artistic director, Robin Phillips, to build Stratford into a major production company, maximizing the use of three separate performance spaces and numerous workshops. Apart from the reorganization of the design department, Daphne Dare's main administrative contribution lay in her sustained efforts to train younger designers – to work at first as design assistants and later as designers of their own productions. While her own designs, usually for plays that Phillips directed, were beautifully realized and instantly identifiable, her generosity to other designers was remarkable. Best remembered for the seeming ease with which her designs accommodated the period transpositions that were one of Phillips's hallmarks, her exquisitely drawn sketches give a vibrant sense of her mastery of tone, period detail, and colour range. She often used a very subdued palette, which was particularly suitable for the many Victorian and Edwardian period switches of Shakespeare's plays upon which she and Phillips collaborated. A good example is the almost monochromatic greys, whites, and dull blues of *The Winter's Tale* (1978).

Typical of the new designers brought to Stratford at this time was Phillip Silver, who designed a very imaginative set for Edna O'Brien's *Virginia* for the Avon Theatre. This set was so evocative, so deceptively simple, with its beautifully controlled mood changes delicately lit by Michael J. Whitfield, that, at one stroke, it seemed to bring Stratford set design into the age of scenography, or integrated set and lighting design. Since then Silver has become an established designer working in many parts of the province, particularly at the Shaw Festival, Young People's Theatre in Toronto, the Grand Theatre in London, and the National Arts Centre in Ottawa. Silver seems to have an instinctive feeling for light and its relationship to location and mood. In *Virginia*, Dare found a perfect vehicle to showcase Silver's particular strengths.

Another young, but highly experienced, designer who flourished under Dare's leadership was Susan Benson, who eventually replaced her as head of design in 1981. Benson had previously worked in many theatres in Canada and the United States, and, since coming to Stratford, has shown considerable versatility in being able to design successfully with the great resources of Stratford and, at other times, with the limited budgets of such venues as the Young People's Theatre, Toronto. Her most spectacular achievement was the 1976 design for Robin Phillips's production of *A Midsummer Night's Dream*, which delightfully realized the director's concept of the play as an extended fantasy relating Queen Elizabeth's splendid court to the wedding celebration that frames the play. Describing the design concept, Benson states: 'Gold expressed the glory of Elizabeth's court, and black and white the reality and the dream, the positive and the negative aspects of Elizabeth's life.'[10] A prolific designer herself, Benson continued the tradition established by her predecessor of training younger Canadian designers: 'I feel my main responsibility here is to help young Canadian designers progress ... I hope that when designers leave the Festival to work in regional theatres, they will, if need be, phone up our wigmakers and bootmakers and find out how to solve any problems that they can't themselves work out.'[11]

This sense of Stratford as the centre, the place from which to come and the source of all problem-solving, would not go unchallenged, particularly by the Shaw Festival. Founded in 1962 at Niagara-on-the-Lake, the Shaw was for many years seen as a pale imitation of Stratford. Since then, it has clearly established itself as a production facility in which designers can achieve great satisfaction. At first many of the same

Heartbreak House (director Val Gielgud, designer Maurice Strike) at the Shaw Festival, 1968. Bill Fraser (Boss Mangan), Jessica Tandy (Hesione Hushabye), Patrick Boxill (Mazzini Dunn), Diana Leblanc (Ellie Dunn), James Valentine (Randall Utterword), Kenneth Wickes (The Burglar), Paxton Whitehead (Hector Hushabye), Frances Hyland (Lady Utterword), Tony van Bridge (Captain Shotover, concealed), Eleanor Beecroft (Nurse Guiness)

designers employed at Stratford also worked at Niagara-on-the-Lake. The main difference was that the nucleus of design activity at Stratford has always been the festival stage with its main emphasis on costume design, whereas the main activity at Shaw has centred around proscenium productions, so that set, costume, and lighting design have had equal prominence. During many of the early years, most of the design duties were shared by Hilary Corbett and Maurice Strike. With the building of a new theatre in 1973, and its greatly improved facilities, the Shaw Festival entered a new era. Several internationally famous designers, whose work had also been seen at Stratford, were employed: Leslie Hurry and Brian Jackson, among others. Since 1980, when Cameron Porteous became head of design, there has been a concerted effort to achieve unity of visual effect by employing designers who have created both sets and costumes for their individual productions. A major feature of the planning of each new season has been long-range anticipation of the years to come, so that each year greater confidence is achieved with

Caesar and Cleopatra (director Christopher Newton, designer Cameron Porteous) at the Shaw Festival, 1983. David Hemblen as Rufio, Marti Maraden as Cleopatra, Herb Foster as Britannicus (in back), Douglas Rain as Caesar, and Roger Barton as Lucius Septimus

the tackling of texts that are more and more difficult to mount; for example, the complexity of staging *Camille* and *Cyrano de Bergerac* made it possible to produce *Cavalcade* in a later season. Not to be outdone by Stratford, Cameron Porteous, himself a gifted designer, has also employed many young Canadian designers; and in some ways, perhaps, his choices have been more adventurous. Thus, the work of both Jim Plaxton and Michael Levine has been particularly innovative. In the designs of both these artists there has been a consistently humorous theatricality, which has marked recent Shaw productions with a very contemporary, self-reflective style. Describing the dream-like fantasy of his designs for *Too Good to be True* (1981), Plaxton says: 'These cartoon clouds. They're not anywhere. Anyone who knows Magritte's work will look at the set and say, "AH, ha! There is a copy of one element of a Magritte up there." I don't try to disguise it.'[12] In a similar fashion, Michael Levine's designs play with the audience's sense of the uncanny with a sinister, almost surreal, humour. His *Heartbreak House* designs for the 1985 production amplified Shaw's grim dream play with touches reminiscent of *Alice in Wonderland*, hinting at the disturbing underside of Edwardian innocence, in an entirely fresh, yet appropriate, fashion.

While Stratford and Shaw have, with their respective resident design heads, allowed for sustained design continuity of approach on a scale that is rarely found in theatre, they did not exist in a vacuum. During the years when they were establishing their reputations there was also considerable growth both in smaller regional theatres and in opera, ballet, and television drama in Canada. Because many designers worked in several fields, as well as at Stratford and Shaw, there were also some new design procedures as a result of these developments.

While it might be argued that, especially in the early years, Stratford looked to England and Shakespeare, theatre in Toronto seemed to look to Continental Europe and Brecht, in particular. The effect of Brechtian ideas on theatrical design in Toronto has generally been stimulating, both in productions of Brecht's own works and in plays by others in which Brechtian techniques were used for design purposes. A major contribution was made by the designs of Murray Laufer while he was resident designer at the St Lawrence Centre for the Arts. Perhaps the most revealing of his works in this respect was his design for Brecht's *Galileo* in 1971. The set consisted of two perfect circles. The playing space was a flat white surface with several entries cut into it. Over this hung a huge bronze disc representing the sun, decorated in bas-relief with repeated, Gothic representations of the crucified Christ, each image slightly different from the next, mutilated or distorted in some way to give a feeling of variety in multiplicity. This massive burnished circle dominated the action and seemed to bear down upon the characters, making their struggles seem both futile and inescapable. Laufer's design concept was also very successful during the riot scene, when huge puppet effigies of the principal characters were rushed across the stage by the ordinary citizens, mocking the complex antagonisms of the famous. Another excellent touch was the fact that the passing of each minute as Galileo struggled with his decision was marked off by the clicking of an actor's heels as his dark figure marched round the perimeter of the circular stage, seeming to turn the white surface into the face of a clock. Since this production, Laufer has moved increasingly towards an integrated approach to design, in which he takes control of all aspects of production. He is particularly interested in Brecht's ideas about the texturing of costumes and has experimented in this way, for example, in his designs for Edward Bond's *Narrow Road to the Deep North* (1972) and Brecht's *The Good Woman of Setzuan* (1974). This is an entirely different approach from the layering effects so typical of Stratford designs, discussed above. For his costumes in Brecht and Brecht-like plays, Laufer tries to distort costumes in a quite non-realistic fashion. The garments are often painted, but the paint is obviously paint, the lumpy paddings are obviously padding, in order to draw attention to the theatricality of the work presented. Related to this is Laufer's use of unusual materials in his set designs: 'I have consistently tried to utilize as many three-dimensional materials as possible. The isolation, abstraction and lonely purity of *The Three Sisters* (1972) was achieved by the use of metal piping while the coarseness of *Puntilla and his Hired Hand* (1971) ... was realized with decaying corn stalks, straw, hay and snow fencing. This quality was suggested in still another Brecht – *The Good Woman of Setzuan* (1974) by using a corrugated metal structure.'[13] One of the most highly esteemed of contemporary Canadian designers, perhaps especially in Europe, Laufer has also designed for the Canadian Opera Company. Increasingly in recent years, he teaches design students at the Ontario College of Art.

Another group of designers developed in the province during the early years of television drama. While these designers were not, strictly speaking, theatrical designers, they should be considered here because of the extensive cross-fertilization of ideas that has existed among television, film, opera, and theatre in Ontario. One such designer who has been able to arrange her work periods between television drama and opera is Suzanne Mess, whose costume designs, not only for the Canadian Opera Company, but for opera companies throughout North America, have created a wide familiarity with the high quality of Canadian design. It would be true to say that almost all theatre designers and craftspeople in Ontario have spent some time either at the Stratford Festival or in the Canadian Broadcasting Corporation design departments. The advantage of this unofficial system of shared apprenticeships is obvious, not only because of the exchange of ideas and methods, but also in that it greatly increases employment opportunities: when the CBC is having a thin season, many craftspeople will probably be able to find employment at Stratford or vice versa.

Television design in Ontario undoubtedly reaped the benefits of several European political upheavals in the 1950s and 1960s. The Iron Curtain diaspora that followed political upheavals in Czechoslovakia and Hungary resulted in an influx of artists and craftspeople to Canada that is reflected in the ethnic composition of the work-force at CBC, Toronto. These artists brought with them not only their creative skills, but an awareness of the political and satirical possibilities implicit in theatrical design and a familiarity with the major dramatists of eastern Europe, which has resulted in some very fine television productions of such dramas and also, perhaps, in some new Canadian plays influenced by such works.

One example of such a new Canadian is Val Strazovec, who came to

Canada in 1968. Besides designing such memorable productions as *The First Night of Pygmalion* and *Sarah*, he was the founder and principal instructor of the CBC's short-lived Institute of Scenography, which tried to break down the traditional separation in design training into set design, costumes, and lighting in order to stimulate a way of thinking about production design as an integral process and 'to assure a successful realization of the audio-visual concept, by understanding the convection of visual information through the optical process.'[14] This radical approach to the training of design students was stimulated by similar courses in Europe, where the idea of an integrated design discipline was well established. Several young designers graduated from the institute, but it became clear, almost immediately, that the CBC was too rigidly departmentalized to be able to employ the institute's graduates without causing major bureaucratic turmoil. Some of the graduates were absorbed into individual departments; other young designers, like David Moe, moved on to freelance production design and now work only occasionally for the parent body that trained them.

To be fair to the CBC, one has to say that the Institute of Scenography years came just at the end of a period of economic expansion and at the start of an era of recession. Perhaps it is not surprising that a government-funded television agency should be seen as one area in which cutbacks could be made at that time. Considering the many new, live, theatre companies that had been founded throughout the country, and in Ontario in particular, there might have seemed to be less need for television drama. Throughout the seventies it was in these new theatre companies that the next generation of designers, many of them with links to Stratford, the Shaw, or the CBC, were to exercise their talents.

One of the most consistently interesting of this group of rather maverick designers has been Mary Kerr. She has worked in a wide variety of media – television, ballet, opera, and film – and in all kinds of theatres, from a delightful *The Way of the World* for the tiny University College Playhouse in the University of Toronto to a highly imaginative *Candide* at Stratford. Her work is characterized by an explosive celebration of colour and pattern, firmly based in her highly personal – rather than merely repetitive – interpretation of period. Over the years she has maintained very trusting, collaborative working relationships with several directors, particularly in the newer production companies.

Another designer outside the mainstream who has based much of her work on collaborations with specific directors or companies is Astrid Janson. Some of her best design work was created for George Luscombe at Toronto Workshop Productions. One of her most successful achievements was the design for Rick Salutin's *Les Canadiens*, which combined convincing realism and deliberately alienating fantasy; some members of the 'real' audience were, in fact, dummies, which kept the rest of the audience popping in and out of 'that willing suspension of disbelief' every time their enthusiasm for the play forced them to take a sideways glance at their silent, frozen-faced neighbours. At the Shaw Festival, one of Janson's most imaginatively simple designs was for *The Cherry Orchard*, in which she replaced the walls of the house with dozens of great flying panels of white lace, which, combined with a series of chandeliers and clusters of huge white balloons, gave the right impression of fragility, decay, and futility, while reminding the audience always of the delicate vulnerability of the orchard, the one beautiful feature of that endlessly featureless landscape.

While the many smaller theatres in Toronto and other cities have provided new design opportunities, the major theatrical venues remain Stratford, the Shaw, the St Lawrence Centre for the Arts, and the National Arts Centre in Ottawa. This last theatre enjoys the benefits of mounting productions in both English and French. Perhaps because of its very proximity to Quebec, it has always seemed somewhat apart from the major centres in the southern part of the province. Yet a study of its programs indicates that many of the same designers who have worked in southern Ontario have also been employed at the NAC: Brian Jackson, Michael Eagan, and Susan Benson, among others. One senses that the sheer distance from the various southern centres frees the spirits of certain designers when they make the journey to the capital. Thus, Susan Benson, best known for the exquisite elegance of her period designs at Stratford, took great enjoyment in designing *The History of American Film* for the NAC, because it allowed her to use 'really tacky, brassy fabrics' for this amusing production.[15] True to its name, the National Arts Centre has also provided several fine touring productions that have left strong impressions throughout the country. One of the most memorable of these was Michael Eagan's design for the Mirbt Puppet troupe of Strindberg's *The Dream Play* (1977/78), which also played at Toronto's Tarragon Theatre and several other venues. The chorus figures, magnificently dressed in rich, oriental costumes, captured all the essential mystery and ambiguity of Strindberg's text, while guiding the audience effortlessly through the more obscure passages. The design decisions led the audience into the fantastic world of this strange play, allowing its genius to touch them, without in any way trivializing or reducing its meaning. Such transfers from Ottawa to other centres provide a means of keeping the province in touch with the capital, and Ontario has been lucky enough to enjoy several such movable productions.

At this point, it might be useful to consider the background, training, and working conditions of some successful Canadian designers. 'Can one make a decent living as a designer in this thinly populated nation? How are Canadian designers trained? Are all designers gypsies, or can they have a settled life?' These are the questions frequently asked of working designers such as Suzanne Mess, Michael Eagan, and Mary Kerr.

Suzanne Mess, whose costume designs are principally known in the field of opera, was trained at the Ontario College of Art and was among the very first group of young artists employed by the CBC in its television design department in Toronto. Because of the international cachet that her name now lends to the CBC, together with the fact that she is a most patient and encouraging supervisor of apprentice designers, she has, for many years, been able to work out a modus operandi that allows her to maintain her staff position in television, while enjoying considerable freedom to take up freelance contracts whenever convenient.

Michael Eagan also enjoys a double function: as a freelance designer and as a professor of design at the very school in which he trained – he is one of the many fine designers to have graduated from the three-year program of the National Theatre School in Montreal. Other successful working designers trained at the National school are John Ferguson, Debra Hansen, Roy Robitschek, and Christina Poddubiuk. Michael Eagan's base is Montreal, yet he carries on a successful freelance career throughout Canada. His designs are seen at the National Arts Centre, Stratford, and many other theatres.

Mary Kerr was trained at the University of Manitoba and moved to Toronto; in the first instance, to undertake graduate studies in medieval drama, where she almost immediately became involved in theatrical design, both on and off campus. She is a prolific and versatile freelance designer working in theatre, television, and film.

Established designers in Canada work very hard, but they are fairly well rewarded for their artistic achievements. Because there has been such immense growth in theatrical activity in this country, designers often find that they have more than the normal share of responsibility for such dramaturgical activities as play selection and season planning – which gives such experienced designers a sense of the esteem in which their expertise is held. Some designers – such as Astrid Janson, Martha Mann, and Phil Silver, who teach at universities – choose to have the security of a permanent base, together with flexible arrangements for freelancing when such opportunities seem interesting and rewarding. Others maintain their freedom and, much like actors, juggle job offers, lean periods, and tantalizing leads, often using the services of a professional manager or agent. Generally, freelance designers earn slightly less than the director or principal actors in a major production. The material demands for productions vary greatly from one show to the next, yet one would not be far wrong in estimating that, on average, 20 per cent of any production budget is likely to be spent on the design and construction of sets, costumes, and lighting.

Conditions for Canadian designers improved considerably following the formation in 1965 of the Associated Designers of Canada. Among its activities, this organization establishes suggested salary scales for the various types of theatres in Canada. With the growth in the number of theatre companies in recent years, trained theatrical designers have found ample opportunities and challenges, which are reflected in the high standing they have achieved in international design exhibitions. Participation in such competitions has also been facilitated by the formation of the association.

Given the diversity of theatrical talents in theatres throughout the province, can one really speak of an Ontario style in theatrical design? Certainly some of the same methods and even the same designers can be found in the great national theatres of the world – one would not wish things to be otherwise. Although there is no one look that unifies the work of such a varied group of individuals, there are some things that can be said to distinguish design in this province. There is a feeling of permanent anticipation of new opportunities built upon the solid foundation of such well-established places as Stratford, the National Arts Centre, the Shaw Festival, the St Lawrence Centre, and CBC, Toronto, with their respective training programs. Despite the budgetary constraints that all these centres have experienced recently, audiences still expect that they may continue to see theatre of a high level of design excellence in such centres. This public confidence is also reflected in the sense that all Ontario designers have that such great production houses are repositories of expert advice, superb crafts work, and new talent. In most cases, designers in Ontario have this feeling about one or more artistic home bases, to which they can turn for guidance, assistance, and, indeed, employment. In this way each centre of excellence is surrounded by many satellites, in the form of those smaller theatres that employ their former apprentices. It is this sense of overlapping loyalties and friendly cooperation that gives theatrical design in Ontario its remarkable quality, its stability despite economic vicissitudes. In his recent study of John Neville, the American theatre historian Robert A. Gaines defines this spirit of cooperation with particular reference to Stratford, though he might as easily have been describing the whole situation of interdependence in theatrical design throughout Ontario: 'The Festival combines the classical theatre tradition with what Professor Ronald Bryden calls essentially the English repertory system of production. But the Festival defines and particularizes both the tradition and the system with the sensitivities and experiences of the primarily Canadian artists, designers, directors and administrators employed by it. The resulting Canadian stamp has been carried by those who have worked there to all parts of the country.'[16]

NOTES

1 Yashdip Singh Bains, 'Painted Scenery and Decorations in Canadian Theatres, 1765–1825,' *Theatre History in Canada / Histoire du théâtre au Canada* 3:2 (Fall 1982), 113

2 Eugene Benson and L.W. Conolly, *English-Canadian Theatre* (Toronto: Oxford University Press, 1987), 15

3 *Theatre Arts* 1953

4 Archives, National Ballet of Canada

5 Jonathan Rittenhouse, 'Herbert Whittaker: A Theatre Life,' *Theatre History in Canada / Histoire du théâtre au Canada* 3:1 (Spring 1982), 55

6 James R. Aikens, 'The Stratford Stage: The Setting for Design,' in *Made Glorious. Stage Design at Stratford: 25 Years, an Exhibition* (Stratford: The Gallery, 1977), 8

7 Aikens, 'The Stratford Stage,' 12, 14; Brian Arnott, 'Artists not Craftspeople: An Interview with Susan Benson,' *Canadian Theatre Review* 3 (Winter 1986), 36

8 Keith Garebian, 'Desmond Heeley: Premier Designer,' *Performing Arts in Canada* 21 (Winter 1984), 51

9 *Leslie Hurry: A Painter for the Stage* (Stratford: The Gallery, 1982)

10 Thérèse Beaupré, 'Susan Benson: Designing the Stratford Festival,' *Scene Changes* 9 (June 1981), 15

11 Ibid., 18

12 Paul Millikin, 'Jim Plaxton Brings a New Visual Innocence to the Theatre without Walls,' *Performing Arts in Canada* 19 (October 1982), 39

13 Murray Laufer, 'Designing at the Centre,' *Canadian Theatre Review* 3 (Summer 1974), 43

14 Canadian Broadcasting Corporation, *I.O.S. Program* (n.d.)

15 Arnott, 'Artists not Craftspeople,' 37

16 Robert A. Gaines, *John Neville Takes Command* (Stratford: William Street Press, 1987), 321

8 *Theatre Criticism*

ANTHONY STEPHENSON

In October 1950, in an essay in *The Critic*, Nathan Cohen's short-lived arts journal, E.G. Wanger wrote: 'Giraudoux in his play *Song of Songs* refers to a man as being like "an aviator before the invention of airplanes." That describes fairly accurately the plight of the Canadian theatre critic.'[1] While this statement betrays the general ethnocentricity of anglophone writers in Canada in that it ignores the relatively healthier climate in French-Canadian theatre at the time, it was certainly applicable to the situation in Ontario. Until theatre exists there can be no theatre criticism. Until an indigenous theatre exists, a theatre of some seriousness and achievement that has its roots in the life of the community and that feeds and is fed by that community, there can be no theatre criticism worth much consideration.

Perhaps the best theatre criticism occurs in periods when the theatre of a particular culture is emergent or in transition. In Ontario theatre, the period between the early 1950s and the mid-1970s was a significant one, and the critic who best reflected that period (though he did not live to see some of its finest achievements) was Nathan Cohen. Cohen fought against the dominating force of external cultures and proselytized for a theatre that was more than passive entertainment. It is arguable that he was the only theatre critic in Ontario and indeed in Canada who attained international recognition and respect, leaving aside such sometime Canadians as Ronald Bryden, Beverley Baxter, and Milton Shulman.[2]

To suggest, on the other hand, that Nathan Cohen was an Everest surrounded by vast plains of mediocrity would be inaccurate. Both before him and since there have been theatre critics of intelligence and integrity writing in the newspapers and periodicals of the province, among them Fred Jacob, B.K. Sandwell, Robertson Davies, Mavor Moore, Oscar Ryan, Vincent Tovell, Urjo Kareda, John Fraser, Martin Knelman, and Herbert Whittaker. That these writers have not had more impact both within Canada and abroad has had more to do with the vicissitudes of Canadian theatre and with the sometimes mystifying editorial policies of Canadian journals than with their particular qualities as critics. Cohen himself seems to have been valued by the Toronto *Star* as much as a creator of controversy and a provider of good 'copy' as for his critical acumen. Theatre criticism, if approached with some sense of responsibility and honour, is no easy profession. As Harold Clurman pointed out in *On Directing*, the reviewer in a large-circulation daily is hampered in his or her true function as 'an enlightened go-between for artists and audiences' by the concern of the newspaper for the review's impact on theatre as a business. Ideally, the critic – he goes on to say – should be an artist with a particular aptitude for the 'optics' of the theatre, with knowledge, experience, and understanding of the craft so that he may serve as 'the audience's knowing eye and conscience.'[3] One might add to this that the periodical reviewer has an advantage over the daily newspaper reviewer in that he or she has more time for reflection and for refining his response. Unfortunately, with very few exceptions, Ontario's weekly and monthly magazines have not seen theatre criticism as being very high on their list of priorities.

In the nineteenth century and the earlier part of the twentieth, the popular theatrical fare was provided chiefly by touring companies from the United States and Great Britain, and only rarely by Canadian-based troupes. The material they offered had already been evaluated in its country of origin and advance publicity had often created a particular expectation in the minds of theatre-goers. This fact, together with the economic importance of theatre advertising to the newspapers, meant that much of what passed for theatre criticism in the period was simply the paraphrasing of press releases. Where the reviewer incorporated any comment of his own, it was usually dutifully approving, and even in the notices of local amateur productions, negative comment was rare, though less deadly than the condescending commendation usually offered. The common practice was for theatre reviews to be unsigned, and one example from the London *Free Press* in December 1910 of Maude Adams's appearance in *What Every Woman Knows* may be taken as typical: 'The play is a big literary effort and the actress is a big natural interpreter. Neither can be done justice at a glance. And it was not only Miss Adams that delighted London. Every member of the company bore his or her part in the general artistic effort and added his or her part to the pleasure of the occasion.'[4]

This passage is no more banal, nor is it less informative, than the great majority of others that could be culled from contemporary sources. Indeed, when one comes across a review in which any kind of standard is being applied, one is apt to overvalue it. Here, from *The Globe* (Toronto) in 1904 is another anonymous writer who is prepared to go a little further than the usual bland back-patting: 'The play is of the kind that is dear to the hearts of the masses, having plenty of lofty sentiment for the humble characters and a prodigality of stupid villainy for the well-dressed man of the cast. The criminality of the villain seems perverse because there is no apparent reason why he should want to make away first with his own child and secondly with the woman he had deceived.'[5]

The first regular theatre reviewer who was identified by name in an Ontario newspaper appears to have been E.R. Parkhurst. Edwin Rodie Parkhurst was born in Dulwich, England, in 1848 and emigrated to Canada in 1870. In 1872, he joined the Toronto *Daily Mail* as a reporter. Until his death in 1924, he divided his career between the *Mail* and the *Globe*, eventually becoming editor of the *Weekly Globe* and music and dramatic critic for the daily edition. His chief interest, however, was music rather than theatre and for some years he published and edited two monthly journals: *The Violin* and *Musical Canada*. As a theatre critic, Parkhurst seems to have taken the same kind of conservative stance as Clement Scott in England. At much the same time, they were both resisting the plays of Ibsen. Realistic problem plays in general seemed to distress Parkhurst, nor for that matter were the very different dramatic experiments of Maurice Maeterlinck to his taste. Typical of his enthusiasms were the plays of Avery Hopwood and A.A. Milne. Of a Hopwood farce, he wrote that it would 'make the most confirmed cynic and the self-deserted [sic] dyspeptic consign their pain and sorrow to oblivion.' In a similar vein, A.A. Milne's sentimental whimsy, *Mr. Pim Passes By*, is described as 'that brilliant English comedy,' which makes one wonder what description Parkhurst would have applied to *The Way of the World* or *As You Like It*.[6]

In assessing performers, Parkhurst's standards seem to have been equally lax. A minor American actress is given the following accolade: 'Miss Sarah Padden in the role of Maggie Schultz in *Kindling* this week at the Grand Opera House is a character actress of the highest order. [She] held the audience breathless with her consummate skill.'[7] The following month, the most he could say about Sir Frank Benson in *Much Ado About Nothing* was that 'as Benedick [he] gave a vivid portrayal in stage action of naturalness and significance of elocution and a deportment that carried the assumption of ease and naturalness.'[8] There are generalities of a respectful but not notably enthusiastic nature about the Benson ensemble, but Parkhurst makes no comment at all about sets, costumes, lighting, or directing.

On the whole, Parkhurst reveals himself as a critic with little knowledge or appreciation of theatre and drama. Nor, as can be seen from some of the above quotations, was he a writer who handled the English language with any degree of grace or skill. To be fair, however, in a period when theatre in Ontario was suffering first from the popularity of vaudeville and later from the boom in movie-theatre construction, Parkhurst had little to exercise his pen on. In a typical week in 1913, the chief offerings in Toronto theatres were *The Garden of Allah*, *Oh, I Say!*, *The Girls of Starland*, *The Firefly*, and *Toddles*.

By 1918, in Toronto newspapers and others across the province, more and more space once occupied with writing on music and drama was being taken up with information about and comment on silent films. In the *Border Cities Star*, a publication serving Windsor, Walkerville, Sandwich, Ford, and Ojibway, the main entertainment feature was titled 'On Stage and Screen,' but even where, as in the Hamilton *Spectator*, the name 'Music and the Drama' was retained, the contents were a mix of comment on movies, melodramas, burlesque shows, and vaudeville performances. Serious reviewing of any of these entertainments was, not surprisingly, at a minimum, and the anonymous, and in some cases pseudonymous, writers – the Hamilton *Spectator* had a 'Jenny Wren' and the *Border Cities Star* an 'Annie Oakley'[9] – were certainly no more impressive than E.R. Parkhurst in Toronto. Not even the Ottawa *Citizen* seems to have produced much intelligent writing on theatre, despite the formation of the Ottawa Drama League, whose existence attested to the fact that there were those in the city with more than a passing interest in the art of the stage. One exception to the general rule was the London *Free Press*, which by 1920 had a reviewer under the name of 'Fanfare' who was capable of the occasional astute observation. In an account of Walter Hampden's performance as Shylock, 'Fanfare' wrote, 'the term "comedy," attached to the play, must be taken in its primary form as meaning not necessarily a humorous piece, but rather a drama primarily concerned with "life," as the term "tragedy" means a drama primarily concerned with the things of death. It was a custom with Edmund Keen [sic] and other classic actors who played *The Merchant of Venice* chiefly for the role of Shylock, to omit the fifth act and by so doing to close on a tragic note instead of the note of comedy: the idea of the eternal rushing forward of life beyond and despite of even the most tragic happenings.'[10] This shows at least a sober and painstaking approach to entertainment journalism, in marked contrast to the mainly glib and often ill-informed efforts of the writer's contemporaries.

That theatre criticism in newspapers was of a generally low standard is not surprising when one realizes that it was almost always assigned to non-specialists. Nor indeed had the situation changed totally by 1970, when Dr John A. McPherson complained in a brief to the Senate's special-committee enquiry into mass media: 'There is probably not a newspaper of even modest size which does not take the reporting of sports, professional or amateur, with some seriousness ... But it would seem that the performing arts, especially drama, whether professional or amateur, do not enjoy such benevolence.'[11] One notable exception among editors in the early part of the twentieth century was Walter J. Wilkinson, news editor of the *Mail and Empire* from 1897 to the mid-1920s. He appears to have been more inclined than most other Canadian editors to stress the importance of dramatic and musical events as news. However, even with his encouragement and support, Hector Charlesworth, who followed Parkhurst as the next important theatre critic, was unable to concentrate solely on theatre criticism. An article in the *Star Weekly* in 1926 had this to say about Charlesworth's career as a newspaper reporter: 'That phase of journalism was forced on him by circumstance. Most successful newspapermen in this country, not least in Toronto, have been trained in the same school of necessity. There was no market for cultural writing ... And, as a rule, the man who criticized music and drama did it as a side line to the daily grind of reporting the news.'[12]

Hector Willoughby Charlesworth was the son of an Ontario small businessman of Methodist background, and was born in Hamilton in 1872. He joined the staff of *Saturday Night* in 1891 and then worked for a variety of Toronto newspapers before becoming city editor of the *Mail and Empire* in 1904. Having returned to *Saturday Night* in 1910, he became its managing editor in 1926 and in 1932 was appointed chairman of the Canadian Radio Broadcasting Commission, from which post he retired in 1936. He then returned to journalism, contributed to *Saturday Night,* and was music and drama critic for the *Globe and Mail* until his death in 1945. In addition, Charlesworth proved his commitment to the development of Canadian theatre through his involvement with the Earl Grey Dramatic Competitions. By 1910, Earl Grey, then governor-general of Canada, had come to rely on Charlesworth 'both as a friend and an adviser on matters theatrical.'[13] His leadership of the adjudication team so impressed Grey that he appointed him sole adjudicator of the 1911 competition.

If Parkhurst was a Canadian Clement Scott, Charlesworth – in manner at least – was a Canadian James Agate. He was a bon vivant, whose resemblance to Edward VII was frequently remarked on, and he cultivated the port-wine-and-cigar manner of an Edwardian clubman, as far as was possible in the Toronto of those days. At his best he could bring a saltiness to his copy that was almost Shavian, as in this *Saturday Night* review of Jules Eckert Goodman's *Mother* in 1910:

No doubt there are many old women in the world who are as silly as Mrs. Weatherill, the middle-aged heroine of Mr. Goodman's drama, and no doubt the Lord in his mysterious way has permitted many of them to become mothers of large families. In *Mother* we are asked to applaud all the follies of the old lady because, as the dramatist intimates, they spring from mother love. Now, mother love is a great and noble emotion that approaches the human concept of the divine but in reality it is only a beneficent sentiment when its results are beneficent. In real life, a woman who could not bring up her sons better than does Mrs. Weatherill would deserve to have them taken away from her by the Superintendent of Neglected Children.[14]

Charlesworth could also occasionally manifest a crusading zeal against small-minded bigotry and in favour of free expression in the drama, as he did in the case of Legrand Howland's *Deborah*. The play was presented in Toronto in 1913 and was promptly prosecuted at the instigation of the Reverend John Coburn. Judge Morson dismissed the case, at which point the Reverend T.T. Shields launched another attack on the play, denouncing it from his pulpit as 'fit only to be witnessed by the population of hell.' Charlesworth defended the play in *Saturday Night* and pointed out to the overwrought clergyman that the main theme of the play was to be found 'in several of the legends of the Jewish patriarchs, as recorded in the Book of Genesis.'[15]

Later in his career, however, Charlesworth seems to have become less trenchant, and sometimes even began to adopt a fulsomeness of tone reminiscent of Parkhurst. In reviewing Walter Hampden's *Othello* in 1922, he called it 'one of the rarest achievements in the whole history of the English drama.'[16] A journalist of Charlesworth's experience should have realized that such a statement invites the reader's disbelief, since it could clearly only carry conviction if Charlesworth had witnessed Burbage, Quin, Betterton, Garrick, Kean, et al. giving their finest performances.

Perhaps the essential flavour of Charlesworth's personality and the best sense of his relationship to the theatre of his time are most fully captured in his volumes of memoirs: *Candid Chronicles* (1925), *More Candid Chronicles* (1928), and *I'm Telling You* (1937). Gossipy and anecdotal, they reveal a man who was as much celebrity-struck as stage-struck and who obviously enjoyed his role as a man of letters who was also a man about town.

Roughly contemporary with Charlesworth was another critic who was associated with both newspapers and periodicals. In general, Fred Jacob seems to have had a more acute sense of the way in which Canadian theatre could be measured from both a historical and an international perspective than either Charlesworth or Parkhurst. Born in Elora, Ontario, in 1882, Jacob joined the *Mail and Empire* in 1903 and became dramatic editor in 1910. From 1925 to 1928, he conducted a department called 'The Stage' for the *Canadian Forum*. In 1928, while entertaining friends for dinner at his home, he suffered a severe asthmatic attack and died of a heart seizure. He was forty-six years old.

Like Charlesworth, Jacob did his best and most considered work for a periodical rather than a newspaper. Indeed, because of the lack of bylines, it is not easy to tell whether Jacob did all or only some of the reviewing for the *Mail and Empire*, and so many productions, including vaudeville bills, were dealt with in so little space that, from the 1920s onward particularly, there was little opportunity for expansive treatment of theatre in that newspaper. In *Canadian Forum*, however, Jacob had the space to provide considered, reflective writing, and much of this was devoted to commentary on the developing Canadian drama.

Hart House Theatre at the University of Toronto was already six years old when Jacob began writing his essays for *Canadian Forum*. In his October 1925 'Stage' column, Jacob commented on the theatre's future. It had just been announced that the theatre would be under the direction of Mr and Mrs Vincent Massey, and Jacob drew a comparison with the Manchester Repertory Theatre under Miss Horniman. He went on to say that he had always felt that 'Hart House Theatre and similar institutions must be the hot-bed for the native drama in the dominion' (p. 28). It was an idea that he restated many times, yet he seemed aware that the 'little theatre' movement in Canada was not quite the same as the one 'fathered in Paris nearly forty years ago by André Antoine, and developed in other lands by men like J.T. Grein, Maurice Browne, Stanislavski, and Kenneth McGowan.'[17] Toronto audiences, judging by the fate of Ibsen's *The Wild Duck*, which played for seven nights only to small houses, were still more interested in escapist spectacle than serious problem plays. At the same time, the supply of escapist spectacle was being cut off. New York producers no longer found the Canadian market a profitable one and the economic incentive for home-grown producers to develop their own native commercial product was insufficient. The 'little theatres,' Jacob felt, would have to fill the gap, even if it meant that their fare would grow 'more commonplace.'[18]

The efforts of Canadian playwrights in the 1920s to balance seriousness with commercial viability were, on the whole, disappointing to Jacob, and the hopes he had held for Hart House Theatre were not often fulfilled. In a retrospective essay on the 1926 Hart House season, he commented that the 'purely conventional pieces' done there 'did not add to the prestige of the playhouse' and went on to single out a particular play, *The Ship*, which he said was 'awkward in its technique, muddy in its ideas, uncertain in its purpose, and generally futile as drama.'[19] One of his last comments on Canadian drama, written in the year of his death, a review of Mazo de la Roche's *The Return of the Emigrant*, reflects Jacob's continuing disappointment. He called the play 'a little drama that lacked all the qualities that a score of Irish playwrights have taught us to expect in pieces about Ireland,' and went on to say: 'There was no music in the language, and no suggestion of half-humorous poignancy in the ideas; the occasional Irish phrase lacked authenticity. Regarding the literary skill of Miss de la Roche there cannot be two opinions, but where she failed any writer, except an Irishman, would have failed. Why Canadians insist upon writing of things about which they have no first hand knowledge, I cannot understand.'[20]

Apart from his reflections on Canadian drama, Jacob's columns covered a variety of other topics, and the impression one gets is that he often approached his subject from a morally conventional standpoint. He disapproved of the manners and morals reflected in Maugham's *The Constant Wife* and Coward's *This Was a Man*, was shocked by the depiction of the Reverend Davidson in *Rain*, was concerned about what he saw as the violence and indecency of much Broadway fare, and praised the U.S. actor-manager Henry Miller because he 'never did an unworthy play to shock the well-bred public and amuse the sensation hunters.'[21]

If Jacob was sometimes the voice of conventional morality, he was also the voice of the future in that his perceptions about the decline of professional touring theatre and the consequent importance of the amateur movement were confirmed by the pattern of development in the late 1920s and through the 1930s. More and more, theatre in Canada began to mean amateur theatre as, rising on the ashes of the Earl Grey Competitions, community theatre organizations like the Ottawa Drama League and the Edmonton Little Theatre Association began to emerge all over the country, culminating in the founding of the Dominion Drama Festival in 1932 and its first annual festival at Hart House Theatre the following year.

Among the critics who were importantly associated with the festival both as commentators and adjudicators, was Dr Lawrence Mason of the *Globe*. Mason came to the paper with impressive credentials. The son of a prominent lawyer, he was born in Chicago in 1882 and was awarded his doctorate by Yale in 1916. He remained there as an assistant professor until 1924, when he was appointed to the faculty at the University of Minnesota. Meanwhile he edited two plays for the Yale Shakespeare

Series: *Julius Caesar* and *Othello*. In 1924, in an abrupt and somewhat puzzling career change, he left academia for newspaper work, succeeding E.R. Parkhurst as music and dramatic critic of the *Globe*.

As a daily newspaper reviewer, Mason clearly had less scope for considered and reflective writing than Jacob had in *Canadian Forum*, but it is surprising, nevertheless, that with Mason the reviewing of drama became skimpier than it had been under Parkhurst. The section Mason edited, headed 'Music in the Home – Concerts – the Drama,' contained much more music, and later film and radio reviewing, than theatre reviewing. But, to be fair, theatre was in decline, and Mason proved himself not indifferent to the development of Canadian theatre. In the *Globe* as early as 1928, he argued for the establishment of a provincial drama league on the model of the British Drama League and the Scottish National Theatre. Indeed, when the Canadian Drama League was founded in 1930, its chief instigator, Brownlow Card, acknowledged his debt to Mason.

Mason was also the first Ontario critic to travel widely and bring back reports from Britain and Europe as well as other Canadian provinces. This suggests an open-handedness and an openness of mind on the part of the editorial board that has not always been a feature of the newspaper industry in Ontario. The *Globe*'s readers consequently were kept informed of what was going on at Stratford-on-Avon, at London's theatres, at the repertory companies of Liverpool, Birmingham, and Bristol, and in the theatres of Germany and Austria. The intention behind these 'Letters of a Globetrotter' was admirable; the execution often was not. In his letter for Saturday, 6 November 1926, for instance, Mason reports that Raymond Massey, after directing Phyllis Morris's *Made in Heaven*, is to appear in Noel Coward's play *The Rat Trap*. 'Neither would be welcome in Ontario,' sniffs Mason, 'and both are being considered for the West End. Both give realistic depictions of matrimonial unpleasantnesses' (p. 9). By this criterion, *Hedda Gabler* presumably would have been equally unwelcome in Ontario.

In Mason's reviews generally, there is little serious analysis of text or performance and even less consideration of other theatrical elements. When he becomes expansive, his style is a mass of clichés and unreflective superlatives, as in his comments on the Abbey Players' presentation of T.C. Murray's *Autumn Fire*, which he calls a 'powerful play, brilliantly presented' to be ranked 'among the greatest in their splendid repertoire,' and then describes it as 'the old story of a vigorous but vain old man and a mere slip of a girl,'[22] a summary that might apply equally well to *King Lear* and *The Blue Angel* and that would tell us as much about them as it does about Murray's play.

By the end of his career, Mason's style had become, if anything, lusher and less disciplined, and his judgments showed even less of the intellectual rigour that one might expect from a former Yale scholar. Editorial policy at the *Globe* also seems to have shifted to the extent that a relatively important theatrical event, Sir Cedric Hardwicke's appearance in Paul Vincent Carroll's *Shadow and Substance*, was allowed only three paragraphs, buried at the bottom of the 'Suburban Toronto' page. Perhaps the curious mixture of social reporting and uncritical adulation explains its placement: 'Sir Cedric Hardwicke opened the local showing of Paul Vincent Carroll's startlingly beautiful play ... on Monday night before a capacity crowd which included the Lieutenant-Governor and many literary, artistic and social leaders. The audience paid this extraordinary production "the perfect tribute" of motionless, spellbound attention, punctuated by rippling laughter, fervent applause and heartfelt tears ... Sir Cedric as the austere churchman of Rome's great tradition adds another matchless portrait to his gallery of superb stage creations.'[23] What precisely was 'beautiful' about the play, 'extraordinary' about the production, or 'matchless' about the performance is not discussed.

This kind of criticism, far from being flattering to the artists involved, which is presumably its intention, is insulting in that it refuses to pay them the serious tribute of detailed critical assessment based on clearly articulated principles. Shortly after he joined the *Globe*, Mason wrote, in 'A Critic's Annual Report to His Readers,' that he saw his function as being to help the public form sound standards of judgment.[24] The standards he habitually applied, however, seem to have been moral rather than intellectual or aesthetic, and one of the obituaries on his death in 1939 praised him for exerting 'his influence for a clean stage.'[25]

While Mason was writing for the *Globe*, the Toronto *Star*'s chief critic was Augustus Bridle. Born in Dorset, England, in 1869, he was educated partly in England and partly in Ontario. After a varied journalistic career, beginning with the Stratford *Herald*, he became associate editor of the *Canadian Courier* in 1908 and editor in 1916. In 1922, he was appointed music editor of the Toronto *Star* and the following year also took on responsibilities for book, film, and drama reviewing. One of the founders of the Arts and Letters Club of Toronto, he became its president in 1913 and later achieved some public fame as the organizer of the Toronto *Star* concerts and for staging his pageant, *Heart of the World*, at the CNE Colosseum in 1927. After a long and impressively active life, he was knocked down by a slow-moving truck at the corner of Bloor and Sherbourne streets in December 1952, and died of bronchial pneumonia in hospital at the age of eighty-four.

Like several of the other critics mentioned, Bridle's chief interest was

music, which dominated his column for many years. The relative importance of music and theatre to Bridle and the Toronto *Star* can be seen
from the fact that music was included under the lofty feature-page heading 'Literature, Music, Life and Art,' while theatre was lumped together
with film under the brusque formula 'Theatres, Movies Reviewed.' The
content of 'Literature, Music, Life and Art' was less lofty, however, than
its title suggests. On a typical page in October 1934, there are several
short, two- or three-paragraph stories: twenty lines on Evelyn Waugh's
A Handful of Dust, twenty lines on Grace Moore demanding $3500 for a
concert, and sixteen lines on Canadian poet Gertrude Lang Miller. In the
same issue in the stage and screen section there is a brief comment on
theatre: 'Toronto wants plays and can't get them. Toronto has hundreds
of players and can't give most of them stage room.'[26]

Granted the poverty of offerings in the mid-1930s, it is excusable that
Bridle wrote so little about theatre. Given the right opportunity, however, his pen could flow copiously and idiosyncratically. A good example of his lively but muddled style occurs in his review of Shaw's
Geneva, which opened in Toronto just after the outbreak of the Second
World War: 'More clearly than ever this cinema of wit is seen to have no
drama plot at all, a Jew for a hero, no heroine except either a deaconess
or a Spanish murderess, two chief goats of satire – League of Nations
and the Established Church – no action whatever, and no finale except
the last curtain that stops everyone talking. Yet ... [the] play spotlights
more human truth in the gigantic hocuspocus of international politics
than all the war scribes and radio talkers have done since the war
began.'[27] This kind of writing is clearly not in the Parkhurst/Mason
mould. One has the sense of an unabashed personality reporting his own
honest if eccentric reactions to a theatrical experience. At the same time,
one has the unkind suspicion that the reason Bridle was allowed to
devote so much space to *Geneva* was that it was newsworthy on two
counts: first, it presented on stage the major combatants in the conflict
that was occupying the front page of the newspaper; second, it had
attracted to Toronto representatives of New York's Theatre Guild,
which was interested in staging the play for Manhattan audiences.

Bridle's eccentric style reaches a kind of apotheosis in a 1945 review
of Elissa Landi in Coward's *Blithe Spirit* at the Royal Alexandra: 'In
spite of these handicaps [her ectoplasmic costume], aided by a wonderful ballerina glide and her phenomenally vibrant, flexioned soft voice,
she was a marvellously spookish apparition, draping herself silently over
the furniture. Her ectoplasmic vitality is in the sheer expressive art of
acting. More spectral envelopment and a more plastic monologue would
make this conjugal spook much less cutely clever and more of an inge-

nue blithe spirit.'[28] By 1949, the woozy syntax and grasshopper thought process had developed into a manic stream-of-consciousness: 'B'way – by some said to be the greatest theatrical in the world (oh, never know what cloudraker penthouses do to magnify 'tout ensemble') has now 11 play hits. A soon-extra by Miller, scripter of *All My Sons* – will take a bit of beating to equal P. Muni starring in that O'Neill way-back *Knew What They Wanted*.'[29] At that point, Bridle was eighty, so he can be excused for attributing Sidney Howard's play to Eugene O'Neill, and for referring to Arthur Miller as a 'scripter.' When he died, to be succeeded by Jack Karr, something strange and colourful and spontaneous disappeared from the world of theatre criticism in Ontario.

While the names of Charlesworth, Jacob, Mason, and Bridle were becoming familiar in Toronto publications, the newspapers in the rest of the province were still relying on unsigned reviews, where any appeared at all. In the Ottawa *Citizen*, the London *Free Press*, the Hamilton *Spectator*, and other local journals through the 1920s and 1930s, there was sporadic coverage of mostly amateur theatre, but no reviewing of any great distinction. The remaining Toronto newspaper of importance, the *Evening Telegram*, also relied on unsigned reviews, the only bylined comment on theatre being Leo Miller's reports from New York and Lucy S. Doyle's show-business gossip column.

Meanwhile, in the field of periodical publication, *Saturday Night* and *Canadian Forum* continued to carry responsible coverage of the theatre scene. At *Saturday Night*, after Charlesworth became managing editor in 1926, several other writers were employed as theatre critics, though Charlesworth still wrote the occasional review. Hal Frank, John E. Webber, and Mary Lowrey Ross were among the most frequent contributors. In 1932, however, B.K. Sandwell became managing editor and also took on the role of drama critic for the magazine. Born in 1876, Sandwell was, like several of his precursors, a native of England. After graduating from the University of Toronto in 1897, he worked for the Toronto *News* and later became assistant editor and dramatic editor of the Montreal *Herald*, where he signed his reviews with the archly whimsical pseudonym 'Munday Knight.' He moved on to editorial positions at the Montreal *Financial Times* from 1911 to 1918, and then temporarily abandoned journalism to take up a series of academic appointments before joining *Saturday Night*.

Throughout this varied career, Sandwell had maintained an interest in theatre, and in the Canadian theatre in particular. As early as 1911 in the *Canadian Magazine*, he made this plea for an indigenous drama: 'Canada is the only nation in the world whose stage is entirely controlled by aliens ... It is true that at the present time we have no plays of our own,

for the excellent reason that we have no machinery for producing them
... But we are not Americans, in spite of the fact that we live in North
America.'[30] In his early days at *Saturday Night*, however, Sandwell
seems to have chosen to cover the imported productions at the Royal
Alexandra: *Rookery Nook*, *Bitter Sweet*, *Roberta*, *Mourning Becomes
Electra*, leaving the 'little' theatres in the hands of other writers such as
Mary Lowrey Ross, W.S. Milne, and Margaret I. Lawrence. One of the
reasons for this is perhaps revealed in a piece he wrote in 1935: 'The
business of theatre is to entertain. The business of the little theatres, it
has been rashly concluded by many of its adherents, is to do very little
entertaining. It is possible that the theory has been too much in evidence
at the Hart House Theatre in the past years.'[31] This passage occurs in the
context of praising Hart House for reversing their normal policy and
mounting a commercial success – Emlyn Williams's *A Murder Has
Been Arranged*.

Sandwell's attitude to the Dominion Drama Festival was also, initially, discouraging. In April 1933, on the eve of the finals, he wrote: 'It
may be doubted whether a Canadian drama can ever be developed on a
purely amateur basis ... A Canadian drama whose sole impelling motive
is a rather self-conscious patriotism is not likely to get very far.'[32] By
1936, however, he had changed his opinion to the extent of writing that
Canadian playwriting had 'embarked on a second period of fertility'
comparable to that which followed the establishing of Hart House Theatre, and that the 'fertilizing force' is the National (sic) Drama Festival.
He elaborates his metaphor somewhat unfortunately when he goes on:
'As the fertilizer is so much more widely spread it is not surprising to
find the crop coming up over a wider area.'[33]

Among the plays Sandwell commented on in the festival was an
experiment in 'symphonic drama' by Herman Voaden. This play, *Murder Pattern*, was a work in which Voaden tried to combine realistic,
expressionist, and poetic elements, together with music, ritualistic
movement, and innovative set and lighting design. Sandwell wrote that
although it was an improvement over earlier efforts, it contained only
one character and that one so 'dimly drawn that the audience was left
mystified by his motivation for the killing which is the central event of
the play.'[34] Among the other critics who wrote about *Murder Pattern*,
Lawrence Mason felt that the play 'sweeps us along in a kind of aesthetic ecstasy,' while Augustus Bridle, after venturing that it was 'as
much like an average play as a mob resembles a quilting bee,' added
that, for originality in theatre, 'Voaden and his players and their menage
of mechanics are just about first in America.'[35]

If Sandwell seems tepid in comparison to the others, this was his usual tone when dealing with amateur theatre in the 1930s. Later, though, after the hiatus of the war years, during which time the festival was suspended, he saw in its revival some very positive aspects: 'The great value of the Dominion Drama Festival consists in the fact that it brings together in one place and for a single event, once in every year, many of the ablest and most self-devoting workers in the theatre from all over Canada, in conditions which give them a most favourable opportunity to profit by one another's knowledge and skill.'[36] But it was with the growth of indigenous professional theatre after the war – from the New Play Society to the Canadian Repertory Company – that Sandwell, often using the quirky alias 'Lucy van Gogh,' turned his attention more seriously to Canadian plays and playwrights. His comments, though not always favourable, were usually shrewd and scrupulous. Speaking of Morley Callaghan's *To Tell the Truth*, which was presented by the New Play Society in 1949, he put his finger neatly on its flaws: 'The play has two sources of weakness, both of which would probably be greatly mitigated by a working over at the hands of an experienced dramatist. There is too much statement of the thesis in terms of philosophical discussion rather than action. And there is an extravagant amount of machinery required to operate such action as there is. Mr. Callaghan writes with the loose and scattering hand of the novelist, not the economy of the practised playwright.'[37] In his last years at *Saturday Night*, Sandwell seems to have felt that there was real hope at last for a professional theatre in Ontario, using the talents of local playwrights, directors, and actors. He continued to praise seriously the work of the New Play Society, which he described as having 'in three years achieved an amazing record of successful and highly artistic production of great classics and great contemporary plays, the latter actually including two works by Canadians.'[38] One of his last reviews for *Saturday Night* celebrated the arrival on Broadway of a Canadian play – Gratien Gélinas's *Tit-Coq*.

Before Cohen, Sandwell and Jacob seem to have been the most consistently serious and intelligent critics in Ontario. Their best work, however, was done for periodicals rather than newspapers, which tended to diminish its influence. Given the nature of periodical publication, with its early deadlines for copy, and the nature of Ontario theatre at the time, when a run of more than a week was a rarity, their reviews often appeared after the fact. Their influence on the box office was therefore considerably less than that of the daily-newspaper reviewers, whose opinion of a production would appear the day after it opened. The less-considered criticism, consequently, had more effect than the more reflective, a state of affairs that continues to some degree today.

Another problem with some periodicals was a lack of continuity in their reviewing staff. At the *Canadian Forum*, after Jacob's death, a variety of writers undertook the reviewing of theatre, some distinguished and some less so. In the late 1920s, the theatre column was renamed 'The Little Theatres' and was edited by Carroll Aikins, then director of Hart House Theatre, and later by R. Keith Hicks. In 1931, the column became 'Stage and Screen,' reflecting the increasing dominance of the film. Between 1928 and 1934, during the regimes of Aikins and Hicks, several well-known Canadians contributed pieces on theatre to the magazine, including Herman Voaden, urging the development of a National Drama League (December 1928), Rupert Caplan, on the 'ultimate national theatre' (January 1929), and Robert Ayre, on 'Les Chauves Souris' (December 1929). The 'Stage and Screen' column was dropped altogether in December 1932. In December 1934, a new column, 'Footlights,' under the editorship of Brian Doherty, later founder of the Shaw Festival, made its appearance, but this too disappeared altogether in April 1935. After that, during the later 1930s, the orientation of the magazine became more overtly political, and coverage of theatre on a regular basis did not resume until after the war.

The postwar period was a significant one for theatre criticism, not just in Toronto, but in many smaller communities, where – in the late 1940s and the 1950s – signed reviews began to appear in local newspapers. In the London *Free Press* in 1949, F. Beatrice Taylor was celebrating the return of stock theatre to the city for the first time in twenty years. Commenting on the Shelton-Ames Players' production of a play called *Cradle Snatchers*, she wrote: 'The situations are sure fire but the lines are weak. To make up for the lack of wit there is a great deal of action and jumping about and we get the impression of quick comedy. But the playing is good right through, direction is fast, the set is gay and effective, the gowns of the women are wonderful and if you don't mind the obvious you have a good time anyway; the Shelton-Ames Players are nice, and they are fun.'[39] This may not be penetrating analysis, but it offers some sense of judgment being applied and some inkling that in reviewing a production there are several elements besides text and performance that should be dealt with. Altogether, it marks an advance from the rehashed press releases that were a common feature of earlier coverage of the theatre in local publications.

For the St Catharines *Standard*, Betty Lampard covered theatre from 1950 to 1980. New-York born, she had little of the New York hard edge as a critic. Her credo was: No production or performance is so terrible that you can't find at least some good things to say about it; this helps balance the negative comments you have to make. The Ottawa *Citizen*, in the 1940s and 1950s, had Isabel C. Armstrong, and later Lauretta Thistle, but looming disproportionately in the world of provincial newspaperdom, there was the numinous presence of Robertson Davies at the Peterborough *Examiner*. Davies, born in Thamesville, Ontario, in 1913, had attended Oxford University, acted with the Old Vic, and been employed as literary editor of *Saturday Night* before becoming editor and publisher of the *Examiner* in 1942. His comments on theatre in that publication, together with his reviews for *Saturday Night* and his books on the Stratford Festival (in collaboration with Tyrone Guthrie), represent some of the best evocations of performance, on the model of William Hazlitt's theatre essays, ever written in Canada. His witty submission to the Royal Commission on National Development in the Arts in 1951, cast in the form of a Drydenesque dialogue, had long-term effects on official attitudes to patronage of the theatre, and his Alexander lectures on nineteenth-century melodrama, published as *The Mirror of Nature*, spiritedly defend a neglected theatrical form, offering some Jungian insights into its appeal. Since his death in 1995, Davies's importance as a critic has been far overshadowed by his achievements as a novelist of international reputation. Nevertheless, he has particular interest as a critic in that, unlike many of those dealt with in this chapter, he had practical experience of the theatre both as a performer and as a playwright.

Robertson Davies was also connected with what was perhaps the most significant postwar event for Ontario theatre, and perhaps for Canadian theatre generally: the founding of the Shakespeare Festival at Stratford, Ontario. What was significant for the theatre was also significant for theatre criticism. A new sense of professionalism was born in both areas of endeavour. The realization of the dream of a local Stratford man, Tom Patterson, aroused international interest and prompted the foundation of other professional theatres in Ontario and across the country. The extraordinary success of the venture raised the consciousness of editors, and the media generally began to pay more serious attention to the theatre during the 1950s and 1960s.

At the three major Toronto newspapers by the late 1950s, three important critics were in place. Herbert Whittaker at the *Globe* had succeeded Colin Sabiston in 1949. Nathan Cohen replaced Jack Karr at the Toronto *Star* in 1959, after two years at the Toronto *Telegram*. Mavor Moore came to the *Telegram* in 1959, supplementing the work of Rose Macdonald, who preferred to concentrate on reviewing amateur theatre. With these writers offering their opinions after each opening, it was perhaps the first time that serious theatre-goers could turn to all three newspapers for indications of success or failure. It is also completely coincidental that from this time on, theatre critics in Toronto, and to some extent performing-arts critics generally, began to arouse more than usual hostility in professional performers, directors, producers, designers, and other theatre workers. Having for decades little more to dread than the occasional admonitory slap on the wrist, while more usually experiencing the rhapsodic prose of Mason or the avuncular encouragement of Charlesworth, they began to suffer the sharp edge of critical dissecting tools.

Of the three daily-newspaper critics, the one most responsible for this new hard-edged style of criticism was Nathan Cohen. Unlike the majority of his predecessors, Cohen was not a member of the Anglo-Saxon Protestant establishment in Ontario. His parents emigrated from a small Jewish community in Eastern Europe to Nova Scotia, where Cohen was born in 1923. In 1939 he entered Mount Allison University, New Brunswick, and became involved in undergraduate theatre, journalism, and politics. His first professional assignment was as editor of the Glace Bay *Gazette*, a small local newspaper. By 1945, he was in Toronto, writing for *Vochenblatt* (Canadian Jewish Weekly), the *Canadian Tribune*, Canada's Communist Party weekly, and *Today, an Anglo-Jewish Weekly*. In 1946, he became associate editor of a new Jewish monthly, *New Voice*, but the magazine ceased publication a year later. Meanwhile, he had written his first piece of professional theatre criticism, a review of the New Play Society's production of O'Neill's *Ah, Wilderness!*, for *Vochenblatt* in December 1946. In it, he praised the production and acting, but condemned the play as weak and berated the society for wasting its talents on it. This review sets a pattern for his later critical work: demanding excellence of Canadian theatre workers while simultaneously urging them to end their reliance on external materials and influences.

In 1947, Cohen became drama critic for CBC Radio, creating a particular impact on a weekly program, *CJBC Reviews the Shows*. It was in those ten-minute segments in which he reviewed both drama and the dance that Cohen polished his style and developed his standards. In 1950, while continuing to work for the CBC, he began his own magazine of the arts, *The Critic*, which lasted until 1952. What made Cohen a national figure, however, was his radio, and later television, show devoted to controversy, *Fighting Words*, for which he was moderator from 1952 to 1962. The Toronto *Telegram* hired him as theatre critic in 1957, and in 1959 he moved to the Toronto *Star*, where he remained until his death in 1971. Throughout his career, Cohen was an uncompromising, opinionated, strong-minded critic of the arts, and a considerable presence on the Canadian scene. He was not universally loved, but those who speak their minds regardless of individual susceptibilities seldom are. Nevertheless, he was a salutary force in a profession that had been marked too long by genteel restraint or jovial back-patting. Cohen never formulated his principles in a book-length manifesto, but scattered throughout his writings are clear indications of the standards he applied. At his most extreme, he applauded Bernard Levin of the English weekly, the *New Statesman*, who voiced the following opinion about criticism:

1 A critic has no duty to the theatre or the film industry.
2 Those at the receiving end have no right to serious consideration of their work, since most of their work does not merit serious consideration.
3 The purveyors of entertainment are in no way different from purveyors of bootlaces, cheese, reproduction antique furniture or depilatories; that is, they are trying to sell something to the public and they have no claims beyond reasonable access to the markets.[40]

In a somewhat less provocative mood, in a letter to Louis Taube in 1970, Cohen wrote: 'It is of no interest to me whether other people like or dislike the show that I see since I have not been hired to tell people what they may like or dislike. I have too much respect for people's individuality and judgment to do that. A critic who presumes to advise the way you propose is not a critic at all, but a stockbroker, who should be giving his services to theatre producers who want infallible guides at the box office.'[41]

Generally, Cohen's stance was pro-Canadian and anti–foreign influence. In his early days as a critic, his enthusiasm for the New Play Society was apparent, and in later years he declared that it represented a healthy development of Canadian theatre that was killed by the foundation of the Stratford Festival.[42] He was also emphatic about the central importance of the Canadian playwright, insisting that the art of theatre could only be strengthened by writers who viewed the world from a Canadian perspective. At the same time, he was often scathing in his condemnation of U.S. playwrights and believed that the U.S. theatre was crippled by its reliance on directors and designers at the expense of encouraging innovative playwriting. O'Neill, Williams, Miller, and Albee, he felt, had all been ruined by the indiscriminate praise of critics and by the commercialism of the Broadway theatre.[43]

Cohen was equally antipathetic to much modern British theatre, as can be seen from his regular condemnation of the repertoire at the Crest Theatre in Toronto, from their opening production in 1954 of Gordon Daviot's *Richard of Bordeaux* to the *Hay Fever* presented during their last season in 1965–6, which he described as being without 'crispness – or subtlety ... wit or inventiveness.'[44] When the Crest Theatre finally closed its doors, an angry controversy broke out in the theatre community about Cohen's effect on the theatre's fortunes. The controversy was rehashed in the *Canadian Theatre Review*, which depicted the clash between Cohen and the Crest as one between a disadvantaged Jewish outsider and a family of well-to-do WASPs (the Davis family, who ran the theatre). However, in the same issue, Donald Davis, one of those chiefly involved, stated categorically: 'I would say definitely that Nathan Cohen did not close the Crest ... I don't think we can blame Nathan for that.'[45]

When it came to dealing with Canadian playwrights, Cohen – though always anxious in the beginning to encourage – did not relax his standards if their work fell short of his idea of excellence. In 1950, in *The Critic*, he described Mavor Moore as the person who had done the most to 'raise Canadian theatre to a level of excellence' and the only one to whom 'the word "genius" can be honestly applied.'[46] In the same year, however, while referring to Moore's *Who's Who* as 'the most important play so far produced by a Canadian writer,' he goes on to say that its 'proposals are undistinguished,' are 'vague generalities,' and that the 'deliberate obliteration of character and crisis' make it 'fundamentally a variety show, or a vaudeville.' Robertson Davies, as a playwright, received less kindly treatment than that at Cohen's hands. Of *Fortune, My Foe*, he wrote that it was 'defective in structure and feeble in characterisation' and that its satire was 'topheavy with abuse'; 'the entire play is very immature, very sad.'[47] Though he found *At My Heart's Core* an 'attractive comedy,' he condemned most of Davies's drama as being more concerned with ideas than with people.[48]

Cohen was kinder, generally, to Quebec dramatists, particularly Marcel Dubé and Gratien Gélinas, but a later generation of anglophone playwrights, including Jack Gray, James Reaney, and George Ryga, were condemned along with Davies. By contrast, John Herbert's *Fortune and Men's Eyes*, Canada's first international success since Patricia Joudry's *Teach Me How to Cry*, was actively promoted by Cohen, who helped find it a New York producer. He recognized that the play, naïve and overwritten as it was in many ways, was based on first-hand experience and that it had the potential of disturbing the complacency of the typical theatre audience. Its theme of dehumanization and brutalization in an Ontario prison was certainly a far cry from the middle-class preoccupations of much Canadian playwriting up to that time.

Nathan Cohen was a wide-ranging critic physically as well as intellectually. He took over the globe-trotter role from Lawrence Mason, but performed it with a great deal more seriousness. He travelled extensively in Europe and the United States, even venturing to the Far East, in addition, of course, to visiting theatres across Canada. He considered the

Toronto *Star* an enlightened newspaper for providing national and international coverage of theatre, and certainly, from a critic's point of view, the opportunity to have access to the theatre of other cultures can help to give a perspective on one's own country's theatre. What was unusual and indeed useful about Cohen's criticism was that it insisted on the same standards for Canada's emerging and struggling theatre as for the theatre of more mature cultures. Some found this discouraging and condemned him accordingly, but the record of Canadian theatre since he began his career as critic proves he was no blight. His stance was always the essentially sound one that to be indulgent to mediocrity encourages it to flourish, while to demand the best will sometimes goad the best into manifesting itself.

Mavor Moore, who became the Toronto *Telegram*'s critic in the same year that Cohen arrived at the *Star*, admits that he and his colleague were at loggerheads. 'Nathan believed in dogmatism,' Moore has said. 'We pushed the same things: Canadian playwrights for example. But I believed in variety within the theatre, while Nathan attacked foreign influences.'[49] Moore was born in Toronto in 1919. His mother, Dora Mavor Moore, was one of Ontario's theatrical pioneers, and Moore himself has had a busy and productive career in Canadian theatre, radio, television, and film. He has written plays and musicals, as well as revues (like the successful *Spring Thaw* series), worked for many years as a professor of theatre at York University in Toronto, and was for several years chairman of the Canada Council.

Moore remained drama critic of the *Telegram* for a relatively brief time, and in the early 1960s moved to *Maclean's* magazine, where he wrote regular monthly articles on broader theatrical topics, such as the summer-festival phenomenon and censorship. Even during his brief tenure at the *Telegram*, his columns, which appeared almost daily, were not confined solely to reviewing. He commented on new acting styles, on specific individuals who seemed to reflect general trends, and on a variety of other topics related to theatre.

When he focused on a particular production, his perceptions were often sane and shrewd, as in these comments on Powys Thomas's production of *Under Milk Wood*: 'With 16 actors impersonating 60 characters only the most skillful differentiation can prevent confusion. The switching of hats is not enough, nor is the adoption of a different dialect by a cast which with a few exceptions adopts an indifferent Welsh to begin with ... In his direction, Powys Thomas was ingenious and imaginative with patterns of movement, but when it came to mood and pace gave us little variety – which we need in an evening long on talk.'[50]

On the whole, Moore's daily newspaper and monthly magazine criticism has been less important for Canadian theatre than his work as actor, playwright, librettist, and teacher, or for that matter as a director of large-scale studies for government agencies. However, after his retirement from York University, he wrote some of the most interesting commentary on the arts then available in Canada in his regular columns for the Saturday *Globe and Mail* in the late 1980s.

Cohen's other notable contemporary is Herbert Whittaker, who wrote for the *Globe and Mail* from 1949 to 1975 and continued into the 1980s as critic emeritus for that publication. Whittaker was born in Montreal in 1911 and worked chiefly as drama and film critic for the Montreal *Gazette* before coming to Toronto. Like Moore, he was actively involved in theatre and, after coming to Toronto, continued to direct plays at the Crest Theatre, Hart House Theatre, and the University Alumnae Theatre. He also reviewed occasionally for such publications as the *New York Times*, the New York *Herald Tribune*, and the *Christian Science Monitor*. Whittaker has always been among the most gentlemanly and generous of theatre critics, and while Moore and Cohen may have been at loggerheads, Whittaker and Cohen sat at opposite ends of the critical see-saw. Reading a review by Whittaker, one would get, usually, an even-handed mixture of negative and positive comments, but little sense of a final weighing of the two. Whittaker has, in fact, admitted that this approach was calculated: 'I developed an ambiguous style; I developed it deliberately; quite deliberately. Two readers could respond in two completely different ways. I gave guidance, but I didn't get between the reader and the play. I gave my views by implication, by degree, by shading, by admitting the good points. The harsh review paralyses some.'[51] This is an interesting technique, but some readers might well have been excused if the implications and the shadings did not always convey to them any recognizable opinion. Certainly, the approach is antithetical to Cohen's.

It would be difficult to single out any one of Whittaker's reviews as distinctive. Often his style resembles that of a toned-down Lawrence Mason, as in this passage: 'Juliani's *Glass Menagerie* often glowed with lovely images ... In the last moments Juliani has provided a stunningly beautiful film sequence with Tom reaching back for the lost Laura.' While later in the same review, a sudden aside, almost in the style of one of Bridle's baffling non sequiturs, appears: 'Michael O'Reagan, too much the hippie to have known Berchtesgaden, understands Tom's sardonic humour for which we forgive him anything.'[52] In a long retrospective piece on the Crest Theatre, in which Whittaker offers a corrective to Cohen's long catalogue of disappointments, this passage occurs: 'In 1957, a distinguished visitor, J.B. Priestley, met the Crest's distinctive ruling family and wrote a play for them. *The Glass Cage* took Murray and Donald Davis and Barbara Chilcott, along with ... the rest of its Canadian cast over to London.'[53] What it neglects to say is as important as what it says. There is no sense here that *The Glass Cage* was not one of Priestley's more interesting or successful plays or that its London reception fell short of the ecstatic. What it does say – 'the Crest's distinctive ruling family' – suggests an attitude to theatre that approves of the idea of hierarchies, of a monarchical caste, in which the Davis siblings are somehow the Barrymores of Toronto. In a culture that has suffered heavily from the insider/outsider syndrome, this is a less helpful attitude than Cohen's iconoclasm.

Ironically, another of Cohen's contemporaries, Oscar Ryan, whose left-wing critical perspective might have put him at odds with the founding family of the Crest theatre, was often its supporter. In 1956 he described the Crest as 'one of the few groups in Canada that is bringing good theatre to the public week after week without a break.'[54] But like Whittaker, Ryan was a supporter of Canadian theatre, and valued the Davises' efforts at least partly for that reason. A founding member in the 1930s of Toronto's Workers' Experimental Theatre and the Theatre of Action, Ryan was also one of the co-authors of the controversial and highly effective play *Eight Men Speak*. From 1955 to 1988, he was theatre critic for the *Canadian Tribune*, most of the time writing under the name Martin Stone, adopted probably to deflect anti-communist reaction against himself, particularly in the fifties. Backed by a capable mind and extensive reading of Marxist theory, Ryan was able to reconcile his socialist perspective with bourgeois, mainstream theatre by chastising its deficiencies as well as praising any evidence of a play's commitment to the fight for social change; for example, in dealing with the Stratford Festival, he notes that a theme of 'the struggle for political power [must] have fascinated William Shakespeare, for in play after play this theme dominates the action.'[55] *Romeo and Juliet*, for instance, he saw as a struggle of 'bourgeois humanism against feudalism.' At the same time, he decries the importing of stars and the absence of Canadian writers and directors in the festival program. Overall, he loved what he called the 'magic' of theatre and was highly aware of theatre craft, which allowed him to comment with sensitivity and insight on acting, design, and directing. Towards the end of his long career, which has tended to be neglected by the broad theatre public and scholars alike, Ryan's views seemed somewhat out of fashion, more in line with early twentieth-century socialist attitudes; but a reading of his work will quickly show that intelligent, vigorous newspaper criticism was not exclusively the province of mainstream voices.

While Ryan was with the communist weekly and Cohen and Whittaker were writing for two of Toronto's major dailies, the periodicals were continuing to offer somewhat uneven coverage of the theatrical scene. At *Saturday Night* after Sandwell's passing, a number of writers undertook reviewing chores, including Robertson Davies, Kildare Dobbs, David Lewis Stein, and Tom Hendry, though more often than not the essays they wrote were not so much criticism as background pieces or studies of specific developments like Hendry's piece on the appointment of Robin Phillips as artistic director of the Stratford Festival in 1974.

At the *Canadian Forum* from the 1950s onwards, there was a similar succession of names, including those of Milton Wilson who wrote chiefly about recorded music, Doris Mosdell whose main field was film, Wendy Michener, Jack Winter, Philip Stratford, W.J. Keith, Antony Ferry, and Paul Levine. One writer whose work as a theatre critic was sparse but effective was Vincent Tovell. Born in Toronto in 1922, Tovell was a lecturer in English at the University of Toronto and active in both stage and radio work, as well as in the university theatre. From 1947 to 1948, he contributed to *Here and Now* magazine. There, on one occasion, he made the shrewd and prophetic statement that 'theatre only emerges at the vortex of a culture, in an intense atmosphere where issues are sharply contrasted and feelings run high.'[56] That period finally arrived some twenty years later when, in the wake of the Vietnam War, social revolution, and Canada's jubilant Centennial, a renaissance took place in the Canadian theatre, the after-swell of which we are still experiencing.

Among other magazines in the period that were important for the development of theatre criticism was *Performing Arts in Canada*, founded in 1961 and edited and published by James C. McIntosh. In 1970, Stephen Mezei (later the founder and editor of *Onion*, a newspaper of the arts) became editor; Antony Ferry (one-time editor of the British theatre magazine *Encore*) was his associate editor. By 1975, *Performing Arts in Canada* had come under the editorship of Arnold Edinborough, who was also importantly associated with *Saturday Night* as editor and publisher from 1963 to 1970. Edinborough, born in England in 1922, former editor of the Kingston *Whig-Standard*, is one of the few remaining Canadian 'men-of-letters' of the Charlesworth school. From 1979 to 1982, when it ceased publication temporarily, *Performing Arts in Canada* went through several changes of editorship, but during its twenty years of existence, while never establishing a high-profile identity with the public, it provided a forum for a number of noteworthy critics, including Peter Hay, George Jonas, and Boyd Neil. The Canadian Theatre Centre's house magazine, *The Stage in Canada*, arrived on the scene four years after *Performing Arts in Canada*, beginning – under the editorship of Tom Hendry – as a monthly bulletin of theatre, opera, and ballet. An interesting feature of this magazine was a segment called 'Theatre Criticism Canada,' which provided extracts from reviews and critical writing across the country. Under various editors – Harvey Chusid, Don Smith, and Raynald Desmeules – it continued until 1973, when the affairs of the Canadian Theatre Centre were wound up and the magazine died with it.

In 1971, *Dialog*, the house organ for the newly formed Theatre Ontario, appeared. Theatre Ontario itself was founded as an association to serve, equally, the professional, community, and educational theatres of the province. *Dialog* (later *Scene Changes*) initially concentrated more on amateur community theatre than on professional theatre. In 1977, however, under the editorship of Jeniva Berger, it broadened its appeal and began to report regularly on the professional theatre, not just in Ontario, but across Canada, and eventually outside of Canada also. Berger actively encouraged young and relatively untried critics, and on average the magazine devoted one-quarter of its content to reviews of current productions. It became the only regularly produced periodical in Ontario, devoted to theatre, that focused importantly on the criticism of performance. Unfortunately, as its popularity with the public grew, its support from Theatre Ontario declined. It suspended publication in 1981.

Another theatre publication with a respectable past is *Canadian Theatre Review*. Founded at York University in 1974 by Don Rubin, a professor in the theatre department and former reviewer for the Toronto *Star*, it grew out of the *York Theatre Journal*, a student-edited-and-written magazine that began in 1971. The *Canadian Theatre Review* was notable for trying to achieve a balance of professional and academic reportage and criticism. Many original Canadian play-scripts were published for the first time in this journal, and it recorded much Canadian theatre history and addressed such important issues as politics in the theatre, arts funding, and theatre training in its opening thematic section. However, owing to the infrequency of its appearance during the year, it did not regularly review plays. In 1983, it was acquired by the University of Toronto Press and Robert Wallace became editor. Currently, it is edited by Alan Filewod from the University of Guelph and Natalie Rewa of Queen's University.

Other university-sponsored publications that have significance for theatre criticism in Ontario are *Canadian Drama / L'Art dramatique canadien*, which originated at the University of Waterloo in 1975 under the editorship of Rota Lister in response to the 'lack of material on our playwrights and their works,'[57] and *Theatre History in Canada / Histoire du théâtre au Canada*, co-sponsored by the University of Toronto Graduate Drama Centre and Queen's University, which began publication in 1980 under the joint editorship of Ann Saddlemyer and Richard Plant, with Leonard Doucette replacing Ann Saddlemyer in 1987. *Canadian Drama* was conflated with *Essays in Theatre* of the University of Guelph in 1991, and *Theatre History in Canada / Histoire du théâtre au Canada* is now known as *Theatre Research in Canada / Recherches théâtrales au Canada*, and is edited by Hélène Beauchamp, Stephen Johnson, and Robert Nunn.

Some publications that aimed at a wider audience appeared in the 1970s and 1980s. A few like *Toronto Theatre Review* and *Onion*, both in newspaper format, flourished briefly and disappeared. Others like *Now, Toronto's Weekly News and Entertainment Guide*, founded in 1981, still survive, as does *Toronto Life*, which began in 1966 and later absorbed *Toronto Calendar* (also founded in 1966). Both magazines originally covered theatre chiefly in the form of brief monthly listings and capsule reviews, but later *Toronto Life*, which was mainly a general-interest magazine rather than an arts publication, began to publish some substantial theatre criticism, mostly by Martin Knelman. Perhaps the most interesting of the more recent publications devoted to theatre, however, is *Theatrum*, founded in 1985. Like *Canadian Theatre Review*, it addresses itself to a wide range of topics concerning theatre in Canada and around the world, as well as publishing original play-scripts, but also, under the heading 'Glimpses – Recent Productions That Caught our Eye' – reviews productions across Canada.

Much of this activity in the fields of theatre journalism, criticism, and scholarship is due to the boom years of Ontario theatre, attended by the development of interesting new playwrights, the formation of vital companies, and the recruitment of a new, younger audience. Of the critics of the '70s who stand out as making a particularly useful contribution, two are especially memorable: Urjo Kareda, who took over from Nathan Cohen at the *Star*, and John Fraser, who succeeded Herbert Whittaker at the *Globe and Mail*. During the early days of the theatrical renaissance, the Toronto *Telegram* died; its last reviewers in the early 1970s were Ron Evans and Dubarry Campau, who brought her own brand of cosmopolitan wryness to the profession. The *Sun*, a tabloid that apes the minor excesses of such British equivalents as the *Daily Mirror* and the *Daily Sketch*, employed McKenzie Porter, who handled his reviewing chores with his own brand of right-wing populism, and more recently Bob Pennington, who brings a sense of conviction and honesty to his work.

Urjo Kareda perhaps came closer than any other critic to Nathan

Cohen in combining a forcefulness of opinion with genuine intelligence and knowledge. A former film reviewer for the same newspaper, he assumed Cohen's mantle with confidence and style and – like Cohen – championed Canadian playwriting, welcoming in particular the stable of young writers Bill Glassco developed at the Tarragon Theatre. Ironically, there came a point when Kareda felt that the balance had tipped too far in favour of the Canadian playwright. In the Toronto *Star* of 2 September 1972, he wrote that what was lacking was 'the good worthy new play which happens not to be Canadian' (p. 109). It was a loss to criticism when Kareda was lured away, first to become literary manager at the Stratford Festival under Robin Phillips, then to CBC Radio Drama to undertake script development, and most recently to Tarragon Theatre as artistic director.

The *Globe and Mail*'s John Fraser, a much more establishment figure than Kareda (educated at Upper Canada College, Lakefield, Memorial University, Oxford, and the University of East Anglia), was music and dance critic for the Toronto *Telegram* from 1971 to 1972, dance critic and features writer for the *Globe and Mail* from 1972 to 1975, and drama critic from 1975 to 1977. He began tentatively, but grew in skill and judgment to the point where he showed every sign of becoming a critic whose opinion the reader could respect and trust. Unfortunately, this assignment proved to be only a stepping-stone to the upper reaches of power in the journalistic world. In 1977 he became Peking correspondent for the *Globe and Mail*, and later wrote a successful book about his experiences. In the mid-1980s he moved to *Saturday Night* as editor, and in 1995 became the fourth master of Massey College in the University of Toronto.

The replacements for Kareda and Fraser did not on the whole earn such respect and trust. In 'Stage Write,' a piece in the March 1983 issue of *Toronto Life*, at the prompting of Don Obe, these critics undertook to review one another – an eccentric, if not foolhardy, enterprise. Gina Mallet, the new critic at the Toronto *Star*, made the following comments on her counterpart at the *Globe and Mail*, Ray Conlogue: 'I have to say, well honestly the nicest thing I can say is: appalling. I just don't think that the person on the job has any experience of life or the theatre. He writes politically, which I find terrible – no real feeling for acting, and he never gets the plot right' (p. 14). Conlogue, in his turn, had this to say about Mallet's reviews: 'I find it difficult when I read her reviews to recognise the production I saw. She will dwell at great length on matters which I find to be peripheral ... The temptation if one desires fame or celebrity is to be notorious, and I have no doubt that this is the policy which Miss Mallet is undertaking very deliberately' (ibid). The personal feuds of critics have little to do with criticism itself, but this public airing of them surely indicates a malaise in the world of daily newspaper reviewing.

From the beginning, the Toronto theatre community had a stormy relationship with Gina Mallet. As she put it in her farewell to the Toronto *Star*: 'I was cast as a villain the moment I arrived.'[58] Her complaint had some justification, since many members of the profession made no secret of the fact that they were dubious about her background, her qualifications, and her knowledge of Canadian theatre. Mallet, who was of Anglo-American parentage and had worked as a researcher and journalist in the United States, seemed an unlikely choice for a position as one of Canada's premier theatre critics, but as the opposition to her grew more vocal the resolve of the Toronto *Star*'s management stiffened. The *Star* would not be dictated to by outsiders. Besides, Gina Mallet was controversial, and controversy sold newspapers.

It seemed, indeed, as if her employers were encouraging her to be as confrontational as possible, and she took up the challenge with relish. Not since Nathan Cohen had a theatre critic ruffled so many feathers. Typical of her style are these retrospective comments on her early exposure to Canadian theatre: (on the tradition of collective creation) 'a theatrical vision of Canada as a barnyard full of co-operative actors taking the homely roles of milkmaid, and sometimes milk-churn'; (on the Shaw Festival) 'a nice country-club kind of theatre, where the parties on opening night far outweighed the performances ... [and] parts were assigned on the tennis-court'; (on the Stratford Festival) 'a kilt ... set the evening's social tone. It was at odds with the work being done on the stage by Maggie Smith.'[59] It sometimes appeared that Mallet's notion of her role as theatre critic was based on faint memories of Sheridan Whiteside and Addison de Witt.

Indeed, in a round-table discussion on the CBC's *Morningside* with host Peter Gzowski, Tom Kerr, and Robert Enright, she dismissed most Canadian theatre criticism as too bland, challenged the idea that theatre critics should be 'analytical,' and suggested that good theatre criticism was 'off-the-cuff,' personal and subjective, and above all entertaining. While this approach can certainly produce lively journalism, it also runs the risk of fostering a kind of reviewing that is ill-considered and trivial. Gina Mallet's strengths were less apparent in her daily reviewing than in the more reflective pieces she wrote occasionally for the Toronto *Star* and other publications. For instance, in the Fall 1983 issue of *Canadian Theatre Review* she gave an account of Toronto's civic theatre, the St Lawrence Centre, which analysed the problems of that institution shrewdly and proved that she had assimilated a great deal of knowledge about the workings of the Canadian theatre establishment.

Her successor at the *Star*, Robert Crewe another expatriate English journalist, marked a return to a less controversial style. Chatty, amiable, workmanlike, he seemed to see the work of a theatre critic as being to reflect the standards of the average undemanding audience-member. Others who have shared the reviewing chores at the *Star* in recent years – Vit Wagner, Geoff Chapman, and Henry Mietkiewicz – have maintained a lower profile than such earlier critics as Cohen and Mallet.

At the *Globe and Mail*, Ray Conlogue was initially a much less controversial appointee than Gina Mallet at the *Star*. Conlogue came to the job with the kind of credentials that many readers had pleaded for. He was not a journalist seconded from the sports or travel pages, but a recent Master of Arts from the University of Toronto's graduate drama program. The expectation was that there would be a certain breadth of reference, a depth of understanding, and above all a sense of scrupulous accuracy. The reality fell somewhat short of these expectations. Conlogue's reviews seldom aroused the passion that greeted a great many of Mallet's. They tended on the whole to be painstakingly descriptive, but often marred by errors that were surprising coming from a former theatre scholar. In a piece on the Shaw Festival's production of *Back to Methusaleh*, for instance, Sir Barry Jackson emerged as 'Barry Jackman.'[60] Again, like Mallet, he seemed more at ease writing pieces that survey the overall output of a theatre. In fact, an interesting comparison between his work in this area and Mallet's can be made by reading his contribution to the *Globe and Mail*'s 'Stage Canada' supplement, 'The St. Lawrence Sins Go Back to Birth' side by side with Mallet's survey of the same theatre in *Canadian Theatre Review*. Her piece is more pungent, his more even-handed.[61]

Conlogue's career as a theatre critic in Toronto ended much more controversially than it began. In May 1987, he wrote a piece on the Stratford Festival in which he claimed that a director of the Young Company did such poor work that he was asked not to return. The director sued Conlogue and his employer, Canadian Newspapers Company Limited, and in February 1992 a judgment was handed down in the British Columbia Supreme Court finding for the plaintiff. The judge in the case commented that Conlogue had used sources that he knew at the time were unreliable and unobjective, and characterized him as 'a person of strong opinions, of single-minded purpose, and of arrogance in the correctness of his views.'[62] Conlogue subsequently moved to Montreal, continuing to write for the *Globe and Mail* as their Quebec cultural correspondent.

A number of second-stringers who had begun writing for the *Globe* while Conlogue was still premier theatre critic continued to cover the theatre after he had departed for Montreal, chiefly Liam Lacey and H.J. Kirchhoff, but the most notable was probably Robert Cushman who, like Robert Crewe at the *Star*, was an expatriate Englishman. Cushman wrote for *The Observer* in England from 1973 to 1984. On coming to Canada in 1987, he freelanced as theatre critic for *Saturday Night* as well as the *Globe and Mail*, and reviewed theatre on CBC Radio for programs like 'State of the Arts' and 'Arts Tonight' with skill and intelligence. A third arrival from England with a distinguished record was Ronald Bryden, who had been theatre critic for the *New Statesman* (1964–6) and *The Observer* (1967–71) and play adviser to the Royal Shakespeare Company from 1972 until his return to Canada in 1976. Though his main occupation since then has been as a professor of theatre at the University of Toronto's Graduate Drama Centre, and more recently as literary adviser at the Shaw Festival, Bryden has contributed some judicious reviews to several Canadian publications, including *Maclean's*.

As a result of the growth in Ontario theatre from the late 1960s onwards and the corresponding increase in press coverage, more and more writers were attracted to theatre criticism as a profession. Consequently, in 1972, the Toronto Drama Bench came into existence. It is an organization of theatre critics, founded by, among others, Herbert Whittaker, Urjo Kareda, Don Rubin, Dubarry Campau, and Janine Manatis of the CBC. Originally confined to Toronto theatre critics, it expanded to include critics from other parts of the province, including Audrey Ashley of the Ottawa *Citizen* and Lyle Slack of the Hamilton *Spectator*. Its principal function has been to jury the Chalmers Play Awards, and among its avowed aims has been that of raising the standards of theatre criticism among its members. Out of the Drama Bench has grown a national organization of theatre critics, the Canadian Theatre Critics Association, established in 1979 with Herbert Whittaker as chairman and Jeniva Berger as president. Another development sponsored by the Drama Bench has been the annual Nathan Cohen Award for the best piece of critical writing on theatre; the first award was won in 1981 by Martin Knelman of *Saturday Night* and *Toronto Life*.

With this growth of a sense of profession, and a growing awareness of the need for higher standards, theatre criticism in Ontario has clearly advanced considerably since the days of E.R. Parkhurst. However, whatever the benefits of creating a professional association may be, theatre criticism will only continue to be an attractive profession to the Jacobs, the Cohens, and the Karedas of the future as long as there is a significant theatre in Ontario to write about and publications to write for that regard theatre criticism as a serious responsibility.

NOTES

1 *The Critic*, 1:5 (October 1950), 2. The quotation is from Jean Giraudoux's play *Cantique des Cantiques* (1938).
2 Sir Beverley Baxter (b. Toronto 1891, d. London 1964), theatre critic in England for the *Daily Express* and the *Sunday Express*. Milton Shulman (b. Toronto 1913), theatre critic of the London *Evening Standard* from 1953. Ronald Bryden (b. 1927 Port of Spain, Trinidad), educated at University of Toronto and King's College, Cambridge, theatre critic *New Statesman* 1964–6, *Observer* 1967–71, professor at the Graduate Centre for Study of Drama, University of Toronto.
3 Harold Clurman, *On Directing* (New York: Collier Books, 1974), 162
4 13 December 1910, 10
5 6 November 1904, 12
6 *The Globe*, 17 September 1918, 8; ibid., 18 September 1923, 15
7 Ibid., 6 September 1913, 13
8 Ibid., 28 October 1913, 8
9 *Border Cities Star*, 7 September 1918, 6
10 30 November 1920, 5
11 Report in Toronto *Star* (CP, unsigned) datelined Ottawa, 9 April 1970
12 Toronto Public Library Scrapbooks, 'Biographies of Men' (TPL T686.J, vol. 9, 1)
13 Betty Lee, *Love and Whisky* (Toronto: McClelland and Stewart, 1973), 73
14 *Saturday Night* 23 (3 September 1910), 6
15 Ibid., vol. 26 (14 June 1913), 10
16 Ibid., vol. 38 (2 December 1922), 6
17 *Canadian Forum* 6 (February 1926), 160
18 Ibid.
19 Ibid., vol. 6 (July 1926), 320
20 Ibid., vol. 8 (April 1928), 625
21 Ibid., vol. 6 (May 1926), 256
22 *Globe*, 14 February 1933, 11
23 Ibid., 11 October 1938, 7
24 Ibid., 22 May 1926, 6
25 TPL T686.J, vol. 7, 755
26 Toronto *Star*, 20 October 1934
27 Ibid., 7 November 1939, 4
28 Ibid., 23 January 1945, 4
29 Ibid., 12 February 1949, 11
30 *Canadian Magazine*, 38 (November 1911), 22–3
31 *Saturday Night*, 19 January 1935, 10
32 Ibid., 8 April 1933, 19
33 Ibid., 4 April 1936, 11
34 Ibid.

35 'Murder Pattern and the Critics,' *Canadian Theatre Review* 5 (Winter 1975), 61–2

36 *Saturday Night*, 15 May 1948, 2–3

37 Ibid., 25 January 1949, 19

38 Ibid., 22 March 1949, 2

39 London *Free Press*, 4 October 1949, 8

40 *Star*, 29 April 1968, 23

41 Letter to Louis Taube, 27 November 1970, Nathan Cohen Papers, National Archives of Canada, M2218 (MG31, D27)

42 'Theatre in Canada: An Expendable Commodity,' NAC, Cohen Papers, M2218 (MG31, D27)

43 *Star*, 20 March 1963, 36

44 Ibid., 6 January 1966, 27

45 Vol. 7 (Summer 1973), 42

46 'Drama,' *The Critic* 1:24 (September 1950), 4

47 'Critically Speaking,' 15 January 1950, NAC, Cohen Papers, M2219 (MG31, D27)

48 'Drama,' *The Critic* 1:2 (April 1950), 4

49 Interview with the author, August 1982

50 *Telegram*, 15 October 1959, 49

51 Herbert Whittaker, interview with Allan Mendel Gould, 8 December 1977; See Gould, 'A Critical Account of the Theatre Criticism of Nathan Cohen,' Ph.D. thesis, Graduate Programme in English, York University, June 1977.

52 *Globe and Mail*, 3 September 1968, 20

53 'Recollections of an Achievement,' *Canadian Theatre Review* 7 (December 1975), 13

54 *Canadian Tribune*, 9 January 1956

55 Ibid., 5 July 1965

56 Vol. 1:1 (December 1947), 80–1

57 Rota Lister, Editorial, *Canadian Drama* 1:1 (Spring 1975), 3

58 7 July 1984, G3

59 Ibid.

60 *Globe and Mail*, 9 August 1986, D11

61 'Stage Canada' supplement, *Globe and Mail*, 28 November 1983

62 Vancouver *Sun*, 2 March 1992

9 Resources for Theatre History

HEATHER McCALLUM

The lot of the theatre historian is a hard one anywhere, for stage people are of all artists the most bemused, careless and creatively mendacious in their records and recollections; the writer who attempts to bring even the most elementary kind of order to the story of the theatre in Canada deserves our special sympathy, for he must make what he can of the imperfect chronicles of touring companies, and the hardly traceable histories of ill-fated native ventures; he must piece out and weigh scant and often contradictory evidence.

Any discussion of the nature and state of Ontario theatre resources must be essentially a set of variations on the themes so genially announced in the foregoing quotation from Robertson Davies's 1969 piece 'Letters in Canada' in the *University of Toronto Quarterly.*[1] Theatre historians are not quite *of* the theatre; their plumage is gray rather than dramatic peacock. For theatre people it is the show that must go on, but once it *has* gone on, only the box-office receipts are of further interest to them. On the more practical, business side of theatre, accountants and managers have their time-honoured reasons for keeping records close and not adding further to expenses by the maintenance of elaborate archives of what is, after all, among the most ephemeral of human activities. In short, the theatre historian, whether he or she approaches the theatrical company itself or those members of the public who have preserved the memorabilia of an early idolatry or a glorious occasion, is something of an unwelcome intruder. Further, the theatre historian's role seems to be inimical and paradoxical – preserving the ephemeral, reducing to dull record the flamboyant and transient.

What follows will deal with the problems of theatre resources as they affect the study of Ontario cultural history. But since that study is still in the stage of modest beginnings, there is some point in treating quite general considerations of attitude and method that will be of help to what one hopes will be the increasing number of those concerned with the preservation of this province's cultural heritage. Subsequent paragraphs will, then, contain general comments on the 'state of the art' of theatrical collections that can be – one hopes – applied specifically to local collections.

Since the art of the theatre is a transitory one, no record of a production, however lengthy, can faithfully portray the fleeting impression created by a performance on the audience. No art is as evanescent as that of the actor. For one thing, the very finest of actors constantly grow in their roles and – at the very least – vary their performances. Unlike television or the screen, which freeze for all time the single version of a role, the theatre thrives on the varied and spontaneous interaction of troupe and audience, giving us each night a unique effort. Despite their ambiguities, the records of the achievement remain, not only in accounts of performance but in the programs, photographs, and stage designs generated by a theatrical production. The artistic record is created – unwittingly – by the director, the designer, and the stage manager, and any such record will include (in varying degrees of completeness, depending on the scale of the production) the designs and models created for the set, the costumes, and the properties. In addition, there are the stage-management and prompt copies of the script, which supplement the director's copy, stage-management records, lighting designs and workshop files, architectural plans and blueprints for each scene, audio- and videotapes of the performance, and music scores. These are only the most obvious sources of information.

Administrative activities in the theatre centre on the office of the general manager, which generates records such as financial files, annual reports, correspondence, and tour books. The numerous efforts to publicize productions produce the most prolific files. Frequently these are the easiest to acquire: production photographs, publicity photographs of the director, designer, and cast, house and souvenir programs, posters, press releases, and files of reviews.

It is the responsibility of a theatre collection to acquire and organize as much of this diverse material as seems relevant to its collections policy and to its public. For the scholar wishing to re-create the past, it is obvious that the widest possible gathering of all information constitutes a proper collection. But for the director or actor interested in how the play he or she is reviving was once performed, a more limited collection is sufficient. Three quite different principles have shaped the nature of current theatre collections: first, the needs of users; second, the problem of location and acquisition; and third, the logistical facts of available funds, storage space, and trained staff.

The public using a collection largely determines its nature and the lines along which it will develop. This public will include those who are involved practically in aspects of a production: the director seeking a suitable play, the designer doing costume research, public-relations staff investigating earlier productions. There will be researchers and scholars who require historical accuracy, biographers, historians, critics, and journalists. There will be professional students of theatre as well as university faculty, graduates, undergraduates, and secondary-school students who require background for courses. There will also be actors auditioning for parts, as well as members of the theatre-going public who seek information about a play or its actors before or after attending a performance. In short, there are five possible publics for theatre collections: the professionals, the scholars, the professionals-to-be, the students, and the interested general public.

For all the evocative nature of the materials in theatre collections, one must recall the rather plodding necessities. The basis of any theatre collection is the plays, theatre histories, biographies, technical and architectural works, critical writings, and periodicals. However, no collection can be omnivorous. It must attempt to acquire and supply information on theatre activity in a defined area. Inevitably, the archival part of the collection must rely on the producing companies in its chosen area to supply the printed record of their work (programs, posters, photographs, press releases). Where there is a stable publicity staff and an adequate budget for materials, such items may be retained, well organized, and easily accessible. In many cases, however, sketchy records only have been kept, to the disadvantage of the company and of the institution receiving copies of this material.

Any archival collection also relies on private donors to build up the theatrical record. Private donors can provide such material as scrapbooks, diaries, photographs, correspondence, playbills, programs, and other ephemera too varied to describe fully. However, much material collected by private individuals can be haphazardly accumulated, and even more haphazardly – alas – destroyed. To the uninitiated, such material is considered unimportant or of a private nature. As a result, there can be frequent, casual, and uninformed destruction. There is the case of a stage doorman at Toronto's Royal Alexandra Theatre who had built up a sizeable collection of autographed photographs of the stars who had passed through the stage door over a period of many years; the collection was destroyed by his wife, who had tired of the accumulation of cartons underneath the connubial bed. This is only one of many instances of neglect. Every archivist has such a tale on which to dine out and weep. Since much of this material survives – as it perishes – by chance, the record is tantalizingly incomplete.

Most important to observe, and almost impossible to codify, is the etiquette of acquisitions. The owners of theatrical memorabilia should not be persuaded to part with the material until they are ready to do so. The idea of eventual giving is sometimes more important to convey than a direct request, since the material is often of a personal nature as well as of broader, social significance. In instances where material has been located and is not yet available to the collection, the archive may be able to make photographic or microform copies, thus safeguarding the original documents while permitting access to researchers.

It is important to remember that some of the most relevant items are hidden away in heaps of memorabilia not specifically theatrical – in family papers, in historical records of churches and congregations, of governments and businesses. In such cases, especial tact must be exercised, and perhaps microform copies are all that can be hoped for.

After the acquisition of the material comes the more exact examination and analysis of what has been received. This involves selection, identification, and organization in order to bring together the background of a particular personality, or the history of a theatre company or building. In recent years these procedures have been greatly refined and elaborated by archivists and others. Anyone interested in theatre collections should become familiar with the work of archivists, some of which is cited in the bibliography.

Materials making up a theatre collection are uniquely related to the profession of theatre. They do not have their counterpart in other print and non-print collections. So the methods of arrangement for the use of this varied material depend on the type of institution, on the organization chosen for its materials, on the period when it was organized, and on the purpose served by the institution. Books and periodicals present no difficulties of handling in a well-organized collection. The care of photographs, playbills, posters, engravings, and stage designs is handled in a well-defined and scientific manner by galleries and museums, as are costumes, stage models, and properties. Indeed, in some cases involving such items as costumes and stage models, museums *are* the logical places for such materials. But when library, archival, and museum resources are combined in one location, new problems arise, since each type of material has its own organization, conservation, and storage requirements, some of them unfamiliar and difficult for conventional library and archival venues. Techniques for managing such a great variety of materials are among the chief responsibilities of a curator, and the techniques are not necessarily the same for all institutions. A close cross-indexing scheme – often unique – is required and, frequently, in order to avoid the initial handling of fragile and unique materials by the public, a photographic or filmed record is desirable. Further protection through professional restoration of fragile materials (photographs, newspaper clippings, original designs, engravings, correspondence, account books) is necessary in many cases.

The theatre collection should be active in publicizing new acquisitions of importance, in emphasizing strengths and special items, and in making selected items available for display both within its own building and in secure and relevant locations elsewhere.

Collections of material relating to Ontario theatre history are held principally by government archives and by university and public archives, as well as in two significant theatrical collections. The most important of the government archives is, of course, the National Archives of Canada in Ottawa. The broad mandate of the National Archives permits this institution to acquire official and historical records and documents of institutions and individuals of national significance. The National Archives produces the *Union List of Manuscripts in Canadian Repositories*, a comprehensive list of significant manuscripts and records in Canadian archival institutions. Its Manuscript Division has a well-established program for acquisition of papers of national arts organizations and of Canadians prominent in the cultural field. Archival collections relating to theatre in Canada include the records of the Dominion Drama Festival (later Theatre Canada), the Alliance of Canadian Cinema, Television and Radio Artists (ACTRA), and the Canadian Actors' Equity Association. The papers of such personalities as Andrew Allan, Robertson Davies, John Drainie, Timothy Findley, Amelia Hall, John Hirsch, Joseph Schull, and Lister Sinclair are also available to be consulted.

The Documentary Art and Photography Division of the National Archives has the largest collection of historical photographic records in Canada. It produces the *Guide to Canadian Photographic Archives*, which lists and describes collections of photographic documents in more than one hundred Canadian archival institutions. The Audio-visual and Cartographic Archives (formerly the National Film, Television and Sound Archives) acquires and conserves all forms of moving images and sound documents of national historical significance, and its collections include well over 100,000 film, radio, and television titles, an important source for the theatre researcher. The Government Archives Division is the repository for the extensive records of the Canadian Broadcasting Corporation and the National Arts Centre in Ottawa.

The material retained by archives relates to many aspects of Canadian history and social and cultural life. The student of theatre history will find many important items hidden in family papers, diaries, correspondence, and scrapbooks belonging to individuals whose careers were in fields other than the performing arts. It is necessary for the researcher therefore to follow up all possible leads and to make inquiries as specific as possible. The National Archives of Canada – one should recall – houses its collections by type of material, so that items such as architectural plans, photographs, posters, and tapes are to be found in the appropriate division. Hence, theatre programs and theatrical publicity posters are maintained in different areas; the researcher must become alert here – as elsewhere – to the details of classification, however elaborate the system of cross-indexing.

The basic objective of the Archives of Ontario is to preserve knowledge of Ontario's historical heritage; apart from government records, it also acquires non-published documentary records that are of enduring significance. Contemporary theatrical material consists principally of the records of Theatre Ontario, the provincial theatre organization, and the Eaton Auditorium Archives, part of the T. Eaton Company Papers. In addition, the tapes and transcripts for approximately two dozen interviews with contemporary theatre personalities have been deposited in the Sound and Moving Image Portfolio.

Municipal archives in cities such as Toronto, Ottawa, London, and Hamilton are responsible for acquiring, preserving, and making available historical materials that relate to the city. Documents of theatrical significance will be found in the City Clerk's records, in assessment records, as well as in collections of photographs and architectural plans.

Universities and their constituent colleges frequently have theatrical collections in their own archives. Sometimes these collections are the result of a close relationship with the community; sometimes the material has been passed on from faculty or alumni. And in recent years, university libraries across the country have acquired the papers of prominent Canadian writers, many of whom have written for the stage, for radio, and for television. The University of Toronto, for example, has a number of such collections, notably the records of its own Hart House Theatre and of Toronto's New Play Society, in addition to the Dora Mavor Moore papers. The CBC Television Drama collection in York University's Archives and Special Collections includes the scripts, production, and financial records of English-language, national network presentations for the period 1952 to 1989. York University has also acquired the papers of several theatre personalities: actor, writer, producer, and theatre administrator Mavor Moore; playwright, theatre director, and teacher Herman Voaden, a leading exponent of Canadian drama during the nationalist period of the 1920s and 1930s; Canadian composer and music director Louis Applebaum, whose work has included periods at the National Film Board, Stratford Festival, and

National Arts Centre. In many cases, papers relating to a specific group or individual are spread through several institutions. The situation encountered by the researcher concerned with the New Play Society, for example, is not untypical. Information about this theatrical group is located at York University, at the University of Toronto, and among the theatre materials in the Metropolitan Toronto Reference Library.

The Division of Archives and Research Collections of Hamilton's McMaster University Library has concentrated on the scripts and working papers of such Canadian playwrights and personalities as John Coulter, James Bannerman, Leslie MacFarlane, Austin Clarke, and Pierre Berton. The Regional Collection at the University of Western Ontario in London has extensive files of programs for London's Grand Opera House dating from the 1890s. Queen's University in Kingston has also taken a regional archival responsibility; its archives houses items from the city's nineteenth-century opera house. The B.K. Sandwell papers and the large collection of Merrill Denison's papers, including typescripts of his plays for stage and radio, may also be consulted here.

The University of Guelph Library's collecting activities in theatre materials began in 1983 when the Shaw Festival at Niagara-on-the-Lake deposited its extensive archives. Records of the festival since its founding in 1962 include prompt scripts, performance files, programs, posters, stage designs, set models, and scrapbooks of newspaper clippings. Toronto's Tarragon Theatre, founded in 1971 to produce new Canadian plays, has also made the University of Guelph the repository for its records, as have numerous other Ontario theatres, notably, the Canadian Stage Company, Theatre Plus, Factory Theatre, Théâtre Français de Toronto, Young People's Theatre, Toronto Workshop Productions, and the Blyth Festival. These materials are available in the Theatre Archives, Archival, Rare, and Special Collections and they offer a major resource for the study of the history and development of contemporary Canadian theatre. Le Centre de recherche en civilisation canadienne-française at the University of Ottawa maintains archives containing manuscripts, photographs, sound recordings, and printed material with a particular emphasis on the Franco-Ontarian community.

The theatre collection in the Metropolitan Toronto Reference Library was started in 1961 in response to public interest in Canada's quickening theatrical activity. Based on an established book collection and supplemented by the resources of all other subject areas in the library, it is the most comprehensive public library collection of theatre resources in the country. Since the library is situated in Toronto, the major centre for English-language theatre in Canada, the collection is in an advantageous position to acquire and supply information on theatre activity in Canada, past and present, through the acquisition of the fugitive materials that exist to document a theatrical performance. Such materials include playbills, programs, posters, newspaper reviews, photographs, original stage designs, and architectural plans, in addition to scrapbooks, account books, and correspondence for theatre companies active in the nineteenth and early-twentieth centuries.

Public libraries are traditionally the repositories for collections of local history material. Long-established regional collections in the London and Hamilton public libraries contain material on past theatrical activity in their areas. Special Collections at the Hamilton Public Library continues to enlarge its archival holdings, which include programs, clippings, photographs, and scrapbooks documenting the city's theatre activity early in this century; the Grand Opera House and Summers Mountain Theatre are well represented. Local history museums such as the Perth Museum, which contains memorabilia of the Marks Brothers, an early-twentieth-century touring company, often take responsibility for acquiring documents of their particular region.

An understandable concentration on forthcoming productions, and the restrictions of staff, space, and funds have frequently prevented theatre managements from keeping a full record of their activities. Yet the theatres inevitably produce the principal sources of material on a production: prompt books, production and publicity photographs, programs, posters, lighting designs, and so on. Since it is impossible to re-create anything as fleeting as a stage performance, those materials that can be preserved should be organized in the best manner possible to provide a record for the future. It is advisable for a company to retain its material as long as space and suitable staff are available. If these conditions cannot be met, the record is best maintained by an institution that is willing and able to organize it for use. Not the least important effort of library and archival staff is that directed towards alerting theatre managements to the value of their records and, where possible, offering sympathetic and practical advice for preserving what is useful to those who are researching the cultural history of a place or period.

The Stratford Festival and the Canadian Opera Company are the major companies in the province that collect and organize their own records. The Stratford Festival Archives was founded in 1967, fifteen years after the festival began. A full-time archivist was appointed in 1971 and in 1977 formal policies and procedures were established for preserving and making available this important and carefully maintained collection of materials generated by the festival. Virtually complete files of administrative papers, prompt books, production files, programs, posters, production and publicity photographs, and press clippings present a comprehensive record of the theatre's activities. A collection of original costume designs for festival productions has been built up over the years, with wardrobe bibles supplementing the finished artwork. Films and videotapes of productions since 1968 are on file. Each season a number of costumes and properties are selected for permanent retention; this archival collection of over two thousand costumes is used for research and display purposes. The archives has also initiated a professionally conducted oral-history program to create interviews with prominent personalities associated with the festival. In addition, a comprehensive on-line catalogue-index to the archives' holdings and thus to the festival productions is now available.

The Archives of the Canadian Opera Association was established in 1974 with a volunteer custodian. The records go back to 1950 and include those of the Royal Conservatory Opera in collaboration with the Opera Festival Association of Toronto, the Canadian Opera Association, and, since 1977, the Canadian Opera Company. There are substantial holdings of administration, production, and publicity records in textual, photographic, and taped form. There is also documentation of Toronto operatic performances other than those of the Canadian Opera Company since 1825.

While not directly concerned with theatrical activity (as it is most narrowly defined), the archival record of the Canadian Broadcasting Corporation is extremely important. CBC Radio in particular produced admirable work in a period when theatrical activity had nothing like its intensity today. Writers such as W.O. Mitchell, Len Peterson, Lister Sinclair, and Gwen Pharis Ringwood did much fine work for the CBC and, later, for the legitimate stage. Under an agreement with the CBC, the National Archives of Canada acquires all types of documents relating to CBC radio and television administration and programming. The Centre for Broadcasting Studies at Concordia University in Montreal supports a bibliographic, research, and publishing project that is currently organizing and housing some fifteen thousand CBC radio-drama scripts.

Several important theatre collections outside the country contain material that relates to Canadian theatre activity. Such material includes programs, newspaper clippings, and photographs of actors who, although Canadian-born, spent much of their professional career elsewhere. These records also include much information on the careers of American and British actors who toured Canada. The New York Public Library's Theatre Collection, part of the Library and Museum of the Performing Arts at Lincoln Center, is one of the most important collections on the English-speaking theatre and thus will be a primary source of information for the researcher, particularly for material on the nineteenth and early-twentieth centuries. The Harvard Theatre Collection, one of the world's most distinguished collections, was established early in the century. Among its very rich holdings are a substantial number of nineteenth-century playbills that document productions in eastern Canadian cities. While the theatre collection in the Metropolitan Toronto Reference Library has photographic copies of these broadsides, a diligent researcher will find much else of Canadian interest in this collection, such as scrapbooks of the North American tours of Henry Irving and John Martin-Harvey. Brown University's collection of American and Canadian poetry and drama is considered the most extensive in North America, and contains copies of plays that are unavailable elsewhere. In London, the Theatre Museum, part of the Victoria and Albert Museum, in its new space in the converted Flower Market in Covent Garden, reveals scrapbooks, programs and photographs of English actors who toured Canada early in this century.

The 1975 Symons report on Canadian studies, *To Know Ourselves*,[2] indicated that the future quality of Canadian studies is directly linked to the condition and resources of Canadian archives. The study of Canada's theatre and drama as an academic discipline has – unfortunately – not kept pace with the expansion of graduate studies in the other fields of the humanities despite some notable individual and group achievements. Research and publication have been slower to develop than one would have liked. But the study of Canadian theatre is now among those aspects of Canada's past that is being treated systematically. Yet Canadians have been slow to appreciate and to collect records of their cultural past. Researchers are still hampered by a severe shortage of primary source materials and those that are available are frequently scattered and fragmented, inaccurate and contradictory, and often buried among other papers of social importance. The present scene is one of private generosity, haphazard growth, and technical and administrative difficulties. As a result, with much primary material still unlocated, a great deal of the country's theatrical history is still undocumented. There is a very great need for well-researched, published accounts of Canadian theatre history to satisfy and stimulate further the growing interest in this aspect of our cultural life.

However, the picture is not simply one of needs stated and then ignored. Increasingly, the situation is being acknowledged beyond the circle of specialists. Various studies produced in recent years (*To Know Ourselves, Canadian Archives*[3]) emphasize the importance of archives in Canada and the need to improve present conditions of acquisition and access. Government at all levels and institutions such as the Canada Council and the Social Sciences and Humanities Research Council of

Canada that share in the responsibility for Canada's cultural development have become aware of the present serious situation. Nevertheless,
a recommendation that I first proposed in 1973 is still valid two decades
later: the responsibility of the Canada Council should include the
requirement that all funded theatre companies deposit copies of relevant
printed documents with an appropriate designated archives, preferably
in the region, while continuing to retain their own records. Eventually,
such material should be passed to a suitable institution for preservation
and organization, or the company should be offered assistance to keep
its own records. In addition, there are several urgent steps yet to be taken
to improve the use and further acquisition of theatre resources in
Ontario. There should be a clear understanding and an established policy
among institutions collecting in the field as to what is appropriate for
each institution to acquire.

The development of a cooperative plan to coordinate archival activity
would involve several areas: surveys of holdings, joint copying projects,
use of specialized technical facilities, and improved archival education,
particularly for the staff of small archives. Many institutions currently
housing archival material lack facilities, equipment, and conservation
programs, which leads to disintegration of the collections, a process that
is accelerated by increased use. Encouragement is needed from the provincial government for small archives in particular.

One important sign of momentum in Canadian theatre studies was
the establishment in 1976 of the Association for Canadian Theatre
Research / Association de la recherche théâtrale au Canada, an association of individuals and institutions formed to encourage and develop
research and publication in the field. Members work to maintain a network for the exchange of information and of work in progress and are
also concerned to improve the collection and preservation of Canadian
theatre materials. The generosity of scholars who share their research
with others working in the field and with institutions requiring information or materials has been a noticeable feature of the membership. The
association has a journal, *Theatre Research in Canada / Recherches
théâtrales au Canada*, dedicated to the recovery and publication of documents and research about theatre in Canada.

NOTES

1 Robertson Davies, 'Letters in Canada: A Stage in Our Past,' *University of Toronto
Quarterly* 38 (July 1969)

2 T.H.B. Symons, *To Know Ourselves: The Report of the Commission on Canadian Studies* (Ottawa: Association of Universities and Colleges of Canada, 1975)
3 *Canadian Archives: Report to the Social Sciences and Humanities Research Council of Canada by the Consultative Group on Canadian Archives* (Ottawa: SSHRCC, 1980)

Select Bibliography

A Note on Sources for Ontario Theatre History

A comprehensive bibliography covering Ontario theatre between the First World War and the early 1970s would occupy far more space than is available here. With that in mind, we have compiled the following list of published reference works, articles, and books, as well as theses, specific to Ontario theatre. Individually they cover a broad range of subjects, and together they provide a substantial introduction to the theatre of the period. For more extensive coverage, readers are directed to sources such as *The Bibliography of Theatre History in Canada: The Beginnings through 1984 / Bibliographie d'histoire du théâtre au Canada: Des débuts – fin 1984*, *The Brock Bibliography of Published Canadian Plays in English 1766–1978*, the *Canadian Newspaper Index*, the *Canadian Periodical Index*, and others listed in the 'Bibliography and Reference Works' section.

Experienced researchers already know that materials for the study of theatre go much beyond published sources and encompass an exceedingly broad range of types, from playbills and company financial records, through artists' correspondence and handwritten reminiscences, to prompt books, designers' maquettes, and stage props or costumes. They also know that these materials are scattered about in places as various as theatre cupboards, house attics, village halls, and school or church basements. There is no guide to the holdings of private individuals, civic authorities, or associations and clubs. However, Heather McCallum and Ruth Pincoe's *Directory of Canadian Theatre Archives* offers a guide to the theatre collections in various institutional repositories. In particular, the National Archives of Canada, the National Library, and the Ontario Archives have substantial collections including such materials as private papers, photographs, audiotapes, and architectural drawings. The provincial archives has microfiche or microfilm copies of almost all existing Ontario newspapers. Municipalities, cities, towns, villages, and regions normally have museums, archives, or less formal aggregations of valuable documents. Local or regional public libraries usually have theatre-related documents. The Metropolitan Toronto Reference Library houses the largest theatre collection, including vertical files on hundreds of theatres and artists; Hamilton Public Library has special holdings for the Hamilton-Wentworth area. Universities and colleges also have significant resources, often with a local or regional focus.

Books, Chapters in Books, and Articles

Aikens, Jim. *For the Record: A Guide to Archive Management.* Toronto: Ontario Arts Council, 1980

Anthony, Geraldine. 'Coulter's *Riel*: A Re-appraisal.' *Canadian Drama* 11 (Fall 1985), 321–8

Anthony, Geraldine, ed. *Stage Voices.* Toronto, Garden City, NY: Doubleday, 1978

Averill, Harold. *Dramatis Personae: Amateur Theatre at the University of Toronto 1879–1939.* Toronto: University of Toronto Archives, 1986

Baillie, Joan Parkhill. *Look at the Record: An Album of Toronto's Lyric Theatres 1825–1984.* Oakville: Mosaic Press, 1985

Balan, Jars. 'Ukrainian Theatre in Canada: Scenes from an Untold Story.' *Canadian Theatre Review* 56 (Fall 1988), 35–9

Beasley, David. 'McKee Rankin: The Actor as Playwright.' *Theatre History in Canada / Histoire du théâtre au Canada* 10 (Fall 1989), 115–31

Benson, Eugene, and L.W. Conolly. *English-Canadian Theatre.* Toronto: Oxford, 1987

Bessai, Diane. *Playwrights of Collective Creation.* Toronto: Simon and Pierre, 1993

Book, Sam H. *Economic Aspects of the Arts in Ontario.* Toronto: Ontario Arts Council 1973

Book, Sam H., and S. Globerman. *The Audience for the Performing Arts.* Toronto: Ontario Arts Council, 1975

– *The Audience for the Performing Arts: Highlights of a Study of Attendance Patterns in Ontario.* Toronto: Ontario Arts Council, 1975

Bossin, Hye. *Stars of David: Toronto, 1856–1956.* Toronto: Jewish Standard, 1957. Jewish theatre in Toronto

Bouissac, Paul. 'The Circus's New Golden Age.' *Canadian Theatre Review* 58 (Spring 1989), 5–10

Brault, Lucien, and John Leaning. *La Salle Academy: A Heritage Building in Black and White.* Ottawa: Ministry of State for Urban Affairs, 1976. See 'The Theatre,' 43–5.

Breon, Robin. 'The Growth and Development of Black Theatre in Canada: A Starting

Point.' *Theatre History in Canada / Histoire du théâtre au Canada* 9 (Fall 1988), 216–28

Bridle, Augustus. *The Story of the Club.* Toronto: Clarke, Irwin, 1945

Brown, Mary. 'Ambrose Small: A Ghost in Spite of Himself.' In L.W. Conolly, ed., *Theatrical Touring and Founding in North America.* Westport, CT: Greenwood Press, 1982

– 'The Canadian Connection.' *Theatre Studies* 24/25 (1977/78; 1978/79), 107–18

Bryden, Ronald, and Boyd Neil, eds. *Whittaker's Theatre: A Critic Looks at Stages in Canada and Thereabouts, 1944–1975.* Greenbank, Ont.: The Whittaker Project, 1985

Campbell, Douglas. 'Canadian Players on the Snowplough Circuit.' *Theatre Arts* 39 (April 1955), 71–3, 88

'Canada's Clowns.' *Canadian Theatre Review* 47 (Summer 1986), 63–72

'Canadian Breweries Backing O'Keefe Centre in Toronto; Figures of Cost and First Deficits.' *Theatre Arts* 45 (October 1961), 78

Canadian Theatre Review. 'A Chronological Commentary.' *Canadian Theatre Review* 7 (Summer 1975), 17–23. The Crest Theatre

– 'The Crest: A Photographic View.' Ibid., 24–33

– 'Crest Chronology.' Ibid., 45–51

Card, Raymond. 'Drama in Toronto: The Forgotten Years 1919–1939.' *English Quarterly* 6 (Spring 1973), 67–81

Carroll, Jock. 'Played Straight "The Drunkard" Is Very, Very Funny.' *Saturday Night* 64 (16 October 1948), 2. Brian Doherty, New World Theatre

Carson, Neil. 'George Luscombe and the Theatre of the "Cabotin."' *Canadian Drama* 15:2 (1989), 149–58

– 'Playing the Piper: The Experience of TWP.' *Canadian Theatre Review* 58 (Spring 1989), 75–9

Charlesworth, Hector. 'Music & Drama.' *Saturday Night* 37 (July 1922), 6. Fire destroys Royal Lyceum Opera House, Toronto.

'The Chester Mysteries.' *Canadian Theosophist* 18 (15 January 1938), 338–9. Drama Guild of the Toronto Theosophical Society

Collins, Richard. *Culture, Communication and National Identity: The Case of Canadian Television.* Toronto: University of Toronto Press, 1990

Conolly, L.W., ed. *Modern Canadian Drama and Its Critics.* Vancouver: Talon, 1987

– *Theatrical Touring and Founding in North America.* Westport, CT: Greenwood, 1982

Crean, Susan. *Who's Afraid of Canadian Culture?* Don Mills: General, 1976

Davies, Robertson. 'Mixed Grill: Touring Fare in Canada, 1920–1935.' In L.W. Conolly, ed., *Theatrical Touring and Founding in North America.* Westport, CT: Greenwood Press, 1982

– 'Renaissance of Professional Theatre in Toronto.' *Saturday Night* 56 (31 May 1941), 23

Davis, Donald. 'Interview: The Davis View.' *Canadian Theatre Review* 7 (Summer 1975), 34–44

Davis, Murray, and Sidney Katz. 'How (and Why) We Run the Crest.' *Mayfair* 29 (September 1955), 28–9, 49–50, 52, 54

Dean, Malcolm. *Censored! Only in Canada: The History of Film Censorship – The Scandal Off the Screen.* Toronto: Virgo, 1981

Drainie, Bronwyn. *Living the Part: John Drainie and the Dilemma of Canadian Stardom.* Toronto: Macmillan, 1988

Duval, Paul. 'Toronto Theatre Group Begins Experiment.' *Saturday Night* 61 (17 November 1945), 25. Toronto Civic Theatre

Edinborough, Arnold. *The Festivals of Canada.* Toronto: Lester and Orpen, 1981

Edmonstone, Wayne E. *Nathan Cohen: The Making of a Critic.* Toronto: Lester and Orpen, 1977.

Edwards, Murray D. *A Stage in Our Past: English Language Theatre in Eastern Canada from the 1790's to 1914.* Toronto: University of Toronto Press, 1968

'Eight Men Speak.' *The Varsity* (Toronto), 19 January 1934, 2

'*Eight Men Speak* Is Cancelled Due to Political Interference.' *The Varsity,* 12 January 1934, 1, 4

Eyman, Scott. *Mary Pickford, from Here to Hollywood.* Toronto: Harper and Collins, 1990

Ferry, Joan. 'Experiences of a Pioneer in Canadian Experimental Theatre.' *Theatre History in Canada* 8 (Spring 1987), 59–67. Toronto Workshop Productions

Filewod, Alan. 'Between Empires: Post-Imperialism and Canadian Theatre.' *Essays in Theatre* 11 (November 1992), 3–15

– 'National Theatre / National Obsession.' *Canadian Theatre Review* 62 (Spring 1990), 5–10

– 'Critical Bodies 4: Professing a Profession.' *Canadian Theatre Review* 57 (Winter 1988), 51–2

– *Collective Encounters: Documentary Theatre in English Canada.* Toronto: University of Toronto Press, 1987

– 'The Ideological Formation of Political Theatre in Canada.' *Theatre History in Canada / Histoire du théâtre au Canada* 8 (Fall 1987), 254–63

Fink, Howard, and John Jackson, eds. *All the Bright Company: Radio Drama Produced by Andrew Allan.* Kingston: Quarry Press / CBC Enterprises, 1987

Fortin, Marcel. 'Le Caveau d'Ottawa: Une troupe amateur en quête de légitimité (1932–1951).' *Theatre History in Canada / Histoire du théâtre au Canada* 7 (Spring 1986), 33–49

Frazer, Robbin. 'Sixty Years of Memories: The Ottawa Little House.' *Performing Arts in Canada* 10 (Summer 1973), 25

Frick, Nora Alice. *Image in the Mind: CBC Radio Drama 1944–1954.* Toronto: Canadian Stage & Arts Publications 1987

Gaines, Robert. *Neville Takes Command.* Stratford: William Street Press, 1987

Gardner, David. 'Charles Jolliffe (1913–1991).' *Canadian Actors' Equity Association Newsletter,* September 1991, 8

- 'A Young Canadian Tackles London's West End, 1957–58.' *Theatre History in Canada / Histoire du théâtre au Canada* 11 (Fall 1990), 163–67
- 'Canada's Eskimo "Lear."' *Theatre History in Canada / Histoire du théâtre au Canada* 7 (Spring 1986), 99–118
Garebian, Keith. *George Bernard Shaw and Christopher Newton: Explorations of Shavian Theatre.* Oakville: Mosaic, 1993
- *William Hutt: A Theatre Portrait.* Oakville: Mosaic Press, 1988
Goodwin, Jill Tomasson. 'A Career in Progress, Part 2: Donald Davis, Canadian Actor and Director, 1959–1990.' *Theatre History in Canada / Histoire du théâtre au Canada* 12 (Spring 1991), 56–78
- 'Andrew Allan and the "Stage" Series.' *Canadian Drama* 15:1 (1989), 1–24
- 'A Career in Review: Donald Davis, Canadian Actor, Producer, Director.' *Theatre History in Canada / Histoire du théâtre au Canada* 10 (Fall 1989), 132–51
Grace, Sherrill E. *Regression and Apocalypse: Studies in North American Literary Expressionism.* Toronto: University of Toronto Press, 1989
- 'Herman Voaden's *Murder Pattern*: 1936 and 1987.' *Canadian Drama* 13:1 (1987), 117–19
- 'Another Part in the Brooker Quartette.' *Canadian Drama* 11:1 (1985), 251–79. Bertram Brooker
- 'The Living Soul of Man: Bertram Brooker and the Expressionist Theatre.' *Theatre History in Canada* 6 (Spring 1985), 3–22
Gross, Gerry. 'Matters of Conscience: The Radio Dramas of Reuben Ship.' *Canadian Drama* 15:1 (1989), 25–38
- 'A Palpable Hit: A Study of the Impact of Reuben Ship's "The Investigator."' *Theatre History in Canada / Histoire du théâtre au Canada* 10 (Fall 1989), 152–66
Hall, Amelia. *Life before Stratford: The Memoirs of Amelia Hall.* Toronto: Dundurn Press, 1989.
Harron, Don. 'Remembering "Spring Thaw."' *Toronto Life* (April 1979), 52–3, 107–10, 113, 115, 117
Harron, Martha. *Don Harron: A Parent Contradiction.* Toronto: W. Collins and Sons Canada, 1988
Helleur, Stan. 'Farewell to Shea's.' *Mayfair* 31 (March 1957), 23–5, 61–3
Hengen, Sharon. 'Ontario, Canada.' *American Review of Canadian Studies* 21 (Spring 1991), 55–69
Hicklin, Ralph. 'The Theatre Season in Toronto 1961–62: A Survey.' *Tamarack Review* 25 (Autumn 1962), 60–8
'Hit Target in Private Drive to Help Theatre Group.' *Financial Post* 58 (10 October 1964), 13. Canadian Players' Foundation
'Hungary's Loss, Toronto's Gain, a Theatre in the Budapest Manner.' *Maclean's* 76 (1 June 1963), 63
Jackson, Dorothy N.R. *History of the Three Schools: The School of Expression, The*

Margaret Eaton School of Literature and Expression, The Margaret Eaton School, 1901–1941. Toronto: n.p. 1953

Johnson, Ken. 'The Canadian Players.' *Mayfair* 30 (February 1956), 38–9, 54–5

Johnston, Denis W. *Up the Mainstream: The Rise of Toronto's Alternative Theatres 1968–1975*. Toronto: University of Toronto Press, 1990

Joliffe, Marlynn. 'Victoria Playhouse, Petrolia: The Building Burden.' *Canadian Theatre Review* 6 (Spring 1975), 32–40

Kerr, Lois Reynolds. 'Lois Reynolds Kerr Recalls the Playwrights' Studio Group.' *Theatre History in Canada / Histoire du théâtre au Canada* 5 (Spring 1984), 98–109

La Salle. Ottawa: Ministry of State for Urban Affairs, 1976

Laurence, Dan H., comp. *Shaw Festival Production Record, 1962–1990*. Guelph: University of Guelph Library, 1990

Lawrence, Robert G. 'Lillie Langtry in Canada and the U.S.A., 1882–1917.' *Theatre History in Canada* 10 (Spring 1989), 30–42

– 'Vaughan Glaser on Stage in Toronto 1921–1934.' *Theatre History in Canada / Histoire du théâtre au Canada* 9 (Spring 1988), 59–80

Lee, Betty. *Love and Whisky: The Story of the Dominion Drama Festival*. Toronto: McClelland and Stewart, 1973

Leslie Hurry: A Painter for the Stage. Stratford: The Gallery, 1984

LeVay, John. *Margaret Anglin: A Stage Life*. Toronto: Simon & Pierre, 1988

Lindsay, John C. *Royal Alexandra: The Finest Theatre on the Continent. The Old Vic: The Most Famous Theatre in the World*. Erin, Ont.: Boston Mills Press, 1986

– *Turn Out the Stars Before Leaving: The Story of Canada's Theatres*. Erin, Ont.: Boston Mills, 1983

Litt, Paul. 'The Massey Commission, Americanization, and Canadian Cultural Nationalism.' *Queen's Quarterly* 98 (Summer 1991), 375–87

Lyle-Smith, Alan, Arnold M. Walter, and Frank Chappell. *The Shakespeare Festival: A Short History of the Initial Five Years of Canada's First Shakespeare Festival, 1949–1954*. Toronto: Ryerson, 1954. Earle Grey Players

McClellan, Scott. *Straw Hats and Greasepaint: Fifty Years of Theatre in the Summer Colony. Vol. 1: The Actors' Colony Story 1934–42*. Bracebridge: Muskoka Publishers, 1984

McKay, D.G. 'Western Ontario Drama.' *Waterloo Review* 2 (Summer 1960), 15–19

– 'Western Ontario Drama.' *Waterloo Review* 2 (Summer 1959), 13–16

McPhie, Susan. 'A History of Theatre at York.' *York Theatre Journal 31*. North York: York University Theatre Department, 1989

MacSkimming, Roy. *For Arts' Sake: A History of the Ontario Arts Council 1963–1983*. Toronto: Ontario Arts Council, 1983

Made Glorious: Stage Design at Stratford: 25 Years, an Exhibition. Stratford: The Gallery, 1977

Marsh, D.G. 'Professional Theatre Reviving This Year.' *Saturday Night* 62 (October 1946), 24–5

Meiklejohn, J.M.C. 'Theatre Education in Canada after World War II: A Memoir.'
Edited with an introduction and notes by Denis W. Johnston. *Theatre History in
Canada / Histoire du théâtre au Canada* 12 (Fall 1991), 141–68
– 'Theatre in Ottawa in the 1930's: A Memoir.' Edited with an introduction by Denis
W. Johnston. *Theatre History in Canada / Histoire du théâtre au Canada* 10 (Fall
1989), 167–88
Michener, Wendy. 'Before Compiègne.' *Tamarack Review* 31 (Spring 1964), 96–7.
Toronto Workshop Productions
Miller, Mary Jane. *Turn Up the Contrast: CBC Television Drama Since 1952.* Vancou-
ver: University of British Columbia Press / CBC Enterprises, 1987
Moon, Barbara. 'Canadian Theatre's Fairy Godmother.' *Maclean's* 71 (15 February
1958), 18–19, 52–3. Dora Mavor Moore and the New Play Society
Murray, Heather. 'Making the Modern: Twenty Five Years of the Margaret Eaton
School of Literature and Expression.' *Essays in Theatre* 10 (November 1991),
39–57
'The National Arts Centre Ottawa.' *Opera Canada* 7 (May 1966), 17–24. Includes
letter by G.H. Southam to 'Opera Canada,' goals of NAC, architecture of NAC,
activities
The New Play Society: An exhibition at the Thomas Fisher Rare Book Library 1979.
Toronto: University of Toronto, Thomas Fisher Rare Book Library, 1979
New, William H. *Dramatists in Canada.* Vancouver: University of British Columbia
Press, 1972
Nipp, Dora. 'The Chinese in Toronto.' In R. Harney, ed., *Gathering Place: Peoples and
Neighbourhoods of Toronto, 1834–1945.* Toronto: Multicultural History Society of
Ontario, 1985
Noonan, James. 'The National Arts Centre: Fifteen Years at Play.' *Theatre History in
Canada* 6 (Spring 1985), 56–81
O'Keefe Centre for the Performing Arts 1960–1975. Toronto: O'Keefe Centre, 1975
Olsheski, Constance. *Pantages Theatre: Rebirth of a Landmark.* Toronto: Key Porter
Books, 1989
O'Neill-Karch, Mariel. *Théâtre franco-ontarien: Espaces ludique.* Vanier, Ont.: L'Inter-
ligne, 1992
'On stage with the Canadian Players.' *On Stage* 2 (Winter 1963), 14
'Ontario's Multicultural Theatre Preserving Languages and Cultures.' *Scene Changes* 5
(April 1977), 5
Our Stage: The Amateur Performing Arts of the Ukrainian Settlers in Canada. Ed.
Peter Krawchuk. Toronto: Kobzar Publishing, 1984. Translation of *Nasha Stsena*
Panzica, Norman. 'The Crest: Quo Vadis?' *Performing Arts in Canada* 1 (Spring–
Summer 1962), 5–6, 63
Patterson, Tom. *First Stage: The Making of the Stratford Festival.* Toronto: McClelland
and Stewart, 1987
Pettigrew, John. *Stratford: The First Thirty Years.* 2 vols. Toronto: Macmillan, 1985

Phillips, Ruth. *The History of the Royal Canadian Navy's World War II Show 'Meet the Navy.'* Willowdale: Author, 1973

The Pictorial Stage: Twenty-Five Years of Vision and Design at the Shaw Festival, Niagara-on-the-Lake. Niagara-on-the-Lake: Shaw Festival, 1986

Pressman, David. 'The New Actor.' *Guide* 1 (December 1937), 7. Toronto Theatre of Action

Reaney, James. 'Stories on the String. It All Started in London, Ontario in the Mid-1960's (Part 1).' *Theatrum* 18 (April/May 1990), 7–8

Relke, Diana M.A. 'Killed into Art: Marjorie Pickthall and "The Wood Carver's Wife."' *Canadian Drama* 13:2 (1987), 187–200

Rubin, Don. 'Evolving to Professionalism: Theatre London.' *Performing Arts in Canada* 9 (Winter 1972), 25

Rudakoff, Judith, and Rita Much, eds. *Fair Play: 12 Women Speak, Conversations with Canadian Playwrights.* Toronto: Simon and Pierre, 1990

Russell, Hilary. 'The Great Canadian Movie Palaces.' *Canadian Review* 3 (January–February 1976), 24–5

– 'All That Glitters: A Memorial to Ottawa's Capitol Theatre and Its Predecessors.' In *Canadian Historic Sites: Occasional Papers in Archaeology and History*, vol. 13, 5–125. Ottawa: National Historic Parks and Sites Branch, Parks Canada, Indian and Northern Affairs, 1975

Russell, Matthew. 'The Stagestruck Queen on King Street.' *Mayfair* 28 (March 1954), 24–7, 66, 68–9

Rutherford, Paul. *When Television Was Young: Primetime Canada 1952–1967.* Toronto: University of Toronto Press, 1990

Ryan, Oscar. 'Two Plays Make a Hit.' *The Worker* (22 October 1935), 2. Toronto Theatre of Action

Ryan, Toby Gordon. *Stage Left: Canadian Theatre in the Thirties.* Toronto: CTR Publications, 1981

Saddlemyer, Ann, ed. *Early Stages: Theatre in Ontario 1800–1914.* Toronto: University of Toronto Press, 1990

– 'Thoughts on National Drama and the Founding of Theatres.' In L.W. Conolly, ed., *Theatrical Touring and Founding in North America.* Westport, CT: Greenwood Press, 1982

Salter, Denis. 'The Idea of National Theatre.' In *Canadian Canons: Essays in Literary Value*, 71–90, 209–15. Toronto: University of Toronto Press, 1991.

– 'Declarations of (In)dependence: Adjudicating the Dominion Drama Festival.' *Canadian Theatre Review* 62 (Spring 1990), 11–18

– 'Ibsen in Canada: The Critical Reception 1910–1980.' In Jorn Carlsen and Bengt Streijffert, eds, *Canada and the Nordic Countries*, 285–97. Lund: University Press, 1988

– 'At Home and Abroad: The Acting Career of Julia Arthur.' *Theatre History in Canada / Histoire du théâtre au Canada* 3 (Spring 1984), 1–35

Sandwell, B.K. 'New Society Is Smooth, Plausible.' *Saturday Night* 63 (4 October 1947), 26. New Play Society's 'What Every Woman Knows'
- 'Callaghan Premiere.' *Saturday Night* 64 (25 January 1949), 19. Morley Callaghan's 'To Tell the Truth,' New Play Society
- 'A New Quality on the Canadian Stage. By Lucy Van Gogh, pseud.' *Saturday Night* 64 (22 March 1949), 2–3. New Play Society
- 'Ottawa's CRT.' *Saturday Night* 65 (22 November 1949), 30. Canadian Repertory Theatre
'Shakespeare Festivals in Canada: The Earle Grey Players.' *Food for Thought* 13 (May–June 1953), 8–12
Shaw Festival Theatre Foundation. *Celebrating!: Twenty-Five Years on the Stage at the Shaw Festival*. Erin, Ont.: Boston Mills Press, 1986
Sidnell, Michael. 'Centennial Play: New Canadians for Old.' *Canadian Forum* 46 (November 1966), 187–8
Souchotte, Sandra. 'Canada's Workers' Theatre.' *Canadian Theatre Review* 9 (Winter 1976), 159–72
Sperdakos, Paula. 'Dora Mavor Moore: Before the New Play Society.' *Theatre History in Canada / Histoire du théâtre au Canada* 10 (Spring 1989), 43–64
Sterne, Richard L. *John Gielgud Directs Richard Burton in Hamlet: A Journal of Rehearsals*. New York: Random House, 1967. O'Keefe Centre
Stuart, Anne. 'Hart House Theatre: A Living Tradition.' In *Ontario Playwrights' Showcase Festival*. Toronto: Theatre Ontario, 1980
Stuart, Euan Ross. 'The Crest Controversy.' *Canadian Theatre Review* 7 (Summer 1975), 8–11
'Students Protest Suppression of Play.' *The Varsity*, 17 January 1934, 1, 4. *Eight Men Speak*
Sudbury Operatic Society, Sudbury a Musical City? Sudbury: Sudbury Operatic Society, 1947
Sutherland, Harold. 'Toronto Enjoys a Summer of Flesh and Blood Drama.' *Saturday Night* 55 (27 July 1940), 13, 19. Royal Alexandra Theatre
Symons, Thomas Henry Bull. *To Know Ourselves: The Report of the Commission on Canadian Studies*. Ottawa: Association of Universities and Colleges of Canada, 1975
Task Force on the National Arts Centre. *Accent on Access: Report of the Task Force on the National Arts Centre*. Ottawa: Government of Canada, 1986.
Tepper, Bill. 'The Forties and Beyond: The New Play Society.' *Canadian Theatre Review* 28 (Fall 1980), 18–33
Terry, Pamela. 'Six Days and a Dream by John Volinska: Drao Players.' *Alphabet* 4 (June 1962), 6–7
Theatre Spaces: An Inventory of Performing Arts Facilities in Ontario. Toronto: Ministry of Citizenship and Culture, 1986
Le Théâtre du Nouvel-Ontario – 20 ans. Sudbury: Edition TNO, 1991

Tippett, Maria. *Making Culture: English Canadian Institutions and the Arts Before the Massey Commission*. Toronto: University of Toronto Press, 1990

Usin, Lea V. 'Creon's City: A History of Ottawa's Town Theatre.' *Canadian Drama* 12 (Spring 1986), 8–17

Usmiani, Renate. 'Roy Mitchell: Prophet in Our Past.' *Theatre History in Canada / Histoire du théâtre au Canada* 8 (Fall 1987), 147–68

– *Second Stage: The Alternative Theatre Movement in Canada*. Vancouver: University of British Columbia Press, 1983

Voaden, Herman. *A Vision of Canada: Herman Voaden's Dramatic Works 1928–1945*, ed. Anton Wagner. Toronto: Simon & Pierre, 1993.

Wagner, Anton. 'Infinite Variety or a Canadian "National" Theatre: Roly Young and the Toronto Civic Theatre Association, 1945–1949.' *Theatre History in Canada / Histoire du théâtre au Canada* 9 (Fall 1993), 173–92

– 'Herman Voaden and the Group of Seven: Creating a Canadian Imaginative Background in Theatre.' *International Journal of Canadian Studies* 4 (Fall 1991), 145–64

– 'Elsie Park Gowan: Distinctively Canadian.' *Theatre History in Canada / Histoire du théâtre au Canada* 8 (Spring 1987), 68–82

– 'A National or International Dramatic Art: B.K. Sandwell and *Saturday Night* 1932–1951.' *Canadian Drama* 12:2 (1986), 342–50

– 'Herman Voaden's "New Religion."' *Theatre History in Canada / Histoire du théâtre au Canada* 6 (Fall 1985), 187–201

– 'Dr. Lawrence Mason, Music and Drama Critic 1924–1939.' *Theatre History in Canada / Histoire du théâtre au Canada* 4 (Spring 1983), 3–14

Wagner, Anton, ed. *Contemporary Canadian Theatre: New World Visions*. Toronto: Simon & Pierre, 1985

Waldhauer, Erdmute. *Drama at Queen's: From Its Beginnings to 1991*. Kingston: Queen's University Drama Department, 1991

Wallace, Robert. *Producing Marginality: Essays on Theatre and Criticism in Canada*. Saskatoon: Fifth House, 1990

Wallace, Robert, and Cynthia Zimmerman. *The Work: Conversations with English-Canadian Playwrights*. Toronto: Coach House, 1982

Warnken, Wendy. 'A Study of Ontario's Performing Arts Resources.' *Theatre History in Canada / Histoire du théâtre au Canada* 9 (Spring 1988), 110–23. Ontario Arts Council

'Workers' Theatre Group.' *The Masses* 1 (December 1932)

'Workers' Theatre in Action.' *The Masses* 2 (May–June 1933), 2, 13

'Workers' Theatre in Action.' *The Masses* 2 (September 1933), 13–14, 16

'Workers' Theatre in Action.' *The Masses* 2 (January 1934), 13

'Workers' Theatre: Ontario in the 1930's.' *New Frontiers* 3 (Summer 1954), 28–30

'Workers' Theatre: The Ten Day Campaign.' *The Masses* 2 (March–April 1934), 13

'Workers' Theatre Tours Ontario.' *The Masses* 2 (September 1933), 13

Theses

Behl, Dennis Lorman. 'Tanya Moiseiwitsch: Her Contribution to Theatre Arts from 1935–1980.' Ph.D., Kent State University, 1981

Birch, Jane Kathleen. 'The Broken Window Pane: A Study in the Creative Imagination in James Reaney's Listen to the Wind.' MA, McMaster University, 1973

Bishop, Carol. 'The Artistic Life of Maud Allan.' MFA, York University, 1989

Blom, Patricia Vandenberg. 'Tanya Moiseiwitsch, Costume Designer: The Creative Process.' Ph.D., University of Michigan, 1982

Brissenden, Constance. 'Canadian Plays Produced Professionally During the 1960's in Toronto.' MA, University of Alberta, 1971

Campbell, Nora Rene. 'The Stratford Shakespearean Festival of Canada: Evolution of an Artistic Policy (1953–1980) as a Basis for Its Success.' Ph.D., University of Wisconsin, 1982

Carr, James. 'The Will to Live: Subverting Maleness in Plays by Canadian Men from Herbert to Fraser.' MA, University of Alberta, 1991

Clyde, Douglas J. 'Merrill Denison: The Dramatist of the Unheroic North.' MA, Dalhousie University, 1930

Day, Arthur R. 'The Shaw Festival at Niagara-on-the-Lake in Ontario, Canada, 1962–1981: A History.' Ph.D., Bowling Green State University, 1982

Day, Moira. 'Children and Reaney's Dramaturgy.' MA, University of Alberta, 1980

Endres, Robin. 'Plays and Politics: An Analysis of Various Models of Twentieth Century Poltical Theatre.' Ph.D., York University, 1976

Filewod, Alan. 'The Development and Performance of Documentary Theatre in English-Speaking Canada.' Ph.D., University of Toronto, 1985

Fortin, Marcel. 'Le Théâtre d'expression française dans l'outaouais.' Ph.D., Université d'Ottawa, 1986

Fuhr, Arlene Lorraine. 'An Archetypal Pattern in Reaney.' MA, University of Alberta, 1974

Goldie, Terry. 'Canadian Dramatic Literature in English 1919–1939.' Ph.D., Queen's University, 1977

Goodwin, Jill Tomasson. 'An Analysis of Ten English-Canadian Radio Plays (1944–56): The Social Comic Vision of Andrew Allen's "Stage" Series.' Ph.D., University of Toronto, 1987

Gould, Allan Mendel. 'A Critical Assessment of the Theatre Criticism of Nathan Cohen with a Bibliography and Selected Anthology.' Ph.D., York University, 1977

Groome, Margaret E. 'Canada's Stratford Festival 1953–1967: Hegemony, Commodity, Institution.' Ph.D., McGill University, 1987

Hankins, Dilys Rosalind. 'Toward a National Theatre: The Canada Council 1957–1982.' MA, The American University, 1984

Haynes, Nancy Jane, 'A History of the Royal Alexandra Theatre, Toronto, Ontario, Canada, 1914–1918.' Ph.D., University of Colorado, 1973

Hiritsch, Basil. 'The Development of Ukrainian Theatre and Its Role in Canada.' MA, Université de Montréal, 1961

Johnston, Denis W. 'The Rise of Toronto's Alternative Theatres, 1968–75.' Ph.D., University of Toronto, 1987

Kotyshyn, Terry. 'Jupiter Theatre, Inc., 1951–1954: The Life and Death of Toronto's First Professional Full-time Theatre.' MA, University of Alberta, 1986

Krieg, Robert. 'A Study of Forest Theatre.' Ph.D., University of Western Ontario, 1978. Six Nations pageant plays on the Grand River Reserve

Lau William. 'Chinese Dance Experience in Canadian Society: An Investigation of Four Chinese Dance Groups in Toronto.' MFA, York University, 1991

McDonald, Ian Arnold. 'The London Little Theatre, 1934–1956.' Ph.D., Ohio State University, 1962

McGill, Robert Emmett. 'Stratford '55: The Establishment of Convention.' Ph.D., University of Michigan, 1972

McNamara, Timothy. 'Innocence and Experience in the Dramatic Works of James Reaney.' Ph.D., Queen's University, 1984

Minsos, Susan F. 'Towards a Myth of Community: Structure and Style in James Reaney's Donnelly Trilogy.' MA, University of Alberta, 1983

O'Neill, Mora Dianne Guthrie. 'A Partial History of the Royal Alexandra Theatre, Toronto, Ontario 1907–1939.' Ph.D., Louisiana State University, 1973

Parkhill, Frances Neily. 'The Dominion Drama Festival, Its History, Organization and Influence.' MA, Emerson College, Boston, 1952

Plant, Richard. 'Leaving Home: A Thematic Study of Canadian Literature with Special Emphasis on Drama, 1606 to 1977.' Ph.D., University of Toronto, 1979

Pope, Karl Theodore. 'An Historical Study of the Stratford Ontario Festival Theatre.' Ph.D., Wayne State University, 1966

Reid, Gregory. 'James Reaney's Ritual Theatre.' MA, Carleton University, 1978

Rae, Elizabeth. 'Christopher Newton's Years at the Shaw Festival, 1980–1993.' Ph.D., University of Toronto, 1995

Scott, Robert Barry. 'A Study of English-Canadian Dramatic Literature.' Phil.M. University of Toronto, 1969

– 'A Study of Amateur Theatre in Toronto: 1900–1930.' MA, University of New Brunswick, 1966

– 'Professional Companies and Performers in Ontario, 1914–1967.' Ph.D., University of Toronto, 1995

Seaver, Richard Everett. 'Douglas Campbell: A Study of His Artistic Accomplishment as an Actor and Director at Selected Theatres in England, Canada and the United States to 1979.' Ph.D., Wayne State University, 1981

Siversky, Sandra. 'The Role of the Designer in Canadian Theatre.' Ph.D., University of Toronto, 1995

Sperdakos, Paula. 'Dora Mavor Moore: Her Career in Canadian Theatre.' Ph.D., University of Toronto, 1990
Stillwell, Henry Le Vern. 'An Analysis and Evaluation of the Major Examples of the Open Stage Concept as Initiated at Stratford, Ont. to 1964.' Ph.D., University of Michigan, 1969
Stuart, Euan Ross. 'An Analysis of Productions on the Open Stage at Stratford, Ontario.' Ph.D., University of Toronto, 1975
Wagner, Anton. 'Herman Voaden's Symphonic Expressionism.' Ph.D., University of Toronto, 1984
Wiens, Esther Ruth. 'Archetypal Patterns in a Selection of Plays by William Robertson Davies.' Ph.D., Northwestern University, 1984
Warrick, David. 'The Toronto Stage History Database of Canadian Professional Theatrical Productions in English 1968–1980: Checklists and Searches.' Ph.D., York University, 1986

Bibliographies and Reference Works

Ball, John, and Richard Plant, eds. *Bibliography of Theatre History in Canada: The Beginnings Through 1984*. Toronto: ECW, 1993
Benson, Eugene, and L.W. Conolly, eds. *The Oxford Companion to Canadian Theatre*. Don Mills: Oxford University Press, 1987
Canadian Archives: Report to the Social Sciences and Humanities Research Council of Canada by the Consultative Group on Canadian Archives. Ottawa: Social Sciences and Humanities Research Council of Canada, 1980
Coad, Luman. *An Index to the Puppetry Journal*. 2 vols. Vol. 1: 1944–82. Vol. 2: 1982–87. North Vancouver: Coad Canada Puppets, 1983
Craig, Barbara L., and Richard W. Ramsey, eds. *Guide to the Holdings of the Archives of Ontario*. 2 vols. Toronto: Archives of Ontario, 1985
Dick, Ernest J. *Guide to CBC Sources at the Public Archives / Catalogue des fonds sur la Société Radio-Canada déposés aux Archives Publiques*. Ottawa: National Archives of Canada, 1987
Fink, Howard, and Brian Morrison, eds. *Canadian National Theatre on the Air, vol. 1, 1925–1961. CBC-CRBC-CNR Radio Drama in English: A Descriptive Bibliography and Union List*. Toronto: University of Toronto Press, 1983
Fink, Howard, ed. *Canadian National Theatre on the Air, vol. 2, 1962–1986. CBC Radio Drama in English: A Descriptive Bibliography and Union List*. Kingston: Quarry Press, 1992
Garay, Kathleen, and Norma Smith. *The John Coulter Archive*. 2 vols. Hamilton: Mills Memorial Library, McMaster University Library Press, 1982–1983
Guide des Archives du Centre de recherche en civilisation canadienne-française de l'Université d'Ottawa. Ottawa: Université d'Ottawa, 1985

Literary Manuscripts at the National Library of Canada. Ottawa: National Library of
Canada, 1990
McCallum, Heather, and Ruth Pincoe, comps. *Directory of Canadian Theatre Archives.*
Occasional Papers Series no. 53. Halifax: Dalhousie University, School of Library
and Information Studies, 1992
MacDermaid, Anne, and George F. Henderson, eds. *A Guide to the Holdings of Queen's
University Archives.* 2 vols. Kingston: Queen's University, 1986–7.
McPherson Library, Reference Division, University of Victoria, BC, comp. *Creative
Canada: A Biographical Dictionary of Twentieth Century Creative and Performing
Artists.* Toronto: University of Toronto Press, 1971
National Archives of Canada. *Guide to Canadian Photographic Archives.* 2nd ed.
Ottawa: National Archives of Canada, 1984
National Archives of Canada. *Union List of Manuscripts in Canadian Repositories.* 2
vols, 1975. Supplements: 1976, 1977–8, 1979–80, 1981–2. Ottawa: National Archives
of Canada, 1975–1985
National Archives of Canada, Manuscripts Division. *Literary Archives Guide.* Ottawa:
National Archives of Canada, 1988
O'Neill, P.B. 'A Checklist of Canadian Dramatic Materials to 1967. Part I: A to K.'
Canadian Drama / L'Art dramatique canadien 8 (Autumn 1982), 176–303
– 'A Checklist of Canadian Dramatic Materials to 1967. Part II: L to Z.' *Canadian
Drama / L'Art dramatique canadien* 9 (Autumn 1983), 369–506
– 'Unpublished Canadian Plays Copyrighted 1921–1937.' *Canadian Drama / L'Art
dramatique canadien* 4 (Spring 1978), 52–63
Playwrights Union of Canada. *Catalogue of Plays.* Toronto: Playwrights Canada Press.
Several published since 1972
Rubin, Don, ed. *Canada on Stage: The CTR Yearbook.* Downsview: Canadian Theatre
Review, 1974
Rubin, Don, and Alison Cranmer-Byng, eds. *Canada's Playwrights: A Biographical
Guide.* Downsview: Canadian Theatre Review, 1980
Somerset, J.A.B. *The Stratford Festival Story: A Catalogue-Index to the Stratford,
Ontario, Festival, 1953–1990.* Westport, CT: Greenwood Press, 1991
Stewart, Charlotte A., and Carl Spadoni, comps. *The Research Collections at McMaster
University Library.* Hamilton: McMaster University Library, William Ready Division
of Archives and Research Collections, 1987
University of Guelph Library. *Theatre Archives.* Guelph: University of Guelph, 1991
Wagner, Anton, ed. *The Brock Bibliography of Published Canadian Stage Plays in
English 1766–1978.* Toronto: Playwrights Union of Canada, 1980

Illustration Credits

Julie and Don Schnurr, Schnurr's Hall, Linwood: exterior (4); interior (5)

Hamilton Public Library: Savoy Theatre (15); Charmed Rope (136); *Whizz Bang Revue* (186); Cockpit Theatre (257); *The Upper Room* (264); community theatre voice session (272); Hamilton Community Players (286); Amelia Hall Collection: Amelia Hall (75); Superior Engravers Collection: Minstrel Show (134); 'Plant and Lord Mayor's Play' (180)

Metropolitan Toronto Reference Library: Catherine Proctor as Hermia (26); Julia Arthur as Saint Joan (35); Cosy Lee (41); Photo by Harrison Scheak: Arden Keay as Elizabeth the Queen (55); Alexander Knox (63); Herbert Whittaker design for *Galileo* (68); John Drainie as Galileo (69); *The Glass Cage* (78); *Champagne Complex* (82); *The Good Soldier Schweik* (93); Ed Kotanen design for *Fiddler on the Roof* (98); The O'Connor Sisters (147); Beatrice Lillie (161); Josephine Barrington (175); 'Chess Is Hell' (190); Photo by J. Fleetwood Morrow: Earle Grey Players (225); Actor's Colony Theatre (226); *Mandragola* design (230); Peter Mews (237); Ivor Lewis (268); *A Jig for the Gypsy* (342); Eric Aldwinckle's design for *This Mad World* (369); Photo by Gilbert A. Milne & Co: *The Lady's Not For Burning* (371); *The House of Atreus* (370); *The Ottawa Man* (372); *Christmas in the Market Place* (373); 'Anna in Hell' (377); 'Quayside in Alexandria' (378); Mae Edwards Collection: Novelty Orchestra (29); Margaret Anglin Collection: Margaret Anglin as Ophelia (19); Nancy Pyper Collection: Vincent Price and Judith Evelyn (54); Ned Sparks Collection: Edward (Ned) Sparks (162); Ralph Hicklin Collection: Garden Centre Theatre (239); Tremain-Garstang Collection: Maurice Colbourne Company (33); Tremain-Garstang design (368)

Moorland-Springarn Research Centre, Howard University: Richard B. Harrison (50)

Agnes Etherington Art Gallery, Queen's University, Kingston: Robert Christie (53); Ted Follows (152); International Players (235); Eleanor Stuart (242); Frances Hyland (246); Judith Evelyn (314)

Thomas Fisher Rare Book Library, University of Toronto: Radio Drama (65); New Play Society (67); Stratford Festival tent (244); *God of Gods* (312); Dora Mavor Moore (319, 320); *The Prize Winner* (337)

Index

St Lawrence Summer Playhouse
(Gananoque), 253
St Marys (Ont.), 146; St Marys Little
Theatre, *271*
St Nicholas Hotel (James Reaney), 354–5
St Peter's Players (Brockville), 279
St. Sam and the Nukes (Ted Johns), 256
St Simon's Anglican Church (Toronto),
131
St Thomas (Ont.), 16, 47, 126, 146;
Bennett's Theatre, 146; Duncombe's
Theatre, 146; St Thomas Little
Theatre, *289*
Saints Alive (Ronald Bryden), 167
Salad Days, 79, 194
Sales, Sammy, 70, 83
Salomé dance, 154
Salter, Denis, 20
Salt-Water Moon (David French), 362
Salutin, Rick, 388
Salverson, George, 65
Sampson, June, 194
Samuel French: play catalogue, 11; Tor-
onto branch, 273
Sanderson Centre for the Performing Arts
(Brantford), 143
Sandwell, B.K., 169, 393, 404–6, 430
Santa Claus Parade (Toronto), 170, 269
Sanvido, Guy, 90
Sarah Gibney Stock Company, 30
Sarnia (Ont.), 173; Drama League
(Drama Club of Sarnia), 286
Sarracini, Gerry, 68, 237
Sarrazin, Michael, 90
Saturday Night, 404, 415; Hector
Charlesworth, 397–8; Robert Cush-
man, 420; Robertson Davies, 408;
John Fraser, 418; Martin Knelman,
421; B.K. Sandwell, 404–5, 406
Satyricon, The, 208
Sault Ste Marie (Ont.), 146; Algoma Col-
lege, 299; Algoma Theatre, 146; Sault
Theatre Workshop, 299, *299*

Savoy Musical Comedy Company
(Hamilton), 39, 165
Savoy Stock Company (Hamilton), 59
Savoy Theatre (Hamilton), *15*, 40, 43, 59,
155, 191, 288
Saxe, Al, 90
Scarborough Theatre Guild, 298
Scarfe, Alan, 249, 254
scenic design. *See* design and designers
scenic studios, 272–3
Schafer, Lawrence, 254
Schipper, Steven, 253
Schnurr's Hall (Linwood), *4, 5*
School Show, The (Ted Johns), 256
School of the Theatre (Toronto), 38
Schull, Joseph, 65, 326, 428
Schwartz, Ernest, 95
Scopp, Alfred (Alfie), 66, 196
Scott, Munroe, 252
Scott, Sandra, 66
Scott Park (Hamilton), 49
Sears Collegiate Drama Festival, 330
Second City (Toronto), 209
Second Lie, The (Isabel Ecclestone
MacKay), 333
Second World War. *See* wartime theatre
Seitz, Ernest, 149
Semple, Goldie, 250
Sennett, Mack, 128
Servos, Lancelot Cressy, 178
Sewell, Bill, 135
Seymour, Hal, 183
Seymour, Jane, 42, 43
Shakespeare Society (Toronto), 270
Shatner, William, 76
Shaw, Harold Nelson, 23, 25, 316–17
Shaw, Joseph, 80, 84, 199, 207
Shaw Festival, 9, 191, 247–50, 377, 420,
421; archives, 327, 430; company
tours, 249, 250; Court House Theatre,
250; design and designers, *378*, 381,
383–6, *384, 385*, 389; Festival The-
atre, 248–9, 384; financial problems,

Willan, Healey, 296
William, David, 247
William A. Grew Players, 42
Williams, Minnie Harvey, 173
Williams, Norman, 298
Williams, R. Hodder, 309
Willis, Austin, 228, 233
Willis, Frank, 66
Wilson, Dick, 148
Wilson, Milton, 415
Wilson, R. York, 296
Wilson, Warren, 202
Windsor (Ont.), 98–9; Allen/Palace/
    Loew's Theatre, 146; Border Theatre
    Guild, 271, 288; International Theatre
    Festival, 98–9, 241; University of
    Windsor, 99, 241, 329–30
Winnipeg Kiddies, 31, 176
Winter, Jack, 92, 328, 415
Winter Garden Theatre (Toronto), 140–1,
    142, 144, 145; amateur productions,
    133, 164; vaudeville, 148; wartime
    revue-musicals, 163
Wolvin, Roy, 192, 234
women: acceptance on commercial stage,
    22, 318; in amateur theatre, 260–1;
    dramatic training for, 318, 320; in
    Dumbells' shows, 158; in minstrel
    shows, 128–9; at Stratford Festival,
    74; in student theatre, 307; in wartime
    entertainment, 180–1
Women's Art Association, 260
Women's Canadian Club, 265
Wood, Lauriel, 227
Wood, Ted, 199
Woodhouse, Alfred, 26
Woodland Players (Ben Greet), 318
Woodstock (Ont.), 42, 288, 327; Capitol
    Theatre, 56; Little Theatre Guild, 271,
    290; Peerless Players, 56
Wordsworth, Roy, 202
Workers' Experimental Theatre (WET), 7,
    8, 57, 172, 270, 414

Workman, Eric, 74
Workshop Productions (Toronto), 91–2
Worth, Irene, 243
Wray, Fay, 64
Wright, Priscilla, 198
Wright Players (Hamilton), 44
Wurlitzer organ (Shea's Hippodrome),
    142
Wyckham Hall (Toronto), 320
Wylde, Peter, 233
Wyle, Florence, 270, *300*, 301

Yeats, William Butler, 7, 17, 104n14, 318
Yee, Mark, 59
Yeo, Leslie, 240, 249
Yiddish theatre, 10, 58
YMCA, 156; Barn Players, 298; Prisoners
    of War Service, 122
York Community Theatre (Toronto), 298
Yorke, Bruce, 236, 240
York Theatre Journal, 416
York University, 254, 327, 416; Archives
    and Special Collections, 429, 430;
    Drama Club, 328; Theatre Program,
    328–9; York University Players, 328
Young, Alan (né Angus Young), 61, 174
Young, H. Wilmot, 28
Young, Leonard, 155
Young, Roly, 60, 71, 158, 181, 187, 201
Young-Adams Stock Company, 28
Young Judaea Drama Group, 295
Young People's Theatre (Toronto), 95,
    206, 383, 430
Young Theatre (Loew's, Toronto), 140
Young Thespians (Belleville), 280
You're Gonna Be All Right, Jamie Boy
    (David Freeman), 358
Yule, William, 46

Zanorin (Catherine Brickenden), 294
Zastrozzi (George F. Walker), 356
Ziegfeld Follies, 154, 157, 158
Zone (Marcel Dubé), 79

THE ONTARIO HISTORICAL STUDIES SERIES

Peter Oliver, G. *Howard Ferguson: Ontario Tory* (1977)

J.M.S. Careless, ed., *The Pre-Confederation Premiers: Ontario Government Leaders, 1841–1867* (1980)

Charles W. Humphries, *'Honest Enough to Be Bold' : The Life and Times of Sir James Pliny Whitney* (1985)

Charles M. Johnston, *E.C. Drury: Agrarian Idealist* (1986)

A.K. McDougall, *John P. Robarts: His Life and Government* (1986)

Roger Graham, *Old Man Ontario: Leslie M. Frost* (1990)

John T. Saywell, *'Just call me Mitch' : The Life of Mitchell F. Hepburn* (1991)

A. Margaret Evans, *Sir Oliver Mowat* (1992)

Joseph Schull, *Ontario since 1867* (McClelland and Stewart 1978)

Joseph Schull, *L'Ontario depuis 1867* (McClelland and Stewart 1987)

Olga B. Bishop, Barbara I. Irwin, Clara G. Miller, eds, *Bibliography of Ontario History, 1867–1976: Cultural, Economic, Political, Social*, 2 volumes (1980)

Christopher Armstrong, *The Politics of Federalism: Ontario's Relations with the Federal Government, 1867–1942* (1981)

David Gagan, *Hopeful Travellers: Families, Land and Social Change in Mid-Victorian Peel County, Canada West* (1981)

Robert M. Stamp, *The Schools of Ontario, 1876–1976* (1982)

R. Louis Gentilcore and C. Grant Head, *Ontario's History in Maps* (1984)

K.J. Rea, *The Prosperous Years: The Economic History of Ontario, 1939–1975* (1985)

Ian M. Drummond, *Progress without Planning: The Economic History of Ontario from Confederation to the Second World War* (1987)

John Webster Grant, *A Profusion of Spires: Religion in Nineteenth-Century Ontario* (1988)

Susan E. Houston and Alison Prentice, *Schooling and Scholars in Nineteenth-Century Ontario* (1988)

Ann Saddlemyer, ed., *Early Stages: Theatre in Ontario, 1800–1914* (1990)

W.J. Keith, *Literary Images of Ontario* (1992)

Cornelius J. Jaenen, ed., *Les Franco-Ontariens* (1993)

Douglas McCalla, *Planting the Province: The Economic History of Upper Canada, 1784–1870* (1993)

A.B. McKillop, *Matters of Mind: The University in Ontario, 1791–1951* (1994)

R.D. Gidney and W.P.J. Millar, *Professional Gentlemen: The Professions in Nineteenth-Century Ontario* (1994)

Edward S. Rogers and Donald B. Smith, eds, *Aboriginal Ontario: Historical Perspectives on the First Nations* (1994)

James Struthers, *The Limits of Affluence: Welfare in Ontario, 1920–1970* (1994)

J.E. Hodgetts, *From Arm's Length to Hands-On: The Formative Years of Ontario's Public Service, 1867–1940* (1995)

Paul Craven, ed., *Labouring Lives: Work and Workers in Nineteenth-Century Ontario* (1995)

Ann Saddlemyer and Richard Plant, eds, *Later Stages: Essays in Ontario Theatre from the First World War to the 1970s* (1997)